VICTUS

VICTUS

THE FALL
OF
BARCELONA

ALBERT
SÁNCHEZ
PIÑOL

TRANSLATED BY
THOMAS BUNSTEAD
&
DANIEL HAHN

HARPER
An Imprint of HarperCollinsPublishers

VICTUS. Copyright © **2014** by HarperCollins Publishers. All rights reserved. Printed in the United States of America. No part of this book
may be used or reproduced in any manner whatsoever without written
permission except in the case of brief quotations embodied in critical
articles and reviews. For information, address HarperCollins Publishers,
195 Broadway, New York, NY 10007.

HarperCollins books may be purchased for educational, business, or
sales promotional use. For information, please e-mail the Special Mar-
kets Department at SPsales@harpercollins.com.

FIRST EDITION

Victus first appeared in Spanish, copyright © Albert Sánchez Piñol, 2012.

Designed by William Ruoto

Library of Congress Cataloging-in-Publication Data has been applied
for.

ISBN: 978-0-06-232396-5

14 15 16 17 18   OV/RRD   10 9 8 7 6 5 4 3 2 1

PUGNA MAGNA VICTI SUMUS.

TITUS LIVIUS

(We have lost a great battle.)

CONTENTS

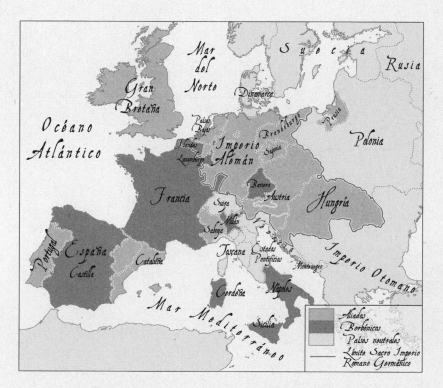

The Political Landscape in Europe 1705

Veni

1

If man is the only being with a geometrical, rational mind, why is it that the poor and defenseless take up arms against the powerful and well equipped? Why do the few oppose the many, and the small resist the great? I know the reason why. One word.

We, the engineers of my age, had not one office but two. The first, which was sacred, consisted of building fortresses; the second, sacrilegious, their destruction. And now that I have become like Tiberius, allow me to reveal the word—that one Word. For, my friends, my enemies, insects all, in the trifling circumference of this universe of ours, I was the traitor. My actions led to the storming of my father's house. I surrendered the city that had been given to me to defend, a city that stood in defiance of two imperial allies. My city. The traitor who delivered it over was me.

What you have just read is a first draft. Writing it, I must have been in a melancholy mood or drunk. When I read it back, I wanted to tear up the paragraph in question, affected and simpering as it was. More the kind of thing one might expect from a cock-sucker like Voltaire.

But as you can see, the Austrian elephant to whom I dictate these memoirs is uncompliant, will not tear it up. She likes it, for some reason, such epic words, so sublime a tone, and so on. *Merda*. Or, as they'd put it: *Scheisse*. But who's going to argue with a Teutonic woman—and, to boot, one with a quill in her hand? Her cheeks are rosier and more swollen than the apple that deceived Adam, her rear end is fat as a regimental drum, and, evidently, she does not understand Catalan.

The clot taking down my words is an Austrian called Waltraud something-or-other; these Viennese names all sound like chewed-up stones. At least she knows French and Spanish. Well, I have set myself to be sincere, and shall be. Poor Waltraud. As well as transcribing these lines, she has the task of sewing me back together from time to time, taking needle and thread to the nineteen wounds that furrow the terrain of my sorry, battered body; wounds from the bullets, grapeshot, and bayonets of fifteen different nations: the broadsword of a Turk, the cudgel of a Maori, arrows and javelins of the natives of New Spain, the New Beyond, and the New Even Further Beyond. Dear, vile Waltraud dabs the suppurating seventy-year-old wounds on my half face, which reopen like flowers with every season's change. And to round it all off, she has to darn the holes in my behind. Oh—oh, the pain! Some days I cannot tell which of them I'm shitting from. And all this for a miserable pension of eight kreuzers a month, for the emperor's purse can stretch no further. It pays for her, and for this drafty garret, but it's all the same to me. Chin up, never mind!—as I always say.

Always, the hardest part is always the beginning. What was in the beginning? Information I am not privy to . . . Nearly a hundred years have passed. Do you realize, gentle reader, the sheer enormity of these words? I have been about the sun so many times, I struggle to recall my mother's name. There's another enormity for you. You'll surely think me a blatherer and a muckabout.

I'll skip the childhood sob stories. Forced to elect the moment when it all began, I would opt for the very day: March 5, 1705.

First, an exile. Picture, if you will, a lad of fourteen. A chill day breaks over the road to Bazoches castle, in French Burgundy. All his worldly effects fit in a knapsack on a stick over his shoulder. He has long legs and is slender about the chest. A sharp nose. And hair straighter, blacker, and more brilliant than the wings of a Burgundian crow.

Well, this lad was me. Martí Zuviría, "good old Zuvi" to some, or even "Longlegs Zuvi." The castle's three spiraling towers, with their black slate roofs, came into view. Fields of barley lined the path, and it was raining so hard you could almost see frogs taking to the air. It hadn't been four days since my expulsion from the Carmelite college in Lyon. For bad behavior, of course. My last hope was that I might be admitted at Bazoches as a pupil of a certain Marquis de Vauban.

The previous year, my father had sent me to France, concerned as he was about the political stability in Spain. (Well-founded concerns, as you'll agree should you read on.) It was by no means an elite school, not by a long shot, but rather a Carmelite venture aimed at the children of families neither rich nor poor, commoners with pretensions but not the means to rub shoulders with aristocracy. My father was what is known in Barcelona as a Ciutadà Honrat—an Honored Citizen. Strange, these titles we give ourselves. To be an Honored Citizen, one must have attained a certain level of wealth—my father was at that level, but barely. He never stopped lamenting the fact. When he was drunk, it was not uncommon to see him tug his hair and exclaim: "Of all the Honored Citizens, I am the very least!" (And he was such a somber man, he never saw how funny the joke was.)

The Carmelite college had a certain renown, at least. I shall not bore you with a full list of my excesses at that place, but proceed directly to the last and definitive.

At fourteen, I was already quite the little man. One night I and the other older students went drinking and scandalizing through the taverns of Lyon. We didn't even remember to return to our dormitories to sleep. It was the first time in my life I had been on such a spree, and the wine had made me barbarously euphoric. The sun was already coming up when it occurred to one of my companions that we ought to return to our lodgings; it was one thing to go back late, quite another not to go back at all. I spied a carriage and leaped up beside the driver.

"Driver! To the Carmelite residence!"

The man said something, I did not understand what, and, my wine-addled brain combining with my juvenile energies, I pushed him into the road."Won't drive us? Very well, we will drive ourselves!" I took the reins. "Forward, boys!"

My ten or dozen roistering companions surged onto the carriage like pirates boarding a ship, and I cracked the whip. The horses reared up and set out along the road. I was having a whale of a time, oblivious to the cries at my back, which had suddenly turned to alarm.

"Martí, hold up!"

I turned to look: My friends, not having had sufficient time to seat themselves, were falling from the vehicle left and right. The carriage hurtled along, and they toppled from it like ten pins. "So drunk they can't even sit in a carriage?" I said to myself. But there was more: We were being chased, I saw, by a furious mob. "What have I done to them?"

The two questions converged in a single answer. My friends weren't able to get up on the carriage properly because it was not, indeed, a carriage, but a casket on wheels. Like all funeral carriages. I'd mistaken it for any ordinary conveyance. As for our pursuers, they were the dead person's family, the cortege. And from the way they were howling, they didn't seem overly pleased. All I could think to do was flee—in any case, there was little else I might do, for the horses had turned hellcats, and I had no idea how to rein them in. I pulled uselessly, succeeding only in making them gallop harder. I sobered up somewhat when I saw, as we took a corner, sparks flying from the wheel edges. We entered a square at breakneck speed. One of the most famous glass shops in Lyon, in all of France, was situated in this square. With the morning light, the frontage, which was all glass, must have appeared to the horses like the entrance to a passageway.

Quite a pretty dustup. The horses, the carriage, the coffin, the dead person, and I were hurled, as one, across the interior of the shop. The shattering of the windowpane was a sound unlike any other. Twenty thousand glasses, lamps, bottles, mirrors, goblets, and vases exploding at once as well. What I still do not understand is how I came out of it alive and, more or less, in one piece.

Getting up on all fours, I peered around at what was now a glass hecatomb. The mob appeared at the mouth of the square. The carriage had come undone at the back, and the coffin was on the floor, with the lid open. And it was empty. "Where might the dead person have gone to?" I asked myself. Anyway, it was hardly the moment to try and find out. I was still stunned by the impact and found myself crawling into the coffin and shutting the lid after me.

My head throbbed horribly. All night drinking, one tavern after another—we'd come to blows at one point with a group of young Dominican monks, even more devout than we Carmelites—then this headlong rush and the bump on the head. "To hell with it all," I said. If I stayed quiet, maybe things would sort themselves out. I laid my cheek against the velvet coffin lining and let oblivion settle over me.

I do not know how long I was in there, but had I stayed a little longer, it would have been forever. A movement awoke me; my closed bed was lurching around. It took me a good few moments to remember . . .

"Hoi! Open this!" I began shouting. "You whoresons, open up!"

My coffin was swaying on account of its being lowered into the ground. They must have heard my cries, for it began to ascend once more (very slowly, or so it seemed to me). Several hands opened the top and out I shot like a scalded cat. What anguish!

"You almost buried me alive!" I cried, justifiably indignant.

It wasn't difficult to surmise what had happened. The family, finding the coffin, had simply placed it back on the carriage and set out again on the road to the cemetery; it hadn't occurred to them to check whether it was their kin or good old Zuvi inside. That was a little too close for comfort.

But the next day I had to deal with the consequences. Eight of my fellow classmates were in the hospital with broken bones, and several ladies who had fainted at the funeral were yet to recover. The glass shop owner was threatening to take me to court. What was more, when rounding up the damage to his business, he had found the cadaver of one of his fellow burghers hanging from a chandelier, which was where it had ended up after the crash. I had gone too far this time. The prior gave me two options: return home with a note explaining my disgraceful conduct, or be sent to the castle at Bazoches. Home? If I went back to my father in Barcelona, having been expelled, I would not come away alive. I opted for Bazoches. From what I was able to find out, a certain Marquis de Vauban was offering to take on students.

2

But enough of the nonsense of children. I was saying: That March 5, I was approaching the castle at Bazoches, on foot and with a knapsack at my back.

The edifice was stately rather than military, attractive rather than pompous. Three round towers soared up out of the ramparts, topped by pointed cowls of black tile. Bazoches castle was beautiful in its antiquated sobriety. In that plain landscape, the eye couldn't help but be drawn to it, magnetized, even, to the point that I didn't hear the coach approaching and nearly running me over.

The road was so narrow, I barely had time to jump clear as the coach wheels splashed mud all over me. This to the great amusement of the two jokers who poked their heads out of the coach windows, a couple of boys my age. The coach carried on toward the castle, their laughter at my misfortune ringing out.

And misfortune it truly was, given that I had planned to present myself in my very best attire. The tricorn hat and the morning suit I wore were the only ones I owned. How could I show myself to a venerable marquis when covered head to toe in mud?

I barely need tell how low I felt arriving at Bazoches. The gates were still open from the arrival of the coach, and a footman came out and began rebuking me. "How many times do I have to tell you people, *alms day*, *Monday*? Get out of here!"

I could hardly blame him. What else was he to think but that I was a beggar come at the wrong time?

"I am here as an engineering candidate—I have a sealed accreditation to prove it!" I said, fumbling with the knapsack.

The man did not even want to listen. This must have been a common occurrence for him, because straightaway he brought out a cudgel. "Away, knave!"

Do you believe in angels, oh German buffalo of mine? I do not, but in Bazoches I met three. And the first appeared just then—just as that footman's stick was about to crack my ribs.

By the look of the girl, she was a servant, but by her air of authority, I imagined she must have boasted some office. And for all they say that angels have no gender, I can assure you this one was female. My goodness, that she was.

I struggle for words to describe that creature's charm. Given that I am not a poet, I'll be brief and simply say that, as a woman, she was everything you are not, my dear vile Waltraud. Don't be like that—I only mean you are broader in the beam than a honeybee, and she was no more than a handspan and a half across. You seem as weighed down as a mule with a heavy load; her movements were those of a certain kind of select woman, noble or not, who could flatten empires under-foot. Your hair always looks fresh-dipped in a barrel of grease; hers was fine, shoulder-length, and watermelon-red. I have never seen your breasts, nor do I ever want to, but I would wager they hang off you like eggplants; hers, you could fit perfectly inside a cup. I do not say she was perfection. Her lower jaw, which was firm and angular, bestowed perhaps a little too much personality for a woman. Well, and since I have begun in this direction, I might as well go all the way; you, you had your chin stolen from you at some point, consummately rounding off your cretinous mien.

What else? Ah, yes, small ears, eyebrows thin as brushstrokes and the color of russet, and as with most redheads, freckles splashed across her cheeks. She had precisely six hundred and forty-three freckles. (Later I'll speak about the academic regime in Bazoches and how it was that I came to count those freckles.) If you had freckles, it would make you look like a leprous witch, whereas she resembled a creature out of myth. And now I come to think of it, one of the few heroes of this age I haven't actually met is your henpecked husband, who puts up with a monstrosity like you every night. Why the tears? Have I said anything that is not truth? Come, take up the quill again.

The maidservant listened carefully to what I had to say. I must have been convincing, because she asked to see my accreditation. She could read, confirmation that she occupied a high position in the servant hierarchy. I told her what had befallen me, which put her in a position to help or have me thrown out. And she helped me. She went off some-where. I waited for a little while (though it seemed forever). She came back with arms full of clothes.

"Take this morning suit," she said, "and hurry. They're starting already."

I ran off in the direction indicated, and didn't stop until I reached a perfectly square room with a low ceiling. For furniture, there were only a couple of chairs, and a door was set in the wall facing. And, next to that, the two lugs responsible for my muddy state. They were on foot, waiting to be admitted.

The first was thickset and had a squashed nose, the nostrils facing more forward than down, not unlike a pig's. The other was tall and scrawny, with legs like a flamingo. His rich boy attire did nothing to hide his ungainliness; instead of having grown gradually, he seemed to have been suddenly yanked from above with tongs. Porky and Stretch, I christened them in my mind.

The fact that they greeted me indifferently, casually, as if this were the first time we'd laid eyes on one another, is not so strange as it seems. Word to the wise, my dear orangutan: People tend to be poor at looking and worse at seeing. The first time Porky and Stretch saw me, it had been fleeting, and now they didn't recognize me. Wearing this wonderful morning suit, I looked completely different. When Stretch spoke, his competitiveness was plain to see.

"Another cadet? Good luck to you, but just so you know, I've been studying the principles of engineering for, oh, *years*. Only one student is going to be admitted, and it's going to be me." He emphasized the word *me*.

"My dear friend," said Porky, interceding. "You forget that I have been awaiting this chance just as long as you."

Stretch sighed. "I cannot believe Vauban himself is about to walk through this door," he said. "A man responsible for the building or re-modeling of three hundred strongholds. Three hundred!"

"That's right," said Porky. "To say nothing of the one hundred and fifty acts of war he's been involved in, great and small."

"The fairest and greatest of which," insisted Stretch, "was taking fifty-three different cities. Harder to penetrate than Troy, each and every one!"

Porky murmured in agreement. "*Greatest, greatest, greatest.*"

"Wonderful," I said to myself. The prior had said nothing to me about any selection process. Or there being only one place. How could anyone be expected to choose me over these two bookworms?

After the Marquis de Vauban's description, I was expecting someone battle-hardened, Herculean, covered in scars. The man who came in, though, was a short, distinguished, and irritable-looking nobleman. He wore a sumptuous wig, the hair wavy and with a central parting. In spite of his advanced age, as shown in his jowly, angular cheeks, his whole being emanated an impatient energy. On his left cheek, there was a vi-olet patch, the result of a bullet that had grazed him at the siege of Ath.

Sebastien Le Prestre Marquis De Vauban

Sebastien Le Prestre Marquis De Vauban

We each stood to attention in a line. The marquis cast his eye over us, saying nothing. He stopped in front of each of us and regarded us for scarcely one or two seconds. And with what eyes! Ah, yes, that Bazoches glance, unlike any other. When Vauban looked at you, it was as though to say: *I know you, imperfections and all, better than you know yourself.* And that was true, in a certain sense. But this was only the man's harder side.

Vauban also had a paternal streak. Though severity might have seemed the most visible facet of his character, no one could fail to see that its aim was both benign and constructive. He was the sort of man whose rectitude is beyond question.

Finally, he deigned to speak. He began with the good part: The royal engineers were the crème de la crème, a select few. So few, in fact, that the kings of Spain and of Asia were prepared to pay any price for their services. This was sounding better . . . French francs, English pounds, Portuguese cruzados. I'd earn, plus get to see the world!

Then the exposition took a turn. Vauban turned serious and said to us: "Be aware, gentlemen, that an engineer risks his life more often in a single siege than an infantry officer will in an entire campaign. Still interested?"

The pair of nitwits at my side assented in unison with an emphatic "Oui, monsieur!" I barely knew which way to look. The military? Rifles? Cannons? I mean, what on earth were they talking about? When I thought of an engineer, I thought bridges, canals. Though Porky and Stretch had mentioned sieges and battles, presumably the men at the helm were always well placed—particularly if their role was to draw up blueprints—in the rearguard, with a wench on either knee.

Look, I had bargained on coming away from Bazoches with some kind of qualification, even in ditch planning. Anything, just something I could use to justify myself to my father. And here was this old loon talking nonsense, endless nonsense, on and on.

For it went from bad to worse. Much worse. Before I realized it, he was already on to "The Mystery."

I've been trying to understand the twinkling lights of *le Mystère* (write it down like that, Waltraud) for the better part of a hundred years, and still I consider myself a novice. So why don't you, my readers, tell me what a lad of fourteen was supposed to think hearing about it for the first time, in that small side room in the castle at Bazoches?

Almost every other word was *Mystère*, and Vauban's tone was so reverential that in the end I thought it must be some cryptic moniker for God Himself. But then again, why bring God into it? By the way Vauban was speaking, God could be no more than a featherbrained stepson to this *Mystère*.

I quickly gave up any hope of being accepted at Bazoches. As I say, I hadn't the faintest notion where it was all headed. Porky and Stretch seemed enthused. They had a good idea what was in store, were as prepared as possible—given their standing and their schooling—and their lives' only objective seemed to be devoting themselves to the rare cause being invoked by the marquis.

Very abruptly, Vauban fell quiet and left the room. Porky and Stretch looked at each other in bafflement. A minute later, someone else came out in Vauban's place. It was her. The redheaded beauty from the courtyard. She proceeded to introduce herself . . . as the marquis's daughter.

The possibility, or anything like it, had not occurred to me. What a fool I was—no serving girl could possibly move with such aplomb. This time she was far more elegantly attired, with a long skirt that covered her feet. She made no sign of recognizing me. She was serious as death and nearly as frightening. She came and stood before us.

"My father wishes to form an idea of your aptitudes. Knowing that his presence can be intimidating to young cadets, he has asked me to carry out the test." Opening a folder, she took out a print. "The test consists of a single question. I will show you designs, one by one, and you must describe them to me. Please be concise in your answer."

She turned to me first, showing me a picture. I still have a replica of the original. (You, you brutish blondie, insert it here, after this page, nowhere else! Get it? Here!)

If she'd shown me a poem in Aramaic, I would have had a better idea what it meant. I shrugged and said the first thing that came into my head. "A star. A star that looks like a flower, with spines instead of petals."

Porky and Stretch, who had already managed a sidelong glance at the drawing, broke down laughing. Not her. She remained impassive, moved two paces along, and showed the illustration to Porky, who answered: "A fortress with eight bastions and eight ravelins."

When it came to Stretch, he merely said: "Neuf-Brisach."

"Of course!" exclaimed Porky. "How could I fail to see it? Vauban's crowning work!"

Stretch, confident he'd won, couldn't help but assume the victorious expression of someone the gods have smiled upon. He even commiserated with Porky, laying the crass amiability on thick. The image in the print was that of the fortress at Neuf-Brisach, wherever that was.

Vauban's daughter asked us to wait while she went and passed on our answers to her father. When it was the three of us again, I said: "The next time we lay eyes on one another, you would be better off minding your manners."

They were taken aback by my aggrieved tone.

"Ah, yes. You're that beggar," Stretch said, finally working out who I was. He was the cleverer of the two. "And might I ask what you're doing here?"

My intention was merely to needle them a little before I left, what with the mud and the fact that I never have been able to stand conceited little snots like them. But my insults were sufficiently choice as to make their faces drain of vim—and they piled right in to me!

There were two of them, but two's not so many, and I kicked them in the shins and poked them in the eyes. Porky came up behind me and started strangling me, and we fell to the floor. I bit him on the arm and aimed a few defensive kicks at Stretch, who was raising a chair over his head, ready to crack mine open. I don't know what would have happened if Vauban and his daughter hadn't come in and interrupted us.

"Gentlemen!" she exclaimed, scandalized. "This is Bazoches castle, not a common tavern!"

We got to our feet and stood up straight, our clothes crumpled, Stretch with a bashed-in eye and Porky nursing his arm where I'd bitten it. The marquis's glare was indescribably severe. And I'm not being rhetorical when I say the silence was such that you could have heard the woodworms eating the chairs.

"You have brought violence into my home," declared the marquis. "Get out."

There was nothing more to be said. The daughter addressed the other two boys. "You and you, come with me." As she was leading them from the room, she turned her head and said to me: "You, wait here."

I was alone with the marquis, who kept his probing eyes upon me. We could hear the protests of Porky and Stretch on the far side of the door. Then, these having diminished, the girl came back into the room.

I thought Vauban's daughter was going to throw me out as well but was staggering our departure; after our punching, biting, and scratching spectacle, it was only logical to separate us to avoid a repeat.

But what the marquis said next, though unyielding in tone, did not fit with a goodbye: "Our first conversation takes place after an act of violence under my roof. Does that seem to you to augur well?"

Better not to answer. He paced around a little. Coming back over to me, he stopped and prodded me on the chest with two fingers. "I am now going to ask you a question," he said, "and I want you to answer honestly. What happened with the Carmelites?"

"Well," I said, "it's complicated. The Carmelites are, how can I say it, they're real disciplinarians."

I could see Vauban wasn't one to beat about the bush. I had no way of knowing what it said in the prior's letter, so I simply decided to present the facts without twisting them too much.

"One day I got in a carriage to return to the college. I was in such a hurry, I failed to notice that, though indeed a carriage, it was meant for a funeral. The Carmelites took it very badly."

"For a funeral?"

"The family was unhappy at the change of route," I said, avoiding as best I could the most disagreeable parts.

I heard lively laughter start up behind me, growing louder; it was the daughter, sitting behind me. The most unexpected thing to me was that the marquis joined in the joke. His stony face suddenly crumpled, and there he was, guffawing. Father and daughter, laughing, exchanged looks.

"Now I understand why the prior sent you to me," said the marquis, explaining: "I studied with them as a youngster, too, and committed a nearly identical error. They must never have forgotten it!" Still laughing, he turned back to his daughter. "Have I never told you about it, Jeanne, my dear? I took a seat next to the driver and said: 'To the Carmelite college!'"

She was beset by laughter, louder and louder, as the marquis continued his tale: "And the driver said: 'Young man, do not be in such a hurry to arrive at the place where this vehicle is destined.' So I understood that it was going to the cemetery. My face must have been quite the picture!"

They broke down laughing. The marquis pulled out an enormous white handkerchief to dry his eyes. When he spoke again, laughter punctuated his words. "Dear Lord God . . . And they got angry at a peccadillo like that?" More laughter. "When one finds oneself in a bit of a spot, lying under a carriage like a boob, that's all there is to it . . ." Laughter, ho, ho, ho. "But honestly . . . I mean . . ." Hee, hee, hee from Vauban, ho, ho, ho from Jeanne, "The Carmelites have many virtues, but a sense of humor has never been one!"

The private man seemed altogether different from his public persona. At that point I did not know that, for Vauban, the idea of "private" included only Jeanne, the youngest of his two daughters, in whom he had complete trust. As he looked at me, the marquis's face turned stony again. "There's still time for you," he said. "Should you choose to remain in Bazoches, your life will undergo radical changes."

Who'd have thought it? When Jeanne passed on our test answers, she must have told her beloved father that good old Zuvi, not Stretch, had hit the mark. She'd seen something in Martí Zuviría . . .

"The Carmelites' letter also makes reference to certain little defects of character: pride, disobedience, a dislike of authority. Want to know what I think? I think the prior has relieved himself of a difficult student."

Almost a hundred years have passed and still, still I see Jeanne Vauban in that moment, seated beside me, head askance, chewing strands of red hair. In her eyes, a look that suggested everything—or nothing. If it had been just the two of us, I believe I would have pounced on her there and then.

Vauban again prodded my chest. "Think you're here merely to become a simple 'engineer'? Wrong. Bazoches is the fount of certain secrets known to very few. Know this: By the time we finish with you, you will no longer be any old commoner. True: You'll touch the gates of glory with fingers of lead. But the rewards will be few. And for you to become an engineer, Bazoches will take everything you've got out of you before we put it all back in. You'll feel as though you've swallowed your vomit a thousand times. And only then will you be worthy of *le Mystère*." He paused to take breath into his old lungs and then asked: "Do you feel you're up to such a task?"

Part of me was saying, Get out of here. Go whistling out and don't stop till you hit the Pyrenees. Drop *le Mystère*, leave the Great Marquis-Engineer-Leanwit to cook in his own sauce, don't get caught up in affairs not your own . . .

Then again, I thought, why not? Though it wasn't what I'd been expecting, I didn't have much of an option. As I hesitated, my gaze turned away a little, toward Vauban's daughter. My giddy goodness, that redhead.

I stood up tall to give my answer: "Ready and willing, Monsieur!"

He nodded lightly. But his blessing contained something slightly troubling, in that he turned to his daughter and said: "What are you waiting for?"

When it comes down to it, the most important decisions in our lives are not made by us, they happen to us. Was it *le Mystère*'s invisible aroma that did it? Possibly. Or it could have been my cock talking. Also quite possible.

3

What led the great Vauban to adopt me as a student? Even now, I cannot answer with any certainty.

His only male child had died at two months old, meaning that Vauban had to make do with two daughters. Was there some form of never exercised paternity that he needed to feel? Don't believe for a moment I was that important. And, as I was later to learn, to a man with Vauban's ideas about the world, he cared little whether his offspring were boys or girls. He sired a good many bastards with local peasant women. This was common knowledge, he never made any effort to hide it, and in his will went so far as to leave each a good stipend. But in life he never paid them the slightest bit of mind.

In March 1705, he was precisely two years shy of death. He knew the end was not far off. A privileged few had gone before me, and I would be the final student. The only way I can put it is sometimes, a few times, I felt like the piece of parchment upon which the castaway writes his last message before inserting it into the bottle.

Naturally, I did not see Vauban each and every day. He was often away traveling, in Paris or elsewhere. Let's say he concerned himself with my progress as he did the majority of his fortification works: in the capacity of supervisor general.

They allocated me a room in a tower at the top of a winding staircase. It was small but light, neat and tidy, and smelled of lavender. The next day I breakfasted in a corner of the kitchens, which were larger than my whole house in Barcelona. I ate alone, the servants all busy with other tasks. I expected I'd see Jeanne afterward—or at least I hoped to. Instead of her, a venerable old man appeared, beaming and delicate-looking.

"So, you're the new pupil?"

He introduced himself as Armand Ducroix. "Have you managed to get your bearings at Bazoches?" he asked before answering his own question. "No, of course not, if he only arrived yesterday. All in good time, hmm, yes."

I was yet to learn that this was Armand's habitual way of speaking. He thought out loud, as if he believed it the most normal thing in the world that his thoughts should flow freely, without hiding in silences and conventions.

"Good lad," he went on, "spirited-looking, built like a greyhound. Yes, he could go far, who knows? But let's not fool ourselves. All is in the hands of *le Mystère*. That sharp nose indicates liveliness of spirit, hmm, yes, and those shoulders look made to bear great burdens. Now to see about fortifying his muscles and his spirit."

He took me to the library. Seeing the rows and rows of shelves overflowing with books, I was astonished.

"Wow!" I exclaimed. "But if each one has fifty books and more? Can any one person possibly have read so much?"

Laughing, Armand pulled up a chair. "Dear cadet," he said. "You will have to read far more before you become a Maganon."

"A Maganon?"

"That was what the ancient Greeks called their military engineers."

As Armand bowed his head to write, I was afforded a view of his cranium, bare and magnificent, in all its glory. A curiously spherical head. With most bald people, their cranium is freckled or has blue or pinkish veins on it, or ridges adorning it, like on a nut. Not Armand. His skin, a healthy pinkish color, was tight as a drum. What hair he still had formed a white halo around the base of his skull, like a crown of laurels that then joined in a beard tapering down to a goatee. Everything about him was slight, concentrated, and compact. The apparent fragility of his bones in reality hid the vivaciousness of a squirrel. His thinness was not a reflection of old age consuming him but a rare vital tension. I never once saw him in bad humor, and he never needed an excuse to laugh. Yet with all that, this bonhomie never obscured his gray eyes, his wolf eyes, constantly watching you. Even out of the back of his head.

He had sat down to write a note. Finishing it, he bade me come closer. "This will be your program of study," he announced. "Read it back to me, if you would."

I no longer have this note—nor do I need it. I remember it down to the last letter:

6: 30–7:	Wash. Chapel. Breakfast.
7–8:	Drafting.
8–9:	Mathematics. Geometry. Lemon juice.
9–10:	Spherical Room.
10–12:	Metrics of Fortifications. Topography.
12–12:30:	Lunch. Lemon juice.
12:30–14:	Fieldwork.
14–15:	Obey and Command. Tactics and Strategy.
15–16:	History. Physics.
16–17:	Surveying. Ballistics. Lemon juice.
17–19:	Mineralogy. Fieldwork.
19:00:	Dinner.
19:30–21:	Architecture.
21–23:	Fieldwork. Chapel.

This was my study schedule, although in reality I was never required to pray, and I never set foot in chapel.

"Sundays you'll have for yourself," Armand said with that perpetual smile of his. "Are you in agreement with the general plan?"

Was I really in a position to refuse?

"Perfect, then," he said, pleased. "We'll make a start. Go next door, if you would, and bring me *La nouvelle fortification* by Nicolaus Goldmann. And *De Secretis Secretorum* by Walter de Milemete."

The library continued in an adjoining room. I could not believe that anyone could be so eccentric as to store such quantities of printed paper. I entered through a doorless recess—and there was Armand once more! At the top of a stairwell, organizing books, with his splendid bald pate and white goatee. The same black breeches, the same white shirt. He looked over at me. Those same gray wolf eyes, and that same kind but shrewd smile. "Can I help you with anything, young man?"

"You . . . you yourself know very well," I said, dumbfounded. "I'm looking for *La nouvelle fortification* by Nicolaus Goldmann and *De Secretis Secretorum* by Walter de Milemete."

Descending the stairs, he handed me the books.

"How did you do that?" I asked.

"Using the index. This library is governed by a principle known as 'order.'"

I was utterly baffled. I retraced my steps, coming back through into the larger room, the books under my arm. And I found Armand sitting at his desk!

The mystery was solved only when my librarian came in and joined us. They were identical twins, as difficult to tell apart as crabs. Even the wrinkles on their cheeks were the same. They began to laugh. Later on I found that confusing the servants at Bazoches was a pastime they greatly enjoyed. They found the range of jokes permitted by that particular corporeal fusion endlessly amusing.

"But you're so alike!" I exclaimed, a little disturbed.

"I can assure you that it won't be long before you can tell us apart."

At that moment the only difference I could see was that one was called Armand and the other Zeno—or vice versa, so impossible did I find it to distinguish them. The first made me sit at a table. He placed Goldmann and Milemete in front of me and, now deeply serious, gave me an order: "Read. And if you understand any of it, let me know."

A strange directive. They left me to read uninterrupted for a while. I did so with the best will. Milemete was my chosen starting point; the title seemed promising. Secrets upon secrets—I was hoping for dragons, founts of eternal life, carnivorous ox-eating plants, that sort of thing. Not in the slightest; it was dry as could be. The only thing that appealed were the prints of some kind of Roman amphora that had four legs and vomited fire. As for Goldmann, again, the pictures were the most interesting thing. They looked to my eye like the illegible scrawls of a person so hopelessly bored that he had resorted to filling page after page with maniacal geometric shapes. After a little while, the twins said: *"Et alors?"*

I looked up. Better to be honest."Not a word," I admitted.

"Perfect. Herein lies today's lesson," said Armand. "Now, at least, you know that you know nothing at all."

The next day the Ducroix brothers continued to indulge me. They limited themselves to assessing my knowledge so they could establish where to begin. I was not very focused—my thoughts were all of Jeanne.

"Something bothering you?" asked Zeno.

"Absolutely not," I said, waking from my daydream. "Merely, I have so recently arrived and do not yet know my position in Bazoches."

"But how can that be?" said Armand. "Are you yet to be introduced to the inhabitants of the castle?"

He himself brought me before each of the servants. I must say, both Zeno and Armand were courtesy personified. With them, there was nothing of the usual distance affected by nobles toward common folk. The latter knew perfectly well their station, of course, but the twins comported themselves with a cordialness that occluded any difference.

To their right, they had me, and to their left, Vauban. They had been with him for decades; they knew all his engineering secrets and shared in his philosophy. They helped in the early stages of his fortification projects, and helped bridge Vauban's military and worldly affairs. Truly, I was lucky to arrive at Bazoches in the autumn of great de Vauban's life. At any other time, the Ducroix twins would have been too busy to lavish such attention on me.

"Now for the marquis's daughter."

Hearing these words, I had to adjust my breeches so no one would notice my upstanding member. I was, however, disappointed, as I was henceforth brought before an altogether different creature: Charlotte, Jeanne's sister and Vauban's eldest. She had a little peach face, red cheeks, a mouth shorter than a tortoise's tail, and a nose oddly positioned, a set square that commenced somewhere above her eyebrows. She had a laugh like a parrot, *clo, clo, clo,* and jowls that shook like the bag of a bagpipe.

And if you, gentle reader, think me a clown for describing her in such terms, how wrong you are. The fact is, I found it distressing to make her acquaintance: How could nature be that cruel? Sisters they were, but all virtue had fallen to Jeanne. Intelligence, great beauty, wit, while Charlotte had always been a simple soul, not a bad bone in her body.

"I believe you have met Jeanne already," said Armand. "She is in town at the moment, occupied by some charitable affair."

Wonderful.

"Her husband is hardly ever in Bazoches himself," remarked Zeno. "When you make his acquaintance, please behave kindly and . . . with a certain delicacy. He is an unusual character."

"What Zeno means to say," clarified Armand, "is that his mind is not all there."

At the end of the day, I retired to my lovely lavender-smelling quarters. What, I, to bed? Not on your life.

During the Ducroix brothers' tour of the castle's living quarters, I had learned which was Jeanne's room. I waited for everyone to be abed before approaching. In any case, I would not have been able to sleep. I let a little time pass before leaving my room, barefoot and carrying an oil lamp. I came to Jeanne's door and knocked softly. Nothing happened. I was vacillating— knock again or withdraw—when finally she came to the door.

Perhaps it is owing to my tender years, but I had never suffered an impression such as that. And I say "suffered," for love, I say, is quite capable of provoking physical pain. My lungs shrank; my mind, usually agile, became suddenly muddy. The lamp flames were less atremble than I.

My first sight of her had been in the attire of a common country girl; next, she had been made up like a queen; now, in a nightgown and with her red locks tumbling loose. And we were alone in the dark. The faint light from the two flames, mine and hers, revealed the outlines of what was beneath her gown. I had been rehearsing two or three phrases but merely stood, slack-jawed.

"Well?" she said.

"I wanted to . . . to thank you," I said, eventually reacting. "I wouldn't be here if it weren't for you."

"Do you deem it appropriate to be calling at a woman's door at this hour?"

"Why did you choose me? Of the three, I was least well prepared—it was plain to see."

"I like to wear comfortable clothing when we are not receiving visitors. Those two walked straight past me, didn't even notice a servant; they saw nothing." Something in her aspect altered. "You asked for help." Regretting having spoken with such frankness, she sought to change the subject. She glanced up and down the passageway to see if anyone was coming. "How old are you?"

I was a few months short of fifteen. "Eighteen."

"So young?" she said, surprised.

As a youth, I always looked five years older than my true age, and when I became a man, twenty less. My theory being that le Mystère was in a hurry to make me grow, because it had designs on me to die before my time, in 1714. This was followed by certain unforeseen cosmic occurrences; a number of decades passed with le Mystère neglecting to add years to me, and here you have me, gentle reader, here you have me.

"I care not a jot for engineering," I said. "Since the moment I laid eyes on you, I have thought of nothing else."

She laughed—she hadn't expected this. "If you knew what was in store for you, you'd change your priorities."

I did not take her meaning.

"The previous cadet lasted three weeks," she explained. "That was not so bad; the previous one went home after day five."

"When I came to Bazoches, I did not know what I was looking for," I said. "Now I do."

She wasn't having any of it. My feelings were sincere, but my ways of presenting them straight out of a cheap theater.

"To bed with you," she said. "Believe me, come tomorrow you'll be happy of some rest."

And she shut the door in my face.

4

Jeanne couldn't have been more right, as I very soon found.
   We began with Drawing, the Ducroix view being that ink and line awoke the senses. Next came Physics and Geometry. That was

when I learned what a privilege it is to have a tutor dedicated entirely to you. And I had two! I'm no pedagogue; I would not know how to go about evaluating their methods, so all I can say is that they applied to me a unique combination of indulgence, discipline, and acuity of spirit.

Next, a break and the lemon juice. "Drink."

It was an order. Until I grew accustomed to it, they had to watch that I did not empty the glass into some nearby plant pot. Because "lemon juice" wasn't truly accurate; Vauban, altogether the polymath, had invented a brew composed of root extracts, beeswax, various juices, and goodness knows what else, so congealed and sickly sweet that it was hard to stomach. In his view, it awakened the brain and fortified the muscles. Well, it didn't *quite* kill me.

Possibly the most curious discipline at Bazoches was the one they called the Spherical Room. The name was closer to the reality than that of the juice, because it really was a room without any corners, egg-shaped, a gigantic globe with matte, pure whitewashed walls. Even the floor was concave, so when the door shut behind you, you were confined in this immaculate sphere. The Spherical Room was at the top of the castle. There was a skylight in the center of the roof, which let sunlight in to flood the space.

"You have five minutes exactly," said the Ducroix twins the first time they pushed me inside.

I felt taken aback the first time. And not because I expected something malign; I simply did not know what to expect. Ever since I'd come to Bazoches, I'd had the sense of a world of marvels surrounding me: strange books, wise twins, beautiful women. And now this spherical, light-filled room, and me inside it, alone, bemused by the majestic silence.

There were objects up ahead. Dozens and dozens of white threads hanging from the ceiling, invisible at the point where they merged with the far walls. And from the threads, hanging at different heights, the most diverse array of objects: a horseshoe, a theater mask, a simple nail. A wig! A goose feather hard to see against the white walls. A gold clock revolving at the end of the small chain.

Five minutes later, they opened the door.

"Speak," said Armand. "What did you see?"

"Things hanging," was my flustered response.

Zeno was behind me. He dealt me a slap to the neck. I turned defiantly and exclaimed: "You hit me!"

"The objective is not the blow itself but to wake you up," Zeno said by way of justification.

"Cadet Zuviría!" called out Armand. "You are blind. Any engineer who does not know how to use his eyes properly is no engineer. If you had been paying attention, you would have given a worthier answer than this vague 'things hanging.' Useless. What things? How many? In what order, height, and depth?"

They made me enter once more—more accurately, they flung me back in. I committed what I could upon my retinas and to memory. When I came out, I had to describe the objects in detail and according to position. I began with the things that had been at the front and detailed the following ones using these as reference. They listened attentively and did not interrupt at any point.

"Pathetic," was Armand's view. "There were twenty-two objects, and you have described only fifteen, and those poorly. There was a horseshoe, yes. But how many holes did it have? Which side was it hanging on? How high up?"

I opened my mouth, but no words came out.

"Do you not understand?" said Zeno, cutting me off. "When you are attacking a bastion or defending one, and you have only a few seconds to form a picture of the situation, how are you going to take responsibility for the lives of those under you?"

"Paying attention is essential," said Armand. "Always, at all hours and in all places. Otherwise you'll fail to see things, and if that happens, you'll be no use in this role. From now on, you'll remain constantly attentive, both awake and asleep. Clear?"

"I think so."

"Sure?"

"Yes."

"Sure you've understood?"

"Yes," I cried, more out of frustration than belief.

Before I'd finished saying "yes," Zeno instantly said: "Describe the buckles on my shoes."

Instinctively, I looked down.

Zeno lifted my chin with a finger. "Answer."

I could not.

"Since you have been with us, I have been wearing the same footwear. And in all that time, you have failed to notice they have no buckles."

In Bazoches, I realized how blind people are. Most men, when they look around, do so in a hurry, alighting briefly on single objects, guided by the base instincts—this I like, this I do not—like children. The Ducroix brothers divided the human race into two: moles and Maganons. Ninety-nine out of a hundred were blind as moles. A good Maganon would notice more things in one day than a mole would in a year. (You yourself, you blubbery mole, how many fingers do I have? Do you see? All this time together, and you have failed to notice that the tip of one of my pinkie fingers is missing. Shrapnel, Gibraltar. I say, it served well: The siege scuppered them, and I enjoyed making life difficult for a Bourbon.)

That day they put up twenty-two objects; others, thirty, forty, even fifty. Sometimes just one, which was mere mockery, for I then had to recount its every detail. My personal best was describing one hundred and ninety-eight objects hanging from a panoply of white threads. And I had to remember everything about each and every object: the number of holes in the flute, pearls on the necklace, and teeth on the saw. Have you, gentle reader, ever tried such a thing? Do so, do, and you'll discover in small details the vast complexity of our world.

These would all have been no more than quaint and stimulating drills, part and parcel with the brothers' eccentricity, had it not been for the discipline known as "Fieldwork." I imagined this was going to be some form of bracing exercise in the open air. Wasn't it just!

We went to a field a mile or so away from the castle, a rectangular field that looked as though it hadn't been tilled in many years. The Ducroix brothers began to hold forth on the lovely views. This was very much the way they went about things; their academic activities never drew them away from their principal motivation in life: to take pleasure in the sight of a bird in flight or a beautiful sunset.

"Well, Cadet Zuviría," said Armand, finally turning to face me.

"Let us suppose—and a wild supposition it remains—that you have become a member of the engineering corps. And let us then suppose that a ditch needs making. What would you do?"

"I suppose order the sappers to begin digging," I answered, caught somewhat off balance.

"Very good!" said Zeno, applauding sarcastically.

Four servants from the castle approached. They were carrying stakes, ropes, and small bags containing lime, and these they deposited at our feet. Also some voluminous round wicker baskets, which, I would later learn, were known as *fajinas*. As well as these, an iron helmet that looked two hundred years old, a leather cuirass of a sort, and a rifle. They also left a pile of sticks, clubs, and a thousand digging implements. There are more kinds of shovels in the world than butterflies, was one of the things I learned that day.

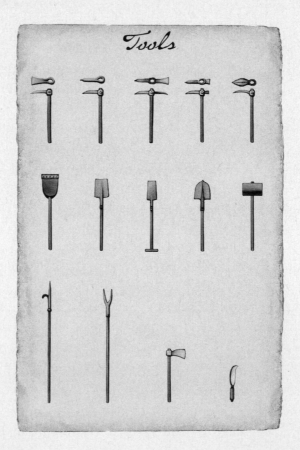

"What are you waiting for?" said Armand.

"What's the rifle for?" I asked, a little worried.

"Oh, don't you worry about the rifle," said Zeno, picking it up, walking a little way away, and loading it.

The first lessons I'd received had been on the metrics of fortifications. I took a stake and inserted it deep into the earth. I then took a rope, tied one end to the base of the stake, unspooled it to a length of sixty or seventy feet, tying the other end to another stake. I then sprinkled lime over the rope; the powder that fell either side marked a straight line for the excavation. Then I heard the report: A bullet had just flown by, whizzing past my helmet like a bumblebee.

I let out a shrill cry. "Eeeh!" I could not believe it; Zeno had shot at me! He stood a hundred feet away, reloading the rifle.

"The other way around," said Armand. "First you smear the lime onto the rope. Then unroll it. If the rope is covered in a good amount of lime, laying it out will leave a clear line. That way you save having to move around the field a second time, and give your enemy less time to shoot at you.

"Zeno can reload and fire every two minutes," he continued. "Lucky for you. A young rifleman, if he's at all handy, will be able to do it in less than half that time. If I were you, I'd hurry up and start digging."

I grabbed a pick by the handle—it weighed more than a dead man—and attacked the strip of lime for all I was worth.

"If you please!" said Armand. "Adjust your chin strap and the cuirass."

"But why was your brother shooting at me?" I cried.

"Because it was his turn. Now it's mine." And he went to take the loaded rifle from Zeno.

The helmet they had given me was more like something from the fifteenth century than our own, with a visor and long earflaps, also made of iron, all extremely heavy. I was still struggling to adjust the cuirass when I heard another report. I nearly jumped out of my skin. "Promise you'll only shoot with caps!"

They both laughed.

"Truce!" I said, raising my hands in the air. "I stop digging, you stop firing, and you can give me some coaching in that *Mystère* you keep mentioning."

"And what do you think *le Mystère* is?" asked Armand.

They fired at me again. I hastened my digging. If I could make a sufficiently deep hole, at least I would have some protection from the bullets. Once the earth was fairly well broken up, I grabbed the shovel.

"Other way, cadet!" shouted Armand. "Shovelfuls are cast in the direction of the enemy. That way you'll have a mound of earth to conceal you more quickly."

I said nothing for a moment as I took in the instructions. Another shot. I began digging even more frenetically. It isn't until you try making a hole to fit an entire body in that you realize what a task it is. Roots as thick as arms appeared.

"Roots!" I cried in desperation. "How do I cut them?"

Everything I said struck the brothers as hilarious.

"Well, of course there are roots! So it goes with this strange French soil of ours: The roots grow beneath the ground, not over it," said a laughing Armand, thrusting the ramrod down the rifle's barrel.

"No scissors?" shouted Zeno, getting in on the joke. "No? Shame! Well, now you know what your job is before bedtime: Sharpen your spade, precisely for this hallowed task."

I continued to dig, down on my knees now so as to make a less visible target of myself. More shots. One so close that soil erupted over my helmet. I finally managed to open up a cavity into which I could just about fit. I was gasping and exhausted.

Armand came over. "Cadet: Change out of those clothes, wash your face and your armpits, and to the study room."

I was defeated. And that first day, after Fieldwork, I still had to carry on paying attention in class.

"Obey and Command" had to do with a classical precept of Quintus Ennius, Appian, or some such Roman or Greek: "Before you can command, you must learn to obey." The subject came to be an addendum to Practical Fieldwork, the idea being that the blisters on your hands would help instruct you about what you might reasonably expect from men.

History classes. For the Ducroix brothers, "Universal" History was the history of France; France and who else? Ah, yes, don't forget

France. Then there was a trifling corner, somewhere beyond the king's borders, an unimportant wayside known as "the world." This far-off land merited a tenth of the lessons, and then only when the Parthians were laying siege to Palmyra, or when Cato said to the Roman senate that in order to ensure a good crop of prickly pears, Carthage would have to be sown with salt. To begin with, I made my skepticism clear, but one day, when Zeno claimed that Arquimedex (they pronounced and wrote it like this, with an X at the end) had Gallic origins, I did not stop him. In general, the French are more open-spirited than people think. True, you shouldn't ever attempt to convince them that perhaps, only perhaps, and according to the opinion of some cartographers who know a little about the subject, Paris is not at the geographical center of Planet Earth. They will not argue with you but simply think you are a poor lost soul.

Being the good Frenchmen that they were, they started with the siege of Alesia. Caesar surrounded Alesia with a twenty-mile-long palisade and then another around that, twice as long, to stop reinforcements from getting in. What did I care about Alesia, Caesar, and Vercingetorix? Hard as I tried, at that point in the never-ending day, my eyelids began to droop, and my arms became deadweights. I rejoiced when supper was announced! Before going to the dining hall, I asked them: "Were you really shooting *at* me?"

"Well," said Zeno, "we try to create a situation with the haze of smoke, and the havoc, of an actual war. We don't necessarily aim at the body."

"But you could have killed me! At a hundred feet, a rifle is hardly accurate."

Shrugging, they continued their conversation. Those Ducroix! What a pair.

Usually, I ate on my own in the kitchens. By the time I came to sit, the servants had been abed a good while. In my corner were fruit and a small cooking pot; I served myself. My fingers were trembling from wielding those hulking picks and spades. The edges of the helmet had chafed my temples, as though I'd been wearing a crown of thorns. At around midnight, when I was just biting into an apple, Armand appeared. "Cadet, outside."

"You're joking," I snapped. "But I'm more dead than alive!"

"I believe I remember you yourself agreeing to the study plan," said Armand. "Do you think your enemy cares a jot as to your physical and mental state?" He examined my head. "I suggest that you put some wadding around your head before putting the helmet back on. That's what wadding was invented for. Go on, then, *allez!*"

And back to the field we went.

Once I was in the hole, I had to dig following the line of lime. I don't think I could have covered even ten feet in an hour. The pick, the spade, the helmet. Those round wicker baskets, which I had to call *fajinas* or be punished. *Fajina, fajina,* more *fajinas.* And the brothers' rifle. Each time a *fajina* appeared, full of earth and forming a parapet beside the trench, Armand would take aim. And those were the conditions I had to work in! I learned very quickly to hide my hands, holding the *fajina* by the base and from behind, so as not to give the shooter a target.

Next day, more of the same. Drawing, studying, fieldwork, studying, fieldwork, retreat practice. And back to the beginning again. I did not have it in me to try and importune Jeanne, I was that shattered. I fell leadlike into bed every night and woke only when the castle bells rang out—very sonorous they were, and positioned (by design, no doubt)—directly above my room. And this was merely the beginning.

As tutors, I have to say, the Ducroix brothers were the best; their methods, the most demanding. *Pay attention!* Spherical Room. *Be constantly attentive, whether in there or in any other place!* Geometry. Ballistics. Mineralogy. Fieldwork. *Allez!*

One day, a fortnight in, I came close to insurrection. It rained the whole day through; plainly, that was no obstacle to the unaltered continuation of field drills. The pick sank into the trench wall, but the earth, compacted by the rain, didn't budge. My body was covered in a thick sludge, a ballast of viscid mud I had to haul around, becoming heavier and heavier. The rain came down ever harder, torrential cascades pouring over the edges of my helmet. There was a foot of water covering the ground, and my shoes were full up. To top things off, the drill lasted half an hour longer than usual. I remember looking skyward, up at those filthy weeping clouds. The skies of France, ah, yes, that gray so sweet and cruel. A shot hitting the cylinder of one of the *fajinas* brought me back to reality.

By the end, I was so destroyed that I could not lift myself out of my hole, which had been growing deeper, wider, and more than anything, longer. Armand did not deign to help me out. I managed to get my arms and head out, complete with that cumbersome helmet, the thick drops of rain bouncing off it.

"And you want me to be constantly attentive?" I protested. "But dear God! Do you not see, if I die, there is little chance of my paying any attention to anything!"

Armand knelt down on the edge of the trench, his nose right up close to my iron visor. The delicate man I thought I'd met that first day had quite disappeared. Even the rain seemed to fall on him in a re-spectful manner, running down the bald sphere of his head and, when it reached his cheek, draining neatly off through his goatee.

"As long as you are alive, you must pay attention. And as long as you pay attention, you'll stay alive. Now, out of the trench."

"I cannot." I held out my hand to him. "Help me, I cannot."

"Not true. You can. Do it."

"I cannot!"

He shrugged and got to his feet, shouldering the rifle. "Given that you insist on this laziness, I hereby suspend my academic powers. I can give orders to a thinking mind, never to a stomach or a back. And given that your belly prefers fasting over dinner, and your back the mud rather than a decent bed, well, I wish you a very good night, my dear cadet."

Lightning and thunder. Off he went, while I fell asleep where I was, snoozing in the rainy mire. I was so broken, I didn't have the energy to take off my helmet.

Next morning, I was awakened by a kick, and thus another day began, just the same as if I had enjoyed a refreshing sleep.

Drawing. *What's that ink stain?* Slap. *Pay attention, always pay atten-tion*, ma petite taupe, *my little blind mole!* Physics, mathematics, this, that, the other. Languages, a hateful subject, according to the Ducroix brothers, but essential, given that certain unfortunates hailing from

England, Spain, Austria, and in general, the backwaters of the world, bizarre as it may have seemed, had yet to learn French. As ever in Bazoches, the titles of the disciplines had shades within them, because aside from English and German, they were also teaching me the language of engineers.

Among the Maganons there was a gestural code they could use to communicate secretly among themselves in public. They spoke using signs, and it was a language so elaborate that there was nothing, neither technical nor worldly, that it couldn't be used to express. I was introduced to this unwillingly, not to say discontentedly, but later learned how useful it could be.

In the deafening clamor of battle, to be able to communicate with one's hands is a very helpful thing. "Pull back," "Ammunition!,," "Get down, there's a sniper to your left." These, the Ducroix brothers told me, from small beginnings had become ever more sophisticated, developing into a great Maganon secret.

Now, gentle reader, picture an engineer about his work. His superior officer (an engineer) introduces him to the fortress commander. In public, the chief of engineers proclaims to the recent arrival: "General so-and-so, to whom not even Corbulo in his sieges of Armenian strongholds could have held a candle!" But at the same time, by moving his fingers and hands around, he is saying: "This man, here to my right, is nothing but a know-it-all. Pay him no mind. Any silly order he gives, agree to but be sure to disobey; come and ask me, and I'll tell you what really must be done."

I had to learn this sign language at a rate of twenty signs a day. This to begin with. Then it went up to thirty, forty, and even fifty. *What was that? Still can't make yourself understood in the arsenal? How are we going to make sure the artillery has what they need when munitions are running low?* Slap! *Wake up! Out to the field!* Spherical Room.

I do not believe anything could be so enervating to a man as that systematic and uninterrupted combination of physical and mental exertion. And even if I shut my eyes, I had to be just as attentive at all hours. Take that! *Back in the Spherical Room, open your eyes!* Cadet Zuviría, when will you learn the simple thing that is to use your eyes! *To the field! Allez! Allez!* And so on, day after day after day.

5

The first month in Bazoches was like a nightmare I awoke into every day—I have no other way to describe it. You might ask: How did I bear it? My answer is, the best way to make the unbearable bearable is a combination of equal parts love, equal parts terror.

The terror, I barely need say, was provided by my father. That was his function; I never had the sensation of being treated as a son. As a child, I felt only aversion for him. When he was called away on business, farther into the interior of the Mediterranean, I couldn't have been happier. I later came to learn the underlying reasons for his embittered character, and this softened my memories of him.

Peret (more on him later) said he had never seen a man so in love as my father had been with my mother. Hard for me to believe, for I knew the man in two moods only: irate and very irate. Always that dour face, taciturn, bearded, off elsewhere in his thoughts, especially if it was the two of us dining together in the meager candlelight. Such a miser he was, he even scrimped on wax.

When I arrived into the world, his life plummeted. Not because of me but because my mother died giving birth to me. He never forgot her. Bitterness was a ballast weighing him down inside—a visible tumor, constantly there. He took refuge in his work, otherwise he wouldn't have been able to carry on.

The port of Barcelona was a very active one and had trade links with the whole of the western Mediterranean. My father, a minor stockholder in a maritime company of twenty or thirty members, a widower and therefore with fewer familial responsibilities than the other associates, often sailed to finalize contracts and strengthen ties with their counterparts—in the Balearic Islands, and in Italy and its surrounding islands. In a business like his, in which client and stockist saw so little of each other in person, it was vital that ties of friendship and business be constantly maintained and renewed. (Everybody knows what Italians are like, forever prattling with their kisses, smiles, embraces, and feeble promises of eternal friendship.)

Let us simply say that, in legal terms, he put himself in a position of care toward me without ever having the slightest involvement with me as a human being. At least that was my experience. He beat me often, though for that I never blamed him; I deserved all those clouts, and many more besides. Curious, but a child will never complain so much about the beatings given as the embraces withheld. He embraced me only when it was my birthday—though I knew full well it wasn't me he was drawing close to him but, rather, my mother. On that day he would become bestially drunk, would weep and squeeze me tight— like a bear mumbling her name—hers, never mine.

I shall say that, to his credit, in this world of illiterates, he spent everything he could on my education, though even the best schools in Barcelona were all a calamity. For professors, we had curmudgeonly priests who, in their own words, treated us pupils as "sinning, rot-destined sacks of flesh."

My father spent half his time at the port or away on voyages, so he contracted the services of Peret to take care of me. The logical thing would have been for my father to find a buxom nurse for me and, since he was master, have his way with her every now and then. But it ended up being Peret, simply because no one cost less.

Even the Italians have sayings about the stinginess of the Catalans. But if my father were the measure of our nation's stinginess, I can assure you, they didn't know the half. I got a beating one day for throwing out a candle that had less than half a thumb's length of wax remaining. Ah, and there was the time he learned of a ship that, because of issues with the cargo, had weighed anchor with six tenths of the hold empty— bluer than a duck egg he turned that day.

Peret was a scraggedy old wretch. Before I was born, he had worked as a stevedore at the port for my father and his associates. All he earned, he spent on drink. When he became too old to carry bulky things, they kicked him out of the shipping company for a layabout and a drunk. He had a long, wrinkled neck and a bald head, like a vulture's. After leaving the company, he circulated the alleyways and lanes of Barcelona's Ramblas, peddling knickknacks, his back so bent he gave the impression of being a mushroom forager. In return for a bare room and a miserable wage, my father brought him in to take charge of me and the household.

Poor Peret. I do not believe there can have been a human being more ill treated by a child. He'd go to bed and I'd fill up his shoes with dung; this he'd find out when he put them on the next morning. He had to wait to go out in the street before realizing I'd painted his enormous hooked nose red. If he ever threatened to hit me, I'd threaten to tell my father about him pilfering from the domestic allowance.

In spite of all, Peret was the only substitute for my mother whom I ever knew. It was impossible for me not to feel fond of the man who combed my hair, dressed me, and showed me affection—far more than my father ever did. I remember that Peret cried a lot—that being his only defense against my abuses and extortions.

When I turned twelve, my father considered what to do with me. The normal thing would have been to send me to one of the Carmelite colleges in Barcelona, but they persuaded him to send me to their headquarters in France, a far more adequate place. He agreed, as it truly was a good school for the son of a businessman; also, it would put me out of sight. I did not blame him. The mutual distance was a relief to us both. At twelve, I looked seventeen, and at some point soon it was going to come to blows between us.

I have already related what passed with the Carmelites in France. Given that for two years now, our only contact had been through letters, when I got to Bazoches I wrote to tell him the news and to let him know my new address. (The expulsion I kept to myself—it would only lead to further questions—I told him it had been a decision made with my future interests in mind, and so on.)

His reply arrived soon after.

What's all this about castles and a marquis? What makes you want to be an engineer all of a sudden? The bridges over the sea are boats, and we have these in the company. You were supposed to be learning numbers. If I find you are playing tricks on me, young man, I'll tear you limb from limb.

Next came the friendliest part of the letter:

Precocious boy that you are, you're doubtless beginning to

have feelings for girls now. Beware. Father a bastard, you'll get not a single peso from the grandfather. Are we clear, *cap de lluç*?

Cap de lluç is impossible to translate; literally, it means *head of hake*, but in Catalan is more along the lines of *hopeless idiot*.

The good part was the surprising mildness of his tone. Being the man he was, if he had been truly angry, he would have ordered me to return immediately to Barcelona, where the belt and a blessed beating would await. As it was, he enclosed the money to cover my studies for several months to come. In my letter, I'd said that Bazoches was twice as expensive as the Carmelites, in theory to sound him out, but to my surprise, he let me have the money with no complaint.

Well, he hit the nail on the head in suspecting me of tricking him. On the first day, I had asked the Ducroix brothers what payment was expected for my schooling. It was the only time I ever saw them take offense.

"Cadet! What, think the marquis needs funding by *you*? It is he who shall remunerate you during your stay. Thereby, you will be seen as very knavish indeed should you ever choose to criticize this house once you have left its walls."

A very noble stance—I couldn't have agreed more. If an aristocrat's honor proved lucrative to others, who was I to complain? While in Bazoches I'd receive money from Vauban and from my father, double what those Carmelite dolts were getting before. I could make a *little corner* for myself, as the Catalan saying goes. (Though, given my circumstances, there wouldn't be much for me to spend it on!)

I'm feeling sorry for myself, and I would not want to be thought a complainer. Because Bazoches was a veritable Noah's Ark, but one that was filled with guides to thinking instead of animals. And I was sufficiently clever to realize this.

Beneath the Burgundy sun, I grew into a good-looking, muscular youth. My efforts were tempered by the strains of pick and shovel (and lemon juice, *gah!*). After a few months in my pit, I was handling the sapper's instruments like kitchen utensils. And most important: I was absorbing rare know-how.

There might have been one or two hundred people in all the world

with a better knowledge than mine of the subjects pertaining to Bazoches. The Ducroix brothers, to their great credit, made my education
involving for me, and soon it was me pestering them to tell me everything, everything. Tiredness converted to hunger; the more exhausted
I was, the more keen to get on with the next lesson. Once I'd gotten
my head around the rudiments of engineering, I began to seek alternatives and improvements myself. More than that: Love has the underap-
preciated merit of also spurring a desire to learn.

For Jeanne was the other thing motivating me, keeping me alive
and awake. With regard to the educational value of desire, I here present an example:

I was walking in a small wood one day alongside Armand. In
Bazoches, the cultivation of "attention" was by no means limited to
sight. Sometimes, on walks in the countryside, I was made to list all
the sounds I could hear. Until a person concentrates, the sheer amount
of detail our ears offer us goes totally unnoticed. The air, the murmurs
of hidden water sources, the noise of invisible insects, the ringing out
of the tools of some faraway labor . . .

Armand slapped my nape. "And the bird? You've missed that. Are
you deaf?"

"But I've counted six different birdsongs!"

"What about the seventh?"

"Where?"

"Behind on your left, a hundred and fifty feet or so away."

At times, I must say, his demands upset me. "How am I supposed to hear
a tiny sound like that, coming from behind me, and at such a distance?"

"By focusing on it. This is why you were given ears." Armand then
turned his hearing in the direction of this invisible bird—"a hundred
and fifty feet or so away"—and when I say "turned," I mean physically
moving his ears, as would a dog!

"Learn to use your muscles" was his answer to my look of surprise.
"That they are atrophied does not mean their use may never be recu-
perated. Let's go."

He obliged me to do it. We spent a good while standing silently in
those woods. I tried moving my ears under Armand's watchful gaze.
No easy thing—don't believe me, try it for yourselves! What did move

were my cheeks or my crinkled-up forehead. Nothing, only ridiculous expressions. I gave up.

I sat down at the foot of a tree with my hands on my head. There was a mushroom a foot to my right. It was the only time I came truly close to giving up. That which two months of hard disciplinary exercises had not managed, this infantile one nearly had.

What was I doing there, in that corner of France, taking orders from a couple of old lunatics? Breaking my back in some pointless trench, my brain chock-full of drawings, angles, geometry—and for what? To be duped out in the middle of some wood, pouring my all into the sublime, halfwit art of waggling my ears.

"I'll never be an engineer, never," I said to myself—thinking out loud, like the Ducroix brothers.

"Martí, lad," Armand said, "you've made decent progress."

He knelt down beside me. It was unusual for him to use my name and not the typical scathing "cadet" or "blind mole." The Ducroix brothers knew when they'd gone too far, and then, only then, would they show me a little affection.

"Not true," I protested like a child. "I see nothing and hear less. How am I ever going to build fortresses or defend them?"

"I said you've made decent progress," he said. And putting on a sudden barracks tone, he gave me an order: "Cadet, on your feet!"

I had sufficient respect for the Ducroix brothers to jump up, desolate though I felt.

"What is behind you, immediately behind the tree you were sitting beneath?"

I described the vegetation, including every single branch: those snapped and hanging down, and those that stood straight up, including the number and colors of leaves on each. I didn't think this any great thing.

"Very good," said Armand. "Five hundred feet straight behind you, what else is there?"

I answered immediately. "A woman. Strolling, carrying flowers. She has a bunch with red and yellow buds in one hand—forty-three flowers, I think. At the speed she was going, I believe by now she'll have picked forty-five." Sighing, I whispered: "She has red hair."

A natural thoroughfare in the woods led to the clearing we found ourselves in. A few hundred feet beyond this, the trees opened out onto a green field in which, half a minute earlier, I had seen Jeanne walking.

"Do you see?" said Armand. "When we want to, we can pay attention. Your problem is that, had it been a lame old woman with a hunchback and no teeth, you wouldn't have noticed her. But, and I'm sure you'll agree, each is just as visible. And for carrying messages between enemy lines, the enemy will always choose the hunchbacks over the redheads. Precisely because no one notices them."

The Ducroix brothers had realized my feelings toward Jeanne from day one, of course. Armand sighed and clapped me on the cheek twice, though I didn't know if this was meant as consolation or recrimination.

"If you want to become an engineer," he said, "you have to be constantly paying attention, and for that, what you need to fall in love with is reality, the world around you."

That night I went down to Jeanne's room. I knocked twice, lightly. She did not open the door. I went back the following night. I knocked three times. She did not open. Another night: I knocked three times and then, leaving an interval, a fourth. She did not open. I didn't go back the next night. But the following night, I gave five little knocks.

Now is when I describe how Jeanne and I fell into each other's arms. How I seduced her, or she seduced me, or how I believed I'd seduced her when in truth it was the other way around, or vice versa, or how it all happened at once. You know, love, all that. The thing is, I've never felt comfortable with love poetry, and I have no notion of how to tell it prettily.

All right, listen: Between the practice field and the castle, there stood a hayloft. Picture Zuvi and Jeanne up in the top, on a bed of dry straw, nude and one mounting the other, and vice versa.

So there you have it.

The Vauban family rarely gathered at Bazoches all together. When they did, curiously, those were the days when I was afforded most time with the marquis. And, using the excuse that he was giving me some practical guidance, he was able to free himself from his dull relations, of whom the only one he could bear was his cousin Dupuy-Vauban. Sometimes they allowed me to accompany them on long walks through the countryside.

Dupuy-Vauban, whom I will henceforth call "Dupuy" so as not to confuse my imbecile of a transcriber, was one of the five greatest engineers of the century. If anything can explain the fact he has, unjustly, not gone down in history, it's his close kinship with the marquis, who inevitably eclipsed him. He was an exceptional, loyal, modest, and unassuming man, virtues of no use in gaining earthly glory. At the end of his military career he had sixteen wounds upon his body.

I always liked seeing him. Dupuy was to me an example and an inspiration, as well as a link between Martí the student and the great marquis. Though far the younger of the two, the marquis treated Dupuy as an equal. I felt like a child in their company—a child growing up amongst geniuses. Just as newborns understand nothing of their parents' speech, to begin with the idiom of engineering was gibberish to me. But as my studies progressed, I began to join in the discussions. One of my most satisfying moments at Bazoches was afforded me by Dupuy, during one of these country walks. Halting, he said to the marquis: "My God, Sébastien! I do hope you inserted the clause into this young snip's study contract!"

"The clause?" I said. "What clause?"

"The one prohibiting him from taking part in any siege in which Dupuy is on the other side!"

They both laughed. As did I. How could I ever possibly take aim at men such as these?

On one occasion, Dupuy was unable to attend one of the family reunions; he was taking part in a siege, in Germany. Vauban must have thought I was sufficiently advanced to accompany him, for the two of us strolled out together, alone.

"Well then?" he said to me. "Do you find your studies to be coming along adequately, cadet Zuviría?"

"Fabulously well, *monsieur*," I replied—and meant it. "The Ducroix brothers are exceptional teachers. I have learned more in these few months than my whole life."

"I can sense a 'but' . . ." prompted Vauban.

"I'm not complaining," I replied, again sincerely. "Only, I don't see how Latin, German, and English apply. And even Physics and Surveying strike me as having hardly anything to do with engineering. *Monsieur!* I spend hours with a bandage across my eyes trying to guess, just by the texture, the kind of sand or stones they place in my hands. Though I have almost grown eyes in my fingers, I fail to see the use to my learning as a whole . . . "

"The whole is you," he interrupted. "Let us walk."

In Sébastien Le Prestre de Vauban's view, all of military history can be summarized as an eternal dispute between attacker and defender. The invention of the cudgel was followed by that of the breastplate; that of the sword, the shield; the lance, armor. The more powerful the projectiles, the more stalwart became the means for defending against them.

If there's one thing men have sought to protect more avidly than their bodies, it is their homes. If we look carefully, the great battles have all been attempts to keep combat at a distance from the hearth. Cain mashed Abel's head with a lump of stone, this is true, but what the Bible omits to mention is that the following day Cain attacked his brother's home, stole his pigs, violated his wife, and put his children into bondage.

Fire versus caves. Ladders versus wooden stockades. Siege towers versus ramparts made of stone. However, one day this unsteady equilibrium was thrown out of kilter.

A moment came when defense turned into a form of attack. Fortification techniques had outstripped those available to the attacker. However large the rocks hurled by catapults, onagers, and trebuchets, any city—if its engineers had the resources to erect sufficiently stout ramparts—would be invulnerable. That city existed, and its name was Constantinople: the last, splendorous stronghold of the Eastern Roman Empire. Over centuries, each emperor would pass on to his successor a widening of the ramparts.

From the point of view of a military engineer such as Vauban, classical Constantinople was ancient civilization's crowning achievement. Its megalithic stone ramparts stood three hundred feet high, and towers and storehouses studded the inside edges.

Decadent Byzantium was invaded on many occasions, but those Herculean ramparts were never breached. All peoples, from East and from West, attempted it, and all were unsuccessful. Over the centuries it resisted twenty-five sieges! Germans, Huns, Avars, Russians—even the Catalans tried in medieval times, lest we forget. But in 1453 something happened that changed the course of engineering, war, history, and, therefore, all humanity.

In Turkey, or thereabouts, there lived a sheikh who got it in his mind to take Constantinople. Vauban had a portrait of the man on a wall at Bazoches. He said this was so as never to forget that one must always respect one's enemy, little as he may merit it, and, should he indeed merit it, one must go so far as to admire him. In the portrait, the Suleiman in question wore a turban on his head and was smelling a flower. He had a cruel, spine-crumbling gaze.

The story goes that, when he was still a young man, he fell in love with a Greek woman who was being held prisoner. He kept her with him inside his tent for three full days and nights. The soldiers began to mutter among themselves, calling him henpecked, a milksop, that sort of thing. Once he had spent a while enjoying the girl, the sheikh found out about the rumors. He dragged the poor Byzantine girl out of the tent and—pam!—slit her throat with his scimitar. Then, with the army in formation before him, he bellowed the words: "Who out of you will follow this sword of mine, so powerful it severs even the bonds of love?"

The sheikh's onslaughts initially comprised the usual: thousands of Janissaries roasted, scalded with boiling pitch, and to a greater or lesser degree, taken to pieces at the foot of the ramparts.

But then a small group of Hungarian and, mainly, Italian engineers (those Italians, always making trouble!) offered their services to the Moorish king. And this sheikh charged them with designing the largest cannon ever known.

Gunpowder was in use by that time, although in battle merely as fireworks, which would frighten the less battle-hardened and aid the morale of one's own side, but little else. But this Turk was very—very—serious about cannons. The result was the Great Bombard, a thirty-foot-long cannon. Once it was assembled, a team of three hundred bullocks was needed to pull it to Constantinople. They covered no more than a mile and a half of ground a day, it was so heavy. But they got there in the end.

The Great Bombard fired half-ton balls of stone. As hard as the Byzantines tried to fill the breaches, what could they do against this? One discharge would be followed by another and another. And though it was hard to be accurate with the Bombard, it was impossible to miss ramparts that high and vertical.

Everybody knows the rest. The Turks poured through the breaches, the Byzantine emperor died fighting on the front line. Throughout Europe, engineers shuddered—for, from that moment on, what use were ramparts? Fortifying a city was a very costly affair, and kings were not prepared to spend fortunes on useless works. The big question was: Now how to protect our cities? (And in private: Now how to conserve our wages as royal engineers?)

Formulas were devised, proposals made, the majority of them unreliable, confused, doubtful. And the only mind ever to succeed in solving all aspects of the problem was the man strolling at my side: Sébastien Le Prestre de Vauban.

Given that pyroballistics had become the principal threat to city ramparts, in order to protect against them, everything had to be reinvented. Vauban glanced at me inquisitively. "Well? What would you do in such a case, Cadet Zuviría?"

What a question. I had not the faintest idea. "I'm afraid I don't know, *monsieur*," I mused aloud. "How to avoid a bombardment by artillery? Only two formulas occur to me: attacking the cannons or hiding from them. Attacking would seem like suicide. If cannons can destroy the strongest ramparts, what would they do to human flesh? As for fleeing, that would save the garrison but condemn the city. And there is no way to hide ramparts."

Vauban clicked his fingers. "The last one you said. You were on the right track."

I had to stop myself from laughing. "But *monsieur*, how to hide the entire walled perimeter of a city?"

"By burying it."

6

I n the Middle Ages, city ramparts were tall and vertical. The thicker the ramparts and the taller the battlements, the stronger the defenses. And to make them even stronger, there you had your turrets all the way around.

The might of medieval ramparts was there for all to see, and to this day, they are so associated in people's minds with the idea of what a fortress is that if we ask a child to draw a picture of a rampart, he'll do one in the old style, even though he has never seen one like that, rather than a modern one, the kind he spends every day playing at the foot of.

Vauban turned traditional fortress-making principles on their head by introducing more of a slope to his ramparts, at times to an incline of sixty degrees; the angle meant that cannonballs would bounce off rather than punch through. Given that cannonballs tended to skew off in all directions, they were extremely inaccurate. Moreover, the height of medieval ramparts had become a disadvantage, so that the Vaubanian

Traditional Wall

system built them behind a very deep concealing moat. In certain of Vauban's projects, the fortifications stood even lower than the town buildings. This produced a curious effect: An army approaching the city would barely be able to make out the defenses, but the civil buildings behind would be in plain sight.

I include a print to give a better idea. (This one, you German flabber face. Here! Not before, not after. Here!)

The medieval turrets, at intervals along the walled enclosures, came to be replaced by bastions. A bastion was a sort of smaller fort embedded in the walls, normally five-sided. See, in this next image, the spear point construction sticking out from the ramparts?

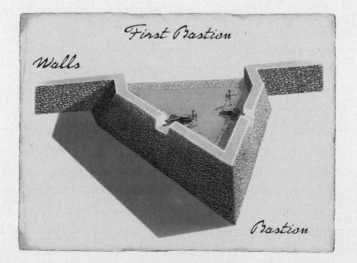

This is a basic bastion, in fact a rather unassuming one in terms of its size. The bastions in the larger fortresses would be gigantic, immense bulks garrisoned by up to a thousand men, with dozens of cannon and underground ammunition stores inside. In the fortifications built by the modern Maganons, thus, the ramparts were protected by bastions, and these in turn provided one another with covering fire.

Let us imagine that an invader decides to try to take the stronghold. The bastion has been expressly designed with five sides. The attackers will have no choice but to scale one of the outwardly projecting bastion walls. Whichever they choose, the adjacent bastions will cover their fellow defenders with sustained fire. As the attackers advance, arrows and cannonballs will rain down from the ramparts and the bastions, as well as thousands of liters of burning pitch.

If, rather than the bastions, they attack one of the rampart's central portions, they'll have an even worse time of it. The poor fools who go down into the moat will never get out. They'll be fired on from three sides: from the rampart, and from the covering bastions to the left and right.

Cross fire. Two words that, on paper, are just an engineer's design concept. But when ink becomes stone, these two words become the light of a very hell.

Cross fire! Hundreds, thousands, of uniforms descending into and rising out of an everlasting ditch, fired at, bombarded, exterminated by an invisible army. The ditch may have been flooded or, as in most cases, packed with sharpened stakes over five feet in length. Those who impaled themselves would have to be clambered over by the rest until, finally, any advance would become impossible. If the attack were by a small troop, not a man would be left alive; if it comprised thousands, the ditch would fill up with writhing bodies.

This callous marvel to which Vauban gave his name could be multiplied infinitely. For still more protection, a "moon" or "half-moon" fortification could be set before one of the flat sections. Before they could attack the rampart's first line, the invader would have to expend thousands of projectiles to demolish the half-moon. And in the unlikely case that it was taken, the defenders would draw back to the next rampart, raising the drawbridges after them. And the game would be-

Bastion Front

A   Curtain wall   E   Glacis
B   Bastion   F   Covered way
C   Moat   G   Tenaille
D   Ravelin   H   Cavalier on the Bastion

gin again, the fallback still viable. The attackers would have succeeded in taking only an outcrop—at a cost of hundreds of dead. What resources could they call on to resume the attack? Moons, half-moons, ravelins, pincers . . . an endless variety of defensive architecture that does not bear describing to the uninitiated. In any case, anyone who wants to can look up the technical details of a fully equipped armature.

Undeniably, the fortified architecture of our time has a certain charm. Ours is the art of making the useful beautiful. Geometric lines, clear-cut and clean. Formally ascetic, they conceal nothing. They are what they are: defenses. And all the beings in this trifling universe of ours seek security in a hostile world. In peacetime, civilians may stroll beneath them, happy and safe, secure in the feelings offered by these bastions with their angular defiles, these colossi crouching like immutable sentinels. It is not that the Vaubanian fortification tends toward beauty but, rather, that beauty approaches its forms, yielding to them. Because when we contemplate them, that doubtful principle appears before our eyes, that unfounded faith: that there is order in the world, an order of goodness.

And in the following print, if this careless windbag puts it in the right place, allow me a poetic detail.

See the little sentry box at the top of the bastion, which looks like a figurehead? In French, this is called the *échauguette*. It is a sentry nest, safe from the elements. Beyond the purely functional, military engineers are not unaware of the aesthetic value of their work. And the *échauguette* is something like the cherry on the cake. The sole detail into which the designer could allow some vain expressiveness. Sometimes it would be delicately conical roofs with black or red slate tiles; at others, ramparts decorated with intricate stone carvings. I was passionate about a great many of them; their artistic value was far from negligible. I knew a Hungarian engineer who drew wonderfully well and whose hobby was sketching these *échauguettes*. And he was quite good at it.

What, when the enemy nears, is the first defensive measure to be taken? You blow up the *échauguette* with gunpowder, to deprive the enemy artillery of a reference point.

This always caused me a unique, inexpressible, ambivalent kind of pain. A city prepares to defend the homes contained within it, and what's the first act? The sacrificing of the most exposed point of beauty.

A city before a siege is like an anthill that has been stepped on. *Annibal ad portas!* The churchbells ring out in warning. Farmers from the neighboring countryside come to take shelter, with family and livestock in tow. The garrison has soon taken up position. Munitions are distributed, the covers taken off the cannons, gunpowder deposits safeguarded.

But even in the midst of this uproarious tumult—when the duty officer shouts out for people to stand clear, that the *échauguette* is about to blow—every time, and I mean every time, the same happens: Everybody stops. Misty-eyed looks in the direction of the *échauguette*—the silence such that you could hear a match being lit. And then, *boom!* An instantaneous shift from the state of peace to the state of war. This *boom* is to a siege as Genesis is to the Bible. We Point Bearers (and, with heavy Miss Waltraud's assistance, I'll come directly to the meaning of the Points) had to be a cut above—we couldn't be like other people. I hated the blowing of the *échauguettes*, but at the same time experienced the joy, the pleasure of the pain, to come.

Bazoches's great error was to believe that the task of the warring Maganons could be dignified—elevated, even, to the saintly status of civilian art. Vauban's belief was that by making war more technical, lives would be saved. Now, with the time that has passed, a great many massacres later, this altogether puerile notion seems sordid. But the marquis believed in it. Truly he did. I can't blame him.

Coming to the end of our stroll, on which he related the history of Byzantium, he asked me a question. We had passed through green secluded meadows, wet with rain, on the outskirts of Bazoches. Crows squawked above our heads. Vauban stopped. "And you," he said, "in this never-ending war, which side are you on? Are you for cannon or for bastion?"

"*Monsieur*, I do not know," I replied, surprised. After hesitating for a moment, I added: "I suppose I am for whoever's cause is just."

He took hold of my right hand and turned it over as if about to tell my fortune, and then rolled up my sleeve. "Tell the Ducroix brothers they are to give you your first Point."

I have summarized a good amount of Vauban's teachings, but please do not think they were limited to one single walk in the country. In reality, there were many meetings, with him stopping in from time to time when I was in lessons or me being called to his study when he had a free moment or felt like enlarging on something or other. In any case, most of my learning was left to the Ducroix brothers to instill. They composed the text; Vauban applied the finishing touches.

Let us go back a little. These Points bear explaining. (At least my German mammoth seems to think so; chatterbox cockatoo that she is, she interrupts and demands that I go back to the mention of the first Point.)

The twins announced my first Point once I had made substantial progress. I stretched out my right arm on a table, palm up, and they applied the tattoo using irons—these seemed part scalpel, part torture instrument. They placed the first Point on my wrist, just where hand and forearm meet. "Point" is one way of putting it. The first was precisely that, a simple circle of indelible ink, dark violet in color, the application of which hurt like anything. The next, an inch higher up my forearm, was more sophisticated, like a plus sign but with the points joined by lines, like a weathervane. The third was a pentagon. Each Point was more elaborate than the last. From the fifth onward, the outline of a bastioned fortress began to take shape. If an engineer reaches perfection, the idea is to have ten Points, covering the whole of the forearm up to the crook of the elbow.

To get in ahead of the curious reader: No person on earth has ten Points. That is, no person is a Ten Points, to my knowledge. Which is not to say there is no person *deserving*—merely that the circle of Maganons was so small, so specialized and select, that anyone who might confer the ranking had been dead for decades. Well, I'm still going, a Nine Points. So what? I'm old enough to take on pupils by now. As if that were not enough, the Paris revolutionaries of today, the ones my insufferable Waltraud so admires, are even changing the traditional ways of waging war. On which I would say a few words.

At the beginning of my century, armies were made up of career soldiers (or mercenaries, whatever you prefer). Given that no such king had endless wealth, armies had relatively few men. This was why bastioned fortresses were so important, for they blocked invasion routes. If, instead of attacking them, an army chose to go around, putting the fortress at their rear, their lines of communication might be severed, and they would be caught in another kind of cross fire: between the enemy army and the garrison at the fortress, which would come out to attack from behind.

Nowadays Robespierre and his Paris popinjays have invented the *levée en masse*—murder en masse, more like. Armies currently stand ten or a hundred times larger than they were in my day. They can leave a number of regiments blockading a fortress, and send the others off ahead; they need not bother taking the fortress. This was why, in my day, there were twenty sieges to every pitched battle, and the majority of the latter were in order to force the lifting of a siege—or to prevent another. Now battles have become little more than tossing rank after rank against rifle and cannon, like feeding firewood into the flames. He with the biggest woodpile wins. The science of modern warfare brought us to this. Viva progress!

As for the mystery of the Points, in the world of Bazoches, these were a way of recognizing progress.

At a time when a polite greeting took the form of a light nod of the head, it was the engineers who were the first to go back to the Roman handshake. On clasping hands, they would turn the wrist very slightly, inconspicuously. Each would see the other's Points and, in this way, work out where the other was positioned in an already decided hierarchy, saving much long-windedness, dispute, and misunderstanding. And believe me when I say how important this was when laying siege to or defending a stronghold. No matter the rankings doled out by the army, a Three Points was always subordinate to a Four Points, and so on. Career officers would perceive something amiss, but in general the Point Bearers were so practical and inscrutable, and military men such dullards, that the latter never cottoned on. Or it did not matter to them.

The Point Bearers' hierarchy formed a core universal brotherhood. What a wonder, how galvanizing to the spirit, to stumble upon a complete stranger in Berlin or Paris, in the vast dales of Hungary or up in the Andean peaks scourged by blizzards, and suddenly, all this way from home, feel, with a simple turn of the wrist, as though by some magic, all that distance melt: two men joined by a mutual recognition. No thing in this world can replace that unique glance of complicity.

Do you know of what I speak, my dear vile Waltraud? No, of course you do not. But it isn't complicated. Behind you sits my cat, enthralled by the fire. See the way he glances at me? That's it.

And yet I did not fully comprehend the value of my tattoos. The Ducroix brothers gave me my second Point for counting chickpeas. Don't laugh. I was fed up with the Spherical Room. To the back teeth! So much that I had not even realized the progress I'd made.

You have succeeded in becoming truly alert when, even as you are distracted, you remain alert. Do you take my meaning? Of course not. Nor, at one time, did I. It has to be internalized. At a certain point, you'll think your mind wanders, but the alertness mechanisms are still on, keeping close track of things.

For lunch one day, I was given a plate of chickpeas. The Ducroix brothers were eating with me that day, and they noticed the second my mind began to wander. (They were right: I was thinking how the down on Jeanne's cunt was exactly the same color as these chickpeas.)

Armand whacked me on the forehead with a ladle. "Cadet Zuviría! How many chickpeas on the plate? Answer immediately!"

I quickly ate a spoonful before answering: "There were ninety-one. Now, eighty-one."

They were delighted. And I hadn't made it up. I myself was not aware that I knew the answer—until they put the question to me. The mouthful I ate was to vex them, and to demonstrate that I was now being observant continuously, not just from time to time in isolated moments.

Each time I exited the Spherical Room, the question was always the same: "Cadet Zuviría, what was in the room?"

As much detail as I went into about the objects I'd seen hanging up, their distances from the floor, the gaps between them, the verdict would almost always be: "Pass, but not perfect."

Eventually, one day, at the conclusion of my list, I paused and then added: "And myself as well."

They had told me a thousand times that the observer forms a part of what is being observed. To my chagrin, it had taken me months to grasp that I also was one of the things in the room. Maybe this will seem a simple lesson in humility or even a not tremendously witty play on words. However, it was anything but.

As the enemy prepared to attack my bastion, I had to see everything, enumerate everything. Our rifles, theirs; the condition of our defenses, the number of cannons, the lengths and width of their parallels; and my fear. Nothing in the world distorts reality like a dose of terror. If I was unconscious of my fear, the fear would look instead of me. Or, as the Ducroix brothers would say: "Fear will cloud your sight, then *it* will be doing the looking instead of your own eyes." The world is a killer; men die storming or defending ramparts. But in fact, the whole thing is no more than a minuscule white sphere, lost in some corner of the universe, indifferent to our troubles and pains. Herein, *le Mystère*.

I became a Three Points upon completing my long trench.

"Congratulations, Cadet Zuviría. You have earned your third Point," Armand informed me. "Permit us, however, to qualify the value of the task you've completed. Having reached the edge of the field, you continued to dig the trench and place out the *fajinas*. This was well done, even though it meant the destruction of the bordering hedge. We gave no instructions for you to stop, and an engineer must always be obedient and resolute. Even so, didn't you notice that the next field had been sowed for corn?"

"I did."

"Correct. Someone digging a trench in private property, outside his own land, would never be punished—on a war footing, all land is in contention. But when the line of your trench met with the donkey pushing the plow, and the goodly man behind it—who, by the way, protested very vehemently at the incursion—did it not occur to you that the exercise was by now exceeding its teaching objectives?"

"No."

"Correct. Orders are there to be obeyed, not questioned. Nonetheless, when this noble worker insulted you, did you really think it was the right thing to hit him with your shovel and throw him in the trench?"

"I did. The blow merely knocked the man out. To argue with him, I reasoned, would be to waste time. I also did it to keep him safe from the flying bullets. An engineer's work is to protect the king's subjects." I sighed. "I dared do nothing for the donkey; I could, of course, have knocked it over as well with a strong blow to the head, but that would have been to put myself in the line of fire. I also could not have been sure it would fit inside the trench, it being very bulky and the trench narrow. My assessment was that the life of an engineer is worth more than that of a donkey, and so I left it to its fate."

Armand and Zeno looked at each other doubtfully. I added: "The donkey appeared indifferent on the matter."

The fourth Point was given to me after a session in the hayloft, one of the best moments in my long career—well, making hay while the sun shines, as they say.

One Sunday afternoon Jeanne and I were in the hayloft after making love, unclothed, and the rain was falling steadily, languidly, without. Jeanne, eyes closed, was dozing. Here was beauty. Her roseate skin, her red locks, reclining on a mattress of straw . . . a vision in the sweet gray half-light of Burgundy. From out of my mound of clothes, I took a folder.

"I have written you some poems," I said, and placed before her a sheaf of papers.

She opened her eyes, and her face lit up. Be a woman noble and high-ranking, or be she stinking peasantry, like my dear vile Waltraud, it is all one; someone says he has written a poem for her, she's automatically over the moon.

She took up the sheets of paper. "And this?" she asked in amusement and surprise.

"A book of poems. Though there is only one that is worth anything, which is the one I completed yesterday and which won me my fourth Point."

"Poems? But these are drawings."

"And?" I said, offended. "The Ducroix brother school me in design, not versifying. But they *are* poems." I drew closer to her. "They're fortress designs. Are they to your liking?"

She didn't dare make a show of her incomprehension, which was nonetheless plain to see. I laid the sheets out on the straw and went on. "My last blueprint is the best. Can you guess which it is? If you look closely, you'll see it's different from the others."

Her eyes skipped between them.

"Give it a proper look!" I said. "You're Vauban's daughter. If you can't understand it, who will?"

She looked at one of the sheets for a few moments. Then put it aside. Another and another. The rain continued to fall. As she was deciding between the drawings, my mind turned to the rain. It struck me that in wet countries, the rain could be used as a weapon against the besieging army . . .

"This one," she said finally. "Yes, this is the one." She'd gotten it right. Her face resembled that of a child who had just learned to read. "This one is different from the others. They look like identical drawings but are not. It has something extra." She looked at me. "What makes it different?"

"In this one," I said, prodding the sheet of paper, "I created a fortress with the thought of you asleep in the middle of the city. And I defended you."

Of the extensive Vauban family, the one who paid the fewest visits to the castle was Jeanne's husband. It is my understanding that theirs was something of an arranged marriage, and the truth is, I did not find his presence unsettling.

It wasn't out of any particular grievance that he kept far from Bazoches. He had simply turned his back on his wife, whom he paid no mind, but not in a hostile or abusive manner. Protocol stated that they had to sit side by side when eating at the great table. He paid considerably more attention to the saltcellar than to his wife (one of his numerous obsessions was a constant fear of running out of salt). When he passed by me, I could almost see the thoughts spilling from his head like sawdust.

Unless his family was supervising him, the man never washed. When he stayed in Paris for extended periods, not under their control, his nails would grow longer than a wolf's. And his very fine clothing was always in tatters. The moment he arrived in Bazoches, he would have to be hurried out of sight and washed and clothed, for if the marquis saw him in that state, he was quite capable of expelling him. But, this much is true, he was extremely happy, perhaps the happiest man I have ever laid eyes upon. His particular mania was the philosopher's stone. He was constantly on the verge of discovering the final piece in the puzzle. And is any man so happy as he who finds himself on the verge of a scientific revolution? Whichever track he was on would inevitably come to naught, and he'd be depressed for several days. But come the third day, he was back to his carefree, lively, and joyous self again, for he had uncovered another secret formula in some dusty tome.

As is so often the way, the cuckold became very friendly with his partner's lover (unfortunately, but what to do?). I do not think he ever knew about Jeanne and me, and if he did know, he cared not a pepper. Much as I tried to avoid him, it was inevitable that sooner or later, he would collar me in some corner of Bazoches.

"My dear Zuviría!" I heard him exclaim one day before he approached and embraced me.

On this occasion he had been at the castle a whole week, an extraordinarily extended stay, bearing in mind the suddenness of his comings and goings. This was due to an old woman, a spirit medium in the town of Bazoches, to whom he was paying daily visits.

"I believe I have finally alighted on the definitive path that will lead us to the philosopher's stone," he went on. "The path was not in this but in the next world! Thanks to that old witch, I am able to converse with superior souls who give me guidance. Yesterday I set off alongside none other than Michel de Nostradame and Charlemagne."

His liking for my company made a certain sense. His family had made up their minds about him already and sent him away whenever they could, while the servants were not at his level. With me, on the other hand, he could hammer on all he liked; as a student, I was somewhere between the two social extremes. For my part, it would have been highly indecorous of me to send a member of the Vauban family off to fry asparagus. So I had to bear his happy tirades, his mental raspberries, on the subject of the philosopher's stone. Looked at with a little leniency, nor was it the heaviest load to bear. My obligations were limited to opening my eyes wide, every now and then letting out a "Can that be?," a *"How* interesting!," or even a "The world will shake with delight!" when my thoughts were: Enough now, fruitcake, I want to go and lie down with your wife.

The true philosopher's stone was Bazoches. Ah, yes, Bazoches, pleasant Bazoches. The best days of my life; the most tender and full of hope. Joyous. And bear in mind that it is a life of ninety-eight years of which I speak, ninety-eight times around the sun. Though, during that time, something somewhat ominous also occurred.

Jeanne and I didn't spend all our time together in secret dalliances. We were on occasion visited by an infantry captain, Don Antoine Bardonenche. I do not remember what the relation was between him and the marquis, but he was free to come and go at Bazoches as he pleased. A young man, supreme with the sword, he was stocky, with a jaw like an anvil and a very candid manner. His ideal was that of the knights errant, though in place of the tragic aspect, Bardonenche had an uproarious laugh. With his perfect manly deportment, he was one of the most handsome men I've ever seen. Charlotte, Jeanne's older sister, was hopelessly in love with him. Sometimes on a Sunday, the four of us, Jeanne and I, Bardonenche and Charlotte, would go for picnics in the meadows surrounding the castle. The two of them would engage in pretend swordfights, armed with sticks, laughing and tumbling innocently around for hours on end. I turned my Bazoches eyes on Bardonenche, to examine him, to ascertain what was hidden beneath that soldier skin of his, at once so boyishly voluptuous. Nothing—there was nothing. All his life was taken up in passion for weaponry and serving Louis XIV of France, whom the laypeople called the Sun King and his enemies called the Beast of Europe or, simply, the Beast.

One day when the marquis was abroad and—what news!—the Ducroix brothers were as well, we two couples made a carnival of the castle. We were still children, in spite of my studies, in spite of Jeanne's marriage, in spite of the infantry captain's uniform worn by Bardonenche. We played blind hen. When the blindfold was put on me, I followed the others without any difficulty. Thanks to my training in the Spherical Room, it was so easy to find them that I hardly needed eyes. I could smell their laughter, hear their smells. But, pretending I couldn't, I let them get away for a little while. Suddenly, my hands were pushing on a hidden door behind a drape. I didn't know why the door might be hidden like that, but with the blindfold on, it felt like less of an aberration to go ahead and enter.

Behind this door was a thin passageway. My hands felt along some wall brackets. Certain curious figures stood on these. I took off the blindfold; before me were reproductions, to scale, of the fortifications of every one of the cities and citadels of Europe.

Dear Lord, I knew what this place was. In Versailles the Beast had a store of designs, in miniature, of all the fortresses on the continent, *toutes en relief*. Should a day come when his generals needed to storm them, they had a replica so that the engineers could plan the best line of attack. Vauban, unbeknownst to the Beast, had built a similar room. Naturally, the marquis wasn't going to show such a secret to a simple engineering cadet like me. Though my loyalty to him impelled me not to, something made me stay.

I looked at the model nearest to hand, a star shape with twelve bastions. It was beautifully made. Out of plaster, small pieces of wood, and porcelain, reproductions of fortresses from all corners of Europe had been constructed. The scales were exact, as were the angles of inclination for each of the bastion walls, the depth of the ditches . . . Rivers, coasts, and marshes were indicated by a lighter or darker blue, depending on how deep they were and their distance from the ramparts. Elevations and gulleys in the land were depicted in brown, lighter or darker depending on the height. Numerical tables in the margins provided complementary information for the technical experts.

I closed my eyes, as though still playing blind hen. The reproductions were of such excellent quality that they could be identified by touch. Ath. Namur. Dunkirk. Lille. Perpignan. Most of them had been erected or rebuilt by Vauban. Besançon. Tournay. And Bourtange, Copertino, too, enemy strongholds spied on by minions of the Beast. Each fortress was star-shaped, and my fingers ran across their outlines, one after another, as if a Milky Way were contained in that magical room. I heard voices. Without, Jeanne and Bardonenche were calling for me. One last *maquette*, I thought, one more before I go back to them.

Eyes shut, then, I ran my fingers over one last series of medieval ramparts and ancient bastions. Everything suggested a venerable place thousands of years in the making. Interesting. More details: It was a port—no ramparts on the sea side. I pulled up. A shudder. I gulped. I knew those outlines.

For the first time in Bazoches, I was touched by a baleful presentiment. For every single thing at Bazoches was dictated by its usefulness, and if these designs were there, it was because one day, perhaps, they could be used to plan an assault. Opening my eyes, I looked upon this last *maquette*. It was Barcelona.

7

Have you ever hated a person the moment you laid eyes on him? Throughout the course of my life, I have had dealings with enough scoundrels, knaves, and lowlifes that if the devil were to gather them all in one maleficent reunion, they would fill the whole of the Mediterranean Ocean. But only one has merited my constant hate: Joris Prosperus van Verboom. See, here, a copy of his official portrait. Lovely-looking lad, wouldn't you say?

Joris Prosperus Van Verboom

When I met him, Verboom must have been a little shy of forty. His coarse demeanor and doggy cheeks put one in mind of a heartless butcher. I do not exaggerate. He had a bigoted sneer on his face, his features packed together as though he had not had his belly purged in years. Whereas the marquis's severe aspect conformed to ideas of order and justice—strict but ultimately just—that of Verboom spoke of his utter hostility to inferiors.

Considering what happened later on, the world would have been a far better place had this man accepted living like what he truly was: a sausage-maker from Antwerp, with no need ever to really leave home. But leave he did, because what defined Verboom above all was that he was both sycophantic and ambitious—it fitted his demeanor perfectly. This was why so many powerful people clamored after him, and he was offered a great many cushy jobs; kings know that the vultures fly high, but never at the height of the eagles.

He'd never learned how to laugh. A trait that was very useful in his dealings with subordinates, because he intimidated them, but catastrophic when it came to women. To see him act the gallant was a pitiful sight, not to say grotesque. His disharmony with the feminine, with the whole sphere of the world not governed by simple obey-and-command, made him timid as a doe. To qualify: He would happily act the clown provided only his love object, and not his rival, were there to see. For there was Verboom, in the middle of the parade ground at Bazoches, trying to seduce my Jeanne with that ugly butcher's mug of his.

I was on my way back from being out in the fields, looking a wreck, arms full of shovels and picks, when I saw them. The Bazoches observation techniques can be turned upon many facets of life, not just the engineering-based. I was a Four Points by then and needed only a look, a half-look, to surmise what this individual was after. Or, better put, whom.

Years earlier Verboom, the Antwerp butcher, had served under Vauban at a couple of sieges. This justified what was ostensibly a courtesy visit. Good excuse to strut about in his royal engineer uniform—ha! He was after bigger game. Jeanne was beautiful and rich, Vauban's daughter, and married to a man who was close to being locked up in the attic of some merciful institution. As I approached, that sausage seller was asking after Vauban. When Jeanne said he was not at Bazoches, he said: "A shame—I changed my route in order to come and pay my respects."

Spurious liar! All of France knew that Vauban was in Paris at that moment, conferencing with the ministers of the monstrous Sun King. Verboom had come to Bazoches precisely because the marquis was *not* at home—all the more leeway to woo Jeanne.

I came and stood right up close to the pair, staring at Verboom with all the brazenness of a madman. He was surprised at such impertinence from a mud-spattered youngster, but being there on a visit, and in front of a lady, he preferred to pay the lout no mind. Jeanne straightaway realized what this might have led to.

"Martí, go and get cleaned up," she said. And then asked Verboom if he would like a light meal.

I carried on looking at him unblinkingly. And then said: "Don't give him a thing—he will never be satisfied."

In my defense, it was almost the Ducroix brothers speaking through me. Excepting Jeanne and brief talks with the servants, I spent my days with them alone and had caught their habit of thinking aloud. As the

Ducroix brothers never tired of saying: "Children do not speak because they know how to think; they know how to think because they speak." A person trained in keeping a constant grip on reality has no fear of speaking frankly. But high society, I forgot, is governed by falsity and censure.

Verboom's face became inflamed, and by this I mean a physical phenomenon both real and remarkable. Ire affects some people in such a way that their facial muscles dilate outrageously. The thick meaty layers of Verboom's face blew up like red bubbles. I should have been afraid. Instead, I had to make efforts to hold myself back.

Jeanne could see we were teetering on the edge of a disaster. "Martí!"

I had the pick and shovel over my right shoulder, and with my dirty sleeves falling back over my elbow, it meant my bare forearm was exposed. Verboom counted the four Points, and his incredulity made his fury double. He grabbed my wrist in one of his thick hands, brought it closer to his face, and said: "There must be some mistake."

The pick and shovel fell to the floor, wood and iron reverberating as they struck against the stone. I, in turn, whipped around and with my left hand pushed back his right cuff. Verboom had only three Points. I clucked mockingly. "In your case, surely not."

"How dare you lay hands on me, dungheap gardener!" he cried. "Let go!"

"More than happy to. When you let go of me."

Pride meant he could not desist. He wanted to humble me, not let me go. He had a boulderlike strength, that of men born to inhabit naturally thickset frames. My muscles were worked, catlike, not an ounce of fat. In the most absurd manner, we found ourselves locked in a body press reminiscent of Turkish wrestling. Or perhaps not so absurd, for in truth men come to blows far more often over women than over questions of money, glory, or anything else.

It must be the time when I've come physically closest to the Antwerp butcher. Our noses were as good as touching. That close up, his coarse features clearly delineated his avaricious gluttony. The deep, dilated pores, and his dense sweat, like the muck a snail leaves in its wake.

Engaging in a fight with a man like Verboom is like scaling a mountain: You think the summit will never be reached, the ascent is endless. About to give in, you push on. Until, suddenly, there you are, setting foot on the peak.

Before caving in, Verboom let out a muffled cry. He knelt down on one knee and scanned my face in horror. I was about to lay my sapper boots across that pig's head of his when a horde of his menservants pulled me away from him. Verboom was slack-jawed, humiliated. Jeanne tried to patch the thing up as best she could. She presented her excuses, swearing that I was nothing to her but an overly protective guardian. And a little unhinged, she had to add, because even being held back by four men, I continued to shout and struggle.

"Martí! Beg pardon of Sir Joris van Verboom. Now!"

Jeanne's demand prompted the servants to loose their hold on me a little, and I took the chance to launch myself at him again. There was somewhat less swagger to Verboom on this occasion. He turned to run but, unfortunately, slipped and fell flat on the road. I grabbed him by an ankle and dragged him along as the servants tried to hold me back by the legs. Before they carried me away from there, I was able to sink my teeth into his left buttock. You should have heard him shriek.

Youthful impetuousness is, in part, formed by the inability to see the consequences of one's actions. But if you are a student kept according to the grace of the lord of Bazoches, under his guardianship and in his pay, when you shred the pantaloons of a houseguest with your teeth, well, my boy, it makes sense that the master of the house will want to have words.

As if this were not enough, my brawl with Verboom had been badly timed. Vauban's meetings with Louis XIV's ministers had made it clear to him that he had been ostracized. It was purely a matter of form that they had invited him; every one of his suggestions—as to matters of both war and peace—had been rejected out of hand. He returned to Bazoches in a dog of a mood, and the first piece of news he heard was that his reputation as a host had been dented.

Darkly, the Ducroix brothers said to me: "Martí, the marquis wants to see you."

Jeanne had gone before me. In his absence, the marquis left her to see to the running of the castle, and she was responsible for whatever went on. When I went in, they were in the midst of trading insults. I caught Jeanne saying: "But you yourself have stated a thousand times the low opinion you have of Verboom."

"We're not talking about him!" shouted the marquis. "He had crossed my threshold, he should have been provided for! And instead of that, we attack him, we take bites out of him!" Seeing me, he exclaimed, "Ah, here's the brute!"

He marched over to me. For a moment I thought he was going to give me a slap. "What excuse can that deranged mind of yours offer?" he rebuked. "Answer! What led you to abuse a guest in my home?"

"He was a base man," I answered.

The truth is sufficiently powerful that it can shock the most eminent of men. The marquis lowered his voice, though not by much.

"And have you not been taught that certain buffers exist between goodness and evil, namely manners? You left the pantaloons of a royal engineer in tatters!"

I wanted to say something, but he cut me off, becoming extremely vexed again."Silence! I never want to lay eyes on you again! *Jamais!*" he roared. "You will go to your quarters and stay there until tomorrow, when the diligence carriage arrives. You will then travel on it to your home or to wherever you please. In any case, very far from Bazoches. Now, out of my sight!"

Up in my room, I head-butted the wall. Home! Without a qualification, with no credentials. My father would kill me. Worse, at this point I knew how lucky I'd been. Life had gifted me something no amount of money could buy: being the student, the sole student, of the greatest genius of siege warfare ever to walk the earth. At the same time, I realized how far I was from having completed my studies; I had not received even half of what Bazoches had to offer. And the hardest thing to bear was the thought of being separated from Jeanne.

I had behaved like an idiot, a downright idiot. When it came to it, my mistake had been that of a poor student. If I had been attentive—if, as the Ducroix brothers had taught me, passion had not blinded me—I would have seen that Jeanne could never fall for a man like Verboom. But no, the Zuviría in me had gone and ruined everything.

The point being that, from that day on, I held Verboom in enmity until the end of his days. Later on, the Antwerp butcher would see me shackled, tortured, exiled, and worse things. But never did he cause me such harm as on that first occasion. My enmity for him was boundless, flawless, pure as crystal. A mutual enmity, it goes without saying, and one that lasted until that swine of all swines got the end he deserved. Lamentably, that episode lies outside my present account, for when it comes to that man's demise, I relish the tale. He suffered greatly; after that, arriving in hell must have seemed like a Turkish bath for him.

Well, be a good girl and I'll tell you later, my dear vile Waltraud—in one gap or another between chapters. But if your horror provokes you to vomit, at least turn your fat head away from me before you do it! I have heard an old saying from your hometown Vienna, which runs more or less: "Next to a good friend, the best thing one can have in this life is a good enemy!" Pah! If enemies they truly are, there is no such thing as a good one; there are only living enemies and dead, and while they live, they are a constant trouble.

Sponge cake—I shall have sponge cake. Bring it to me.

Thankfully, the angels never sleep. While I was shut in my room, the twins showed Vauban the plans for a project to fortify Arras. They handed him the prints and made comments while the marquis examined them carefully, leaning close to the paper, as his sight was failing. He used a sort of magnifying lens with no handle, a large piece of concave glass girded with iron and held up on three small wheels. It moved around on the paper in search of small errors. In such moments he resembled a simple jeweler.

Arras was a project very close to the *maréchal*'s heart. For one reason or another, he'd had to defer it constantly, but nonetheless ordered the Ducroix brothers to make plans for the most complete, most powerful, and best-equipped fortress imaginable. When Vauban was studying plans, he never spoke. There could be ten, fifteen, even twenty experts around him, and they could be making continuous remarks as to his marvelous projects. But as I say, Vauban was very sparing in his comments. Only his breathing would be heard, for, as with many men who breathe heavily when deep in thought, he turned his nose up at the general chatter.

At any event, those who knew him could guess his opinion by the sounds escaping from him. Silence was a bad sign, very bad. On the other hand, when an idea excited him, he let out the strangest guttural noises; to those not of his circle, these seemed to indicate annoyance, though it was quite the reverse.

As the Ducroix brothers continued to hand plans to him, the guttural grunts and groans grew even louder. At one point, his lens stopped over a bastion. "*Et ça?*" he asked, not looking up. "What are these three rises on each of the corners supposed to mean?"

"Turrets, *monsieur*," they said. "Fortified turrets."

"I don't understand."

"The mortar is the bastion's prime enemy," said Zeno. "The idea is to combat the enemy artillery by using the same weapons: Destroy their mortars using mortars of our own. With the advantage that the mortars inside the bastion will have a solid stone casing protecting them. The enemy must install theirs in exposed positions, making themselves vulnerable to cannonade. Meanwhile, those inside the stronghold, given their iron carapace, will go unharmed."

Vauban's guttural sounds grew louder.

"As you can see, the turrets have only a small opening near the top, in the shape of a half-moon. But the base will have a pinion on which it can turn, a platform allowing one hundred and eighty degrees' turning range; with three mortars up there, any object outside will be covered."

Not a man given to praise, on this occasion, through clenched teeth, Vauban had to acknowledge the Ducroix brothers' good work. Armand then peered close to the final plan, turned stiff, and screeched at his brother: "*Mais tu es idiot!* What is this you've brought to the marquis's table?"

Vauban did not know what was meant until Zeno humbly excused himself. "A thousand apologies, Marquis. I've committed a blunder: These prints are no more than exercise pieces by that execrable engineering cadet, Martí Zuviría."

They moved swiftly on as though nothing had happened, leaving Vauban nonplussed but also angry, for he was sufficiently clever to realize that all this had been a ruse to make him change his mind about me.

That same night, Jeanne tackled him during dessert. She sent the servants out, and even her sister, Charlotte, so that it was just the two of them at far ends of the long table.

"I know what it is you seek!" cried Vauban, pointing a fork in her direction. "And the answer is no! I am a marshal of the realm, I have had the unhappy task of deciding the fate of the lives of many thousands of men. And now, when I send an uncouth youngster back to his home, I find everyone around conspiring against me. Not even on campaigns among generals have I found such opposition!"

"I would never oppose what my father decides on such a trivial issue," said Jeanne. "There was something else I wanted to raise with you."

"I don't believe you. You're bluffing, the lot of you! I'll have you know I'd be within my rights sending him to a galley ship, should that be pleasing to me. How can I be expected to waste my time on an individual who sees fit to bite my guests on their behinds?" He finally stopped pointing the fork. "I never should have admitted him!"

"And I say," Jeanne went on, unruffled, "that there is another issue I wish to raise with you." Getting up from her seat, in all her gracefulness, she went over and sat upon the marquis's knee. "Papa," she continued, putting her arms about his neck, "it's a good idea."

"What are you talking about?"

"Me marrying Prosperus van Verboom."

"What the— . . . "

Jeanne put a finger to his lips and, with her best smile, said: "He seeks my hand, and you know it. It is hardly the first time he's happened by Bazoches. Shall I present his case to you?" She sighed. "My marriage is a farce. We weren't unhappy to begin with, but now he's lost his mind. This affliction will at least allow me to request an annulment of matrimony. With your contacts at the Vatican, it will be given within a year. Oh, Papa! Think of the opportunity. Verboom is one of the most gifted engineers around. Marry him and I will become a lady at court! I'll be the luckiest woman in the world!"

Placing his hands on her hips, Vauban lifted his daughter from him. Then he leaped from his chair as though a demon had poked him with a trident. He began pacing up and down the dining hall, one hand on his back, the other gesticulating wildly. "Verboom's soul is blacker than a dog's! Hear me? The disease of power, money, and vainglory consumes him. Of course he desires the hand of a Vauban daughter! The day after I die, he'll make off with my name, our home, our fortune, all my credit and glory. And my own daughter! That reprobate, that unprincipled mercenary, giving his life in service of all the devils!"

Jeanne showed her indignation, her chin held high, her eyes squinted and choleric. "In service of devils, you say?"

"Aye, I do!"

"A reprobate mercenary, a traitor to any decent cause . . . "

"Exactly! You have understood exactly."

"A man who uses women like sacks of dung and, when he's emptied them, throws them away at any bend in the road."

Vauban applauded sourly. "Very good. I think you take my meaning."

"A creature with a soul blacker than a dog's, if dogs had souls."

"Bravo!" exclaimed the marquis, clapping twice more, sarcastically, wearily.

Jeanne took a breath and, in a neutral tone, declared: "He holds you in the utmost esteem."

"That carbuncle's esteem matters nothing to me! I have only ever shown him a gentleman's customary courtesy. Never have I had a shred of confidence in him, for he does not merit it and never shall have it."

Jeanne cut short the marquis's words like a scythe. "I mean Martí."

The marquis, the marshal, the man, said nothing more. He straightaway saw the trap he, of his own accord, had fallen into.

"He adores you, and I can assure you, his reverence has nothing to do with the titles you hold but, rather, the things you have built." She drew closer to her father, her chin held still higher, and with great calm added: "And you are going to do away with him for a bite on the behind to a black-souled reprobate."

She turned on her heel and left the dining room.

Though the Ducroix twins would later reveal all of this to me, at the time it happened, I was sobbing, cursing, and pounding on the walls of my room, so I could have had no notion of what was going on three floors below. I did not sleep at all that night.

Logically, then, it was with spirits sagging that I came downstairs the next morning. I had packed my bags, not much of a job, for I owned next to nothing. Indeed, the coach stood waiting out on the parade ground. Though I forget which, either Armand or Zeno said to me: "Before you go, the marquis wishes to speak with you."

Vauban ignored me when I came into his study. He had a book before him and was murmuring as though he had never progressed beyond reading out loud. The light of day came from the far side of him, through windows that covered almost the entire length of the wall. Not an elaborate tactic but effective: The light would dazzle the visitor, making him feel immediately inferior in the face of this august, luminous presence.

He looked up and, in a peevish voice, said: "Sit!"

I obeyed, naturally.

"Well? What plans have you made for the future?"

"Your Excellence, I am yet to make any," was all I could think to say.

"Ah, but," he said tartly, which surprised me, "did you ever even have any?"

His tone and my agonizing situation impelled me to blurt out: "I did, Your Excellence, yes! In recent times I have hoped to become an engineer, with all my heart. Though I suppose *monsieur* wasn't aware."

"Impertinent child!" he bellowed. "Or are the words you have just spoken not the very definition of impertinence? Answer!"

I broke down crying. I was only fifteen years old! There before me was Sébastien Le Prestre de Vauban, marquis of Vauban, marshal of the realm, and goodness knows what else. A living myth, the man who had stormed sixty-eight fortresses, the great fortifier. All these things. And I was nothing but a boy, somewhere along the road toward becoming a man.

"You're crying!" said Vauban.

I got to my feet.

"Since you have been kind enough to receive me, Your Excellence, in spite of my subordination, may I make one final appeal?"

He said nothing. I took his silence as a license to continue.

"Allow me to bid farewell to Jeanne."

He took an eternity to answer. I had no notion what to do, pinned to the floor like some scarecrow.

"You and I are going to agree on something," he said at last. "Given that you would be returning home in disgrace, I have an alternate proposal: that you continue your engineering studies in the Royal Academy at Dijon. On my recommendation, naturally. In exchange, I ask only that you never come anywhere near Bazoches or my home again, much less my daughter. You will give the place a berth of thirty miles. Your studies, until they are completed, and all your academic costs will be paid by me. You will want for nothing. Accept."

"May I see Jeanne? It will only take a few minutes."

He got up from the table like a fury. "And you never even bothered to hide the fact you are Catalan, and from the south! I know your kind very well, I worked along that frontier for over a decade, fortifying places against the zealous, rebellious natives. As a matter of fact, I believe I'm more than entitled to ask you a vital question: In your heart, which king do you owe allegiance to? The king of Spain or the king of France?"

"*Monsieur*," I said, "until two days ago, I served only the kingdom of engineering."

"If you would seek to flatter me, know that I am as immune to obsequiousness as I am to wine. We moderate men never get indigestion."

I did not know what reply to make, if indeed the marquis was expecting one. This was all beside the point. It would cost me nothing to persist: "Does it seem so unusual and dangerous to you, sir, that I bid her farewell?"

"Bid me farewell," he insisted, a rare intrigue showing on his face, "and as well as a place at Dijon, and your maintenance, you will receive the sum of one thousand francs—to spend as you see fit."

My eyes brimmed once more with tears, but before my composure fled me entirely, I managed to say: "*Je l'aime.*"

Something inside the marquis gave way. He had provoked me, I realize, in order to find out if I was different from Verboom. That Antwerp butcher had always been an ambitious reptile, and to him, marriage was a means to an end. The person before him now was renouncing everything for the sake of a farewell.

If all was lost, I wanted to see Jeanne one last time. Even if I had to push the marquis himself aside to get to her. But then he softened and, in a voice both calm and resigned, said: "Sit back down, you fool."

He dandled a small bronze figure in his hands for a few seconds. He turned it over in his fingers. It was a twenty-four-point star, a small-scale version of the fortifications he'd built at Neuf-Brisach.

He looked out the window over the Bazoches courtyard, the fields beyond. Without turning to face me, he said: "However, nothing changes the fact that you bit Verboom."

"Yes, sir."

"On the buttocks."

"The left buttock."

"I have received word from him: Your canines went sufficiently deep that he is still not fit to ride a horse."

"I am very sorry."

"You are a liar."

"I mean, *monsieur*, for the trouble I caused you and all of Bazoches."

Another long pause before he spoke again. "Tell me: Do you take me for a dolt?"

"No!" I cried, jumping to my feet. "Sir, no!"

"Often," he continued, as though not hearing me, "I have seen you come to dinner with your back covered in straw. The same straw that happens to also be stuck to the back of Jeanne's dress."

I thought he was about to come down hard on me, but instead, what followed was a sigh.

"Marriage . . . yes . . . that citadel which all without wish to enter, and all within wish to get out from." He looked me in the eye. "But you ought to know, Cadet Zuviría, that of all the fortresses created by man, matrimony is the most impregnable. Do you take my meaning?"

"Can I see her?"

"What you shall do is go to the classroom and apply yourself to a double lesson of strategy. As shown by recent events, tactics are a considerable weak point: If you attack from behind, take note, you ought always to go for the windpipe, not the rump."

8

Clearly, the Ducroix brothers were extraordinary teachers, and Vauban was one of a kind. In the early hours of the day following my reprieve, he took me by the elbow, and the two of us went for a walk in the castle grounds.

He walked with a cane, but it did nothing to alter his haughtiness. Every now and then he stopped before an apple tree, picked an apple with his free hand, and took two or three bites before throwing it to one side. (Nothing wrong with that—the trees were his property.) More often than that, he stopped in order to cough, spit, and then dry his mouth on one of the large white gold-trimmed handkerchiefs he kept in his tunic pockets.

"Up until now, you have been learning about fortifying cities," he said. "And you have not done badly, according to the Ducroix brothers. From now on, you will apply yourself to becoming an expert in the art of laying siege to them."

"But *monsieur*," I said, smiling, "if I've learned anything, it's that, because of your very own fortification methods, well-designed defenses are altogether impossible to break through."

Stopping, he looked at me and smiled indulgently.

I have had the good fortune—undeserved—of meeting a good number of the geniuses of my age—such as in the arts, Mozart (poor boy, I twice destroyed him at billiards), in terms of moral rectitude, Washington (drier than salt cod), and above all, Rousseau. Not Voltaire! Not that upstart, that despicable pipsqueak. Even Franklin and Danton ought to be considered universal geniuses. But, looked at properly, each of these distinguished himself for contributing a single idea to the human race, only one. Vauban had the immense merit of making two. First, he designed the perfect system for immuring cities. Following that, exceeding or, even, in a sense, nullifying his own work, a method for storming them.

I had my folder under my arm and Vauban drummed his fingers impatiently. "A design of yours. Come, let's be seeing it!"

I held the plan up before him, and he considered it for a few moments. . . . "*Ggnnnnn* . . . Yes, fourteen . . . fifteen days. Fifteen, at the most."

"Pardon?"

He looked up at me. "It would withstand a siege of fifteen days. Not one more."

"But Your Excellence," I protested, laughing a little, "that's impossible."

Holding his forefinger in front of my nose, he said: "Never use that word in my presence." Then he asked me, *me,* the person who had designed the project, how I would take over that fabulous amalgamation of bastions, moons, half-moons, and superimposed buttresses.

I shook my head. "I really don't know, *monsieur,*" I said. "The only thing I can think of would be to concentrate a portentous amount of artillery, fifty wide-bore pieces, at a single point, and carry out a bombardment for months. But what king could afford the luxury of so much artillery? And that's without taking into account the logistical nightmare of transport and maintenance, or the astronomical costs for that amount of gunpowder and ammunition, and so forth."

That it was just the two of us permitted an act of intimacy he carried out only when he was on his own or with Jeanne: He took off his wig. I already knew from Jeanne that he'd lost his hair very early in his youth, but I was so accustomed to those artificial curls that I found it difficult to contain my surprise at seeing a man before me balder than a toad.

"Logistics? Astronomical costs?" He sighed and then added, "All you need are picks and shovels. And decent men."

And so it proved: Vauban's siege method was based on something as simple and straightforward as pick and shovel.

Once the surrounding fence had been established, the engineers would decide on the point of attack. The works would begin at a prudent distance, out of range of the defenders' weapons. This act was called, altogether appropriately, "opening the trench," and it marked the beginning of the construction of the Attack Trench.

Like jigsaw pieces beginning to slot into place, the many backbreaking sessions with the Ducroix brothers began to make sense. Because Vauban's method consisted of nothing more than a sapping job, perfectly coordinated. See here, in all its splendor, his siege *méthode.*

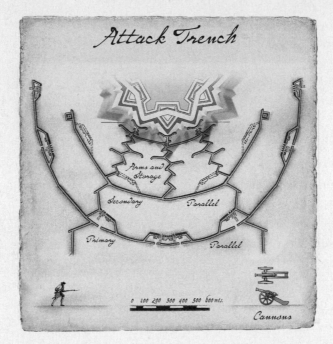

Attack Trench

Arms and Storage

Secondary

Parallel

Primary

Parallel

0 100 200 300 400 500 600 mts.

Cannons

The aim was to make an immense excavation, the so-called Attack Trench, that would lead to the bastions. To keep the sappers from being fired on by the enemy, the trench had to be deep enough to hide them. And to avoid enfilade fire, it had to run parallel to the ramparts. The initial trenches were therefore named "parallels." Three parallels, connected by linking culverts in zigzag, would be enough to reach the ramparts. The work would assume a very distinctive appearance. To take on a perfectly designed fortress, the perfect trench.

Never have such immortal works been so ephemeral. A large trench could be titanic in size and, once finished, would simply disappear, swallowed up by not being used. In a number of months, rain, mud, and disuse would see it buried in the mud, forgotten. Racine himself was once sent as a reporter to one of Vauban's sieges. "There are more corners in one of our great Attack Trenches," he wrote admiringly, "than in all of Paris." And at the very instant the city conceded defeat, the life of the trench was at an end.

Logically enough, an Attack Trench required impeccable command of each of the sciences imparted to me in Bazoches. All in all, it would mean thousands of men working together in a coordinated way.

The trench had to be wide enough for an entire army to be able to move around inside, and that meant the removal of millions of square feet of earth, with pinpoint accuracy and orderliness. The floor and walls were lined with pieces of wood to prevent landslides and flooding. A siege meant the felling of an entire forest! Munitions stores were located in the second line of trenches. Large enclosed spaces would be dug out in certain places with the sole aim of creating refuges for the cannons and mortars whose task it was to punish the point of attack and the defenders' cannons. And when the moment came, the third parallel would become the launch point for the assault.

Imagine a trench advancing not along the exact route laid out for it but going off on a tangent of a few degrees. What would happen in such a case? Nothing serious, if we forget about the sappers *not* digging in parallel to the ramparts, who would be exposed; that is, from the fortress, the vanguard sappers could be seen, and they would find themselves riddled by enemy fire.

Not the ideal situation, wouldn't you say? I've been on one side or the other dozens of times, and if there is a competent officer in the bastion, the most minor error in the progress of the works won't go unpunished. Usually, a sniper will spill the brains of the poor dupe digging away in the open. But as I say, an attentive, observant officer, efficient and highly intelligent (like yours truly), would leave it a day before doing anything, holding fire as the badly dug trench advanced so ill-advisedly, leaving more and more of the men exposed in the open furrow.

The vanguard sappers might have noticed the parallel trench going off track, no longer parallel but perpendicular. And from the nearest bastion, one of the entire trench lines, and all these muddy little ants carrying wicker baskets of earth, comes into full sight. But the engineer on duty, putting his feet up in his rearguard cabin, ignores the warning, refuses to concede he's done anything wrong. Blueprints are blueprints, and after all, though the French have recently chopped off their king's head, the society in which we live is still governed by class. Am I wrong?

Except for those educated by a good Maganon, engineers were spoiled, arrogant brats from some important family, severely indisposed to listening to their inferiors. Well, bear in mind that *I* received my education from the best of the best, and therefore, I naturally consider the vast majority of military engineers for what they are: a band of savages so inept they couldn't find their own rump if they used both hands.

Up on our bastion, looking through the telescope and seeing the peons working with pick and shovel on a trench that has strayed off track, the moment has come to act. Rifle fire? Well, of course not. While the enemy worsens his error, you transfer three wide-bore cannons into position on the bastion wall.

Into one of these, pack a five-kilo ball; into the other two, grapeshot. And adjust the range. First land one fifteen feet to the left of the furrow, then another the same distance to the right. Everything's ready—though the sappers have no idea. First because they're keeping their heads down behind the brushwood breastwork; second because, in the midst of the general harassment, the rifle fire from both sides, the continual exchange of rockets and grenades, the cries of the wounded and the screen of smoke cloaking no-man's-land, it would never occur to the poor idiots that the two explosions have anything to do with them. And so, when a lot of people are gathered there, on the perpendicular that never should have been, you give the order for all three cannons to fire at once.

Ten sappers explode into ten thousand pieces. The trench is furrowed, and the impact is so powerful that their remains won't embed into the far wall but will be blasted back the length and breadth of the trench. The shreds of bone, meat, and viscera will likely spread out over an area of more than five hundred feet.

Much is gained from this. Imagine now the morale of the survivors when the nincompoop engineer sitting in his little cabin says, "Dear Lord, what poor luck," before ordering them to get back to it—all of a sudden they're three days behind schedule. Desertions may follow, some might even rebel; in any case, the siege is delayed. And when you are the defender, you have one objective: to play for time.

Meanwhile, the unfortunate sappers have to go back to their work, advancing on all fours. And the lovely spectacle accompanying them is that of walls coated with pieces of their friends, fragments of cranium, ribs, and femurs split like pieces of cane. Human intestines, by the way, have a tendency to stick to the wooden uprights in a trench like boiled noodles to a wall . . .

You, stop your whinging and *write*! Did you not say you liked the epic tone, all that rot? Well, here's epic for you.

But the example I have just given is hardly worthy of Vauban's genius. If his method were rigorously followed, the defenders would never be presented with such opportunities. He never made a single mistake. Under his command, the parallels advanced implacably, at great speed, as though an army of termites were doing the work. Within a week, two at a stretch, he could be within sixty feet of any rampart. And at that distance, with the trench so close, the besieger had the upper hand.

They could then tunnel under the bastion and, once underneath, pack the tunnel with an enormous explosive charge. *Boom!* The bastion would come down with the defenders inside; the rubble would plug the hole beneath and create a mound for the attacking force to scale. The defenders could always come back with countermines, but with the enemy a mere sixty feet away, who could be sure they had not opened two, three, or even four different underground galleries? In any case, the other option, and the commonest conclusion to a siege, was a grenadier attack.

Grenadiers! My God, the very word brings shivers. The French had the best grenadiers of all; they were, very simply, killing machines.

For the French grenadiers, sixty feet was nothing. They were select men, chosen for being the strongest and, more than anything, the tallest men in the realm. In certain armies, instead of the normal tricorn hat, they wore their traditional brimless cap. Their uniform was spotless white. Trench warfare converts soldiers into an army of ragdolls, but they never let the slightest speck onto that Bourbon white.

And now consider the effect of this: Each side has become a band of scarecrows, faces black with smoke and soot, all military neatness gone. And you, at the top of the bastion, your hands covered in sores from all the carrying and firing, fed up with pissing down the cannon chamber to cool it, half-starved to death because all you've been brought to eat is rancid cabbage soup, your eyes red from tiredness and the gunpowder, half deaf from the explosions, you suddenly see a hundred giants dressed in brilliant white emerging shoulder to shoulder, with aston-

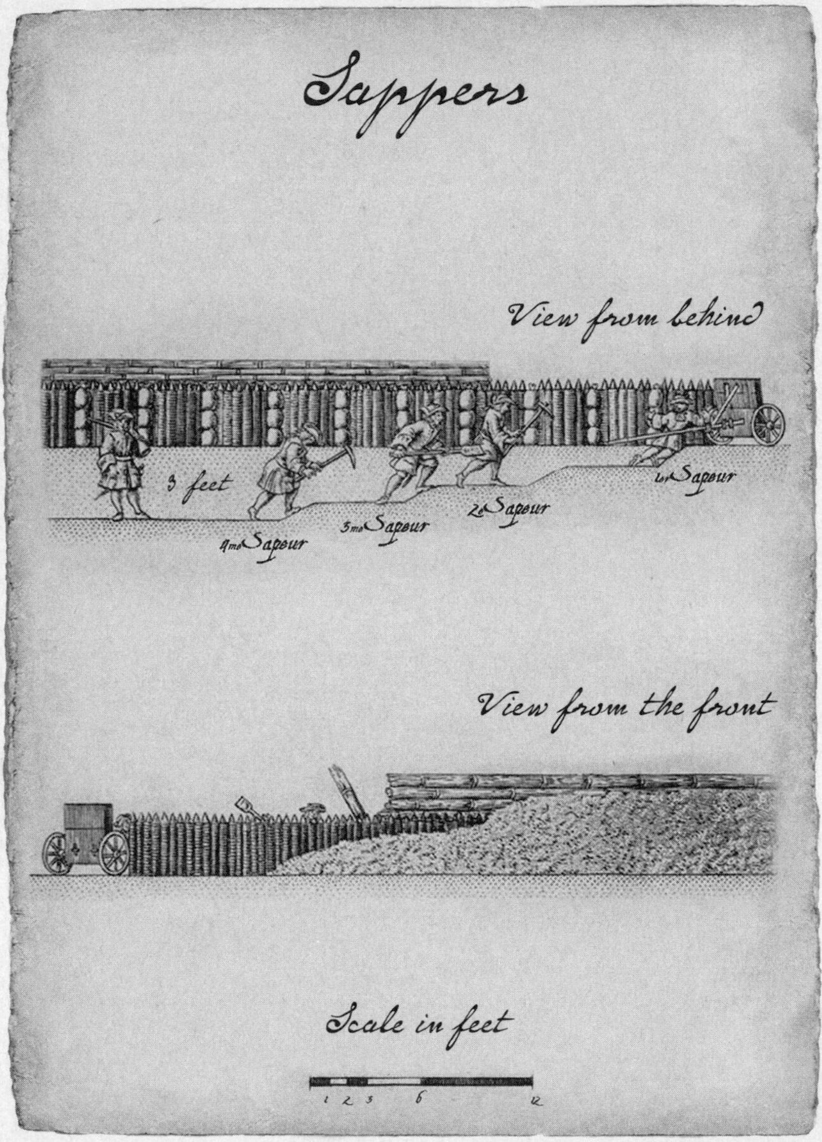

Sappers

View from behind

3 feet

4me Sapeur

3me Sapeur

2e Sapeur

1er Sapeur

View from the front

Scale in feet

1 2 3   6   12

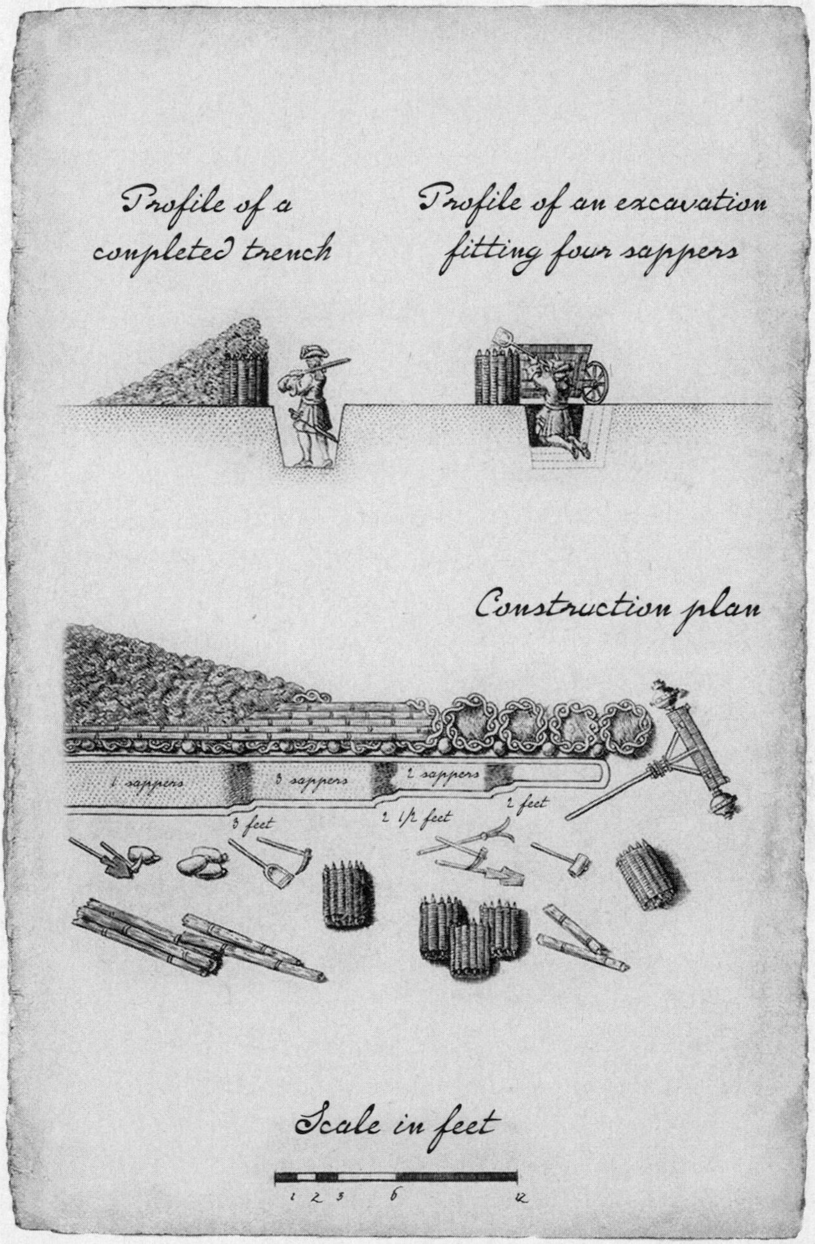

Profile of a
completed trench

Profile of an excavation
fitting four sappers

Construction plan

1 sappers   3 sappers   2 sappers

3 feet   2 1/2 feet   2 feet

Scale in feet

1 2 3   6   12

ishing aplomb, from the enemy trench. It's conceivable that, for all your officer's bawling, you, rather than pulling the trigger, will let your jaw drop. For half a minute, at least—the half a minute it takes the grenadiers to line up at the edge of the trench.

One or two, or five or six, or even twenty or thirty, will naturally go down under the concentrated, desperate fire turned on them by the soldiers in the bastion. But these, *these* stay as still as statues and react only to the voice of their *capitaine*. He gives the orders:

One: *Attention!* And they stand up even taller, for all that the bullets whistle by. *Zip, zip!*

Two: *Grenade!* They put their hands to the grenades in their pouches —a kind of iron and bronze ball, incredibly heavy in relation to its size, and with a short fuse.

Three: *Au feu!* They light the fuse and hold the grenade behind their head, ready to throw.

A terrifying sight—particularly when viewed from the summit of a half-destroyed bastion. All those flickering sparks, suspended in the air, apparently so harmless . . . One may be tempted to stand watching, like the rabbit with the serpent, to see what happens. But if you find yourself at such a point, believe me: Forget Honor, forget King and Country, all such nonsense, and run, run for all you're worth!

Fourth and final order: *Lancez!* A hundred or more black balls curving through the air toward you, landing directly upon the defenders' heads.

Next, a pretty carnival of screams and flying human limbs. Then a bayonet charge, sweeping aside the wounded and any crying out for mercy. Or do you imagine those who have been providing the others with targets to practice on will feel all at once forgiving? Just because the others raise their little hands? No. They will bayonet their livers, they will split them head to behind and move onto the next. As the first to enter a now defenseless city, one that had the chance to surrender and obstinately refused, they are well within their rights to ransack houses, churches, and storerooms, slit civilians' throats, and amuse themselves with the womenfolk.

The problem any defensive perimeter faces is that a chain of fortifications is only as strong as its weakest link. An assailant force need not take the rampart's whole perimeter, just a toehold on a single bastion, just one. Control one bastion, and the city will be yours for the taking. The city has fallen. This is why, once the attack reaches the third parallel, the defenders usually concede. A trumpet will sound, asking to discuss the terms of the surrender. With a rampart destroyed and the enemy trench a few paces away, any sensible garrison opts to negotiate an honorable way out. I have seen surrenders that were majestic in the way they were enacted.

A trumpet from the besieged calls for a truce. The firing dies down. The tumult of war becomes expectant silence. A few minutes later, the garrison commander steps forward in his best regalia, sword in belt, at the center of the breach—which the cannons have made look altogether like a stage in a theater. He is not at risk; to shoot him now would be too dishonorable. The two armies look at him: the besieger in the trenches and those remaining on the fortifications. Should he be a man with a talent for declamations, he will stand proud and tall before proclaiming with a dignified wave of the hand, *"Monsieur l'ennemi! Parlons."*

And they agree terms.

It is not a military manual I'm writing here, so I won't go into the technical aspects (which I had coming out of my ears in Bazoches), measures, countermeasures, appeals, stratagems, and all manner of imponderables that might arise during a siege. But in a nutshell, these were the rules of the game.

Vauban was not the only one to set out a general method for besieging. When he was young, his great rival was Menno van Coehoorn, a Dutchman with a face more elongated than a cucumber.

Vauban and Coehoorn settled their disputes many years before Longlegs Zuvi was even born. In fact, it was already history when I came to Bazoches, with both men nearing the ends of their lives. But two distinct schools of thought came to be named after them, two entirely opposed ways of conceiving a military siege.

The system Coehoorn devised, it might be said, was the obverse of Vauban's. For Vauban, storming a fortified place was a rational undertaking, informed by almost all the disciplines with which humankind has shaped the world. For Coehoorn, it was a stunning act of extreme violence.

Coehoorn is said to have compared the siege to removing a molar—painful but quickly over, the quicker, the better. According to the Dutchman, the besieger ought to concentrate on the weakest, or least well defended, point in the fortifications. Once this had been identified, hurl everything at it and break through it in one savage on-slaught. At night, if possible, using the element of surprise, exploiting any weakness the besieged side has failed to take into account. Nothing else mattered.

Theorists across Europe divided into two camps, and impassioned arguments ensued: the supporters of the attack à la Vauban and those who preferred it à la Coehoorn. Needless to say, I was on Vauban's side; unavoidably, intellectually, we become our teachers' children. And my view has always been that, at root, there isn't much to take from the Coehoorn school. The idea that what the enemy needs is a good cosh to the head—any thug could come up with that. Hard-line Coehoor-nians would come back with the argument that war is simple, radically simple. In reply, I would say this is to negate two thousand years of de-velopments in the science of war. A humanist edifice was constructed upon Vauban's foundations; Coehoorn merely encouraged rashness.

The Coehoornians had another, more scientific argument, which therefore held more weight. They claimed, with reason but unreason-ably, that Vauban's method always drew things out. "Agreed," they would say, "a city besieged according to Vauban's model will inevitably fall within ten, twenty, or thirty days. But in that time a great many things could happen: Epidemics might break out within the besieger's enclosed camp; reinforcements might arrive; the adversary might lay siege to one of our cities, turning it into an exchange of kingdoms, or any other diplomatic imponderable obliging us to suspend the siege."

Coehoorn's detractors, in turn, pointed to the risks involved in such a premature thrust. If successful, it would indeed see an end to the siege before it had formally become that. But if it failed? You ended up with a carpet of dead bodies, the city intact, and the defenders' morale sky-high.

Clearly, the debate turned on certain irreconcilable principles, end-less fodder for the dispute. Vaubanians and Coehoornians, two schools that would never see eye to eye. Once a Maganon was a Coehoornian, he would always be one, and vice versa. The debate never ended. The problem being that these rational theories were also at cross-purposes with individuals' self-interest.

Your young and ambitious general, for instance, would tend to be a Coehoornian. What did it matter to him to sacrifice five hundred, a thousand, or two thousand lives in a reckless attack? Coehoornians sought glory, and after all, they wouldn't be the ones having to cross those labyrinths of stone, those unforgiving ditches and steep scarpment walls. By contrast, and though they were little educated in the matter, footsoldiers were outright Vaubanians. Out of self-interest! The thing is that Vauban was no military man. He never was. The engineer in him always governed the soldier. At the first siege he was in charge of, he addressed not his generals but the rank and file: "Sweat for me, and I will save you having to bleed." Sweat instead of blood. That was the heart of it.

Coehoorn accused Vauban of being spineless; Vauban branded Coehoorn a brute. In private, after the Dutchman's reference to pulling teeth, Vauban referred to him as "the Dentist." And their rivalry went beyond the merely intellectual: Vauban once even laid siege to a fortress commanded by Coehoorn! In 1692, this was, at Namur.

What brought particular renown to the duel was that the Beast was there watching. Louis XIV was there, and as king, he was the attacking army's general in chief. He witnessed the spectacle with his royal buttocks comfortably seated on a litter, an awning over him, and refreshments at hand, since he had delegated command to Vauban. If things went badly, it would be the fault of the subordinate. (Kings, all of them, are callous self-serving swine. Always have been, always will be!)

Well, in spite of the fact that Coehoorn had a heavily manned and battle-hardened garrison to count on, the city fell in precisely twenty-two days. Not a day longer. Driving home the victory was that Vauban had twenty times fewer dead. Vauban once managed to take a city with only twenty-seven dead or wounded! The rank and file adored him. At Namur's surrender, the Beast couldn't help but grimace owlishly when the troops who usually would have been cannon fodder—still alive, thanks to Vauban—cheered far more loudly for Vauban than their own king. Soldiers may be simple, but they are not stupid.

Namurcum captum. Could there ever have been a more total victory or a more humiliating defeat? As a matter of fact, there could. Vauban showed mercy to Coehoorn in the only way a righteous person could: showing such indulgence as to raise up the generous giver and belittle the receiver. The keys to the city were handed to him by Coehoorn himself, whose cucumber face looked longer and waxier than ever. Vauban abstained from unnecessary humiliations; the garrison was allowed to leave Namur honorably. The Frenchman showed extreme courtesy in renaming the citadel where his enemy had made his last stand as Fort Coehoorn. A monument to gentlemanliness. Looked at another way, it could be seen as a way of commemorating his great rival's defeat, wouldn't you say?

A small detail: Have you not noticed? Note that Vauban did not rename this interior bastion Fort Louis XIV. And this although his king had been there at the brow of a hill, watching over the whole siege.

They were great friends—Vauban and Coehoorn, I mean. They shared the same principles, though from opposed angles. Their rivalry had the intractability of intellectual competition about it. An insane rivalry, considering the blood spilled. But given that each, with divergent technical notions, sincerely believed that his principles would lead to less blood being spilled, a moral judgment is difficult to make.

Above and beyond banners, kings, and countries, the devotion to *le Mystère* brought them together in secret brotherhood, one that rose above all conflicts and hierarchies. The departure of the garrison made this clear. The usual protocols of a city in surrender were taken to ludicrous extremes; at Namur's gate, two lines of French soldiers were there to present arms.

The Dutchman with the cucumberish face was at the head of the formation. After him came his men, flags flying. When they passed each other, Vauban and Coehoorn saluted, sabers to nose, dividing their faces symmetrically. Two days earlier they would have used them to spill the other's guts.

"*À la prochaine!*" ventured Coehoorn. (Until next time.)

"*On verra,*" Vauban calmly replied. (Perhaps.)

Magnificent. And the joust didn't end there. Being impartial, I cannot hide the fact that the warning from the man with the cucumber face turned out to be prophetic. As with all eternal contests, the scales were to tip again.

Years later, an army under Coehoorn's command attacked the self-same Namur! He attacked according to his own *méthode;* that is, in brute fashion. And was victorious. Unfortunately for him, on this occasion it was not Vauban leading the defense, leaving the final verdict on the titanic duel undecided to the end of time.

The undeniable fact is that those heading up siege forces were not always rational Vaubanians. They were very often callous and unscrupulous Coehoornians. One of them, an ambitious youth, once had the gall to send the marquis the most offensive of letters.

His name was James Fitz-James Stuart, duke of Berwick. Please remember the name. It features later in our tale. And heavily! If it hadn't been for him, the tragedy of Barcelona, my tragedy, never would have taken place.

In the year 1705, I had yet to hear of Berwick, who, that year, as general in chief of the French forces, had led the attack on the fortress of Nice. From what I have been able to gather, he and Vauban were at odds over an attack on Nice, which the marquis considered a waste of time, money, and above all, good men. Berwick was a most ambitious Coehoornian, and while the siege was under way, Vauban wrote tireless letters urging him to call it off.

Berwick must have taken this badly, because a snide and presumptuous letter came to Bazoches one day from the front.

> As you see, sir, Nice is taken. On the angle you considered impossible to attack, and in very few days. This, I hope, will lead you to conclude that those on the ground, directing operations, ought to be believed ahead of those so bold as to dispense opinions from two hundred leagues hence.

A reproach that was shot through with a victor's disdain. The marquis flew into a rage. "Who does he think he is? Writing to me, *me,* in such a tone! A fatherless little bigmouth whose greatest merit has been to bathe his hands in the blood of others."

No one could go near the marquis for two days; his mood was such that he did not even come down to eat.

An irresolvable paradox lay at the heart of Vauban. Because if I have referred before now, with disgust, to those who disavow the art of war, it must be understood in Vaubanian terms. What *is* war? Guts spilling, pillaging, destruction? The paradox is that, according to the Bazoches way of looking, the art of war, at its most developed, prevented war. A discipline whose goal was to undo itself!

Unlike the Beast he served, Vauban found expansionist desire odious. For the miserliness of it, for being a concept ridiculously detached from the homeland, if you like. For Vauban, France wasn't a good country; it was perfection. So why seek more? All his energy went into conserving what had been inherited geographically. Into fortifying the borders to such a degree that any attack would be aborted before it had begun. He came up with the *pré carré,* the "square field," which is what the frog eaters call their damned estate: France as a perfectly defined monolith, eternal, compact, and peaceable. Genius builder though Vauban was, he was ruled by the moneyed and, if I may say so, shortsighted mentality of a conformist. Vauban perfected Vegetius's saying: *Si vis pacem para castrum* (If you want peace, erect fortresses). If deterrence is at its optimum, who would attack whom? So, an end to all conflict.

Vauban ended badly. In many ways, he was a staunch conservative in a country governed by the modern mania for universal power; in others, an overly audacious reformer. In his writings, he proposed freedom of creed and thought, and in that another tyranny, one that sought to flatten the individual: giving everything to your autocrat. He wanted to recoin hereditary aristocracy as meritocracy. And he hoped to do that in the context of the most absolute monarchy since Darius of Persia! The Beast's ministers thought Vauban harmless enough. His guiding principle was not revolution but reason: He calculated that out of every twenty-four French people, only one was cultivating the land; as a consequence, the other twenty-three were living off his efforts.

They cast him out like an old loon, and if they didn't bother to pursue him, it was because he was too old, hoary, an anachronism. His ingrained idea of loyalty stopped him from ever rising up against his king. Quite the reverse. For all he hated Louis's way of doing things, his misguided conduct and his pretensions, he would have died a thousand deaths for him. His guile in other fields was of no use to him when it came to seeing politics for what it really was. His logic was geometrical and, therefore, overly simplistic. He never came close to understanding that in human relations, endless vectors are at play, juxtaposed, unforeseeable, hidden, and almost always malign.

The end to war! How ironic. Plato already said it: Only those fallen in combat have seen the end of war.

9

If life were divided into stages, mine was about to come to the end of its most profitable and lovely. And in the most abrupt and distressing manner. Although it wouldn't be quite right to say it all came crashing down at once. The day Jeanne's husband miraculously recovered from his mental illness was the beginning of the end.

When a person succumbs to madness, those around him react with a mix of incredulity and indignation, as though the ailment suffered is a personal affront to them. In a way, we associate the lunatic with the figure of the deserter. As with battalions, we press close together when facing life's difficulties, and have no time for anyone who drops out voluntarily. Curiously, when someone who has lost his mind then regains it, this disbelief is even greater. Someone cured of that kind of affliction is as strange to us as a deserter rejoining the ranks.

I had heard he was getting better. But Paris was far from Bazoches, and my studies were all-consuming. When he came to visit, I couldn't believe it. He did not look disheveled, his gait was steady, and his gaze, which once would have been lost for hours in pursuit of invisible bumblebees, was quite normal.

He was as friendly to me as ever. "Zuviría, my good friend!" he exclaimed when he saw me, clapping his hands on my shoulders. "It's been a while, and how you've changed! You've grown a whole foot, when you were already having to duck under doorways. And what character in your face!" he added with an affectionate chuck. "You've grown innerly even more than without."

"Permit me to be pleased," I said in turn. "For I am not the only one showing some remarkable changes."

His eyes turned misty, as though penitent at the thought of his recent past. "You are quite right, *mon ami*."

I could not help but ask as to the medicine or treatment that had brought about his extraordinary recovery.

"Treatment? None whatsoever. Simply, I was off in my corner one day, singeing my fingernails like Paracelsus, when I asked myself a question that was so simple, it had never occurred to me before." He drew a little closer, as though fearing to be overheard, and with wide eyes said: "If I am a hugely wealthy man, married to a hugely wealthy woman, what the devil am I wasting my time trying to convert salt into gold for?"

I noticed a distance in Jeanne. I didn't make much of it until the following Sunday, when, as ever, we met in the hayloft. We would arrive there separately, and normally, she would be undressed, waiting for me, lying down on the first stack of hay. This time she had her attire all on, and she was standing up.

Even my Waltraud, who is denser than a sack of potatoes, would have surmised what Jeanne had to say, so I'll save the telling of it. It pains me to this day.

"The fact that your husband is not out of his mind," I said, "does not mean our feelings have changed."

"My feelings for you, no; my duty to him, yes."

One thing of which I am sure is that great lovers, true lovers, never go in for the kind of little scenes you see in the theater. And do you know why? Well, playwrights can say whatever they please, but love is the most rational thing in the world.

There was a lot I could have said, but I knew in advance the answer. She was a wealthy woman, now happily married (or less unhappily, at least), and the daughter to a marquis. She wouldn't give it all up for a lad with no credentials, some provincial cadet. Changing the subject, she said: "The Ducroix brothers say your Points only need polishing, and you'll be ready to become a great engineer. In fact, they're thrilled with you."

I said nothing; I looked at her. She was not ignorant of my despondency, my mute recrimination, my wordless hurt.

"Tell me something, Martí," she said then. "Between being a royal engineer and staying by my side forevermore, which would you choose if you had to?"

I opened my mouth two, three times, but nothing came out. I had entered Bazoches out of desire for a woman and would be leaving in love with engineering.

This marked the beginning of the end. Things falling apart, the great debacle of my life, March 1707. "Matrimony, that citadel which all without wish to enter, and all within wish to get out from," Vauban had said. Even stiff old Zeno and Armand Ducroix gave me a couple of slaps on the back. I didn't need to tell them what had happened, of course not. They said one day: "No feat of engineering can keep this pain at bay. Take deep breaths, and that's all."

I believe they gave me my fifth Point as a way of lifting my spirits. And because something else was going on, something I didn't know about and which was far more significant for me, for Bazoches, and for half the world: Sébastien Le Prestre de Vauban was dying.

His lungs were giving out. The final phase of an illness that had crept up on him in Paris. The Ducroix brothers kept it from me for as long as possible. When they decided to say something, Armand did so in inimitably stoic fashion: "Cadet, the Marquis of Bazoches is dying."

He would not be coming back to Bazoches—a fact that seemed to have more finality than the death itself. I froze. To me, Vauban had become a figure standing outside of human contingencies. It was like being told fire can no longer be lit, or that the moon would henceforth rise and fall in a matter of seconds.

Zeno was already with the marquis, assisting him with the final act. Armand and I climbed into a carriage and set out for Paris. It was a strange journey. I had never been to Paris, the head of that war-loving religion named France. I tried to stay attentive, and at the same time, I couldn't get Jeanne from my thoughts. Yes, it was as though a cosmic conjunction had forecast these two ruptures in such a short space of time. I was also bothered by uncertainty, something that, out of fellow feeling, I didn't dare put to Armand. He answered my question without my having to formulate it: "The marquis will hold on until he has said goodbye to each and every one of his close relations."

One of the inconvenient things about being a patrician of the first order is that all manner of people will flock to your deathbed. Custom demands that, even in great agony, almost anyone has the right to come and bother you, What's-his-name, Thingamaijig, first and second secretary to the commander at the Hellespont, cousin of your alcoholic father-in-law's other son-in-law. That the person going through those agonies should have to put up with a chattering multitude has always struck me as unnecessary and cruel. But can I truly criticize? After all, I myself went and took up position in that troop of undesirables. In my case, because of something very pressing.

For Vauban was going to validate—or not—my fifth Point. According to Armand, the marquis had expressed an interest in examining me personally. A great honor, even greater considering the circumstances. Perfection among Maganons is based on a rule of ten—so what it meant, the authority that came with reaching five Points, isn't hard to see.

Vauban's Paris home was a small palace but not ostentatious. In the antechamber to his room, there must have been fifty or sixty individuals awaiting an audience. Protocol demanded that he be seen according to a strict hierarchy, and since the least grand personage was the owner of five cannon factories, night had fallen by the time it came to me.

"If I were the marquis," I said with a sad sigh, "I would hurry up and die and not have to put up with all these bootlickers. *Merde!*"

"Keep quiet and follow me."

And Armand made his way through the people. Getting to the door, predictably enough, a servant, primped and preened to the extreme, detained us. "Eh, you! Wait your turn."

"Sir!" said Armand indignantly. "I am the marquis's personal secretary, and my place is at his bedside. Or do you fail to recognize me?"

"Ah, yes, a thousand pardons," the man said. He did not know about Zeno's twin brother. "But were you not inside? Excuse my error, I must not have seen you leave."

We crossed the threshold. Armand grumbled, "Moles . . . The world's full of them . . . They're all moles . . ."

The great Vauban was reclining in a magnificent four-poster bed. His upper half was sunken in a voluminous cushion. He was dying, and no mistake. But even at this final hour, his presence was awesome. His broken breathing was like that of a lion. His family was there. Jeanne was by his side.

Protocol demanded that I approach the foot of the bed and greet the great man with a bow of the head. I could not. To him I owed the two most rewarding years of my life, the shaping of my character and my destiny. I sprang toward his hand and raised it to my cheek, sobbing like an infant. To the Vauban family's credit, no one held me back or reprimanded me. Furthermore, when I raised my head, the marquis regarded me, and if a father's look can say to a son, "You are my creation," that was indeed the most paternal look I had ever been given.

"You have entered this room as a cadet," the marquis said. "My wish is for you to leave it a royal engineer."

He bade his daughters and secretaries leave us, Armand and Zeno to stand at the door. I would have liked to see the face of the servant who tried to stop us from coming in: the personal secretary appearing before him again, now double.

"For obvious reasons," rasped the marquis, "the exam will have to be brief. I am going to ask you one question only." He gazed up at the ceiling for a few moments, mouth open, deep in thought. Finally, without taking his eyes from the ceiling, he said, "Summarize the following: What elements comprise the optimum defense of a besieged stronghold?"

I could not have imagined a simpler question. It was a formality, then. Before he died, Vauban wanted to send his final engineer out into the world, that was it. For all that he might try to hide it, I knew he was extremely proud of this student of his—unruly, quick to answer back, but at the same time, well suited to the office. I began to sketch out the vertical columns supporting a decent fortress with bastions. The glacis, the covered path, the correct distance between bastions to avoid creating blind spots in the areas that took the brunt of the onslaught. I even permitted myself an analysis of the gullet, that is, the bastion entrance, which, to my mind, tended to be built too narrow. But then something unexpected happened. Vauban interrupted me. He still had the strength to raise his voice. "Get to the point, please!"

I was also startled to hear: "No, no, that's not it."

I was on the wrong track? I became nervous. I went into detail on the width of rampart walls, the steepness of their inclines. On making the best of the terrain in erecting defenses. On the moat and the many ways of sealing breached walls. The chagrin on his face said no, this was not what he wanted to hear. He put his hand to his brow, an unmistakable sign of displeasure in the marquis. I spoke about garrisons, about the adequate number of men in relation to the size of the fortification, the necessary weaponry, ammunition, and provisions. I quoted Hero of Constantinople's sage advice to a general defending a stronghold, at which moment a pained look came over the marquis. He half shut his eyes, pursed his lips. He looked up at the ceiling, as if requesting a postponement, then said: "No, no, and no! Get to the point, time is running low." And sighed. "A word. The answer is comprised of just one word."

People who are close to death have no time for being vague, and Vauban was treating me like some dolt. My spirit trembled. Everything I'd learned I now doubted. I went on a little more—perhaps Vauban wanted to hear about the compassionate element of a defense, so I made reference to each and every measure that might be taken to keep civilians safe during a siege. No. Wrong again. I stopped there. I had no notion of what he wanted to hear. I stopped speaking.

Forefinger raised, he uttered something I'll take to my grave. "One word. All you need to do is say one word."

I stepped closer to his bed and leaned over it, resting my fists on the mattress. "But *monsieur*," I said in a tone gentler and more respectful than for anything else I have ever said, "I have just recounted all that Bazoches has taught me."

It was as though Vauban were surrendering. He lifted a hand to his eyes. "No, you haven't done it. You haven't understood. Enough." He took a heaving breath, not looking at me. "I cannot give you my blessing, my conscience will not allow it. Believe me, I am sorry. You are going to have to find a better teacher than I. I have failed you." And he issued his judgment: "You are not fit."

I thought it was me death had come for, not him. He made a tired gesture with his hand, which then fell back onto the bed.

"I have an audience now, one I cannot put off. Go."

I left the room white as plaster. The Ducroix brothers immediately understood what was happening and drew me apart, keeping me from the assembled carrion. I could hardly speak. I rolled up my sleeve in despair. "The fifth Point!" I said, looking at my forearm. "I have it etched into me, but it isn't mine. Who will validate it now? Who?"

As they brought me away, I whimpered like a small dog that had just received an unmerited beating. "But what word did the marquis want?" I said, sobbing. "What was the word?"

I had gone to Paris to take the test, the most important test of my life. I would leave having learned a bitter, useless lesson: When can you tell all is lost? When even those who hold you dear say nothing. For the Ducroix brothers let out afflicted sighs, and the only solace they could offer was to remove me from the sight of others, taking me to the room that was farthest from everything in that death-visited house.

Sébastien Le Prestre de Vauban died on March 5, 1707. Of the rites and the funeral, all I am left with is an indistinct vertigo: "You are not fit."

I was the last creation to come out of Bazoches and, if I may be so bold, the best wrought. A machine made perfect over the course of two years of rigor and discipline. Toward the end of my training, I felt I could do anything; Constantinople had been besieged twenty-five times, and I felt confident I could defend it from twenty-five armies at once. Or to storm it myself, if serving another master. Fifteen days would be all I'd ask, time to make three parallels. And now I was nothing—a nothing that condemned me to life in limbo. "One word, just one." But which? By that judgment, I had been turned into a monster, a stillborn unicorn.

One of the endless numbers who attended the final farewell was Don Antoine Bardonenche, the infantry captain whose company Jeanne, her sister, and I had occasionally enjoyed, playing blind hen on the banks of streams or along the castle passageways at Bazoches. I was sitting on a bench with my hands forlornly folded in my lap, my mind empty except for the pain, when Bardonenche came over, svelte and sporting his white livery.

"You, my good friend, are melancholy," he said, jovial as ever in spite of being in the midst of a funeral. "They tell me you are seeking gainful employment."

I had not the energy to reply. Bardonenche continued: "Since engineering is your subject, you ought to put the knowledge you've acquired into practice. What would you say to joining a brigade of engineers as an adjutant? That way you'd gain practical experience. After a time be ratified as a member of the royal corps, I'm sure."

With the marquis's death, Bazoches had become something quite different. Jeanne would be taking the reins. There was no way I could stay. I gave an absentminded nod. Bardonenche cheerfully punched his left fist into his right palm. *"Rejoignez l'armée du roi!"*

Jeanne had been the anvil and Vauban the hammer. And I, a piece of brass crushed between the two. Nothing mattered. If a vacancy had opened in Anatolia, making fences for Turkish sheep, I would have said yes. As for Jeanne, my final conversation with her served only to further demolish my soul.

"You were the one who let me in to Bazoches," I reminded her. "You lied to your father. You said I knew his work best, which wasn't true. Maybe it was a mistake; maybe we should never have met. We'd all be far happier now."

"But Martí," she said, "I told him no lies. I related to him exactly the three candidates' answers, yours included. 'A stone flower' was how you described his best fortress. To which my father said, 'This one will be my student, it could be that this one has the heart of an engineer.'"

Vauban was buried at Bazoches. The heart, separate from the body, in an urn. A lover of order, he did not want to oppose the conventions of his time. But for any who knew how to look, it was all there: his body to the priests, his heart for *le Mystère*. For those believers among you, know that, of all the human beings who have ever lived, Vauban is the only one I would dare say with certainty made it to heaven. I'd wager anything—anything you like—that on seeing him approach, they opened the gates, opened them wide, not a word. Either that or Saint Peter would run the risk of him coming back with a regiment of sappers. Heaven—I'd bet he'd have taken it in seven days. Well, let us not be impious, even if only so as not to offend the One those gulls believe made this dung heap of a world; eight, let's say.

10

Of the journey from France to the depths of Spain, all I can recall is my feet, so downcast was I the whole way. Nothing mattered to me anymore. My body was a limp piece of hide, untouched even by the abominable jolting of the carriages. *Le Mystère* had abandoned me. The day before Vauban died I had felt full with it; the next, it had evaporated. As many pages as I might dictate, I would never be able to explain the simultaneous horror and apathy this emptiness came with.

I am a human desert, I know it. Every day of my life, a grain of sand is added to the dunes. So much time has passed, so very much, that in my contemplation of the boy Martí Zuviría, it is as though I see another person. I am not indulgent with him, I swear it. But I am able to feel a certain amount of compassion for him. His future, his love, his hopes, those who guided and taught him . . . It had all vanished, suddenly and at once. Who would have emerged unscathed from such a thing? And all for a word, The Word.

I am ninety-eight years old now, so in 1707 I would have been . . . Help me out, oh, sweet swine . . . Yes, sixteen. Bardonenche's regiment crossed the border of Navarra as a column many miles long, on foot, and once in Spain made a hard southerly march for three days. I was allowed to ride in one of the many carriages that brought up the tail of the convoy, and not on foot, like the rugged infantry. We were to join the main body of the army, at which point I would be incorporated into the engineering staff.

If you ever had to partake in those endless marches, day after day, you would understand how fortunate I was in this. The soldiers advanced two abreast, and from sunup to sundown, with the carriages bringing up the rear. The marching pace of the French army was one of the swiftest in all of Europe, a pace taken every second: left, right, left, right . . . *En route, mauvaise troupe!* A week after crossing the border, men began to fall by the wayside, exhausted. The sweeper carriages gathered them up. To pay for this, come the end of the day, they had to see to the tasks around camp. Since these were just as punishing and far more humiliating, only those who genuinely could not go on would allow themselves to drop.

Bardonenche went on a splendid horse, riding up and down, checking the formation of the line. I have already made mention of his pleasant nature. He frequently came alongside my carriage, which was toward the back, and directed a few spirited words at me beside the driver. Navarra was damp, and even when we came down into northern Castile, it was predominantly lush. But the moment we set foot on the southern steppes, it became dry and dusty, and the heat suffocating, though it was still only springtime.

Bardonenche was the most formidable swordsman. In fact, aside from his mania for swordplay, all there was in him was nonsense. As to sword philosophy, he declared: "What the devil is there to say? Strike before you are struck." And he was profoundly disdainful when it came to any weapon propelled by gunpowder, sparks, and flint. "Bullets fly any which way, the tip of my sword at one target only: the enemy's heart."

In some of my lessons at Bazoches, I had noticed likenesses between swordplay and engineering. Certain Maganons aspired to the perfect fortress. I asked Bardonenche if he had ever thought about the existence of the perfect sword, the perfect deathblow, or the perfect swordsman.

He looked at me as though I were some prattler who had just asked about the mystery of the Holy Trinity. "*All* my fights have been perfect," was his indignant response. "As proved by the fact that I'm here to talk about my nineteen duels, which is more than can be said for my opponents."

At any event, I had the consolation that we were on the same side, so I'd never have to face the ire of his blade.

We knew we were drawing closer to the Spanish-French army by the detritus that began to line the route. Difficult to credit the amount of dross left in the wake of a large troop. Unusable pots and pans, pieces of timber, broken carriage axles, pouches riddled with holes, dead mules, tattered apparel, frayed rope, horseshoes. The sun beat down on all manner of things.

We crossed La Mancha, turning west. We stopped for a couple of days in Albacete, a cold and unlovely place, and again set off. We camped for a night in one village, a thousand miles from anywhere, a hundred thousand fleas to every soul inhabiting it. I got drunk on a wine so contaminated that the bottom of the bottle had become a cemetery for insects. I swallowed them down and all. The following morning, when I was sleeping it off, Bardonenche came and woke me.

Before we set out, there was a local he wanted to speak with, and I was to act as translator. Where precisely was the Franco-Spanish Army of the Two Crowns? I asked, rubbing my eyes and not in the slightest bit interested.

"About to have quite a battle," he said. "Marshal Berwick is in pursuit of the Allies, and the Allies are in pursuit of Berwick." He pointed west. In the distance was a hill presided over by an old castle, and a settlement at the foot.

"What is the place called?" I asked, removing sleep from my eyes.
"Almansa."

Thus Martí Zuviría, brazen Martí Zuviría, became involved in the greatest imbroglio of the age, the War of Spanish Succession. The largest war the world has ever known. Dozens of countries were drawn into it; it lasted a quarter of a century and had several continents as its theater. I'm no historian—I wouldn't pontificate as to its causes—but it was certainly so vast, and its influence on my life so decisive, that I must at least sketch a general outline. To save your suffering, I'll be brief.

In the year 1700, Spain's Emperor Carlos II died. The man had been an aberration of nature, a slathering burden who, had he not been king, would have spent his days locked up in some monastery. His Castilian subjects called him "the Bewitched." I'm not so pious, so what say we leave it at "the Loon"? He died childless—how was he supposed to go about begetting them? His mind was so far gone, he probably didn't know that the radish between his legs had uses other than for pissing.

All monarchs are, by definition, loony—or end up that way. The only question is whether their subjects prefer the rule of someone with very limited mental functions or that of a nasty whoreson. When I was young, I erred on the side of the former, for at least they content themselves with eating pheasant and leave the people in peace. The

Loon, for example, was heartily lamented in Castile but wildly popular in Catalonia. Why? Because he did nothing. His atrophied brain was a reflection of Castile and its congealed empire. The Catalans loved it. The less a monarch governs, and the farther away he stays, the better.

It was clear, long before he died, that this human offal of a king wouldn't be leaving behind any heirs. Naturally, all Europe's ears pricked up—all the carrion. A number of years afterward, I met a nobleman who had served in the Spanish embassy in Madrid at that time. He told me the court was so infested with spies, they even "looked into" the king's undergarments! Tests proved conclusive: Carlos never ejaculated. And as the laws of nature state, where there is no semen, nor will there be any progeny.

For the French, it was a golden opportunity. If they could place one of their own on the Spanish throne after the Loon died, two historical objectives would be dealt with at a stroke: creating an alliance with their eternal enemy south of the Pyrenees; and indirectly, the main prize, bringing under its own aegis the decayed Spanish empire, stretching across Italy, the Americas, and a thousand far-flung places across the globe. That monster Louis XIV must have been rubbing his hands together with glee.

But as the saying goes, one thing leads to another. The Loon was part of the Austrian dynasty, the Hapsburgs, and they were there, too, circling the dying king with the same intentions as the French vultures.

By the time Carlos the Loon gave up the ghost with an unhappy gurgle, things were already well and truly a mess. The Beast put forward his grandson, Philip of Anjou, and Austria's Emperor Leopold proposed his son, Archduke Charles, as the future Carlos III of Spain.

Anjou made the English and the Dutch extremely uneasy. If Spain and France joined together (for Little Philip obviously would be nothing more than a puppet controlled by the Beast), the balance of power would tilt. The Spanish empire was something akin to a dying man covered in pustules, and France the local braggart. The Beast had turned France into an autocratic tyranny with a huge stockpile of armaments, unprecedented in the modern world; it did not bother to hide its goal of world domination. Which led England, Holland, and of course, the German empire to declare war on France. The fact that

Portugal and the House of Savoy also formed an alliance showed the Beast's menace—the only reason China didn't send regiments to get involved was because it was a long way to travel, and hiring a boat rather expensive.

As I said, the greatest imbroglio of the century, and all because of some unsoiled undergarments. How did it not occur to anyone to send a stud into the queen's room one night and let them go at it, then decree that the child was the Loon's? What that would have saved us, *caray!*

So, as I said, all the armies of Europe joined the fray. On the borders of Germany, the French and Dutch were going at it hammer and tongs. And in Spain, what truly caused the dispute?

Before I continue, a necessary but brief digression to explain the Spanish Affair, which has a complicated aspect for foreigners like you, my dear vile Waltraud. That aspect simply being: There was no such thing as Spain.

If Caesar described Gaul as divisible into three parts, he might have said of the Hispania existing after the fall of the Holy Roman Empire that it was divided into three strips, each stretching north to south.

One of these vertical strips is Portugal, occupying the Atlantic portion, as any map will show you. The widest strip is Castile, in the center. And then there is one more strip of land, invisible on the maps of today, along the Mediterranean coast. This, more or less, is the Catalan crown. (Or was; nowadays we are nothing).

Though all these kingdoms were Christian, each had distinct dynasties, languages, and cultures. Histories of their own. The mutual suspicion was such that they were constantly at war. No strange thing. Catalonia and Castile had opposed mentalities. Apart from Saints' Days, they had nothing in common. Castile was rain-fed; Catalonia, on the Mediterranean coast. Castile, aristocratic and rural; Catalonia, middle-class and shipowning. The Castilian landscape had produced oppressive signories—there is an anecdote from medieval times that I can half remember, possibly apocryphal, but which explains the thing well.

There is a little princess from Castile, and she marries a little prince from Catalonia. She goes to live in Barcelona, and on the second day, a servant talks back to her. The girl asked for a glass of water, or where they kept the chamber pot, something, and the servant told her to go and look for herself. Naturally, the Castilian princess appeals to her husband: The foulmouth must have a flogging. The prince shrugs: "My lady, I am sorry," he says, "I cannot comply." She, going wild, inquires why. "Here, unlike in Castile," says the husband with a heavy heart, "the people are free."

In the year 1450, more or less, the two kingdoms were joined by a royal intermarriage. Anyone could have seen that, as a marriage, it would end badly, very badly. I compare the union of the two crowns to a marriage that is going badly because the discrepancies that lay in the years to come were very much like those between two individuals who marry wanting different things. The Catalans wanted a union between equals; Castile, as time passed, gradually forgot this founding principle.

All was well in the first couple of centuries because the two kingdoms continued as they always had been, each with its back to the other. Catalonia, governed by the Generalitat (the Catalan government), paying tribute to the common crown more symbolically than anything. Then the Hispanic monarchy, which had been itinerant in the Middle Ages, settled in Madrid. The seat of power shifted to Castile.

According to one of our oldest constitutions, the Catalans were obliged to fight for the king only "in the case of an attack on, and in defense of, Catalonia." In other words, Madrid was not allowed to recruit cannon fodder for its wars in Flanders, the plains of Patagonia, or any one of the fetid corners of Florida. As for taxation, the amount paid by Catalans had to be approved by its own court. Accustomed as they were to their despotic ways, the monarchs now based in Madrid found it intolerable, scandalous, that the peninsula's most prosperous area should not give up anything when there was a war on—against half the world.

Ludicrous! The crowns had joined together in the fifteenth century, not the kingdoms; the same king for all, never the same government, and never under the yoke of Castile. That had been the agreement. In Castile, this independence was always seen as a nuisance, and later a betrayal. Remember what I said about a marriage going wrong? One side had forgotten its promises, the other was feeling increasingly stifled.

In the year 1640, the Catalans had had enough, and the entire country rose up in rebellion. Mobs of angry peasants entered Barcelona.

The Spanish viceroy was apprehended when he tried to flee. They didn't treat him well, it's fair to say. The largest piece left of him would have fit inside a vase.

The uprising of 1640 was followed by a war between Catalonia and Castile, with France caught in the middle. A long, cruel war in which neither party gave any quarter. It concluded with an indeterminate pact that left everything more or less as it had been, Catalonia governing itself according to its own constitutions and liberties, Castile plumbing the depths of decadence.

The ensuing peace was a long intermission, more than anything. Catalonia and Castile exchanged openly hostile glances. Mistrust on the part of Castile had converted into undisguised rancor. Indeed, see what the writer Quevedo had to say on the subject:

> *Catalonia is the grotesque abortion of politics. Its people are a pox on their kings, and all suffer because of them. A nation arming itself with criminals unworthy of ever being pardoned.*

Here he limited himself to expressing a repute we fully justified. Elsewhere, he was more to the point, elucidating the adequate treatment for this treacherous breed:

> *As long as there remains in Catalonia even the one Catalan, and stones in the field, we shall have an enemy, and we shall have war.*

How kind! "Grotesque abortion . . . a pox on their kings." A worthier inquiry surely would have been to ask *why* no one loved us.

Castile's high point came with the conquest of the Americas. Thereafter, it fell into a dull and lethargic stupor. An outcome written in its roots. The Castilian character par excellence is the *hidalgo*, that is, the nobleman, a medieval creation who still lives on. Proud to the point of madness, going out of his way for the sake of honor, capable of fighting to the death over a slight, but incapable of any constructive initiative. That which for him is a heroic gesture, in the eyes of a Catalan is nothing but the most laughably pigheaded error. He can't see beyond the present moment; like dragonflies, he aspires to brilliance, but his wings flutter erratically, carrying him low and to no place in particular. His hands are good only for bearing arms; otherwise, it would mean getting them dirty. He does not understand, much less tolerate, other ways of life: Industriousness is repellent to him. In order to prosper, that same aloof conception of dignity paradoxically impels him to plunder defenseless continents, or to carry out the miserable role of courtier.

Spanish nobility . . . Spanish nobility . . . I shit on their nobility! What did we have to do with that scum? Work, to the true Castilian, was dishonorable; for a Catalan, the dishonor was not to work. I can still hear my father, holding out the palms of his big hands for me to see: "Never trust any man with smooth hands."

Their grubby empire sank into history's dirtiest, lowest slime. Millions of the natives were enslaved, their backs broken in mines across the Americas, but Castile, apart from cracking the whip, was unable to construct a free, or at least sound, economy. Any initiative it came up with was cut short by a monarchy with shades of the Asiatic—as well as being autocratic, also backward and especially corrupt.

In 1700, finally, after the Loon had died, the magnitude of the disagreement between Catalonia and Castile became evident. For the Catalans, a French king was a political aberration, the end of all their freedoms, of their very essence as a nation. France's autocratic regime, which would sooner or later come to apply to Spain, would cancel all indigenous powers. When Castile chose Little Philip, there was no way back from the conflict. In reaction, Catalonia opted for Archduke Charles of Austria to sit on the Spanish throne. (Or a maharaja from Kashmir, if he had come and presented his credentials—anything but a French Bourbon.)

That will do. Now you might understand better the situation in the peninsula of that year. For the Catalans, Spain was merely the name for a free confederation of nations; the Castilians, on the other hand, saw in the word "Spain" an imperial extension of Castile. Or, put another way: For the Castilians, Spain was the chicken coop and Castile its rooster; for the Catalans, Spain was a designation merely for the stick used to beat the chickens. Therein lies the tragedy. In fact, when a Catalan and a Castilian used the word "Spain," they were referring to two opposed ideas—which is what leads to such confusion for the foreigner. See what I am driving at? In reality, there is no such thing; Spain is not so much a place as a failure to meet.

But before I finish, allow me to say just a few words about my nation, Catalonia. Because in the picture painted so far, I might seem to be a Vaubanian enamored of just one side of the Pyrenees, and that simply isn't the case.

Even as a child, I realized what a piece of flotsam Catalonia was, floating along on the currents of history when, by rights, it should have sunk hundreds of years before. The problem was that no one wanted to notice its congenital weakness and, even less, try to remedy it. When our *concelleres*, the Catalan government ministers, held a parade, it was pitiful. A group of silly-looking rag dolls who thought themselves very important—for they never had to doff hats to the king—and their garments and caps were made of red velvet. To the people, they were the "Red Pelts." We were too enamored of the pantomime.

And here you have our worst defect. We never knew what we wanted, beyond having a good time, the last redoubt of the poor and insignificant. Neither one nor the other—neither France nor Spain—but incapable of building our own political edifice. Neither resigned to our fate nor disposed to changing it. Trapped between the slowly shutting jaws of France and Spain, we resigned ourselves to riding out the storm. Which left us adrift, directionless. Our ruling classes, in particular, were the height of chronic indecision, endlessly caught between servility and resistance. As Seneca said: If a sailor does not know to what port he is steering, no wind will be favorable to him. And when I think about our history, what comes to mind is the most nail-biting question: Which excuse is more melancholy, that which harks after "What we might have been" or that which says "We never should have tried"? We suffered both of those harrowings. The Catalans' problem was that they never knew what they wanted, and at the same time, they wanted it intensely.

In 1705 a small group of upstanding Catalans conspired to seek the aid of the Allies in light of an incipient uprising against the Bourbons. The Treaty of Genoa between Catalonia and England was struck. The idea was for an Allied army to disembark in Barcelona. England committed to meeting the cost of operations. For their part, the Catalans would raise a Catalan army of volunteers to support the standard troops. This would open the way to Madrid, where they would place the Austrian ape Charles on the throne and give him the title Carlos III of Spain.

As good lawyers, they demanded every guarantee. The contract went so far as to detail what kind of feed the Allies should give to the beasts of burden. Very Catalan, yes. Oh, and if, by some twist of fate, as explicated in the contract, "any adverse and unforeseen events occur when weapons are drawn (God forbid)," the English crown promised that the Catalonian principality would remain "with all the security, guarantee and protection of the Crown of England, without their Persons, Goods, Laws and Privileges suffering the least alteration or detriment."

And now, excuse me if I explode.

Who did these little lords think they were to speak in the name of the country without even asking the opinion of the Generalitat? Agreed, at that time Barcelona was in the hands of the Bourbon military. Even so, what authority did they have to involve us in a world war as nonchalantly as going out for a stroll in the countryside? Did it occur to no one that we weren't bartering over a bag of green beans or a kilo of salt but, rather, the blood and the future of the entire country, all in exchange for a scrap of paper? Things did not simply go badly for us— they went as badly as could possibly be imagined. We lost the war. In 1713 our last forces were grouped together upon the walls of Barcelona. The foreign troops had boarded their ships, leaving us with our rumps naked in the wind. You can guess what England did next. They did not have the decency to lie to us. When someone brought out the famous little scrap of paper, those windbags simply spat, saying: "It is not in the interest of England to preserve Catalan liberties."

Fabulous! And hard to believe as it may seem, when the Catalan ambassador knelt at the feet of Her Gracious Majesty, begging for aid to Barcelona—which, reduced though it then was to rubble, was still holding out against the Bourbon onslaught—what did she say? That we ought to be thankful for their constant concern, that was what!

In Utrecht in 1713, just as the siege of Barcelona was beginning, all the implicated powers negotiated a general peace. So that the English diplomats would not make an issue of the Catalonian question, France and Spain made them a gift of Newfoundland. This was what, in the eyes of the English, our thousands of years of liberty were worth, as well as the worth of that scrap of paper—the right to fish twenty tons a year of cod.

In the last year of the war, tragic 1714, the defenders of Barcelona had been reduced to fighting for their lives, their homes, their city. For the Catalan liberties, which were perfectly tangible, a regime that was opposed to the horror now raining down. They fought under the orders of Villarroel, Don Antonio de Villarroel. Wait a couple of chapters and you will see my view of this man, how he lifted me out of abjection like a boot out of mud. And if you were to ask me the cruelest of questions—to whom do I owe more, Vauban or Villarroel?—my answer would be: I should rather die than answer.

Of the five hundred or so of us who initiated the charge that day, September 11, 1714, I do not believe more than twenty or thirty survived. Villarroel was shot from his horse. The horse fell on top of him, kicking around in pain, and as the grapeshot flew, it was no easy task dragging him out from underneath. One of his legs had been crushed, and the bone above his knee was protruding from his trouser leg. Even so, he pushed away the men helping him, shouting as if possessed: "Don't stop the charge! Don't stop! No falling back, not as long as I still draw breath!"

When we pushed on, a charge of grapeshot flew from a cannon and took off half my face. I fell to the floor among mounds of dead and wounded. Lifting five trembling fingers to my left cheek, I found it wasn't there; in its place, a cavity had been blown as far as the other side of my mouth, a wettish bloody hole with splintered bits of bone sticking out, and my left jaw was broken. I'd lost half my face. Blinded by my own blood, I became not the most reliable witness to those last few hours of Catalan freedom.

In the intervening seventy years, twenty or so different masks have covered my face. The first was somewhat cobbled together, skin-colored, covering my whole face, and with slanted eyes, as in the visor of a helmet. In America I had a craftsman make me a far better one. It cost me an arm and a leg, but it was money well spent. It came down over just my cheek, my left eye, and half of my mouth. The right side of my face was exposed to the sun, and this is what people have always been able to see; given that it was intact, no reason to hide it. It adjusted at the back with clever bands and invisible catches. My sharp nose could stick out all it liked—I was lucky not to have had that blown off, too. Women began casting admiring glances my way once more, and I felt almost human again.

Many other masks were to follow, a great many, some exquisitely designed. Some I sold, others I lost in tropical climes or in wagers, some were seized from me, others stolen, and many were broken by thumps and kicks and fallings-down from horses. The sixth one I owned was shattered by a stray bullet. I owe my life to that mask, which was made of a robust ivory.

Why am I telling the story of my masks? Why is it important? You, woman, you tell me to be quiet only when it seems a good time to you—not when it is good for the book.

11

I have just given an outline of the Catalan view of their final war, which saw an end to them as a nation. But at that time, April 1707, Longlegs Zuvi, nothing but a young lad who couldn't have cared a pepper for politics and history, was headed into the thick of that French border war on the side he would later come to loathe. And all for the sake of a Word.

When we joined the main body of the Franco-Spanish army in Almansa, we could see for ourselves how bad things were. The two sides, the Allies and the Two Crowns, had spent the previous fifteen days seeking each other out and then withdrawing in a succession of marches and countermarches, indecisive skirmishes and sieges at minor fortresses.

The Allied army was led by the earl of Galway who, despite his title, was French: His name was Henri Massue de Ruvigny, and he was a veteran who had lost an arm the previous year, campaigning in Portugal. This is why, as historians love to repeat, Almansa was seen as a battle between an English force commanded by a Frenchman, and a French force led by an Englishman—General Berwick. The truth of the matter was more complicated.

Berwick must have been the most eminent bastard in all of Europe. The illegitimate son of the ousted James II, England's last Catholic king, Berwick had grown up in France and always served the Beast. (Remember the letter he sent to Vauban in 1705 about the fall of Nice?) As the pompous name "The Army of the Two Crowns" indicated, it was made up of French and Spanish, that much is true, but also Irish (Berwick's personal guard), Walloon mercenaries, Neapolitans (you always find a few of them about the place), and even a Swiss battalion. As for the Allies, aside from the English, Portuguese, and Dutch, there was a small corps of diehard Catalans and another of French Huguenots —to this day, I struggle to understand how a bunch of Huguenots pitched up in those desolate latitudes, a nook off to the west of Albacete.

Morale in the Two Crowns' camp wasn't precisely what you could call high. Everything had been withdrawn in the recent days. It was said that Galway had begun sarcastically referring to Berwick as his "innkeeper," since the latter was continually taking up lodgings where he had slept the previous night. Berwick stopped at Almansa only because he'd run out of provisions.

This delay at least allowed Berwick to group together the reinforcements pouring in from far and wide. Some of these, such as the part of Bardonenche's Couronne regiment in which I traveled, were top-notch. But the vast majority were press-ganged Spaniards—recruits, worth less than nothing.

A sorry sight they were. The day we arrived, they were being given some last-minute training. A regiment, however, is like an oak tree: some twenty years are needed for it to take shape. During the maneuvers, you saw the French advancing in straight lines, while the Spanish twisted about like vines. I didn't want to think what they would be like under enemy fire. They had been given the gray and white uniforms of Bourbon France. Another strike on the part of the Beast: French companies had been given the contracts to provision all Spanish forces—by decree. In other words, your country gifts its throne to a French prince and, on top, has to pay him rent. Quite a racket. (At least the Catalans squeezed the English down to the very last coin.) The majority of the recruits were very young. Poor boys. They were having their heads introduced into the lion's mouth because the textile companies in Lyon could claim their pay for the uniforms only when the bodies wearing them were dead. The encampment was an endless sea of tents—no doubt the canvases were from France as well, all bought at a pretty price dictated by the Beast.

Berwick was lodging at the mayor's house, where the recently arrived officers were going to present themselves to him. Bardonenche wanted me to go with him. He was sitting at a table upon which a large map had been unrolled. Around him were a dozen or so high-ranking officers at a council of war. I found it strange that at a simple council, they would be wearing their armor. It must have been very uncomfortable debating and cogitating with those iron breastplates, shoulder and arm pieces on. Perhaps it was to accentuate their authority, or so everyone would understand the gravity of the situation. Berwick looked up as we came in.

The first, most noticeable thing about Berwick was his youthful mien—not very military. My God, I thought, how can a babe like that command the respect of a whole army? He was thirty-six, and his skin was still baby-soft. He had a perfect oval face. The nose, solid, thin, divided it in two; the lips, though wide, were also wildly sensuous, and the corners rose amiably upward. His fine arcing eyebrows had been heavily plucked. Rarely have I looked upon such black eyes. The right one was squinting somewhat, a feature I attributed to the overwhelming pressure he must have been under.

But James Fitz-James Berwick (Jimmy to his friends) was one of the most frequently depicted people this century (he was by no means immune to vanity). So instead of one plate I'll give you two. You be the judges.

Ho! You like him, horrendous Waltraud? Don't fool yourself. He would have barely glanced at you, for you are as ugly as a keg on legs, you are—well, other things besides.

Word in camp was that Berwick was backing off due to his English roots—he had a treacherous streak, so they said. Codswallop. But in

James Fitz James Duke of Berwick

James Fitz James Duke of Berwick

Madrid they had taken the idea so seriously that crazy Philip V had sent the duke of Orléans to take over command! His opposite number in the Allied army, Galway, was a gruff general, fifty-nine years of age, and his right-hand man, the Portuguese Das Minas, a hoary old sixty-three. They felt certain they'd be having little bastard Berwick for breakfast. Even less flatteringly, Berwick's own army was of the same opinion. I have already said a little as to the quality of the new recruits. Few generals have found themselves on the eve of battle with an outlook so dire.

I turned my Bazoches gaze on Berwick; I couldn't help it. He was making a superhuman effort to try to master his own fate. The dilemma was clear: Brave a battle and his army would most likely be demolished, or shun it, and the duke of Orléans, who was soon to arrive, would wrest command from him. In terms of his personal interests, both outcomes were equally fatal.

Berwick came over to the recently entered officers, greeting them one by one. Bardonenche he knew personally and stopped at him. They were chatting away like old friends, when at a certain moment he noticed me. Pointing to me, acutely interested, he said: "And this handsome, stern-looking youth?"

"Ah, yes," said Bardonenche. "Martí Zuviría, the most promising engineering cadet in all France, Your Excellence."

I had studied at the Dijon academy? he asked.

"No, sir," I answered. "I did my training under one engineer alone."

He wanted to know the name. I didn't want to bring up Bazoches. "Someone," I said with diplomatic sarcasm, "to whom you once sent a missive regarding the happy conquest of Nice . . . "

His gaze grew sharp, and he said: "I was sorry not to have been able to make the funeral. As you can see, I have been somewhat busy of late." Those around him burst out laughing. "Have I said something amusing?" barked the Englishman, turning on them.

His mood swings were dramatic and, as I would later discover, also predictable. It was his way of catching his subordinates off guard, a way of reminding them who was top dog. He waved a hand as though offended, and everyone withdrew. "Not you," he ordered me. "I want you to tell me about the final moments in the great Vauban's life."

Ah! A little one-to-one chat, what about that! I had seen it coming the moment he called me a "handsome, stern-looking youth." Converse about Vauban! If it had really been that, Bardonenche should have stayed, the aristocrat, the old friend, and someone who had been present in the marquis's dying days. He had asked me to accompany him to his private chamber. How was I supposed to say no? Sometimes the predictable is unavoidable.

He led me up some stairs. We entered his room and he said, "Help me with my armor."

The words were friendly, the tone, authoritative. He turned away from me, crossed his arms, and I undid his cuirass at the neck. I couldn't help but let the armor fall to the floor with a clatter. More than asking, he ordered me: "Call me Jimmy."

The brusqueness of the demand infuriated me. I gave him a fierce look. Outside of the field of battle, he was not accustomed to being disobeyed, and my hostility must have disarmed him, because he gave a surprisingly submissive wave of the hand, now saying, *"D'accord?"*

I was thinking about how to get myself out of the situation when something happened. Once he was free of the steel that held and tormented him, he staggered. His knees buckled. He scratched the wall with his nails as he fell. He began drooling like a slug and convulsing.

The convulsions were so violent that I thought to go for help. "Your Excellence, what is it?"

Still kneeling, he turned his head slowly. Something in his eyes was different. He was the private Berwick now, free of the need to be ostentatious. An organism pushed to inhuman limits, a creature lacking all affection.

That power brings with it an enormous public aspect is no secret. And Jimmy was obliged to push his army beyond all bounds. The slightest false move, even blinking at the wrong moment, could be taken as a sign of weakness. An out-of-place gesture and his authority would evaporate. A wrong decision and he'd lose an army. On the night preceding Almansa, he was less than a rag.

I felt for him. I know I may have been wrong to. I got my hands under his armpits and heaved him to his feet. He pushed me away, furious. "I'm fine!" he shouted.

"No, no, you aren't," I said. "Vauban spoke to me of the illness of those with power, and ways of treating them."

He gave me a hateful glance.

"Tea with thyme in it," I said. "And turn your back on the world."

I found out for myself that day that the things I had learned at Bazoches would make me feel love for people more often than was desirable; my sight, my sense of touch, all my senses were too sharp not to see the man suffering underneath that triumphant uniform. That this man was so powerful, and at the same time so defenseless, and that he had to hide his inadequacies from the world, moved me to the point where I couldn't help but take him in my arms. Jimmy, poor Jimmy, he never knew that my love for him was due not to his power but—oh, paradox!—his weaknesses, which made even him human, that demon who would one day annihilate us.

He did not let me accompany him the following day, which meant my experience of the battle of Almansa was from inside the town walls. I hardly lamented the fact; Zuvi wasn't exactly spoiling for a fight. Plus, I had learned about sieges, not battles in open country. I watched the encounter from a window, which is one way of putting it, for the fog, smoke, and clouds of dust combined to form a curtain so opaque that all was reduced to the din of artillery and gunfire.

Against all expectations, Jimmy crushed the Allied army. He came back covered in dirt, worn out, dents all over his cuirass. And yet the demonic part of him was visible in the return, the part that kept him going. For battle had cured all his ills: Victory is the most marvelous elixir. He seemed a different man; more than merely cured, Jimmy was drunk on vitality, exultant, bursting with life.

Seeing me, he said, "You're still here. Good."

And so began an amity that, to put it one way, was far from straightforward. James Fitz-James, duke of Fitz-James, duke of Berwick, of Liria and Jérica, peer and marshal of the French realm, thanks to the victory at Almansa, knight of the Golden Fleece, et cetera, et cetera. Anything you like. Even so, never ceasing to be a bastard; son of James II of England, yes, but a bastard all the same.

Life pushed him into a race he could never win. However many armies he destroyed, fortresses stormed, services rendered, he would always be what he was: misbegotten, a social neuter. Any aristocrat of good blood who had notched up half the accomplishments of his short life would have been held up as more than Olympian. Not him. Son of an outcast king and illegitimate to boot. Hence his constant quest for legitimacy and royalty.

The strangest thing about him was that he was also absolutely clear-sighted. He knew he would never be given the one thing he sought. He garnered honors and praise, duchies, infinite wealth, all the clap-trap awarded by kings, ceremonies with priests in attendance, and the singing of infantile hymns. In private, he scorned such affairs. I know he did. Certain of his supporters have said he made the most of his time on earth, emphasizing the ten children he had with his second wife. Ha! Don't make me laugh. Where do they imagine a person like Jimmy would find time to lie down with his little wife (who, by the way, was uglier than a Barbary ape), even if we're talking about only ten occasions? In 1708 alone, he took part in three different campaigns in the service of that dreadful monster of a king, Louis XIV—in Spain, France, and Germany. Do they want to try and convince me that he went a-wooing to her whenever he could? That he'd trot off to her abode, say, "Sweetie, here I am," have a roll around with her, and then back to the action? I can assure them the only possibility is that he tasked someone else with such matters. On top of the fact that I was with him.

Fine, all right. I said I had set myself to be sincere, and that is what I shall be. I'm too old to care.

We fucked the whole night through. And the next day, we did not leave the room. Why would we? Where could be better than there? Plus, he could allow himself it. There were continual knocks at the door: "Your Excellence, the mayor of Almansa entreats an audience!" or "Your Excellence, urgent dispatch from Madrid!" or "Colonel so-and-so asks about lodgings for the prisoners." At first the door knocker startled me, but when I jumped out of bed, sending the chamber pot flying, all Jimmy did was laugh. The world was at his feet, why should he bother to answer? He had earned the right not to let a door knocker importune him. That's what power is, precisely that: The world seeks an audience with you, and you laugh at it from behind the door.

Now what? Why are you making that face?
I could have skipped this, but you asked for a love scene.
You didn't like it?
I can see you did not.

For a good amount of time, I was very close to being happy. I felt sure *le Mystère* had delivered me into the arms of a teacher who might be a replacement for Vauban. Jimmy was perfectly suited to the role. He was sufficiently distinguished as a Maganon that, a full two years before, he had dared disagree with Vauban in his letter from Nice—and on the subject of a siege, no less. Further, Jimmy included in his criticism of the marquis the statement that it was all very well pontificating from the rearguard, passing judgment on those fighting up front. And this was precisely the thing I needed, the siege experience, the reality of combat, and of life, that would enable me to discover The Word.

Everything was fine to begin with, though little of note took place. Jimmy and the rest of the army had to recover from battle. I understood that. Then winter arrived, and naturally enough, the campaign was put on hold; since time immemorial, armies have never fought in winter.

Jimmy was one of the great personalities of his age. Daring but at the same time sound in judgment, an incongruous mix flowed in him: He was both an utter egoist and extremely generous and indulgent toward others. He was one of the few truly great figures of our century, this tortured and tortuous century, full of sagas epic and inane. But by the spring of 1708, we had been together for almost a year, and I was still to see any action. Some say the great Battle of Almansa was exceptional. For every one battle in open country, there were ten sieges of strongholds, large or small, and the issue for me was that I was missing out on them all. Attacking or defending, what did it matter to me? If I finally got to take part in a siege *selon les règles*, not merely as a theoretical exercise, I might be able to unveil The Word, that Word that had the kernel of knowledge trapped inside it. Validate my fifth Point. I wouldn't let it go.

"Oh, don't worry yourself over that," Jimmy would say. "You're rendering far worthier services: making war pleasurable for me."

At that point, our mutual understanding withered, all the ties that could bind me to him as a man and, especially, as a Maganon. I had erred: People in high office demand everything from those around them, and Jimmy was the most egoistic marshal of all. He used soldiers, engineers, and lovers alike.

He tried to keep me from leaving, began avoiding me. When it comes to powerful men, the best thing is to give them a wide berth: If they grow tall, you will be in their shade, and if they fall, you'll find yourself crushed underneath. With Jimmy, I was kept quiet by an unfathomable force that also kept us apart: *le Mystère*. You do not say no to a marshal of France, not to his face, so I limited myself to trying to leave without him noticing.

When spring came, the Franco-Spanish army split into two. One part was to remain under Jimmy's command, while the other would be led by the duke of Orléans. I asked to be reassigned to the latter's section. Among aristocracy, the envy of others is much to be desired, so you can imagine Orléans' satisfaction when I offered him my services. Vauban's name could move mountains, and Orléans didn't hesitate to accept me in. Indeed, no doubt rivalry between leaders had an impact, a considerable one: Stealing Berwick's little apricot would supply Orléans with endless opportunities to lord it over him.

The day before we were set to leave, I received orders to present myself at Jimmy's field tent. My having "deserted," gone over to his rival in the Bourbon high command, was doubtless an affront. I knew it and made my way there very reluctantly.

He was sitting, writing something, when I came in. The tent was rectangular and very long. His desk was at the far end, and it was as though he were a spider waiting in its web. He bade his servants leave and, once they had gone, thrust his quill into the inkstand like a knife, saying: "You haven't even said goodbye."

I could take refuge in hierarchy for once. I held my nerve, looking straight ahead of me. I spoke in a formal, distant way: "The marshal has sent no order for me to bid him farewell."

"Enough of the silliness!" he barked. "We're alone now. And stand at ease. You're like a pole in the ground." He handed me some papers. "Read. You'll be grateful to me all your days." As though he were doing me a considerable favor, he added: "You're coming with me. It's decided."

It was my appointment as a royal engineer. Or at least a personal petition to the Beast, signed by Jimmy.

This is how powerful people behave. Everything, as far as they're concerned, is agreed without discussion, and on they go. What I might have to say, my interests, desires, needs, mattered not a jot. But I had been educated at Bazoches, and that was a rampart that not even the duke of Berwick could clear. I interjected: "You can't appoint me engineer."

He wasn't sure how to overcome this resistance, whether to employ threats or seduction, but was too clever to go fully either way. "It will be the king of France doing so," he said evasively.

"Not even he has the correct authority." I bared my forearm, showing my five Points. "The king may make what decrees he pleases, but not on my tattoos. You know full well."

"You want us to disagree. Tell me why."

I said nothing. I could have hurt him by saying his only authority over me was carnal, or that his spitefulness was the product of wounded vanity. That was how Jimmy was: He thought he had the right to receive love without giving any back. No, I didn't say a word. What would be the point? It was a good thing I kept quiet: He took my silence harder than any accusation I could have come up with. He realized he was up against a force that was not me but which I was merely representing. He pondered how he might subdue it but was sufficiently intelligent to know it was beyond his powers. He sighed, then barked: "I at least have the right to ask why you don't want to come with me. I'm more than a marshal to you. Which is why I want you at my side."

I interjected for the second time, brusquely rebuffing him. "Of course a marshal is what you are." I looked him in the eye. "Always and wherever. Much as you might want to be, you can't be anything else."

I left without being ordered to. He wouldn't have been able to stop me.

Jimmy, along with half the army, was to go north, and Orléans east, to lay siege to a city named Játiva. Alas, I wasn't allowed to join Orléans's troops. As a farewell of his own, Jimmy left me a poisoned gift: a bureaucratic tangle between his secretaries and those of Orléans that would delay my transfer. He did it simply to aggravate me, as it meant I had to stay in Almansa waiting for my new passport to be sorted out. Very nice. The siege of Játiva promised to be quite the spectacle, and there I was, stuck in that godforsaken Albacete pigsty, a place that—among the wounded, monks, reinforcements, and mounds of provisions that were to be sent out to the new battle lines—would have the smell of death about it for a thousand years to come. They say that, on both sides combined, ten thousand poor souls died at Almansa. Ten thousand, when, at a well-directed siege, the marquis had shown a way of losing no more than ten! The slaughter had been such that the inhabitants of the town had to use the wells as graves. They threw the naked bodies in like sacks. Naked, I say, because the people were so miserable that they stripped the belongings of the fallen, right down to their dirty undergarments.

The Word. My mistake had been not learning The Word. What had been the marquis's question? "Summarize the optimum defense." The days went by with me stuck in a dust-ridden field tent, and my anxiety grew. More than wanting to, I needed to experience the things I had been taught at Bazoches.

By the time my passport came, Játiva had already fallen into Bourbon hands, but the siege of Tortosa was about to get underway. I shrugged it off: The Word might be found in any siege, I thought. Tortosa was also an extremely interesting prospect. One day a supply convoy set out, and I was allowed to go along.

During the march, an incident occurred that would shatter my musings, which until then had been purely to do with siege warfare. The convoy had to stand aside to allow a crowd coming the opposite way to pass, made up of women, children, and the elderly, all of them dressed in rags and wretched-looking. These individuals were all tinted the same: Their clothes, their faces, their feet as they shuffled by, all took on the same grayish, subdued hue. A flock whose tribulation was plain to see, who, in spite of their numbers, went by in silence. Only the youngest ones were bold enough to shed tears. None even held out a hand for alms. They were being escorted by a few men on horseback who cracked the occasional whip to make them keep up the pace. An old woman fell down directly in front of me, and my natural impulse was to lean over to help her. One of the riders spurred his horse over to us. "Stand away from the rebels."

"Rebels?" I said in surprise. "Since when have old women been rebels?"

The man came and stood his beast between the old woman and me. A horse's hooves can be very intimidating, and I took a couple of backward steps.

"Fancy changing direction? We've got plenty of room for more!" bellowed the man, deadly serious.

It isn't exactly prudent to argue with a man who's armed and on horseback when you yourself are neither of those things. Even so, I made clear what I thought of this villainous bully. He looked at me with his beady rat eyes.

The driver of my carriage, an older man I'd chatted with a little in the jib, came up behind me, tugged on my arm, and hissed: "Don't be an imbecile."

"But what can these children and grayheads have done that's so bad?" I cried. "And where are they being taken?"

"What do you want to be?" he said in my ear. "A good engineer or a Good Samaritan?" To try to calm things down, he turned a smile at the man on the horse, saying: "Hi, friend! How did it go in Játiva?"

"No such place as Játiva now," said the brute, spurring his horse away.

So the people were from Játiva, deported to Castile, an express wish of Little Philip's. After the city was conquered, thousands were enslaved, including from the nearby settlements. Even Játiva's name was eliminated, the place rechristened Colonia de San Felipe. Had I not seen this sorry column with my own eyes, I would have refused to believe it.

I spoke very little in the ensuing days. I had been educated to believe in a certain basic idea, that a king fights to defend or win territories— never to destroy them. Such an absurdity could make sense only in the mind of a madman. What use could there be in taking control of a place that has been flattened? Játiva, the city of a thousand wells, wiped from the face of the earth because a king had pointed his finger at a map.

As soon as we crossed into Catalonia, we began to see people hanged from the branches of trees. The convoy's slow advance was now constantly presided over by these oscillating bodies. On the larger trees, there were sometimes five, six, seven cadavers swinging from the branches, some higher, some lower, feet stirred by the wind. Most were men of all ages, but I did see a woman hanged from one solitary oak. They had not even bothered to tie her hands behind her. Beneath her on the ground were a little girl and a dog; its snout thrust in the air, the animal let out heartrending yowls, snorting through its nostrils like a bellows. The dog knew the woman was dead, but most harrowing of all, the child did not.

Official historians limit themselves to official history. They omit to mention that in 1708 the war had reached Catalonia, and thousands of Catalan irregulars joined in the fight. "Volunteers" would be one name for them, "militia," or "mountain fusiliers," but we called them Miquelets. These require a little explanation; otherwise, what was going on will make no sense.

"Miquelet" itself is simply a transcription of the original Catalan word *Miquelet*. The origin is possibly Michaelmas (*Sant Miquel*), when harvesting would traditionally commence. Anyone who didn't find work at harvest would look for alternatives, such as enlisting in the French or Spanish armies. If, for instance, the French were raising war against southern Protestants, the paymasters would hurry to Catalonia to recruit Miquelets. Miquelets were vehemently opposed to putting on army uniforms and footwear, and they even armed themselves. The French and Spanish high command considered them undisciplined hillmen, savages almost, unpredictable and unorthodox—none of which stopped them from appreciating their virtues as warriors. As light infantry, they were peerless. Excellent in forest combat, and as snipers, they always took on perilous roles in the vanguard, ravaging enemy lands. "*Les Miquelets ont fait des merveilles*" was the view of French officialdom. Which was why they were quick to enroll as many as possible: They cost half that of a professional unit and were twice as effective.

The problem was that some of them took a liking to the life of pillaging and slaughtering in the name of others. Whenever demobilized, they'd roam the hills and tracks as bandits, waiting for the next call-up.

Catalan civilians came to abhor them—at least in the cities, Miquelets were thought of as outlaws.

1708 was the first time a Bourbon army had set foot in Catalonia. As was to be expected, the Miquelets took exception to the invaders. Until that point, they hadn't cared a radish for the war, but all that changed when their own lands were advanced upon. Though nominally under the command of the Allied armies, they acted of their own accord. In any case, the fact that they wore no uniforms meant the Bourbons didn't recognize them as combatants bound by the usual treaties, which made hostilities unprecedentedly ferocious.

A captured Miquelet would usually be hanged. For their part, the Miquelets were no less cruel. Any soldiers they took prisoner would have their feet scorched and, before execution, be made to hop around like dancing bears. Sometimes the Miquelets would send them up onto the edge of a cliff or gully, where the enemy could see them. A horn would be sounded to draw the attention of the Bourbon soldiers. The prisoners, in single file, would have their ankles tied together with a long rope. Then the first one would be pushed over the edge. Then the second and the third, until the weight of the fallen, combined, would pull the others over. I was witness to one of these savage reprisals. Ten or twelve soldiers, hands tied behind their backs, ankles connected by the same rope. The more who fell, the harder it would be for those at the top to hold the weight. My God, their shrieks and cries. What a sight, these lines of white uniforms falling, vanishing without a trace. Nothing, I can assure you, could possibly lay a man's heart any lower.

Here's a representative account of the Miquelets, to show what kind of people they were. A case that, unfortunate that I was, I had to experience in the flesh.

Eighty or so Miquelets had at that time made an incursion into an area on the Catalan frontier called Beceite. Typical Miquelet behavior: They'd take out a small Bourbon detachment, then spend a few days in the liberated settlement, living more comfortably than up in the hills. But the fates were against them on this occasion, as the unit I was traveling in to Tortosa was passing very near to Beceite. We came across a couple of fear-stricken Spanish soldiers, who had managed to get away, and they told us what had happened at Beceite.

The Spanish caught the Miquelets with their breeches around their ankles that day. They were out in the town square celebrating their small victory, half drunk, when two cavalry squadrons rode in. The Miquelets fled in disarray, and thirty of their number were killed and one taken prisoner.

When it was all done, our unit took over the town, and I can assure you this was no pretty sight. In one corner, like a pile of discarded horseshoes, lay the soldiers who had died when the Miquelets first attacked; strewn across the square, the thirty Miquelets ridden down and bayoneted by the cavalry. Day was already well advanced, and it was decided that we would stay the night in Beceite, so "hospitality," as the officers put it, was "arranged."

Doors were kicked down and the civilians rounded up in the square. The skirmish was over, but the screaming and wailing had barely begun. Once all the townspeople were there, the officers, in order of rank, began picking out the prettiest girls and taking them back to their houses, where they would exercise what they termed their right to "hospitality." In other words, raping these women, whether they were virgins or had husbands, all in plain view of their families.

Back in the square, the mayor was down on his knees, and one of the captains had a sword at his neck. The town had always been loyal to Philip V, protested the mayor.

"He's lying," said the driver of my carriage.

"How do you know?" I said.

In answer, he pointed at the bell tower, which was empty. "Any town without a bell supports the archduke," he explained. "They were all handed over and melted down to make cannons." He winked at me. "Well, these are Catalans, so no doubt they made a little money out of it. But the end result's the same."

Overhearing us, a corporal came over. "You speak Catalan?" he said. "Because we need a translator."

I got down from the carriage and let him lead me to the sole prisoner. He was the group's leader, a man by the name of Ballester. Before they hanged him, they wanted to extract whatever information they could. His eyebrow was split and had bled profusely. But his broad face had a beauty out of keeping with the situation, and seemed to scorn any pain he might have been in. The ropes binding his wrists were soaked dark red. He had been captured moments earlier, and the blood he'd shed was already dry, as though, the thought struck me, he had been born with old veins.

And he was astonishingly young. Leading a squad of irregulars, and yet he couldn't have been any older than sixteen or seventeen—a boy, like me. He must have had quite the temperament, to be respected as a leader. His features melded nobility and sadness—not so strange, given the situation. But something also said to me that, even in better times, he'd be the distant kind. As for Ballester's gaze? It put me in mind of waves crashing against rocks; sooner or later, they'd overwhelm you. We came from such opposed worlds that I felt uncomfortable having to address him. I told him what his captors wanted. His attitude to me was that of a man listening to rabbits chew grass. He tilted his head and spat blood, and all he said in answer was: "I'm going to die, and that's all."

He didn't lament death, as though, more than an inevitable risk in the militia, it might mean martyrdom. Human instinct leads us to sympathize with the captive rather than the captor, and though Ballester's fate mattered nothing to me, I found myself saying, "Don't be a fool. If you promise them information, they'll keep you alive. Tell them something they'll need to wait to check the veracity of. Meantime, anything could happen. Who knows? Maybe peace will break out."

He raised his hands, bold youth, and looked me in the eye. The words seemed to scrape out from between his teeth. "If it weren't for these binds, I'd rip out your tongue, shitty *botiflero*."

Botiflero is the worst insult one can ever give a Catalan. It means anyone who supports Philip V, Castile, and the Bourbon dynasty. A traitor, a colluder, that is. The *-iflero* part of the word relates to a Catalan (and Spanish) word for *fat*—anyone, that is, all puffed up in his finery. I imagine it comes from the fact that the vast majority of supporters of the Austrian king, Charles, were from the lower classes, and those few Catalans behind Little Philip tended to be aristocracy and clergy.

Anyway, what does it matter where the word comes from? The point is that Ballester had insulted me, and I responded accordingly. "I try to help you, and you insult me!" I shouted. "I'd like to know what my place as an upstanding engineer has to do with the lowly kind of warfare you are engaged in."

A few more insults went back and forth. The only thing to note being how clear was the irremediable distance separating us. For me, war was what I'd been taught at Bazoches: a technical exercise free of ill will, tempered by the nobility of the opposing spirits. War, in this account, could (and ought to) be undertaken without emotions, which can only cloud the rational landscape of engineering; battle was a rational sphere, closer to chess than flying bits of lead. If a soldier had ever said to Vauban that he hated the enemy, no question, Vauban would have answered: "And what has he ever done to you?" Whereas for individuals like Ballester, war was a matter of life and death. Or not—it was more, much more than that—according to what he believed, this war was being conducted according to principles far higher than the brief transition that is life. From my point of view, of course, this was deluded: A military engineer was as far removed from mysticism as a clockmaker.

Yes, I had seen hundreds of people hanged, their feet swaying in the pines. I'd seen the Játiva hecatomb, and the dog and the girl at the woman's feet. But my education was made of stuff too solid to be rocked by a few sad sights. I stopped arguing with Ballester; it wasn't worth the trouble. He seemed to me the perfect mix of bandit and fanatic.

"Very well," I said, "don't tell them anything. You're the first person I've ever met who'd prefer a shorter to a longer life."

The Spanish captain who had sent for a translator was becoming annoyed, not being able to understand the insults. Curtly, he demanded to know what had been said.

"The Miquelets in this area are under orders of General Jones, the English commander in Tortosa," I lied. "Their mission is to take this godforsaken place and then await orders. A courier will be arriving tomorrow, first thing. To speak to this nincompoop, specifically."

As I'd thought, rather than stringing him up there and then, they decided to use him as bait.

"You've got another night to live," I said to him. "Put your house in order."

I had made it all up. No courier would be arriving the next morning, but I was in no danger. The Miquelets had decided against it, was all anyone would think, or they'd worked out it was a trap. Why did I do it? I don't know; perhaps Jimmy's royal generosity—not at all the same thing as generosity—had rubbed off on me. Or because of being a student of Vauban, whose punishment of vanquished foes was always benevolent. I do not believe it was purely out of goodness, as my next piece of conduct demonstrated very well the so-and-so I was becoming: I went after one of our Mediterranean beauties, a young girl, my and Ballester's age, who sparkled even from afar, even with a dirty rag for a head wrap. I saw her passing in front of a squat building, an open-door stable now holding twenty or thirty military horses. She was inside, feeding them hay. When she saw me, she looked away.

Look, I have lain down beside women from a great many latitudes, some of them of the strangest tints and hues. And in the eternal debate over which are most beautiful, I hold with the French. It must be one of the few commonplaces that are actually true. Still, it is a general truth; individually, when a Mediterranean woman is beautiful, she is without peer. And this young girl was bewitching. Her curly locks escaped from under the edges of the head wrap and fell down about her shoulders. The darkest black hair.

A passing sergeant warned me off: "Don't go near that one, she's sick with something. She'll even ward off horse rustlers."

It must be a question of character: If you say to certain people "Don't go," the very first thing they'll do is go. I entered the large stable, stopping a few feet from her with my elbow propped on the back of a horse. Chewing a piece of straw, I looked directly at her. She didn't stop working, piling straw in the mangers, pretending not to notice me.

"Come over here," I ordered.

From closer up, I could observe her in more detail. Sure enough, she was very young. Her nose had a pronounced, graceful curve to it. Slowly, I lifted a finger to her cheek. She turned her face away, but I had her cornered. I brushed her cheek with my fingertip, coming away with one of the ugly black grains. Well, perhaps she was contagious, but not to a student from Bazoches, who notices even the tiniest details. I pressed on the eruption, then put my finger in my mouth and sucked.

Raspberry jam. How clever! Not only had her pretend illness gotten her a job; it acted as a brilliant shield against the possibility of being raped. She knew she'd been found out, and the uncovered areas of her pale skin flushed an irate red.

Don't for a second think I'm going to launch into some discourse about military abuses. I've had dealings with too many soldiers, from all across the world, not to see their side. The common soldier is born a pauper and will die one. And things become available to an armed man that he'd never have the benefit of without a rifle at his shoulder. Spoils, and victims, become defenseless objects; it is then up to the morality of the would-be pillager to protect them. I agree that violating defenseless women is not a nice thing. My point is merely that to condemn the pillagers is easy—as easy as pillaging is difficult to defend.

No, I did not violate her. Perhaps because, if you have been educated in Bazoches, you come to treat women à la Vauban, and not à la Coehoorn. But my case is an exception to what was happening all across occupied Catalonia: At that very moment hundreds, thousands, of soldiers were stepping inside barns such as that one, sword in one hand, woman under the other arm.

The country was too small to provide lodgings for so many soldiers. A number of years later, I met a man who had been the mayor of a town of no more than eight hundred souls, called Banyoles. Practically every single virgin had been deflowered, and seventy-three of them fell pregnant. When he went to the governing authorities to protest, they reacted in the typical Bourbon fashion: by throwing the mayor in jail. Not even the Dutch in the sixteenth century suffered such ignominy at the hands of the duke of Alba's troops.

I asked her a few questions. Her name was Amelis. She did not hail from Beceite, the town where we were. So what was she doing there? She told me that she lived as a camp follower, taking whatever jobs she could find. I was about to push her harder, to try and elicit more information, when I heard shots outside.

It wasn't uniform volleys, like the kind you'd expect from regular troops, but, rather, a scattering of shots, punctuated by inhuman wailing. If there is one thing I have always had in spades, it is the prudence usually associated with beetles; rather than running out of the stable, I went farther in, to the back, keeping Amelis close to me as hostage. We got inside a mound of straw, me with my hand fast over her mouth, and I myself kept very, very quiet. Whatever was happening, I'd be sure to find out later on, without trying to be a hero. Indeed, it didn't take long before I found out what, and who, it was. A soldier burst in, terrified, trying to get away from something—he wasn't given time to hide: A number of Miquelets followed immediately behind. They ended his life as if he were a dog, beating his head in, and then went out in search of more. During the execution, I moved my hand from Amelis's mouth to cover her eyes. She was kind and prudent enough not to scream.

This was the execution I mentioned before, the one I witnessed in the flesh. The unpredictable, what in military terms was irrational, was never clearer than in assaults like the one on Beceite. They themselves had been given a hiding; they'd fled leaving thirty dead and their little *caudillo,* Ballester, in enemy hands. Who could have expected a counterattack within half an hour, leaderless and against superior forces? But their regard for Ballester, and the chance to rescue him, quite simply, drew them back.

The Miquelets revealed a principle that is often ignored but that I have always had much respect for: lunacy. In war, it always lends the element of surprise. And they won the day! The Spanish officials were spread around in different houses throughout the town, each with his breeches down. The rank and file were not on guard and had no one to give them orders. Extremely cautiously, I peeked out of a window. At the end of the street, in the town square, I saw Ballester himself. Free once more, surrounded by his men, he was about to slit the throat of the captain who, moments before, had had him interrogated. The captain, kneeling; Ballester behind him. He lifted the captain's chin with one hand and, with the other, drew a knife across the man's gullet.

I barely need say how nervous that pretty little scene made me. In Ballester's eyes, I was an accursed *botiflero.* I preferred not to think what he'd do if he caught me. The way the captain had been killed, I was sure, would be rather agreeable compared to what they would line up for me; bleeding cleanly to death was sweet in comparison with the inventive torture methods the Miquelets could surely come up with.

The only thing was to hide and await nightfall. Then make myself scarce. The two of us lay there for a long while, on the floor, under that mound of straw. I lay close to Amelis's back, the two of us like spoons. My cheek against hers, my hand over her mouth once more: a forced, absurd intimacy. Her neck smelled lovely, and the straw made me think of Jeanne. This is what human beings are like: people being shot down in the street outside, me possibly next in line, and even so, I couldn't avoid seeing, in Amelis's outline, with all her clothes on, Jeanne naked.

Night finally fell. We were still lying down, and I whispered in the ear of my dark-haired beauty. "If I let you go now, you'll give me away, and they'll be straight after me. I'm going to keep you with me for a little while. All I want is to get out of here alive. Behave yourself and I'll let you go once we're clear of this place. Understand?"

She nodded, and I took my hand away from her mouth. Just to be safe, before I let her go, I spoke the most amorous words imaginable: "And if you cry out, I'll strangle you."

Outside the stable door lay the street, where I would inevitably run into one of those deadly Miquelets. Behind the stable, on the other hand, there was a wood not far off. Slip out of a back window, was my thought. The problem was how; the window was too narrow for us both to get through it at the same time. If she went first, she'd run off screaming the moment her feet touched the ground. If I went first, she'd turn on her heel and escape. She was a sharp girl and could see my problem without my having to explain it.

"Get out of here," she hissed, more disgusted than hostile. "Why would I bother getting them to kill you? I won't say anything to anyone."

"And I'm supposed to believe that."

I picked her up at her hips, lifting her onto the cramped window ledge, and then got up next to her, side by side. It was a thick adobe wall, made far thicker than usual, perhaps to keep the stable cool. That meant the window was reached by a long tube, a few feet in length. We were bound to get stuck with our arms in front, our heads outside, our bellies wedged together and our four feet dangling in the air behind us.

"Don't worry," I said. "I've studied how to deal with situations like this."

"Oh, really?" she replied. "Quite the student you've turned out to be."

"Anatomical theory states that, if a man's shoulders can fit through the width of a trench or a mine, the rest of the body can also get through. And if the cavity is too narrow, all you have to do is dislocate one shoulder. Once through, simply pop the shoulder back into place."

Her large eyes grew even wider. "You're going to dislocate your shoulder?"

"No, of course not," I said. "I'll do yours. I'll put it back in afterward. It won't be hard—both my hands are free, and I know how it's done."

At this point she began buffeting me about the head with her fists. "You've had your grubby hands on me for hours, and now you're saying you want to break my back! I'm not going to let you touch me anymore, not even my shoulder!"

I put my hand over her mouth. "Quiet!"

I have no idea how we did eventually manage it. I believe I may have pulled off the wooden frame, widening the space somewhat, and we then slid out like boneless lizards. We fell to the floor outside, I lifted her up, and into the woods we went.

Beceite was surrounded by mountainous terrain, a delightful natural labyrinth for the Miquelet parties to shelter in. The Army of the Two Crowns was off to the southeast, and that was the way I headed.

It was a pinewood forest, not especially dense, and a full moon bathed everything in an amber light. There is no such thing as war for crickets, and the freshness of the night was a relief after the heat of the summer day. Had that group of senseless throat slitters not been so close by, it might have been a most pleasurable nighttime stroll. Once we were far enough away to make noise, I said: "Quite the friends you've got! That soldier who came into the stable—they beat him to death just to save on bullets!"

Though she was at my side, she made it clear she wanted to get away from me as soon as possible. "I don't have any friends," she said. "And even if I did, who are you to criticize? What does war have to do with the poor?"

"It's possible to be poor and not a savage," I said.

"At least they don't go around raping their enemies' women!"

"Neither do I!" I said, defending myself. "And, so you know, I'm an engineer. We *professionals*, engineers or soldiers, we serve the person who has contracted our services, whichever king it happens to be, and for the duration of the contract, and that's all. Birth does not tie us to any particular sovereign, and therein lies our privilege. I might serve France today, Sweden or Prussia tomorrow, and no one could call me disloyal or a deserter, just as no one would be surprised to see a spider crossing the river by jumping from rock to rock."

"To the Miquelets, you are a Bourbon," she said. "And if the Bourbons go around hanging their parents and children, is it so surprising they want to kill you?"

"I am paid to carry out engineering works. To be honest with you, I couldn't care less either way, Bourbon or pro-Austrian, one side or the other."

Suddenly, she stopped. She looked around, smiling, and said: "Do you not hear that?"

The abrupt change of subject surprised me, but I answered: "You're quite right, it's very annoying having to walk in a pine forest. I supposed it would be pointless to ask you to stop stepping on pinecones; they crunch so loudly, you can hear them a mile off."

"No, engineer," she said, cutting me off, straining to hear. "I mean the music."

Music? There were, of course, only the sounds of the forest at night. Had she lost her mind? The summer moon lent her pale complexion an unreal tone. I thought for a moment that she might have been referring to the two of us; we'd gotten off on the wrong foot, but the forest at night *was* making everything sweeter. Or perhaps not: I reached an arm around her waist, but she got away from me immediately.

As she went, she left me with an almost sad sigh. "No, you do not hear it," she said. "Farewell, then, great engineer."

She had disappeared, but the scent of her lingered in the forest air for a moment. And know something else? I wasn't certain whether she had taken me for a ride or there was something more.

I walked all night to try and put as much distance as I could between me and that Miquelet warren. At first light, I positioned myself on top of one of the large boulders you see throughout that region. From up there, lying on my front, I could see the path without being seen. I had a decent amount of time to think things through. In such moments, the infinite superiority of love over any horror becomes clear, because my mind turned again and again to that girl: Amelis, averting the images of death, Amelis.

After Jeanne, no beauty had moved me as much. And you'll agree when I say that Amelis was at a disadvantage, seeing as Jeanne always had recourse to upper-class cosmetics, whereas when I met Amelis, she was wearing a laughable head wrap and had disguised herself with a pretend disease. Where could she have gone? Her parting words could have meant anything, even that she was a spy, possibly for both sides. . . . She would end up hanged, that was for sure.

At midmorning I made out a dust cloud on the horizon. This was the first time in my life, and the last, I believe, that I was happy to see a detachment of Bourbon cavalry. At least they wouldn't treat me as the Miquelets might have done! I signaled to them with my hat from the top of the boulder and came down to ground level.

At their head was a captain in a dust-covered uniform, the white of it altogether gray now. Without dismounting, he asked me: "Spanish or French?"

"Alive is what I am, and it's a miracle!" I cried, scurrying over to them. "Get me away from here, damn it!"

12

The army set to attack Tortosa was led by the duke of Orléans, nephew to the Beast himself. Orléans had twenty-five thousand men under his command, and a lavishly stocked artillery train.

Thus, after so many twists and turns, I was going to take part in a proper siege. I won't deny that my spirits picked up. Perhaps I would manage to overcome my Bazoches disaster, restore myself, become an engineer. I'd spent two years, the most interesting years of my short life thus far, deep in the task of becoming a Maganon, absorbing both the science and the necessary morals. Twenty-four months, if you think about it, is a considerable portion of the life of a sixteen-year-old. So whenever I was feeling doubtful, I would roll up my right sleeve. I meditated on my five Points, contemplating them in many different lights, in the glowing dawn, or by that of a full moon, when midday embraced us or in the soft violet twilight. My God, I found my tattoos full of beauty, those five sacred Points. I couldn't give up. Tortosa meant the chance to discover a Word that would bathe me in light.

The Bourbon army had pitched tents outside Tortosa on June 12, and I arrived the next day. I joined the engineers' brigade as an aide-de-camp. I could make myself additionally useful with my French and Catalan, and there was a chance that I might be used to liaise between the French and Spanish contingents.

Family ties are even more important in France's army than in Europe's other armies, and the engineers' brigade had been given to the duke of Orléans's cousin to command. He was an innocuous man, phlegmatic rather than lackadaisical, of slender build and cheerful, a daydreamer. He had effeminate tastes, which reflected in the way he carried himself, and indeed his pretty looks, though they were no indication of his carnal preferences. He spent his days inside his splendid field tent, in which Darius of Persia would have been quite at home; its fabric was decorated with large cashmere depictions, and the roof was in the shape of an onion bulb, like orthodox church domes. Spacious and sumptuous—an entire orchestra could have fit inside—it featured nocturnal carousings with throngs of people, the only thing restraining them being his cousin's warnings. This pleasure seeking of his was regularly excessive; one of the things he liked most was to recruit, en masse, whores from the towns through which the army passed, along with a few elderly nuns. The Spanish priests complained to Orléans, who, wanting to avoid a scandal, promptly tried reining his cousin in. Wigs and perfume were his great weakness; he loved to stand before a mirror trying on dozens of different hairstyles. As for perfumes, he had them sent in especially. Always overpoweringly strong. His arrival would be preceded by a great wave of Asiatic smells.

His mind was on Versailles, and he put up with this southern sojourn with an air of ironic resignation. He hoped to go back to Paris saying he'd served *dans l'armée royale.* As for his relationship with the engineers, let us say it was the same as that of a pet fish with its elements: That it inhabits a pond does not mean it understands water. The gravity of the man was such that I have entirely forgotten his name. Let's call him Monsieur Forgotten.

Something good about Monsieur Forgotten, I admit, was that one could be sincere and speak the truth with him, by no means the usual way with French aristocracy. Granted, the impulse behind his tolerance of me was not all that lofty. Why did he put up with me when I criticized and made suggestions and even accusations? Because I was a nobody, less than a nobody. To him I was a fly of the kind constantly buzzing around us in the relentless summer heat, and he treated me as such.

For what it is, or was, worth, the siege we were engaged in seemed an out-and-out disaster to me from day one. I am the first to recognize that war always has been, and will be, the art of negotiating short-ages and imperfections. No campaign or siege has ever been conducted in optimum conditions. Quite the reverse: Something will always be missing. The man-at-arms, or the siege engineer, must have the gump-tion to improvise, to make the most of the situation (and trust that the enemy is on a level, or worse, footing). Vauban knew it, and that was why my technical instructions by the Ducroix brothers were always tempered by that one maxim: *Débrouillez-vous!* Deal with it!

Even allowing for the usual mishaps and limitations associated with war, Tortosa was a complete negation of all I'd learned at Bazoches. It had some value pedagogically: as an example to an engineer of what *not* to do. Ineptitude, in a siege situation, is paid for in blood.

An example. The first day, the very first day, of my studies in siege warfare, the Ducroix brothers etched in my memory the Thirty General Maxims of de Vauban, which pertained to any attack on a strong-hold. Would you like to know what the very first one was? Well, then I'll tell you.

Être toujours bien informé de la force des garnisons avant de déterminer les attaques: You must always be well informed as to the powers of the gar-rison before beginning your attack.

The calculations of Tortosa's defenses proved useless: Orléans had found out that there were some fifteen hundred soldiers, among them English, Dutch, and Portuguese, set to stand against us on the ramparts. Among them, survivors from Allied troops at Almansa. But we noticed, once the attack had commenced, that their forces had multiplied: The civilians were lending enthusiastic support, so enthusiastic that the regular troops themselves were nonplussed. A further fifteen hundred men, the civilian militia, joined in, and everyone else was helping, too: women tending to wounds, children bringing pitchers of water to the bastions. I was dumbfounded. Why didn't they hole up at home and wait for the storm to pass? Why would these simple peasants, to whom dynastic affairs were neither here nor there, risk taking part in a battle, as well as the reprisals in the case of defeat? Fool that I was, I was yet to realize that this was going to be the war at the end of the world—the end of the Catalan world, at least.

In the eyes of an engineer, Tortosa was an unusual city indeed. It had long been a strategically important spot, a military boundary, which meant there were a great many different fortification styles superimposed, from the Arabic rampart all the way to the very modern bastions. It sat on either side of the River Ebro, not far from where it met the sea—hence its strategic importance. In fact, the city was on the west bank, and a bastion stood protecting the east side. As a whole, it was thoroughly fortified. The Austrians had had their best engineers

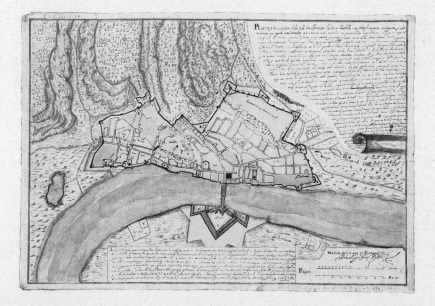

working on the defenses, preparing for a siege they rightly judged inevitable after Almansa. Most of the walls were modern, coming down at a sharp angle. Churches stood at the ends of certain parts of the cities, and then engineers had no qualms about turning these into makeshift bastions.

It made sense that Orléans would come up against such well-prepared defenses. Whoever controlled Tortosa would have the most important river route in Catalonia, and with it all routes south.

We struck the trench on July 20. As I explained in the opening chapters, "striking the trench" was the founding act for attacking any stronghold. Once your point of attack has been chosen, there's no going back. Total defeat for the besieged, or disgrace for the attacking army.

I heard only on the nineteenth that the order had been given. "And the geological report?" I asked the Forgotten.

"Report? What report might that be, dear aide?"

Troops had been posted in the area where the trench was to begin, but no engineer had reconnoitered it. Really, the whole engineers' brigade was full of dimwits, and most of them hardly knew what I meant. At first I thought they must be joking.

"We are going to strike the trench without doing a geological survey?" I asked.

"My, you're meticulous!"

The grand event would happen, I was informed, the next day at eight in the evening. I put my hands to my head and straightaway went to entreat Monsieur Forgotten to hold off. "Sir, I have been told we are to strike the trench tomorrow."

As ever, he was sitting in his tent, trying on a yellow wig in the mirror. He answered without looking at me. "Your information is correct. Which will give us the whole night ahead to dig under cover of darkness."

"It's not advisable, sir."

"Oh?"

"It's June, sir. It's still light at eight in the evening."

"You, sir, are a pessimist, not to mention a panicmonger."

What Monsieur Forgotten did *not* mention was that he was oblivious, not to mention a wanton killer! I'll explain why.

Striking a trench is always a highly delicate operation. Thousands of soldiers are gathered together, converted into peons, and made to line up at certain predetermined points under the cover of dark: rows of stakes joined together by a trail of lime on the ground. (I've participated in setting up the stakes at times, scrabbling along on your knees and in fear of your life.) The closer to the stronghold the trench can begin, the fewer days will be needed for digging. Counter to this, the closer to the ramparts it begins, the more likely it will be noticed. At this point the troops still cannot take refuge beneath ground—it was quite usual for the trench to begin within range of the defenders' cannons—since the digging has only just begun.

Each of the men would have a pick or shovel, and thousands of the *fajina* wicker baskets would already have been lined up. The signal would be given and, as quietly as possible, digging begun all along the line. Each man would work behind the *fajina*, which the first shovelfuls would fill up, creating the first parapet in a matter of minutes, however precarious the situation.

Only a very disciplined troop, or one working at a very safe distance, would be able to move about undetected and at absolutely no risk. Predictably enough, the enemy sentries saw us, heard us, or, I'd say, possibly smelled us, given Monsieur Forgotten's pungent patchouli. And what was bound to happen, happened.

Twilight in the west of Catalonia has an intensity and forcefulness all its own; the throes of the day come erupting into the sky in oceanic blues and reddish ambers. As cannon fire commenced, a strip of maroon lit up the horizon.

There were fifty or so Allied cannons at Tortosa, of all calibers, and they began to pound our positions immediately: 2,200 excavators turned to 2,100, and in no time at all, 2,000. A chronicle I read subsequently referred to that night of horrors with the following lovely phrase: "The cannonade that night was a delight to hear." Those historians might save "delight" for describing royal weddings, I say!

It couldn't have gone any worse. Everything that Vauban foretold, all the possible things that can go wrong in a siege, came about. Another example: As a rule, commanders in the artillery tend to love blowing things up. At the first chance, with a childlike joy, they will commence firing. As happened in Tortosa. The first parallel had not even been dug, and our chief of artillery was already there, ordering fifteen cannons and six mortars be installed—at positions we had not even touched with pick or shovel. The problem being that the first parallel is at such a distance, nearly a mile from the ramparts, that cannonfire won't land anywhere near. If the guns are accurate enough to land any shots on a rampart or bastion, that is. A great many hundredweights of gunpowder and ammunition for nothing. I objected; Monsieur Forgotten didn't even hear. What did it matter to him? The artillery chief was one of his revelers par excellence, and in any case, neither of them would have to cough up for the powder.

The trench a little way advanced, we ran into some monumental rocks under the surface. It was almost as though some had been placed there by the enemy expressly to obstruct the trench. For the largest ones, we had to resort to explosives. But the blasting would also take out a large section of the trench, including the *fajina* parapets protecting us from enemy fire, which would then have to be reformed. And to think my superiors had laughed off a geological survey!

It was also in Tortosa that I had confirmation of another of Vauban's teachings, one he'd told me about in person: Sappers are heavy drinkers; they become drunk before going and getting themselves killed. The front end of the trench moves forward by dint of the work of a small crew—eight or, at most, ten men. However grandiose the overall works, that is the most that can fit into the confines of a trench. The enemy knows this very well and concentrates fire on just that point.

Sappers suffer a disproportionately high number of casualties and deaths. However well they are paid, and though the crews are relieved every three or four hours, the tension will end up destroying their nerves. In order to bear it, they drink, and drink, then they drink some more.

For a young engineer such as myself, Tortosa brought home the gap between lessons and reality. Take the Mantelletta, for instance. If you look at any images of a siege, beside a sapper there will always be a barrow, a contraption with two wheels and a panel of wood. The sapper farthest forward uses this as a shield. Fine, well, you can forget about that—I can assure you the nitwit who drew those pictures has never been present at a siege in all his life. I can remember only one siege

where a Mantelletta was used, and that was because some recently grad-
uated dunderhead forced the sappers to take it. Sapper crews hated the
Mantelletta—why? Because they enrage the enemy, who sees the head
of the dragon and proceeds to rain down upon it all the fire they can.

But of all the gaps between theory and practice, perhaps the most
surprising was something no one had referred to during my studies: the
raft of people voluntarily inserting themselves into the battle situation.

In Vauban's world, the spheres of civic and martial life were at once
overlapping and separate. But the last thing I expected was, as the Attack Trench became a complex web of passageways and surface-level
crypts, that it would also be invaded by civilians. Milling around as
though the parallels were city boulevards, and the lines of communication streets and alleyways.

Naturally, as the trenches drew closer to the ramparts, and the enemy fire grew fiercer, you would see fewer and fewer non-troops. But
even where the vanguard was most exposed, dozens of people who
had no clear place there would be swarming around. Priests above
all. Everyone with something to sell; the whores offering a quickie
up against some outjutting trench corner, lying there with their legs
akimbo, cunt in the air, lifting their skirt whenever anyone came by;
peddlers offering morsels to eat, a break from the usual insipid gruel.
The range of professions that descended into the trenches was nigh on
infinite. Shoemakers, professional gamblers, barbers, people to delouse
your clothing, cobblers, gypsies, prostitutes of all varieties, anything
and everything. Bear in mind that Vauban never would have tolerated
such a sorry spectacle—but Vauban had the kind of clout you don't see
very often. And Orléans was a Coehoornian who had little time for the
idea of a siege being comprised of different facets. I think he initiated
that trench only to give his cousin Monsieur Forgotten a chance to take
the credit back at Versailles.

It was quite a lesson to me, seeing the way man exploits and usurps
undergroun realms. And there in the trench at Tortosa, I met two creatures who caused me profound dismay, the closest thing imaginable to
creatures from the underworld.

The child can have been no older than six or seven years. Even an
animal would clothe itself in a more dignified way. Barefoot, and with

tattered pantaloons that went down only as far as his knees, and a vest that might have been white once but was covered in gray from ash and adventures. And his hair, mother of God, his hair: So much grime and muck had accumulated in it that his sandy locks had turned into rough, ratty clumps. And then, dependent on this child, another being out of fable: a dwarf clothed in the attire of a traveling fairground. His face was squashed together, as though he were suffering some form of mental constipation, not uncommon among his kind. But his compulsive grimacing suggested he was unhinged in some way. Most extraordinary of all was the funnel crowning the dwarf's head—a large round piece of metal, its pointed spout pointing proudly up. You couldn't be sure whether the funnel suited the dwarf or vice versa. Both child and dwarf were the same height.

I will always remember the first words I said to the lad. I took him by the scruff of the neck and asked: "You? Where's your father?"

Father? He looked at me as though I'd said something in Chinese. His Catalan was mixed together with a little Castilian Spanish and much French. As for the dwarf, his chosen form of communication was the grunt. The child was called Anfán, the dwarf Nan; their life stories were contained in these names. Anfán was no more than a spoken transcription of the French word for "child," *enfant*. I assumed therefore that his life until then had been spent in French military encampments, where the men simply called this wayward little creature *enfant*. And "Nan" is simply Catalan for "dwarf." Doubtless Anfán was an orphan with nowhere else to go. Catalonia had been in an almost perpetual state of war for decades. His parents having died of natural causes—or at the hands of some murderer—Anfán, like so many, fell by the wayside. As for the dwarf, his name represented a summary of his life as much as the mystery of it. How had he got there, and where from? No one would ever know. Neither his language, nor his mind, both deficient, would ever be able to express it. One thing was certain: The child loved the dwarf unreservedly, fiercely, absolutely. As he scurried around the trenches, Anfán was always sure to protect the dwarf and provide him with shelter, and on one occasion, when they lost each other, the boy rushed around in sheer desperation. He looked for Nan night and day, and when they were reunited, an outbreak of joyful weeping was heard all around.

I came across them one night, sleeping totally unprotected in their little den: a hole in the ground alongside the first parallel, full of a great number of empty munitions boxes as large as coffins. Seeing some shadows, I entered. And there they were. For a bed, some old rush matting hidden at the back of the rat hole, in among all the detritus. They slept hugging each other, far from the din of fighting without.

Anfán, mewling sweetly, held a protective arm across the dwarf's chest. I got ready to give them the fright of their life—but something stopped me at the last moment: Anfán's unshod feet. I held one of them lightly in my hand. I examined it with the same attention I had applied in the Spherical Room. The scars all over the soles spoke of the harshness of the life he'd led. I was overcome by emotion, something an engineer should always guard against. I did not want to grow attached to this sorry pair, but neither did I feel it in me to trouble them.

There is something sacrosanct in the breathing of sleeping children, as though a sign by nature to say that anyone who harmed them would never be forgiven. I laid a sheet of munition wadding over them, that was all, and left.

We were yet to get as far as the third parallel. The majority of the civilian interlopers didn't go any farther than the first. Even the greediest trader didn't usually go as far as the second, at which point the enemy projectiles fell more accurately; light weapons were in range, too.

One day I found myself at the vanguard, making some calculations on a tablet, looking through my periscope. Ay, yes, the periscope. That Z-shaped lens-tube, so very useful for observing the ramparts from the trenches, the same reason it would always be targeted by enemy fire. The best way of concealing it was in a gap in the ground between two *fajinas*. Alas, there was some Allied whoreson, a Dutchman or a Portuguese, up on the ramparts with a telescope; he had it trained on the trench's cautious advance and must have had a gift for spotting periscopes. Telescope versus periscope: This was trench warfare. Half my life I have spent fighting on the side of the periscope, half on that of the telescope. An enemy officer ordered a twenty-bore cannon to see if it could hit me.

Boom! The cannonball landed right between two large wicker baskets that were above me—orange light exploded all around me. I was saved by the fact that I was crouched down at that moment, leaning right forward and making notes on the distances. A nearby crew of sappers came and dug me out of the avalanche of mud, uprights, and rubble.

I was not the slightest bit just or thankful in the way I pushed my saviors off me—shouting and shoving them away. The periscope, a very expensive piece of equipment, was broken. This made me even more vexed. Finally, an old sapper managed to bring me back to my senses. He gave short shrift to my fit of pique. "Calm yourself, lad. You survived somehow. Now get yourself to the rear, get a strong drink inside you, and they'll soon sew you back together."

He was quite right, not that it stopped me from going away in a foul mood. In that humor, with my face darker than coal, I made my way to the rear. Which was when I saw that pair, Anfán and Nan, up to their tricks again.

You find a multitude of lateral openings in the overall circuit of an Attack Trench: spaces for storing ammunition and building materials, recesses begun in error and abandoned, drainage ditches, false branches to confuse the enemy watchmen, areas for men to fall back into and depositories, branches leading to the artillery platforms. In one of these I saw Anfán on his knees, facing a soldier who was in the process of unbuckling his belt.

What was it about the prospect of this act that so enraged me? All I know is that I howled at the man like a monkey. "Pig! I'm going to send you to the galleys!"

The soldier was startled—finding himself reprimanded by some frenzied stranger, eyes staring out from a soot- and red-mud-covered face. Then I noticed the dwarf was in there, too, behind the soldier. Hearing me, he shot out, followed by the boy. And they didn't go away empty-handed.

"Imbecile!" I said to the soldier. "They've stolen your purse. The least you deserve!"

He ran out after Anfán and Nan—not, of course, that he was ever going to catch them.

Once the second parallel was under way, the mortars and cannons on either side bombarded one another twenty-four hours a day. The besieged sought to impede the forward progress of our trenches and destroy our artillery, we to destroy theirs and to create breaches in the ramparts. The firing from the city rained down on the *fajina* parapet like hail. Near misses would come flying at those of us behind.

For some unknown reason, summer in the south of Catalonia can be even more suffocating than down in Andalusia. Add to this the dozens of dead bodies situated foolhardily above the trench, which no one dared bury even at night, and you can imagine the clouds of pernicious insects that abounded. What a wonderful invention sign language is! We engineers had another way of communicating. Why? Well, because if you opened your mouth to speak any word longer than *oui,* twenty flies would be in there before you knew it.

As for Nan and Anfán, I chased after them day and night, in vain. They were impossible to catch. They scuttled like lizards on six feet and always knew the best fork in the trenches to vanish down.

I decided to try and make a pact with them. I came across them one day in a trench that was particularly long and straight, they at one end and I at the other. Before they ran away, I let them know it wasn't my intention to trap them. I left a folded piece of paper on the floor. I shouted out that it was a pass so they could come into my tent—if they came, I'd reward them with chocolates. Then I withdrew so they could come and take the piece of paper.

It did not work. Perhaps they didn't trust me, but most likely, their natural tendencies simply took over. They were trench rats, born to pilfering and dashing off.

A few days later, I finally got my hands on them. I was lucky enough to run into them on a sharp corner, and they didn't have time to escape. The dwarf managed to evade me, but I got a good hold on Anfán. I lifted him up under my arm as he kicked and screamed.

"Quiet!" I said. "I'm going to make certain you're never seen around here again."

But he somehow wriggled free and dashed away, Longlegs Zuvi following after. I lunged and got him by the ankle. The two of us rolled around on the floor of the second parallel.

Thus, when an enormous man appeared nearby, the two of us were tangled up, tearing at each other like schoolboys. Anfán thrashed around, but I was getting the better of him and didn't pay much mind to the man.

"You!" he growled. "Does no one in this army salute a general?" He pointed to the band on his belt indicating his rank. He must have been around fifty years old, with thick, substantial cheeks. From where I was, like a worm on the ground, he blotted out the sun. I got to my feet. If I had known then how important this man was going to be in my life, I can assure you I wouldn't have given such a wishy-washy answer.

"Apologies, General, I didn't see you. Now, if you'll allow, I'm trying to bring a bit of order to this trench."

I had been in contact almost exclusively with French personnel, and I must admit I had taken on many of their prejudices, and the way they looked down on their Spanish allies. They considered them an army of poorly organized, poorly directed beggars. And they were right. This general wasn't happy about being brushed aside. Obviously, faced with a French general, I would have shown an altogether different attitude, and he knew it.

I made to head off with Anfán by the neck, but the general stopped me, putting his hand on my chest. He'd encountered me tangled up with this whimpering boy, the boy resisting and trying to get away. What could he think? Our eyes met, and then I knew. He got me by my shirt and slammed me against the trench wall. Keeping a hold on me, he brought his face right up to mine. "I know your kind very well! Like abusing trench orphans, isn't that it?"

"Me?" I said as his large hands pinned me back. "I must be the only person in the entire army trying to *stop* such abuses!"

To make things worse, Anfán began weeping like a widow. He was so convincing that even I, in another moment, would have been moved. He spoke his mix of Catalan, French, and a little Castilian, but you didn't need to know languages to understand what he was saying: that I was an underground letch, that I'd made him suck my *pito*, the whole thing. Kneeling now, in a memorable final flourish, he lifted his eyes to the heavens, two tears running down his mud-smeared face, and begged the Almighty to free him from this life of sorrow. Even his sandy locks seemed pitiful. At six years of age, not even the rascal Martí Zuviría was quite so accomplished! I of course protested, but the Spanish general grabbed me by the neck with bull-like strength.

"That's enough out of you, you swine! How can such a vile specimen as you even exist? Abusing children is like sacrilege!" he cried, and with a swipe of the hand, he delivered his judgment. "What is there left to say? I've heard enough."

He was a hefty, well-built man, and in the confines of the trench, his figure blocked out his entourage of Spanish assistants. Within seconds, they all piled on top of me, and I was under arrest.

"Before this day is out," he growled, wagging a finger in front of my nose, "you'll be swinging from a tree."

He meant it; there was no point in my protesting or appealing. My only chance was if the French generalship interceded, but it was clear that this Spanish general had little sympathy with the French. Anfán was very pleased about the turn of events. As three men dragged me away, he followed after, skipping and jumping around me and my captors. His hands by his nose, wiggling his fingers, he mocked me: "What fun!" he said, then went on in Catalan so my captors wouldn't understand. "Don't you want me to clear off? Well, for once I'm going to listen to you. I wouldn't miss it for the world, you getting hanged, stupid old mule!"

Then, by some miracle, someone shouted out: "General! General! Look! Up there!"

Sure enough, something came into sight up above Tortosa: Through the hazy gunsmoke, we saw flares going up. Obviously something other than the usual shooting and grapeshot. Little flashing red and yellow puffs of smoke, against the blue of the summer sky, and the pure white of the clouds, forming a beautiful five-colored painting. Unfortunately, I wasn't quite in the right frame of mind to appreciate it.

"Red and yellow flares, red and yellow!" called out the general's assistant, in high excitement. "The Allies are using the red and the yellow!"

"Let's go, let's go!" ordered the general. "Follow me!"

And he led the way to headquarters. He had one of these Castilian voices custom-built for telling others what to do, so forceful that they brook no reply. When someone like this general said "Follow me," it meant "Follow me," and everything else ceased to matter. The men who had a hold on me immediately let go and simply trotted after their leader.

A red and yellow signal, in Allied code, meant a petition to friendly outside forces for urgent help. So here was a dilemma for Orléans! The flares signified that the garrison in Tortosa was on its last legs, yes, but also that an auxiliary Austrian army was close enough to see the signals in the sky. Which gave Orléans two choices: Lift the siege and head out to take on the external army, or (à la Coehoorn) throw everything he had at Tortosa despite the trenches not yet being complete. In either case, the mountains of earth that had been moved would all be for nothing.

This was what the high command had to reckon with. For me personally, the flares were a godsend, and I let out a sigh of relief like a buffalo. My long legs folded, slack from the fright, and I knelt down. I saw Anfán. It was just the two of us again.

"I'm going to break every single bone in your body!" I roared.

What do you think my dear, vile Waltraud? Did I catch him? Yes or no?

Of course not. A rat scurrying up into the nooks and crannies of a cathedral wall would have been easier to catch.

13

The assault was now down to the infantry, not the engineers. We fell back from the trenches as thousands of Bourbon soldiers took up their attack positions.

I did not see the assault, but I did hear it. I was by one of the entrances to the first parallel, in the rearguard. First came a bombardment at twilight, the attack beginning at exactly the same time we'd begun digging the trench: eight in the evening. Then we heard rifles being fired, and the sounds of the infantry charging up a forty-five-degree incline. The resistance was so fierce that civilians resorted to hurling statues of saints from the ramparts. It was four hours before the Spanish took hold of a single bastion. There was no cease-fire until two in the morning.

Predictably enough, Orléans had opted for a direct attack, cost what it may. And the vast majority of the wounded crying out were doing so in Spanish, not French. I didn't think so at the time, but in hindsight, it's enough to make you spit. What was the point of this war? A French monarch wanting to get his hands on the Spanish throne, with the Spanish army at his service. Any serious encounter, and it was Spanish soldiers who would be sent as cannon fodder into the charnel house. It was hardly as though the Spanish were dying against their will. Not even the Turks would have been obtuse enough to involve themselves in such a shambles as this.

At the Allies' request, there was a truce. Orléans suspected they were playing for time, but he was so intent on taking Tortosa that he put up with it. He lost nothing by it. The auxiliary army was still a long way away, and Orléans had control of a bastion. Well, during this truce, something truly chilling happened.

We heard cries, women screaming. It was still dark when, from inside the walls, a lamentation went up, a clamor that put one in mind of passages from the Old Testament. We later learned that the inhabitants of Tortosa, hearing that the foreign officers had opted to surrender, were in despair.

I couldn't understand it. In dynastic conflicts, the people hid; they never took part in the combat themselves. I remember saying to myself for the first time: "Zuvi, you have been away from your home too long. What on earth is going on here?"

Luckily, I didn't have very much time to consider it. I was approached by a French official, a liaison officer with the Spanish command. He told me I was to go to the bastion we had taken, to tell the troops there they were about to be relieved. Fine, I supposed—falling back from such an exposed position would surely be taken as good news. What seemed strange was for a youngster like me to be sent, to speak with a general, no less.

Seeing my shambolic appearance, the liaison officer said: "Get washed, put a decent tunic on over that. And shine your boots."

"But Captain," I said artlessly, "shouldn't someone with a far higher rank be going on such a mission?"

"Oh!" he said, patting me on the back. "Take it as a great honor, my boy."

A great honor! What this "great honor" consisted of, I'll now tell you.

It wasn't until dawn that I was sent to the bastion, when the sun was already up, warming the living and causing the dead to rot. The path to the bastion was lined with bulging bodies. As I went up the mound made by the rubble of the bastion, my boots raised clouds of flies covering the bodies, like plump, winged chestnuts.

There were hundreds of soldiers up on the bastion, rifles loaded and bayonets drawn, sheltering in the ruins and looking out over the deathly quiet city. The general to whom I was to take my message was also sheltering among the bastion stones. He was the same man who had tried to have me hanged, though, thank heavens, he didn't recognize me just then!

"*Mon général!*" I said in French. "I find you at last." I gave him the order to fall back.

He didn't understand a word of my French. He looked at one of his men and said in the sternest of Castilian voices: "What does this Frog want?"

I repeated what I'd said, this time in Castilian, and with the kind of reverence and smile one reserves for the victors. "An order from the high command, *mon général*: You have carried out your task, gloriously and honorably, and now please allow yourself to be withdrawn. French battalions will take your place until hostilities are complete."

His disdain turned into fury. Turning his head and squinting, he said: "Allow ourselves to be *what*?"

"Leave him to us, my general!" said a nearby soldier, brandishing his bayonet.

I kept up my diplomatic smile, while saying to myself that I never would understand these military types.

What could they be thinking? They'd suffered terrible losses. I had come to them with the good news of being allowed to leave that dreadful spot. And how did they respond? By threatening to spill my guts with the sharp end of a bayonet.

The general launched himself at me. His puffy cheeks flushed dark red. Grabbing me by the collar of my shirt, he thrust me the way I'd come, back down the glacis covered in dead bodies, and said: "Look at them! Look! Do you think they died so that some Frenchie can come and take all the credit? Do you really think I'm going to let some cousin of Orléans come and have the keys to the city placed in his hands?"

I resisted him, aided by the knowledge that I'd done nothing wrong. For all that he was a general, I shouted: "Do you think this mess has anything to do with me? Let me go, imbecile, I'm just a messenger!"

That stopped him in his tracks. He hesitated for a moment—how does one deal with a soldier who would speak to a general in this way?—before exclaiming: "Tell that to the person who sent you!"

What happened next, all the historians must somehow have missed, for it has never seen mention in any of the accounts of the siege.

He gave me such a kick up the behind that it was a miracle I didn't go into orbit. I flew down the slope, bouncing over the rubble like a ball, dislodging stones of all sizes, as well as cadavers, which, in the moment I bumped into them, seemed to come to life for a moment.

I returned to camp with my tunic ripped and my rear end on fire from the kick. I was ready to burst with umbrage. I ran into the liaison officer.

"Ah!" he said cautiously. "How did it go?"

Now I understood why I'd been sent! No one was brave enough to go and tell the general he was being relieved, so to avoid a scene, they'd sent the most insignificant creature in the army.

"How did it go?" I said, infuriated. "Where did you get that Spanish general?"

"Mm, yes . . . ," the Frenchman said apologetically. "General Antonio de Villarroel does have quite the temper."

Yes, dear readers, that's right: This was my first encounter with Don Antonio. It was he who, years later, would go on to drag good old Zuvi out of the most pernicious existence to the highest heights; the same man who, though of Castilian origin, in 1713 would lead the defense of the Catalan capital, Barcelona, and make the ultimate sacrifice for us.

Dear vile Waltraud, weighing heavier on me than an anchor, constantly interrupts. She's finding it hard to understand how, if Villarroel was serving a Bourbon king in the summer of 1708, we'll find him fighting on the Austrian side in 1713.

Let's see, my most horrendous Waltraud: I already know you to be dimmer than a glowworm's fetus, but even so, has it not occurred to you that, in order to be understood, this book must be read in order, all the chapters, and to the very end?

What a tonic a kick up the backside can be! I should really have thanked that mad general.

What on earth was I doing there? Since failing Vauban's test, I had been floundering in inertia. Fine, well, now I had a siege under my belt, and what else? Had I discovered The Word? I had not.

That kick up the backside was going to send me straight home. I would go and apologize to my father, on my knees if I had to. I'd come clean. And he would forgive me—bad-tempered as he was, I was still his only son. I said to myself that however bad a father might be, he could never trump a siege. To hell with warfare, and generals ready to kick you about, and all the Monsieur Forgottens in this world!

I hurried back to my tent. I was ready to cut my losses, grab the few things I really needed, and head to Barcelona.

The whole army was waiting for the terms of the surrender to be agreed, so I wouldn't find a better moment to make myself scarce.

Given the engineers' elite specialism, their tents were surrounded by a makeshift stake fence that separated them from the common troops. Monsieur Forgotten's tent, with its bulbous roof, was in the middle of our precinct. Around that, individual officers' tents, and next, the lower engineers, where aides-de-camp like me slept. There were usually three pairs of soldiers on guard, but that morning, with the conclusion of the siege imminent, there was just one soldier, a youth. He was walking up and down, rifle at his shoulder, and greeted me as I came past. Ignoring him, I went into my tent.

Someone had been through my things, I was surprised to find. All my money, everything I'd saved from Bazoches, plus my wages since I'd joined the French army, all gone! Understandably enough, I shot out of there in a rage, angry even at the fact that anyone had entered the tent, which was bad enough in itself.

"Soldier!" I shouted at the unfortunate sentry. "Are you blind? I've been robbed!"

"Sir, I'm very sorry," he said. "It must have been that pair."

"Pair? What pair?"

"A dwarf wearing a funnel for a hat and a boy with dirty pigtails."

I let out a howl. "So if you saw them, what came over you that you let them enter? Didn't you think they looked suspicious?"

"They showed me a pass, sir, I had to let them through!" said the soldier, excusing himself. "I can't read, but an officer who was passing by helped me. It was fine, according to him. The pass had their names on it, and it was signed by you."

I kicked a fencepost with my sapper boots. Childhood! That time of the soul's innocence! My good friend Rousseau ought to have met this miniature monster Anfán before writing his essays on pedagogy!

They'd employed a brilliant strategy, waiting until the last day of the siege to use my pass, when all eyes were on Tortosa and camp was practically empty. This prompted a thought in me. I ceased my attack on the post and asked the sentry: "Was it long ago they were here?"

"Not at all. They just left. I think I saw them a few minutes ago." He pointed toward the outskirts of camp. "They went that way."

I trotted in the direction indicated. I traversed the camp, coming to the last tents. Beyond these stretched parched fields, only one or two bushes here and there. I spotted the pair. Nearly half a mile away, cutting across the fields at a run, and weighed down with more booty than ants in the Yucatán.

There were thousands of nooks and crannies in the trenches for them to hide in, but in open country, they didn't have a chance against Longlegs Zuvi. I ran after them, accelerating, eating up the distance.

Seeing me coming, they also picked up the pace, though each was weighed down with a sack larger than his own body. They reached the top of a rise and disappeared down the other side.

It was a couple of minutes before I reached that point, and once there, I couldn't see them anymore. Damn it, where had they gotten to? I paused for a moment to catch my breath.

I scanned around, thinking maybe they'd hidden in some hole in the ground. But no, there weren't any. "Come on, Zuvi," I said to myself, "think! Wasn't it the lord of Bazoches himself who taught you to use your eyes?"

A couple of hundred feet to my right: a small construction, abandoned. One of these stone huts where peasants keep tools and suchlike. There was nowhere else they could be.

I circled the place before going in, checking for any escape route. No, the windows were too small even for them. Only then did I approach the door and shout: "Come on, out with you! I know you're in there!"

To my surprise, the door opened immediately. It wasn't either of them, though, but a French soldier.

He was the paradigm of soldiery at its most depraved. His belt was loose, and his uniform was so dirty that its whiteness was a mere memory. He peered out of drunken, sleepy eyes. Leaning lazily against the doorframe, picking at his teeth with a knife, he asked what I wanted. What was going on there? I pushed him to one side and took a step forward into the hut. Once my eyes had adjusted to the gloom, I was dumbstruck.

The dwarf was in there, tied to a beam, his mouth gagged with straw and a rag tied around him. Anfán was seated on an old chair, bound tight at his ankles and wrists. Gagged, too, and with a black hood that came down over half his body. The French soldier had an accomplice, and he was kneeling down finishing tying Anfán's binds. Even the flies had fled that place. Nan looked at me in utter terror. They'd stumbled into an atrocious situation, one of these small hells you'll always find in or near a war, just as cobwebs always inhabit corners.

My first thought was to recover my belongings and get out of there. This perverted pair of maniacs disgusted me, of course. But we were in a time of widespread indiscriminate killing. The sooner I could get away, the better.

There was a small detail, though, something otherwise quite minor, that made me more upset than I ordinarily might have been. Want to know what this trivial thing was? A bead, a bead of sweat, running down the cheek of one of those swine. This little drop betrayed foul desires, a soul gone rancid. His mouth hung half open, and he was staring intently at Anfán, who was desperately trying to free himself on the chair. Like all scavengers, he had large gaps between his teeth, which made him all the more repulsive. Sometimes it's trivial details that spur us into action. It had been a bad day, and someone was going to have to pay for it.

There was a thick, rusty chain hanging from the ceiling. I picked a large stone up off the floor and, stowing this under one arm, reached up and took down the chain with my free hand. I took a step toward the soldier at the door. "Mind holding this stone for a moment?"

"All right," he said, putting away his knife and holding out his hands. "But what do you want me to hold it for?"

The answer was very simple: so he would have his hands full as I brought the chain down across his head, knocking him to the floor. The other man was too much of a coward to take me on. Seeing me coming toward him with the chain, he curled up in a ball, protecting his head with his hands. I'd scared him witless, and I left it at that. Dropping the chain, fed up with Tortosa, with war, with the world, I untied the boy and the dwarf, gathered my belongings, and left the hut.

Anfán and the dwarf followed me out. *"Monsieur, monsieur!"*

Any hostility I'd felt toward them had faded. I'd recovered my money and my effects, and if you have saved a person's life, you do not then give him a hiding. Which isn't to say I cared what happened to them, not in the slightest. Without breaking stride, I said scornfully back to them, "Go and get back in the trench. Turns out you might have been right: With what's going on at the moment, it might be the safest place for you."

They swarmed around me like butterflies.

"Get out of here!" I said again. "You ought to be hanged, you little thieves. Luckily for you, I myself am in too much of a hurry to get back to Barcelona."

But the mention of Barcelona only made them more excited.

"Monsieur!" cried Anfán. "We've wanted to go to Barcelona for so long! We've been saving up to do exactly that."

Saving up! What my father would have said of this pair's ideas about work! I was about to give them a farewell thrashing when I heard the snorting of animals.

A cavalry squadron in the near distance. The rearguard of the besieging army was protected by these mounted patrols. They would escort foragers, ward off Miquelet attacks, as well as rounding up deserters. I could have spoken with them but was too much the fugitive by this point. My first impulse was to dash into a small forest that stood nearby and looked dense enough to make it difficult for horses to enter.

"No, *monsieur!*" said Anfán. "You won't make it in time. Follow us!" They turned in to an abandoned vineyard, Anfán gesturing for me to follow. "Run! Quick!"

The vines were a little above knee height. In such open country, cavalry would trap us easily. They were insane, these two. But do you know what? I followed them anyway.

The patrol came after us. We made a desperate dash, me weighed down with the two sacks, sweating. I cursed myself. But when the horses reached the edge of the vineyard, they pulled up as though obstructed by some invisible force. The riders didn't attempt to spur them on.

Anfán laughed, very pleased with himself indeed. "Horses hate vineyards—they break their legs on the vines."

The riders fired a few shots our way, with no great intent. By the time they went around this vineyard, which was extensive, we'd be well into the forest. They decided against following us.

"Saved your life, *monsieur.* You owe us one," said Anfán when we finally stopped to rest among the trees.

I laughed. "Surely it's I who saved the two of you—from something awful—and you who owe me."

"Let's make a deal!" said the child. "We get you a vehicle, and you take us to Barcelona."

"Vehicle? What vehicle?" I said, intrigued. I'd escaped so unplanned, I hadn't even thought about the next leg of the journey.

"Follow us!" They led me along a small hidden path, the woods and undergrowth becoming ever thicker around us.

"Here," said Anfán after a short time, bringing me through an opening between some trees.

There, nestled against a wall of vegetation, stood a two-horse carriage. The driver was still in his seat. Dead.

There were thousands of Miquelets in this area, harassing the siege army's rearguard; the driver must have made a harebrained attempt to flee from some small skirmish. There was a bullet wound in his back, the dried blood blackening his white uniform. His last effort must have been to try hiding away from the road, and this was where he'd ended up.

In the seat, with his chin on his chest, the dead driver looked as though he were sleeping. Taking hold of him by the shoulder, I pushed him somewhat unceremoniously to the ground. The horses, sensing a living human, brightened up, seemed pleased. Consequently, they were very obedient during the tricky maneuver of turning them around and going back to the road.

"We're going to Barcelona?" asked a gleeful Anfán.

He had such hungry eyes, this child—hungrier-seeming than his stomach itself. I examined the horses. One had a bullet in its right haunch; the other's mane had been singed. Fine, I thought: They needed only to be able to cover the distance to Barcelona, a hundred or so miles. I climbed onto the bay of the carriage, which was full of sacks. Opening one, I found biscuits in it. I lobbed a couple to Nan and Anfán, who gobbled them down, even though the biscuits were the size of discuses, if not bigger. But there was an assortment of things. When I went to open another sack, cylindrical and six feet tall, it fell over, loosing its contents all over the floor of the bay.

Bullets, lead bullets. A torrent of little round bullets that went everywhere. Nan and Anfán, beside themselves with excitement, got down and began gathering them up. What a small thing a bullet is, a tiny globe, apparently so inoffensive. And yet, properly directed, it will kill soldiers and generals, kings and paupers alike. Not that any of this entered Anfán's thoughts. He and the dwarf began playing marbles with them. He was still a child—an accomplished survivor, perhaps, but a child first and foremost. Standing watching them in the carriage bay, I couldn't help but feel a pang of nostalgia.

It was the first natural silence I'd heard in twenty days, the time I'd been in the trenches. Twenty days and nights, putting up with the thundering cannons and the insidious sound of the sappers' picks. And now nothing but forest around me, the trill of birds, and the air clear of artillery smoke and resounding trumpets. Plus a child, and a dwarf with a funnel on his head, playing marbles with the instruments of death. Yes, infancy will always be our time of subversion.

While they amused themselves, I investigated the rest of the cargo. There were two blankets covering something in one of the corners. Lifting them off, I discovered a hefty trunk. It had three locks, which took my breath away: I knew what those three locks signified.

I'd shared a tent during the siege with, among others, one of the army paymasters. One of those asses who reckon themselves important because they rub shoulders with the top brass. He wasn't high up enough to sleep in the officers' tent, but he turned up his nose at sharing with the rank and file. So we were saddled with him. He talked constantly. I'd get back to my camp bed, exhausted from the trenches, and he'd be at it straightaway—blah blah *blah*. It didn't matter if I had been on a day or a night shift, he'd be there waiting—Prattler Paymaster, as we began calling him. His problem was that he worked only one day a week, so he'd spend the rest of his time gossiping and going on at anyone unfortunate enough to be in earshot.

Well, one day this nuisance paymaster was showing off a key he had, which was for the chest that held the army's wages. The money chests, he told me, had three locks, and the keys were held by different people—one by the paymaster, one by the field marshal, and one by the supervisor general. Prattler Paymaster crowed about having met the supervisor general. But you tell me, what other kind of chest on an army vehicle would have three locks?

I didn't have the three keys, but, having studied at Bazoches, I did not need them. I found a mallet and chisel there in the carriage and, employing my acute sense of precision, hammered off the locks. When I opened the top, there inside were dozens of small cylindrical sacks, packed tightly together in two rows. Each with a wax seal bearing the Bourbon fleur-de-lis. I broke one open, and coins came tumbling out. There must have been wages for an entire regiment there, at least. Mother of God.

Have you ever had an abandoned treasure trove fall into your hands? The sensation is very much akin to that of love at first sight: Your heart beats harder, your hands tremble, and a happy nervousness takes hold of you. And you are overtaken by a terrible desire to flee with it.

I slammed the top shut, startled by the discovery. Nan and Anfán were still playing marbles.

"Here, boys!" I said, a Judas smile on my face. "Go back to the driver's body and check his pockets, will you?"

A brazen lie to give me a chance to get clear of them. By the time they'd realized what was happening, I'd already set off, cracking the reins on the horse's backs. Nan and Anfán ran uselessly after the carriage.

"*Monsieur, monsieur!*" shouted Anfán. "Don't leave us here, please. Take us to Barcelona!"

Turning in the seat, I saw his little head, his matted locks blown by the wind, his pained expression . . .

But now, much to my regret, I have to halt my tale, because Waltraud the dunce interrupts, sniveling, whinging, calling me a heartless so-and-so. Why the sudden sentimentality? Can't you see what these two were like? Anfán was a born thief—how could I possibly have him and this chest along on the same journey?

All right, all right. I'll confess something to you, if it'll make you feel any better.

I pulled on the reins and stopped the carriage. The truth is, I felt a pang of compunction. After all, I'd secured myself transport, plus booty, thanks to this pair. Seeing me stop, and with their hopes renewed, they ran harder to catch up. When they got within twenty or so feet, I threw a few coins in their direction.

"All yours! Bread and wine's on me!"

And I cracked the reins again.

Deep down, you see, I've always been a good person.

Departing Tortosa as swiftly as the wounded horses allowed, I was struck by the perilousness of my situation. There were patrols everywhere, from both armies, and constant skirmishes. But in reality, the two armies were the least of my problems. The south of Catalonia had been ravished by war, and there were bands of looters, bandits, and deserters of six or seven nationalities, to add to my beloved Miquelets, who were the worst of all. I was on my own with just a pistol, and for company an altogether appealing chest full of coins. I have rarely been so pleased to see the sun go down. To my right was a narrow path leading through the middle of a field of overgrown wheat. Possibly a place to hide for the night. The lack of recent harvests had left the wheat to grow implausibly high. At the end of the field was an irrigation canal. I couldn't have hoped for anything better: The tall ears of wheat would screen me, and here was water for the horses and me. I took their torturous harnesses off.

I had yet to finish setting up camp when he appeared.

He came into the clearing from the same path I'd taken. He wore an ample black cape. With this garment and his tricorn hat pulled down over his eyebrows, he appeared to float out of the wheat. In alarm, I reached for my pistol, which I had left in the carriage. What was this figure doing here, so far from anywhere, civilization as well as the war? I pointed the pistol at him. "Do you come armed? Identify yourself."

He continued moving toward me and simply said: "Pau."

I didn't know if this was his name or a declaration. (*Pau* means "peace" in Catalan but is also our word for "Paul.") Keeping my guard up, I came back at him, matching him for ambiguity, raising him on the sarcasm: "Fallen off your horse?"

The man flashed a quick smile. He held his cape open, showing himself unarmed. His shirt had wide sleeves that fell back when he held up his arms. What I then saw, my dear vile Waltraud, I have never seen again: ten Points, one after the other, tattooed on his right forearm. The tenth, just beneath his elbow, stood out.

The indelible ink marked skin far older than the man's expression; he had a venerability but also seemed in excellent physical and mental shape. Ten Points! The ideal engineer, a perfect Maganon. My suspicion gave way to astonishment and admiration. Still smiling that inexpressive smile, he came and stood before me.

"And you?" he said, his voice neutral.

"At your service," I said, lifting my right sleeve and showing my five Points.

He drew a little closer. "Where have you come from?"

"Tortosa."

"And where are you bound?"

"Barcelona."

"Why?"

"That's where my father lives?"

"Are you certain about that?"

"Yes."

"Nothing's certain."

It seemed more like an interrogation than a dialogue, but a Point Bearer never questions his superiors, who, in turn, must know all a subordinate has to tell. Nothing must be kept from them. I couldn't take my eyes off his forearm and the tenth Point. He stepped to one side and surveyed my little camp: the carriage, the irrigation canal, the high wheat surrounding us like living walls.

He was every inch the Ten Points. He seemed to listen, rather than look: the objects around, the insects, the general environment, even the transparent air, spoke to him, only too happy to confess all. Then he made a gesture: He raised a hand as though telling an orchestra to stop playing. He looked at my carriage for a few moments. "What's inside your vehicle?"

"Nothing," I lied.

"Exactly."

Though I was a product of Bazoches, even so, I shuddered.

It was a warm night. He took off his cape and rolled up his sleeves. My eye settled on his forearm again.

The world of engineering, its practical spirit in direct opposition to the symbolic, here gave one small concession. For the glorious tenth Point was smaller than the preceding ones. That is, when an engineer reached perfection, his prize was a point that strongly resembled the first: a simple circle.

He asked me, "Who is your teacher?"

"It *was* Sébastien Le Prestre de Vauban. He's dead now."

"A good engineer, yes, a very good engineer," he whispered respectfully. "He lives on in you. Remember him."

"Unfortunately," I said, "I didn't earn this fifth Point. I failed to find a certain Word."

"Well, you'll have to carry on looking."

"I've given up on it all," I said. "Even if I were to persevere, who could ratify my fifth Point? Vauban is dead, I know no other teacher, and anyway, I wouldn't want anyone else to take me under his wing. So, enough."

He smiled faintly. "Everyone says the same thing. Until one day they graze the sky with their fingers. And from then on, they would rather die than give up on that glory."

In spite of my respect for him, I couldn't but smile incredulously. Noticing this, his tone changed, becoming imperious enough to subdue kings. He raised his voice. "If a teacher is what you need, you will find one, whether or not he has the Points. There's no getting away from your search for this Word, and when you find it, you will know you are worthy of your fifth Point."

I wanted to say something but failed to find the right way to express myself—with the proper respect. In any case, he was the one directing this conversation.

"Lay out your mat," he said.

I obeyed.

"Lie down. Shut your eyes. Sleep."

I was asleep before he finished speaking.

It would be very interesting to include here my dream that night. Unfortunately, when I awoke, I couldn't remember it. I was left with nothing but a fleeting trace. The blurry image of a young woman, naked, with violet-colored skin and a very dark pubis, somewhere in a blazing landscape. I spent weeks trying to fully recall the dream. She had the most sorrowful eyes. Suddenly, legions of white beetles attacked her, swarming all around her and running up her ankles. She called out for my help. But everything melted away before the meaning of the dream became complete. Trying to decipher it, I turned the dream over in my mind hundreds of times.

Unfortunately, I was too much of an insomniac in those days. The dream slipped through my hands like a fish. Very frustrating.

The following day, I climbed back up in the carriage and set out again for Barcelona. I didn't bother to check if the chest was where I'd left it. A Ten Points would never bother with such trifles.

Now, eight decades on, eighty times around the sun later, I believe I know who this twilight man was. A moment—I must breathe.

He was no man. He was *le Mystère* itself, traversing this earth with the indifference of a beekeeper seeing a few upset beehives. He came across a curious bee and lingered over it for a few moments.

He must have been at a loose end.

14

All morning long I drove along a route flanked by pine-covered mountains. And at midday came across the thing I'd been looking for, my want and deliverance.

An inn stood on the floodplain that opened out to my right. Its main building was a shoddy adobe construction, a long rectangle with a thatched roof. There was an old man in front of it, digging a grave for a dead mule lying there. Stopping the carriage, I got down and approached him.

I passed myself off as a modest businessman looking to join a civilian convoy. He was almost completely deaf.

"You're looking for protection?" he yelled, holding a hand up to his head like an ear trumpet. "Okay, well, the boys are inside. They escort carriages. The more travelers who club together, the cheaper it ends up. And they've got a gift for negotiating at checkpoints with soldiers, whichever army they're from!"

"Can I get myself something to drink?" I said, handing him a couple of coins. "I'm parched."

"Go in and help yourself—though with this heat, the wine will be warm," he replied, pointing to the main building. "Wait, though: If you help me bury this mule, I'll give you all the wine you want, free. People come along," he complained, referring to his customers, "and as soon as their mounts have a rest, they're so worn out, they drop dead! What am I supposed to do with them? Why don't you tell me that, eh, eh?"

Yes, that was exactly what I needed to do at that moment, bury dead mules. I didn't bother to excuse myself but headed straight into the adobe building.

The table inside looked like the Last Supper. Drinking and talking at the tops of their voices, twelve gruff, very drunk men, half sitting with their backs to me, and those on the other side obscured by the way the light fell. At first I didn't pay them any mind, nor they me.

I went over to a bar made of some rough planks set over a line of casks. There was a pitcher hanging from a post on one side. I took a couple of swigs—it was a rancid-tasting herb wine—and then heard a voice behind me.

"Come and join us, friend! You'll find our liquor far preferable to that vinegar."

It was worth getting off on the right foot with them, so I went and sat at the center of one of the benches. Only then did I get a proper look at their faces.

Scars. Earrings. Beards rough enough to sand rocks with. Heavy bags under their eyes, and eyes that scanned you for where best to stick a knife—in your windpipe or just under your chin? And this was an escort organized by decent citizens? The most harmless out of them all must have been saved from the scaffold five times, at least. And sitting straight across from me, my old friend: Ballester.

I went whiter than blanched asparagus. The look Ballester gave me was thick with hate. He said just four words.

"*El botifler de Beceit.*"

Waltraud has forgotten who Ballester is. He was in the last chapter! That fanatic young Miquelet briefly captured by the Bourbons, an utter animal who'd be only too happy cutting off my two ears and using them as a handkerchief.

Ballester's words brought the revels to a halt. The twelve primitive apostles turned to look at me in unison. I was speechless. Under normal conditions, my Bazoches senses would have picked up on Ballester's presence before I entered the inn. But I'd given up on engineering, and I'd been so eager to find an escort, it had made a common mole of me. I was as ashamed as I was frightened.

Ballester pulled out an enormous and very sharp dagger—likely the one he'd slit the captain's throat with in Beceite. I wanted to flee but didn't make it halfway to the door. I was pushed to the floor by four sets of hands, and Ballester came round and stood behind me. As he brought the point of the dagger to my jugular, I cried out: "Wait! I've got something you want!"

If ever you find yourself in such a situation, do as I say and skip trying to be clever. Go straight for the words that will be most appealing.

"A chest full of money!" I cried, half suffocated by the terror and the blade at my throat. "Right outside!"

All thirteen of us exited the inn, me with my chin up high due to the knife prodding it in that direction. The old man was still digging the mule's grave. Tears began to run down my face.

"Make it easy on yourself," said Ballester. "Spit it out, and I'll let you choose the way I kill you."

"My carriage!" I said, pointing to it. "You'll find something of interest in there. I swear to Christ!"

Three of Ballester's men climbed up into the carriage. The old man dug, murmuring mindlessly to himself, oblivious to everything but the mule. He was too deranged to have a clue what was going on.

Ballester's men found the chest beneath the blankets.

"Fifty rifles!" shouted one of them, joyful, throwing a handful of coins in Ballester's direction. "We can buy fifty rifles with this lot!"

"I stole it from those Bourbon scum!" I said, trying to turn their glee to my advantage. "I'm a patriot, utterly committed. The only thing I want is to topple Little Philip and his grandfather!"

While they rejoiced in the ill-begotten fortune, I came up with a convoluted tale. I was a spy working for the Generalitat, I went around sabotaging the evil Bourbons, my allegiance was with Austria. Attacking me was a mistake, and a crime, too. My mission, secret, meant traveling to Barcelona with the cargo; ministers from the Generalitat were awaiting my arrival. I even asked if they would like to escort me, and said they'd be paid handsomely if they did a good job. Ballester punched me to the ground. "String him up," he said.

I whimpered and wept and begged for my life. I pushed the men off me and knelt down in front of Ballester. My family was dead, I told him, I was my blessed father's only remaining son. A poor, peaceful, upstanding patriot.

Begging mercy from your executioners seems the most pointless pursuit. But in that case, why do men always subject themselves to such humiliation? I'll tell you why: because it works.

"Sir," I implored. "Have you forgotten who saved you from hanging in Beceite? The few hours of grace afforded you by my lenient words gave your men time to come back for you! And this is how you repay me! The one who saved your life, you sentence to death!"

Ballester spat by my nose, which was down on the ground. "It's all right, your chest has brightened up my day," he said. "Get out of here. I won't lower myself to dirty my hands with you."

I can still hear his rasping, stony voice and the words he said: *"Fot el camp, gos."* (Away with you, dog.)

They stripped me, though my clothes were worth nothing. It must have been a symbol to the Miquelets when releasing prisoners. They even took my undergarments, stained though they were with mud and shit from twenty days in the trenches. I instinctively covered up my genitals with my hands. Turning on my heel, I fled, my rear end bare and the men pursuing me with their laughter.

"Hey!" Ballester shouted once there was a little distance between us. "Do you know how to write?" He had shifted to addressing me in the *usted* form, usually reserved for superiors.

I stopped and turned, with my hands still in front of my crotch, and stammered an answer: "Yes, well, of course. In several languages."

He waved to me to come back. I obeyed, what else. He ordered his men to pull a plank from the carriage. He handed it to me, along with a piece of iron with a sharp point. "Write 'I am a *botiflero* dog' on it. In French and Spanish."

"May I ask," I whispered haltingly, clearing my throat, "what the inscription's for?"

"Oh, I've changed my mind," he said in the most amiable of voices. "Seeing as you know how to write, I'm going to string you up, and the whole world will know why. We'll hang the plank around your neck."

The iron and the plank dropped from my hands. Down on my knees again, I implored him, I whimpered, I cried whole seas. He looked up at the sky, sighing as though reconsidering. I thought he might have softened again, but what he said was: "Know Latin, too? Put it in Latin as well."

I scratched out the letters on the plank, moaning and begging all the while. Ballester's men found the whole thing hilarious.

"On your feet, boy!" they said, their voices upbeat, once I had finished. They tied my hands behind my back and picked me up at the armpits. The tallest tree in the vicinity was a fig tree. Someone put the plank around my neck. The old lunatic began shouting from the hole he was still digging: "So many big men, all in one place, and none of you comes to help an old man!"

One of the Miquelets tried to get the rope over one of the top branches but was so drunk that he stumbled and fell flat on his face. More laughter.

"Don't you know how deep a hole has to be to fit a mule in?" continued the old man. "And me, toiling in the sun, in this heat. What a life!"

You only get one death, and mine had fallen into the hands of some drunk, bungling executioners. They finally managed to get the rope over the topmost branch. My head was introduced into the noose, and without any further ado, a couple of the brutes pulled down on the other end of the rope.

"I know you're all good lads! You pay well, and anyone who fetches up without any money, you escort them for free. But I'm poor, too, and old, and tired! And this mule is enormous!"

I was lifted ten feet into the air. The yank on the noose caused my tongue to stick out. You never know how long your tongue is until you get hanged. The rope makes the blood in your head collect; you go bright red. My urine made an arc when I pissed myself. Some of the Miquelets fell down laughing.

They were too drunk to remember the well-reputed untrustworthiness of fig trees. The branches have a tendency to break, and, when I had been raised a little higher, the one bearing me indeed snapped. There was a great noise as I fell to the ground: bones, wood, and bushy leaves all in a heap.

Their guffaws were probably heard in Tortosa. Then, quite simply, they turned around and went off. That's how Miquelets are.

"*Figa tova! Figa tova!*" they called out mockingly as they rode away, taking my carriage and the chest, of course, with them.

(*Figa tova* is untranslatable. *Figa* in Catalan means "fig," and *tova* means "soft"; put together, they mean a whining know-it-all. Like Waltraud here, for instance.)

"Ho, you layabout!" cried the old halfwit. "Instead of lying there, you could at least give me a hand."

Vidi

1

Very well, then, we can agree that my return home was rather less glorious than that of Ulysses. The only attire I was able to procure for myself was a pile of beggar's rags. And thus it was that I returned to Barcelona after four long years away. Defeated by the war, baffled in my wretchedness. And the worst thing of all: with a fifth Point on my forearm that I had done nothing to deserve.

But let us forget about the tragedy of Longlegs Zuvi for just a moment. I was returning to the city of my birth, to old Barcelona. To her noises, her smells, her alleyways. Her harbor, her excesses. The city felt like an invention of my memories, more distant than my mother. All I had retained in my head were a child's recollections—do not forget, I left my home when I was but a child—and I was returning to Barcelona equipped with senses that were far from ordinary, which Bazoches had honed. Everything was new, after a fashion, for my perceptions and the passage of time meant I was experiencing the place as a foreigner would.

At this point I ought to ramble off into a description of Barcelona in the early years of the century. Which would be a very dull thing. Since I have a map from the period, I shall simply attach it and leave it at that.

The city walls are not shown on this plate. Very fitting, bearing in mind my mood at that moment, because the last thing I wanted was to go back to thinking as an engineer. Or about Bazoches, or Jeanne, or Vauban's "You are not fit." Or The Word.

As you can see, the city was bisected by a broad avenue, Las Ramblas. The urban sprawl was much denser to its right, and on its left, vegetable gardens in abundance, something very useful to have in the case of a siege . . .

I had left Barcelona a boy, and I was returning a man. A failure, but a man. I can assure you, this voice speaking to you now has never known a more frivolous port or a city, nor one that was home to more

foreigners. Not even in America! They came, they settled, and their origins melted into the crowd. The day they decided to stay, they'd Cata-
lanize their family names as a disguise, so nobody might know whether
their birthplace had been in Italy, France, Castile, or somewhere more
exotic still. As for the rest, and in contrast to the Castilian obsession
with keeping the blood pure of Moors or Jews, the Catalans didn't care
a fig for their neighbors' origins. If they had money to spend, if they
were pleasant enough, and if they didn't try and impose religious ideas,
new arrivals were left to get on with it. This atmosphere, so passive and
receptive, meant that the people would be transformed in less than a
generation. So it was with my father.

Thanks to his Catholic heritage, every other day in his calendar was a feast day. (The papacy had to have something going for it to have so many followers around the world.) Besides these, we should add the dozens of more or less improvised occasions, such as days of thanksgiving to commemorate the king being restored to health, or because Santa Eulalia had appeared to a drunkard in the street. But make no mistake, if the Catalans encouraged feast days, it was only because they understood that idleness is good business.

The festivities, which the calendar teemed with, cost colossal amounts. Barcelona's festivals and carnivals were spoken of the world over. Those carnivals! The Castilian aristocrats, all so chaste, would return from their visits scandalized. Rich and poor out on the streets, men and women all together in a throng and dancing till the early hours. Just appalling. To a Castilian nobleman, clothing had to be one color only: the severest black. When I was in Madrid in 1710, I was surprised by the blackness of its patricians. It was the opposite in Barcelona. More than three hundred kinds of fabric were imported, and the more money you had, the more colors you would flaunt in your attire and at the dances.

There was a constant flow of merchandise being unloaded at the harbor. You could find a dozen varieties of ginger alone. When I was a little boy, my father once gave me a thrashing because I'd come back from market with the wrong kind of rice—no wonder I was confused about which he'd sent me for: There were as many as forty-three different varieties of rice, something to suit every purse.

In few places have I seen people smoke as much as I witnessed in Barcelona. In the city's *botigas*, it was possible to find an even greater array of tobaccos than there was of rice. Healthy though smoking obviously was, the habit spread to such an extent that the bishop was obliged to pronounce an edict, an ecclesiastical proclamation, no less, forbidding priests from smoking—at least while performing their offices!

In Barcelona in the years before 1714, you always had the impression of a city governed by a tolerant, opulent, libertine kind of chaos. People worked themselves to death and, at the same time, died laughing and merrymaking. On the whole, the government of the Generalitat didn't meddle when it came to popular excesses. Let me give you one example: the *pedradas*.

The line dividing popular revelry and mob violence has always been vanishingly thin. When my father was a young lad, the *pedradas* were the favored pastime of Barcelona's universities. Essentially, these consisted of a contest between two teams, each made up of a good hundred participants. They'd find some expanse of open land to gather in, and with the two teams on opposite sides, when the signal was given, hunks of stone would begin to be hurled. Thousands of stones went back and forth, and if you could strike an opponent in the head with one of yours, so much the better for you! You will be wondering, perhaps, what sort of rules applied to such a noble pastime? The answer could not be simpler: There were no rules at all. The group who finally fled in terror was considered the loser; the one left on the field, the victor. Naturally, the battle would leave dozens injured, many with their heads split open for life, and even some dead.

The real crybabies among the clergy clamored against the brutishness of the *pedradas*. Could the competition not be made a little less rough by at least replacing the stones with oranges? At their insistence, the universities assumed a position entirely typical of the Catalans: agreeing without complying. At the start of the civic battles, oranges would be used, but only until these ran out, whereupon the combatants would proceed with stones. The Church was obliged to hold off on the sermonizing because the *pedradas* were an enormously popular entertainment; crowds came to watch, bets were laid and sides taken. And who among us is unfamiliar with students' playful ways? Very often, when there was an attentive crowd, instead of attacking each other, the two groups, laughing, would unite to bombard the unsuspecting spectators!

Using the *pedradas* as their excuse, the students would sometimes designate the area around the university their "field of honor." Then the two rival groups would form an alliance, feeling fraternal all of a sudden, leaving the building a wreck, outside and in. Lectures would be suspended until the furnishings were replaced, and—who would have thought such a thing, what a coincidence!—it seemed these *pedradas* always sprang up at the university around exam time. No wonder my father sent me to France; always having been head and shoulders above my peers, and always having been a scoundrel, I would have found my place (my father was sure) in the front line of the stone-throwers, on one side or the other, and would have ended up with my skull smashed in. In any case, during my boyhood, *pedradas* had already begun to tail off noticeably. But of one thing I am quite sure: If Christ was able to save the blessed prostitute from stoning, it was only because there were no Barcelonan university students around in Judea at the time.

While I'm on the subject of prostitutes, one of the defects of Barcelona in those days, which demonstrates the fathomless perfidy of the "Black Pelts" (as the bishops were commonly called, owing to the color of their cassocks), is that brothels were strictly forbidden. There was a particular watch kept over boardinghouses and inns, and "suspect" women were constantly kept under observation. As far as I can tell, this disproportionate harassment of the city's pitiful tarts was a kind of concession granted to the Black Pelts on the part of the Red Pelts (the government, in the popular jargon, owing to the crimson color of the robe worn by Catalan magistrates). Since the rich and powerful were quick to ignore sermons against gambling and luxury, the government gave the Church the satisfaction of repressing, at least, those poor, defenseless prostitutes.

Which is not to say there were no whores at all. Of course there were! In cities with brothels, the tarts stay inside and never come out; in cities without any brothels, they spill all over the place and at all hours. With the ancient profession of procurer abolished, aspiring tarts came up with a thousand cunning schemes to allow them to carry out their work in secret.

Anyway, as I was saying, I had been wandering the streets, summoning the courage to return home, when I heard the sound of drums approaching. The crowd, all crushed together on the Ramblas, dropped to their knees.

The news of the fall of Tortosa had arrived in the city before me. On occasions such as that, the Barcelonans carried in procession their most sacred relic: the standard of Santa Eulalia. I hope you will allow me a few words at this point, because the Barcelonans' precious flag most surely deserves them.

As a banner, it was nothing extraordinary. It was, however, quite different from modern ensigns. The whole large silk rectangle was taken up by the portrait of a young woman, her body violet-colored,

with sadness in her eyes. Something about the image was irremediably pagan. The art that had captured the melancholy in her eyes was
wonderful.

According to the dictates of tradition, the flag had to be passed on,
by hand, from Catalan kings to their firstborn and successor. It was said
that an army that flew this flag would never be defeated. (A lie, I say:
Catalan history comprises ten sound defeats to every one victory.) In
any case, what is certainly true is that the flag of Santa Eulalia provoked
feelings of devotion that far outstripped merely military support. As it
passed by, the Barcelonans knelt to cross themselves and ask for protection and blessings. If you will allow me to share a thought with you, I
can tell you that this reverence had precious little to do with religion.
For this ensign was much more than a saint: It was the representative
of the city itself.

I did not kneel. Not through lack of piety but because that violet-
colored young lady reminded me of the one in the dream that *le Mystère*
had provoked in me. The flag progressed, flanked by drums beating
out a dirge for the fall of Tortosa, and when it passed, those saintly eyes
seemed to be asking me something.

Martí Zuviría did not talk to flags, of course, but the sensation of
an encounter with a creature from another world, albeit as real as an old
friend, was so vivid that I simply stood there, agog. And, well, I suppose
you must now be asking the same question as my heavy, vile Waltraud:
"So what did the violet girl ask you?" I'll tell you, then: She didn't use
words; a damsel, when asking your protection, has no need of words.

Since all those around me were on their knees and I remained standing, it was not hard to spot me from a distance. Somebody called out
my name—it was Peret. I believe I have already mentioned old Peret,
that human relic who had taken care of me in the absence of a mother.
He had recognized me, and when Saint Eulalia had gone by, he threw
himself upon me. He was still a sentimental old graybeard, and when I
asked him to stop crying, his response stunned me: "It's you I'm crying
for. Or did you not receive my most recent letters?"

No, I had not received them. My life had been so busy, and any letters had been lost in the limbo of the roads. Peret could not stop himself
from blurting out the news: "Your blessed father is dead."

To my disbelief, to my despair, he also told me that I was a changed man. I was not moderately wealthy but poor. I did not live in my house, as I believed, but nowhere at all. Because I was not the son of a Barcelona trader: I was an orphan. My father had died suddenly. Shortly before, he had married a Neapolitan widow whom he had doubtless met on one of his mercantile voyages. Once he was dead, she and her children had no qualms in setting themselves up in my house. Or, rather, her house, which was what it was now.

Over the course of the following days, my stupefaction gave way to indignation. I threatened the usurpers with legal action to hound them to the end of time. And that was more or less what did happen: Over the ensuing years, I spent everything I earned on the best lawyer in the city, one Rafael Casanova. Oh yes, a splendid fellow for arguing a case in a courtroom. Eighty years have passed, and still I am awaiting justice.

If cavalry charges moved at such a pace, this world would be sorely overpopulated.

2

Peret, who had been my father's old servant, took me into his little den, close to the harbor. Once you were through the door, you had to go down three steps, and at that depth, the rats believed themselves to have the right to challenge us for possession of the territory. The place was something between a ground floor and a basement, and the only windows were slits at street level, small rectangular openings through which we could see the feet of passersby. We had two rooms: One served as a bedroom and the other a dining room, kitchen, toilet, and whatever else we might happen to need. The damp stains came halfway up the wall in grotesque shapes.

Peret took pity on me. Even in his own state of wretchedness, he gave me a little money, just enough for me to get drunk on the cheapest booze and in the most putrid of hovels. I was the unhappiest engineer in all the world.

Once you have acquired the rationality of Bazoches, from then on, that steers your thoughts exclusively, sleeping as well as waking. I very often wanted to free myself from the tyranny known as reality. Rather than having to listen all the way through as atrocious violinists stood on tables chanting bawdy songs. The caterwauling of soldiers of many nations. That laughter, which we could tell, without a word being spoken, whether it came from Germans, Englishmen, Portuguese, or Catalans. The yelling of the drunks, the smoke from the pipes and cigarettes that blackened the vaulted ceilings. I would have preferred never to see the light of the tavern's five hundred candles dripping light into the dark. People laughing, drinking, dancing. The din of humans entertaining themselves, which, to my great regret, kept me at arm's length from this same human condition.

Yes, it was pain, that class of pain. My final meeting with Vauban was torturing me. "The answer is comprised of just one word," the marquis had said. One word, my whole youth ruined by this Word. But which word, which? Night after night I gave in to despair. At lonely corner tables, I downed whole tankards, one after another. The Word, which word? I thought back over them all, from *amor* right down to *zapador*. No, that was not it. I got myself so drunk that the spirals that rose up from the smokers, meandering toward the ceiling, made me feel as though I were doing circuits around an Attack Trench. Very often, drunk, I made my way toward those smokers and set upon them, head-butting their jumbled teeth. I received countless cudgelings, all of them heartily deserved. Thrown out of nameless squalid little hovels, I lay there in the dirty, narrow streets of Barcelona, this modern Babylon.

Drinking to flee the world, drinking to escape your very body. Let us drink, all of us, we insects in the trifling circumference of this universe of ours! Let us drink until our vomiting repeats, returning to us as faithfully as dogs! All in all, how was I to be rid of my Points? At my worst moments, I would bare my right arm and, gazing on those delicate geometrical shapes, I would weep. My misfortune was etched into my very skin.

What might Jeanne be doing? Anything but thinking of Martí Zuviría. I could hardly blame her. I should have said to her, "I love you more than engineering." But I did not, and so lost them both.

*   *   *

One day I was wandering the streets, swigging from a bottle. I had stopped to buy a cabbage leaf filled with fried meat from a street vendor, and as I was haggling, I saw an unforgettable face. She was last in a line of women standing at a water fountain.

The public fountain is one of the great inventions of civilization. A place where women can exhibit themselves while they stand in line, and the young fellows can get to know them with the gallant excuse of carrying their water for them. And guess who was waiting her turn to fill a good-sized pitcher? Right, it was my old friend Amelis.

She threw me a quick look like a little cornered bird. Only fleeting, but strike me down if it didn't suggest a certain interest in the well-groomed Martí Zuviría. Better not to mention the Beceite episode. I offered to carry her pitcher, and in truth, she did not turn me down. A bit of gallantry and a perfect excuse to make conversation. Or to pick up on what we'd been up to in the pine forest before she vanished into the night. We hadn't taken ten steps when I noticed someone lifting the tails of my coat in search of my purse.

I might attribute my particular sensitivity to the acute perceptiveness instilled in me in Bazoches, but the truth was, I did not need to resort to that. A while earlier, I'd detected the presence of another pair of old acquaintances in the area: Nan and Anfán.

They had managed to make it to Barcelona after all. The boy, still with the same indescribably dirty mane; the dwarf with the funnel pulled down onto his head. The two of them were busy watching the passersby like miniature vultures. Noticing them, I handed Amelis the pitcher and grabbed them by the collar. It really felt as though no time had passed, as though we were back in a winding trench, with them running away from me around the bends.

"That's it!" I said. "I've got you this time."

They started to whine and bawl as though I were the aggressor and they the victims.

"Go on, let them go," said Amelis. "They're only kids."

"Ha!" I laughed. "You have no idea what these two are capable of. I intend to hand them over to the first patrol I find."

"You can't do that," my dark beauty said in their defense, "they will get twenty lashes, and with those tender bones, it will surely kill them."

I shrugged. "It's not I who make the laws, I merely carry them out." The lawsuit against the Italians over my father's apartment was very much in my mind as I said that. "And if an honorable man like myself is being given such a hard time, I don't see why I ought to be indulgent toward incorrigible thieves."

Anfán clung to my ankles, weeping and begging. When he saw that the girl was defending him, the weeping became louder. Since I am the greatest fraud of the century, I can recognize my own kind in an instant. And I must concede, the lad was wonderfully good at it. But he did not convince me.

"Off we go, trench pig!"

Amelis grabbed hold of my elbow. "You can't treat these two little ones so!"

It is all very well for women to be compassionate creatures, but this one was starting to sound like Our Lady of the Poor and Defenseless.

"Please!"

I merely said, "I'm sorry, sweetie," freed myself from her grip, and walked on, a pickpocket in each hand, dangling like a couple of trout. What I did not expect was that she would come and stand directly in front of me, blocking my path. She stood with her arms crossed.

"Let them go," she said, then added bluntly: "Very well, what is it you want?"

Truly, this was unsettling. I understood what she was suggesting, but that did not make it any more comprehensible. I stared at her even harder.

Her features had something irremediably sad about them. But nobody can be that generous, so why did she volunteer? Well, it was all the same to me. She was too beautiful, and I was too much of a swine, for me possibly to refuse. I let them go.

"Next time I'll see you hanged!" I shouted. "Your necks will be longer than a goose's, understand?"

Before I had finished telling them off, they had already gone around three corners and were nowhere to be seen. I turned to her: "Where to?"

She took me to La Ribera, one of the most insalubrious and overpopulated neighborhoods in all Barcelona, which is saying something. Solid gray buildings, three, four, even five storeys high, and narrow little alleyways that stopped the sunlight from reaching ground level. It was unbelievably full of people and animals. Stray dogs, chickens living on balconies, milking goats tied to rings in the walls, *meeeehhh* . . . Some of the people living there seemed quite content; they smoked and played dice in the doorways, using a barrel as a table. Others were like the living dead. I watched one man who looked like Saint Simeon the Stylite, the difference being that Simeon spent thirty years on top of a pillar and this man seemed to have been through at least double that, and living on a diet of sparrow shit. To make passersby pity him, he would open his shirt and show his ribs, which stood out like crab claws. He held a beggar's hand out to me. "*Per l'amor de Déu, per l'amor de Déu.*"

Most of the buildings must already have been old when the Emperor Augustus was here. We went into one, I don't know which, but it was even more squalid, possibly, than all the others. We climbed some stairs, up to a door on the third storey.

We walked in. I looked around us. A single shrunken room, a single window. The street was so narrow that if you stretched out your hand, you could almost touch the building opposite. At the back of the room, a straw mattress with no bed frame. Beside it, a little mountain of melted wax topped by a few candles. I imagined that at first the candles had been put on the floor, and that as they'd burned down, the same mass of melted wax had come to form the base for the ensuing ones. The rest of the furniture was comprised of a stool near the door and a basin of water, over which Amelis squatted down to wash. And that was it.

"This is where you live?" I asked as she undressed.

"I live nowhere."

The presence at the back of the room of a little wooden box—made of what seemed to be fine wood—was all the more noticeable in the midst of that destitution; Intrigued by that solitary object, no larger than a shoe box, I walked toward it and, since Zuvi is an impertinent sort of cove, lifted the lid. The moment the box opened, a tune came out, jolly but also mechanical, filling the room. I jumped a little, like a scalded cat. I felt like one of those ignorant savages, as this was the first time I had seen a *carillon à musique*.

"What are you doing?" Amelis snapped in protest.

She had been busy taking off her clothes, and when she noticed my intrusion, she seized the music box. She stood there naked, protecting it with her body, keeping it away from me. I do not believe even she was aware of the beauty of that picture: a woman this lovely, protecting that musical repository.

She closed the lid, and the music died away.

"I've never seen such a thing," I said.

She opened the lid again, and as that mechanical tune filled the air, she said: "Hurry. You have until it finishes."

Well, then, best get to it. I had gone there to do her, and I did. She seemed much more offended that I should have laid hands on her music box than on her body. There was only one moment when she showed any sort of kindness toward me. It was when she said: "Wait."

She picked up the tangle of my clothes that had fallen down and put them on the stool, in order that they should not get dirty on that filthy floor. We went straight back to it, and I soon had her shrieking like a witch on the bonfire.

When it comes to women, I have always followed the same strategy that Vauban used with cities: Assail them, but be not overly hasty. And you can take my word for it—with such spoils in my sights, it was difficult to ease off on the barrage. But then the little tune came to an end, and she pushed me from her body.

"I've done what I said, you're satisfied, and the children got to keep their lives," she said, staring up at the ceiling. "Out."

There was nothing more to be said. I picked up my clothes and hat from the stool, dressed, and walked down the stairs without saying goodbye. Once I was out on the street, I passed the half-dead prophet again. He was still holding out his hand, with the same refrain: "*Per l'amor de Déu, per l'amor de Déu.*"

Everyone is in a decent mood after a good fuck, so I stopped to give him a couple of coins. I rummaged in my pockets. But just imagine—my purse had disappeared.

That whore!

I raced back up the stairs like a wild thing. How could I have allowed myself to be beguiled so grossly, so utterly predictably? Me!

Who, just moments earlier, had been feeling odious and guilty for taking her to bed! I was more annoyed at the deception than at the loss. What would the Ducroix brothers have said? But when I entered the room, I stopped dead.

On top of the girl, on the straw mattress, there was an enormous brute of a man, and he was giving her a thrashing, right and left. And what a thrashing. He had her held between his legs; she was screaming, with no way to escape. It wasn't that the man was especially broad at the shoulders, but his woodcutter's arms looked like hammers. At this rate, he would kill her in no time. He wasn't a customer, as I could tell by the fact that the music box was closed.

"Oi, look here!" I cried, as a reflex. "What's this?"

The big fellow, whose back was to the door, turned and looked at me. An ogre, a one-eyed ogre. Until that moment I had thought the Cyclops lived on islands in the Aegean.

"What's it look like?" he barked, looking at me with his one eye. "I'm giving her a rosewater bath, right? Are you going to stand there waiting your turn? Get out of here, blockhead!"

Was I going to be intimidated by this ruffian, this one-eyed lowlife, however oversize he may have been? Of course I was. I forgot all about my purse and ran down the stairs. "What a piece of work is a man," I muttered to myself.

What happened next is harder to understand. I was on the last run of stairs when a little old woman appeared. She was carrying a pitcher much like the one I had offered to carry for Amelis.

"Allow me, my good woman, allow me," I said, impeccably friendly. "I'll take it up."

I came into the room carrying the pitcher, which did indeed weigh a ton. Don't ask me why I went back, because I do not know. I am no knight errant, and this girl was nothing but a thieving whore.

The one-eyed ogre was still going for it. Nor is it true that I am especially compassionate, but if you had heard the girl screaming! Although she was writhing between the sheets, trying to scratch out his one remaining eye, she was only a few punches from getting herself killed.

So there I was, me, her, and the ogre. And the pitcher filled with water in my hands. And—worth pointing out—the ogre had his back to me. Raising the pitcher high above my head, I hurled it with all my strength at the back of his neck.

The ogre toppled to one side, water and blood everywhere. His body subsided; there was a rushing noise like a landslide. He rolled over on the floor, coming to lie faceup. Amelis was soaked in blood and water, too, a pitiful sight, her lips cut and her hands shaking.

What came next was the sweetest conversation of my life.

Me: "Got anything heavy to hand?"

Her, hugging her knees and furious, as though she were still struggling with the Cyclops: "Do I look like a dockworker to you?"

Me (sarcastic): "Your little friend is waking up, and if I don't do something, he's going to rip us to shreds like a couple of heads of cabbage."

Her, pointing at the four candles: "That, you idiot!"

Me (still more indignant): "It's just a pile of wax! What am I supposed to do, make him swallow it so the poor baby gets a tummyache?"

Her, still with her arms around her knees, rolling her eyes like someone obliged to deal with an inveterate imbecile: "Noooo . . . It's not just wax—pick it up!"

The block of melted wax had a cannonball hidden inside it. God knows whether it was from the bombardment by the French fleet in 1691, the siege of 1697, the skirmishes that followed the landing of the Allies in 1705, or some other battle. Some person with a sense of humor had carried it up here and begun to use it for holding candles. The melted wax had wrapped itself around the ball like a solid shell, making it unrecognizable.

I picked up the iron projectile with both hands and approached the one-eyed ogre. His neck was twisted, his head in line with the wall.

Me: "Turn his neck! Don't you see I can't get a proper shot at this angle?"

"You can't get what?"

"Turn his neck!"

Without leaving her mattress, Amelis grabbed the ogre by the hair and pulled. I stood astride the fallen body and raised the cannonball over my head. At exactly that moment, his one remaining eye opened.

"Wait!" cried Amelis.

Had she suddenly turned compassionate? She pointed at the bomb. "What if it explodes?"

Still half stunned, the ogre understood what was going on. He grabbed my ankle in one hand, his living eye wider than ever.

Well, his final sight of the world was to be a twenty-four-caliber projectile falling directly onto his face. That was too close. Whatever the strategists may tell you, the best tactic will always be a good heavy blow from behind.

I rubbed my hands to remove the wax. "Done. It was his head that did some good exploding, after all."

From her bed, Amelis looked at the dead ogre, then at me, and said: "You aren't planning on leaving me here with that, are you? If they find him, they'll kill me!"

I save her life, and now she asks me to scrub the floor. Women!

"I didn't come back to get friendly with your boyfriends," I said. "My purse," I added, holding out my hand for her to return what was mine.

She laughed and told me she had no purse. I could search as much as I wanted, she said, to prove her innocence, but I would not find it. On the whole, I do know when somebody is lying. And she was so sure of herself that I ruled out the possibility. What was more, in that barren room, there could be no little nooks or hiding places. If she was a thief, she was such a good one that she deserved my respect.

Sometimes you have to know when you're beaten. I made as if to go. But when I was at the door, she said coldly: "Wait."

She poured the water (which she'd been using to wash her cunt) out into the street. She wiped the blood off her face with a rag, got dressed, and the two of us left together. She went ahead of me without saying a word, surly as ever. And whom should we find but Nan and Anfán, sitting on the steps of the Pi church.

When they saw me, they started to run, but she gave a shepherd's whistle and they stopped. We approached them, and Amelis rummaged through Anfán's clothes till she had turned out my leather purse. She handed it over to me as if to say: "Now we're even."

They had planned the whole set piece. While gallant young men carried the heavy pitchers full of water, their arms raised, spellbound by the vision of this dark Helen of Troy, Nan and Anfán would relieve them of the contents of their pockets. If anything went awry, Amelis would intercede. Everyone surrendered to the entreaties of an eighteen-year-old angel as beautiful as she was: everyone except unscrupulous types like me. Those she'd take to the room in La Ribera. While they fucked, Nan would keep watch as Anfán crept into the room, silent as a lizard, to swipe the purse. You'll recall that she placed my clothes on a stool beside the door, very easy to reach. I am sure that the loudest of her amorous wailing coincided with, and provided cover for, Anfán's entrance. After, she could then maintain her blessed innocence, since the booty had gone and no trace of the crime could possibly be found. A fine trio.

The boy, the dwarf, and Amelis stayed in the half-basement in El Raval. They couldn't be seen around La Ribera, at least until the death of the one-eyed ogre had been forgotten. As we learned subsequently, he was neither a procurer nor a criminal from the underworld but a depraved patrician who would occasionally carry Amelis's pitcher and had gone mad with passion for her. Eventually, fed up with his pockets being picked, he'd come straight over to kill her.

They had nothing but the clothes on their backs, except for Amelis, who was carrying her one earthly possession in her arms: that strange box that played a tune, to which she was so attached. It was clear that she used her *carillon à musique* as a shield to protect herself against the sorrows of life. When she appeared, she had that sacred little box swaddled as though it were the baby Jesus Himself.

At first the whole thing was a real nuisance. Peret and I were already finding it a squeeze in that half-basement, and now we had to find room for another three bodies. Amelis and I shared the only bedroom. Peret and that other pair lay on straw mattresses in the room that served as kitchen and dining room. Peret could not abide them. He made my head throb with all his complaints, lamentations, and recriminations.

The dwarf, for example, had very queer ideas about domestic life. When he didn't get his way, he'd express his frustration by shrieking like a speared boar, high-pitched and frantic enough to wake the dead.

If he was ignored, he'd use his own head as a battering ram, butting doors and walls, racing around the house like a spinning top.

If the dwarf seemed eccentric, Anfán's behavior was positively indescribable. The word "thief" is inadequate to describe that lad. He was compulsive, a larceny fanatic. Any time of the day or night, you might find his little fingers in your pockets. Thanks to what I had learned in the Spherical Room, I could see him coming a mile off, and shooed him as though swatting a fly, but poor Peret was robbed as many as five times a day. One morning he awoke early with a candle stuck in his nose and completely naked. Before breakfast, Anfán and Nan had already sold his clothes on the streets.

I tried to reason with the boy. "Don't you understand that while you are here, what's ours is yours?"

"No."

At least he was honest.

Peret, entirely logically, wanted to beat them to death. As usual, Amelis protected them, shouting, hiding them behind her skirts. Peret's opinion could not have been clearer: "Since you live with her, you have the right to treat her as your wife. Put her in her place and give her a good hiding every once in a while!"

Our half-basement was a nest of disagreement. On the other hand, I was in no hurry for Amelis to leave. She soon recovered from the beating she had received. She was infinitely more beautiful than the first day I saw her in the stable of a godforsaken little town. And in short, let me just say that, in bed, she was very obliging. We slept together, and this started to change into a routine that began, bit by bit, to develop beyond mere pleasure into a happy, daily amazement. Love? I do not know. Nobody ever asks whether he loves the air that he breathes, and yet he cannot live without it. It was a little like that. Her thoughts at the time were a mystery. Did she approve of her new condition, or did she go along with it in order to keep a roof over her head—or for the sake of that pair, with whom her relationship was more that of an older sister than a mother? All I can tell you is that one night, before making love, she did not open the *carillon à musique*. And from that night on, while we were still together, she never opened it again.

The thing was, Anfán's thieving habits had to stop. Either the boy changed, or we would all be driven quite mad. I did not even consider beating them, as I was sure that technique would be no use. From what little I knew of his biography, the lad had experienced such treatment wherever he went. The results were plain to see.

The big changes started on the outside. Vauban had been such a stickler for cleanliness that he bathed every week. I am no admirer of such excesses, but Anfán and Nan had never been closer to water than a pair of desert rocks.

The worst was when we wanted to cut the hair of one of them and remove the funnel from the head of the other. The moment they saw the scissors and the clippers (could we have used anything less to yank off that funnel?), they fled and did not show their faces in the house for two days after.

Finally, we reached a compromise with Anfán. We had nothing against his braids, but we gave him to understand that those twisted shapes were made of pure filth. If he washed them, Amelis promised, she would weave his fair hair into natural braids, dozens of blond braids; we promised she would. Much more attractive, too.

Clean, decently dressed in a white shirt and a pair of pants without holes in them, with braids that glowed yellow instead of greasy rags, he even looked like a child and not the cabin boy from a pirate ship.

With the dwarf, we agreed to burn his circus clothes and that he should remove his funnel once a month. We had to swear that, while we washed his hair, he would be allowed to hold on to the funnel with both hands. I refuse to describe all the bugs and pus-covered gack we found in there that first time. Yeuch!

Amelis, Nan, and Anfán were a tight, inseparable trio. It was not quite clear who had adopted whom. However much I asked Anfán about his past, it was as though he had a crater in his memory. Whenever he was abandoned, or whenever his parents were killed, it must have been when he was very small, as he had no memory of them. It was better, perhaps, that he didn't remember. He was aware of no other life than this one, as a piece of floating detritus, ever at the mercy of the tides of invasions that followed one another through that natural corridor of the Mediterranean called Catalonia. His very name, his barracks talk, a mixture of French, Catalan, and Spanish, said it all.

Boys will always be boys. Including that little beast Anfán. Deprived as he was of paternal love, he filled its absence by projecting it onto the dwarf. Deep down, Anfán gave Nan the very thing he himself was crying out for. I began to feel a soft spot for the boy when I understood that.

As far as I knew, not long after the siege of Tortosa came to an end, the pair had run into Amelis (the roads from Beceite and Tortosa met on the way to Barcelona). If a place has a roof, it's possible to call it home; under that roof is the shared hearth, and in the absence of a fire, an embrace, simple and basic, will do. They were her home. The proof being, Nan and Anfán never got used to sleeping far away from Amelis. At any moment of the night, they might leave the straw where they lay and come in to us. That I might have been busy with her made no difference at all to them. They crowded in with us and slept like kittens. To begin with, I protested: "Can't they at least stay outside till we've finished?"

Amelis answered quite simply: "What difference does it make?"

The three of them were shocked by my civilized rules. To them it was much more normal for all of us to sleep together in a tangle of elbows and knees, one person's feet in another's face, or someone's cheeks on someone else's belly. One false move, and the end of that damned funnel could stab you anywhere. And I mean anywhere!

Look, I know it is not really right to be making love and sleeping when you have a kid, a dwarf, and a funnel sharing your bed.

But honestly, what can I tell you?

3

Around that time we received the most unexpected of visits: four porters with three heavily armed escorts, who said that they had come from beyond the northern border and were delivering a letter and a trunk in my name.

The letter was from Don Bardonenche, who begged my forgiveness for not being able to deliver the trunk in person. The Vauban family had entrusted him with the mission of getting it to me. Unfortunately, once he had reached the border, the Allied army had blocked his passage, however strongly good Bardonenche had insisted that he was driven only by personal motives to visit beautiful Barcelona. "This world is going to the dogs," wrote Bardonenche sadly, "as can be seen from the fact that nowadays, men don't even trust their enemies." My dear vile Waltraud is surprised by this, but I can assure you that in my day, at least among career soldiers, such courtesies were not in the least unusual.

Well, when we opened the trunk, our surprise provoked—in this order—stammering, shouting, and fainting, because it contained no more nor less than one thousand two hundred francs. The marquis had bequeathed the sum to me in his will. I won't pretend I wasn't moved: Even from beyond the grave, I remained in Vauban's thoughts. Why had it taken so long? The distance between Paris and Barcelona is not inconsiderable even when there is no war on, and the conflict had increased the number of legal obstacles for such a large sum of money to reach me.

To celebrate my newfound fortune, I went on a binge so monumental that I suffered a hangover for two days. The problem was, that gang took advantage of my lying down a little to squander my treasure: They spent every last coin buying an apartment, a fifth-storey abode in the busy La Ribera neighborhood. Amelis needed a man's signature, so Peret obliged. You will better understand my desire to throttle them when I tell you that the contents of the trunk were insufficient, which meant that, to complete the purchase, it was necessary to secure a loan. Naturally, they arranged to take it out in my name. As for the rest, how could a man trained to put up or knock down city ramparts ever love partition walls? I don't know how I bore it when Amelis showed me our new nest.

It was a common house with just a few pretensions: cheap painting on the ceiling, geometric patterns on the plastered walls, three bedrooms, and a kitchen. It smelled of new plaster. As usual, the fifth storey was the cheapest, since getting there required climbing numerous flights of stairs. At least the height meant there was sunlight in the bedrooms. We had one to ourselves, another for Nan and Anfán, and a third for that parasite Peret (his charge for helping with the swindle by pretending to be me with the creditors). The rear balcony looked out over the bastion of Saint Clara. The fortified pentagon stretched all the way out as far as the foot of the balcony. We could look down and see the bastion yard, the changing of the guard, the whole thing. In our room, Amelis showed me a skylight that opened immediately above the bed. Through the glass, there was a view of the sky, bluer than the Mediterranean itself.

As a matter of fact, the house became a real home the day Amelis installed her *carillon à musique* in our bedroom. Through the skylight, the rays of the sun poured down onto the white sheets, and she would often sit in the middle of the bed, naked, brushing her long black hair, her lips moving in time to that sad melody. The beauty of the sight was enough to turn you to stone. In such moments it was best not to interrupt her self-absorbed nakedness.

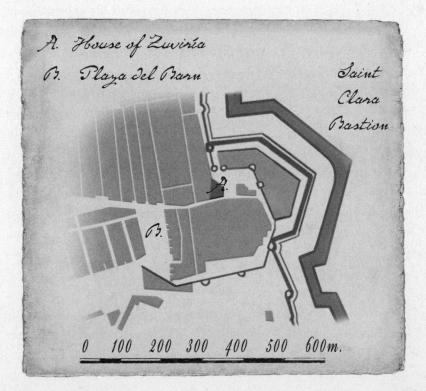

God, how the life we shared had changed! In the past, Amelis had made use of the music box in order to escape during the torments life had subjected her to. Now it served a different function: as though that music—so unusual, so artificial, and yet so sweet—were transporting her back to her most distant memories. No, it was more than that, the music box itself comprised the memories, the way a desert has no borders: The desert is itself the border.

And so, well, we were now the brand-new owners of a home. A problem arose from the fact that the trunk from Vauban had contained one thousand two hundred francs, while the apartment had cost one thousand, six hundred, and twelve. In other words, in less time than it takes to sleep off a hangover, we had exchanged our state from happily well-off paupers to that of happily poor property owners. And indebted ones, at that. We had to pay off the debt, and during wartime all business gets drawn into war, too.

It's about time I recounted my little adventure in Castilian lands. How I was dragged into the 1710 campaign, how I came to witness the rise of Archduke Charles to the Madrid throne, and the fall that followed. Ah, yes, and also how I found—altogether unbelievably—a teacher who would replace Vauban, and that the last individual in the world I ever would have supposed capable of exercising any kind of preeminence in anything.

For this reason, if you will allow me, I will first permit myself a brief digression. My dear vile Waltraud is against it; she thinks I ought to get on. Well, pity for her.

In order to tear me away from the taverns, Amelis insisted that we leave the city, even if for a day, on the pretext of a *chocolatada*. For a reasonable price, it was possible to hire a carriage to take you six or seven miles outside Barcelona. There you would find green expanses, meadows, and beautiful views, and at the end of the day, the carts would return to collect the day-trippers and bring them home. Let me tell you a little about the *chocolatadas*.

A *chocolatada* did not necessarily mean simply going and eating chocolate. Depending on the kind of people taking part, the most peculiar products might be added to the melted chocolate, aphrodisiacs in particular. The priests had declared war on chocolate and were constantly sermonizing against its consumption, which was very much the fashion.

As chocolate is black, nobody could ever be sure what had been added to a mug. The cook could slip his hand in and add a few intoxicants, which, consumed to excess, could cause death. It was just a risk you took. In fact, it was more the danger than anything that excited people about it, because the great majority of *chocolatadas* contained no more than that, some innocent cocoa boiled up with sugar. But since everybody went along with the suspicion, if not the absolute conviction, that some love drugs had been poured in, whenever you put your hand on your daughter-in-law's lovely behind, you could always blame the chocolate. (Yes, yes, everything was always the chocolate's fault, of course!)

Fantasy or not, after a second mug people suddenly felt a passionate urge to dance. They would hold hands in a circle, laughing and singing. And without the slightest decorum! Men and women jumbled in together, with no distinction between generations, status, or kindred! There were always a couple of fiddles to brighten up the party, and shortly afterward, couples of dancers would start disappearing. You can guess what they had gone off to do.

I didn't care a fig what they had done to the chocolate, I was suffering only for my Amelis. The carriages left us on a beautiful green hillock. No sooner had we alit than I started feeling unwell, since I knew that in the dissolute atmosphere of a *chocolatada*, any clown would try to take advantage of her. I remember the exact moment when my jealousy attack struck: I was helping her down from the wagon, my arm around her waist, and as I deposited her on the ground, I felt as though I had lost something. "Oh, *Déu meu*, . . . " I said to myself with something like sorrow. "So that's what it is—I'm in love with her."

There must have been thirty or forty of us sprawled on blankets. Presiding over the plain was an old ruined *masía*, a construction with no doors and half the roof caved in. The *masías*, traditional Catalan mountain houses, were miniature fortresses that took care—great care—of an area's defenses. I wasn't surprised that the former inhabitants of this one should have chosen such a setting: From there it was possible to control any approach, three hundred and sixty degrees around, and from a great distance. Bazoches was certainly not the first place to study the ancient art of defending.

After breakfast came the chocolate, and the revelry began. The fiddles started to play jouncing tunes. People gathered around in circles. Amelis took my hand for us to dance, too. I could not. At that moment something unusual happened: Anfán came up behind me and threw his arms around my neck. It had taken nearly a year for him to get that close. Laugh if you like, but I felt moved. He rested his boyish cheek against mine and whispered: "Can I rob them, jefe? They're all drunk."

"No, no, you can't. They are drunk, but they're also good people."

That line of argument had no impact on him whatsoever.

"All that booty, and I could even buy Nan a new funnel."

"Has Nan asked you for a funnel? No. What you want is to have some fun. Well, go and dance, then. You'll see how much you enjoy that, and no risk of a whipping, either." In the tone Vauban used to employ with me, I added, "You won't understand why, but you have to make sure nobody takes Nan off into the bushes." And I shouted: "*Allez!*"

When it comes to little boys and soldiers, it's always better to charge them with a mission than a punishment.

And you will allow me to become a little emotional now, for I discovered, suddenly, that this was happiness. The green grass, the jolly fiddles. Circles of people laughing and dancing like zanies. Crooked little Peret holding hands with a widow, whispering filth in her ear. Nan and Anfán dancing, Nan as inexpressive as ever but happy on the inside; Anfán, following my instructions, driving off with a kick any woman who approached the dwarf. And Amelis laughing, dancing, her black hair loose in the wind. I don't know how long it lasted. Just a short time, I'm sure; happiness is always fleeting. All at once Peret and the widow came rushing out of a clump of bushes, Peret holding his pants around his calves and the woman running with her hair all disheveled. They must have seen something when they were right in the middle of things.

"Ballester!" cried Peret, terrified. "Ballester's coming!"

Ballester! My old friend who had become one of the most notorious and cruel Miquelets—though I have already explained to you that in Catalonia, the word "Miquelet" could mean many things.

The *chocolatada*, as I have said, took place on a high plateau. I climbed up on a rocky promontory and could see what would soon be upon us: a group of light cavalry, still some distance away. To judge by the dust raised by their hooves, there must have been a good dozen of them.

Panic transforms people into a herd. Everybody was shouting and running. The wealthiest, who had come on their own horses, fled at a gallop, leaving their lovers behind (and most unscrupulously, indeed—ah, love!). The rest didn't really know what to do; animal instinct sent them inside the abandoned *masía*. Nan and Anfán were running, holding Amelis's hands. They, too, went into the *masía*, and I was right behind them.

Inside, people were crushed together like cattle, because even though it was a spacious place, the partition walls had fallen in long ago. The women wept and hugged one another, the men tore their hair. I shouted for silence.

"Anyone planning to do anything," I yelled, "or should we just wait here to be sacrificed like little lambs?"

A gallant in his best glad rags stepped forward. "What are you saying?" he said. "You with your baby face, and the man who's coming for us is Ballester!"

"I was pretty sure it wasn't Saint Peter on horseback!" I replied, and turned to address the whole crowd: "So are we going to do something, or aren't we?"

"Listen to the big captain here!" The gallant was mocking me again. "These people bugger little boys like you for breakfast!"

There was a rotten old table. I climbed up on it. "Listen to me, all of you: If you do everything I tell you, there's a chance we might get out of this alive."

But again the gallant spoke up: "The men coming this way are professional killers, and they have an arsenal. All we've got here are women, children, and doddering old men. The house is in ruins, and you mean to defend it." He pointed at the entrance. "There isn't even a door!"

Something flashed through my head. If I'd had the time to think, believe me, my answer would have been rather different. But the situation was so urgent, and at the same time so desperate, that I could not do it. Which was why I sighed and, emphasizing each word, said: "*We are the door.*"

"They will slit our throats and rape the women!" the gallant insisted.

"That's precisely why we mean to fight, you dolt!" I shouted. "When they see that they can get neither booty nor ransom, nor steal any horses, they will slit a few throats for their amusement and go riding on our women." I pointed to Amelis. "That's my woman, and I swear no one will touch her. They shall not!"

There are many different kinds of silence. The silence of desperation, the silence of reflection, the silence of peace: Every one is different, and that particular one reeked of doubt. Then somebody said, "They raped me once, a long time ago."

It was a little old woman, the kind who still crackled with energy. She looked at the gallant while pointing a finger my way. "And on that day I would have liked to have a 'little boy' like this one around." Then, looking at me, she said: "I'm just an old bag, but if you tell me to, I will stone anyone who sets foot through that door. What have I got to lose?"

Murmurs. That voice, humble but firm, was able to transform fear into anger. Peret came over to the table. He took hold of one of my ankles and said, petrified, "But Martí, lad, whatever do you think we poor wretches can possibly do?"

"First of all, pile up all the weapons we have, here on this table," I replied.

I got down from the table, and the men who were carrying weapons brought them over. As usually happens, the most heavily armed are the most cowardly; the gallant took out two large pistols and a dagger. Altogether, we gathered six pistols and fifteen knives of varying sizes. The most pitiful of arsenals.

"Superb!" I cried, giving a sterling performance. "You see? With all this, we could defend Sagunto itself."

As I've said, Catalan *masías* are designed like miniature fortresses, capable of repelling assaults from all four sides. Walls as thick as the ramparts of a city, windows as narrow as arrow-slits perpendicular to the ground, stone roofs that will not set fire: Even though it was falling into ruin, it remained a significant fortification.

I asked the women to pile up some good-sized stones. The roof had partly fallen in; using the rubble and the remains of the furniture, the men improvised a way up to the top. From there they could shoot, or at least throw stones, at anyone who approached. Others used the rubble to build a barricade—though a more symbolic barrier than an actual one—blocking the door. I told the children to go search in the corners. I squatted down beside Anfán. "Look underneath the floorboards; you're sure to find something."

And they did. Every *masía* has its own arsenal. In the floor of what must have been the main bedroom, Anfán and Nan found a dusty trapdoor. They opened it. Inside were four muskets. Rusty, two of them missing their stocks, but muskets all the same.

"What do you want us to do with this junk?" someone asked.

"Clean the barrels."

"They're here!" It was one of the lookouts; the only thing we weren't short of was eyes.

For some time, the horsemen did not approach. They went round and round the *masía*, sniffing about, little more than that. I was running from one end to the other, asking the people stationed there: "What are they doing?"

"Nothing. Just loitering and looking."

To the defenders, the time spent waiting for an attack is immeasurably worse than the attack itself; we needed to stop ourselves from imagining its horrors, at all costs. I decided to go outside. Amelis tried to hold me back.

"Who do you think should go and speak for us, then?" I said. "That gallant? Peret? You can be sure that Nan and Anfán won't be leaving your side."

"They're bandits! They won't be reasoned with."

She was weeping tears of rage, furious with me, as though I had just confessed to her that I had a lover. She pummeled my chest with both fists. "They'll kill you! They'll kill you!" She turned and walked away.

You see? It is easier to reason with bandits than with women. And as for you, woman, don't give me that look—just write down what I say.

We moved the fragile barricade from the doorway, and I stepped outside.

One of the bandits on horseback approached and then stopped about twenty feet away, scrutinizing me. I'd come up with no better idea than simply looking indifferent. I greeted him with a forced smile, touching the tip of my tricorn hat with my fingertips. He rode off. Then his boss appeared, escorted by four horsemen on either side. Ballester.

He had changed since we'd met in Beceite and at the inn. He'd aged; he seemed more used to that life of assault and flight. I could see that his eyes were sunken, as though their sockets were twice as deep as most people's. He was not especially ugly, since ferocity can have its appeals. But with those sunken eyes, his eyebrows solid and dark like rope, and a thick, incredibly black beard, he had the look of a man who cared little for age or such things. He sported a pair of pistols either side of his upper torso; in a sticky situation, he could cross his arms and draw them in a flash.

I will always remember that look on Ballester's face. His eyes had their own eloquence. And it was contradictory. They said, *I'm going to kill you*, and at the same time, they said, *Let's talk*. Those who could not see the second fled.

What I said was: "Good afternoon."

"It is, a very good afternoon," he replied. His hands were on the pommel of his saddle, and he was looking up at the sky like a country philosopher. "A very good afternoon *indeed*."

"What can we do for you?" I asked.

He took offense. He rode his horse forward and circled me a few times, an act that was obviously most intimidating. I could almost hear people's hearts pounding inside the *masía*. I raised my voice. "It's rude addressing a person who is not mounted from on a horse, even for a gentleman."

Ballester addressed his men: "A gentleman! Did you hear that? I'm a proper gentleman now!"

His fellow outlaws burst out laughing. Ballester made a gesture of mocking condescension and dismounted.

He did not smell bad—a fact I found strange, because as the son of a seafaring trader who lived with his back to the inland places, I had been schooled in the belief that Miquelets were no better than the dregs and overspillings of the brimstone of hell. Ballester gave off a smell of clean ashes, of thyme, and of rosemary. As did his men.

A year had passed since we had met, but he stated rather than asked: "We know each other."

"I do believe we've met," I said coolly. "We engaged in a commercial transaction. I came away with nothing, and you with everything."

He ignored my words, gesturing at the *masía*. "Why have you shut yourselves inside there?"

"Your reputation precedes you."

"Oh, dear—and what reputation would that be?"

Since we had decided to defend ourselves, I stood my ground. "They say Esteve Ballester is a murderous brute, a criminal. That he uses the excuse of fighting for the Catalan fatherland to attack poor defenseless travelers. He robs and kidnaps. If the ransom does not arrive in time, he burns his victim's feet. And that's when he's in a good mood."

He chose to ignore the provocation. "Really?" he said. "And you believe everything people say?"

"I myself happen to know that some people, he strips naked, hangs, and leaves for dead."

He gave a guffaw. "To the best of my knowledge, I have never taken anything of yours." He paused, then said, his voice graver: "And as for you, *botiflero*, you dare to call me a thief?"

If I wanted to bargain with him, it was not good to have him talk down to me like this. Ballester and I were halfway between his men and the *masía*. I took off my hat. It was the sign for all the firearms to be poked out of the door, the windows and the roof, including the barrels of the rusty muskets, which the women had polished up with rags and spit.

"*Señor*, I have twenty rifles pointing directly at your head," I lied. "Our riders have galloped off to notify the guard. They'll be along any moment. You know we are poor citizens; there's no booty to be had here. If this has to be resolved with firearms, there will be no one but you to blame for it."

I had shouted these words so that everyone could hear. It was a simple calculation: If the prospect of raiding the house didn't seem profitable, they would leave. And even if they believed only half of my lies, that was enough to give them good cause for doubt. Unfortunately, the proximity of violence changed Ballester. So it is with all men, but in him it was as though something inside snapped. His deep eyes sank deeper. The blue vein across his right temple swelled and throbbed. Years later, I would discover the small things in him that signaled murderous intent: When he was ready to kill, you could smell that sweating of his, incredibly intense.

His voice hissed horribly, the blue vein as thick as a worm: "If your people kill me, mine will kill you, too, you fool."

"Indeed," I replied, also whispering. "All in all, it's a draw."

Then we heard something: the cries of a terrified child.

One of the horsemen approached with Anfán under his arm. The boy was struggling. When he saw me, he reached out his hands toward me, his fingers splayed open, and began to squeal even more desperately.

Ballester must have seen something change in my expression, because he gave a bit of a grimace, though not a smile, and said: "So it seems that draw of yours has just gone to hell."

We all have dreams in our childhood in which we are swallowed up in a deep tentacle-filled pit. But to Anfán, this was now reality. He was thirty feet away, and those thirty feet were as insuperable as a whole world.

The boy had been with me for a year. I had clothed and fed him. He slept with me and my woman. I had scolded and corrected him more times than I could count, and he was a little better now than when I had first met him. Just a little, but now, for the first time, I saw tears in his eyes that were not false.

I felt a red curtain drop down over my eyes, descending. I didn't recognize my own voice as I said: "You are going to release him! Now! Or I swear by my blessed mother that I will kill you. You and that animal who's holding him." And I added, so quiet as to be almost imperceptible, "I swear it."

For a single, endless moment, Ballester stared into my eyes. Anfán was squirming around, and I was about to lose my mind completely. Perhaps Ballester understood: You can't negotiate with a madman. With a flick of his head—as though the business were nothing to do with him—he gestured for the rider to put Anfán down.

The lad started running, so quickly that he fell and got up and fell again. Even though he was petrified, running with his straw-colored braids in the wind, when he was a safe distance from the horseman, he stopped, stuck out his tongue, and gave him a *bras d'honneur*. Then he was whimpering and running again, and he didn't stop till his arms were clinging tightly around my waist.

Ballester moved away from me. It was an odd moment, because it clearly meant something that, though the barrels of a thousand guns were pointing at him, nobody had fired yet. He walked up and down in front of the barricaded doorway, rage in his eyes.

"You people have such a quiet, happy life," he began. "You think the world is nothing more than *chocolatadas* and fucking. Fools! The sky is going to fall on our heads when you least expect it."

To demonstrate his prophet's disdain, he risked slapping away the barrel of one of the rifles pointed at him. I didn't react. I made a gesture to the people in the *masía*, downplaying Ballester's audacity; better that he give his little speech and then leave. After everything that had happened, it was obvious that at this point, all he wanted was not to look bad in front of his men, with a bit of braggart talk.

"You people all believe the Generalitat's lies merely because they're published in official documents. How many poor people do you know to whom I owe anything? I have paid for hundreds of masses, for the upkeep of orphanages . . . The only people who need fear me are the *botifleros* and the Red Pelts." He was referring to the ministers of the Generalitat, because of their red velvet clothing and hats.

I've told you this already? Oh, damn it all.

From inside the *masía* came an anonymous voice: "You raped my son-in-law's cousin, ill-born swine! They ought to tear you limb from limb up on the fifth gallows!"

"Slander!" replied Ballester, turning toward the voice. "People have been carrying out attacks and *claiming* to be acting in my name. Or does anyone really believe that Ballester needs to use payment or force in order for a woman to join him in bed?"

The lively old lady poked her head out through the doorway. She had half-climbed onto the heap of rubble with a rock in her hand, threatening to hurl it at him. "You or any other Miquelets . . . what difference does it make? You think you're so big and strong just because you sleep around a campfire and dine on the venison you've hunted. You fight for your own benefit, attacking peaceful people, and now you want to persuade us you're some kind of mountain saint because every once in a while you happen to kill a drunk Bourbon? Get hanged!"

Ballester waved a finger at her threateningly, but his voice was more restrained. "*Mestressa*, do not be mistaken. I have killed more Frenchmen and Castilians in this war than any of the king's regiments."

At this point I intervened, Anfán in my arms, his legs around my hips like a little monkey, and clinging so tightly to my neck that he was almost choking me. "If you're so passionate about defending the country, why not join King Charles's army?"

"Because both armies are the same, even if they're wearing different uniforms; flames burn all the same, blue or red."

I thought he was leaving, but he turned back toward us. He whispered in my ear: "I can swear, too. Now listen to me: If I see you again, I'm going to send you flying. Understand?"

Anfán leaned in toward Ballester's face, puffed up his cheeks, pressed his lips together, and let rip with a huge raspberry blown in his ear. I think it was the first and last time I ever saw Ballester laugh healthily.

"And tell your little braided monkey here that if he doesn't learn some manners, I shall come back and take him." He opened his eyes wide, staring at Anfán without blinking, made his lips into an O, and went "*Boo!*"

Anfán clung even harder to my neck, squealing with fear, his back to Ballester, kicking against my hips. Ballester mounted his horse amid laughter from his men, and before leaving, he announced as he turned his mount, raising his hat in greeting: "Ladies! Gentlemen! You have had a good day today." And he offered a polite gesture to the old woman who had accused him: "*Iaia, t'estimo.*" Grandmother, my regards.

He spurred on his horse, and away they went.

Anfán spotted something on the ground. Ballester had dropped his riding whip. Anfán climbed down my body as if it were a tree and handed me the trophy.

I shall carry the happiness on that boy's face with me till the day I die, his satisfaction at offering me Ballester's whip. It was not a gift; it was something that cannot be expressed fully in words. He had been born a thief, and the fact he was now sharing his booty said it all.

I snatched the whip away. "You! I told you to stay by Amelis's skirts and not to move!"

The day wasn't over. Though you may find this hard to believe, the real heroism of the day was yet to come. After dinner, I confronted Anfán.

"After you found those muskets, I told you to stay with Amelis," I said, glaring at him across the table. "And you disobeyed me."

He responded like a wild beast with rational faculties. His innate instincts and his sense of justice joined forces to proclaim in a single voice: "But the bandits were thieves!" He stood up on his chair, defensive and indignant at the same time. "Why can't I steal from thieves?" he added, his eyes wide. "They were thieves!"

Peret shouted: "Stupid boy! When are you going to learn that's the worst insult you can make against anybody? If it weren't for Martí, the Miquelets would be roasting you alive right now. Stupid boy!"

Something snapped when Nan, who was sitting on his chair, swinging his legs and looking down at the floor, repeated Peret's words: "Stupid boy."

"Time for you to be punished," I announced.

I went to my room, returning with Ballester's riding whip. I sat down and said, "Come over here."

It is a very particular expression, the expression on the face of a human being who discovers that he has been betrayed. After a year under the same roof, after so long sleeping in the same bed, I was going to use violence on him. The boy approached, feigning indifference. By the time he had taken those four steps, his expression had changed to that of someone who never wanted to see me again.

I placed the whip in his hand and held out my open palm. "Hit me."

At first he didn't understand.

"Hit me!" I said again.

He did, gently.

"Harder!"

He turned away to consult the others, bewildered, but I put a finger on his chin and forced him to look at me.

The whip cracked against my hand.

"Is that the best you can do? Harder!"

He hit me harder, drawing blood. When he saw it, he took a step back in alarm.

"We're not done yet. Again."

I offered him my bleeding palm one more time. He hit me. The whip had gone deeper into the wound, and this time I couldn't help a grimace of pain.

"That's enough," Amelis pleaded.

"Quiet!" I shouted, and looking straight at Anfán, I said firmly: "Keep going, or get out of here and never come back!"

He raised the whip. I showed my wounded hand, the open groove streaming with blood. "The whip. Use it!"

He burst out crying. He had never cried like this before. In the hands of the Miquelets, he had been afraid, but with this torrent of tears, he was purging himself of all the ills of the world, all the bile that our age had corrupted him with. Amelis put her arms around him.

"Do you understand?" I whispered in his ear. "Now do you understand?"

Anfán learned that night that his pain was ours, and ours his. His learning that lesson meant I learned another: that four human beings can be not merely the sum of a few individuals but an entity conjoined by fondness for one another. That night our full bed seemed to me quite changed. I no longer saw that elbow, that funnel, that mane of hair belonging to another, a nuisance that fell in our eyes as we slept. They were a whole now, like the Spherical Room had been, beyond just the objects that inhabited it. I looked at them, I tell you, with the alertness of Bazoches, undisturbed by feelings, which are nothing more than clouds obscuring the landscape of reason. And yet I never cease to be amazed how methodical observation can turn into tenderness. I heard Anfán's gentle snoring, watched Nan's grimaces as he dreamed, Amelis's closed eyelids, and said to myself that the bed, that tiny rectangle, was surely the most valuable star in our whole universe.

4

S o there it was, the strange home that, in mid-1710, I was forced to leave for a long time. And why did I leave? I should say a little about the military situation in those days.

Despite the frivolity of the Barcelonans, whose lives carried on as though the war were being fought on the banks of the Rhine alone, the truth was that it was coming closer and closer. One might say that by 1710 it was already all around us. The only territory controlled by Charles was the little triangle that was Catalonia, with Barcelona at its center. In 1710 almost all of Spain was in the hands of Little Philip, the Two Crowns' strategy was fiendishly systematic, and our Allies, meanwhile, operated by means of momentary thrusts, followed by long stretches of indolence.

The military situation was going from bad to worse, so the Allied leaders decided that something had to be done. And each time war ground to a halt in the Spanish theater, the Allies made the same choice: to send a new general to Spain to get things moving again. At that time, the latest import was the Englishman James Stanhope. If only we'd had a different Jimmy on our side, James Berwick rather than the boy Stanhope. As bigheaded as he was impulsive, Stanhope was the embodiment of the attitude "I'll sort this out in a trice!" How is it possible that a man who thinks he knows it all should learn absolutely nothing? General In-a-Trice! That's how history should have remembered him!

He arrived in Barcelona well briefed by his government. England had had enough of the war, and his mission would be to put an end to it once and for all. And this was the final effort London was prepared to make to bring about a victorious conclusion. New military contingents arrived with Stanhope, too: Dutch and Austrian infantry, along with the powerful English cavalry corps, with Stanhope himself at its head. These reinforcements, combined with the Allied troops that had remained in Catalonia, were bound to be enough for a great offensive, avenging Almansa and crowning Charles in Madrid as the king of all Spain. And all in a trice!

The offensive raised uncommon expectations among those of us in Barcelona. History books tend to forget the huge numbers of people who travel with an army on campaign. And since the number of civilians following an army convoy often exceeds the number of actual soldiers, it is, you will agree, a rather sizable thing to forget. On the one hand, there are the people providing services, from barbers to cobblers, indispensable functions for such a great contingent of humanity. But there was also the fact that the 1710 offensive was to be the decisive attack. Hundreds, thousands, of pro-Austrian Spaniards in exile in Catalonia joined the military columns, and they did so with the enthusiasm of people who finally see an opportunity to return home, galloping to victory. Matters didn't end there, because in addition to the merchants and expatriates, there came a whole trail of opportunists. After all, Catalonia was the land that had been most faithful to Charles's cause. It would make sense that, upon ascending the throne in Madrid, he would recompense his compatriots with perks and positions. And can you guess who was to be found among the worst of that pack of hustlers? Yes indeed, good old Zuvi. I told Amelis that this was an opportunity unlike any other, that with luck, I might be able to land myself a tidy sum we could use to pay off our debts.

And yet money wasn't the true reason I added my name to the convoy of army followers. I never told Amelis that, of course. She never would have understood that I was risking my skin for a Word.

The trunk from Vauban had been a message from beyond the grave. It was as though the marquis were saying: "Is this the life your teacher prepared you for?" I told myself I could not accept the marquis's fortune, not without making one final attempt to learn a word—The Word.

"Summarize the optimum defense": That was what Vauban had asked of me. Half of Europe's armies were attacking the heart of the Spanish empire. If they wanted to crown Charles, they would need to take the capital, Madrid. Spain and France would do their utmost to oppose this. The greatest leaders would clash on the bare wastelands of Castile; the whole struggle would hinge on Madrid's defense. It promised to be a spectacle both tragic and grand, a clash of cosmic proportions. And within this theater, perhaps I might find a teacher to continue the marquis's work. With his help, maybe The Word would be revealed to me. The recriminations I heard from Amelis made me happy, because there could be only one possible reason for her opposing my departure: love. But I had a debt to another love, and it was every bit as great.

I owed it to Vauban.

I needed to figure out some way to follow the army, so I came to an arrangement with a merchant who was planning to follow the troops with a two-horse covered wagon laden with barrels of stomach-churning liquor. He was calculating that when the army crossed the dry, uninhabited parts of Castile, where it would be impossible to procure any wine, the price of alcohol would soar.

We came to a mutually beneficial agreement. I needed transportation, and his wagon was covered with a bit of sackcloth that would serve as a roof over our heads at night. The merchant was accompanied by his son, a troubled lad whose wits were barely sharper than a dog's. At night the merchant and his lad would sleep in the front section of the wagon, right behind the driver's seat. Another passenger and I would be at the back, defending the rear.

This other passenger said his name was Zúñiga, Diego de Zúñiga. Eight decades have passed, and I still remember him as an altogether remarkable man. What set Zúñiga apart? Well, strange though it may sound, it was the fact that there was nothing about him that stood out, absolutely nothing at all. He wasn't very talkative or very withdrawn; he wasn't miserly or profligate; neither tall nor short; neither merry nor sad. Every man has his own distinctive manner, a certain way of clicking his fingers, an unusual laugh or a particular way of tilting his head when he spits. Zúñiga did not spit, his laughter was always buried away within the laughter of others, and he tended to keep his fingers hidden. A ghost would have seemed much more tangible beside him. He was one of those fellows you tend to forget the moment they have left your field of vision. As a matter of fact, as I try to reconstruct Zúñiga's face now, I find it hard to gain purchase on it in my memory.

According to what he told me, he was the son of a moderately affluent family brought low by the war. Since his father was one of the

few Castilians to have taken Charles's part, the Bourbons and their supporters had expropriated the family's possessions. By then an old man,
he hadn't survived the shock of it all. Zúñiga was a native of Madrid.

The two of us got on well, if only because we had a lot in common. For a start, our families were of a similar social standing, neither
rich nor very poor, and life had brought us down several rungs on the
ladder. We were the same sort of age, added to which was the similar-
ity between our family names. We slept curled up next to each other.
From the first day, it seemed quite natural that we should share our
bread and wine. A shame he was not a more garrulous sort.

Shortly before arriving at Lérida, we caught up with the giant serpent
that was the Allied army, a motley troop of Englishmen, Dutchmen,
Portuguese, and even a regiment of Catalans (a gang of diehard loons, I
must say), led by a high command every bit as diverse. We approached
the main column by a little path that met it at right angles, and we had
to wait hours for all the troops to pass, with their baggage, artillery, gun
carriages, and provisions. Then came our kind: thousands of people who
followed the army like seagulls the stern of a fishing boat.

Knowing that we were in for a long journey, and that there were
gaps in my Spanish, I had brought with me the thickest book I could
find. I would read it before turning in for the night, by the light of the
fire, or even in the wagon. Between one jolt and the next, I'd be taken
by fits of laughter, because it was a most brilliant piece of work and a
delight to the spirit. What follows is a seemingly insignificant episode,
but for some reason, one that has remained in my memory.

We had stopped at some spot or other. It was one of those plains that
stretch out beyond Balaguer, a foretaste of Spain's vast empty stretches,
and to kill time, I began to read that book. Soon I was laughing. On
every page, there were five things to make me chuckle. These out-
pourings attracted the attention of Zúñiga.

"May I ask what you're reading?" He looked at words on the binding and said, with a mixture of distaste and disappointment, "Oh, *that*."

Unable to understand his qualms, I exclaimed, ever so amused: "It
has been some time since I've laughed so heartily!"

"Irony may be divine, but sarcasm is of the devil," said Zúñiga.
"And you will agree with me that this is a book abounding in sarcasm."

"If a writer is able to make me laugh," retorted cynical Zuvi, "I don't much care how he does it."

"The worst part is," he went on, "that the writer reduces heroic feats to their basest, most wretched parts. And if we want to win this war, we need to extol the epic, not mock it."

"I can't see how you can dislike such an engaging, humorous story. I've just been reading a chapter in which the protagonist frees a chain of prisoners. His reasoning is very enlightened: Man is born free; it is therefore intolerable that any man should be chained up by other men, and as a result, any noble soul has an obligation to oppose such a thing. Once they have been freed, of course, the villains express their thanks by stoning him." I burst out laughing. "Sad, amusing, superb!"

Zúñiga didn't laugh, not even a little. "Rather than refuting my argument, you strengthen it. Because the reason for being a man of letters is to convey lofty thoughts, and to do so in a style that elevates the language. What you have there is something quite different: pages filled with cudgelings and frivolity. Is that what the writers' art should be devoted to?"

"Literature can, and indeed should, teach us lessons that, in its majesty, only it is capable of imparting. If someone says, 'There is clarity in madness!,' well, wise words, but also no more than baseless opinion. But when this idea is presented to us plotted out within a dramatic framework, I have no choice but to agree." I shook the thick volume with both hands. "Yes, that's the great truth within this story: that reason is to be found in the irrational."

The day after this literary debate, it was Stanhope and his cavalry ponies that took the role of protagonists in our current tale. We found ourselves on the outskirts of a little town called Almenar. Day was nearly done, and we were readying ourselves to spend the night on the outskirts of the village when word began to spread that the Allied army had met the forces of the Two Crowns. I suggested to Zúñiga that we go on ahead a bit to see what was happening. We left the civilian caravan behind. We came across the sick wagon in the rearguard, and when we asked them what news, they gestured eastward. "They say Stanhope's surprised the Bourbons."

I told Zúñiga I thought we ought to climb a little nearby hill, to watch what was happening.

It was a good walk. To tell the truth, we went because we had nothing else to do. And with the sun already setting, at this time of day, the climb would not be so wearying. It was an ocher-colored hillock, dappled with clumps of rosemary. The smell was wonderful.

Our summit was modest in height, but the views from it were good. A rectangular plane stretched out at our feet, flanked by mountains to the left and a river to the right. On one of the shorter sides of the rectangle was In-a-Trice Stanhope with his horsemen. A single regiment, in battle formation, occupied a space of some two hundred feet. In-a-Trice had arrived in Spain with four thousand strapping lads, selected for their fearsomeness. When not drinking or riding, they were pissing away their "bir" (a drink they spell "beer"), so the Catalans ended up calling them *pixabirs*, which is to say, "piss-beers." And on the opposite end of the rectangle was the Bourbon army. Their infantry had been hurriedly arranged in a line, and their bayonets were fixed. God, what a great spectacle it is, to see thousands of men in formation and poised for battle. And yet, schooled as I was in the arts of Bazoches, I could sense something more than flesh and uniform. Amid that whole human mass, arranged as it was by battalion, I could make out their souls, like the little flames of thousands of candles trembling before the breath of an approaching hurricane.

I remember Zúñiga speaking the thought that was then running through his head: "Dear Lord, how is this going to end?"

In my day, the theorists of cavalry were engaged in a debate that ran curiously in parallel to that between us engineers. They, too, were divided between Vaubanians and Coehoornians, as it were, their Coehoorn being Marlborough. Yes, yes, the very same, Jimmy's cousin: *Malbrough s'en va-t-en guerre, mironton, mironton, mirontaine.*

Up until that point, a cavalry had always followed the most prudent tactics. The riders would approach the enemy infantry, stop at the distance of a pistol's range, and fire. Persistent gunfire could cause the infantry to lose its nerve and run. Then, and only then, would the cavalry draw their sabers to pursue the soldiers as they scattered in all directions.

These formations, which were sly and always had the chance of getting away entirely unscathed, were changed by Marlborough. Essentially, what he proposed was to go back three hundred years in the art of military cavalry, saying: Wasn't the horse itself a hugely powerful weapon? Marlborough took the cavalry back to the Middle Ages: the horse seen not as transportation but as a means of crushing whatever was in its path.

The English cavalry was the first to take on this new tactic. When they came to within three hundred feet of the enemy line, they did not stop: They shifted up from a trot into a charge. They trampled anything that was in their way—problem solved! And—in a trice!

Let's see whether you can guess, my foul little German, which of the two theories In-a-Trice Stanhope subscribed to? Bravo, you guessed! How very clever you are!

The sun was already sinking below the horizon, an orange semicircle surrounded by a violet halo. The great mystery is why the Spaniards did nothing. By the time Zúñiga and I reached the hill, the two sides had already been engaged for quite some time. The Spaniards had had hours to change formation or even withdraw from the field. But they did nothing, they did nothing of anything, at all. They just waited, melting under a summer sun. Perhaps the valley was too narrow for them to maneuver; perhaps they did not know of the tactics used by the English cavalry and thought that the riders would do no more than harass them a little with pistol and rifle. Or perhaps it was just the usual: The Spaniards were led by a pack of incompetents.

We could see the Allies on a bit of headland setting up a battery of six cannons. They began to fire at once, clearly meaning to support the charge of the cavalry. Stanhope had split his forces into two lines. When the order was given, the front line would charge, sabers in the air and howling hoarsely like wolves.

Believe me when I tell you there are few things in life more terrifying than a cavalry charge at twilight. Thousands and thousands of hooves, rumbling heavily against the ground in a multitudinous animal rush; the shaking was so great that, even where we were standing, stones and clods of earth were dislodged and went tumbling down the hillside.

By that time the Bourbon army had been severely diminished. At the start of the year, the French troops had returned to their country as reinforcements for the front at the Rhine, and the Spanish recruits left a great deal to be desired. In any case, you didn't have to be a general or know the weaknesses of the Army of the Two Crowns; you only had to look at that mass of red coats on horseback headed toward the fragile line of little white soldiers, and it was obvious how the affair was going to end.

The Spanish lines quivered like strings of sausages, however much the officers ranted and raved, demanding order. They hesitated. Poor lads. Recruited not four days earlier, they were about to experience a charge from the elite of the English army. I did a quick calculation: four thousand horses, about three hundred kilos per head, plus an average of sixty for each rider, came to a total of over a million four hundred thousand kilos, racing forward at twenty miles per hour against some poor petrified boys. A moment before the impact, I looked away.

In some places, surprisingly, the upthrust bayonets did offer resistance. In others, the formation toppled like an old fence. Even the noise made you think of thousands of timbers splitting. And yes, despite the decisive violence of that clash, I learned one lesson on the field of Almenar, one I often repeated: that most retreats, curious though this may be, begin in the rearguard.

From that moment, the battle was reduced to no more than a human hunt. To a cavalry soldier, there is something magnetic about a back turned to flee. Instinct urges him to go in pursuit and split open the skull with a saber. As for the man being pursued, there are no words to describe the torment of his flight. If the saber doesn't get him, the horses' hooves will.

I have already described the battlefield as a rectangular valley, mountains to the left and a river to the right. To reach the river, it was necessary to climb down a rift in the land, which appeared all of a sudden and went down a considerable way. In their flight, hundreds were pushed into it by their own companions. They bounced down the rocks of the slopes, while the survivors tried to swim across the river. The others scattered eastward.

In the rush, the Bourbons abandoned their artillery and their whole baggage convoy. I called out to Zúñiga, pointing toward the farthest horizon: "Look! Way over there, in that raised copse, don't you see it? It's Little Philip himself, running away with his escort of palatine mercenaries!"

Stanhope's piss-beers were busy riding down the Bourbons. And these had abandoned all their baggage, including the opulent wagons with all the riches that Little Philip had brought with him. I have told you this before: The early bird catches the worm, and in the midst of so much confusion, it wouldn't be hard to get hold of a generous slice. A wagon transporting the royal crockery, fifty pairs of fine shoes, whatever we could lay our hands on. Besides, it was getting dark, which would help to hide us. The groans of the dying began to rise into the air like the croaking of frogs by a pond at dusk. Dozens of looters were there already, hopping between the fallen bodies. I could see that the men were rummaging through the corpses for jewels or coins, while the women tended to take possession of boots and clothing.

"We're better splitting up," I said to Zúñiga. "If one of us finds something, we'll let the other know by whistling three times."

We each went our own way, but before long, I gave up. It was almost completely dark. I stopped at the steep bank that went down toward the river. Perhaps, I thought, some important carriage might have toppled over the edge. If I were a Bourbon bearing the royal crucifixes, or the king's gold chamber pot, I would choose to hurl it all in the water sooner than let the enemy take it.

The slope was very steep, and I climbed down gingerly. I found nothing of any interest, just a few dead bodies scattered across the riverbank. On both banks, there were vegetable patches, destroyed by the passage of the armies. The moon was there to light the way back to our wagon now, and when I happened to see Zúñiga, he was coming out of a little stone hut, a small workers' store.

"Oh, Diego, there you are," I greeted him.

He looked very startled to see me. He'd gone into the house to snoop around a little, he told me; no joy. If it hadn't been for my sense of smell, I would have turned back, and that would have been it. But in Bazoches, they had trained my eyes, my ears, and also my nose: every one of my senses. The moment Zúñiga pulled that rickety old door closed, something happened. That same door, when it moved, pushed a blanket of air from the inside toward my nose. A smell. A very distinctive smell—mixed with other more common smells, like dry grain or old esparto grass. But in the middle of it all, that smell. My nose recalled it, but my memory could not.

"I'll just have a quick look," I said.

"I'm telling you, there's nothing there," said Zúñiga, barring my way. "Let's go."

I brushed him off and went ahead, entering the house. That smell, that smell, unpleasant and yet, at the same time, irresistible. What was it to me, what did it remind me of? It was very dark; the only light was that of the moon, spooling down like threads of silver. The tools were covered in rust, forgotten; rotting ears of corn were piled up. At the back, a shapeless mass covered by a bit of old sackcloth. There. Each of us has a particular smell. And our fear intensifies that smell. I felt a sudden spark: At last I knew to whom it belonged, that smell of greasy pores, of some thick, oleaginous matter.

I pulled back the cloth. And there he was, hidden like a scorpion under a rock: Joris Prosperus van Verboom. And just as one ought to do with a scorpion, before it reacted, I gave its head a good stamp. "Caught you," I said. I turned his heavy body over and began laying in to him with short punches.

"Martí! Leave him, you're going to kill him!"

"Oh, he and I are old acquaintances," I said, catching my breath.

And I gave him a little more. Verboom was shouting out things in French, in Spanish, and in one of those Dutch languages, too.

Zúñiga grabbed me in his arms. "You've told me a thousand times that normal people don't have anything to do with this dynastic war. And now there's this poor wretch, and you're about to kill him!"

"Poor wretch?" I interrupted my beating and looked at Zúñiga, panting. "Did you say poor wretch? This is Prosperus van Verboom!"

Zúñiga saved Verboom's life. When he learned that this was a big fish we'd caught, he begged me not to kill him, saying we ought to take him prisoner and claim a reward. And I was stupid enough to agree.

Verboom had been unseated from his horse by a cannon shot. Slightly wounded, during the defeat, he had dragged himself over to that happenstance refuge. The truth was, they did congratulate us and reward us handsomely for his capture. So much that even In-a-Trice Stanhope wanted to meet us.

My heart gave such a leap that I felt it halfway up my throat. Could this be a sign of *le Mystère*? Before becoming cavalry, maybe Stanhope had served as an engineer. Was he perhaps to be my new teacher? Let me give you the most synthetic answer I can: no. I found him the least likely creature one might ask for moral shelter. All great horsemen look small when they are not in the saddle. Stanhope looked it and he was, short in stature as he was short of brains, as well as conceited and silver-tongued. We had been dragged over to his campaign tent for one reason and one reason only: extolling his own person by appearing to praise us. By the time we left, it had been made quite clear to everybody present that if the Allies had been victorious in battle, if they had captured such distinguished characters as Verboom, it was not down to the combined forces, nor to that little king, Charles, but entirely and exclusively to the presence in Spain of a genius by the name of James Stanhope.

Following our audience, Zúñiga asked me about Verboom: "What has he done to make you hate him so much?"

I was not sure how to answer. Such a long time had passed since our argument in Bazoches. I thought about Jeanne and felt a stab in my breast. But I wanted to believe that my ill will toward the Dutch sausage-maker was led by something more than personal revenge.

Verboom was a bad man. Read those words again, and you will agree they are the worst that can be proclaimed about a human being. It is as if to say: "The world would be much better off without you." In a just world, there would have been no place for Verboom, and finding him in an imperfect world, one should drive him out of it for fear he might make it worse. I did not do that, and soon repented bitterly, as always happens when we choose profit over justice.

And what do you think? Is this a note too moralistic on which to end the chapter? Right—you like it. Well, in that case, there's no doubt about it at all: Strike it out. I'm sure it's better without.

5

Almenar was a decisive victory. Nobody doubted that the Two Crowns would seek to join further battles. But the number of casualties, which was not too great, did not reflect the turmoil in their ranks.

Without the French contingent, Little Philip could count on only the Spanish recruits, who, as you have seen, had proved themselves greener than grass. The next encounter took place in Zaragoza, a city on the banks of the River Ebro. And this one went even worse for Little Philip than Almenar. By the time the day ended, eighty flags had been captured, six hundred Bourbons taken prisoner, and the infantry suffered twelve thousand casualties.

After the victory at Zaragoza, the Allies paused to decide what to do next. They were in a place called Calatayud, and the council of war that met there was made up of nine generals from a variety of nationalities. The Portuguese, naturally, were keen to keep going and join up with Portugal; Lisbon and Barcelona would be united through the two armies physically joining. Other generals wanted to take control of the north. If they could take Navarre, they argued, they could seal the border with France, and Philip would be cut off from reinforcements from his grandfather. Charles was having doubts. But now Ina-Trice Stanhope intervened. Navarre, to the north? Portugal, to the west? What the devil were they talking about? He had arrived with the express mandate to place Charles on the throne as Carlos III of Spain and return home. And that was precisely what he intended to do. Apparently, he thumped the table at this point: Either the army marches to Madrid, or he and his piss-beers go straight back home. So, Madrid it was!

The pro-Austrian army was never such a precise military machine as in the lead-up to Zaragoza. As for the troops, nobody had seen such a ragtag army since the days of Hannibal. After spending whole months with them on marches and roads, I can tell you I came to know them very well.

The English officers were true gentlemen, while to a man, the rank and file were louts, the worst in Europe. In the Portuguese forces, it was the other way around: The soldiers were a delight, always shy and obedient, but under orders from officers who acted like slave traders. Among the Dutch, there were two categories of soldier: the drinkers, and then the bad drinkers.

The attitudes of the different national groups toward one another could be defined as "let them have a drink, but don't let go of the bottle." The English looked down on the Portuguese with infinite contempt. They took them for worse than the Spanish, which is saying something. As for the Portuguese, as you can imagine, they had different ideas. If the English were so rich and such know-it-alls, they asked themselves, why did the final victory never follow?

Well, it looked like it was finally coming now, because that autumn, in 1710, the Allied army was making its juggernaut advance on the heart of Castile. Now, you might be wondering how the capital defended itself against the Allied army. The answer is very simple: It didn't.

On September 19 two English dragoons reached the outskirts of Madrid. They were astonished to learn that between them and the city, there was no opposition in place, not so much as a single scraggy battalion of conscripts. I was just as astonished as that pair of dragoons. So there wasn't going to be a fight? No, there would be no such thing. Not a single shot fired! Had we ridden across half the peninsula for this? When the city was in sight, Zúñiga explained to me that Madrid was not a fortified city. It was just surrounded by a ring of masonry whose only purpose was to drive traffic toward the customs posts that charged a levy on products entering the city. Good work, Zuvi!

While Charles was preparing his triumphal entrance into Madrid, Zúñiga and I got in ahead of the troops. My first impression of Madrid was that it was a bare, charmless city, all its streets empty. I was wrong. We did not know yet that Little Philip, when he had withdrawn from the capital, had been followed by up to thirty thousand courtiers and supporters. He hadn't left them much choice: Any nobleman or adviser who didn't follow him in his flight would have been considered a traitor to the blessed Bourbon cause.

The best lodgings we were able to find were in the attic above a tavern. The ceiling sloped down so steeply that to move about where it was lowest, we needed to crawl on our hands and knees. And the furniture was no more than a couple of straw mattresses, two washbasins, and a window. Well, we couldn't complain. We had entered Madrid before the mass of the army. To celebrate his return to his home city, Zúñiga took me to one of the most popular taverns, and as we were putting away a few jars, the innkeeper heard us talking.

"But really, gentlemen," he said, "it is possible you don't know? The Allies are about to enter Madrid." He glanced left and right as though afraid we were being overheard. "Ten days ago, all French subjects received the order to leave the city. Where were you? How could you not have known? There's not much love lost between the Allies and the French!"

Zúñiga and I exchanged a glance. The innkeeper, it seemed, had mistaken my Catalan accent, taking me for a Frenchman. Diego shrugged as if to say, *Well, why disabuse him?*

"Oh, damn," I replied, "I was sure my accent would go unnoticed."

"Oh no, not at all!" said the innkeeper. "And you might find yourself in a real pickle."

"The *real* pickle," I interrupted him, "is that I cannot leave Madrid. Actually, I've only just been sent here. You do understand, don't you?"

I let him come to his own conclusions. People like you to think them cleverer than they actually are. Finally his eyes lit up: What I have here, he must have thought, is a spy for King Philip.

It was only then that I added: "Hush! The city will be filled with Austrians in a flash. And our arrival was so hurried that we have not resolved the matter of our lodgings."

And so, thanks to the patriotism of this innkeeper, we got ourselves a free bed and a roof over our heads in the attic. Once we had settled in, we caught up with the latest news on the situation. According to what we were told, Little Philip had decided to add to his arsenal a weapon unknown in modern warfare: the cunt.

The innkeeper explained it to us in the most confidential of tones: "When it became clear that Madrid was sure to fall, the government brought in all the sickly whores from Castile, Andalucia, even Extremadura. Bodies in thrall to the most invisible and contagious of ailments. Thus, they hope to inflict thousands of casualties upon the Allies. However much you may want to, be sure not to come anywhere near the tarts!"

Madrid is not the most beautiful capital one might hope to visit. Its streets spread out in an arbitrary fashion, a horror for any engineer. The uneven ground robs buildings of their perspectives, and their facades are of an ugliness that frankly defies belief. Public decoration is at a minimum. Madrid has no ancient relics, though this is a failing that one can excuse given that it is a new city. It was not until the court was established here (which happened only a century before the arrival of Longlegs Zuvi) that this little one-horse town began to assume the grand position of capital. What one cannot excuse, however, is that, being a new city, it was extended with no advance planning, streets improvised on sloping ground, narrow, dark, and winding. I'm telling you, when it was being built, Madrid's engineers must have been off erecting fortresses in the Caribbean. The streets are absolutely filthy, and the road paving, where there is any, is poorly kept, broken up, and sticking out. According to the Madrileños themselves, the worst torture the Inquisition could conceive of would be to put the offender in a carriage and send him rolling over this city's cobblestones.

But I am giving a one-sidedly glum impression of Madrid. My senses, sharpened in Bazoches, got even more excited when confronted with something new, and given that this novelty was an entire city, my eyes and ears were experiencing a feast. Yes, my studies in Bazoches had made my visit to Madrid an exploration. To a good student of *le Mystère*, everything shines, and everything is lit by close observation. Natives and foreigners united to praise the Madrid skies. The air was always fresh; its light in winter was sweet and beautiful, while in summer, unlike in the Mediterranean Barcelona, its sun never hurt your eyes. Your typical Madrileño was a lover of all chilled drinks, which obliged him to load up a thousand beasts of burden stocked with snow. In Barcelona, the trade in ice was a lucrative one; in Madrid, it made millionaires. There is no more pleasant way to waste one's time than strolling along the banks of the city's river, the Manzanares, with a little sweetened ice in your hand, admiring the beauties. On the whole, the marriageable young women will sit there like flowers, chaperoned by relatives, under a parasol, showing off the latest fashionable attire. The young gallants who walk past slow their pace and offer compliments, which are met with a little wave, or a snub, or a wave that is also a sort of snub.

Madrid's main square is a constant bustling revel. It is the last staging post on the road to the capital of the empire, which is why people gather to hear and comment on the latest news. The same square is the site of autos-da-fé, bullfights, and executions. A happy triple confluence, as spectators can marvel at the penitent, before the bullfights then take over, and the spectacle is rounded off with all the fun of a beheading. The audience members are still chatting about the condemned man's last words when messengers arrive from the far reaches of the empire to recount the slaughter carried out by the Mapuche Indians in some colony or other, or an attack on a Caribbean port.

Spaniards are not too greatly enamored of their dominions. So very far away, after all, and they get so little real benefit from them, that the good news is received with the same indifference as the bad. I found this mild nature extremely appealing. To a Barcelonan, Madrid seems like the most peace-loving of places. We Catalonians live in a state of war, war that is dormant but also constant, everyone against everyone else. Poor against rich, those from the wealthy coastline suspicious of the mountain barbarians from the interior, Miquelets against foreigners and the Guard against the bandits. On the sea were the Berber pirates, whose particular business was kidnapping travelers and demanding ransom. And to complete the picture, hordes of stone-lobbers otherwise known as students. All this, not to mention the dynastic wars, which are the only ones historians consider worth recounting.

For many, varied reasons, it was different in Madrid. The presence of the court restrained any violent challenge to established power; the city was far from the path of any invaders, and by nature, the Madrileños are not much inclined to rebellion. Like every court, Madrid was a honeycomb that attracted a huge mobile population. People who—like any opportunists—were interested not in fighting but in huddling together. Perhaps the strangest thing was that in Madrid, popular aggression issued solely from one particular class: the *emboscados*, or Stealthy Ones, young noblemen who wore cloaks covering their faces and bodies and spent their days looking for any excuse to duel.

As if life were not dangerous enough, all Madrid needed was these lunatics, a strange mixture of a knight-errant and a night jackal. The merest slight would be cause enough for them to demand a duel—to the death, no excuses. The nighttime belonged to them, which was why, when the sun set, Madrid was transformed into a much duller city than Barcelona. I very quickly learned that the best thing to do was to appear poor and pitiful, since, for an *emboscado*, there was no value in killing just anybody. And since good old Zuvi was always less dignified than a shaggy Indian, I managed to avoid their attentions without too much trouble.

Now for the best part of all. If you ask me where this little soldier stood to attention the most times, he would surely answer you two places: Cook's Tahiti, and Madrid in that autumn of 1710. Definitive proof that there's something wrong with the world lies in the fact that whores charge money to screw. And you can just shut up and write, sanctimonious old cow. However, when the rumor spread that they were all Bourbon agents, the poor Madrid tarts had no choice but to lower their prices, then lower them again. And when they were right down near ground level, lower them again. It was obvious that it was all a lie dreamed up to torment the Allies. And yet the occupying forces swallowed it completely. Considering Little Philip capable of the lowest acts, they shut themselves up in their quarters in search of consolation, replacing the whores with the bottle. A soldier's mind can be unpredictable.

Anyway, I was saying that, for Longlegs Zuvi, at least, those were incredibly happy days. The army had entered Madrid, but Charles was on the outskirts, attending to his little bits of business and preparing his great triumphal entrance. In the meantime, I was spending my days screwing low-cost beauties.

To begin with—I hold my hands up—I made a real novice's mistake.

On the first day, as I walked through the southern part of the city, I stopped to look at one of those horrible windowless facades. A friendly Madrileño who appeared to be at a loose end came over to me. "What are you looking at with such interest? Are you planning to set up a house of mischief?"

"Not to set them up or manage them," I replied, ever the innocent. "I would be satisfied with enjoying them myself. Do you know whether visiting a 'house of mischief' is very expensive?"

"Lord, no," the good fellow replied, "why should it be? Here in Madrid, we are all very welcoming. Go in, go in, ask the owner anything you like."

The door was indeed ajar, showing no sign of fear or caution as regarded passersby. I climbed a narrow flight of stairs. On the second storey, there was a fine woman darning clothes. And what a discreet first floor it was! Not so much as a window, doubtless to hide the office carried out there.

"Hello!" I greeted her. "How many girls are there in the house?"

The woman gave me a strange look. Perhaps she'd taken me for a constable, and I wanted to reassure her. "Don't worry," I said, "I'm only a customer."

At that moment, a man came in. I repeated my question, and although the fellow looked confused, the woman gave him to understand that I was a rather illustrious visitor.

"Well, I've got my wife here," he replied, somewhat disconcerted, "whom you've already met, my three daughters, and my blessed mother. But might I ask who you are? And why are you interested in the women?"

"You employ your own daughters? Is that normal in Madrid?" I said, a little scandalized. "Well, your customs are no business of mine. Mind showing me them? And how much do you want for me to enjoy them for a while? Nothing unusual, just a quick bit of rough-and-tumble. You must understand, I've come from a long way away, and I have my needs."

The man turned livid and wanted to throw me out.

"Oi, look, I'll pay my way!" I protested. "Your outrage is a bargaining ploy, I'm guessing, eh, but do name your price first. Take Catalan money? I haven't had time to visit the money changer."

To my surprise, he furnished himself with an ax—and raised it above his head!

"Look, you will never meet a tougher negotiator than the son of a Catalan trader, so you can calm down," I said. "All I want is to go to bed with your daughters, all three at once, if that will get me a discount."

When I saw him charging toward me, ax ready to swing, I told myself that the best thing would be to race back down the stairs.

"Your loss," I shouted as I fled. "And you should know, sir, you have just put a considerable dent in this city's once great reputation for hospitality!"

When I told this story to Zúñiga, he roared with laughter. "Houses of mischief" were not brothels but the name by which people in Madrid referred to a particular kind of legal ploy. According to the city's laws, the king had the right to charge taxes on the second storey of every building. In order to avoid paying, people would build their houses in such a deceptive way that the first floor had no external windows and looked like an extension of the tiled roof. Houses of mischief! For the love of God, what did they expect me to think? And who would even think of imposing such a foolish tax? Truly, playing host to a court would never be good business.

All the same, putting aside such minor misunderstandings, which can happen to any visitor, it didn't take me long to get used to the sweetnesses of the city. I would spend the day flitting from flower to flower, and when I returned to my attic, the patriotic innkeeper would be waiting for me: "You always come home so exhausted! I wouldn't trade my job for that of a spy, no sir, I wouldn't. You have such deep bags under your eyes, my friend. I can see that the comings and goings of an agent to the king must consume both body and soul."

At this point, my dear vile Waltraud gets annoyed, protests, and starts to squirm, calling me a bad husband, depraved, and a libertine. Of course, this is the female view and could never be a man's. Whatever can you be thinking, my little wood louse, do you really believe Amelis was waiting for me, quietly spinning like a Penelope? In spite of everything, we loved each other, which is something that your blond pigeon brain will never understand.

On September 28, Charles finally made his entrance into Madrid. The plan was that the king should attend mass at the Atocha sanctuary and subsequently make his triumphal entrance into Madrid. Some triumph! Ha! And ha again! Here, write down a good deal of mocking things, write laughter and jeers, a thousandfold!

Charles came in on a white horse, wearing an extremely elegant black suit. You should have seen the look on his face. Because out on the streets, there was nobody to be seen, absolutely nobody, apart from good old Zuvi and a one-legged man who hadn't had time to hide.

He wasn't their king. The Madrileños hated Charles just as much as the Catalans hated Little Philip. The previous day, an order had gone around that the people should wash the route clean of the usual city filth, and deck the balconies with garlands. Naturally, they did no such thing. The streets were as thick with dung as ever, if not more so. He found the balconies empty and shut. The bells seemed to be tolling rather than chiming. When he was still only on Alcalá Street, he turned back without reaching the palace and supposedly uttered the words: "Madrid is a desert!"

I cannot confirm this, because by that point in the procession, I had already gone off with some dire prostitute or another, so you will understand that Charles's tantrums were of no interest to me. But right behind Charles, on another white horse, rode In-a-Trice Stanhope, and his face spoke volumes, even more eloquently than that of the king.

They're all the same, these foreign generals, they never get it. They didn't want to acknowledge that Castile and Catalonia were at war in just the same way as France and England; that Spain was a name that hid a reality more powerful than politics, trade, and even, if I may say so, common sense. A pitched battle between two opposing ways of understanding the world, life, everything. I tell you, I was watching the look on Stanhope's face very closely; at last the man had understood what a fine mess he'd gotten himself into. Never had a commander failed so roundly after having completed his mission so perfectly. He had conquered Madrid, but doing so *as an invader* had lost Castile; he had crowned Charles, but Charles was an interloper on the throne and, as such, apt to change.

The English might come to accept a French dynasty reigning in London, or the French an English dynasty in Paris. The Madrileños would never put up with Charles as their king, never, and not because he was Austrian but because he was king of the Catalans. And Stanhope thought a couple of cavalry charges would fix the whole business. Don't make me laugh! Yes indeed, my dear vile Waltraud: As you people would say, *schöne Schweinerei*, a fine old mess.

For the whole war, the Bourbons had been strategically superior. The Allies had conquered Madrid with a madcap kind of medieval cavalcade. The Bourbons always behaved according to the most methodical rules, like a slow, detailed snare. The Allies were in Madrid, but the French and Spanish were firmly anchored in Tortosa, in Lérida and Gerona. I'll sort this out in a trice! I would laugh if it weren't for the fact that the Allies' tragedy would end up becoming ours, too.

Over the next few days, Charles attempted to appeal to the Madrileños, a thousand persuasions and flatteries. Free bullfights, gifts, and perks for the city. Nothing doing. He paid for three days of illuminations to which nobody showed up; until that time, I had never known how depressing a fireworks display without spectators could be. A people's dignity cannot be bought, as monarchs are always forgetting.

He even went so far as to hand out money, in the manner of the Caesars. Several horsemen rode around the city with bags filled with coins that they would toss up into the air. The Madrileños did bend down to pick them up, naturally, because it's one thing not being pro-Austrian and quite another being a fool. They did so, but did not forgo their most caustic sense of humor. Charles had proclaimed himself Carlos III of Spain. They would kiss the coins and proclaim sarcastically: "Long live Carlos the Third, while the money keeps coming!"

So as you can see, the conquest and occupation of Madrid was not as epic as the phrase suggests. And since Vauban's question had been about the optimum defense, this was hardly the optimum setting for finding myself a teacher, nor for learning The Word. Meanwhile, the clamor against Charles was starting to grow. Not that people were plotting an uprising. It wasn't that. The vast majority of Madrileños have one thing in common with the vast majority of Barcelonans: As long as their life continued unaltered, they were as little inclined to fight for Philip V as they were to fight against Carlos III. The Allied soldiers stayed shut away in barracks and had little contact with the people, so there was not too much provocation. And the Civil Guard was made up of Catalans, whose reputation for heavy-handedness struck dread into people. In any case, one might say that they had reached a state of perfect balance. When they caught a miscreant, they would give him a thrashing, force him to cry "Long live Carlos III!" and take him to a dungeon. And when they caught an innocent passerby, just the same: If they didn't like the look of him, they'd give him a thrashing, force him to cry "Long live Carlos III!," and *he* would be taken in, too.

It was the stealthy *emboscado* Bourbons and the fanatical priests who were having the most trouble. As far as I could make out, they were squandering their labors. On the one hand, they had no need to bribe the people of Madrid for their loyalty, for they had it already. And on the other, however much they might be induced, the Madrileños were prudent enough, or responsible enough, not to be so crazy as to rise up against an army. (Furthermore, why would they want to mutiny as long as there were bags of money raining down?) As for the Spanish priests, they are the very worst of all Catholics. Their interests are always allied with the interests of human stupidity, each of which they foment with every sermon, and neither a sense of the ridiculous nor the power of reason is enough to stop them.

One day I was sitting in some tavern when a beggar came in. Instead of asking for alms, he began to hand out leaflets. He left a couple on each table, including mine. Having nothing better to do, I read it. By the third line, I was unable to contain my laughter.

Some sly agent of Philip's must have employed the beggar to hand out those scraps of paper, which gave a clear picture of the Bourbon mentality. The pamphlet did not attack the English, the Portuguese, or the Austrians. Not at all. Their entire rhetorical charge was aimed against the "rebels," which is to say the Catalans. According to their author, the blame for the enemy having occupied Madrid did not lie with the Allied forces or in Bourbon incompetence but with the Catalans and their plotting. Even I ended up convinced that in their free time, the Catalans had invented crab lice, bunions, and piles. That the Catalans also suffered from these evils was no excuse, just as the Jews were damned, however much of a Jew Christ Himself may have been.

I don't remember precisely the points made in the pamphlet, and perhaps it's better that way. All I have retained are the main charges against us. When the war ended, we would rape all the women in Castile and murder their husbands or send them off to the galleys. According to this pamphlet, the Catalans were behind a plot to take power and monopolize the trade with America (from which Catalonia had always been strictly excluded, being from a separate kingdom). Taxes on the Castilians would be not merely extortionate but would make slaves of them, with all the money ending up in Barcelona's coffers for the rebels to enjoy. Natives of Catalonia would supplant the whole of the army's high command, and all Castile's judges and jurists. To be certain of maintaining a hold over Madrid, a fortress would be erected, which would keep its inhabitants enchained until the end of time.

I laughed and laughed. I should not have. What I was reading on that piece of paper, that little scrap, was the worst that humanity is capable of. And not because of its malice toward the enemy, not that. It contained something far more terrible, as time would tell.

What was so diabolical was that only a few years later, this little scrap of paper would be transformed into a reality, but applied to Catalonia, and on a biblical scale. The Bourbons, projecting their own fears, punished imaginary offenses so thoroughly that no stone was left unturned. The mass murder began long before the war ended. After September 11, 1714, the legal framework of Catalan order was pulled down and Castile's installed in its place. For decades Catalonia would be considered a land under military occupation. All of its rulers came from Castile. The once rich country was ruined by taxes, and the majority of its population reduced to penury. Finally, to keep Barcelona under control, they erected the Ciudadela, the most perfidious Vaubanian fortress ever conceived. Can you guess who its author was? Nail on the head, first time: your man Joris van Verboom, the Antwerp butcher. Such was his reward for his part in the siege of Barcelona. Have I already told you how I killed him?

But who would have imagined all that in 1710, with the Allied army in Madrid and Charles boasting—however nominal it may have been—the title of king of all Spain. Evil is at times impossible to see, and I sensed no animosity at all. People were pleasant, even obsequious; the war remained something being played out at a dynastic level, far from the day-to-day wretchedness of Spain's various peoples. I tore the pamphlet into pieces. What at first had made me laugh, on more careful reading made me furious. I had seen the outrages of the Spanish forces at Beceite, Catalan forests full of nooses and hanged men. Now I could see the source of their soldiers' and officers' murderous bile.

I returned to my lodging in a stormy mood. I would have liked to break someone's skull, but whose? Whose? The blame didn't fall on any person in particular, but on something like an invisible mist. Evil is like a black cloud; it forms high above, out of our reach and beyond our understanding, and when it pours down upon us the cloud itself is unseen, and we merely suffer its torments.

I didn't want to share a table with anyone that evening. I went up to my attic room furious, with a hunk of bread and some cheese. Zúñiga wasn't there. Just as well. As I say, this wasn't a day to be shared with anyone, friends even less than enemies. I sat down on my straw mattress. The cheese was dry. Since I had no knife, I started to rummage around in Zúñiga's effects for one. Next to his straw mattress was his round leather bag. On a different day, I would have been more restrained with other people's belongings, but I needed a knife, and besides, we were friends. I turned the bag upside down, tipping its contents onto the floor.

There was nothing solid inside, only sheets of paper. Hundreds of pamphlets, quarto sheets identical to the one I'd been given to read moments earlier in that tavern. I had a bunch of them in my hands when Zúñiga came in.

I had previously been friends with a man, a man called Diego Zúñiga, and through that door some other man came in, a stranger about whom I knew nothing, apart from his mission: to give his life for Philip V, the most loathsome man of the century. His watery nature now made sense, that way he had of looking without being seen, his discreet, almost insubstantial profile. Earlier images of Zúñiga flashed though my mind. In Almenar, I had caught him coming out of the little workers' house where Verboom was hidden. He must have hidden the man there himself. Yes, until that moment it had never occurred to me: Some people are born spies.

I flung the handful of leaflets in his face and shouted: "This trash is yours!"

He didn't bat an eyelid. This was Zúñiga, invisible Zúñiga, and he never let his passions betray him. He simply went about picking up the bits of paper, acting as though I weren't there. I kept on at him.

"You ask me why I have served my king? Is that what you wish to know?" he replied at last. "Why I have risked my life, spent years and years hiding out among the enemy? Two words, I suppose: fidelity and sacrifice."

"A king's privilege is that we will uphold him, not hate for him," I said. "Only a barbarian could wish to confront peoples and nations as though they were armies."

He smiled. "When your government ministers violated their oath of fidelity to King Philip, who was it that set up the Catalan people on a collision course with their king? And what did you think would happen next? That Castile would look upon such a slight to their sovereign unmoved—a sovereign who, if we're being quite accurate, is yours, too? That, after you had brought war to Spain and betrayed us, we'd just stand there, arms crossed, doing nothing? We have an empire to preserve, Martí, and in Barcelona, all they want is to bleed it dry. Castile has supported itself for three hundred years, while you people concerned yourselves with other matters, hidden beneath the skirts of your liberties and constitutions."

"Oh empire, empire . . . What have you gained by conquering a world? The American Indians hate you; your European neighbors don't envy you, just hold you in contempt, and maintaining that myriad of possessions overseas has ruined Castile's exchequer. And you think you have the right to demand that other kingdoms take part in your excesses, and do so for the glory of Castile! I took you for an intelligent man, Diego."

"I also hold myself as such," he responded coolly. "Which is why I regret having been unable to comprehend the Catalan soul. Can you explain the reason for this unreasonableness? Why do you wish to destroy a mighty union that would make us powerful and well respected? Why do you so detest a common scheme that should have unified the peninsula centuries ago?"

"Because what you people call unity is in truth oppression! Tell me: Would you move the court to Barcelona? Would you allow Castile to be ruled by Catalan kings? Your ministers to be chosen from among Catalan government ministers alone? Would you like the idea of your villages and towns occupied by Catalan troops, having to bear them, take them into your homes, offer them up your wives?" I waved some pamphlets under his nose. "According to what I've read here, I imagine not!"

"Natural law dictates that big will consume small, the weak yield to the strong. Despite everything, that is not Castile's position. You could be a privileged part of a whole, and instead you choose to be less than nothing. It's incomprehensible."

"Maybe what's incomprehensible is measuring honor in terms of a hunger for war. That road has led you to nothing but defeat and bankruptcy. Every prosperous nation flows with money and sweat, not weapons and gunpowder. But you people insist on stubbornness, obtuse heroism. Every ship that is filled with cannons instead of barrels is one more ship lost to trade; every regiment trained and armed, an industry wasted. At least that is what my own fellow citizens feel."

To Zúñiga's credit, he knew how to listen, I'll give him that.

"I understand now," he said. "Greatness doesn't move you, only riches. Not glory but wealth. You detest the Spartans for the same reason you love the Sybarites." He took a step toward me. "But tell me, Martí, what's the point of a life bereft of epic desires, shorn of exploits to pass down to the next generation? Your scheme for life is no different from that of an earthworm. No light and no dreams, always under the earth, never rising above your times. Better to lose your life in battle than waste it in some tawdry backwater." He concluded with this pronouncement: "Mediocrity of spirit, that's what's wrong with you."

"And what's wrong with you," I replied, "is that you are drunk on books of chivalry. The bad ones!"

The little laugh he let out was as powerful as it was contemptuous. He had hidden from me his role as a spy, even used me as camouflage. Who would have suspected such a thing from the companion of a harmless libertine like Longlegs Zuvi? I grabbed him by the neck and pushed him up against the wall.

"Someone scribbles this shit, off in some unseen corner, and then, before you know it, the forests are full of hanged men," I said. "I've seen it! A pile of falsehoods like this gets written down, and the next day, people who have nothing to do with writing have their throats slit and their bodies thrown off cliffs. Just tell me you don't believe the travesties written in these pamphlets. Tell me!"

I looked him in the eye and, in that same moment, understood something terrifying. I cursed my blindness, for his smile told me that he, my good friend Diego Zúñiga, had written or dictated those words.

"Castile has conquered a whole world," he said. "And now four bloodsuckers show up from Barcelona, shielding themselves behind Archduke Charles, and want to take everything our forefathers died for. Never. And believe you me, Martí: A lot of people are going to pay. The king's power may not extend as far as Vienna or London, but you can be sure every last corner of Spain is within his reach."

I let him go. Good old Zuvi never liked things to be too definitive, but my voice has rarely been firmer than when I said: "Diego, you and I are no longer friends."

That really was not my best day in Madrid. I spent the night going from tavern to tavern, not to find new whores but to drink. Very well, I'll tell you the truth: What I really wanted was to bash someone's face in. I'm no great brawler, but I would never deny the value of a good fight. When everything is going wrong, the best thing a man can do is throw a few punches, if possible in the face of someone who deserves them. And if not, well, then the next fellow who happens to be passing. Man against man. It hardly matters who gives and who receives: Venting your anger is ample.

I felt guilty, too, very guilty. I had accompanied the army in the hope that something bad, a war, would do me good, bring me a teacher, but how was I to find Maganons in Madrid? In my drunken madness, I started rolling up people's right sleeves in search of Points. Unfortunately, the tavern patrons gave me a wide berth. With my Barcelona accent and my cursing of Philip V, they took me for an agent playing drunk in order to flush out Bourbons. Even the most foolish believed I was a pro-Austrian provocateur. I could find nobody to comfort me, nor to confront me. I can still see myself there, slumped against the penultimate bar, drunk, alone, and shouting: "How can it be that in the whole of Madrid, I cannot find one single friend, nor one single enemy?"

It was already the early hours of the morning when I found my way to a dive full of rowdy drinkers. If I couldn't get a beating there, I never would. I was so far gone, I could barely stand. The place was packed, not a single seat free. I saw five men sitting squashed around a table. The one in charge was in his fifties, a big fellow, authoritative-looking. At any other time I would have recognized him at once, but wine is no friend to memory, may the Ducroix brothers forgive me.

I grabbed the smallest of the five by the neck and yanked him from his seat. I sat down on it, put my feet up on the table, and said to that man in his fifties: "Mind if I join you?"

He didn't rise to the provocation. Instead of throwing the first punch, he nodded to his men to ignore me. They were arguing about military matters, and one of them made reference to something defensive.

"What you have just said, *señor*," I interrupted him, "is utter nonsense. Sticking stakes in glacis only gives your attackers steps to use. Well, idiots speak idiocies, I suppose that's no surprise."

The man in his fifties must have had considerable authority, because even after that, he managed to rein in the man I'd offended. Looking at me, he said: "Before you find yourself trading blows with Rodrigo, who, by the way, will demolish you, it would be interesting to hear you back up your insults with argument."

"You should know, *señor*, that it was not I who spoke," I said, defending myself, "but the great Vauban, who speaks through me."

"Oh, damn," said the big man sarcastically. "So you're in the habit of breakfasting with French marquises of a morning?"

"I was," I replied, to his disbelief, and qualified it: "Sometimes."

Now that the argument was between him and me, I could take him in more fully and, despite the wine, did at last recognize him. "Wait a moment, I know you! Since I saw you, it's been going round and round in my head; I was confused by your lack of uniform, but I've remembered at last." I waved a finger toward his nose. "Tortosa! Yes, that's right, Tortosa! You're General Rumpkicker! You sent me flying back down the glacis!" I got to my feet and challenged him, circling my fists in front of his face. "Come on, then, seeing as you're so brave. See if you dare to give me a kick now that you're not in your general's uniform!"

The old man looked at me as an old dog looks at a bluebottle.

"Shall we shut him up once and for all, Don Antonio?" his men intervened.

"Just try it!" I laughed. "In case you hadn't noticed, Madrid has been occupied by the Allies. I just have to step outside and whistle. The Guard will be delighted to arrest our friend the general, especially bearing in mind what happened at Tortosa, added to the fact that the Guard is made up of Catalans."

The whole group gave a laugh so unanimous that everyone else in the place stopped and looked over. What was funny? I didn't understand it at all. Quite unnerved, I dropped my fists and scratched the back of my neck.

"I'd be very happy to take you down a peg or two," said this general. "But first, sit beside me and tell me what you made of that siege."

I did. Maybe it was a way of letting off steam, as useful as coming to blows. I spent a long hour drinking and discoursing on the flaws and defects of the Tortosa siege. That Attack Trench, an incomplete joke. Our rushed, shallow digging. Inadequate materials, inadequately applied. An Attack Trench *en règle* is a more sophisticated construction than a pyramid! And that one was no better than an absurd collection of galleries going nowhere, walls braced with green pine instead of proper uprights. The earth that should have been compacted kept spilling down. And what did it lead to? All those unnecessary deaths. Thousands of lads murdered, but it was politics that killed them, not the enemy, *cojones*. The trench only had to make it as far as the city walls. The English commander, a sensible man, would have surrendered. But, oh no, that pig Orléans wanted glory in a hurry. What did a few thousand deaths matter to him? I say again, *cojones*!

I was incredibly drunk. Once I had vented all this, I looked at the general. The wine was coming out of my ears. "And as if that wasn't enough, you gave me a kick on my behind!"

I wanted to use my hand to pick up my glass. But my eyes could no longer calculate distances, and my fingers passed through it as though it were a ghost-thing. I was seeing triple: Three generals sat before me now.

My disquisitions on Tortosa were of some interest to him, because he grabbed me by the lapels and, shaking me hard, asked: "Where did you learn all this? And why did you mention the French engineer?"

The alcohol had defeated me. I looked at him. I opened my lips, very slowly, to tell him something about Bazoches. I gave up, couldn't, didn't want to. And what was more, why should I have? My mouth all furred up, I moved closer to the general's ear and moaned sadly: "Tell me something, I beg you. Do you know The Word?"

He looked at me with a frown, his mouth open. "Word? What damn word?"

He went on asking me questions. But in my condition, I was beyond any authority. I said: "It's a load of shit, all of it."

My head sagged as though I were a rag doll. My forehead was dropping onto the table like a neck under the executioner's ax.

Some hours later, I was awakened. I'd been left on my own, and the place was closing. My right cheek was glued to the table, stuck there with dried wine. I left reeling. A patrol that was going past saw me having trouble.

"Hey, lads," they said to each other in Catalan, "let's have a bit of a laugh with that drunken sot." They surrounded me and pressed me to shout the much repeated "Long live Carlos III!"

"Long live Madrileño stew!" I shouted.

"Huh? Show a bit more respect for your king!"

"Respect? Kings are all the same! Self-centered child-snatchers! And now that I think of it, how have you managed to get yourself lost in Madrid? Go home and stop fucking with good drinkers."

I think it was the most comprehensive thrashing I have ever received. I was so flattened that when they were done, there was little difference between good old Zuvi and a Ceuta rug. Once they were done, they also stole my boots.

At first light, I was rescued by the patriotic innkeeper. He was walking past on his way to open up the tavern. He saw me stretched out in the road and carried me, one of my arms over his shoulder.

"But for God's sake, man, I did warn you!" he scolded me. "Whatever made you get mixed up with those Catalans?"

6

I was so shattered that even two days later, I still couldn't get up from my straw mattress. My only joy was to see that Zúñiga had left the attic. Many years later, we would meet again, and he would spend decades pursuing me across three continents. He never stopped hating me. But that's another story.

I got to my feet, all my bones aching, and dressed. In an inside pocket, I found a passport that must have been put there on the general's behalf by his men:

> Please go to Toledo and report at once to General Don
> Antonio de Villarroel.

As soon as I had read it, I understood a number of things. No wonder they laughed at me when I threatened to turn them in to the Guard! Despite Little Philip's threats and coercion, some Castilians had taken advantage of the 1710 occupation to switch sides. This General Villarroel was evidently one of them. Those men around him must have been his staff officers. Most likely, they were in the tavern to celebrate Charles having allowed them into the pro-Austrian army with full pay and rank.

And so I headed for Toledo. To be honest, I wasn't sure why my legs were taking me there. To be interviewed by that general? The same one who, back in Tortosa, had sent me rolling down the glacis with a kick in the behind? Anyone could see that the fellow had the nature of a resentful mule, that he was clearly one of those military types who swallows hammers and shits out nails. What business could good old Zuvi have with someone like him? Well, shall I tell you something? I did go to Toledo, and I went more directly than the flight of an Indian's arrow.

I found Villarroel in the Toledo citadel, in an extremely somber-looking study. He got right down to business. He was indeed serving as a general in the pro-Austrian army, and he wanted to have an expert in siege warfare among his staff officers. He was no fool: He'd picked up on my comments about Vauban and knew at once that this kid was much more than a hopeless drunk. We started to haggle over the terms of my recruitment, though the money was the least of my interests.

Call it intuition, call it *le Mystère*, call it what you like. As we negotiated, I took advantage of the opportunity to examine that man's inner recesses, bringing all my Bazoches faculties to bear.

There was something about him, though I could not have told you what exactly that something was. "If you need a teacher, you will find him, whether he is a Points Bearer or not." Still, would he be the man to continue the teachings of Vauban? Not an engineer but a military man, and a Castilian to boot, while I was a Catalan? "Well, and why not?" I said to myself. "Did the Marquis de Vauban not take me in despite the French hatred for the Catalans?"

I resolved the conflict between my head and my heart by means of a compromise: I would give the general a chance. If he showed himself worthy of Vauban, I would follow him. If he let me down, I would desert him at the earliest possible opportunity.

As usual, my dear, extremely vile Waltraud stops the narrative with an ignorant inquiry. First she asks whether my plan to desert at the earliest opportunity wasn't dangerous. I answer yes, it was, but much less than it might seem. In my day, such a large proportion of men deserted, and from every army, that one might rather ask the opposite question: Why were there any men who didn't? Some clever-clogs soldiers used it as a way to make a living, the fraudulent practice of enlisting in those armies that paid best and then deserting. The result was such a bloodletting that recently formed armies would sometimes reach the front reduced to half their number. That's as far as the troops were concerned. As for the generals, my fat Waltraud is surprised that Villarroel had begun the war on one side only to switch halfway through. Well, we should make it clear there was nothing unusual about that. Times change. Nowadays the French army is made up of Frenchmen, and the English army of Englishmen. It wasn't like that in my day. A career soldier was a qualified professional not much different from, say, a medical specialist. A French doctor could be employed by an English king, and no Frenchman in his right mind would criticize him for treating a foreigner. And so any sovereign might hire soldiers of any origin, and what gave a soldier his distinction was meeting the terms of the contract, not whose contract it was. In 1710 Villarroel rescinded the contract that bound him to Little Philip, leaving him perfectly free to serve any other sovereign who might make him a good offer. Is that clear now, my blond walrus? Let's go on, then.

In the early days, what a terrifying man commander Villarroel seemed to me, a veritable tyrant on horseback. Cavalry was his great strength; he would take his squadrons out to the outskirts of Toledo, and "Off we go, lads!," riding more often, and better, than the Macedonian royal guard. As an engineer, I managed to avoid most of the exercises, though not all. Hup-hup! Up and down, down and up, till your rump was square-shaped from the saddle. He was more like a sheepdog than a general. Whenever a rider strayed, there the general was, *woof woof!*, barking and bothering the dimwit who had gotten out of formation. And as the dimwit in question tended to be good old Zuvi, I did get some tremendous tellings-off.

"I've got a contract as an engineer, not a dragoon!" I protested one day, wobbling about on my saddle.

"And what do you expect me to say to that?" he shouted. "Accept it! God made you for a monk rather than for a soldier, just give thanks you haven't been promoted any higher!"

Don Antonio drank only one little glass of wine at lunchtime. He was satisfied with a dish of half-cooked pap and wasn't interested in any women but his own wife. On the nights when he didn't sleep in his marital bed, which were about three hundred and sixty-four nights a year, he preferred a wooden board to a mattress. How could good old Zuvi possibly get on with such a man?

Engineers have never felt comfortable in the structures designed for military types. Those martial salutes, that respect for hierarchical superiors, I never took to any of this myself. I sneaked away from the pack whenever I could. Toledo was so dull that when I got drunk there, it was no longer to satisfy my vice but because I had nothing better to do. Once I was called to a meeting of the general's staff officers, to which I reported late and jollier than usual. Don Antonio gave me one of his looks, silent and incredibly fierce.

They were arguing about the situation as a whole, which was dark with storm clouds. While the Allies sat rotting in Toledo, Little Philip was gathering thousands of recruits for his army. As if that were not enough, the Beast had sent him French reinforcements under the command of the Duc de Vendôme. Villarroel shared his fears that Toledo was being transformed into a giant trap. He asked my opinion: Could the city survive a siege?

The wine laughed for me. "Ha ha ha! What a silly question, Don Antonio—I mean, General. Heh heh heh, if the Bourbons besiege Toledo, there won't be any siege. Supplies getting cut off, the people taking against us, the city walls becoming so rotten that even the stones have maggots in them. Hee hee hee, bearing in mind that they are likely to exceed our number by three to one, it would be best to quit now while we still can, ho ho ho . . . ”

I was locked up in the cells for a week, on bread and water. And not because he disagreed with my opinion but because I had said exactly what he thought, but said it rudely. I thought my dungeon would be so deep that they'd have to send my food by catapult. No. The truth was, the incarceration was not too tough—apart from the diet, which purged me.

During my brief incarceration, something of relevance also took place: Charles fled Toledo, and Castile, and made a discreet return to Barcelona. The fact that he had gone before the army tells you everything you need to know about his confidence in a military victory. He left before anybody else, to hell with us all. The road to Barcelona was riddled with Castilian irregulars ready to cut his balls off, which meant that he had to travel surrounded by an escort so strong that it weakened the army further. A heroic example!

As for the Castilians, he had only complaints and recriminations: “I found many people in Madrid who asked me for things, and nobody to serve me.”

What did he expect? Castile and Catalonia were at war; being king of the Catalans excluded him from reigning over the Castilians. He of all people should have known this. And he did, in fact.

While he was in Castile, he drank milk only from goats that had been transported from Barcelona. His bread was baked from Catalan wheat, and even the sugar in his confectionary had been brought over from Catalonia. All his supplies were watched over by the regiment of the Royal Catalan Guard, an elite corps made up entirely of staunchly pro-Austrian Catalans, fanatics so fanatical that you could hear a “Carlossssss” when they broke wind. I scarcely exaggerate.

When he crossed the border from Castile to Catalonia, he alit from the royal carriage, exclaiming, “I am back in my own kingdom at last.”

He was loved by as few people in Castile as Philip was in Catalonia. If he had faced facts, he might have negotiated an end to the conflict. An end to the war. And if things had gone that way, I would have had

at least one country in which to bury my bones. But no, His Majesty
King Karl, our meringue-faced Charles, needed to rule over an empire
and couldn't settle for less. He did get his empire in the end! Though
not as we expected, and through a stroke of chance and at the expense
of his Mediterranean subjects. I will tell you of that anon. Let me first
explain what happened on the final day of the Allied occupation of
Toledo and the retreat, the painful retreat, to the land of the Catalans.

Good old Zuvi got out of his cell. If you will allow me at this point
to make a confession: The very mildness of the punishment made me
reconsider the man who had imposed it upon me.

What little experience I had with Don Antonio told me he was a
good general, firm but fair. He had done the right thing, locking me
up, absolutely the right thing. Vauban would have treated me just the
same, as he should. Thanks to that incarceration, I became aware of
how dulled I had become since leaving Bazoches. Perhaps Don Antonio was a kind of walking Bazoches.

Once I was out of my dungeon, I reported to him. He noticed the
change he had wrought in my spirit, and his behavior toward me softened a little.

The thing is, with Villarroel, you always ended up paying for your
failings, one way or another. And the last one, the last sin of youth that
I committed while under his command, very nearly cost me my life.

I wanted to celebrate my newfound liberty with whores, and the
binge lasted so long that I awoke late, worse for the wear, and not in
the barracks.

"The archduke's army! They're finally off!" cried the whore who
woke me. "They left at night so they could slip away unnoticed. Long
live King Philip!"

The whole fucking army was returning home, and me rubbing the
sleep from my eyes! Even though, at Bazoches, I'd been taught to remain alert even in my sleep, the notification hadn't reached me because
I'd spent the night outside the barracks. I got dressed so quickly that at
first I tried to put my shirt on over my legs.

The Allies were not exactly beloved in Toledo, and as soon as I
was outside, I could see that the atmosphere was warming up. As the
news spread and neighbors began to wake, their bitterness awoke, too.

You could already see small groups shouting: "Long live King Philip! Viva!" and brandishing improvised weapons above their heads. God, anything could happen now.

I hastened toward the citadel. I thought there might be some reserve battalion left behind that I might join. What I found was a little band of drunkards, so drunk that even the most imperious orders hadn't been able to get them out of their bunks. There was a bit of everything: some Englishmen, Portuguese, Dutch . . . Alcohol makes no distinction between origins.

"What are you still doing here? They've all left for Barcelona!" I cried. "The Toledo mob is going to kill us!"

It was useless—they didn't respond at all. I felt as though I were at the bottom of a monstrous Atlantic whirlpool, with the only ship that could save me, the Allied army, receding farther and farther into the distance. No sooner had I left the citadel than I began to hear shouting and gunshots. People were looking for the last stragglers, and there were plenty of them. At the end of the road, I saw an Englishman on his knees, being kicked and stabbed by a yelling crowd of men and women. It was as though people had lost their reason.

Toledo is a relatively small place. I ran through the streets, heading east. So as not to arouse suspicion by my haste, I gave the occasional enthusiastic cry: "Long live King Philip! We're free at last! Viva, viva!"

And you—why are you making that face? What would you have liked me to have shouted? "Long live King Charles! I'm a fucking Catalan rebel, and I eat truffles and Castilian babies for dinner!"? Use your brain, my little cannonball-head.

The last street led to a few kitchen gardens beyond which scraggly vegetation stretched toward the horizon. I stopped a moment to look behind me. Over there, up at the top, the citadel was wreathed in smoke. A few desperate rifles appeared through the small windows, but it was obvious there was nothing to be done. Poor bastards. Before being quartered alive, they would do better to turn their final bullets on themselves.

Good old Zuvi has always had luck on his side, because as chance would have it, there was a priest arriving in the city. He was riding a decent-sized horse, Amazon-style, with both legs on the same side because of his cassock. I knocked him to the ground, climbed onto his saddle like a monkey onto a coconut palm, and tore off at a gallop, so fast it felt like the horse had eight legs. Toledo! You're welcome to her.

7

The Allies had Don Antonio's light cavalry as their rearguard. His horsemen acted as a protective screen for the rest of the army, who moved more slowly, as they fled Toledo for Barcelona. I met them at a crossroads from where they were scanning the horizon. Don Antonio, their leader, was sitting at the foot of a solitary tree, eating, surrounded by his staff officers.

By the time I reached them, the priest's horse was a wreck. I was sweating horrors and distress, and I didn't climb down from the horse's back so much as dropped onto the thin yellow grass. And there I stayed, lying there gasping like a dying fish.

"Here's the little engineer," said Don Antonio by way of greeting, entirely indifferent. "We thought you'd disappeared, you know."

My hair was on end after the shock. Someone poured the contents of a jug of water over Don Antonio's hands, and he gave them a cursory wash and said: "Right, off we go."

"I've only just arrived!" I protested. "Even the shadow of my soul is weighing me down!"

He shrugged. "Very well, stay if you'd rather."

"What about all the stragglers?" I protested again. "Back in Toledo, there are dozens of soldiers getting massacred. Why are we abandoning them?"

"Because they're layabouts."

At once he was back on his splendid white horse. One of Don Antonio's officers spoke for him: "With Vendôme upon us, you really think the whole fucking army is going to sit and wait for a handful of drunkards? They had their chance. Things like this are useful for purging the troop of its undesirables."

Yes, this from Don Antonio de Villarroel Peláez. And to think I believed he might replace the mastery of a Vauban!

Criticisms aside, if you ever want to know whether a general is one of the good ones, don't even think about blood-soaked victories—tell him to lead a retreat; if you want to make it even more difficult, a retreat in winter. It's much easier to defeat than to defend; it's easier to attack than to retreat in an orderly fashion. A retreat never brings laurels or decorations.

An army in flight can come dangerously close to panic, threatening to disintegrate. We find ourselves in enemy territory, which is the main reason for keeping our ranks closed. As I've said, the Castilian country-folk did not exactly love the Allied troops. If a soldier left formation, worn out, if he fell asleep under a tree, *thwack!*, he would end up with his gullet sliced through with a sickle. Our flanks were surrounded by gangs of irregular killers, and behind us we had the Duc de Vendôme, the old marshal whom France's Beast had sent to Spain to help his idiotic grandson. The whole Allied army was a single body, pressed together as tightly as a frightened herd, *meeehhhh . . .*

And the cold! That winter, 1710, was the coldest of the century. Just picture this: One day I stopped my horse at the foot of a solitary tree, looking at a branch that had frozen in the frost. The weak sun was reflected in it with the rich colors of a rainbow. Then I heard *plop, plop, plop* hitting the ground very nearby. They were birds, dozens of them, falling from the branch, frozen.

The Allied army was transformed into the largest gathering of chil-blains ever. My fingers were constantly purple; my lips were a maze of cracks. Since I had fled Toledo in whatever clothes I happened to be wearing, I needed to find some way to get something warmer: gloves, hat, blanket. Comradeship among soldiers? Ha! *Débrouillez-vous*, more like! I stole it all. And a scarf—old, but long enough to go three times around my neck and even covering my nose like an *emboscado*.

What followed was an interminable march across an endless land-scape. Not just level but absolutely, perfectly flat. Not just dry, arid. In spite of the winter cold, neither the mist nor the rain managed to dampen it. God, how hard the Castilian soil is; there's not an invader's boot that can soften it up. We crossed distances that went on forever; towns would emerge like atolls on an ocean horizon. What is Castile? Get a big expanse of wasteland, plant a tyrannical regime upon it, and there you have Castile.

Vendôme was a great soldier. The Bourbon army was pursuing us relentlessly, with no hesitation, no letup, always in search of the perfect moment to destroy the Allied army, but also in no hurry. If you ask me, the only thing that spared us any unpleasant surprises, including getting ourselves completely surrounded, was Don Antonio's cavalry.

Villarroel made no exceptions. I might have been nominally an engineer, but I had to ride, patrol, and fight like anyone else. I tried to make claims for my special expertise.

"We're short of men" was his reply.

"Not least because we abandoned them in Toledo after they'd had one drink too many!" was mine.

"It's only that lack of men that prevents me flogging you." He handed me the reins. "Get on your horse."

It was during that terrifying retreat that good old Zuvi became an expert horseman. Not through any love of horses but out of the strongest imperative that exists: You learn or you get killed.

But I'm not being fair to Don Antonio. You might not believe me, but that apocalyptic retreat from a hostile Madrid to Barcelona—the Retreat, as we veterans would come to call it—taught me to respect him, then to admire him, and eventually to love him.

He censured my manners, never my opinions. I was no more than a mouthy lad, and he was a proper general forged in cauldrons of iron and gunpowder. Who was I to argue with him? At the time, I couldn't see the vast tolerance he extended to me. In his eyes, I was exempt by virtue of my youth and my office. No other general would have been so indulgent.

His motto was the same thing I'd been taught at Bazoches: Know what you need to do, and be where you need to be. He worried about his troops. Actually, that was the only thing that guided him. Vauban saved lives by means of numbers; Villarroel, by example. If you will allow me to simplify a little, I would say that to me, Vauban was theory and Villarroel was practice. Even during mobile wars, there are many things for an engineer to do: Find the best place for a ford when the bridges are inaccessible, build pontoons or provisional defenses. It was only then that I was able, as it were, to make use of my studies. And with this I earned the great general's respect.

I suggested that we leave a small provision of dragoons to our rear, in some one-horse town that had a few battlements standing. When Vendôme approached, he would be forced to stop the whole army, to consider whether to attack the place, besiege it, or surround it. Our dragoons would mount their horses and race out under cover of night. Yes, the following day, the Bourbons would discover that the place was empty, but by then the Allied army would have gained a day's marching on them.

The next trick from the Bazoches list was really rather cruel. We gathered all the inhabitants from down in Villabajo and sent them up to Villarriba—these were two settlements located on the north-south axis separating us from the army we had in pursuit. Simultaneously, another Allied squadron would force the inhabitants from Villarriba to head down to Villabajo. It often happened that the two populations would meet—amazed—on their way, bringing their goats, wagons, and chattel with them. The ill feeling between these unfortunate people illustrated the scale of our disgrace. The fact was, the Bourbon scouts wouldn't spare the horses to notify Vendôme: "Marshal, the inhabitants of Villabajo have been moved up to Villarriba!"

From which Vendôme would deduce that the Allies were divesting themselves of mouths to feed as they converted the place into a center of resistance. Then another group of scouts would come to him saying the exact opposite: "Marshal, the inhabitants of Villarriba have been moved down to Villabajo!"

What was going on? Things became clear only when the Bourbons, having taken many precautions, entered the town square of each of the two villages and found, hanging on the door of the town hall, a polite note, written in perfect French, from good old Zuvi.

À bas Villabajo
Le maraud!
À bas Villarriba
Le gros Verrat!
À bas Vendôme,
Ce sale bonhomme!

Which might be loosely translated as:

Neither Villabajo nor Villarriba. Oh, Vendôme, but what a fool you are.
Well, it obviously sounded better in French, because it rhymed.

The Retreat of 1710 can be summarized as one long, unending logistical nightmare. Geographers can say what they like, but having experienced the Retreat, I can tell you that in my opinion, Barcelona will always be farther away from Toledo than the Land of Saturn.

Stanhope and his Englishmen insisted on marching parallel to the bulk of the army. Maintaining communication between the two bodies of men complicated everything. An army advancing or retreating lays waste to a huge area around it for its own maintenance. With the Castilian land being so poor and the winter so harrowing, it is understandable that the two columns needed to be moving very far apart from each other. "Close together when in combat, far apart when on the move," so says the military maxim. But not quite that far apart, *caray*!

On December 8, Stanhope—that conceited ass Stanhope—allowed himself to be surrounded in a small town by the name of Brihuega. He didn't know how near or far behind the enemy was. Unbelievable though it sounds, he stopped in Brihuega for three whole days so that his army could rest and he could have himself a nice little cup of hot tea. Before he knew what was happening, Vendôme was upon him. He dug himself in at Brihuega. He sent the bulk of the army as many as six desperate messages, begging them to come to the rescue of the English.

How could he have allowed himself to get trapped so easily? The explanation is simple. Stanhope didn't have Don Antonio's eyes. His heavy cavalry did not move easily in that war of feints and dodges. And Stanhope was a great Coehoornian brute, capable of heavy frontal batterings and nothing else.

After some conference between the senior command, Don Antonio came out of the tent to tell us how things were going. When we asked his opinion, he shook his head. "There aren't enough of the English to survive a mass assault. Vendôme knows that, and he'll throw everything he's got at the attack. They'll never make it."

But the Allied army went to their aid. The trumpets sounded, and the whole army turned tail and headed for Brihuega at a forced march. The political and military consequences of losing the entire English contingent would be equally serious. After so many protracted maneuvers, after making such efforts to put some distance between us, we turned around and headed of our own free will into the battle we had striven so hard to avoid. Well, Lord In-a-Trice, thank you very much!

Oh, but let us be a little more indulgent; perhaps it was not such a senseless maneuver after all. The Allied army was hastening to the rescue; if In-a-Trice could hold out a little, we would be able to catch the Bourbons between the devil and the deep blue sea. While we were driving our mounts to their limit, Vendôme surrounded Brihuega and demanded the surrender of the English forces. Stanhope responded with a most peculiar note: "Inform the Duc de Vendôme that my Englishmen and I shall defend ourselves to the bitter end."

Somebody ought to have explained to In-a-Trice that heroic proclamations only become a source of perpetual ridicule for anyone who fails to live up to them. By the third attack, he was having doubts. Why die in some godforsaken Castilian village in the middle of nowhere if he could spend that night dining on pheasant with his opponent general, Vendôme? When we approached the outskirts of Brihuega, the sound of cannon fire had already stopped. It wasn't hard to guess what had happened: The English, the entire English force, had surrendered.

Four thousand veterans taken with all their weapons and all their equipment! And General Stanhope at their head, the same man who had arrived in Spain so very generously supplied with arrogance and with horses. I'll sort this out in a trice! And now his four thousand Englishmen were marching toward captivity, heads lowered and with a bayonet escort.

Well, we planted ourselves on the outskirts of Brihuega, gasping for breath. And who should be waiting for us, rubbing his hands in glee? Only Vendôme and the entire Army of the Two Crowns, in perfect battle formation.

The Bourbons exceeded us in number by two to one. Our men and horses were exhausted after a day and a night's marching to rescue Stanhope. And with the enemy so close, we had no way to retreat. Never has a battle been so unlooked for and yet so unavoidable.

An engineer will never be a soldier. Our mentality differs in one fundamental point: Why are human beings so keen on killing each other out in the open when we've invented such marvels of self-preservation as trenches and bastions? In case it comes in useful to you one day, let me cite *Martí Zuviría's Brief Instruction Manual for Surviving a Pitched Battle*. Thus it goes:

CHAPTER ONE: Devise some good excuse to separate yourself from your fighting formation.

CHAPTER TWO: Drop to the ground facedown, feigning death, with your head behind the biggest rock you can find, and don't move till your ears inform you the shooting is over.

CHAPTER THREE: Instruction Manual concludes.

I can assure you, it has been of great use to me, as evidenced by the fact that at the age of ninety-eight, here I am, with half my face missing and three holes in my ass but still dictating my memoirs to my dear vile Waltraud. The only defect of this guide is that in certain circumstances, such as in Brihuega, it is not possible to put it into practice. And do you know why? Because of all the generals in the world, I had to be serving the only one who used his rank not to hide behind but to make himself more exposed.

Villarroel had been born in a uniform, and for a fellow like that, dying in battle was one more perk of the job. That particular battle had been lost before it was even begun; anyone could see that. My own war vehicle was a horse who had been worn out by the cold, the deprivation, and his exertions. His ribs were so prominently visible, his flanks looked like a bellows. My horse stood beside that of Don Antonio, who, without looking at me, gave me a telling-off: "Sit up straight, Captain Zuviría! Any soldier who happens to glance to one side should see his officers proud and ready for the attack. And you look like a limp head of lettuce."

I did not answer. He gave me a sharp blow to the kidneys with his riding crop and added: "An officer is the spirit and the mirror of the troops. If an officer has doubts, the men will collapse."

I straightened up a little, not much. I, too, spoke without looking at him. It was as though we were in a horseback confessional.

"I'm not an officer, sir, you know that as well as I do," I said sadly. "*Merda*."

That Catalan word, *merda*, made him smile. "You might not know it, but I was born in Barcelona."

I looked at him, astonished. Villarroel, the epitome of Castilian virtues: severe, inflexible, and just. That piece of news simply astonished me.

"My father was also a soldier, and he was posted there," he explained. "Which was why my mother gave birth to me in Barcelona. Beautiful city."

While Villarroel made a happy speech about the beauties of Barcelona as seen through the eyes of a Castilian, the fighting stretched all the way down the line. From where we sat, we could just hear the din of the gunfire, see the injured men pouring back toward the rearguard, hear the yells of the sergeants trying to maintain order in the ranks.

"Don Antonio," I groaned, "this is madness. There's no way we can possibly win this battle, you know that already."

In reply, he stuck his riding whip under my chin, raised it, and exclaimed: "You will address me as 'General'! My staff officers are allowed the familiarity because they are men who have shown their valor under my command. That is not true of you."

At that moment, a messenger on horseback, sweating despite the cold, approached us. "General! The enemy is breaking through on the left flank! Marshal Starhemberg requests that you return to the front."

Villarroel put the crop away, drew his sword, and cried: "It was about time, damn it!"

Half the Allied cavalry followed him. I did, too, in spite of myself.

And so, a day of suffering. When the Bourbons broke our line, there was Don Antonio's cavalry, ready to close up the breach. I spent the whole battle riding side by side with that man.

"I'm your faithful squire, Don Antonio!" I shouted, for want of anything better to say.

"In that case, tell me," he retorted, laughing, "why is it that when the enemy is to our right, you ride to my left, and when we have them on our left, you switch sides and position yourself to my right? You wouldn't happen to be using my body as a moving *fajina*, would you?"

Have you ever had a nightmare that lasted five whole hours? That's what Brihuega was like. From noon until sunset, the Bourbons tried to break through the Allied lines. Our officers tightened up the battalions, rebuilt the walls of bayonets. The regiments were sturdy but badly depleted, nervous exhaustion visible on their faces. By around three in the afternoon the infantry were so desperate that they began to form squares.

My dear vile Waltraud, who knows nothing about anything, asks me to explain. How easy that is! Basically, we were giving up.

When an infantry battalion is cornered, it literally forms a human square, with the soldiers pointing the bayonets outward and the officers, the drummers, and the wounded in the center. It is an agonizing method of resistance, especially against a cavalry. A troop who resorts to that is admitting that they are abandoning any kind of attack. (Do you understand me finally, my little blond she-bear?) And back they come, the Bourbons, and again, and again. When a breach is opened, there goes Don Antonio and his cavalry, closing up the gaps with a charge of scrawny old nags, again and again.

If you ever find yourselves compelled to take part in a cavalry charge, do the following: The most important thing is to avoid the violence of the impact. At the last moment, dip your head down behind your horse's neck to hide a sharp tug on the reins that will stop the animal. In the confusion, nobody will notice what was holding back the momentum. Throw all the strength in your body into your calves, squeezing them to the horse's flanks as though they were forceps. Position yourself between the first and second line of attacking riders. If the enemy flees, spur on your mount and go for it, yelling as though you've broken through the line alone (thereby allowing yourself much vaunting about the battle afterward). If they stand their ground, swing your sword above your head, cursing your fellow riders who are getting between you and your adversaries. But do not advance! In the case of a retreat, turn tail and flee shamelessly. The front line of idiots you allowed to go ahead of you will protect your back.

The battle of Brihuega was decided by exhaustion. Or, rather, not decided. The Bourbons had thrown all their wood on the fire without breaking the cohesiveness of the Allied army. Some regiments suffered up to a dozen consecutive assaults. And when they faltered, there was Don Antonio charging over with riders to drive the enemy away.

In the last countercharge the momentum took us out beyond the Allied infantry. When we stopped, we were surrounded by the bodies of the enemy dead, a real carpet of white uniforms. I gave a childish howl: "What a sight, Don Antonio! Look at this slaughter!" I leaped off my horse and stared around me. There were so many dead bodies, I had to take great strides so as not to tread on them. "You were right after all! We haven't lost! And Vendôme thought he had us. Ha!"

Then the general dismounted, came over, and with fury in his eyes, gave me a resounding slap. And left.

I was dazed, but more by the offense than by the pain. I couldn't understand it. Villarroel had spent the whole day scolding me for my lack of military spirit and enthusiasm, and when I showed a bit of fire, he struck me. No, I still hadn't understood that war, his occupation, increased Don Antonio's pain and his contradictions. With one hand on the offended cheek, I protested, "What have I said now?"

One of his adjutants explained for him: "You imbecile, not twelve months ago these were the lads under Don Antonio's command."

8

Don Antonio called for me at the first chance the army got to pause for breath after Brihuega. It was late, the retreat had already been sounded, and the night was so cold that just to cross the short distance to his tent, I had to wear my whole arsenal of warm clothes.

The staff officers were delighted; the official report of the battle praised my great general to the skies. But I had never seen him in a good mood. And as for his relationship with me, the most recent episode we had shared had been a slap in the middle of the battle.

His campaign tent was more Spartan than Leonidas's. His mattress was thinner than a plank of wood. The rest of the furniture amounted to a folding seat, a small table, and a couple of candles shivering at the icy air that sneaked through the thousand cracks in the canvas.

He wasn't looking good. He wasn't sitting on his chair but on the camp bed, drinking straight from a bottle. I'd rarely seen him drink. Well, all warriors are familiar with the melancholy that arises after a battle. He looked at me with eyes hooded by red, drooping lids. Outside, the Castilian wind howled like a monster calling out to you from your nightmares.

"I struck you," he said, skipping past any formalities. "I was wrong to do that."

I wasn't sure how to respond.

"My apologizing has nothing to do with your foolishness," he went on, "only with your uniform, however provisional it may be. You don't strike an officer. It's ugly, degrading to the rank."

"Yes, Don Antonio."

"General, damn it! Address my person by the rank I hold."

He looked up, and I saw he was half-drunk. "Yes, General."

"As for the rest, I have signed up a man who is mean and selfish. All armies have blisters popping out all over their ass, and you are the fattest, most pus-filled in the entire Allied coalition."

That is an "apology" as understood by Don Antonio de Villarroel: He summons me to ask for forgiveness and ends up calling me a purulent blister. He pointed at me with the mouth of the bottle and added: "I ought to hang you."

"You're right, Don Antonio."

"But as an engineer, you do have a certain competence. I've seen you carry out maneuvers that might lack grace, though they are amusing." He sighed deeply. "It's my fault; engineers are no use on horseback. No. Your skill is hiding away between chunks of stone."

"Yes, Don Antonio. I mean, no, Don Antonio. Whatever you say."

He looked at me a moment, his eyes glassy with wine. He patted the mattress a couple of times. "Sit here!"

I obeyed, and he put an arm around my shoulders. He smelled of sour wine. And then, to my surprise, he showed an affection toward me that I had known nothing of. "You needn't worry, son. You're a coward, I know that, but few men are born brave. Bravery is something you learn, just like a child learning to speak. Do you understand?"

"I'm not sure, Don Antonio."

He squeezed me a little tighter, jostling me like a wisp of straw. He waved a fist under my nose. "The good Lord has placed a barrier between each man and his destiny. Our mission in this life is to get past it, to go beyond it, to have the courage to learn what there is on the other side." He stopped, pensive. "Whatever that may be."

"But Don Antonio," I replied, shriveling up, "that does sound rather dangerous."

I shouldn't have said that. He stared at me with his drunken pop eyes and, with his booming Castilian voice, let out some words that I can remember down to the last drop of saliva: "So what the fuck did that French engineer teach you, then?"

"How to fortify, storm, and defend fortresses, Don Antonio."

"And what else?"

I hesitated. "What else, Don Antonio?"

He shook me. "Yes, yes! What else?"

I must have been brought low by the carnage, by being far from home. By that night, one more night camped out in the cold. The wind howling like a pack of wild hounds. The post-battle melancholy had struck me, too.

"Don Antonio," I confessed, "I've lied to you. I'm not an engineer. The French marquis never approved the fifth Point that was to make me an engineer."

He didn't hear me, or if he did, he didn't care. "Damn battle," he whispered. "Damn it . . . The world is a thousand souls lighter. And what for? Nothing has changed."

The wine had gone to his head much more than I had realized. He curled up his knees like an old man, arms folded, and lay down on the camp bed. I stayed where I was for a few minutes, watching the great man sleeping after his victory. In Bazoches, I had been taught to look at objects that hung from invisible threads, to decode them and understand them in their vast humility. How could my eyes not be drawn to the human enormity of Don Antonio?

I felt a rush of pity toward him. That night, as the man snored, sleeping like a fetus, I would have given my life to protect his rest. His whole life was service, discipline, a just measure of rigor. I saw each of the pores on his mature cheeks, everything I knew about him, and told myself that this cavalry general had chosen his own path to *le Mystère*. Then I understood his most deeply hidden secret, perhaps better than he understood it himself: that ever since he had started, he had sought to die in a heroic cavalry charge, so beautiful in its despair.

It wasn't a simple, senseless death wish. For somebody so self-denying, so possessed by the spirit of chivalry, to fall before his men did not signify the end of an existence but the perfecting of one. At Brihuega, he had spent the entire battle right at the front of every single Allied charge and countercharge. But death had eluded him, stubbornly, mockingly. As for me, I found myself at the opposite end of the moral arc. And yes, thanks to the senses I had developed at Bazoches, I understood, or at least respected, his code of intransigent rectitude. For this very reason, what a tragic irony in his life! In 1705 he had begun the war on the Bourbon side and, in 1710, had moved over to the pro-Austrian side. A path on which the view of the enemy had changed places and faded away, stripped of any meaning. To protect today's friends, he would kill yesterday's. Sad, sad, sad. It might be that *le Mystère* was keeping him for that apex of all dramas that was Barcelona on September 11, 1714. Like it was keeping me.

It was the coldest night of the whole Retreat. A pitiless wind whipped at the thin canvas of the tent. I took off his boots and covered his body with the only blanket there was in the tent. I went out, stole a couple more blankets, and came back to wrap him more warmly. He was snoring. Before I left, I kissed his cheek. Just as well he was sleeping deeply. If he had realized, he would have struck me on the head for being a pansy. Then I went and got myself drunk on what was left in the bottle.

Don Antonio. My battle-running general, my good Don Antonio de Villarroel Peláez, the most anonymous hero of our century. Things ended badly, very badly. Not many great men came out well from that war of ours. That leech In-a-Trice Stanhope was certainly one of the lucky ones.

Owing to his high rank, the Bourbons treated him with kid gloves, and four days later, he returned to London like a greenhorn coming home from an outing. Without glory, but without dishonor, either.

Instead of hanging him, the English exalted him, perhaps as a way of disguising the failure of their continental strategy. He married the daughter of the governor of Madras and thrived in politics. Some men are born covered in a patina of moral oil: Misfortune slips off them like water. But those same men stain everything they touch. A decade later, his government was foolish enough to give him the reins to the faltering English economy. I'll wager anything you like that, as he took on the post, he exclaimed, "I'll sort this out in a trice!"

As we already know, England's finances ended up the same way as their expeditionary forces: destroyed in a trice. It took him only two years to devastate trade with America and the savings of a million shareholders, and to bring half the country's industries, banks, businesses, and warehouses to the point of bankruptcy in what has come to be known as the South Sea Bubble. From my own exile in England, I recall some delightful heads, such as Swift or Newton, a wise astronomer who looked like a libertine priest. Newton always had one eye on the heavens and another on his purse. During the crisis, he lost thousands of pounds in shares, and measured though he surely was, even he wanted to strangle Stanhope. I can still see him now, shouting, "It's infinitely easier to predict the motion of a heavenly body than the lunacies of these secretaries of finance!"

As for Marshal Vendôme, our enemy at Brihuega, in those last days of 1710, Little Philip named him governor-general of Catalonia. A premature title, you will agree, since at that point, most of Catalonia remained in the hands of the Generalitat. The truth was, he never got the chance to enjoy the post. In 1712, as he was travelling through one of our towns to the south, Vinaroz, he stopped—to everyone's horror—to have dinner. To make him happy, they served him the local delicacy, fried prawns.

"How good these prawns are!" Vendôme crowed.

The people of Vinaroz were scared to death, naturally, so they just kept serving him trays and more trays of prawns. The glutton wolfed down sixty-four prawns. No one dared to tell him that they were served in their shell but that you eat them without. Vendôme was such an exalted aristocrat that it never would have occurred to him that a servant would bring him in a shell something that was eaten peeled, and that his noble little fingers were being smeared with grease from the sea.

That very night he died of indigestion.

In the days that followed Brihuega, we became intoxicated by a false sense of security. Since we'd left Toledo, the cry that had united the army had been "Return to Barcelona or die!" After the failure of the great Bourbon attempt to annihilate us, everybody let go a little.

We were already on Aragon land, barren like the Castilian but at least an Allied kingdom. Don Antonio was in command of a motley troop made up of a few hundred Dutch, Portuguese, Palatines, Hessians, a real ragtag bunch. (Italian mercenaries, too! They were everywhere!) Most were ill or bore wounds from Brihuega, and we carried them in wagons that were full up and groaning heavily. So as not to be a burden on the march of the army, we took a parallel route.

Although I didn't like the idea at all, I went with Don Antonio. From the very first, I knew that looking after this little troop of invalids, riding apart from the main army, was a bad idea. I was anxious as I rode alongside my great general, asking myself what good old Zuvi was doing there. The answer, as you can imagine, is that I had grown to feel a loyalty for this man very similar to that which had bonded me to Vauban. The marquis taught me what I needed to do; Don Antonio went further, filling the work with moral meaning. That same day he would be practicing what he preached.

Being so far away from the army, we were easy prey. Nine out of ten of these wounded men couldn't lift a rifle. If we were attacked by a decent-sized force, we would be condemned to disaster. I had a bad feeling about it all. I was constantly turning in my saddle, scanning the horizon, or racing up and down the short column of wagons chivvying the drivers. What we hoped was that the Bourbons would not pay any attention to these little crumbs of the army and we would be able to get ourselves lost on minor roads. We couldn't.

The Castilian warriors attacked us on both flanks at once. The diminished mounted escort charged—led by Don Antonio—then charged again, and a third time. The Bourbons avoided them like wolves escaping a shepherd, but they were soon back in pursuit of the defenseless flock, and there were more of them each time. Those in the wagons who were in a fit state had armed themselves and fired from where they were on the flatbed of the carts. Don Antonio gave the order to take refuge in the nearest settlement, a small place called Illueca that we could make out on the horizon.

I was desperate. "Don Antonio! Please don't do it! You know as well as I do what that order will mean. Please!"

He didn't answer. We entered Illueca like a mouse into a trap. Don Antonio's logic was absolutely impeccable: The Bourbons exceeded us in number; if those of us on horseback fled, the injured in the wagons would be annihilated in the excitement of the fighting.

As an engineer, I knew that Illueca was impossible to defend. We had neither the provisions nor the arms to defend it. And we knew, furthermore, that there was nobody to come to our rescue. But once we had dug ourselves in, when all the smoke had cleared and the siege begun, Don Antonio could agree to a reasonable settlement with someone in the Two Crowns' command. At least they would have respect for the lives of the wounded. That was what duty and sacrifice meant to Don Antonio: to lose the warrior's most sacred possession, freedom, if in doing so, he could save the lives of his men.

But I could not forget two details that were crucial to my own interests: that good old Zuvi was neither ill nor wounded, and that the prospect of captivity was unbearable to me. I tried, exasperated, to reason with Don Antonio. As the gates to the town were closed and some improvised defenses set up, I asked him to reconsider: "Let's flee while there is still time, leaving the command in the hands of some lame officer who can negotiate the terms of the surrender." I had plenty of tactical reasons for this: he was a general, the finest commander under Karlangas. Was it worth the army losing his talent for some hundred invalids?

Nothing doing. He would never abandon men under his command, never. I had escaped a razed Toledo, the cold Retreat, the battle of Brihuega. And now, because of a stupid question of honor, I was going to fall into the hands of an intransigent enemy. His example was an admirable one; more than that, it was heroic. But Longlegs Zuvi wasn't yet ready to grasp The Word, as evidenced by the fact that I exploded in frustration.

"You're more stubborn than a deaf mule! You hear me? A fucking mule in a general's sash! That's what you are."

Anyone else would have had me hanged on the spot. But he didn't do it. Why?

He was fond of me, there was no other explanation. He and his adjutants just left me alone there, stamping on my tricorn hat in utter fury. After a while I was called into his presence. I had calmed down a little and I could recognize my insubordination. I went to meet him like a lamb to the slaughter.

He was in the castle. I had to climb a spiral staircase to get to the top of a solitary turret, whipped by the four winds. From there you could keep an eye on the whole landscape all the way to the horizon.

Although I wish I could, I know I never shall forget that sight. Our good general standing alone, wrapped in a long, ragged, rat-colored cloak. He looked like a human *échauguette*, impassive at the gusts of wind that shook those heights. He was using his spyglass to watch the Bourbons' movements. The warriors of Castile had already called for the French regular troops. Seen from where we stood, they looked like little white roaches. Soon they would have Illueca surrounded. Soon our sacrifice would come to a head.

"What am I to do with you?" he said, still looking through his spyglass.

Resigned, I allowed my gaze to follow the direction of the spyglass and just answered: "I suppose it doesn't much matter, Don Antonio." I sighed. "We are going to fall into their hands."

"Do you have a family?"

"I think so."

He lowered the spyglass. "You think so?" he boomed. "Either you have a family or you don't!"

"I do." I hadn't the slightest idea what he wanted.

"I need a messenger to tell the king what has happened," he said. "I have served under the Bourbon flag. It might be thought that I took advantage of the situation to commit treason."

"But anyone thinking that, Don Antonio, would be an idi—" I shut up, suddenly understanding that this was just an excuse he had dreamed up to spare me from captivity. "Forgive me, Don Antonio."

"General! Address me according to my rank."

"Yes, General."

He went back to his spyglass and said: "Take saddlebags filled with plentiful provisions. And my horse. It's in the best condition. I don't want it to end up with some French fop."

I wanted to thank him, dizzy with delight, but he prevented me with a shout: "Now get out of my sight before I change my mind!"

I withdrew. All the same, when I reached the staircase, something made me turn. I couldn't go just like that.

"Don Antonio, I want you to know that I have been thinking a lot about what you said that night. I don't have the courage to take on that invisible border which God has put in front of us. And you, what's more, you seek it out with tireless tenacity."

He looked me up and down. He noticed how moved I was. "What are you talking about? When did we have that conversation?"

"A few nights ago, Don Antonio. In your tent."

He didn't remember.

"For me, you're a teacher who has come to replace the person I have most admired in this world," I went on. "From the first day you have made me a gift of your example. And today you have given me freedom."

Don Antonio didn't expect me to fall to my knees, nor that, my shoulder leaning against an old battlement, I would confess: "For the second time in my life, I have failed in a decisive test. In the first, I didn't have the heart to understand what was being asked of me. In this second, I haven't the courage to take it on."

I couldn't hold back my tears. I cried so much that my hands, covering my face, were wet as sponges. I cried so much, hugging that cold Aragon battlement, that for a moment I forgot what we were doing there.

Villarroel looked through his spyglass once again and immediately said, in a gentle reprimand, "They've nearly completed the siege. Stand up."

I got up on my long legs, and as I was leaving, ashamed, he was the one who stopped me for a moment. On that cold, windy day, in that distant place, Don Antonio's eyes took on the brilliance of Vauban's.

"Zuviría," he said, "don't be mistaken. You will be able to run away today. But for good or for ill, this doesn't end here. Neither the war nor the tribulations of your soul. Now go."

I fled at a speed that was meteoric, if not very heroic. Villarroel's horse was every bit as reluctant to be taken prisoner as good old Zuvi. What was more, my body was lighter than his master's, and within moments we had become accomplices in our flight. And just in time! Once we were out of Illueca, we came across the enemy troops as they closed the siege and had to drop behind some bushes to hide. I lay down on the animal's body and covered its mouth with my hand. It was very docile.

As chance would have it, the Spanish irregular forces were beginning to be relieved by French soldiers and officers. And knowing how much Don Antonio liked the Frog-eaters—and now he would have to negotiate the surrender with them! But it was for the best. The French would be satisfied with taking the garrison prisoner without any executions. While the Bourbons kept their eyes trained on the city walls, I—behind them—took advantage of the moment to head off in the opposite direction.

Free, in flight, on horseback. And yet the joy of the survivor remained outside me. Because of what I had left behind and what was yet to come. I crossed places where rejoicing and happiness had no reason to be. Poor old Zuvi on an animal's sore back, his clothes filthy, his tricorn and scarf in tatters. Across every hill, natural cones of earth as low as Moghul tombs. I was whipped by a constant wind that cut my lips. In those few moments when the wind fell silent, it felt as though rider and mount would be turned to stone then and there. And always, at any time when there was some light, that enormous sky covering my head and out toward infinity. Blue, a limpid, huge blue, vaster than the whole Spanish empire. I couldn't stop thinking about Don Antonio.

My hopes of finding The Word in the lands of Castile had died there. How would I find it in a country that tolerated only empty spaces? Indeed: I had found a teacher capable of taking Vauban's place, and what was more, a man of Castilian origin. But that same land had taken him captive, had trapped him inside, perhaps forever. I owed him my liberty, perhaps my life. I could have shared in his luck, and I didn't, while he made the teacher's supreme sacrifice: to give his life for his student's. Thanks to Don Antonio, I could return to Anfán and Amelis. Wretched but free. I cried like a baby, big, slow tears that slipped down my cheeks.

Illueca, for anyone interested in historical trivia, is the resting place of a pope, Pope Luna, a dramatic type who, in the fourteenth century, challenged Rome. After Don Antonio capitulated, the French soldiery demolished the man's tomb in the hope of finding great treasures. They found nothing in the casket but bones, and the Frog-eaters took this badly. They dismantled the mummified body, played football with the skull, and ended up hurling it out of a window.

9

As to what happened between my return from the Allied offensive in 1710, to settle back in Barcelona, and the vile summer of 1713, it's not worth the telling.

We owed a great deal of money from the purchase of the house in La Ribera. Amelis and I argued about the debts, we argued about her poor skill in cooking (great lovers do not tend to be good cooks), about a thousand silly things. When the subject of the debt came up in conversation, and its generous twenty percent interest, it was like the rolling of thunder that precedes a storm. Peret, Nan, and Anfán would vanish down the stairs. Then I would scold her for having bought the fifth-storey apartment in La Ribera. She would laugh at my scruples. Amelis didn't know how to read, she didn't know how to add, she knew just one thing: You survive in this world only if you can learn to walk on broken glass. Any of you husbands reading this, however good-natured, will be asking yourselves an extremely reasonable question: Why didn't I just give her a good hiding? Look, it all came down to two things: If I wouldn't use violence when in service and against people I didn't know, how could I with her? And the second reason: I loved her.

It wasn't hard to find out that she had gone back to selling herself. I had been schooled in Bazoches, after all. When things were particularly tight, bags filled with money would appear. She thought she could keep it a secret from me because she was very skillful at measuring out the flow of the money. Besides, she didn't spend much time renting out her body. I noticed that when she disappeared, her violet-colored Sunday dress was also missing from the closet. I had no doubt whatsoever: She was the luxury whore of some Red Pelt who paid her well for her attentions. I kept quiet.

That's enough for today. Pass me the cat and the bottle. And go.

For lack of anything else to occupy my time, I took on the role of home teacher to Nan and Anfán. To my surprise, the dwarf turned out to be very good with numbers, although sitting still was not his forte; after a while he would start squirming as though the chair were covered in nails. At this point, I ought to mention something that makes me sad. My lessons had one unpredictable effect, and a deplorable one. The brotherhood between Nan and Anfán began to break down. I can remember one particularly pitiful day.

I had given Nan a big spinning top that had numbers all over its surface. Anfán came into the little room I sometimes used as workroom and saw Nan with the top in front of him spinning. They argued. The dwarf clasped hold of the top, unwilling to give it up. Anfán was offended and cried: "You and those numbers! Have you lost count of how many crusts of bread I brought you when we were sleeping in those tarts' hovels? Have you forgotten that already? Nan *merdós!*"

That he should aim such a strong insult at Nan was so unusual, so unthinkable, that I didn't even respond. The dwarf did. He chased after the boy, crying with remorse and kicking him out of sheer helplessness. To try and console him, Nan gave him the big spinning top. Anfán tried its weight, hesitated, and ended up throwing it out the window. A bit farther and he would have killed a knife sharpener who was outside on the street.

Anfán understood somehow that a comfortable life, modern education, all that, was destroying the fundamental bond that held them together. They were reconciled, but it wasn't like before.

Between us, Amelis and I had given them a roof, clothes, food, and even affection. With the best will in the world, we'd tried hard to make sure they had something like a family. So they were no longer exposed to shrapnel or to the rigors of the elements, but you got the sense that all the pain from before, rather than being driven away, had filtered beneath their skin. During the siege of Tortosa, I had never seen them sad. On the contrary. They mocked death every bit as mercilessly as they mocked me. And they always came out on top. Nowadays, Anfán was no longer stealing, no longer interrupting us in bed to throw his arms around our necks, purring. Now, during his long afternoon tea, he would just sit on the rear balcony, his legs hanging through the bars, on his own, with the low, languid appearance of a savage who has been ripped out of the jungle. Eating a hunk of fried bread soaked in oil, he would watch the people on the street and beyond, in the Saint Clara bastion, and farther beyond still, in the outside world. We were tormented by the same question: Wouldn't it have been better if they had never left the Tortosa trenches?

In order to temper the hours we spent in lessons, I increased the frequency of our walks. The truth was it made scarcely any difference whether I taught them at home or on foot, and Anfán was a little creature who needed fresh air. Something happened during one of those walks that demonstrates how an excess of civilization transforms upright people into simpletons.

As I was saying, I had taken Nan and Anfán out for a walk, this time into the outskirts of the city. Anfán was exceptionally interested in my military adventures. I was always reticent when it came to recounting that collection of carnage, mud, and bayonets, but my resistance only intensified the boy's interest. We were already outside the city walls, on a small path flanked by scattered houses and kitchen gardens, when he asked me about the generals I had known.

"If you're talking to a French general, you have to stand up really straight. Like this," I said, standing to attention, arms parallel to my body and my chin up, "as though you've swallowed a broom. And whatever nonsense they say, you have to click your heels—like this!— and reply with a shout: '*Mes devoirs, mon général!*' Then they order you to attack a given position. You reply, even louder: '*À vos ordres, mon général!*' and in the middle of the commotion, you race off in any direction other than the one they sent you in."

"And is that the same with Spanish generals?"

"Oh no, with the Spanish ones, it's completely different!" I exclaimed. "With them, you have to cry '*A su servicio, mi general!*' and run off in exactly the opposite direction than the one they've told you to go in."

They must have been growing up, because they took this as a joke, while I was being entirely serious.

"Well," I said, acknowledging the truth, "I did serve under the command of two great men whom I would have obeyed blindly, whatever madness they ordered me to do. Not because they were great generals but because they were great teachers."

"And of those two great men," asked the dwarf, "which was the greater?"

To Anfán, the greater was the one who had taught me to survive, because if you're dead, you can't learn any more secrets. To the dwarf, who had great lucidity in that little frame of his, the greater was the one who had taught me secrets, "because if you don't know the secrets of life, you can't survive," he said.

We walked on, and Anfán climbed a fence that was surrounding a small cottage and a kitchen garden. All he wanted was to examine the cedar that rose up at one end of the fence. I had been talking to them about the qualities of different kinds of wood, and the fact that cedar is one of the most valued by various kinds of artisan. Anfán wanted to see what it felt like and climbed up the trunk like a monkey.

"The same tree is used to make both fiddles and rifle butts," I said. "Strange, isn't it? At this moment, inside there, you can find both a fiddle and a rifle. If it were up to you, which of the two would—"

I was interrupted by a yell from the gardener's cottage, and it sounded furious with Anfán: "Oi, you! You bunch of petty thieves! Scram, or you'll see what's what!"

"I haven't stolen anything!" said Anfán, defending himself with uncommon vehemence because just this once it happened to be true.

But the young man—who was brandishing a stick—came over the fence accompanied by a little dog, which hurled itself at the dwarf. I let the four of them battle it out for a bit. Then I stepped in. "All right, all right, that's enough now."

I talked to the young man courteously. I admired his fruit trees and how well kept the garden was. His attitude changed. His father appeared. We chatted, and he ended up giving us a string of garlic and a few ripe tomatoes.

"You see how being honorable can do you good?" I said to Anfán as we walked home, arms full.

"Good?" he protested, rubbing his face, which was still red from the blows he had received. "I don't see any good in it at all! The one time I'm not stealing, and I get attacked by a great beanpole like that. So much for being honorable!"

"Then you're quite wrong," I replied. "What's the first thing you do after you've stolen something?"

"What do you think? Race off like a cannonball!"

"Exactly. Meanwhile, today you were attacked by a fellow five years older than you, armed with a stick and a dog, and instead of running away, you defended yourself."

My rhetorical flourish must have had some impact on him, because he was listening closely.

"Honesty lubricates the muscles of your soul," I went on. "It protects us in the face of injustice and strengthens our will to fight. You were the weaker party, and you were unarmed. But you were right, and you knew it. That was why you stood your ground.

"On the other hand, righteous souls are complemented by calm speech. Look at this garlic and these tomatoes I'm carrying. Free and obtained in simple good faith, which is hard to find nowadays. And why? I didn't steal them; I didn't even have to lie. When I was admiring this good man's vegetable garden, I was telling him a great truth: that his noble work transforms the world, and that puts food on his table. And he, to repay me for this precise flattery, wanted to share his food with some total strangers. Why settle for an exchange of bad things when you can exchange good ones? He's given us much more than we would have been able to get ourselves by stealing!"

A good speech, don't you think? As a teacher, I was never much of a Rousseau, but not bad for an amateur.

As we approached the city gates, I saw a strange group of people. Five men, four of them armed with rifles over their shoulders. And the fifth was him—it was him! The Antwerp butcher!

Joris Prosperus van Verboom. Under escort, happily walking about outside the city, making his way around the foot of the city walls. I knew he was a prisoner of the government (I'd captured him myself, remember?), but I hadn't realized he was here in Barcelona. I left Nan and Anfán, made straight for him, got my hands around his neck, and tried to strangle him. The guard intervened and parted us.

"Hey there, just take it easy," said the captain understandingly. "I can tell you don't like the big fish of the Bourbons, but we've all got to be civilized about it. We have to treat our enemies nobly until it's time for them to be exchanged."

"Exchanged?" I screamed. "What are you talking about? This scum can't be exchanged! And now you've been stupid enough to let him go for a walk! He mustn't be allowed out of the city again till the war is over! Leave him to me."

Most men get to their deathbeds without ever understanding that war is not a matter of brute force. That the outcome of a conflict is settled in a higher sphere made up of ink and volumes and calculations. Verboom was a Points Bearer. No doubt he'd suggested the walk in order to examine our defenses, our precious bastions. It was quite clear that Verboom would be calculating information that would be worth a score of regiments. I at least had to rebel against the idiocy of the government and its good manners.

There he was, not even in chains, measuring out the distances between the walls, their thickness and height and the depth of the moat. The best place for a huge, threatening Attack Trench. Verboom was the spy who took the fewest risks in all of history—they couldn't arrest him because he was arrested already; he was living as his enemies' guest, and they were blithely showing him whatever he wanted to see. We were right at the foot of the Saint Clara bastion. Only a few dozen meters away was my home, the home I shared with the kids, with Amelis.

I hurled myself against the Antwerp butcher one more time. This time I was restrained less subtly. I was so furious that I smashed in two or three noses. Eventually, they knocked me down with their rifle butts, to the laughter of Verboom, who spoke in French so that the guards should not understand him: "*L'homme avisé est toujours sur ses gardes même quand il se trouve emprisonné."* A watchful man is on his guard even when he is a prisoner.

It was a line from Livy, I think, often cited in Bazoches, I'm sure, in which the word "asleep" had been changed to "a prisoner." My own side was beating me, and he had the luxury of standing there laughing. Always the same, going around in spirals like a Venetian dream: Whenever I confronted the Dutch sausage-maker, there would be a screen of authority figures stepping between us who were entirely incapable of understanding why it was necessary to eradicate him from the world.

I spent the night in a dingy cell, partly underground, surrounded by whores, drunks, thieves, and other riffraff. Verboom spent two years as a captive in Barcelona. And there wasn't one day or one night when he didn't sleep in a bed that was fluffier than that of most Barcelonans, and when he didn't eat better than we did, too. The Red Pelts suckled him with our blood, kept him in silk and cotton. Just as I was saying: We brought the serpent's egg into our home and lulled it gently until the viper was born.

While I was being beaten and arrested, Nan and Anfán made their way calmly back to our home in La Ribera. My absence was not in the least bit strange, as I might have gone off to the tavern for a while, or anywhere. But at dinner, Amelis asked after me.

"The captain gave him a beating, and he's in jail," replied Anfán, eating his soup without a pause. "He gave us a speech about honesty, and the effect of speaking well, and the uselessness of violence when there is no just cause for it. Then he saw an unarmed gentleman who was a prisoner and went off and started punching him. When they dragged him away, he was screeching like an animal, cursing the virgin, the government, and the idiot King Karl. I'm sure they'll hang him."

Ah, the candor of a child.

Another subject that occupied me during those days was the liberation of Don Antonio. Rescuing him from the claws of the Bourbons had become an obsession for me. You might say that securing his freedom was the only thing that remained of my engineer's spirit. Since I hadn't been able to get to The Word, at least Vauban's successor could be freed. That was my poor consolation. There were prisoner exchanges happening all the time, but there was little that a starveling like Martí Zuviría could do. I tried to take advantage of my tavern friendship with a Dutch agent who worked on exchange deals. He was always coming and going, crossing the lines, and anyone unaware of what he did never would have guessed that he was involved in such high-powered intrigues.

Prisoner exchanges were a kind of cross between a game of chess and a secret auction. A colonel was worth three captains; three colonels could get you a general; and you could round up by offering amounts in hard cash. Meanwhile, both sides had an interest in recovering their most valuable technicians (like the swine Verboom, whom I wouldn't have given back until I'd ripped out his tongue and his eyes—it still makes me crazy to think of how foolish we were). The process of negotiation was a torturous one, because nobody wanted to acknowledge the real value of their best-loved pieces, nor reveal what they'd be prepared to pay for them.

In the middle of 1712, Don Antonio de Villarroel had been a prisoner for a year and a half. It was an outrage that a soldier of his caliber should be in enemy hands for so long. I bought the Dutchman all the drinks I could, to try to exert my influence, and to coax some information out of him. But the man was an artist in the ways of "mini-diplomacy," as he called it. Whenever the subject of Don Antonio arose, he would give a little laugh. The only stories I could get out of him were contradictory ones.

"The problem with Villarroel," he sometimes said, "is that he's too good a general. There's a rumor that they've been tempting him with the offer of a good position in Philip's army. But Villarroel is resisting them. They say he has unhappy memories of the Bourbons and wants nothing more to do with them. To tell the truth, I don't really understand. After all, he's served the Two Crowns in the past. He could go back to the Bourbon side unblemished, since his enlisting in King Carlos's army was entirely legal. As for the Bourbons themselves, they aren't stupid: They don't want to release him if it will restore his talents to the enemy."

Other times, however, he would smack his lips and offer a quite different version. "Your poor general has an enemy back home. The government is not choosing to prioritize his exchange, so he will rot in captivity."

When I started to get worked up, the Dutchman would shrug. "Tell me," he would say. "On this subject, King Carlos is very much led by his counselors. These things don't get decided without the blessing of the Generalitat. And the government isn't interested. They say Villarroel 'isn't one of us.'"

To what could they be referring? Well, no man is ever free of his past. In Barcelona, the fall of Tortosa had stung, and very badly, and they remembered that it was Don Antonio who had led the final assault that took the city by storm for the Bourbon forces. Besides, he wasn't Catalan.

I was in such a bad mood in those days that my domestic relationship with Amelis was getting worse. We couldn't have a meal in the same room without an argument breaking out. Or worse still, there would be a long, tense silence that hurt everybody. It moved me to see Anfán and Nan suffer. They looked at us with the expectant gaze of someone who doesn't want a fight but cannot say so.

Until one night Amelis said to me, "You can stop growling, complaining, and sniffing the air as though everything smelled rotten. Your little general is free."

I was flabbergasted. "How do you know?" I asked.

"What difference does it make?"

"Is it anything to do with his exchange?"

She replied with the cruelest, most mocking tone of voice she could, emphasizing every word: "Yes, 'course it is! Your fucking *Mystère* asked me for it."

I couldn't coax any more out of her.

However it had come about, at the end of 1712, Don Antonio was at last exchanged. The bad part was that Verboom got his freedom, too. The negotiations happened in secret, and I assumed that the Antwerp butcher had been included in the contingent that was exchanged. He left fatter than when he'd arrived, and his head filled with data. I don't like to brag of my skills as a prophet, but facts are facts: The first thing he did when he got back to Madrid was to write a thorough account of the city's defenses. As for Don Antonio, he naturally took the road in the opposite direction: from Madrid to Barcelona. He was offered a post as a cavalry general, which he finally accepted.

He was a man who had always worn tragedy engraved on his brow. I believe he took on the new charge for the simple reason that there was nothing else he could do. He was a career soldier; the army was his life. Why had he spurned the last, generous offer he had received from Philip V? Pride, perhaps. Don Antonio was a very Spanish man. You know how it is, that lofty idea of pride, so very Castilian, constantly at the crossroads between utter heroism and the most sublime stupidity.

10

Meanwhile, there were things happening far beyond our horizons that would overturn the war entirely, bring fate into our lives, and place me—contrary to all my predictions—face-to-face with The Word itself.

In 1711 a scrawny young lad by the name of Pepito died. A devastating attack of smallpox, and straight off to the grave with him. His death caused the war to take a dramatic turn and condemned all Catalans to perpetual slavery. You'll be wondering how it's possible that such a banal event, a simple death from smallpox, could have had such decisive effects. Well, due to the fact that this particular sickly lad, this Pepito, was Joseph I, the young emperor of Austria and brother to King Charles. With Pepito dead, the Austrian throne came into Charles's hands; he still had aspirations to reign over all Spain and was now the emperor of the Germanic Holy Roman Empire. As you will recall, the war had started because England was against the dynastic union between France and the Spanish empire. London would never countenance the creation of such a strong continental power; hence their support for Charles as an alternative to Little Philip. But the solution they had imagined created a new problem, with Charles uniting Spain and Austria under a single scepter, thereby threatening to create a kingdom that was every bit as powerful as anything they'd feared. In other words, the situation that had triggered the conflict in the first place was simply shifting position.

Pepito's death sealed our condemnation. On that very day, England's diplomats began to look for a negotiated solution to the situation. And—just look how things turn out—this time they really did find their solution in a trice: Charles was to renounce the Spanish throne and remain in Vienna forever; Little Philip, in turn, should renounce his claims to the French succession (in the event of the Beast's death) and stay in Madrid forever. War over. Move along, please, nothing to see here.

France dragged its heels, but it was exhausted; Charles objected, but his heart wasn't really in it. Without military support from England, and especially without her financial backing, he wouldn't be in a position to keep fighting for long, not as much as three months. So everybody accepted the English proposal, more or less. From then on, it was only a matter of haggling and pinning down the minor details.

And the Catalans? Surely you're joking! Neither Charles nor the English deigned to inform the authorities in Barcelona. As you can imagine, even the Red Pelts would have expressed some outrage! And so our Miquelets went on dying in the mountains, our citizens went on paying exorbitant taxes to support a war they could never conclude, and all the while our own king was digging our grave. Diplomatic negotiations move slowly, all the more so when you've got a world war involved, and between 1711 and 1713, the Catalans kept on fighting, like dumb pawns, for a king who had already sold them out to their executioner.

I can't help a brief digression here. The chroniclers have written that Pepito died from smallpox, a story I've always thought sounded rather fishy. There's no such thing as a single victim of smallpox; either you've got an epidemic or there's no smallpox. Imagine the coincidence that it should be Pepito, of all the people in Vienna, who was the only person to contract the illness.

Relations between the two brothers had been sour for some time. Out of fraternal solidarity, Pepito had been spending vast sums on a distant war, and he was as fed up with the conflict as all the other chanceries in Europe. According to what I heard from an old Viennese courtier, the final letters that Pepito sent Charles took this tone: "My dear brother Karl, enough of this endless war! So the Catalans love you and the Castilians hate you? Well, how would this be for a solution—how about Philip as king of the Castilians and you as king of the Catalans?"

The fact that this option was not merely a comment between brothers but an official policy was demonstrated by the fact that all the Austrian newspapers published the proposal as a definitive solution. Charles didn't think the idea was the least bit funny, and he sent the next letter to his brother via an agent who put arsenic under his fingernails. Smallpox! What do you think, my dear vile Waltraud? Did he kill him like Cain killed Abel? Well, shut up, then, your opinion isn't worth a damn anyway.

Where were we? Oh yes, Charles being named the new emperor of Austria. He packed his bags and raced over to Vienna for the coronation ceremony. He left his little queen—now also the empress of Austria—back in Barcelona as a pledge of eternal fidelity to the Catalans.

I say it again: An excess of civilization transforms upright people into simpletons. Because it was quite clear that Charles was never coming back and that the queen—who, to tell the truth, had been left as a political token—would use the first opportunity she got to follow him. She spent a year in Barcelona, yawning her way through the opera. And then, when the time looked right, a very goodbye to you! What still gives me shivers, and riles me no end, is the reason that the old tart gave for leaving. In her own words, she needed to go, owing to "the great matter of the hoped-for succession." In other words, that great matter was urging her to open her legs to her Charles, which was much more important than the destiny of an entire nation.

Now, would you like to guess what the Red Pelts did when Charles's little queen announced her noble reasons for leaving us in the lurch?

They let her go without a word of complaint! Those very men, the Red Pelts, the gents of the noble ruling class! The only card that a nation without a king might be able to play; the final guarantee that an entire country would not be disemboweled alive. And they waved it goodbye with full honors! The entire government went off to the docks, and the only thing they cared about was getting a place near the queen so as to be seen during the farewell.

Let me tell you what they *should* have done! They should have sent a sealed letter to Vienna swearing that we were going to put Her Majesty in the room with all the rats, and that she wouldn't change her petticoat until Charles had worked European diplomacy to achieve every political, diplomatic, and military guarantee that Catalonia would remain free and safe. But that was not how it happened; the Red Pelts were too civilized for that. The world was going to slit our throats, and they were busy fretting about powdering their wigs!

With his hands free now, Charles signed the ominous Treaty of Evacuation with the Bourbons. According to its terms, the Allies were to withdraw all the troops they still had on the peninsula, that is, in Catalonia, which was the only territory under their control. From then on, things happened fast. When the queen fled to Vienna, the post of viceroy of Catalonia was filled by an Austrian soldier, Marshal Starhemberg.

It was on Starhemberg's shoulders that the burden fell of carrying out the most heinous and monumental mass execution in recent times. Early in 1713, the drama was ready to come to a head, all the cogs in the machine set for the sky to fall in. All that was needed was for the lever to be activated. And Starhemberg was that lever.

The Beast and the Allies had formalized their agreement behind the scenes. The messenger arrived in Barcelona: Starhemberg should order and direct the evacuation of all Allied troops from Catalonia. Dutch, Germans, and Portuguese boarded the English fleet anchored at Barcelona. Didn't this mean handing over this most faithful of countries to slaughter and butchery? Of course it did. And so what? *It is not in the interest of England to preserve the Catalan liberties.* Nor their lives.

Just imagine the astonishment of the Barcelonans when the news was made public. At first no one wanted to believe it. A wave of fatalism silenced every soul. On streets and in taverns, the inevitable was being discussed, and drunks sang the most gruesome ditties:

> *The Portuguese have signed the deal!*
> *The Dutch will soon comply.*
> *The English up and left us here . . .*
> *It's time for us to die.*

The walls of Barcelona were covered in posters, some of them of the very blackest humor:

The Comedy of Evacuation

DRAMATIS PERSONAE

Spain, as the friar's ass; our freedoms, as a toilet
brush; slavery in a number two role; and all the Allies
playing the part of shit.

The positions, titles, and boons that Charles had signed lost all their value overnight. There was one clown who would go around ringing a bell, throwing confetti over passersby, shouting: *Es venen senyories a preus d'escombaries!* Titles for sale, at the price of wastepaper!

The thing is, sarcastic humor has always helped people keep control of their fear. One day I ran into Nan and Anfán very close to our home, in the popular Plaza del Born, where they were acting as street performers. The dwarf was performing in the nude—if you don't count the funnel on his head—like a deformed Adam. He had bent his left leg back as though he were one-legged. He had tied a ham bone to his knee, extending the apparently mutilated leg. From the front, he looked like a creature with a pig's leg and trotter. He was using a penknife to scratch the bare bone in search of the last little bits of flesh. He was feigning terrible pain, and as he swallowed the minuscule pieces of ham, he seemed to be weighing the pleasure he got from tasting it against the torture he was inflicting on himself. Meanwhile, Anfán walked among the spectators, holding out an open bag, asking for contributions, and singing a little rhyme that was very popular in those days: *Entre Carlos tres i Felip cinc, m'han deixat ab lo que tinc!* Between Charles number three and Phil number five, they've left us with barely enough to survive!

Ah, laughter, that great outlet for fear, which buries it but does not drive it away. Because the third phase is terror.

Terror arrived in the city like the plague, brought in by travelers. Everyone fleeing from the interior of Catalonia converged at Barcelona. And whenever they came in through the city gates, the Barcelonans would pounce on them, questioning them about what was happening inland. They always gave the same answer: "All the horizons are on fire."

And it was true. If a place did not surrender at once, it was blasted by cannon fire and attacked by the cavalry. The Bourbon columns that had followed the Allies in our retreat were not content with riding into the towns and cities. They demanded that the mayors come out to meet them and offer their submission.

Terror can play out in opposing reactions. Submission to the threat, most commonly. But sometimes, just occasionally, it incites a mood as uncommon as it is dangerous: collective rage.

The last columns of Allied soldiers retreating toward the coast were no longer being begged to stay; the civilians threw stones at them. The height of indignation came when proof emerged that there was treachery in addition to desertion—not only were they going, but as they beat their retreat, the Allies had handed the keys to cities and strongholds to the Bourbon commanders!

In the closing days of June 1713, Barcelona was seething with indignation. People are not stupid; they know full well whom to blame for their misfortunes. Hundreds of furious people gathered outside the residence of Viceroy Starhemberg and stuck chicken talons and feathers to the door. They were wrong in one respect: Starhemberg was no chicken, nothing of the kind, just as executioners are neither cowardly nor brave; they are simply despicable.

The Red Pelts came to ask him for an explanation as to why the Allies were retreating, why they were abandoning defenseless cities to such a cruel enemy, and finally, what Charles meant to do to prevent the execution of an entire population who had been faithful to him ever since the war started.

Starhemberg's answer should go down in the history of cynicism: "My finest feelings and affection are with you, Excellencies."

And he left. That same afternoon he climbed into his coach, leaving through the back door, on the pretext that he was off on a hunting party. He never came back. The truth was that he had gone to join the Allied troops who were about to embark at the mouth of the Besòs River, to the north of the city. The English fleet was there to prevent trouble in case of altercations in the port of Barcelona. Our loyal allies!

They say that Starhemberg did not even resign his post as viceroy. It's hard to imagine any greater ignominy. Even men condemned to death are allowed to receive extreme unction.

And while our allies were departing, leaving us on the palisades, and the Bourbon columns made their implacable approach toward Barcelona, what did the Red Pelts decide to do? Nothing. Even as Starhemberg was packing his bags, up till the very last moment, they were still sending him dispatches for signature. According to their twistedly legalistic logic, that Austrian vulture was still viceroy. The machinery of state really ought to keep up appearances. The fact that Starhemberg was in league with the enemy, that he was handing over our homes and our freedom, well, heavens, that hardly seemed important!

Among the Allied regiments boarding ships were a few Catalans, though not many, who in their day had been enlisted in Charles's imperial army. They weren't Miquelets, halfway between hell and the law, merely men who wanted to make careers in a regular army. They knew exactly what was going on. They weren't at the heart of government, they didn't have daily dealings with the executive and their elevated politics, and yet they understood what was up and to whom they owed their fidelity. Right up until the final day, there were men who abandoned the ranks of the Allied forces, even some who leaped overboard from ships to head for Barcelona. Starhemberg exceeded mere rigor, ending up in cruelty: He gave orders that deserters should be executed, when the truth was that throughout the whole war, he had been quite unenthusiastic in his pursuit of deserters. And so our most generous young lads were left hanging from trees, dotting the path of retreat, and all the while the Red Pelts were bowing down before these boys' murderer.

Toward the end of 1713, the Red Pelts decided to call the Catalan parliament. They were so disconcerted at the situation that the session could be summarized in one single point: How to face the Bourbon advance, submit or fight?

I should clarify that our parliament was divided into three groups, or branches: One was made up of the nobility; the second represented the common people; and the third, inevitably, consisted of the cockroaches from the Vatican.

As for you, woman, you are not to interrupt me or correct me when I pick on the priests! I'm perfectly aware of what I'm saying, and I'm going to speak my mind.

I am not saying that all priests are bad people. It's not that. During the siege, you could see certain priests who were thinner than cypresses, fragile as glass, still and impassive as they faced enemy fire. With no earthly possessions but their cassock, they had bullets buzzing past their ears and they remained imperturbable on their knees, administering the sacrament to the dying on the front line. Their bishops, however, were like the Red Pelts, but black. You need only to look at the behavior of the cardinal and bishop of Barcelona himself, the wretched Benet Sala.

On the first day of discussion, the secretary to the parliament asked the ecclesiastical branch their view. As theirs was the smallest group of the three, it seemed logical that this should be cleared up before the others. Their answers were evasive. Not a yes, not a no. They just contended theological abstractions, according to which war is itself a bad thing, and when it breaks out between Christians, the good Lord weeps blood.

A fine bunch of Philistines! To the best of my knowledge, the Vatican has blessed dozens of wars, and they have never been too bothered that people have died in them. What was more, up till now, for thirteen long years of world war, it had never for a moment occurred to them to think that war was a very unpleasant thing. And then came the knife in the back.

Benet Sala had a good pretext for leaving Barcelona. Around that time, he had been called to Rome. And in one of those ruses so very typical of the Vatican, he had coordinated with Starhemberg to set sail the same time as the Allied forces.

Suddenly, the Barcelonans found themselves abandoned by the army who had been protecting their bodies and, simultaneously, by the shepherd who was meant to be caring for their souls. Naturally,

Benet's aim was to demoralize the very Christian people to whom he owed spiritual service, so that they would waver, surrender, and go into the slaughterhouse as docile as lambs. When I die, I hope to be able to have a few words with Benet Sala. Because I have no doubt we will both roast in the cauldron of Pere Botero, that devil of legend, but I can swear that Sala will also be drowned in it, strangled by yours truly in the soup.

Meanwhile, in the city, emotions were running higher and higher. What happened next is hard to explain.

Religious expression has always been a good outlet for feelings of powerlessness. The streets were filled with processions praying for the city's salvation. They were an absolute nuisance, making trouble under our window day and night. While they were no more than murmuring crowds at first, their excitement grew with the city's. The procession that caused the greatest impact was the one made up of the dozen young women who went off on pilgrimage to the holy mountain of Montserrat in a quest for divine intervention. (Montserrat is a very curious mountain to the northwest of Barcelona. It looks like a blunt-edged handsaw, at the summit of which is kept a strange virgin with black skin.)

Call me an unbeliever, but processions made up of pretty young women with tight-fitting bodices do seem rather better attended than the ones with people in hoods flagellating themselves. That vision, at a certain moment, prompted a thought in the minds of the people: "Well, actually, now that we think about it, why do we have to put up with girls this delightful going off to be sacrifices?" And in that way, religious processions were transformed into proclamations of rejection of the surrendering of the city. Eventually, the cries for the city's saint, Saint Eulalia, were transformed into a clamor against Philip V.

And good old Zuvi? What was he up to while all these civic convulsions were going on?

What I was interested in, in those days, was reviving the legal case concerning my inheritance. I had plenty of free time and often stopped by the lawyers' offices. The only thing that occurred to me that might speed up the case was talking to Casanova himself—he was the lord and master of that office. Nothing doing. Casanova was never to be

seen there, and his employees just dizzied me with dispiriting circum-
locution. That Señor Casanova had a senior political position now and
couldn't offer me his support, that the courts were overflowing with
all this unrest, that this, that that, and the other. Other times the door
wouldn't open the whole day, so chaotic was everything. When that
happened, I'd be in a filthy mood. When I was arguing with some
pettifogging junior, I could always rail at him and get some of it off
my chest, even if it did no actual good. But what can you do with a
closed door? If they gave me a good brigade of sappers, I could storm
a twenty-bastion fortress in twenty days. But the house of a lawyer?
There was no point in even trying.

"Hey, Martí, want to see something fun?" Peret said one day.

The debates in parliament had started, and Peret had invited me to
attend.

"You're planning to go in?" I said scornfully. "There's a triple guard
on the door; the Plaza de Sant Jaume is full of hotheads. Can't you hear?"

Through our windows, we could hear the howling of the indignant
people as they gathered there.

"Just follow me and keep quiet. And put your Sunday clothes on."

I had nothing better to do, so I followed him. It took us some time
to get there, because Sant Jaume was indeed overflowing with a noisy
mob. They weren't revolutionaries, exactly; they weren't crowding up
against the doors and the guard. Their eyes were on the balcony. The
people didn't want to topple the government, they wanted to be led.
Their cry was: "The *Crida*! Publish it! Publish the *Crida*!"

By the *Crida*, they were referring to the legal call to arms. Only the
Crida had the sacrosanct power to call up Catalan adults in defense of
the country, and anyone who rose up without its support found himself reduced to a Miquelet—that is, an outlaw, however patriotic his
intentions may have been. That was why it was so important that it be
published according to legal procedure. And the raison d'être of the
Red Pelts was, naturally, to prevent it.

Peret walked me around the building to the door on Calle de Sant
Honorat, which was much narrower and more discreet. There he muttered a few words in the ear of the two soldiers who were standing

guard, and they let us in. I was surprised by the soldiers' attitude, at once complicit and suspicious.

"A certain gentleman has offered me some money in exchange for my support for the cause he is defending," Peret explained as we climbed the stairs.

The parliament was split into two opposing camps: those in favor of releasing the *Crida*, gathering an exclusively Catalan army and resisting, and those who would prefer us to submit ourselves to the approaching army of the Bourbons. As I have said, the Red Pelts had no interest in protecting the constitutions, and without a legal *Crida*, there could be no call to arms. So I followed Peret, and before I knew it, we were in the Chamber of Sant Jordi itself.

Imagine a large rectangular hall, high-ceilinged, with stone walls. Three of the walls were covered by grand chairs upholstered in velvet—red, naturally—in strictly kept rows. On the main table, there was nothing but a book of oaths and a small bell, all on top of a big crimson cloth. In theory, the bell was to begin and end different people's turns to speak. I say "in theory" because when debates became more heated, the speakers didn't care a fig for that bell.

On paper, the whole of the Catalan territory had the right to send representatives, which was impossible, when you bear in mind that three quarters of that territory was already occupied by the enemy. Things had moved into a new phase that day. With the voting rights divided out and all sewn up, both groups were concentrating on finding other ways of exerting pressure. Yes, you've guessed it: hiring mercenary throats to yell out their slogans and disturb the opposing speakers. Peret was a suitable candidate, because his age meant he could pass as an old patrician and because he would have sold his mother's grave for a dish of fried squid. And the Chamber of Sant Jordi was every bit as stormy as the country itself. Not everyone who was supposed to be there was there, and not everyone who was there was supposed to be. Many members were unable to attend (they had good excuses: they were rowing in galleys or hanging from trees); others had simply abandoned their obligations.

If I remember right, this great day was July 4 or 5, and it was hot as hell. The spokesman for the pro-submission band was one Nicolau de

Sant Joan. Before he started speaking, he was already being applauded. He urged people to be quiet. Solemnity was one thing, at least, he wasn't short of.

"When strength is lacking, the natural thing is to consider the moral impossibility of resistance against power. Christian law and the law of nature both teach us, and persuade us, not to expose to the ultimate rigors of war our temples, those people of vulnerable age, those people whose lives are devoted to God. The fury of military license is no respecter of churches; nor does it have consideration for those of tender years; nor does it leave intact the sanctuary of virginity."

At this point he was interrupted by a loud laugh. "Nor do we! Bring us a virgin, and we'll show you how it's done!"

It was Peret, of course. His impertinence, so inappropriate at that moment, confused Sant Joan. The Red Pelts were none too happy. "Rascals! Rebels! Silence!"

Sant Joan resumed his speech. "Our country finds itself between Castile and France; the ports to the sea, shut off by the French navy. As for the English, who have handed us over, we should feel apprehension and legitimate misgivings. So I ask you: Where does the king, our lord, have an army naval force superior to those two powers to bring us assistance? And even if they did arrive, what sums of money could he allocate to our aid, considering the war under way on the Rhine?"

"What we need are fewer rich people lining their pockets, and more *cojones*, you dunderhead!" shouted Peret. There were plenty of people behind him: "Boooo, boooo!"

"Enough! Rascals, rascals! Out of the hall! Out!"

Those words came from the Red Pelts' claque, who were stamping their feet and waving their arms around. To the Red Pelts, common people were little better than riffraff who served only to get in the way between their office and the wise decisions they made. But they forgot that not everyone of their class thought the same way. And among them, sticking out like a beacon anchored in a desert, was one Ferrer. Emmanuel Ferrer.

Ferrer was a member of the minor nobility, but very popular because of the way he had distinguished himself in the administration of the city. This human rat addressing you now may have as much the makings of a hero about him as a horseshoe, but that doesn't mean he can't recognize those qualities, in all their magnitude, when they appear over the horizon. Ferrer lived a comfortable, peaceful life; he was wealthy and he was happy. He had nothing to gain from voting for resistance, and everything to lose. As soon as he spoke, he would have committed himself openly to one side, and when the Bourbons arrived, they would come after him with all their despotic bile.

When his turn came, Ferrer stood up and said: "I have a question: Is Catalonia any different now from what she used to be? Do our laws and privileges not give us the ability to oppose the Castilians who want unjustly to oppress us? What reason does the Bourbon have for oppressing us so severely, wanting to make our open and free people into a nation that is subjugated and enslaved? So who could possibly agree to Castilian vanity and violence being enthroned over the Catalans, that we should serve in the same ignominy they force upon the Indians?"

"You're all crazy, irresponsible!" replied those on the side of the Red Pelts. "You're going to bring our whole nation to ruin!"

I should like to be impartial. I would never say that the noblemen who voted to submit were all corrupt. By no means. There were more than reasonable justifications for not offering resistance. We had been abandoned; we were being attacked by the entire might of the Two Crowns, the French and Spanish empires combined. Voting for a negotiated solution, however little we might expect from such a thing at this point, did not necessarily imply serving Little Philip.

Ferrer invoked the name of the king of Portugal, a kingdom that was fearful of following the Catalans down the same route and who surely would help us; if we resisted, Emperor Charles wouldn't be able to wash his hands of us without his international prestige being tarnished. England had signed a long-standing agreement; the Catalan ambassadors were traveling around all the courts of Europe arguing the case for a people who wanted nothing more than that most basic of rights: survival.

He was interrupted several times. Ferrer remained deaf to the voices of friends and enemies alike. He went over Catalonia's history, of the pernicious dynastic alliance with Castile, and continued: "For all these reasons, let us at once take up arms and raise our flags, let us enlist soldiers without a moment's delay. May the Fidelísimos Brazos Generales, our three honorable branches, use all the authority that God has placed in their hands; may they immediately draw up manifests to make our justice and our proceeding absolutely clear to all of Europe, and let our enemies discover to their cost that the spirit and honor of the Catalan nation has not declined a jot."

Deep down, though, not even Ferrer was very hopeful. It was such a desperate play that it could almost have been mistaken for a noble suicide.

"May our nation meet her end with glory," he went on, "for a glorious end is worth more than accepting demands and violence the likes of which even the Moors were never guilty of."

My dear vile Waltraud interrupts me here, raising her great head like a cow who can't find her pasture and asking, again and again, what my own opinions were at that time. They were not of the least significance, but very well, I shall summarize them.

My point of view sought to be as dispassionate as possible, and this was it: Both sides were right. To submit would mean losing the liberties that had ruled us for a thousand years, being transformed into one more province of Castile and its empire, sharing its people's yoke, suffering merciless repression. Resisting, as the Red Pelts kept proclaiming, meant ruin and massacre. We were faced with a choice between two options, each as bad as the other.

There was a vote. Submission won. By a sizable majority. Ferrer gave a leap, went over to the secretary with the small bell, and insisted that his name be noted, that there be a specific record of his vote against. It was like signing his own death warrant. When the Bourbons arrived, that would be evidence enough to hang him. And yet other nobles got to their feet and went to follow Ferrer's example!

I was amazed. Why would people do such a thing?

We ought to examine the other side of the coin, too. Just as admirable or even more so, strange though it may seem. Because there were noblemen like Francesc Alemany, Baldiri Batlle, Lluís Roger, or Antoni València, whose consciences led them to vote for submission, and so they did. Later, things would take a turn. And they fought. They followed the will of the majority, setting aside their personal opinions in favor of the general good. Waltraud asks me why I have tears in my eyes. I can tell you: because these men, who never chose resistance, fought unfaltering for a long year of siege. They acted in support of other people's ideas, even those people who were opposed to them. And at dawn on September 11, 1714, they sacrificed their lives. All of them. I can see València now, attacking a wall of bayonets, saber in hand, swallowed up by a sea of white uniforms.

To give you some idea of the significance of the resolution, I'd say that the noblemen's branch of the parliament was similar to that of the English lords. More important than the number of votes, it had an intangible moral weight, and it was very common that the people's branch simply ratified their decisions.

"It serves you right that your side lost," I said to Peret as we headed home. "Aren't you ashamed of having sold your opinion?"

"No, lad, not at all," he replied. "The Red Pelts paid me to join the claque in favor of submission, but they were foolish enough to pay up in advance."

"In any case, they're currently at two–zero," I snorted as we made our way across a packed Plaza de Sant Jaume. "Priest and nobility, in favor of submitting. Tomorrow the people's branch will follow the ruling from the nobles. It's over."

I have never been so wrong. We were still in the square when a spokesman came out onto the balcony and did indeed inform the crowd that the noble branch had voted for submission. It was as though a frozen downpour had fallen. No one objected. Of those thousand throats, not one rose up in an angry shout. But instead of going home, they continued to camp out where they were, there in the Plaza Sant Jaume!

In my opinion, that was the real turning point. Not an act of rebellion but a deaf noncompliance. The people down there were so disconcerted by what they had heard, just as the nobles up on the balcony were disconcerted by that mass stillness and silence. What could they do? They couldn't expel all those people. Nobody would dare, nor did they have enough troops to try. Besides, an act of violence like that could lead to just the kinds of disturbance that the Red Pelts were trying so hard to avoid.

That whole night nobody moved from the packed square. The following day, the people's branch of the parliament assembled. The atmosphere out on the street, and Ferrer's speech, had so fired them up that their vote went in favor of resistance, and by an overwhelming majority. This time the Plaza Sant Jaume did react, with an explosion of joy: "Publish the *Crida*! Publish it!"

There was so much shouting, and it was so passionate, that they were no longer merely expressing a desire. It was a threat and an order; fail to comply and anything could happen. And more of the noblemen changed their votes! But it didn't end there. The most intransigent of the Red Pelts placed a thousand legal obstacles in the way. They alleged that the branch of aristocrats had expressed the change in their intentions out in the corridor, not in a session that had been convened legally, and as such, it was not a binding decision. Their strategy, as it's not hard to deduce, consisted in drawing out proceedings for so long that the people outside grew tired and went home. They did not succeed. Two days and nights had gone by and the Plaza de Sant Jaume was as full as ever, or fuller. Generosity always has this bitter side to it; those most willing to give everything are those with the least to gain by a victory and the most to lose from a defeat. Over the course of those two days, the debates ran aground.

On July 9, Peret wanted to go back to the Chamber of Sant Jordi.

"Again?" I exclaimed. "I can't believe the pro-submission party has been so foolish as to pay out again to people who betrayed them at the last minute."

"No, lad, no—you see, I gave such a convincing performance the other day that now those on the side of resistance have offered me a bit of money to yell even louder."

"But the pro-submission party knows you; they'll stop you from getting in!"

"No, they won't, because I've informed the submitters about the offer from the resisters, and they promised me twice as much if we join the claque in favor of peace. I shall vote for submission. Long live peace! Want to come?"

When we went in, we found the Chamber of Sant Jordi a madhouse. The blessed altar of Catalan parliamentarianism transformed

into a grocer's store! As they were sitting in rows in front of one another, the yielders and the resisters were protesting, waving their hands
before them like the tentacles of an octopus. Those in favor of fighting
were shouting from their seats: "The constitutions and our freedom!
Let's draw up the *Crida*!"

"Peace and good sense!" came the reply from the other side.

Ha! As a spectator, I was getting irritated at the Red Pelts and
their oafish sycophants. Hadn't the vote gone for resistance despite
all their schemings? Well then, if that was the freely expressed will
of the people, the *Crida* would have to be drawn up. (As far as I was
concerned, this would mean dashing out of the city as fast as I could
go. No one needed to tell me, of all people, what a siege of such a big
stronghold would mean!)

"*Seny!*" yelled those who favored submission. "Have you lost it?
Seny!"

I should explain this *seny* business, the *seny* they were invoking. Isn't
that so, my dear vile Waltraud?

The Catalans are the world experts in useless spiritual inventions.
You might describe *seny* as an attitude of calm, reasonableness, peace-
fulness. In theory, when faced with a serious problem, a man who is
assenyat should react with a restraint altogether opposed to the chiv-
alrous passion of the Castilians. The problem was, there was an army
bearing down on us, and it was led by Castilian *hidalgos*. To their warrior mentality, *seny* was incomprehensible, a despicable trait of Jews and
hucksters who sought to resolve their differences with words because
they lacked the bravery to do it with swords.

As I said, the Chamber of Sant Jordi was overtaken by a cacophony
of roaring. The Red Pelts had kept two *coups de théâtre* for that final day.
They took the first one out of the grave.

An old nobleman, nearly blind, tottered into the chamber, one
hand on a stick and the other leaning on the arm of his great-grandson.
Did I say old? Ancient! He must have gotten up from bed at least four
times a night to pass water; and just think, I get up three times myself.

His name was Carles de Fivaller. As with those old senators from
the Roman republic, his moral potency came not so much from any
position as from his experience and the respect he had earned over a

long life of public service. Fivaller had an honorary seat in the chamber. Being such a wreck, he had not been present in any of the debates. But the Red Pelts had gone to fetch him out of bed, which he never left, to come in and advocate on behalf of *seny*.

There was something much more than a crooked old man entering the chamber. With Fivaller came Catalan parliamentarianism itself. Rather than taking his seat, Fivaller stopped in the exact center of the Chamber of Sant Jordi. Everybody knew his words would have a tremendous impact. Both sides stopped, reverent.

"My sons. The ruins of my age prevent me from being of use to my country," said Fivaller, looking around in the way the blind do, at everyone and no one, his chin up. "Which is why I beg, I implore, this august chamber to grant one final wish, which I hope will be granted me."

He had to stop to get his voice back. There was such silence that even the shameless Zuvi avoided swallowing so as not to make a sound.

Fivaller brought a trembling hand to his face to wipe away a tear and finally said: "Now that my hands can no longer bear the weight of a rifle, I ask you, please, in this fight we are forced into, to use my body to take the place of a *fajina* in the battle."

Oh, the cry that went up then! Unexpected joys are the noisiest kind of all. Even some of the Red Pelts were moved, giving in. Perhaps Fivaller wasn't quite so senile after all. Or so blind or so deaf. As he had crossed the Plaza de Sant Jaume, the square filled to bursting, he must have understood what was going on.

A subversive hand opened the balcony doors. Seeing them open, the people downstairs thought the matter had been decided: "The *Crida*! Announce the *Crida* once and for all!"

But the most inveterate Red Pelts still had one cartridge left. Together with their friends the Black Pelts, they had drawn up a list of theological-legalistic arguments. You can guess which way these were arguing.

Their Vatican eminences enjoyed considerable respect. They were perfectly capable of turning the tables. The nobles had already changed their minds once. Nothing prevented them from coming back. And a little sermon from the priests might be enough to make many delegates on the people's branch have a bit of a think.

In order to have the greatest impact, they decided that the text should be read by their most talented rhetorician, a marble Demosthenes. He was admired by those of his profession, the men at law, and he had only lately decided to enter politics. Well, this great man was none other than Rafael Casanova, the lawyer who was dealing with my house, and who now walked into the chamber wearing the long red gown of the Catalan magistracy.

"You!" I cried the moment I clapped eyes on him. I leaped up, and with three strides I was beside him. "Damn it, Casanova! I'm absolutely fed up! Do you hear? I put my father's inheritance in your hands! And I want the inheritance from my father! I have a right to it! Defend the damn thing once and for all!"

Since most of those present were educated people, when they heard "the inheritance from my father," they interpreted this as a reference to "the inheritance of our forefathers," a frequent theme of these debates. Those who were not yet on their feet were spurred on by my attack.

"The lad is right! Enough is enough! A hundred generations of Catalan heroes are looking down upon us from heaven. It's time we drew up the *Crida*!"

Despite the high passion, the two sides had been jeering from their seats. But now, following my example, dozens of people piled in around Casanova, either to rebuke him with me or to shield him from me. Casanova, losing his balance, tried to straighten his red velvet cap, but I got away from Peret, and from everybody who was getting in my way, and I went back to jostling him.

"But this is violence!" protested Casanova, like Caesar receiving the first stab wound.

"Violence my foot!" I cried, indignant. "We pay you to defend our interests, and all you do is fob us off!"

"He's right! Enough of this delay! The lad is right!" shouted all those opposed to submission. "We should be ashamed that we need a kid to show us the way. The enemy is approaching at a forced march, and we're wasting our time on useless debates!"

At this point, Emmanuel Ferrer took the initiative. And it was a shrewd, brilliant initiative, as he was the first person to notice that the decision was hanging by a thread, a thread that was within reach of only the boldest. He walked away from the commotion and over to the bespectacled secretary with the little bell, who had remained in his place, with a haggard expression, and ordered him, pointing a finger, imperiously: "Write!"

The man needed to choose between chaos and a firm guiding spirit. For a moment the secretary thought about it. Then he dipped his pen in the inkwell.

Ferrer dictated a few hurried lines. Before the ink had dried, Ferrer stamped it with the government seal, grabbed the piece of paper from the secretary, and raised it in the air, proclaiming: "The *Crida*! I have it!"

Debate over. Ferrer was lifted into the air and carried out into the street. Outside, he was given an ovation from the crowd, frenzied and ecstatic. I could see this all perfectly, because rather than following them out into the Plaza Sant Jaume, I stepped out onto the balcony.

I saw Ferrer carried aloft on someone's shoulders, showing the paper with the *Crida* to the crowd, who swirled around him like a wheel on its axis. I simply couldn't understand it: They were weeping for joy because now they could go to a desperate war.

All those people carried off Ferrer—or, rather, the *Crida*—plunging into the city streets. The square was left deserted, covered in debris after the prolonged encampment.

The mentality of your average Catalan shelters one single moral principle, which is as flawed as it is endearing: They are always certain of having right on their side. They aren't the only people to feel this way. What is extraordinary about the case of the Catalans, however, is what they deduce from this: Given that they are in the right, the world will end up realizing this. Naturally, things aren't like that. The movement of a train of artillery depends not on truths but on interests, and they are not up for debate: They impose themselves on you, they crush you.

I remember that there were just two sentences. The first of them, to my mind, being the most exquisite, limpid, and beautiful yet written in the Catalan language.

Having on this sixth day of the present month advised this city council to resolve to defend the Liberties, Privileges and Prerogatives of the Catalan people, which our ancestors gloriously achieved at the cost of their own blood, we shall on the ninth day of the present month make order of the public proclamation for our defence

Marshal Starhemberg was surprised to hear the call to arms when he was right on the beach, just about to set sail. From the mouth of the Besòs River, he could see Barcelona's western walls. He asked the reason for such a ruckus of shouts, drums, and trumpets. "A reckless enterprise," he said, apparently, "but brave."

He struck the ground twice with his walking stick and boarded his ship.

He ought to have formulated his words the other way around: a brave enterprise but reckless. And how! Or, rather, he should have said what he was really thinking: "You're staying here, poor bastards."

11

The historians tell us that at the start of the Third Punic War, the city of Carthage went through a military fever. All alone, with no friends and hurtling toward a certain end, the entire might of the Roman Empire was hurled upon them. And yet its citizens threw themselves into laboring for their defense with frantic ardor.

Something similar happened in Barcelona in 1713. A warrior passion overtook the whole city. The foundries beat out a frenzied rhythm. The workshops were turning out rifles, bayonets, projectiles of every size. Most surprising of all: The Barcelonans faced up to their dangers with a happiness that was quite in opposition to their circumstances. Children ran about the battalions, and—in an inversion of the natural order of things—women threw compliments to the soldiers.

There was a reason for this new mood. Barcelona's popular classes had always felt that dynastic war between Austrians and Bourbons was something basically apart from them. But now war was approaching their walls and threatening to destroy the regimen of freedoms they had maintained for as long as they had been Catalans.

I'd add one more thing besides: By attacking the Barcelona of people like Amelis, Philip V was committing the most unforgivable mistake a tyrant can make: attacking the houses of people who have no houses. They will defend home tooth and nail, for that is the final redoubt of those who have nothing else. My Amelis had spent her life as a wanderer, her sex as her only refuge, and now that she finally had a home, this lunatic despot was threatening to cut her future short. And not just my Amelis; Barcelona was the refuge for the dispossessed from all over. The place where they had at last found four walls and a wage. How many of the heroes born in our siege were foreigners! And now that all the doubts about whether the fight was just and necessary had been dispelled, Barcelonans of all kinds were throwing themselves into this war, their war, with the kind of revelry that doesn't happen even during carnivals. Just this once, rich and poor, men and women, were united in common cause. The happy were fighting for their happiness, while the unfortunate joined this common cause hoping that, in the struggle, their afflictions would disappear.

We should be impartial: Enthusiasm makes it impossible to see anyone but enthusiasts, and not everybody shared that uncommon euphoria. The indifferent, the fearful, the uncertain, the reluctant, even the occasional pro-Bourbon would keep quiet or hide themselves away, in the hope that times would change. But all the same, what a sense of unity! Fear is contagious—but hope is, too. Because a man like Zuvi, whose senses were so alert, couldn't but be moved when his Bazoches eyes fell on the smiles of the poor, the wretched, the hungry who—at last—had found a cause to give their whole lives meaning.

Nobody could be more aware than a Bazoches student of how miraculous such a transformation is. Those of us in the business of war, who end up wedded to violence, have always been a tiny minority. In normal conditions, you don't see anyone bearing a rifle. Actually, human beings are such cowardly creatures that for the most part, they aren't prepared to risk their lives, even if it's in order to save them.

One of the days of greatest jubilation was when the reluctant rich abandoned the city. The wealthiest, as one might imagine, didn't want anything to do with that madness. They'd rather get to the Bourbon lines and throw themselves on Little Philip's mercy. He wouldn't deny them. The rich are always welcome.

They gathered in a convoy, like a herd finding safety in numbers. What exactly were they afraid of? The government of Red Pelts had always protected them. They were abandoning their civic obligations; it was public knowledge that they were thinking about heading to the town of Mataró, a well-known refuge for *botifleros*. And after they were gone, the Red Pelts did not expropriate their homes—inexplicably— but posted guards outside to prevent them from being looted.

On the day of their flight, their opulent carriages gathered on Calle Comerç. Since the convoy had been preannounced, the people were congregating along the roads that led out of the city, jeering and bombarding the vehicles with rotten vegetables. Those crowding onto the balconies scoffed at them and mocked them. But that was all. No acts of violence, nothing more than sarcasm and blackening potatoes launched at the wigs of the poor coachmen. Had the situation been reversed, the Bourbons would not have hesitated to resort to summary executions.

I happened to meet the convoy in its slow progress. The city's children were using their whole repertoire of taunts on it, which could be tremendous. But the whole thing was a social act in which the festive prevailed over the punitive, and there was three times as much laughter as there was insult.

I was filled with sorrow. Those people fleeing were going to be spared an imminent terrible siege, and I and mine should have been in those carriages, those life rafts amid the shipwreck. All of a sudden I noticed the last carriage stopping beside me.

"Martí!" I heard my name being called. "Well, if it isn't you, Zuviría's son!"

It was Joaquim Nadal, the richest investor in my father's company. When he saw me, he ordered his coachmen to stop his carriage. He opened the door and leaned halfway out and said: "What are you still doing here? Come on, get in! You can see my carriage is the last. What luck I spotted you, lad!"

When he saw that I was hesitating, he looked at me, confused. Carrots and turnips bounced off the roof of the vehicle. "*Botifleros, botifleros!*" cried the crowd. "*Foteu el camp!* Bugger off!"

Nadal insisted: "Come on, kid! What's up with you? This is your last chance. Come with me, or you're staying here at the mercy of this rabble."

I excused myself and said politely: "But this isn't rabble, Señor Nadal. They are the same people they always were; they're our neighbors."

He stared at me as though I were a lunatic. "I see," he said thoughtfully, as vegetables continued to rain down, and after a moment he said again, "I see." He closed the door and told the coachmen to drive on.

That night, at home, Peret spent dinner praising the new battalions and their banners, which had been blessed in church. Some of the units were in blue uniforms, while others wore the most beautiful garnet. There were even some as yellow as lemons. When he started talking wonders about the works that had been carried out on the city walls, I could no longer contain myself. I interrupted him so sharply that he did indeed shut up.

"Has the entire city lost its mind?" I protested to him and Amelis. "Dreamers like you haven't the slightest idea of what's happening on the other side of the Pyrenees. None at all!" I banged the table. "How many Catalans are there in the world? Half a million, give or take a few. There are more people living in Paris alone. The French are born with a bayonet under their arm; they are the most aggressive people in the world. And they're heading this way, the army of the Spanish empire reinforced by battalions from France. And we have been abandoned by all our allies—all of them! Oh, well, that's just splendid!" I exclaimed, applauding my own sarcasm. "So, now tell me: If the city arms itself and closes the door, can you imagine for one moment what the consequences of such lunacy would be? Spain can devastate the city by land and France by sea, but I'm not going to let them destroy my house."

An uncomfortable silence fell. I didn't expect Amelis to be the one to speak. Quietly, in a voice that for her was unusually subdued, she asked: "And if the city were to give itself up, would everything be all right then?"

I rubbed the back of my neck and answered: "I don't know. No one can know. That's why we're going to go. The five of us. You, me, Nan, Anfán, and Peret. We'll come back when things have calmed down. It's decided."

I expected an argument, shouting, but they offered neither dissent nor agreement. Amelis shut herself up in the bedroom. Peret wandered over toward the fireplace, rekindled the fire, and started to roast peppers. Their docile behavior made me feel empty inside, as though I were throwing punches at the air. I followed Amelis and closed the bedroom door behind me.

"Anfán's only a boy," I said. "Nan is such a troubled little fellow. Peret has only ever left the city to go out on *chocolatadas*. But you know as well as I do what the advance of the Bourbon army really means. You've seen the woods filled with hanged men, the outrages perpetrated in the occupied towns. If I enlist, you know what difference there'll be between your destiny and mine?" Before she could answer, I announced, "I'll just be killed."

If she had only resisted or replied. Whenever that particular sadness of hers took her over, I was rendered speechless. It was as though she were crying on the inside and I could not dry her tears.

She walked over to the music box and opened it. She looked up at the sky through our glass skylight and said: "Very well, you're in charge. We'll go. But tell me, Martí—where? The whole country's at war. Are we going to set sail for Naples? And once we get there, what then? There's war in Italy, too. Are we going to Turkey? Farther still?"

"No," I replied, "there's no need. We just have to get to Mataró. It's not two days' walk from here."

"With the *botifleros*?"

There was no recrimination in her tone, but that didn't stop me from feeling insulted. "With people who want nothing to do with any of this!" I replied.

"And how do you know they won't attack Mataró? The pro-Austrians, the Bourbons, the Miquelets. And if, somehow or other, pro-Austrians do win the war, how will we come back to Barcelona then? Every finger will point at us and call us traitors." Her gaze still fixed on the skylight, Amelis went on: "I told you I used to live by following armies on the march. I lied. It's the armies who have always followed me. I lost my virginity to a French soldier when I was thirteen. I bled for eight days. On the ninth, there was a Spanish captain. The ones who came afterward, I don't remember too well, I don't want to. A lot of Miquelets. At least they would give me something to eat after doing it. After that, I just wandered." She looked around her. "I've never had a home."

For the first time since I'd come into the room, she looked at me, very sad. "Let's go, then, Martí. But just tell me: Where? Where?"

I couldn't bear that she agreed with me: Whenever she did, it disarmed me. As for me, the question I was asking myself was a different one. What right did a king have to change my life? Anyway, what did I really care about in this insignificant life, this paltry crumb of *le Mystère*?

The thing I most loved in the world was the sight of Amelis getting out of bed every morning, naked, squatting down over the washbasin to clean herself. Her black hair fell as far as her nipples. She always parted her knees wide. And she used a lot of water, perhaps because the place between her legs was the refuge for a thick black bush. From bed I would watch her, and we'd exchange a smile. Despite all my woes and all my impudence, nobody had the right to interrupt that sequence of everyday actions that allowed me to recognize happiness. Nobody.

A sigh. I raised four fingers till the tips touched the glass of the skylight. What would Ten Points have said? "Once you have grazed this sky with your fingers, you will never want to pull your hands back again." There are moments when life positions us in just the right place where morality and necessity converge. Why would anyone decide to tackle a fight that would be desperate and fatal? For eternal glory? For the perpetual comfort of the human race? No, my friend, not that. *Le Mystère* has already told me.

People allow themselves to be killed at Thermopylae for an apartment with a skylight.

Having served under Don Antonio, I didn't find it hard to secure an audience with him. Because, unbelievable though it may sound, the

Red Pelts had chosen him as commander in chief of our forces. An unexpected decision. There were two other candidates from older families who were, thank God, rejected. They were Catalans, they had no shortage of military experience, and naturally, their titles in the nobility surpassed Don Antonio's—he was, as we know, a Castilian national, born to our sworn enemies. Why, then, did they choose Villarroel? Your guess is as good as mine. Perhaps, out-and-out defeatists that they were, the Red Pelts were not all that optimistic and wanted to avoid one of their own being responsible for the disgrace of the inevitable disaster. Or perhaps the reason was simply that he was the best of the best, and having the option to choose such a competent general, even they could not deny him the position.

In truth, I approached his office with a mixture of contradictory feelings. My dear vile Waltraud asks me how it's possible that I had never paid him a visit, given that he had been free for a year. The answer is very simple: because my joy at his return was combined with my shame at having abandoned him right before his capture.

He offered me a seat and was polite to me, too polite. In Don Antonio, this was not a good sign. Why? Well, because he was never, not ever, agreeable to those under his command.

"I am most grateful for your offer," he said at last. "But I am going to turn it down."

I stopped, frozen. Had we not shared the 1710 Retreat? Had I not proved my worth as an engineer? Within Barcelona's walls, there were few qualified engineers. Did he not think me competent, as he had three years earlier, and then out in the open?

"Of course I do. Despite your youth, as an engineer, you have mastered techniques that are unprecedented and always effective."

"But?"

He thought for a moment before answering in that booming voice of his: "I'm turning you down because you don't have what you need to have."

I wanted to throw some punches, to take it out on the walls. Naturally, I asked what he was referring to.

"Our last conversation, in Illueca," he said. "I offered you the chance to leave, and you left."

"That's right, Don Antonio," I replied, offended. "But it was you, as I recall, who offered me the chance to run away."

"Indeed. And so you fled with no dishonor. But that's just it. If you had stayed, your captivity would have been glorious."

I saw red. "Oh, for the love of God, Don Antonio! What use would it have been if they'd captured me? I still think it was a mistake for you to allow yourself to be taken prisoner, thereby depriving the army of your skills as a commander."

He smiled. "Come now, Zuviría, be honest with yourself. Your flight wasn't motivated by rationality but selfishness. You weren't driven by your love for life but your fear of death."

"They were just a little band of cripples!" I protested. "And do you want to know something sad, Don Antonio? When I got back to Barcelona I went for help. Well, nobody wanted to listen to me, no one in the army even remembered the wagons that you and I had been escorting. The worst thing of all is that they might have been right: Four wagons of invalids were not going to win the war."

"You see," he interrupted me. "You served under my command, but you understood nothing, nothing at all."

I was so hurt that I didn't say a word. I got up and walked toward the door.

Looking back now, from so many years later, I think Don Antonio had set up the whole scene. Because when I already had my hand on the doorknob, he said: "One word. If you'd said just one word in Illueca, I would consider you an engineer."

I stopped. One word. Perhaps on some binge, drunk on cheap booze, I had confessed my tragedy to Don Antonio. One word! In any case, that phrase set my insides on fire. I turned—furious—and banged my fists down on his oak table.

"Everyone in this city has gone mad!" I cried. "Everyone! Every person from the council down to the last beggar is supporting a defense that is idiotic! I've fought against the opinions of my family, of my friends, of my neighbors. And now that they've finally persuaded me to take part in this preposterous defense, here you are—you of all people—refusing to enlist me. No! You have no right to do this! This is my city, it's my home, and you are going to let me into your fucking army whether you like it or not!"

He allowed me to vent for a while, and when I was out of breath from all those words, he said: "That's already an improvement. At least it's some progress." After a pause, he added: "I told you in Illueca, son. The war is not yet over, and nor are your tribulations."

That night, at home, we had a goodbye dinner to bid farewell to peace. At least to the fake peace the city had been living through over the past few years. When we reached dessert, I called for a minute of everyone's attention.

"After some tough negotiating with Don Antonio, he has bestowed the rank of lieutenant colonel upon me. Did you hear that? You're talking to a lieutenant colonel, so from now on, I'll expect you to address me with appropriate respect! The youngest lieutenant colonel in the army! And that's not all. My pay will increase by ten percent, because in addition, he has hired me as his own private aide-de-camp." I couldn't help a smile of triumph. "What do you think?"

"A lieutenant colonel!" cried Amelis. Though she then asked: "So what's one of those?"

"You see, my love," I explained between puffs on the cigar I was smoking, "in an army, the rank immediately below a general is a colonel, who leads a regiment. A lieutenant colonel is an officer pending the assignment of his own regiment. Do you understand?"

"So you don't have your own regiment yet?"

"Well, no," I confessed. "But what does that matter?"

Anfán was sitting beside me. He tugged on my sleeve and asked: "*Jefe*, how many soldiers do you command?"

"None in particular," I replied. "I will be taking charge of higher matters. The reality is that I will be working as an engineer. But Don Antonio, valuing me so highly, believed I ought to have a rank fitting with my authority, to carry more weight among the soldiery."

"Well, I think it's a pretty shitty rank if you aren't commanding any soldiers, *jefe*," Anfán concluded.

"I'll be earning twenty-six pesos a month!" I announced very proudly. "That's without counting the extra ten percent as aide-de-camp."

At this point Peret intervened: "So tell us, Martí, this aide-de-camp thing, what exactly does it mean?"

"I've told you, it means I'll be completely available to Don Antonio for any crisis or anything that happens to come up. He values me very highly!"

"So you mean you'll be Villarroel's errand boy." He burst out laughing. "You've allowed yourself to be duped. Your working day is going to be twice as long, if not more."

"In exchange for which you've only got another ten percent," Amelis pointed out. "Some negotiator you are!"

They had succeeded in casting gloom over my mood. "You're right, maybe I'm not the best businessman in the world!" Like anyone who finds himself at a loss for an argument, I resorted to patriotism. "But when the enemy is approaching, we shouldn't lower ourselves to pecuniary baseness."

"What color will your uniform be?" asked Amelis.

"None. I won't have one. In practice, as I said, I'll be working as an engineer. And the engineer corps are not required to be in uniform."

"Not required to be in uniform!" exclaimed Peret, laughing. "Have you ever heard of a general who is—as you put it—*not required* to wear a uniform? You haven't even gotten them to pay for one of those for you!"

They were ruining my party, the lot of them. This wasn't the triumphal march I had been expecting.

Peret asked: "And your name will be signed up to the lists of which regiment?"

"Signed up?"

"Yes, man, on the payroll of which regiment?"

I gave a dismissive wave of the hand holding my cigar and said: "Oh, I don't need to be troubling myself with those little details. Don Antonio is the most honest man in the city. It's inconceivable that he would not make sure I appear on somebody's payroll."

"Very well," Peret insisted, "but in which regiment?"

"I don't know!" I gave up, cornered and deep down rather annoyed at myself for not being able to give a different answer. "When I was in France, I learned to build, defend, and attack bastions. Nobody taught me what kind of bureaucratic paperwork is required by rearguard secretaries!"

"Fantastic!" They all roared with laughter, including the dwarf. "They aren't buying you a uniform, and you'll be spending your days racing this way and that. You're a lieutenant colonel, which is a provisional rank; you have no provisional regiment, and you don't know which one you might have."

"Very well!" I said, defending myself. "I think I remember Villarroel saying something about an imperial regiment. He has already sent letters to Vienna asking for confirmation of his own position and, while he was at it, doubtless asking for me to be enlisted in one of Charles's units. We can take that for granted. Do you think the emperor isn't going to listen to the request of his only general in Spain?"

This time the laughter was so thunderous that the neighbors banged on the walls in complaint.

"But how very stupid you are, Martí! That's not how things work. If they sign you up to an Austrian regiment, it'll be months before you get your rank recognized. And now you're being paid out of Vienna, not Barcelona. Until the imperial funds arrive, you won't get a salary. The French fleet is blockading the port, so it's quite possible you'll get nothing."

They had spoiled my dinner. Worst of all, they were right.

"Fine!" I said, addressing Peret. "Maybe I'm not going to get rich, but you've enlisted as a private, and the salary for privates is nothing to write home about."

"And who says it's the Generalitat who's going to be paying me?" he replied, laughing at my bewildered expression. "Martí, you know what the Barcelona rich are like. You think people like that are going to be prepared to join battalions, climb bastions, or stand guard night and day, to risk getting shot at or bombarded? Of course they aren't. It's one thing being in favor of constitutions and liberties, it's quite another gambling their own skin for them. And so I showed up at the home of some of the particularly reluctant ones."

"A commercial visit," said Amelis, understanding at once.

"Precisely," said Peret. "The government wants complete units, but they don't give a damn about the identity of the people who make them up. So I have offered myself to fill the place of the biggest shirkers. In exchange for a small gratuity, naturally."

"You've taken the place of a rich person who doesn't want to fight!" I cried, outraged.

"Only after a strict auction," said Peret.

They spent the rest of the night mocking good old Zuvi and his poor commercial sense. By the end of it, I was so dejected I couldn't even finish my cigar. Of all the sieges I've taken part in over the last seventy years, the one government by whom I wasn't paid a cent was that of my own country. Still . . . I didn't know it at the time, but that was actually our last night together and happy. Why does it cost so much to see how happy you are, when you are?

I can remember Peret laughing at my naïveté; I remember his wish to fight, at his age, and I think how fortunate we human beings are that our destinies are hidden from us. My friend Peret was killed after it was all over.

By the end of the siege, the only healthy Barcelonans were the cannibals. You could recognize them because their skin was an unnatural pinkish color, their pupils shone repulsively like the eyes on a fresh fish, and their lips were frozen in a perpetual smile. The rest of the city's inhabitants were a beggarly mass, dusty bodies, as though they had been shut away in some dark attic. For weeks, months, after the siege, the Barcelonans who traveled outside the city could be recognized by their deathly complexion and their crestfallen gait. One day Peret went out to get some food. Perhaps simply because he was Barcelonan, some spiteful soldier shot him. But it's more likely that they cried halt at some roadblock. He didn't hear their voices and they fired.

What is a fortress? Bring together a handful of people ready to fight, an enclosed space, and a standard, and there you have a fortress. In the summer of 1713, the military situation was as I am about to describe it to you, and I will begin with the good part.

As we know, the Red Pelts had named Don Antonio commander in chief of the army. A huge task was expected of Don Antonio, if not an impossible one: to organize, drill, and lead an army that did not exist, with the mission to defend a city that was indefensible.

Besides the staff officers, the most outstanding thing we had was our artillery. This was under the command of Costa, Francesc Costa. Quite a fellow. The best artilleryman of the century. To give you an idea of his skill, I shall set down just one piece of information: When the Bourbons entered, Costa was the only senior officer they did not detain. (Well, Costa and good old Zuvi, to be precise.) Jimmy, being of a rationality that was as superb as it was entirely without scruples, knew what he was dealing with and offered him various perks and an extremely well-remunerated position, four doubloons a day, if he joined the French army. Costa did not hesitate for a second. He said yes, that he would be very honored to make a career in the army of Louis XIV. That same night he disappeared.

Costa's best artillerymen were from Mallorca. When it came to Costa's lightning flight after September 11, I would bet anything that it was his Mallorcans who had met him to set sail for the Balearics.

Costa was a small, quiet fellow. He didn't walk; rather, he slid along, head down and hidden between his shoulders, eyebrows raised as though he was always astonished or apologizing. He never spoke unless spoken to. It was most wearing having to deal with him; the fact is, people who are so shy unnerve any interlocutor. His favorite words were "yes" and "no," and while concision is highly desirable among technicians, Costa's excess of reserve was out of all bounds. Let us forgive him. Let us admire him. If anyone could understand him, it would be me. We had parallels that connected us: On paper, command of the artillery fell to General Basset, just as that of the engineers fell to Santa Cruz the elder. In practice, I led on the engineering, and Costa on the cannons. These functions above our rank wove a complicity between us. To people like Costa, reality was no more than the angle and distance at which a bomb fell.

His shyness was innate, and he concealed it by chewing on parsley all day long. By the end of the siege, everybody was chewing on weeds so as to deceive their hunger, no choice in the matter, but for Costa it was a natural impulse. As for the possibility of making conversation with him, as I said, you had to drag every word out of him. I remember the first time we met. I asked him how many artillery pieces we had at our disposal.

"Ninety-two."

I had expected some complaint or request. But nothing. "Have you set out the pieces according to Don Antonio's orders?"

"Yes, with a few adjustments."

"Do you think we'll have enough?" I asked, still faced with this parsimony of his.

"It depends."

I waited for some further comment. None came. "And what does it depend on, in your opinion?"

He looked at me wide-eyed, as though only my judgment mattered and not his. "On the ones the enemy's got."

"To the best of our knowledge at the moment, bearing in mind that our spies have been giving us reports that don't all match up," I said, "their convoy is made up of a hundred and fifteen. We can assume that there will be reinforcements coming in future."

"Well, then," he said.

"Well, then?"

"Yes."

His terseness was irritating me; he must have noticed, and he added, raising his eyebrows higher still and chewing his parsley: "My Mallorcans will keep them at bay as long as they do not outnumber us by a ratio of more than five to three. Beyond that, I cannot give any assurances." He took more sprigs of parsley from his pocket and began to chew on them like a bored rabbit.

As to the general situation, the good part ends here, and there wasn't much to it. And so begins the bad bit.

A fortress without troops to defend it is as useless as a garrison in a stronghold without walls. Even you, my dear vile Waltraud, can understand that. Well, we had neither one nor the other. Neither an army nor walls.

The first time I went over the rolls of the army, my soul plummeted into my feet. Villarroel wanted a precise calculation of the resources and forces at his disposal. One day he came through the door while I was discussing matters with Costa. He interrupted us as brusquely as usual. He wanted to know why he hadn't seen the list of all the units.

"I'm sorry, Don Antonio," I said, "I haven't been able to calculate the totals because of a mistake." I couldn't help laughing while I showed him some papers. "Some idiot in the government has sent us this. I ask them for the army rolls, and they send us the plans for a proposed new market."

As Villarroel was reading the papers, I laughed again. "They must have muddled the documents," I added. "What you've got there must be the layout for positions for sellers, suppliers, and traders. As you know, they're saying that, after the war, they want to restructure the market in Plaza del Born. I'll go myself to the Generalitat in person today and demand the correct rolls."

But Villarroel was looking at me with those frowning eyes, saying nothing.

"That can't be." I swallowed. "Tell me you're joking."

Until that day, I had thought we would be making war like any other European kingdom (albeit with no king). The government would hire professional forces wherever they could be found, or would bring them in from elsewhere by making them a reasonable offer. The local militia would be there for support and supplies. What else could you expect from civilians who were barely more skilled than old Peret?

The only professional troops the city had were remnants of the Allied army, the odd individual who, for one reason or another, had decided not to go when his fellows were evacuated. The best little group were the hundred Germans. They were together in a unit of their own, led by eleven officers of the same origin. And such compact ranks! I had to bring them countless messages, which they obeyed with a watchmaker's precision. Professional soldiers will always have a bit of the adventurer about them. I say this because Waltraud, who has less imagination than an ant, couldn't understand what some of her compatriots were doing in Barcelona between 1713 and 1714. In those days, it was hardly the most pleasant place in the world to be, though an adventurer isn't looking for what's safe but what's exciting. Many of them had reasons for not returning home, and the Generalitat paid reasonably well; others, in short, had good reasons for staying.

You must understand, my dear vile Waltraud, that in this world, there is such a thing as mutual attraction between male and female genitals, also known as love. Barcelona was full of beautiful women, either single or married to seamen who were practically never home, and . . . Well, need I go on? As for the other enlisted foreigners, there were so few, they're not even worth counting. Yes, we did have a bit of everything, from Hungarians to Irishmen (even Neapolitans, who were still everywhere). I met one who was from the Papal States.

But as I say, the bulk of our army was made up of simple civilians. I had left my city when I was very young, and was only vaguely aware of what was considered the traditional way of defending it. It was based on the Coronela, the local militia. Each trade was assigned its own unit as well as one of the city gates. This was all very well by the military standards of the thirteenth century, but this was five hundred years later, and we were living in Vauban's technical age.

To give you an idea of my distress, I shall describe to you the entire roster of the Fifth Battalion.

First company: attorneys-at-law. (And they didn't even know how to take care of my case! How could we expect them to fire a rifle or man a bastion?)

Second company: blacksmiths and tinkers.

Third company: market gardeners.

Fourth company: potters, upholsterers, and makers of pots and pans. (At least these latter are easier to understand: When the hunger sets in, there will be empty pots and pans aplenty.)

Fifth company: belt-makers.

Sixth company: butchers. (Another group who'll be out of work before long.)

Seventh company: cobblers.

Eighth company: silk weavers and dyers.

Ninth company: students of theology, medicine, and philosophy. (A fine graduation awaits them.)

And with this, we had to face dragoons and grenadiers trained through experience in a thousand battles: with companies of coopers, innkeepers, and velvet-makers; booksellers, glovers, rope-makers, grooms, tailors, stevedores, legal clerks. As I recall, the Sixth Battalion had an entire company made up of people who resold things. Yes, you read that right, they weren't people who sold things; they *re*sold them. What could they have been thinking when they signed them up? Reselling to the quartermaster the bullets that had been used by the enemy?

The total came to fewer than six thousand armed men. Fewer than six thousand against forty thousand. Some of those forty thousand were tied up trying to hold back our Miquelets from the interior, but even if there were only thirty thousand, the math didn't lie: As far as troops were concerned, for each defender of Barcelona, there were five Bourbons. To complicate matters still further, our problems began before the siege had even been formalized.

The only scenario in which the running of a military dictatorship is permissible, indeed necessary, is in a city under siege. It isn't a matter of politics but common sense. Because the worst position for a military stronghold is trying to face an attack while under a split command. And that was precisely what happened to us.

Villarroel was supposed to be the commander in chief of all the pro-Austrian troops remaining in Spain. But as I have already explained, the problem was that the vast majority of the soldiers belonged to the Barcelonan militia, under the control of the council. Furthermore, Don Antonio always bore the burden of having been named commander in chief by the Catalan government, who considered him a general there to do their bidding. Villarroel insisted that his position be ratified by Vienna, which finally happened in November 1713. But this only made matters worse, because according to the terms of the Treatise of Evacuation between the Two Crowns and the Allies, imperial troops were not allowed to remain in Spain. The Red Pelts considered him a foreign subordinate; to the enemy, he was a rebellious Castilian.

The Red Pelts always guarded their prerogatives very jealously, and Don Antonio had to ask their permission if he even wanted to transfer the company of the *Impedits*, made up of former soldiers who had lost limbs. Going to war with people missing an arm or half a leg might seem a little absurd, but I can assure you, they were tremendously useful fellows. They had experience and extremely high morale. I remember one of them, with one leg that went down only as far as the calf of the other, raising his crutch as Don Antonio walked past, exclaiming: "General! I shall not retreat, I give you my word!"

During a siege, garrison work is a terrible drain on troops. Even if a system of rotation is used on the bastions, tiredness, bombardments, and sickness lead to a trickle of losses that we couldn't allow to happen. The *Impedits* would be useful covering bastions and stretches of walls that were not under the most severe threat, allowing those being relieved a bit of rest.

There were disgraceful scenes. Don Antonio in a council of war with the Red Pelts, screaming his head off—flushed with rage—demanding, protesting, that they allow him a hundred men? Even fifty? Pitiful. A commander in chief being denied the right to move a handful of cripples. All we needed at that point was for Villarroel's aide-de-camp to be one Martí Zuviría, a fellow universally known for his diplomacy. More than once—and more than twice—I nearly smashed in some councilor's spectacles. It was infuriating. More than infuriating, because in certain situations, stupidity can come to resemble pure treason.

Let us recall that when it all began, in that ominous summer of 1713, the enemy was approaching Barcelona at a forced march. The Allies' garrisons were handing the keys to our cities to the killer. Deceived, disconcerted, with no authority giving them orders and all taken completely by surprise, it had never occurred to the Miquelets scattered around the countryside that such a stab in the back was possible. They came down from the mountains and, from one day to the next, found friendly sites occupied by Bourbon troops. There was nothing they could do but remain on the horizon watching the fires, the looting, the executions. The final uproar.

In those circumstances, some drastic decisions were essential: extending the *Crida* right across the country, proclaiming the legitimacy of Barcelona's government, and bringing together disparate fighters under a single banner. They had to prevent more towns and cities from falling into Bourbon hands. And for this, it was inescapable, desperately urgent, to show some symbol that would unite those who were longing for a voice to lead them. Villarroel ordered a military delegate to leave the city immediately with the silver mace and the banner of Saint Eulalia and travel across the country proclaiming that the struggle was not over.

"Take the sacred banner of Saint Eulalia beyond the Barcelona walls?" The Red Pelts were not sure. "That is most unusual. This will require a debate first."

They weren't joking! Solemnly, they gathered in council. Was it fair and fitting within the law and tradition that the sacred banner should be taken outside Barcelona's walls? What honorable escort would accompany it? As for the few noblemen who were still in the city, were their titles sufficiently worthy for them to carry the pole and its braids? The debate stretched on; it was resumed the following day and then the next, and the next, without arriving at a definitive legal conclusion. Villarroel was absolutely incensed. By the time they had decided, the enemy would have taken control of all of Catalonia, with the exception of Barcelona and a few isolated sites like Cardona, those places where the most determined native commanders had refused to comply with the imperial orders.

Let us now examine the fortifications of Barcelona, which so often used to make me turn away, unwilling to judge them so as not to relive my past as a student in Bazoches.

The first order Villarroel gave me, his first commission, was to produce a report on the general condition of the defenses. I obeyed. I walked around the whole site. I cried. And when I say that, I am not, to my shame, speaking rhetorically.

As well as being an engineer, I happened also to be a Barcelonan. And when you examine the walls of your own city, knowing with certainty that they are going to be attacked by armed men ready to burn down your house, kill your children, and rape your wife, you see things somewhat differently. According to *le Mystère*, I ought not to feel emotion. A Maganon without a cool head is not a Maganon or anything at all. To justify my dismay, however, I should tell you that what I found was a complete and utter disaster.

Comparisons can be useful. Look at the next illustration. Put it in the place where it's supposed to go, or you can forget that you and I ever met, you fat old magpie.

If by any chance, destiny had seen good old Zuvi commissioned to fortify Barcelona, this would have been the optimal result.

As you can see, the city walls and the inner bastions are protected by a series of staggered half-moons or ravelins, perfectly arranged and three meters deep. Each one would have to be taken in separate attacks, without this ever affecting the main line of defense. By the time Jimmy managed to reach our final redoubt, the number of his dead would form such a tall mountain that the top ones could be buried on the moon. In fact, and following Vauban to the letter, the very existence of such fortifications would discourage any assault. Jimmy was a sly fox and would have graciously declined the honor of leading a siege of such complexity. And if not Jimmy, who else could vanquish us?

Now compare the previous plate with the sad reality, on the following page.

Devastating. Incongruous. Dislocated jaws, a heap of shapeless lumps. Or, as Vauban would have defined it technically, more circumspectly, a "composite fortress"; that is, an ancient site that has been patched up to meet the demands of modern warfare.

The old city walls had been supplemented with a few pentagonal bastions. There was no small number of them, and each had its own name, its own story; in themselves, they were real characters who were dear to the Barcelonans. But all those bastions had been built in different periods, with no overall plan and as though merely patched up. A few stretches of the wall were so long that the gunfire from one bastion could not serve as backup for the next, being too far apart. As for the dry moat that had to stretch around the outside of the fortifications, the less said about that, the better. It was so full of waste and debris, and so shallow, that you could see the ears of the pigs that grazed in it. A bankrupt government would find it hard to allow for whole squads of cleaners. The sieges at the end and beginning of the century had damned whole stretches of the perimeter. Amazing as it may sound, nobody had bothered to repair the holes. That is the position we found ourselves in. And now we had the barbarians *ad portas*. A devastating military machine, ignited by a hatred toward the "rebels" and trained through their experience in a long decade of campaigns. In under two weeks, they would be pitching camp outside Barcelona.

One might want to formulate this entirely legitimate question: If war came to the peninsula in 1705, and between that date and 1713 there were eight long years to fortify the city, how was it possible that the Catalans, who had their own government, never took care of the defenses of their city? This is one of my private torments, an argument that fills my nightmares and the distress of my wakeful hours. What could have happened? You should never have recourse to an "if . . . "; that "what if . . . ?" can kill. Because the answer, curiously, is neither political nor military. It doesn't even have anything to do with matters of engineering.

Vauban was indeed the greatest military engineer of all time. But he was also French. In his study, using only ink and paper, he could create fascinating systems of defense, optimal and perfect, overwhelming in their geometric beauty. There was one problem with Vauban's system of fortification and one only: It cost a lot of money.

Human imagination can develop at no cost, right up until the point at which it comes into contact with contractors. Tons of material, thousands of stonecutters, carpenters, and laborers, dozens of local specialists—or, more frequently, foreign ones, charging astronomical fees. Suppliers cheat, swindle, and defraud the government's finances. The work drags on, the budget increases by a factor of three or four. And once the work has begun, how can it be suspended? A site that has been half-fortified is more useless than a half-built cathedral. You can praise God in a potato patch, but you cannot defend the city until the very last *échauguette* has been erected, humbly proud, on the point of the bastions. Even the most slow-witted of vegetable sellers understands that a wall needs to be closed up. Progress on a wall is in plain view of everybody, which puts considerable pressure on those in charge. They resign themselves to corruption. Opportunist agents in league with the technicians, the former supplying inadequate shipments and the latter signing for the receipt in exchange for an illegal "commission." Money, always money. Themistocles was already saying as much: War is not a matter of weaponry but of money—whoever is the last person holding a coin. (All right, maybe it wasn't Themistocles, it might have been Pericles, I don't remember, but really, what difference does it make? Put any name you like to that quote. Anyone but Voltaire!)

There was another significant reason for this utter defenseless-
ness. In 1705 there was every indication that the war would be over
in a matter of months. After their troops had landed at Barcelona,
the Allies would advance on Madrid, they'd depose Little Philip, and
Charles would become the king of all Spain. Castile would learn, at
last, that it was not the cock of the walk, and the Catalans would
make Spain a confederate kingdom, modern and prosperous, with
an English parliament, a Dutch fleet, and a bourgeoisie competent
to hold the reins of the finances. But it didn't happen like that. The
war dragged on. Charles, from his base in Barcelona, asked for more
and more loans from the Catalan authorities to defray the costs of
his multinational army. Wars are won in attack, not in defense, and
the government gave in. The ultimate result of this was the drama
of 1713 and 1714.

I did my calculations that very night. An unusual calm reigned at
home. Nan and Anfán were playing together, strangely pacific, next to
the fireplace, in which we were roasting peppers and green tomatoes.
Next to them, in a rocking chair, Peret was reading by the light of the
fire. He had never learned to read in his head, and he was muttering
aloud like a monk. They were lines of verse by Romaguera, and they
were shockingly bad, and they seemed worse given our situation. Perhaps that is why I remember them.

> She envies you, the butterfly,
> For being happy so,
> For her love's destined soon to die
> While yours can live and grow . . .

Amelis was more affectionate than usual. She wanted to set aside
the calculation tables, the paper and inkwell, and take me to bed. I
brushed her away with a burning feeling under my skin. They hadn't
realized what was awaiting us; they didn't want to, as though ignoring
the future might make it disappear.

According to my most optimistic calculations, the city would be
able to resist exactly eight days of actual siege conditions. Not a day
longer. And after that, blackness.

12

The weeks immediately preceding the arrival of the Bourbon army were very useful ones. The Coronela companies paraded up and down the Ramblas—more than anything, to raise the people's morale—and did shooting practice. The conscripts took it all as a terrifically fun exercise, revelry that was hardly military at all. They got hold of two large dolls of semi-human shape, filled with straw, behind which they erected a three-meter-high wooden barricade. They called one of them Lluís and the other Filipet, Bourbon scum. Every day a hundred rifles would shoot at them ten times. Without that much success, if I'm honest. To the question of how accurate they were, all I need to tell you is that the surrounding windows were boarded up.

It is impossible in such a short space of time to transform companies of tinsmiths and tanners into professional units. That was not the aim. The bonds that hold men together are much more important than the quality of their marksmanship. And that camaraderie, in turn, has to be knitted together with confidence in the officers. In this regard, Don Antonio was unique. Nowadays an insurgent France is scattering an endless supply of revolutionary generals right across the world; from one day to the next, they have gone from wearing a tavern apron to a marshal's sash. But in my day, the senior officers were quite different. In my ninety-eight years, I have encountered dozens of colonels and generals who knew nothing of their regiments but the color of their coats.

Don Antonio was a real soldier, a man of battle and trench. His love for the army came from his family. In fact, Don Antonio having been born in Barcelona was an accident, as I've told you, since around that time, his father was posted in the city. I'm telling you: a man with a destiny. Because to the Red Pelts, he never stopped being Castilian and, as such, an intruder, while the Bourbons did not even recognize his status as Catalan. Years later, Jimmy showed me a copy of the list of the main players to be arrested once the city had fallen. (He did it to persuade me that he'd had nothing to do with the repression, as they had been detained after he left Barcelona. He was lying. If he didn't give the order, neither did he prevent it, well aware of what would happen.) By Don Antonio's name, they had not written "Castilian" but, very significantly, "not Catalan."

The thing was, Villarroel quickly realized that this army was not like other armies. The Coronela was a collection of armed civilians, and the usual conventions could not be applied to them. He would get much further with encouragement than with strict discipline.

I've never seen a commander in chief who spent so much time among his troops. He would show up all of a sudden and unannounced at some post or other on the walls, then another, then another. He was in the habit of calling the soldiers "my boys," which they loved. On one occasion when most of the armed citizens surrounding him were his own age or older, he corrected himself in the middle of his sentence: "My boys—I mean, sorry, I meant to say, my brothers . . . "

The soldiers burst out laughing. And the old codgers among them were allowed to pat him affectionately on the back! In any other army, that would have cost you fifty lashes.

This would have been all well and good were it not for the fact that, since I was so young, in public he would call me *fillet*. That is, "son." It must have been the only Catalan word he ever learned, the stubborn old thing. What's more, he pronounced it wrong, which I think he did on purpose, because instead of *fillet*, he would pronounce it *fiyé*, emphasizing his Castilian accent, which the soldiers found hilarious.

Decades later, I served under that Prussian, Frederick. And—my God—the difference between Barcelona's conscripts and the regiments of Prussia! To Frederick, a soldier was less than a dog. Much less! I can assure you—and this is no exaggeration—that any German soldier would have jumped for joy to be treated like a dog. Just one detail: When the Prussian regiments were on the move, in order to prevent desertions, the soldiers were forbidden from getting more than six meters away from the formation; this was surrounded by horsemen armed with carbines, with orders to shoot to kill. Can you imagine the Prussian tyrant addressing a soldier as "my brother"? Please! That was the difference, the big difference, between our army and any other. Don Antonio was a real military man, but he was able to see the nub of the truth: that the Coronela was made up of free men defending their freedom, and you cannot lead men like that by watering down the principles that drive them.

Right, enough of this sentimental rot.

More often than I would have liked, Don Antonio called me to attend meetings of his staff officers. My main concern was the engineering works, so my presence at these meetings felt like a waste of time. The Bourbons were approaching, and I have described to you already the state in which our defenses found themselves. Normally, I didn't say much. But one day the discussion turned to the troops and how few of them there were. Somebody—I do not recall who—suggested incorporating groups of Miquelets into the official soldiery. The government of Red Pelts was prepared, reluctantly, to grant permission. Ballester's name was the first to crop up in this argument. My notional superior as head of the engineers was one Santa Cruz, a man well connected among the Red Pelts whom Don Antonio had no choice except to tolerate, but whom he ignored. Santa Cruz was radically opposed to raising Ballester up to the honorable state of a soldier. Don Antonio asked my opinion.

"No, I don't believe Ballester is a mere bandit," I said with certainty. "A fanatic, yes, and bloodthirsty. But deep down, he is a man of great nobility. It may be that he has kidnapped the odd Red Pelt—excuse me, the odd wealthy gentleman from the government—however, he is ruled not by a desire for profit but by hatred of the Bourbons, be they French or Spanish."

"General . . . ," Santa Cruz interrupted me, "seeing as we already have discipline problems among the Coronela men, what would happen when they have these people of such dissolute morals as their examples? And we all know how lenient I am when it comes to using those words, 'dissolute morals.'"

"With Ballester or without him," I argued, "discipline will never be the Coronela's forte. And if Ballester agrees to join us, it will always be in his natural role as part of the light cavalry. We could use him as a link to the Miquelets on the outside, to reconnoiter the terrain or cause trouble for the enemy's foragers. We will hardly see him, since he will be as little use to us posted on a bastion as a Coronela battalion on horseback."

Don Antonio was staring into the void, saying nothing, lost in his ruminations. At that moment, I realized just how much good old Zuvi wanted Ballester brought in. My old arguments with him no longer meant anything; I could judge Ballester as he was, a shrewd, capable leader, whether in a uniform or not. And we were desperately short of men with experience.

It was an age before Villarroel pronounced his verdict. Finally, he passed judgment: "We're so short on troops that we have nothing to lose by offering him the chance to join up to serve in the armed forces, and now with honor. If he turns down the offer, well, then it's between him and his conscience."

"Very well said, Don Antonio!" I cried.

His eyes drilled into me. It was very hard to bear that look of disapproval, severer than any words he could have spoken. Don Antonio needed to attend to some dispatches, and the rest of us officers turned to leave. I remember Santa Cruz shaking his head, disapproving.

"Zuviría." Don Antonio stopped me when I had already reached the threshold. "One more thing: You are to take charge of making Ballester this offer yourself."

I thought I was going to have a fit. "Me? But Don Antonio, that's just not possible! I have a mountain of work to do, reinforcing the walls and bastions."

"Well, I believe it is indeed possible," he interrupted me. "Because I am your superior, and that is what I have ordered you to do, and because it has become clear that you are a great supporter of Ballester's. Doubtless he will be more sensitive to your requests than anyone else's."

Sensitive to my requests? What I naturally could not tell him was that Ballester had laid siege to me in a *masía*, and that before that he had robbed me, he had stripped me naked and hanged me from a fig tree.

"Come on, *fiyé*, what's that face for?" Villarroel said consolingly. "You think I'm going to risk losing an aide-de-camp when the enemy is just six days' march away? I'll make sure you are supplied with an adequate escort."

The "escort" consisted of two gentlemen, one of them very thin on horseback and the other smaller and sitting on a mule. The one on the horse apparently knew more or less where the Bourbons' advance guard had gotten to, and the one on the mule knew all the habitual hiding places used by Ballester and his villains. They were every bit as terrified as I was. The quartermaster's store loaned me the uniform of an infantry lieutenant colonel. To make me more respected, according to Don Antonio. I doubted that very much. Ballester was perfectly happy slitting the gullets of officers, and he absolutely didn't care which side they were on. What was more, the coat was so tight on me that I couldn't do up the front. Still, this was hardly a time to start seeking out a good tailor.

We rode out of Barcelona, passing through a number of towns, finding nothing visibly changed. The countryfolk were on our side and gave us news about the advance of Philip's army, then under the command of one duke of Pópuli. Pópuli! Another name to consign to the bonfires of history. And when I tell you why, I'm certain you will agree with me.

They had seen only a handful of Bourbon patrols on horseback, only fleetingly, no sign of the columns of infantry or convoys of artillery. They were moving at that slow pace because they wanted to secure all the towns as they went. The *Crida* notwithstanding, the Bourbons didn't think the Barcelonans so crazy as to close their city walls to such an impressive army.

As for Ballester, finding him was easier than we had anticipated. He didn't bother to hide. With the evacuation of the Allied troops, especially outside Barcelona's walls, any last trace of authority had disappeared.

We found him in an opulent country mansion, a residence that had been abandoned by a notable *botiflero*. Through the windows, we could hear the sounds of a frenzied party. Men singing and shouting, wild laughter from the women, and the crash of bottles smashing against the floor or the walls.

"Are you really planning to go into that den?" asked my escorts.

"There's no need for you to come with me. If all goes well, we'll see each other again soon. And if not . . . " I gave a resigned sigh. "In that case, inform Barcelona."

No sooner had I walked through the door than I found myself in a very spacious hall. Everything was turned upside down. And there, like a gang of drunken monks, were Ballester's men. The drunkest of them was a great hulk of a man. Around his neck, he was wearing a curtain as though it were a cloak, and he had a chicken spitted on his sword. I can see it now, that chicken with its beak half-open, its eyes closed.

I counted five women and ten men. One of the men was in women's clothing and was dancing with the body of a dead Bourbon soldier. The dead man's head swung like a pendulum, falling backward or leaning forward onto the cross-dresser's shoulder, and the man hugged him, lavishing caresses on his cheeks. Another fellow was suspended from the big chandelier on the ceiling, making howling noises. He must have been the joker of the group. His audience laughed, simultaneously reprimanding him and egging him on. Everyone but Ballester.

He was sitting in a corner, on a sofa that had been disemboweled by bayonets. On either side of him, a couple of tarts from the town had their arms around his neck, one of them laughing like a madwoman, the other, who was drunk, with her head resting on his chest. Ballester was the first to see me.

At that moment, the lamp gave in to the weight of the man who was swinging from it. Man and lamp fell together in a thundering of broken glass. The great roars of laughter stopped dead: The monkey man had landed right at my feet.

The hulk approached me with sword and chicken raised. He wanted to babble some kind of threat, but he was so drunk that he tripped on what was left of the lamp and he, too, fell flat on his face.

Ballester made a clicking sound with his lips, sarcastically. "What bad luck you seem to be having with me!" he said, not deigning to stand up. "You come here to rescue your little *botiflero* friends, and look who you find."

"I have found," I replied, "exactly the person I was looking for."

One of his men approached me, dagger drawn, to eliminate me without further ado. I held up the tube in which I was carrying the rolled-up documents, with the seal of the Generalitat on the outside. "This," I announced, "is an official commission and in the interests of all those present. Would you like me to read it? I'm sure you would, because if you slit my throat, I don't imagine anyone here can read."

At least they hesitated long enough for me to add: "The government has decided to confer the rank of captain of a volunteer regiment to Señor Esteve Ballester. With uniform and remuneration as befits this position. In addition, Captain Ballester shall have the right to enlist whichsoever men he chooses, who will be admitted into service as honorable soldiers of the emperor and on a wage from the Generalitat."

For a few moments there was silence.

"Now!" one of the less drunk ones shouted at last. "Now they show up to lick our asses! Now that the Red Pelts find themselves with theirs suddenly on the line!"

I chose not to reply. Not least because he was right. They surrounded me—everyone but Ballester—screaming right up close to my face. One of them was telling me the story of a farm that was repossessed because of the high taxes; another showed me his back, striped with lash marks from the Red Pelts.

If you want to talk to mutineers, you need to be above them. And I'm not referring to a position of morality. I circled around a table, climbed upon it, and holding up the tube, said: "It may be that this was signed by the Red Pelts. But this"—grabbing hold of the front of my uniform—"is a principle that is higher than all of them. It was sewn by a woman in La Ribera for her husband, an officer in the Fourth Battalion. The man is a carpenter. Who was it that whipped you? The carpenters of Barcelona or agents of the government?"

"Go to hell, you and the fatherland!" they jeered, surrounding the table. "What did you do for us when we needed help? You sent us to the guards! Persecuted us! Put us to the rack!"

"Shameful wretches!" I yelled, and even I was impressed at my own audacity. "What kind of child, seeing his mother threatened, instead of defending her, reproaches her for a slap she gave him years earlier?" I shook my head as though a profound sadness had taken hold of me, but I made a joke. "It's like they say: When a child falls down a well, his mother throws herself down after him. When it's the mother who falls down, the child goes off to tell the neighbors."

Incredible as it may sound, there were a few bursts of laughter. I didn't wait for them to die out, and resumed my reproachful tone. "Well then, the bad news is that our neighbors are called Castile and

France, and they are the ones who are trying to drown us in the darkness of that well."

"And they've sent you here to tell us that? We are the ones with the least to lose when the French and Castilians dine on the constitutions with a side helping of turnips. Go to hell!"

"You can go to hell yourself!" I roared, beside myself. "Even you know it's not really like that. If Barcelona falls, we all fall with her. What would happen if the Bourbons razed everything to the ground? Even if you've run away from your homes, I'm sure you have relatives and friends somewhere. Don't you care about them? No more random ballots: The new mayors will be handpicked by Little Philip, and they will be confirmed *botifleros*. All young men will be forced to serve under his banner, including in that ghastly place they call America, for decades to come. Our judgments will depend on their judges, who may be no better than ours but are certainly farther away, and they hate us. And if the rates of taxes seem exorbitant to you now, wait till they're set at the court in Madrid by our enemies, without the branches of our parliament having any sacred right to veto them." I had gotten myself so worked up that I paused only to catch my breath. "Are you all blind? You should be the first to see that it's the Red Pelts with the least to lose in the event of catastrophe. They'll always rise back up to the top, whoever's in charge. And if you truly are so indifferent to all this, tell me, why are you dancing with Bourbon corpses?"

They settled a bit. I was completely overtaken by my passion. How peculiar: Up until that moment, I hadn't realized how closely my ideas tallied with my speech. I had gone there to persuade them, and in reality, I was the one being most persuaded.

Someone asked: "What kind of man is your commander?"

That was very typical of the Miquelets' mentality; they cared less about the cause they were defending than the man who would lead them.

"You can work that out for yourself," I replied with a bitter smile. "He was the one who ordered me into this den, and whom I did not hesitate a second in obeying."

Up to that point, Ballester had not spoken a word. He got up off his broken sofa and said: "And what I believe is that if we go into Barcelona, we will never come out again. Tell these men if that isn't so. Tell them!"

"No, I can't tell them that," I replied, weighing my words carefully. "That may well be the way things go. They will kill us all. All I can assure you," I added, moderating my voice, "is that if that happens, I will not survive any longer than you will."

Ballester gestured with his thumb toward a door at the back of the room. "Get in there."

It was a rear patio enclosed by high walls. So I might feel more at ease, I was sharing the place with a couple of dead bodies in white uniforms. I tipped out their bags, which were full of letters between officers: They had been messengers for the Bourbons. I imagined what had happened. They'd been riding between units carrying messages when they saw this delightful-looking mansion on the way and came in for a little rest. Ballester was passing by and had the same idea. Bad luck.

Through the door, I could clearly hear the Miquelets' arguments, which all happened at the top of their voices. Some wanted to accept the offer from the government; most were in favor of slitting my throat. Best not to listen to them.

It was strange the way my thoughts were going in those days. All the means I had acquired at Bazoches were still active. The siege had not even begun, and yet it was already shaping and guiding my mind. Martí Zuviría, Prince of the Cowards, was eclipsed when Engineer Zuviría was awakened. I remember that my only thought was: If they kill me, I have to make sure these letters get to Barcelona one way or another.

The door opened. I went back into the great hall. All the eyes of the men and women were on me. It would be best to take the initiative myself.

"It may be that you do not want to take part in the defense of Barcelona," I said, holding out the letters to Ballester. "But I presume you are not against it, either. Please take these letters out to the man who brought me here."

During a pause that went on forever, Ballester stared straight into my eyes without taking the papers I was holding out toward him. His men were even more expectant than I was, since I had at least prepared my share of resignation. Despite all my time at Bazoches, it took me a whole year to understand the full significance of that look of Ballester's.

"Take them yourself," he answered tersely, without the slightest trace of sympathy despite what he was saying. He went over to the table, picked up the tube holding his commission as captain of the volunteers, looked at it, and said sadly: "These lads are getting soft. Softer than the branch of a fig tree."

Men and women all gave a roar of jubilation. As though the last person to make up his mind had been their leader and the final decision had depended on him. Today I'm sure that's not how it was, that Ballester had been the first to favor that fateful option. That he had kept his opinions to himself so as not to interfere in the others' judgment, not to seem too mild or force them into an act of suicide.

They were going into death and doing it gladly. Within a moment they had vanished, getting on their horses, the women clinging to their sides. The sounds of hooves and neighing seemed to disappear into the distance in a moment. Ballester moved more slowly; a leader does not run. We were left alone. He was very self-absorbed, far away from me, from everything. I noticed that he had the same expression from that day in Beceite, with his hands tied, awaiting death. We left the mansion. As we mounted up, his horse and mine were alongside but facing in opposite directions, the two riders face-to-face.

"One other thing," I said. "If you agree to subordinate yourself to the imperial army, from this moment you have a duty to rank and to discipline. I am a lieutenant colonel and the aide-de-camp to our commander in chief, and you must obey any orders you are given. Without exception."

He gave a little smile, which always looked ghoulish in that face with such a thick beard and such black bushy eyebrows. "I said to you in that *masía* that if we met again, I would send you flying."

He closed his hand into a fist and brought it with all his strength into the middle of my chest. I hadn't yet put my feet into the stirrups, so I was flung from the saddle and landed on my back. It was just as well that I fell on some tall rosemary bushes that cushioned my landing. All the same, it was quite a punch.

When I looked up, Ballester and his men had already gone. Out of the undergrowth came the skinny gentleman and the tiny one, who helped me to my feet.

"Holy Mother of God!" they exclaimed, while my hands tried to alleviate the pain in my kidneys. "You're alive. And Ballester on his way to Barcelona. What did you have to give him?"

"Something those people have always been denied," I replied. "The truth." They looked at me, hoping for more details, and I added: "I gave them my word that we were all going to be killed."

And so we come to July 25, 1713. The enemy will be arriving any day now. The work of building and repairing the city walls was not finished, very far from it. After talking to Don Antonio, we decided to stop it all, apart from the work on the palisade.

When there is time to anticipate a siege in advance, the garrison will surround the fortified enclosure with a screen of sharpened stakes pointing out toward the besieger, immediately outside the moat, the first line of defense of the walls and bastions.

There is another interruption from that bag of lard by the name of Waltraud. She tells me that from what she's learned so far, a palisade would seem to be a useless measure. Artillery fire would certainly destroy a few simple wood contraptions sticking out in front of the walls. So why waste time sticking in more and more and more rows of stakes?

A palisade makes it harder for an infantry to advance, and it intimidates the enemy. A forest of thousands and thousands of pointed stakes constitutes a quite considerable obstacle. At least if you look at it from the point of view of someone who has to cross it while being shot at from all sides. Officers need a lot of authority if they are to drive their men against a sharpened barrier.

All right, so the artillery bombardments will smash most of the stakes into splinters. But even that is not as decisive as it might appear. The stakes are two or three meters long. They are sunk very deep into the ground, at an acute angle, and with a buttress at their base. So that only a meter or a meter and a half is sticking out. The grapeshot and the bombs will indeed destroy them, but even if only a few inches are left, that is enough to injure feet and calves. The same explosions help to break and sharpen the points. A thick forest of solid spikes is no small matter to contend with. When the attackers advance en masse, it breaks up their formation, injures hundreds, and slows down the assault. And then they have the moat awaiting them, and the walls. Sometimes the simplest defenses are the most effective.

What I will not deny is the great transformation to the landscape that a palisade implies. The city, our ancient, frivolous Barcelona, suddenly seems to be surrounded by a halo of prickles, hostile and grim. The perimeter of a fortress can be vast, and I have seen enclosures circled by eighty thousand stakes. This static wood, worked by hands that wish to cause somebody else pain, is an announcement of death. When it is soaked by the rain, it is even more dismal than when it is covered in snow. When it is somewhere as sunny as Barcelona, its intention to cause harm is laid bare.

In our stores, we had sixteen thousand stakes. According to my calculations, we needed a minimum of forty thousand. We didn't have them. Well, what was I to do? Go sit in a corner and cry? *Débrouillez-vous!* I focused on covering the most exposed areas.

At least we were not short of enthusiastic help. The government could not pay for all the work that needed to be done, but thanks to the prevailing civic fervor, we were joined by six thousand volunteers. I spent long hours with them, out on-site, where the work was being undertaken. I showed people how they ought to be digging in more deeply, anchoring the foot of the stake well for when the sticking-out part is blasted into the air by the effect of the artillery fire; I made sure they were leaning out at an angle of forty-five degrees; that the end was well sharpened, all of that. We were short of the stakes, tools, workers, and above all, time we needed to transform Barcelona into a hedgehog-city.

I was spending that July 25 supervising the works on the palisade when Ballester and his men came past. They were leading their horses behind them, and they were happy and flushed with wine. A lot of the whorehouses that were best supplied with the strongest liquor were outside the walls, waiting for travelers before they entered or left the city. They were doubtless returning from just such a brothel. It wasn't hard to understand. There was an end-of-the-world mood in those establishments. When the Bourbons showed up, the party would stop.

It was four days since they'd arrived, and they had become famous for how profligate they were in taverns and brothels. And for their fistfights with the guards. Each time I heard news of them, I shook my head, disappointed. Perhaps recruiting them hadn't been such a good idea after all.

When I saw them, I addressed their leader. "Ah, Captain Ballester," I said, not thinking, prompted by the urgency of the situation. "Leave off what you're doing and help us with these stakes. We need all the hands we can get."

I should have seen his answer coming. They all burst out laughing, saying they had come to fight, not to work. This was bad, as their refusal to comply forced me into a confrontation.

I had told Ballester quite clearly that if he was joining an organized defense, he consequently had a duty toward discipline. If I allowed him to ignore me once, and in front of everybody, I would never have his respect again. I was in my shirtsleeves because of the heat. It was not the ideal attire for intimidating a gang of killers. Yes, this was bad. To make matters worse, when they recognized Ballester, the workers who were closest put down their tools and waited expectantly, holding in a gasp of fear. All the same, Longlegs Zuvi walked up to the Miquelets and said: "That's an order. Here everyone works." And pointed a finger all the way down their line. "Everyone."

"Really?" Ballester answered. "Because I don't see any Red Pelts here sticking in stakes."

"We're not out in the field now. Here we fight differently." I took a few steps back and took one of the workers by the arm, a very young girl. I tugged her over and showed her open palms to Ballester. "Look at the blood flowing on her hands. These scratches are decorations every bit as worthy as any you can earn from some heroic deed in war."

Ballester moved his face close to mine and, with barely contained hatred, whispered: "If what you wanted was manual laborers, why the hell did you ask us to come?"

"When are you going to understand," I replied in the same tone, "that all of this is not for me but for the common good?"

"What I am beginning to understand," said Ballester, "is that war is a good excuse for the Red Pelts to subjugate us even more than they used to."

I was going to answer when we heard a terrific noise: All the bells in Barcelona were ringing the warning bell. Dozens of wild belfries, announcing the bad news. We looked up. The sentries on the walls had been warning us for some time. So absorbed were we in our squabble that we hadn't even heard them. From the top of the bastion, they were shouting: "They're coming! They're coming!"

When news that is so long awaited is finally confirmed, it becomes somehow unreal. They were here. Although for weeks we had thought of nothing else, the fact stunned me. Ballester, the palisade, everything was suddenly meaningless faced with the danger that was so imminent.

"What are you waiting for?" shouted the sentries. "Get to the nearest entrance. Get inside or they'll close the gates!"

They were a couple of very young lads, poorly armed, one of them wearing a pince-nez. On that day, this particular sector was being guarded by the philosophy students. They looked more fragile than the paper in their books. The one in the spectacles pointed toward the horizon.

"Run! There's a whole army heading this way!"

Victus

1

You! Yes, you! How dare you set foot in my home? I've just been reading what we've been writing until now.

What do you call this? What do you call it? You've *transcribed* everything I've been saying! Word for word!

That's what I asked you to do? Well, yes, it was, but even you can surely understand that some things aren't to be taken literally. When you tell a visitor to "make themselves at home," do you really mean that? No! Naturally you do not!

When I began my tale, I assumed you'd sprinkle a little sugar about; I wanted a nice, straightforward book, like the ones Voltaire wrote, silly *Candide*, that whole thing. Well, not as puerile as that, perhaps, but properly laid out on the page, so people can read it, right up to the *señoritas* in their salons. And look at this! Do you not know what you've done? You, yes, you! You are to literature what Attila the Hun was to grass!

Així et surtin cucs pel nas, filla de . . . !

What I'm about to say isn't to do with my tale, but it's important you all know: Waltraud has left me.

That's right. Odd, wouldn't you say? That deceitful, big-assed ninny of a cockroach, she mutinied two weeks ago, altogether unexpectedly. I've seen neither hide nor hair since. Well, not nothing: She put a note under the door the other day, containing some ridiculous allegations to justify deserting. That she was very sorry, all that rot. She was shameless enough to accuse me of acting improperly!

And you, reader, haven't gotten the full picture of our relationship.

Don't for a moment think she was working on this book out of the goodness of her heart—not at all! That was her excuse! Deep down, she thinks she's the author. Like the sheepdog that grows so accustomed to biting the sheep, it begins to think it's the shepherd. Although . . . I don't mind admitting there have been times when she altered the course of the story as it was getting a little out of hand. Now she thinks I won't be able to carry on without her, that there's no way for me to recount the bitter end of the siege of 1714. Well she's wrong, very wrong! She wants me to get down on my knees and beg her to come back! Vanity! Women! Which idiot invented the second word when we already had the first? I'll never ask that letter-sucking magpie back!

I, Martí Zuviría, Engineer, by the Grace of *le Mystère,* Bearer of Nine Points, Lieutenant Colonel under His Majesty Carlos III, engineer in the Army of America's Rebel States, and in the Austrian Imperial Army, and in Prussia, the Turkish Empire, for the Tsar of Russia, the Creek, Oglala, and Ashanti Nations, Aide-de-Camp to the Maori King Aroaroataru, Comanche, *Mystériste,* expert in siege warfare, ducker and diver, frightened of swimming, et cetera, now, always, and in summary, human scum:

HEREBY CONFIRM, before God and such men as wish to heed my words, the following capitulations:

One: that my behavior toward Waltraud Spöring, since she entered my service and up until this day, has not always been entirely appropriate, especially in handling her efforts to tend to my poor health.

Two: that I beg her forgiveness, publicly and privately, humbly beseeching that she come and work (not too hard) for me again.

Three: that she has never asked to share in my literary glory, nor earthly vainglory, and that all her efforts with regard to this work are for the benefit of historical commemoration, for what it might be worth. (Less than nothing, by the way—but you are to *leave this bit out.*)

Four, a further and freely ceded capitulation: that Waltraud Spöring is not ugly but has an especial beauty. She is beautiful *inside,* and that's what counts (in the eyes of God). (Very nice, though not even you would believe it.)

Happy now? Now that you've got your quill back, I imagine it makes no difference what I say, you'll write whatever you feel like writing. This book is going to end up more disfigured than my face because of you! If you were honest, you'd include the fact that this has all been a horrible kind of extortion, a humiliation beyond compare.

No, I never insulted you! What did you expect? To be treated like

a forest nymph? You're more like a German forest bear, the only difference being that there's no such thing as a bear with blond hair . . .

Don't leave! Wait, please, my best beloved vile Waltraud. Who am
I going to talk to if you leave?

Sit. Pick up the quill, I beg of you.

Better, much better. Help yourself to a coffee with honey, if you
like. Don't forget I'll be taking it out of your fee, though.

So then, July 25, 1713, finally, and the Bourbon army under the duke
of Pópuli arrived outside Barcelona. The palisade soldiers, led by Zuvi
Longlegs, went down into the bunkers. The good thing about cap-
taining a retreat is the distance you can put between yourself and the
enemy.

Predictably enough, Pópuli's army was welcomed with a barrage
from our cannons. In fact, when we palisade soldiers dropped back into
the city, three cavalry squadrons galloped out past us. A skirmish with
the Bourbon advance party took place, and the Catalan cavalry came
away with a number of prisoners.

Pópuli took this defeat as badly as if he'd lost a regiment. In war,
morale is everything, and when the cavalry rode back into the city,
they received a hero's welcome. The prisoners looked bewildered, as
befits anyone who has just suffered a sudden defeat. They couldn't believe they'd gone from conquerors to captives in such a short space of
time.

"Planning to enter Barcelona, were you?" crowed the people lining
the streets. "Well, here you are now!"

Pópuli's full name was the not at all pompous Restaino Cantelmo
Stuart, prince of Pettorano, gentleman at the court of Camara, and
goodness knows how many other surnames and fluffy titles. Little
Philip's choice of general to defeat the "rebels" was very deliberate:
Pópuli was even more pro-Philip than Philip himself, and he hated
old Barcelona with a vengeance. Should the Allies choose to pull out,
Pópuli would be only too happy to take charge of the occupation of
Catalonia. And he quickly had a chance to show his affection for hei-
nous acts of war.

Before reaching Barcelona, as his army had been advancing through

Catalonia, upon taking control of a certain locality, Pópuli had two alleged pro-Austrians brought before him. "You two are going to play dice," he said to them. "The winner gets to keep his life."

An abuse, of course, but perfidious, outrageous, and arbitrary to boot. Also, he went on to pardon the loser: Acquaintances of the man claimed he was actually a Bourbon and had only feigned loyalty to Little Philip. (There's something that now might seem laughable in this. For seasoned gamblers like the Barcelonans, honesty in the game was sacred. What really infuriated them wasn't Pópuli's tyrannical cruelty but that he hadn't hanged the loser.) But this was only a small, if macabre, side story. His truly atrocious act was to hang every single prisoner taken after a skirmish near Torredembarra. Two hundred prisoners, that is.

In this, he followed Madrid's logic. The ministers there, after the Allied withdrawal from Spain, said that anyone opposing Bourbon forces was to be considered a rebel and treated accordingly. The view from Barcelona was obviously quite different. With the foreign troops gone, the Generalitat had hurriedly formed an army, paid for out of its own coffers. So they had regulars at their disposal, uniformed and on the Catalan government's payroll. The spiral of reprisal and counter-reprisal between Bourbon and Miquelet—we've covered that. But for Pópuli to do that to two hundred men at a stroke was beyond atrocious. Two hundred regulars hanged! Don Antonio sent a missive to Pópuli asking if he'd drunk away his senses. Pópuli answered by saying the same treatment would be meted out to any prisoners taken from that day hence. Don Antonio was especially offended that Pópuli addressed him as the "Rebel Chief." Don Antonio, a career soldier, and the most respectful gentleman when it came to the courtesies and conventions in war! This time Don Antonio replied, very well, he was then obliged to accord the same treatment to any prisoner taken by his side.

The men hanged from the city walls, in sight of the enemy encampment, comprised his answer. A dismal sight if ever there was one: below, the sharpened stakes of the palisade; above, the hanged men.

This opening exchange was more than enough to warn Pópuli's army to take precautions. The regiments installed themselves two thousand yards from the city walls, just out of range of the artillery. They

Trapping Barcelona by Cordon

immediately began building a cordon, an enormous circuit of parapets to surround the entire city, blocking it off between the River Llobregat to the south and the River Besòs to the north—the idea being to isolate the city until the engineers had planned their line of attack.

A military cordon, in and of itself, is no great secret. A hastily dug ditch, basically, along which barricades are thrown up with compacted earth, planks of wood, stones, sticks, and anything else the besiegers can lay their hands on. They put any unevenness in the land to their advantage, making extra obstacles out of hummocks or natural ditches. As far as possible, they create scaled-down versions of the five-sided bastions. Needless to say, the besiegers will flatten any buildings in the vicinity, no matter how small, for matériel.

The building of the cordon was under way when three messengers arrived bearing Pópuli's surrender ultimatum. The mood in the city was such that these were more likely to be strung up than welcomed—a double guard, bayonets drawn, had to form to protect the men from the baying crowd.

That night Don Antonio called me in to see him. As soon as I came into his study, he addressed me: "I want you to go with the emissaries bearing the reply."

"Me, Don Antonio?"

"You're my aide-de-camp, if memory serves. And this is precisely the kind of occasion when aides-de-camp come into play. It isn't only the city's honor that's at stake here but, since I am commander of the garrison, mine, too."

"Certainly, Don Antonio."

"I already know you're not a soldier, just an engineer in uniform, and the most basic rudiments of militariness are quite beyond you. But do you think you could be so kind as to address me as 'General'?"

"Yes, General."

"I need to know you won't be discourteous in any way with the enemy. Their army has just pitched, and in war, appearances are as important as in matters of the heart."

"You're right, Don Antonio."

"They're constantly labeling us seditious, countryless, kingless, and dishonorable. What better way of refuting such charges than to be courteous with them, with their troops looking on? You mustn't let anyone spoil this. Graciousness, good deeds, gentlemanliness, gallantry, neatness. This is your task."

"As you wish, Don Antonio."

Honestly, it seemed like a waste of time to me. The Bourbons were in place, they were here for our blood; no amount of talking was going to change that. But that was the way with military honor in my time: a bloodbath with spotless manners.

A young Pelt was charged with taking the city's answer to Pópuli. Evidently from a good family, he appeared proud to have been given the job, and had dressed in his best attire. He received me with a smile. "I'm told you'll be acting as my second," he said. "Do you know the protocol?"

"Well, no."

"I go first. You stay to my right, a pace behind. After you, the Bourbon messenger, and bringing up the rear, two standard-bearers, one with the royal standard, the other with parliament's. Be sure to adhere to the conventions."

"As you wish."

"We'll bow to their officers—amicably but never submissively. Remember, we're at war!"

He was the one, it seemed to me, who had forgotten we were at war.

"And when exactly," I said, "does bowing go from being amicable to submissive?"

"Don't worry about that. All you have to do is, once we get there, hand me the missive. I unroll it, and I read it out." This little Pelt was indeed proud to be leading the delegation. "I haven't slept all night," he said, beaming. "I've been working on memorizing a few immortal words to add to the government's missive. Today, sir, we shall make history."

The location of the Bourbon encampment, just out of range of the city's artillery, meant it was quite a walk to get there. For my part, I was deep in thought the whole way, and not altogether happy thoughts.

We halted very close to their front line. There were thousands of soldiers working away on their ditches and barricades, all the way from Montjuïc to the mouth of the River Besòs. As far as the eye could see, men were chest-deep and shifting shovelfuls of earth.

The dimensions of the ditch, the sight of so many thousands of men working so systematically, intelligently, to bring about our destruction, left me feeling stricken. I'd been on the other side in Tortosa, so I hadn't comprehended how distressing this all was from the point of view of the besieged.

A few minutes later, a podgy colonel came out to meet us, with four officers alongside. Coming a little way past the half-finished trench, this colonel addressed us brusquely: "You took your time."

All the buggering about preparing for ceremony, and the Bourbons didn't even bother to greet us.

"The reason for our lateness," I said, stepping to the front, "is explained in the first paragraph. Here, read it for yourself." I handed over the missive, somehow forgetting the protocol, and the Pelt's immortal words.

The colonel, seeing that it was written in Catalan, thrust it back into my hands. "Tell us what it says in Castilian!"

The colonel and the men he had with him seemed cast from the same mold: dark eyes, pompous-looking mustaches, and a studied haughtiness to them all. I took a breath. There are a thousand ways to offend one's enemy—now that I was going to have to read, I chose to do it in a chirpy tone, enunciating slowly as though reading to the village idiot—as if I doubted his ability to comprehend the civic composure of the people of Barcelona.

The enemy's letter, delivered to this City by a messenger, required such attention that we considered it proper not to reply immediately.

I looked up from the sheet of paper. "Shall I go on?" I said. "Or do you already have an idea of what comes next?"

"Read on!"

I felt like I was breathing fire. This fat little colonel was really getting on my nerves with his self-important tone; I wasn't there to take orders from him. I hesitated: to read or not to read? That was the question. I resolved to follow Don Antonio's orders.

I filled my lungs so that the thousands of white uniformed soldiers digging the trenches would hear. Curious to know what was happening, they'd put down their picks and shovels to watch the scene. They viewed me thoughtfully, without any animosity. Their officers were so absorbed that they gave no order to go back to work. "Read it," I said to myself, "like Jimmy announcing his own arrival at the gates of heaven." I summoned my most stentorian voice:

This City will resist the enemy at its gates.

This City, and the whole Principality, innately loyal to its sovereign—whose charge it would be to declare peace—remains at war.

The unjust and extraordinary threats against us are not daunting, but rather give great heart to the vassals upholding their oft-stated oaths of allegiance.

And because this City is not accustomed to changing the terms of civility, it returns the messengers as safely as it received them. In view of this reply, the Duke of Pópuli should proceed as he judges best, for the City is resolved to oppose all invaders, as he is about to learn.

Barcelona, 29th July 1713

A long moment passed—longer than their execrable cordon—with the Army of the Two Crowns standing looking at us, as though *le Mystère* had turned us to stone. I lowered the paper brusquely, and only then did the greasy colonel turn indignant, or at least made a show of indignancy.

"What kind of farce do you call this?" he cried. "Do you know you are welcoming a siege?"

"What does it look like?" I said, rolling my eyes. "Think we've got cannons up on our bastions just to welcome you in with flowers?"

"Such folly can only be that of criminals who know they are guilty and are afraid of royal punishment."

"Sir!" I said. "Show some respect."

"Your ramparts are far from fit for war, and His Majesty's army has forty thousand hardened soldiers!"

I raised my balled fists above my head. "And we have fifty thousand! Each and every city dweller, plus all the unfortunates who have fled to us seeking refuge!"

"Zuviría, please!" interrupted the Pelt, the first time he'd spoken.

But that colonel had succeeded in irking me, and I let him have it: "And for you to call us criminals! When we occupied Madrid in 1710, the worst we did was to hand out a few bags of coins. And you thank us by setting fire to villages and cities, hanging women and old people, and now setting camp before our walls, ready to scorch us with thousands of pounds of gunpowder."

"No one raises his voice to me, least of all a rebel to the king!" roared the colonel. "The only thing stopping me from teaching you a lesson is the hospitality required by the rules of war! It's not too late for you to come to your senses. Do you really think you can resist the most noble duke of Pópuli? He has already covered himself in immortal battlefield glory and is a descendent of the most august Neapolitan families."

A Neapolitan! Now, there was a way of pacifying me! Their commander in chief, Pópuli, Neapolitan! See how they get absolutely everywhere?

"Neapolitan, did you say?" Making a show of moderation before I exploded.

"From Naples, yes, and of its most distinguished stock."

But before he could finish, I bellowed like a hippopotamus. "Know the real reason why your little Italian general hasn't attacked yet? Because he's scared stiff! His rectum is clenched so tight, a beetle's antennae couldn't fit up there!"

"Please, Lieutenant Colonel!" cried the scandalized Pelt, who had turned green and white, rather like a chard.

"We're going to give Pópuli such a kicking that he'll go flying, all the way over the Mediterranean and back to his Italian boot!" Then, turning to the officers alongside the corpulent colonel, I said: "As for you, come any closer and we'll riddle your bodies so full of holes, you'll end up more like cream sieves, you bunch of blockheads!"

It goes without saying that there ended the courtesies. The Pelt was so dismayed that he didn't say a word during our walk back to the city. For my part, when Villarroel asked how it had gone, I merely replied: "Mission accomplished, Don Antonio."

2

So began the long, cruel, and singular siege of the city of Barcelona. Within a few days, the Bourbons had closed their cordon, just about, from one side of the city to the other. Following that, they were so occupied in applying the finishing touches that they didn't bother to begin firing at us.

The mood inside the city fluctuated more than the London Stock Exchange; very quickly, the Barcelonans shifted out of euphoria and into the monotony of a never-ending standoff. Neither did the city consider surrender, nor did Pópuli attack. There were some routine artillery exchanges between the cannons on the bastion tops and the besiegers, more colorful than dangerous, the occasional cavalry sortie into no-man's-land, and some desertions from either side. Strange as it may seem, more soldiers flowed in the direction of the city than fled it. The Spaniards tended to desert more regularly than the French, doubtless because they were given worse food. The defectors usually exaggerated the hardships they'd undergone—to win our sympathy—but we could see that the soles of their boots had rotted, and that spoke volumes.

Things were increasingly strained between the French and Spanish. The French accused their allies of being good for nothing, incapable of looking after their own allies in a siege. The Spaniards retorted by pointing out that the French navy was as good as pointless. (And right they were; the naval blockade was a constant source of embarrassment for the French, at least until Jimmy arrived.)

As an engineer, I couldn't have been happier with the way the siege was going. Let me remind you that when a city was besieged *selon les règles*, even if everything went as well as it could for the attackers, they still had only thirty days. All an engineer in my position wanted, therefore, was to draw things out. What the government chose to do with that time wasn't my concern: negotiate a respectable peace, bring in foreign reinforcements, or wait for other world powers to intercede with diplomacy. Any of these. If Barcelona's cries were heard in the rest of Europe, sooner or later, someone would have to do something. Thus I reasoned, vaguely. Everyone did. Meanwhile, the months passed, and Pópuli never embarked on his Attack Trench, and so to us, every new dawn was like a victory.

A curious *drôle de guerre*, yes. Consider it: Most of us soldiers did a shift on the ramparts or in a bastion and would then go home for dinner or breakfast, often a stone's throw from our battle post. I myself, within five minutes of being up on a bastion observing the Bourbons with the telescope, or directing defense works, would be back at my table with Anfán on my lap and Amelis putting a plate in front of me. "How was your day, darling?" "Great, sweetie, they sent out a patrol, and we dropped our breeches and showed them our bare behinds."

People would go down to the seafront parade for aperitifs. Sometimes becoming the audience for exciting skirmishes between the two navies, our own ships sailing out into the bay to slip past the blockading French ships, who could do little to stop them. The crowds cheered and clapped, as though it were some kind of stage play on water going on, and not a siege.

News and provisions came into the city by boat. From what we could piece together, it sounded as though, outside the city, far bloodier fighting was taking place. The Red Pelts were also keen to hear any and all news—some of the boats bore Archduke Charles's letters from Vienna. I believe I've already made mention of that swine having sold us out, but in his royal little letters, his message was always: Well done, my boys, keep it up, keep on smiling at your executioner.

Between the city and the enemy line, there were a few workers' cottages, inns, and in the lanes near the city, brothels. Through the course of the siege, these gradually fell to pieces and were destroyed. By the artillery and, mainly, because both sides sent crews of foragers to bring back tiles, bricks and slabs. They needed anything they could lay their hands on to reinforce the cordon, and we, to bulk up the ramparts.

Usually, a patrol, one of ours or one of theirs, would occupy an abandoned building midway between us and the enemy. They'd dismantle anything of interest as quietly as they could and then, when the sun went down, return to their own side, arms or sacks full of whatever they'd plundered. If possible, we'd keep out of sight by making our way back along a dry riverbed or a disused irrigation channel. Logically enough, skirmishes were commonplace. Truth be told, they usually happened suddenly and confusedly more than out of any great desire to fight.

Pillaging is generally associated with an outbreak of savage brutality when, really, methodically taking apart a building is one of the most tedious tasks known to man—particularly, say, when you're charged with leading a certain Ballester and his men in the operation. (This fell to me, of course; other officers declined such a great honor.) To begin with, rather than keeping their heads down, the Miquelets tried to provoke the enemy. They couldn't, or didn't want to, understand that we'd gone to that abandoned farmhouse, or that stable, to gather matériel for our side, and to keep it out of Bourbon hands. I became incensed, seeing them wasting time—pulling women's clothing out of trunks and japing around in it. And instead of staying silent, it would be a noisy jamboree, with petticoats for scarves. Good old Zuvi—he was like a hen trying to order a dozen wolves about. And more often than not, they simply found my orders incomprehensible.

"The frames! Pull the window frames out!"

"Why the *cojones* do you want us to take wooden window frames with us?"

"Do as you're told!"

"You engineers have very strange ideas when it comes to war."

We'd fall back, and always, always, one or two of them would have a petticoat draped around his neck. With six or seven large window frames weighing them down, they'd run along at a stoop.

I brought the scrapping schedule forward. To try and get in before the Bourbon crews, and because if we went out later in the day, the Miquelets were sure to be drunk. Not that I could stop them from coming back drunk; in the early days of the siege in particular, wine and liquor were still being found in abandoned larders.

I was sometimes less harsh with them when they seemed downcast. Those rooms, now empty, had been occupied not long before by people like them. Or at least the people they'd been before joining the Miquelets. Their thoughts were plain: If we're here to defend a city, what are we doing destroying its houses, outside the walls though they may be?

It fell to me to teach them a few things. "Your life is no longer your own! It belongs to the city now, and it is for the city to decide what you do and when you shall give your life. As long as the siege lasts, we cease to exist as individuals. Accept it!"

Ballester would come back with some retort, and we'd have an altercation. A very isocratic form of command, of course, though that didn't make it any less tiring. I felt snared—Ballester closing on me from below and Don Antonio from above.

I finally understood the usefulness of all those hours in the Spherical Room. It was akin to living inside it, to serve under a commander like Don Antonio; oversights were not tolerated. When would the fortification works be complete on this part of the ramparts? Why that blunt angle on the Saint Père bastion? What's that gap in the stockades doing there? How many bricks do we have in our provisions? My brain, along with every one of my muscles, was pushed to its limits. And this was even though the siege remained nothing but a series of small skirmishes.

Don Antonio would usually have a cohort of officers and assistants around him. But one chilly morning, he and I bumped into each other, just the two of us, up on the ramparts. Wrapped in a bedewed cape, looking out through a telescope, he resembled one more rock in our defenses.

"Don Antonio," I said, breaking in on what he was doing. "Something's been troubling me." I took the fact that he didn't shout at me as permission to speak. "You criticized me for not having what it takes," I went on. "And yet you let me serve you."

"*Fiyé*," he said, still peering out through the telescope. "You had an education with the greatest engineer of our age, and I cannot do without such knowledge."

"But I didn't complete my studies. I didn't pass the test." I rolled up my sleeve. "See these tattoos. They tell my story—the fifth one, that I'm an imposter. There's something I'm missing, Don Antonio, but I don't know what it is. Perhaps you're the person to tell me."

Villarroel didn't react. He continued scanning the enemy positions and said: "Let me ask you a question, my boy. If the entire Bourbon army were bearing down on your house, would you hold the last redoubt to the bitter end? Answer."

"I would, sir," I said, and not in the least enthusiastic tone of my life.

Notwithstanding, he replied: "We generals spend our whole lives hearing people saying 'Yes, sir!' And do you know what? The words I've just heard don't fill me with great confidence."

I said nothing. He lowered the telescope.

"Zuviría. Your learning is ample. In France, they taught you everything you need to know. What's holding you back, what's keeping you from what you're looking for, is something else. A tremendously simple thing, in reality."

Then a strange phenomenon took place. Something came over Don Antonio's gaze, a sort of leniency or mildness, a look of compassion. Until that day I had seen such a look in the eyes of only two people, only two: Amelis and Ballester. And he said to me: "You haven't suffered enough." He paused for a moment, as if waiting for that something to quit his body, and when he spoke again, he was the great general once more. "I'm going to notify the general staff of something tomorrow, the start of a crucial, potentially decisive maneuver. All our hope, more or less, lies in this play. And you're going to participate in operations. Perhaps you'll be able to resolve the doubt that lingers in your soul. That is," he said grimly, "if you survive."

I was about to take my leave when he caught sight of my bare belt. "One other thing," he said. "An officer without a sword isn't an officer. Find yourself one."

The quartermaster was so tight, he wanted me to pay six pesos for a sword. I flat refused. That same night, while Peret was sleeping, I stole his. It had so many chips and nicks in it, it was more like a saw than a sword, which didn't bother me, as it would be sheathed most of the time. Peret was deeply upset and badgered me all the way through the siege to give it back. I pretended not to hear. "Six pesos!" I said.

Don Antonio's maneuver consisted of sending out some ships, well stocked and carrying a little more than a thousand men and companion cavalry, and disembarking behind the enemy's rearguard. Their mission would then be to raise recruits throughout the land and, when the numbers were sufficient, to come in and attack the far side of the Bourbon cordon. This, coordinated with a charge by the Coronela, would pincer Pópuli.

Bazoches had taught me about all the possible ways out for a garrison under siege, and this must have been among the most audacious, imaginative, and well planned I'd come across. Or it would have been, if there did not exist on this earth a race of pernicious, gluttonous dilettantes known as the Red Pelts!

Waltraud beseeches me to calm down, to carry on, but I don't want to calm down, I don't have the slightest interest in calming down. For the French and Spanish—they had to be killed mercilessly—they were the enemy. But the Red Pelts, those lordlings with their powdered cheeks, turned everything we were fighting for into an empty husk. Deep down, they didn't believe in Catalan liberties, or in our constitutions. In the end, they were faced with an enemy who sought to exterminate their people, something so unprecedented and ferocious that they did carry on fighting, but only because there was no choice. Out of earshot, their motto was: "Chaos before slavery." I'll describe everything that happened! How they hindered General Villarroel, how they managed to make defeat out of our victories. For until now, only the victor's version has been told, or that of the complicit Catalan upper class: empty lies, the lot. And as everyone knows, an empty cup makes more noise than a full one.

Schnapps, bring me more schnapps. May the harshness of it strip our throats but never quench our hearts! Chin up, Martí!

Back to the story. Where were we? Ah, yes. The expedition.

The government wanted it led by the deputy of the military estate, the very noble, and also profoundly Pelt-y, Antoni Berenguer. Not the ideal man for such a complex and risky venture: In spite of his title, he was a politician, not a soldier, and he was also very old. He was confined to a wheelchair, complete with a chamber pot attached underneath. His lower eyelids hung down like wet bloody tongues. Yes, credit where it's due, his white eyebrows and beard, cut by one of the city's finest barbers, did confer upon him an air of venerability.

Deputy Berenguer had a retinue of upstanding citizens to underline the solemnity of his post. They were nothing more than a crew of bootlickers, and very quickly, our name for them—"Berenguer's oafs"—stuck. There was no point to them unless they were with the deputy; away from him, they were nothing but a herd dressed in silk.

I wasn't sure about Berenguer from the start. True, as deputy of the military estate, he was the institutional incarnation of the spirit of the struggle. He, and only he, had the sacred right to bear the silver mace symbolizing the Catalans' right to oppose any invader. This was a large silver truncheon with baroque inlay, affectionately referred to by the people as "The Club." Any neighborhood the deputy passed through with this in hand, all the local inhabitants over the age of sixteen were obliged to drop what they were doing, to leave their lives behind, and to give everything in defense of their country. But, so my thinking went, was it really necessary to put this sanctimonious old fart aboard a ship? And that isn't a metaphor, by the way; his guts really were in poor order.

As for Colonel Sebastià Dalmau, who was also part of the expedition, words cannot describe the talents of that giant of a man. Of all the anonymous heroes of this century, Dalmau was one of the greatest.

He descended from one of Barcelona's grandest families. When the Allies withdrew from Catalonia, he immediately came in on the Generalitat's side. In fact, he was one of the few in the upper classes who responded to the *Crida*. His whole fortune went to underwriting the Catalan War, every last peso. The Sebastià Regiment was financed entirely by his family; the soldiers' wages, weapons, provisions, and uniforms all came out of his pocket. The infantry on the expedition was to be formed of this regiment, which consisted of non-nobles and non-guild members. Tavern and brothel dwellers, scum—the government trusted them less than they would a converted Jew. From my point of view as an engineer, I didn't judge them on where they came from or their prestige but on their military effectiveness, and in that respect, they struck me as an altogether magnificent unit. The Red Pelts worked by a different logic and were relieved to see the back of Dalmau's troop. (Why risk decent young men when the dregs were offering themselves up?)

Some men are born to be happy, just as others might be born lame or with blue eyes. Dalmau had one of those smiling "all will be well" countenances, and coming from him, it seemed like certainty rather than wishful thinking. He had a very Barcelonan way of looking at things. War, to him, was at root a transaction, with one's homeland as a business and one's family as shareholders. Properly considered, in a civilian army, he was the ideal kind of commander.

As for the other officials who boarded ships on that expedition, we need mention only one other, a German colonel. And the less said about him, the better. In siege situations, dark things happen.

This colonel was one of the few, the very few, who chose to come over and serve the Generalitat when the Allies withdrew. But he wasn't motivated by any noble cause. Various common crimes—including looting from dead bodies—meant his reputation preceded him. Word had it, he'd led a troop who had stripped dead soldiers of their possessions before burying them en masse.

His position in the Allied army had therefore become untenable, and when the *Crida* went out, he defected, claiming that the Catalan cause was close to his heart. For the Generalitat's part, it was short of officers and admitted him without asking questions. Even so, he was such a scoundrel that the German volunteers in Barcelona refused to serve under him. Don Antonio set out for him, in no uncertain terms, his choices: Either he could restore his reputation when the bloodiest fighting came, or pack his bags for Vienna, where the hangman would be waiting. He had no choice but to join the expedition.

His favorite word was *Scheisse*. He said it so often, the men ended up calling him Scheissez. Just so you know, my dear vile Waltraud, in Spanish surnames, the ending *-ez* means "son of." Perez, son of Pere; Fernandez, son of Fernando, et cetera. What the Barcelonans didn't know was that *Scheisse* means "shit" in German. So every time they addressed him, they were calling their superior officer "Shitson." Shitson himself wasn't amused, but since Don Antonio had made it clear he wouldn't tolerate the man abusing his authority, he had to grin and bear it. He was always looking at you out of the corner of his eye. During the voyage, we were constantly glancing at each other. He was like any of the other rats on board, the one difference being that rats are the first to abandon a sinking ship, whereas Shitson was looking for a way off as soon as possible, whether the vessel was seaworthy or not.

For my part, I couldn't seem to shake that look Don Antonio had given me just before the order to join the expedition. Now the outcome of the war depended on the thousand men sailing with me. Perhaps I was on my way to learning the definitive lesson. That of The Word.

Ballester and his crew of ten were also with us. They'd be sure to come in handy as scouts. As for the French flotilla blocking our exit, that was the least of our worries. Our ships were dodgers, built to hug the shore; theirs had deep hulls and could never get anywhere near the coast. The journey to Arenys wouldn't take long, not over six hours if the winds were favorable, and we wanted to be swift so we could travel under cover of dark. As for the embarkation, I'll save the details: forty-seven ships of all different sizes, a thousand infantry, and several cavalry squadrons boarding them. The voyage I'll skip as well—owing to my rank, I spent the duration alongside Berenguer, his farts, and his oafs.

As with the voyage, disembarking was a tedious affair. There weren't many barges to transfer the troop to dry land, and since the bay at Arenys was shallow, the majority of the men jumped over the sides and waded to shore, powder and rifles above their heads. The horses were simply thrown into the water; instinct sent them inland. I was one of the first to get down after Ballester and his men. It wasn't bravery but, rather, that I couldn't stand being on the ship a second longer. When I set foot on dry land, I felt like someone had replaced my head with a whirligig. The sea! Here's a question: What's big and useless like the sea? Only one thing: my dear vile Waltraud! Ha! Oh! Not laughing?

To make things that bit more complicated, the people of Arenys welcomed us as though we were liberating them. Lovely, but if you want to create a huge amount of confusion, mix together a soaking-wet regiment, barges with men and equipment being off-loaded, horses running up and down the shore, officers raw-voiced from shouting, and then add in hundreds of old people, women, and children running and hugging a thousand dizzy soldiers. Great care was required with Deputy Berenguer; carrying his wheelchair to dry ground provided quite a spectacle. Since no adequate barge could be found for the grand so-and-so, someone came up with the brilliant idea of carrying him instead, the porters wading waist-deep with him on their shoulders. First the wheelchair was handed down to them, then the deputy. What they hadn't accounted for was how heavy the flatulent general was. He settled into the chair and the poor porters sank up to their necks. A little more and they'd have gone under. Berenguer, though, was very happy, going along the surface of the water like Jesus of Nazareth in a wheelchair.

Almost recovered from the seasickness, I walked up to the top of a dune from which the whole beach could be seen. I caught sight of Ballester, his men around him on the rocks having breakfast, him standing looking pensively out at the sea, his horse's reins in one hand. For mountain folk, the sea will always be a mystery that stirs them. It was going to be a good while longer until everyone had disembarked, and I went over for a chat.

"Tedious. Shall we head out? A race?" I said, challenging him. "Bet you anything you like I can get to Mataró before you."

Mataró was under enemy occupation. It was as though I were daring him to a harebrained race to a cliff edge—whoever stops, loses. He snorted contemptuously. "The army up to its neck in water," he said, still looking out, "and you talking about horse racing."

It was precisely his gruffness that made him so much fun to needle. "You're just afraid to lose!" I said. "I bet a peso."

He abruptly turned to face me, the blue vein on his forehead standing out.

"You have to obey my orders, remember?" I added. "Well then— mount up!"

And up we got. In no time at all, we were galloping at breakneck speed. I know, it was sheer stupidity, as well as an affront to all common sense. But know something, my dear vile Waltraud? We were only young.

We entered a pine forest on a narrow path. His horse was black, mine a dun white. They were neck and neck for a good long while. Every so often I turned my head and stuck out my tongue. This enraged Ballester—sense of humor not being his strongest suit—and he spurred his horse to go faster. I don't know what happened with mine—perhaps it saw a snake, perhaps a hoof struck a pine root—but it pulled up suddenly, and I went sailing forward over its back. Luckily, it had rained recently, and the muddy ground cushioned my landing.

I got up, assessing the surrounding greenery with all my sharpened senses. It struck me how foolhardy we'd been. We'd gone a good way south, and it couldn't have been over two or three miles from Arenys to Mataró. There was no way the Bourbons wouldn't have garrisoned a place like Mataró, so near to Barcelona.

"Strange," I said. "Nobody about. No checkpoints on the road, no horseback patrols. Not a soul."

"We've stolen a march on them," said Ballester, whose ears had pricked up as well now. "They weren't expecting us to disembark behind their rearguard."

I mounted up again and rode a little farther on. Not a trace of human life. Only the thick and deathly silent forest on either side of the path. We came to a steeply rising bend. "Look!" I cried.

Startled, Ballester put his hand to the hilt of his sword. But I meant only the butterflies—hundreds of orange butterflies were swarming around in a clearing to the left of the bend in the path. Dismounting, I walked forward into that cloud of orange wings.

Thoughts of Bazoches came into my head, memories of the Ducroix brothers' rational magic. No, I felt no desire to harm those butterflies. Quite the opposite. The world was at war, it was a time when everything was close to tumbling into the abyss, and submerging myself in those fluttering wings felt cleansing to the spirit. They understood; they came and landed on me. Dozens and dozens alighting on my outstretched arm, covering the sleeve of my uniform like a resplendent wreath.

"Thinking of eating them?" said a laughing Ballester from up on his horse.

"Don't be barbaric! They're resting on my hand precisely because they know I won't do them any harm. Listen: When a person observes a scene with all his attention, he becomes a part of that scene. Plus, insects love new things."

"Mother of God," groaned Ballester, his hands on his saddle pommel. "We're the expedition scouts, and here you are, wasting time trying to tame winged maggots."

"Come on, dismount," I said. "Come on, man, get over here. I'll show you a trick."

He rode on a little way to check that there was nobody beyond the bend. Then he came back and dismounted.

"Hold out your arm," I said, showing him. He looked at me, unconvinced. "Come on! What's the problem? Ballester the Brave, happy to take on an army of Bourbons but afraid of a few butterflies?"

"It's me who frightens insects. My men will tell you the same. We were sleeping out one warm night, and they all woke up crucified with bites, whereas I hadn't been touched."

Eventually, I got him to hold out an arm, palm up. For all the butterflies swirling around me, dozens and dozens of them, as Ballester had predicted, they gave him a wide berth.

"See?" he said, somewhat triumphantly lowering his arm again.

"It isn't just a case of holding your arm out," I said. "You need to offer them all of yourself. The hand has to be both messenger and message."

He let out an annoyed snort. But instead of answering, he lifted his hand again, though in the manner of someone accepting a tiresome bet. To his obvious surprise, a butterfly flew toward him. Fluttering around a little, it came to rest on his rough and calloused hand.

Ballester's face softened. He looked childlike for a few moments, regarding the butterfly that had landed on him; an unthinkable transformation. For once, here was a creature, albeit a maggot with wings, that didn't fear him. We glanced at each other. And began laughing. I'm not sure why, but we laughed.

The spell was broken when we heard a faint noise, measured, like brass on brass. Ballester turned and looked toward the bend in the path. Half a dozen soldiers came into sight; the sound was that of their canteens clanking against buckles and straps. Their uniforms were white. The vein on Ballester's forehead dilated once more.

They came to a halt—though they had been advancing with rifles at the ready, this was a surprise they hadn't been ready for: two men standing in the forest, playing with butterflies. A long moment passed, Ballester standing there with his arm still outstretched. Then his butterfly flew away.

That was his signal: He launched himself at them with his sword drawn. The six of them had advanced two abreast, and Ballester aimed for the middle. He slashed at their necks, left and right, and all I remember is the animal cries—Ballester's and those of the men as they fell. In the blink of an eye, six Frenchmen were down, either dead or wounded.

Gasping after that remarkable burst of energy, Ballester braced his arms against his knees. The look he gave me—was he begging forgiveness or arraigning me for frolicking with the butterflies? I was gasping, too, though in my case, it was from the shock.

Four more soldiers appeared on the path. They came at a pace and with their rifles up. They shouted something in French. They surely couldn't believe what they were seeing: six of their colleagues dead and two men standing there.

"Drop your sword!" I said to Ballester.

He did so, but I already knew what was he was thinking: about freeing up both hands to draw his pistols. Better to be taken prisoner than die, I thought.

"Ballester!" I cried. "Don't draw! Much as you want to, don't do it!"

Everyone started shouting and screaming, everyone except Ballester. The French just about to pull their triggers, me saying we'd surrender. Ballester kept his arms across his torso, a hand on each of his pistol hilts. *Ne tirez pas, nous nous rendons!* A silly thing to point out, but one thing I remember is that all the butterflies were gone.

When I heard the shots, I threw myself to the ground and curled up in a ball, shielding my head. Three reports—*crack crack crack*—followed by three more, then another three.

But when I raised my head, I found that Ballester wasn't dead, nor indeed was I; it was the four Frenchmen who had been shot down. From a bluff to our right, a dozen Miquelets were advancing, emerging from the thick woodland with the barrels of their rifles smoking.

And they were suspicious of us. "Who do you serve?" one asked.

"Emperor Charles," I answered, on my knees and trembling. "And you?"

"Busquets. Hands up," said the man who seemed to be their leader, pointing his rifle at me, "and keep them up. Elbows to ears."

I did as he said, but I protested. "We're with the army of the Generalitat!"

He only became more suspicious. A number of the others swung their rifles around in my direction. "You lie! And if you speak Catalan, that must make you a *botiflero*."

As they waited to see what I'd do next, Ballester took the opportunity to finish off one of the dying Frenchmen next to him. A bullet through the nape of the neck—I remember it exiting through his mouth, as though he'd spat it.

Ballester's relationship with death was something I could never get my head around, never. The Frenchman was certainly dying, nothing could have saved him, and I agree, the most humane thing was to end his suffering. But for Ballester, shooting a man was like tying his shoelaces. A trivial act, devoid of reflection or consequence. There I was, whey-faced, kneeling, arms to the heavens, whereas Ballester's response was to take out his pistol.

"Take me to the man leading your unit," he said to the Miquelet interrogating me. "He owes me twenty pesos." Looking over at me, he said: "Busquets is terrible when it comes to dice."

They led us to a clearing in the woods containing a group of men. There was something in the air, a tangible despondency, the leadenness that is the mark of a defeat. Those not injured and grumbling looked downcast, like scarecrows whose supports had been removed. It had begun drizzling.

Unlike Ballester's men, hardened in a thousand battles, Busquets's were civilians only recently incorporated to mountain life. They still had shoes on their feet, and not the rope-soled sandals; they didn't have the usual blue hooded knee-length cloaks; and their weapons seemed cobbled together, kitchen knives and old muskets that made you think they must have grabbed whatever they could on the way out the door.

None of this was of the slightest interest to Ballester. He walked straight over to a man sprawled on his back against a saddle, with a blond beard and mane of hair. The gold earrings he wore suggested he must be the leader, the previously mentioned Busquets. He'd been shot in the left shoulder, and there was a man next to him delving into the hole with a pair of pincers. Not the easiest task, given that Busquets, in between slugs from a bottle of liquor, was squealing like a boar in a trap, spraying out mouthfuls of liquid when the pain became too much.

Recognizing Ballester, Busquets thrust the bottle in his direction. "You! What on earth are you doing here?"

Ballester held his hand out. "You owe me twenty pesos."

Busquets looked baleful, fit to murder; Ballester just kept his hand outstretched. I feared the worst and glanced around at the rest of the men. But then Busquets burst out laughing, with his good hand grabbed hold of Ballester's forearm, and called him "whoreson," in a nice way. The surgeon, who had retracted the pincers, looked at me as if to say: *Do these seem like adequate working conditions to you?* Anyway, this was how it was with the Miquelets.

As for me, Busquets seemed skeptical. "Lieutenant Colonel? How wonderful." He drank another slug and let out a howl at the surgeon. "Trying to treat me or finish me off?"

Not knowing how best to address him, I opted for the most formal and generic. "If you wouldn't mind, Captain Busquets, could you tell us what's been going on in the locality?"

Busquets didn't seem to think I could be trusted. Tilting his head to one side, Ballester said: "I know he acts like one, but he isn't actually a Red Pelt."

Sighing, grumbling at the surgeon throughout, Busquets told us what had been going on. "We made an attack on Mataró. You know, all the *botifleros* in Catalonia have taken refuge there. And they force the town to feed and shelter them. Which helps us—more recruits. Those damned *botifleros*, so conceited, so insufferably arrogant . . . They pitch families out of their houses or use the inhabitants as servants. They're being served from silver platters while the people starve. Forced to cook for them, empty their pisspots." He became angrier as he went on. "Who do they think they are? Taking over our houses, treating us like slaves, and—the cheek!—they accuse us of rebellion!"

The surgeon was still digging around, and Busquets let out another howl. "So," he said when he'd recovered, "someone blabbed, or maybe it was just that they were sent some reinforcements, I'm not sure." He took a breath. "Infantry came for us, but they had cavalry, too. We don't do so well against cavalry. We were trounced."

"When?" I said.

"Just yesterday."

"They've had more patrols out," said Ballester. "Trying to surround you."

"I know. They don't have enough troops to surround a forest as big as this, though. Plus, I've sent a company to their rearguard to monitor their movements. Now I'm just waiting for the last of my men to join up with us so we can get out of here." Liquor all over his chin, he turned to the surgeon. "And for this sawbones to patch up the wounded!"

"Shut it," said the surgeon. "You're not making this any easier. Taking bullets out isn't exactly what I was trained to do."

"Isn't that what surgeons do?" I said.

"Surgeon?" the man said back, matching the sarcasm of my tone, not stopping what he was doing. "I fled Mataró because I was afraid I might slip and cut some *botiflero*'s throat." Looking over at me, he said: "I'm a barber."

I took Ballester to one side. "Busquets hasn't done anyone any favors," I whispered. "If everyone was fighting their own little wars, there's no way we'd win the main one. Do you see that now?"

"Busquets did well," Ballester said. "This is his home, and he fought to protect it. What did you expect? For him to sit there waiting for us to show up? Until last week, not even we knew we were going to come to Mataró."

Despite the distance between us, Busquets had overheard. "At least I tried, damn it. We gave it a go!" he shouted, leaning on his elbow against the saddle. "And now you show up, from God knows where, and start criticizing."

I went over to him. "I have no issue with you killing Bourbons. But you've also been making it easy for them to kill patriots." I gestured around us. "Look at your men, torn to shreds, holed up in the middle of some dreary forest. And Mataró still in Bourbon hands." I crouched down so we could speak eye to eye. "These men will listen to you, Busquets. Order them to join the Army of the Generalitat." I turned to Ballester to try to get him to help. "Say something, man."

He held out his hand. "You owe me twenty pesos."

"To hell with you," shouted Busquets, his blond mane and long gold earrings shaking, "you and your twenty pesos! And you"—he pointed at me—"can leave off. The deputy! My men don't trust the Red Pelts, to them they're as good as *botifleros*. We've no grand strategies, all we want is to get the enemy out of our homes, and have a home again. No, we won't go running around all of Catalonia, we won't abandon our families." He sighed bitterly. "And what kind of leader would I be who orders his men to do something they don't want to?"

His invective was interrupted by one last howl. The barber had finally extracted the bullet. "For you," he said, placing a bloody red ball in Busquets' hand. Kissing it, Busquets then introduced it delicately into a small leather pouch. Lead against lead—that was the sound it made dropping in.

Ballester whispered in my ear: "Busquets collects all the bullets that enter his body. Saint Peter told him he'd only open his gates when the pouch was full."

"And you," said Busquets, addressing Ballester now, "I'd like to know what you think you're doing running around doing the deputy's bidding. He's one of the worst Red Pelts around."

Ballester's look became more sarcastic still. "Twenty pesos," he said.

Same old story. Put three Catalans in a room, and you'll have four different opinions. Shaking my head, I said to Ballester: "This is pointless, let's go."

"Fine, go, then!" shouted Busquets, incensed, as we made our way out of the clearing. "I expected nothing more from Red Pelts! We'll keep up the fight though! You hear? We'll carry on fighting as long as one of us remains alive!"

I wafted my hand in the air, not turning around, as though bidding farewell to an incurable madman.

"And yet we're supposed to follow you!" Busquets ranted. "Well, I'll have you know: We're going to liberate Mataró, and its storehouses, and its sixty thousand cuarteras of wheat!"

I stopped in my tracks as though I'd walked into an invisible wall. I strode back over to Busquets. "What did you say? Say it again? Sixty thousand cuarteras of wheat? Are you sure?"

"The storehouses are full to bursting. Mataró's the natural place for the Bourbon army to keep their provisions. Very close to their cordon at Barcelona, and the patriots all fled from the town. No fear of sabotage."

I stood staring ahead, my jaw on the ground. Sixty thousand cuarteras of wheat! The besieging army's entire supply, a stone's throw from where we were. The Two Crowns had no idea about the deputation having disembarked. Which explained their having placed only a few cavalry squadrons at Mataró, sufficient to keep a few flighty Miquelets at bay and nothing more.

"Captain Busquets!" I cried. "You are under orders from the deputy now, and you will obey them. Work with the army, and we'll have taken Mataró in no time."

Busquets screwed up his pained face even more. "But you yourself said a second ago that we would have to follow where you went, and that taking Mataró was a useless enterprise!"

Ballester and I led the horses away, crossing through the thick undergrowth, crestfallen. When we reached the path again, I couldn't

keep myself from hugging Ballester, who was taken aback by my enthusiasm. "We're going to turn the siege of Barcelona into a latter-day
Cannae!"

"What do you mean, 'can I'?" he said, annoyed. "Explain yourself,
damn it! I haven't read as many books as you."

"Think about all the prisoners and deserters who come over to our
side. They all say the same: They've got no decent footwear, they're
eating insipid gruel day after day. Which is to be expected—the Bourbons have ravaged the country so badly, there's nowhere to get supplies. They're like the gluttonous fox after it's eaten the whole chicken
house."

"And? You have no idea what hunger is. When push comes to
shove, people will always resort to stealing."

"That's your view; you lead a small crew of mountain men. But at
Barcelona, there are forty thousand mouths to feed, and they're stuck
there. We've got enough to feed them all right here: the foodstuff in
Mataró. The Bourbons are doubtless thinking they can starve Barcelona into submission."

"And what about can I?"

"Cannae was Imperial Rome's worst defeat. Hannibal was facing a
Roman army that had twice his number. When battle commenced, he
let his frontline buckle back, drawing the Romans in, and, meanwhile,
had his Carthaginian cavalry come down the wings and encircle the
enemy. Our cavalry will be the wheat they've stolen. If we deprive
them of wheat, and the deputation is situated at the Bourbon cordon's
rear, all will be lost for them. The besieger, besieged."

There was a hint of a smile on Ballester's face. He took my meaning. "Forty thousand men can't survive for weeks and months on empty
bellies. They'll have no choice but to lift the siege."

Before we mounted up again, I hugged Ballester. "Setting up a new
siege will be totally impractical for them. Their morale will be rock-
bottom; the military coffers in Madrid, empty. Europe's sick of war.
Little Philip will come under pressure from all different ministries to
sign a pact with the Generalitat."

We rode as hard as we could back to the deputation. They'd posted
themselves inside an old country house. Deputy Berenguer, Dalmau,

and the other staff officers were holding a council of war. Shitson was there as well, which meant we'd arrived just in time.

I was so excited, I could barely get my words out straight. Deputy Berenguer was annoyed. "This Busquets you speak of, he's nothing but a petty tyrant! He has neither title nor uniform. We can't be sure to whom he owes loyalty."

"But Your Excellency," I said, "the man's wounded. I saw him with my own two eyes."

"You've been fooled, then," retorted Deputy Berenguer. "You just don't have the brain to see it. How can we be sure his reports are accurate?"

"Because Busquets and his men are from Mataró," said Ballester dryly.

Dalmau stood up and, with his usual congenial smile, made a proposal: "Leave them to me, Your Excellency. We lose nothing by moving out a little from our current position."

We led the cavalry and the whole regiment to Busquets's wood. When the Miquelets saw us, they erupted in sheer delight: a whole army come to rescue them! War, that great pendulum. A few hours earlier, Busquets was wounded and far from help in some forest, and now here was an army, well equipped and ready to go. Mataró would open its gates to us, the enemy storehouses would be ours, and, with a little luck, the final victory, too. Busquets's Miquelets were over the moon. They embraced Dalmau's men, weeping with pure joy. It was the first time I had felt at all optimistic during the war—and it would be the last. We didn't need to win it; it was good enough not to lose.

At midafternoon I was called in to join the general staff. Members of the senior military were posted in the country house down near the beach where we'd landed. A debate was going on, a most heated one, between Deputy Berenguer and Dalmau. The former nestled in his pisspot throne, the latter with his fists thrust against the table, leaning forward.

"Our objective is to raise recruits and then go and liberate Barcelona!" bellowed Deputy Berenguer.

"Our objective is to win the war!" replied Dalmau from his side of the table. Seeing me come in, he said: "Ah, Zuviría. You, I believe, interrogated a couple of French prisoners whom Busquets was holding."

"I did, Colonel."

"And they corroborated the information on the storehouses?"

"In every respect, sir," I said, not understanding the argument.

Dalmau turned to face Deputy Berenguer, his energies renewed. "Do you hear that? If you don't trust Busquets, at least have faith in his enemies. Four and a half million kilos of wheat! Their whole food-stuff supply! We're past harvest now, the land's going to be producing nothing more; they'll have no way of feeding their army! Plus, imagine what it'll do for morale to take control of those stores. We can easily sail a portion into Barcelona as a trophy. Or better still: Transport all we can and share it out among the most needy! They'll enlist in droves!"

Deputy Berenguer, though listening, was clearly annoyed. "And I say again," he said, "the decision's been made by our superiors, quite apart from the circumstances we're faced with here. Obey orders! Your attitude is near insubordinate!"

I couldn't help but get involved. "Your Excellence, may I ask what you mean by a decision made by our superiors?"

Dalmau had subsided into a chair, looking like he'd given up. He passed a tired hand over his face. "We're not going to be attacking Mataró," he said dispiritedly. "The deputy's against it."

I was astonished. "Mataró will open its gates to us!" I cried. "No blood need even be spilled! We lose nothing by attacking and gain everything. It might even mean the end of the war!"

"You will obey my orders, as I will obey those of my superiors," said the deputy before I had finished. "I have instructions from the government not to enter Mataró. And that's how it will be."

I was speechless. This was beyond me. Our own deputy refusing to use force against the enemy. "Your Excellence," I said, my mouth dry. "Your opinion may be down to the fact you've never seen our lads in action. They'd storm Paris and Madrid, given the order. Have faith in them, I beg you."

"Come now, you don't fool me," he said with disdain. "I may be old, my legs may not work anymore, but my eyes still do." Pointing at me, he addressed Dalmau once more. "The man who accompanied Lieutenant Colonel Zuviría before, was that not the infamous Ballester? Ballester! A country bandit, a prince among brigands! I myself sent out a decree to have him hunted down a couple of years ago, calling for him to be hanged, drawn and quartered, and his body displayed as an example." He took a breath. "War indeed inverts and subverts the natural order of things. And you, Dalmau, know very well, better than anyone, that the men in your regiment are little different. The lowest of the low and, as such, prey to the basest urges."

Dalmau protested. "My men fight like lions!"

"And I congratulate you on that," said the deputy. "Your regiment has only recently been assembled, and they've very quickly shown themselves to be hardy. But Dalmau, tell me something: Have you ever given them an order *not* to use violence?"

"If you are referring to discipline, all the officers here will back me up in saying there have never been any issues."

"In Barcelona!" specified the deputy, wagging a finger. "Under the watchful and paternal eye of the Generalitat. But once inside Mataró, can you guarantee that discipline will hold?" He turned and addressed me once more. "Lieutenant Colonel Zuviría, I hear you served as an engineer in His Majesty's army in 1710?"

"Yes, sir."

"Tell us, in that case: Is it reasonable to suppose of a place that has been turned into a general storehouse, and in which a huge quantity of grain has been gathered, that other goods and stuffs will also be gathered in that place?"

"Of course, Your Excellence," I said, because it was true, and because this way there would be more arguments in favor of an attack. "Weaponry, munitions, material that can be used for sapping and for building trenches, certainly, and possibly carts and horses we'll need to transport it all away—"

That old graybeard with his drooping eyes was both canny and astute, because before I could finish, he cut in. "What about wine? Cheap liquor?"

"Well—" I hesitated. "Possibly."

He raised his voice. "Possibly? They'll have food enough for an entire army and not a drop of filthy alcohol? Lieutenant Colonel! Before an attack, what do men use to calm their nerves?"

I gave in, to my great regret. "A little alcohol, doubtless."

"Not a little, a lot!" he said scornfully. Taking a couple of breaths, he turned back to Dalmau. "The first thing your men will do is to get drunk. And once they've turned into a drunken mob, any discipline you've instilled will melt; nothing will hold them back. There are very many of the most noble families in Mataró, lineages going back to King Jaume I. Ill-advisedly, they've betrayed their country, but we can't allow them to be massacred, least of all without any kind of a trial! We have here the ideal conditions for the lowest plebes to wreak the lowest vengeance: stabbing noblemen and taking advantage of ladies. Need I tell you what our enemies would do if they heard news of such an atrocity? Spread it around Europe, debasing Catalonia's blessed name! We're a small country; international consensus matters to us. No, sirs, I will not allow a minor victory to annihilate all our possibilities."

I was so riled by all this that I myself took the floor. "Don Antonio would never approve such a decision! Quite the reverse."

"Our commander in chief is at the government's command, and my orders come from the government," shouted the deputy. Like any Red Pelt, he was immediately incensed by any discussion about the Generalitat and Don Antonio's competing influence. "It isn't a military dictatorship!"

"Don Antonio, a dictator?" I said, becoming animated. "I've never heard such bilge in all my days!"

My tone forced Dalmau to intercede: "Lieutenant Colonel Zuviría! Act in a manner more befitting your rank—that's an order!"

But I couldn't control the frenzy taking hold of me. "If Don Antonio loved the saber regiment so much, he'd be fighting for the Bourbons; they offered him far higher wages than Vienna now pays him! And if our lads get their hands on a few *botiflero* petticoats, where's the harm in that? That's how it is in war, and these cowardly, self-serving so-and-so's abandoned their people to join the butchers. What should we do with them? Pin medals on their chests? Extol their honorable virtues? We could exchange them for patriots! Take this many *botifleros* and we'd stop the execution of hundreds, thousands, of Miquelets!"

A number of the officers in the room wanted me arrested. When I put my hand to my sword hilt, Dalmau came and pushed me to the door. "Easy, Zuviría," he said as he led me out. "You'll achieve nothing, speaking to people like that."

I still had time to shout over his shoulder: "What *is* this war, anyway? Let clockmakers make clocks and politicians politic—soldiers should be left to do what they do, make war!"

All there was for me to do then was sit at the foot of a tree with my head in my hands.

The pendulum of war, indeed. Lose, win, lose again. Everything changed within minutes, incomprehensibly, and on the basis of decisions that seemed divorced from the military. How were we to stand any chance of winning with this kind of people leading the way? They cared more about their own kind, even if they were *botifleros*, than their own soldiers.

Before I realized it, Ballester had come up and was standing next to me. "I've just come back from reconnaissance with my men," he said. "Mataró is impossible to defend, and the garrison is a trifle. Should I report to someone with the details?"

I didn't answer but kept my head buried in my hands. Ballester hit me on the shoulder. "Are the battalions ready?" he asked. "There are three entry points. I don't even think we'll need them; they'll surrender as soon as we come into view."

I could hardly look at him. "There isn't going to be an attack," I said. "Mataró isn't going to be taken."

An eternity seemed to pass before he spoke again: "But why not? Why not?"

It was one of the few times when I saw him become upset. I found this show of vulnerability unbearable; I felt responsible.

"Ballester," I stuttered, "I'm sorry. You're right about the Red Pelts. I shouldn't have made you come." I got to my feet, avoiding eye contact. "You should take your men and leave. Or join up with Busquets. Do what you like."

He took me by the scruff of the neck and slammed me against the tree. "Who do you think you are? Who, damn it? You've as little right to eject me as you had to make me join up! Now tell me: Why no attack on Mataró?"

I didn't even try to resist. In my confusion, I was as sincere as I could possibly be: "I don't know why."

Just then a couple of officers came by. "Ho! What's happening here?"

"What's happening," said Ballester, letting go of me and beginning to walk away, "is that there are some people who have no idea what's truly happening."

3

There is perhaps only one thing sadder than watching fortune slip between your fingers, and that is to be moving away from it out of your own free choosing. It had been decided: The expedition would move on, no attempt would be made to take Mataró, and so we went on, like a treasure seeker who, having orders to bring back gold, discards a diamond as big as a rock. The cavalry went first, with the infantry bringing up the rear. A late-summer Mediterranean downpour began to fall.

The Miquelets under Busquets watched the army leave; despairing, grievous looks they gave us. Their silence was an accusation. I'd met them after a defeat—this was worse still. It was as though their souls had been extracted from their bodies. Even in victory, they'd suffered a defeat, and yet none could tell at whose hands.

The only one to raise his voice was Busquets. As the rain came down, he rode alongside the ranks of blue-uniformed soldiers.

"Why, why go?" he cried. "Victory's right there!" He gestured in the direction of Matarós. "We only need to knock on the door, and the whole rotten building will come tumbling down!"

I have stored up a great array of memories in my life, and the image of Busquets then is one of the most pathetic. His arm in a sling, his long blond hair wet with rain, his useless entreaties.

Ballester and his nine Miquelets were in the column's rearguard. They looked up at Busquets impassively, but I knew them, I knew that inside they were on fire. I spurred my horse over to where Ballester was. "If you want to leave," I said, "do it now. It wouldn't be good for the officers to catch wind of it. Legally, they could have you for desertion."

He turned his head and spat by the feet of my horse. "You're the deserters," he retorted.

Busquets came over, bedraggled and weeping. "Ballester!" he said beggingly. "If we joined forces, maybe we could try it ourselves?"

Ballester just shook his head. "They'll have been warned by now," he said. "And they'll be getting reinforcements soon enough." Then he flashed a rare smile. "Anyway, what would be the point of staying here with you? You'll be dead before you ever pay me back."

"It's for Saint Peter to decide how long we're for this earth," said Busquets. "And my bullet pouch is still only half empty."

"Or half full," said Ballester.

Busquets and his men made their way away from the column. I had no notion where they were headed. They didn't even bid us farewell.

And what about me, why did I carry on under the orders of that insect Deputy Berenguer? I don't very well know. Don Antonio had ordered me to go with him, and I found it unthinkable to disobey Don Antonio. I believe I may also have been moved by the impulse, latent in every person, to drink a bitter cup to the very last dregs.

It rained for the rest of that day.

Things went from bad to worse after Mataró. When Pópuli learned of the expedition, having recovered from the fright, he threw all he could at us. Thousands of Spanish and French were sent from their posts across Catalonia to seek us out and crush us. Pópuli went so far as to take a handful of battalions away from the cordon to join the hunt; he knew very well how dangerous a mass uprising would be to him. Sad to say, but our enemies had more faith in the Catalan peasantry than our own leaders did.

With such inferior numbers, the expedition soon became the fox trying to outrun the pack of hounds. We'd enter a town or village with trumpets blaring and the silver mace up front. Deputy Berenguer had given the order for us all to wear our finest attire, to make a stronger impression. To begin with, the order was obeyed. Then we ran out of changes of clothes. Soon enough we became unkempt, had no foot-wear, and our blue tunics were covered in mud and patches. In spite of everything, the marching band always had a full complement; its upbeat songs contrasted with our general aspect. *Pu-rum pum pum!* We'd come into a town square and the *Crida* would be read out, along with a little oration from Deputy Berenguer. And the following day, or the one after that, we'd have reports from our patrols that entire enemy regiments were approaching, and we'd have to take to our heels— Deputy Berenguer aloft, truly almost shitting himself.

Well, all this was more or less to be expected. (The Bourbon attempts to pin us down, I mean, not Deputy Berenguer's flatulence.) Evading ambushes became our specialty; we traveled light and had a thousand eyes to inform us of the enemy's positions. But the true disaster had already happened, and its name was Mataró.

Word of the *Crida* from Barcelona spread, along with news of the fiasco at Mataró. People aren't stupid. With precedents like that, how could they trust the deputy? When he harangued them, his argument was based around three things. One, that Archduke Charles was a pious man, deeply, deeply pious. (As if it mattered in the slightest that a king, in some far-off place called Vienna, loved God.) Two, that they should trust in Our Lord God, for He would come to devout Catalonia's aid. (If everything was in God's hands, and if God was on our side, why had He stood by and watched the country's current plight?) Three, so as not to scandalize the upstanding Christians in the crowd, he would keep quiet about the enemy's iniquitous outrages. (No, man, no! *That* you want to shout from the rooftops! Let even the deaf know that we share their pain!) I remember Dalmau, during Deputy Berenguer's speeches in the town squares, looking to the heavens and showing his opposition with the occasional snort.

One of the worst things was seeing how self-confirming Deputy Berenguer's social prejudice was. All the zealous patriots had already joined groups of Miquelets like those of Busquets. Our presence was meant to encourage town councils to resist and govern in the name of the Generalitat, and to let the clergy know how treacherously their superiors had acted. But above all, we were hoping to win over the undecided majority: those who weren't prepared to become outlaws but would happily oppose tyranny if it were done under the banner of a free and legitimate power. Deputy Berenguer's speeches, full of as much hot air as his bowels, brought only excuses and tepid responses.

Those who did join were the dregs of society—the dregs of the dregs. The usual layabouts, or folks so starved that they joined up simply for the meal. And thus Deputy Berenguer's recruitment drive served to confirm his opinion about the lower classes. If any doubts remain as to what that man was like, here are a few more examples.

One day we found ourselves faced with several Castilian battalions. They were occupying a town we wanted to take, and when they came out to engage us in battle, once the firing had begun, a group of patriots inside the town scaled the bell tower and began firing at them from behind. Our men waved their tricorns to salute the men's efforts, and our standard-bearers waved the flags joyfully. There are few sensations as exhilarating as finding kinship with complete strangers. This put the Castilians on the back foot; you could feel them vacillate for a moment, and that was the moment to sound a charge and sweep them aside. Instead of that, what we heard were the trumpets sounding the retreat.

Not believing what I was hearing, I pushed the soldiers nearest to me. "There must be some mistake," I said. "Keep firing! Don't stop!"

Shitson himself had to come riding over and gave me the order to fall back. "Didn't you hear the retreat being sounded?" he howled at me from up on his horse. "We're leaving! We've had word from the scouts that a full regiment is on its way to hem us in."

"We've got *them* hemmed in!" I shouted, beside myself. "We could get to Portugal and back before that regiment arrives."

Shitson had it in for me in particular because we were the same rank. I tried to make him feel less envious by saying it meant nothing, Don Antonio had promoted me only so my orders to do with engineering would be obeyed. It was pointless. All that happened was, as well as considering me a pen pusher, he also decided I was an imposter. He was obsessed with being promoted to colonel. That would happen only if a new regiment was formed, or if an existing colonel was killed, and that made any other lieutenant colonel a rival. Leaning out of his saddle, he prodded my nose with a finger. "You'll never make a soldier, Zuviría. Your problem is you fail to see the bigger picture."

The bigger picture! Let me tell you about the "bigger picture" of that day.

After we left, the Bourbons didn't take the trouble to capture the snipers in the bell tower: They simply set fire to the church, and the men burned alive. The tactics they used against us were proof of the straightforwardness of the Bourbon approach. Any town that had taken us in would have its houses burned down, and one in ten inhabitants would be shot. Straightforward indeed.

Not long after that, the expedition forces divided into two. It was Dalmau's suggestion, it being his view that there was no way for us to tackle such great numbers head-on; the best thing was to split the column. The main unit would stay under the deputy's command. A secondary but well-stocked column would be under Dalmau, and a number of other, smaller units would go farther afield and try to raise troops.

Not a bad plan. If we split up, it would make it harder for the Bourbon patrols to track us, and in the first place, they'd be delayed trying to work out how many units we'd split into. They'd have to divide their forces, too. The large-scale war had become one of smaller encounters, so it was advantageous to try and reduce the numbers. Also, Pópuli's terror tactics had other impacts. Once people knew their towns would go up in flames the day after we left, they became less willing to open their doors to us. By splintering, we'd move into a great many more towns, and not even the commanders of the Army of the Two Crowns would be brazen enough to burn down every single town and city in Catalonia.

That day I found out about the sheer sickening perversity that underlies all war. The deputy, emerging at one point from his musings, looked up and, with eyes full of hope, said: "Well, if that were to happen, at least the peasantry, stripped of menfolk and places to live, would join our side."

The other men there seemed not to notice. Dalmau because he was concentrating on the maps on which he was explaining his plan, and Shitson because he was Shitson. But the words made a strong impression on me.

Politics are bad; war is evil. There's only one thing worse than these two: a hybrid known as war policy. I'd been educated in a world where engineers were the hinges separating politics and war. A world based on the idea that politics merely shadow the armed forces: following behind, defining the outer edges. Coming into the new century, however, the noxious fumes of war took over the whole corpus. And here were the consequences: the overall thrust of our elevated mission being to protect citizens' lives and homes. Turning the moral principle on its head, for Berenguer, the enemy burning and killing was no bad thing as people's helplessness and feelings of revenge would play into our hands.

It goes without saying that Dalmau was extremely fed up with the deputy, his senile speeches, his constant gas from the other end, and this was another reason behind his proposal. Dalmau wanted to see what he could achieve on his own. I implored him to let me be in his column, but he refused.

"When we get back, Don Antonio will want an account of things," he argued. "And without me around, the only reliable witness is you. Or do you think we should leave it to Shitson?"

The following weeks and months are a whirlwind of images in my memory, always the same, always changing. The Army of the Two Crowns hounding us. Us fleeing, attacking, counterattacking. March, countermarch, nights out in the open. Rain. Sun. Mud. Always on guard. Towns for us, towns against us, towns being put to the torch. The landscape there became a kind of cement in which past and present merged, as one's senses were dulled by the sheer monotony of repeated cruel acts. We'd retrace our steps and find yesterday's supportive town had become today's ashy ruins. Mud. Sun. More rain. Sleet and hail, we'd make our way into ravines and hidden paths, later emerging in a forest. To our right, seven trees, each bearing three hanged men. Hadn't we been there the day before? No, the day before it had been three trees, each bearing seven men. Change of direction; the scouts as our antennae, the column shuffling along like a thousand-legged insect. We were being defeated by a paradox: There was no way for us to recruit new troops because we were constantly fleeing, and we were constantly fleeing because of our inability to raise recruits.

Nor would I wish to suggest that it was the same everywhere, with each and every inhabitant prepared to make sacrifices for the constitution and Catalan liberties. Far from it! Many were the instances of betrayal, debility, and self-serving behavior. War also allows man's most atavistic instincts to flourish.

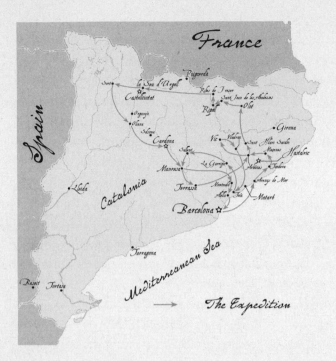

I found myself at the vanguard of our unit one day, riding with the cavalry, when we came under fire from a hillside strewn with boulders. We could hear our assailants calling out encouragement to one another, and they were talking in Catalan. I thought it must have been one of these lamentably regular cases of mistaken identity you get in war. "It's local militia," I said to myself, "they've mistaken us for French or Castilian troops." I gave the order to the other riders not to return fire, and moved forward, waving my hat to greet them. But the firing only intensified. As I moved closer on my horse, I could make out one of their men loading his rifle up on the top of a boulder.

"What the . . . What are you *doing*?" I cried. "We're with the Army of the Generalitat!"

To which the man said nothing. His elbow moved frantically as he thrust the ramrod up and down, and then I could see it in his eyes: He was just praying that my confusion would last long enough for him to have an easy shot at me.

When the Allied army disembarked at Barcelona in 1705, a great many municipalities declared themselves supporters of Charles. But it wasn't unanimous. It wasn't at all unusual for two neighboring towns to have opposing sympathies. Why? Because the priest had said God favored Little Philip? Not at all! They'd simply plump for whichever side their detested neighbors had not. Everyone must know stories about eternal disputes over rights to a well, or ownership of a windmill, anything. While Charles had been on the up, they'd kept quiet, said nothing. But now, with the Army of the Two Crowns occupying almost all of Catalonia, enthused, they took up arms and had no qualms about gutting one of their neighbors and using their political affiliation as an excuse.

As for the peasants shooting at us from the hillside, they couldn't have cared less about constitutions, Austrian monarchs, Bourbons, and the like. The global war gave them a chance to institutionalize local conflicts. Europe's apocalypse, to these people, became a story on which to hang the one thing they did ardently believe: that the next town along was a pack of whoresons. Catalonia's freedom, the future of the land, the necessity of shrugging off the yoke of foreign tyrants, all was secondary to the noble calling of going and bashing in your neighbor's head and, while you were at it, his son's as well.

It's as I say: War was the fire beneath the boiling pot, unleashing those atavistic fumes, pulling back that slight and insecure lid called civilization. Rousseau was right: Savagery isn't without, it's underneath; savagery isn't to be found in far-off exotic places but in our own recondite depths. At the slightest excuse the savage in us will come storming to the fore, bowling down the civilized part like a cannonball.

Not that Voltaire ever understood, that insufferable dandy!

Deputy Berenguer was becoming less and less physically able. But his mental faculties were as good as ever: He could see that we hadn't recruited very many men, certainly not enough to attack the Bourbon cordon with. But that didn't stop him from sending letter after letter to Barcelona. Something about this made me sick. The Two Crowns army was closing in around us. To get through their net, we had to send some of our best riders—their loyalty had to be beyond question—and they'd be laying their lives on the line, trying to break through to the coast. Coordinating their arrival with that of a ship secretly sailed in from Barcelona made it triply dangerous. And what for? So Berenguer could send missives saying there was nothing to say.

An impasse had been reached, impossibly disheartening. The 1705 insurrection had begun in a place called Vic, a little over thirty miles north of Barcelona. We had to overcome many obstacles and make many detours to reach it. Quite the saga, for the Bourbons pursuing us were growing daily in number, and it took considerable maneuvering to get our unit to its destination intact. At least we were sure to have a warm welcome, given that Vic had been the first place to rise up in support of Charles. That's what I thought then—I laugh to remember it!

They wanted nothing to do with us. Their elders urged us to turn around and leave the very same day, so as not to compromise them. "Bear in mind that, because we were the first to side with the emperor, we're bound to receive the harshest punishments."

The deputy, always indulgent with his own, went easy on them. Not me. "Given that they were the first to go on the attack," I said, "that ought to make them the last to quit the defenses."

Ordered to hold my tongue, I obeyed. It was pointless anyway. We still weren't to know at that point, but it was the most futile of discussions. During the meeting, we later learned, Vic's representatives had sent some namby-pamby local official, one Josep Pou, to ask for clemency from Little Philip's army. Fabulous! The ones who had struck the match, accusing us of arson.

In the end, it became as though all our to-ing and fro-ing was merely to keep Deputy Berenguer from falling into Bourbon hands. Coordinating ourselves with the other columns—which were moving around as constantly as we were—and with Barcelona, too, was no easy task. A large number of our messengers never came back. Each time one galloped away, I found it hard to hold back the tears. If they were caught, they'd be tortured to death—itself a useless act, as the messages were written in a code that only Berenguer knew. The one thing he could be praised for, the clod.

It was a most ingenious code, with numbers standing in for letters or symbols. So, A was 11, M was 40, and E was 30. Other numbers stood in for whole things—70, for example, meant Barcelona; 100, bombs; 81, Philip V; 53, grenades; 54, Pópuli; and 87, Miquelets.

A rumor went around among the men that Deputy Berenguer kept the message hidden deep inside. The Bourbons would never decipher the code, because the numbers and letters were all nothing but a ruse. In fact, Deputy Berenguer would fart holding a cylinder to his behind. The implement didn't, in reality, decipher written signs but, rather, the whistling sounds made when the cylinder's top lifted.

Well, mob humor never has been that refined.

One day, early in the morning, the sentries sounded the alarm. Everyone scrabbled to arm himself, thinking it was a dawn attack by the Bourbons. No. To our relief, it turned out to be compatriots of ours—Ballester and his men, to be precise.

The sight of Ballester returning to us was one of the few happy ones during the whole expedition. I ran over and embraced him. I'm sure now that Ballester did appreciate my effusiveness, even though he couldn't show it at the time. I put my arms around him; his stayed pinned to his sides. I didn't mind. I could tell by his bewildered expression that he was having feelings he had no way to express.

Looking him in the eye, taking him by the shoulders, I said: "I knew you wouldn't abandon us. I knew it."

He pushed me away. "You were the ones who abandoned us. Don't you remember?"

Looking around, I saw that only seven of his nine men were with him. "What about Jacint and Indaleci?" I asked.

"What do you think?"

We both fell silent for a moment. I was the next to speak. "And in spite of everything, you've come back?"

"It's you who have come back," he said, pointing behind him. The Miquelets had been scouting ahead of a far larger body of men: Dalmau's whole troop. Plus three thousand men newly joined! Dalmau had recruited them himself, addressing the matter very differently to Deputy Berenguer. Not so strange, if you think about it. They were two poles: Deputy Berenguer's apathetic moralizing and Dalmau's levelheaded enthusiasm couldn't have been more different. For Deputy

Berenguer, the homeland meant the past, and protocols; for Dalmau, the future, and people's rights.

A war council was held. Dalmau wanted to put forward some ideas he'd formed while expeditioning alone.

All told we could bring together five thousand men now. He wanted to proceed in line with the original plan: Attack the Bourbon cordon at Barcelona and raise the blockade. The disparity in numbers meant outright victory would be impossible. To start with, we were surrounded by thousands of Bourbons who had been deployed throughout the area. If they realized where we were marching, they would simply form a wall between us and Barcelona.

"But if we *were* to evade them," suggested Dalmau, "we'd be in a position to attack the cordon's right wing." He spread a map out on the table. Everyone present came closer in.

"The Bourbons have divided the cordon into three sectors," Dalmau explained. "The right wing is made up of Spanish troops, and the area they're positioned on is swampland. We'd be at an advantage attacking there. Spanish troops are less well trained than the French. And on such uneven terrain, our Miquelets would move around far better than regiments accustomed to fighting in formation." He rubbed his eyes. "Coordinating the attack with the troops inside the city will be no easy task. Particularly if we decide to strike at night, which we'd need to do to compensate for our lack of numbers—use the element of surprise. But if we do our part and Villarroel does his—no doubt he will—I don't see why we shouldn't succeed."

Well, this was the point of the expedition, to free Barcelona from the Bourbon siege. Everyone agreed that it was risky but not impossible. There was still the issue of the deputy: an attack by night, among five thousand men in swampy terrain, would be too much for old Berenguer. It would be fraught with danger. In the tumult of battle, and in the dark, anything might happen. That Deputy Berenguer was a good-for-nothing blackguard didn't make him any less important a personage. He'd be quite a prize for the Bourbons, and it would be a heavy blow to the Catalans to lose him. No, he wouldn't be killed. But they'd be in a position to mount him on a donkey and ride him around with a cylinder on his head.

Berenguer put his hands to his face and, in a pitiful performance, said the last thing he wanted was to be an obstacle for the fatherland. Finally, he had realized that's what he was. The attempt must be made, he said. All he required was four trustworthy soldiers to be his body-guards. If the situation became ugly, these four would have the blessed job of slitting his throat before the enemy kidnapped him.

The cheek of the man! For the duration of the expedition he'd been cowering, and now he wanted to make himself out as the hero. It was the height of imposture, and that in an era when heroism was the commonest currency. Men like Villarroel and Dalmau, warriors like Ballester and Busquets, would never make proclamations about their willingness to lay down their lives: They took it for granted, and would do it without a second's hesitation. And there we had Deputy Berenguer, measuring his every word for its epic qualities, for how it would sound in the annals.

I stepped forward. "Oh, don't worry about four men to slit your throat, Your Excellency. One would be sufficient. Me."

"Zuviría!" he cried. "I've had enough of your insolence. Think you're the army joker, don't you? When we get back, the first thing I'm going to do is have you thrown in the Pi dungeons!"

Next, one of Berenguer's oafs made a proposal: Try and reach the coast, and from there send the deputy off in a ship somewhere, before tackling the cordon. Everyone was happy—Dalmau because it meant being free from Berenguer, and Berenguer because it meant he'd be out of harm's way.

Ballester and his light cavalry were sent ahead as an advance party, as usual, to be sure the nearby paths and trails were clear of Bourbons, and that the deputy could therefore be evacuated. I went with them. We reached a place called Alella by nightfall; to avoid unpleasant sur-prises, we chose to camp on the beach rather than trying at a house in the town.

During the ride, Ballester had seemed more on guard than usual. I put my sleeping mat next to his, the sand for a mattress. We bedded down a stone's throw from the sea. The day had been clear, and the stars shone in the sky above. Like that poetic detail, my dear Waltraud? Pish, I say! If it was night, and there weren't any clouds, why on earth wouldn't the stars be shining? Anyway, you can keep it in—it will help give an idea of our melancholy mood that night. We were engaged in a cruel war, but the gentle cadence of the waves and the sound of the crickets cradled us for one peaceful moment: a feeling that moved me to speak.

"I want you to know something. I thought Mataró was an outrage as well."

Ballester didn't answer. Offended by his silence, I protested: "I'm trying to apologize! Though I'm hardly to blame."

"Your Cannae went to the dogs," he said finally.

"True. And the way we're headed, there's more bloodshed to come. Even if things go according to plan," I lamented, looking up at the sky, "thousands will die. If only Vauban were alive . . . "

"What are you complaining about? It's a war, people die. If they didn't, it wouldn't be war."

I decided to change the subject. "Are you married, Ballester?" I asked.

"No, I have some women, but none of them are my wives. You?"

"There's one who's as good as my wife. I think she was a whore before me. Something like that."

"Are you being serious?" said Ballester, taken aback—and not much could surprise that man.

"Whore, mischief maker, thief . . . What does it matter? Needs must, these days. I live in a house along with her, an old man, a dwarf, and a young boy. You've met the boy."

"I have?" he said, again surprised.

"Yes, when you laid siege to us in that *masía*."

Ballester pulled his blanket over himself. "I only remember," he said, yawning, "that I'd never seen such a soft lad."

"You're right there," I said, and with the thought of Anfán, a daft feeling of happiness rose up my neck. "Though I'm not his father."

"But you treat him as a son," Ballester pointed out, yawning again.

"Well, let's just say that, to him, I'm the one who makes the rules. That's all."

We were both tired, and Ballester's eyes began to fall shut, but I pushed his arm again. "Do you have children, Ballester?"

Opening his eyes again, he looked up at the stars. "I think so. Maybe one or two. Difficult to know for certain. Women are always claiming I'm the father, though all they really want is the leader's money."

"But you're not bringing them up."

He sneered. "How could I? Their mothers don't want for anything. I take care of all that."

I tugged on his sleeve again, more earnestly still. "Ballester, I want to ask you something. Something between you and me."

He lifted himself half up, suspecting some trick, his usual forest animal cautiousness. But all I wanted to know was: "Why do you fight?"

He meditated for a few moments, taking a fistful of sand and letting it drain away. As a prompt, I said, "I don't need a long speech, you can keep it short," before adding: "A word, please, just a word. It's all I ask."

But to my disappointment, he lay down again and, with a sigh, said simply: "If you haven't understood it yet, what would be the point of telling you now?"

4

Perhaps I should not have been so surprised by the aberration that next took place. The full extent of Red Pelts' mad legalism, the false emptiness of their patriotism—which was about to become apparent on the beach at Alella—anyone would have been hard pushed to surmise. My only thought at the time was that, finally, we were about to be rid of Deputy Berenguer and his clot-headed retinue.

The body of the army arrived early in the morning, without incident. Meanwhile, Ballester and I negotiated with some locals over requisitioning a boat, one of a decent size but light and swift. The plan was for Deputy Berenguer and his advisers and assistants to depart at twilight, and sail away under cover of dark.

The old man kicked into life for once. He ordered a security perimeter be established, with the men positioned at the high points that dominated the bay. Five thousand men on guard struck me as excessive, but I shrugged and got on with it. All Pelts esteemed protocol very highly, and I just thought Deputy Berenguer wanted to make a show of his eminence.

Ballester and his men were the only ones exempt from guard duty. While the rest of the army took up positions on hilltops and where any paths entered the area, they hunkered down in a fisherman's tavern in Alella, on the outskirts of the town and about a hundred yards away from the beach. I could see what they were about, but I was supposed to be taking part in seeing Berenguer off.

"Don't forget to pay for what you drink," was all I said. "We're not Bourbons."

Coming back to camp, I found Berenguer sprawled in his chair with five or six of his officers around him, Dalmau and Shitson included. They'd begun without me, the babe of the expedition. Dalmau was making a florid farewell speech.

"Excuse me for interrupting," said Berenguer as I came in. "But I ought to point out, you and all the rest of the senior officers will also be setting sail with me."

I was standing behind Dalmau and, like him, was stupefied by this.

"Pardon me?" said Dalmau, as though he'd misheard. "How can we come with you? If I and the other officers aren't here, who's going to give orders to the men?"

"Everyone from lieutenant colonel up," Berenguer said. "All are to return with me to Barcelona. It's an order. No discussions."

Abandon five thousand men! Not carry out the attack on the cordon! All these months of hardship and sacrifice for nothing! We found this injustice, this monumental lunacy, so hard to digest that neither Dalmau nor any of the other officers reacted.

"But Your Excellence," Dalmau finally said, extremely disconcerted, "this isn't possible. Who will lead the attack on the cordon?"

"I believe we have a commander eager to gain his stripes in war," said Berenguer. "The troops will be in good hands."

He meant Shitson! It was tantamount to discharging the troops. There hadn't been time for the new recruits to forge bonds with their leaders by taking part in any conflict. Now, if their leaders abandoned them, they were also sure to go back on their promises. Dalmau's regiment would disintegrate; since they were light on veterans, personal

ties were extremely important to them (as they are in any army, to be
fair). What would they do if their commander left them on some beach
in the middle of nowhere, without any explanations, and now to take
orders from some reprobate? We might as well hand them straight over
to the Bourbons.

The other officers, though speechless, complied, following Berenguer and his oafs aboard. Not Dalmau. He stood where the gangway touched down on the beach, refusing to go aboard, and becoming
increasingly vocal in his opposition to the decision. One of the men
who'd already gone aboard rebuked Dalmau. An order was an order.
Did he think he was the only one who felt this to be an affront to his
dignity?

"Not at all," said Dalmau. "But again, it isn't just or reasonable to
leave my regiment, as well as other equally dignified officers, at the
orders of a man who has shown himself to be anything but."

While Dalmau and Berenguer continued to argue, I ran back up to
the tavern, barging open the door. Seeing me in such a state, Ballester
thought we were under attack. If only that had been so!

"They want to leave!" I shouted. "Tell the lads!"

At first he didn't take my meaning.

"They want to leave," I said again. "Not only Berenguer and his
aides. The order's been given for all officers to sail, all except Shitson!
We have to put a stop to it! Get the men together! The deputy might
change his mind if we kick up enough of a fuss."

Ballester promptly did as I said, for once. He and his men left the
tavern and rode out to the perimeter positions. I went back to the boat,
another wearying dash down the beach. The argument had gone up
a few notches, with Dalmau still refusing to board and all the other
officers already having done so. I'd never seen the usually affable Dalmau so furious. I began shouting and screaming as well, using far less
decorous language than Dalmau, as you can imagine.

Up in the surrounding hillsides, the news began reaching the
troops. They turned to the sea to look, when they were supposed
to be looking out for a possible attack. Dozens, hundreds, of men
began streaming down to the beach, none of them fully understanding what was happening. Up on deck, one of the officers beseeched

Berenguer to order Dalmau to embark. "Otherwise," he said, "we're all done for."

Berenguer shouted at Dalmau from his wheelchair: Either he embarked immediately, or he'd be tried for insubordination. For a few moments, Dalmau gazed out at the waves as they broke on the shoreline, before turning to me: "Come, Zuviría." Still I refused. He took me by the elbow and added: "A direct order from the deputy of the military estate cannot be disobeyed." And then he whispered: "Plus, someone has to be there in Barcelona to say what's gone on."

I'm neither proud nor ashamed to say I was the last to take the few steps up that wooden gangway and board the ship. Seeing their entire high command getting into this small ship, leaving them behind, the men came careering toward the beach. Five thousand armed men, coming after us from all sides; Berenguer's oafs nearly pissed themselves. Berenguer called out for the anchor to be weighed—"Posthaste!"—and what happened next is something that has stayed with me all my many days.

In spite of the misdeed, those five thousand men did not come and try to kill anyone. They gathered in the bay, looking out at us not with hate so much as the incomprehension of an abandoned dog. If I couldn't understand why we were leaving them, how were they supposed to? I saw Ballester and his men, grouped on a ridge to one side of the beach. *He* knew what was going on. Their centaur silhouettes, lit by the Mediterranean twilight, filled me with an unbearably weighty feeling of shame.

Before we had sailed two hundred feet, I saw a fair-haired youngster wade out up to his knees. He stood out to me because of the blond plaits he wore on either side of his head, which reminded me of Anfán. He was waving something above his head. Then the rest of the troops began chanting. At that distance, the noise of the sea and the wind made it difficult to hear. I was the only person aboard looking back at the coast. I listened harder. When I realized what it was, I thumped the deck four times with my fists. "Turn back! Turn back!" I cried. "Damn it all, turn the ship around!"

The oafs came over, ordering me to be quiet. For once I was able to say what I thought about them to their faces: "Imbeciles! The deputy's forgotten the silver mace!"

And so it was. The men were shouting, "The Club, the Club!" Berenguer and his oafs had been in such a hurry to get away from their own men that they'd managed to forget about the supreme symbol of Catalan resistance.

How is it possible for a people to be so brave and at the same time so submissive? I'll tell you: It's possible because, as Alella demonstrated, they had far more faith in their free institutions than in the people running them. Berenguer had left behind the silver mace, while the ragtag army he'd shown so much contempt for had remembered it. And it didn't even occur to them to hang him—they just wanted to make sure the Club was safe.

The boat made a slow and humiliating about-turn. All those aboard were so ashamed or so afraid that they didn't want to disembark to go and fetch the mace. Because I'd raised the alarm, they seemed to think I was the man for the job. Pish! I understood how unsettled the deputy was when his oafs came over, again imploring me: "Please."

I didn't even have to get down from the boat. Its hull wasn't deep, and as we came back to shore, the lad waded out to meet us, up to his chest in water. I leaned over the side and took the outstretched Club. As soon as I had it, the boat pushed off again. I shouted back at him: "What's your name?"

He replied, but the wind must have changed direction, and I didn't hear. I rue that wind so, so very much that it makes me feel like never saying another word. What's the worth of a book that contains Berenguer's name, the abominable Antoni Berenguer, and not that of the young boy?

I spent the return voyage seated in a corner between two barrels, my arms crossed and a blanket over my head so that I wouldn't have to speak to anyone. My first thought was that the whole thing was a conspiracy, that Berenguer was secretly taking orders from the Bourbons. In fact, after Barcelona fell, the word was that he did serve the new government, immediately and with servile acquiescence. But I'm not really one for conspiracies. He was a weak man, that's all, and when a man is in a position of power, weakness and treachery are apt to merge. Perhaps he made all the officers set sail with him so they'd have a share of the shame, or perhaps he was worried that an attack on the cordon would cost too many officers' lives. Being from good families, the Red Pelts would have been unhappy if so many of their own had been led to slaughter. Who knows. It's hardly the most important thing.

We were willing to wage war on the Two Crowns for the sake of our constitutions and liberties, a single city against the immense might of two allied empires. But, I ask, how are you supposed to fight your very own government?

As for the upshot of our disastrous expedition, the less said, the better. When we arrived back in Barcelona, Don Antonio wasn't exactly the calmest he'd ever been. Thank goodness I wasn't there when the news of Berenguer's cowardice reached him, the Mataró disaster, the calamity of abandoning an entire army on a beach. Apparently, Don Antonio threw his staff of office to the floor, proclaiming: "An offense to God! A disservice to the king! And ruination for the homeland!"

Don Antonio demanded explanations, and when he came to us, Dalmau and I made no bones about what had happened. He wanted Berenguer hanged from the city walls. As was to be expected, the Red Pelts rushed to Berenguer's defense. But his conduct had been so dire that even they couldn't keep him from being put on trial. I kept my thoughts to myself; honest justice would be out of the question. He came away completely unscathed. Don Antonio didn't have jurisdiction over public figures, so Berenguer was merely placed under house arrest. Given that he couldn't get out of his wheelchair anyway, will someone please tell me what kind of punishment this was? The justice of the Red Pelts, that's what!

With Berenguer off, exiled in his gilded cage, what happened to the five thousand men who had been abandoned? The moment Dalmau touched down in Barcelona, he chartered a return flotilla—out of his family's coffers—to go and rescue them. It got there too late. They'd scattered, unsurprisingly. Some had joined Busquets's group, or others'. Hundreds had been captured by the Bourbons, and you can guess what treatment they received. A good many more simply returned home. Who can blame them? The rest carried on harrying the Bourbons on the outskirts of Barcelona, of their own accord. But the expedition's strategic objective had failed utterly.

Amazingly, some were willing to go on to Barcelona and made it there, forcing their way through the cordon. Small groups of cavalry, with the darkness as cover, charged in like berserkers. In the middle of the night, we saw part of the cordon light up with flashes of rifle fire, and heard the wild riders howling. They crossed the less protected swampy areas and, when they reached the open encampments, hurtled in like meteors. A little while later, ten, twenty, thirty men shot through into the city . . .

We never heard another word about Shitson. Either the Bourbons hanged him, or those troops he'd been left to lead did it themselves. If you want my view, knowing what Dalmau's men were like, I'd say it was probably the latter. But this is all supposition. If I ever did find out, I've forgotten. Thanks be to forgetfulness!

Come on, enough of the weepy bits. Chin up, never mind! That's what I say. Or, as we said in Barcelona, *via fora* to the sadness. At least I made it home in one piece—no mean feat. Having embraced the members of my odd little family, I collapsed into an armchair, gazing on the walls as though civility were a distant memory. I didn't talk much. I looked out from our balcony, which had a view of the city walls. The cooper company was on patrol up on the Saint Clara bastion. They'd lit several small bonfires to cook their dinner over. It was good to know they were there, and to know that it was for one reason: so that I could sleep safely in my home that night. By this point I had far more faith in these coopers-turned-soldiers than in any unit of regulars.

Nan brought in a pot containing hot water and left it at my feet: his way of celebrating my return. And Amelis dropped a handful of salt in—my God, a hot footbath, surrounded by your nearest and dearest. This was a home. Anfán bade me tell them about my heroic exploits . . .

As I took off my boots, I turned my mind to those interminable marches, day and night, all those thousands of men with threadbare espadrilles on their feet, or simply going barefoot. I thought of the smell of burned gunpowder, and of the dead we'd left behind, to no end. I could still smell the stench of rusted bayonets and old leather. And all of it for what? So that that swine Berenguer could sit in his little palace, surrounded by his dozens of oafs, denying that he'd had anything to do with anything.

"Heroic exploits?" I said. "Know the one thing I've brought with me to say? That the reason I went was so you might never have to."

I wasn't fully happy until I laid my head down on my pillow. Amelis joined me a little while later. The room was dark and I couldn't see her, I only heard the door. She came in and got on top of me, both of us unclothed. Food had begun to grow scarce in the city, and she was thinner than before. Through the window came the occasional far-off explosion, illuminating the room, accompanied by sounds of artillery. Bourbon artillery, not ours, but I felt sure we had nothing to fear. They were only calibrating their cannons in case they decided to attack the Capuchin convent one day, and that was outside the main walls. Amelis's hair fell over my face, and I could smell the mint tea she'd drunk before coming in. Running a hand over my face, she said: "Do you want to go to sleep?"

Sleep? I hadn't heard anything so funny in a long while. Chin up, Martí Zuviría, never mind! There are few things as intense as making love to the sound of a cannonade. And in this life, take it from me, there's only one thing that ranks above first love, and that's the second.

I forgot to say anything in the last chapter about the expedition's very last upshot. Well, I'll do so now, and that'll be that. *You* put the chapters in order as best you can, that's what I pay you for.

I found myself up on the Saint Clara bastion early one morning, involved in a cannonade, when Francesc Castellví appeared. He was the captain of a Valencian company, with pretensions to be a historian. But there are some who don't know when it's the right—or the wrong—time for courteous greetings.

From time to time, our sentries would spy a group of enemy foragers in no-man's-land. The alarm would be raised across the bastion tops and our cannons trained on the foragers. From the cordon, the Bourbons would use their longer-range artillery to provide cover, and an artillery exchange would commence.

I thought it the most ridiculous waste of ammunition. At that distance, our cannon fire almost never reached the besiegers' positions, and vice versa. But so things go in war. Our chief gunner, a man named Costa, asked me to authorize returning fire. We were still well stocked with gunpowder, and his Mallorcans could use the chance to train the city gunners.

"Great that you're back in one piece!" said Castellví, shouting to make himself heard over the detonations.

"Right, yes," I said, otherwise occupied and as good as ignoring him. "Thanks."

"And you look well. A little thinner, yes."

"Haven't you got a company of men to be looking out for?"

"No, not today. Today's a rest day for us. I'm going around visiting friends."

There I was, giving orders to the munitions carriers, verifying hits and misses, and keeping a close check on how much gunpowder was being used. And here was Castellví asking after my health.

Most of the enemy's shots fell short. One or two would reach the walls, but so tired by that point that they'd bounce off the walls, to the rumbling, scraping sound of stones. *Crrrack!* The cannonballs would roll slowly back down the rampart walls, wreathed in smoke. Each army used the same caliber, which meant each could also use the other's; the same cannonballs would end up going back and forth time after time. Some became airborne letters. Using chicken blood or carbon, the Bourbons would write, for instance, "Up yours, rebels." To which our men would reply, on a different part of the cannonball: "Stick this up your Bourbon behinds." That sort of thing, with pictures of cocks, anuses, and mouths to match.

"And you must be happy your little friend's back, too!" persevered Castellví.

"Friend? What friend do you mean?"

"What friend do you think I mean? Ballester! Along with his men!"

"No!" I cried. "There must be some mistake! They stayed in Alella! We'll never see them around these parts again!"

"It's true, I tell you! They crossed the cordon in the night! On horseback, just before dawn, a few hours ago! They're here in the city!"

"You're wrong, I say! It can't be him! Ballester will never forgive us for leaving them the way we did!"

The Mallorcans were shouting out orders, and what with their devilish accents, the noise of the cannons, and the commotion of the carriers, it was almost impossible to hear. We'd have lost our voices soon enough. Where were the Vaubanians to teach the Valencians sign language?

"It was Ballester!" Castellví insisted exasperatingly. "This war must be recounted afterward, down to the very last detail! And I am determined to do that!"

"Fine! Recount the war, off you go. I'm rather busy just now waging that war!" Before he left, I added: "But you're wrong! Ballester hates us! What on earth could move him to risk his hide getting back into Barcelona?"

I stopped midsentence. Very often it's the words themselves that clarify thought, and not the other way around.

"What's wrong?" said Castellví. "You've gone completely white! Cannonballs frighten you?"

"Stand in for me, would you?" I shouted at the top of my voice. "I'll owe you one!"

"But I'm infantry!" he protested. "I haven't the first clue—"

And now I'm going to leave you to guess the reason for my haste and where I was headed. My dear vile Waltraud knows. But how clever you are, my lovely little buffalo!

There could be only one motive for Ballester to come back: to murder Berenguer. According to his Miquelet logic, the aberration at Alella wasn't down to politics but to real individuals, and as such, the only answer could be to slit real throats.

I ran all the way to Berenguer's home and arrived panting and just in time. Ballester and his men were coming around the corner of a thin street alongside the residence, and they had knives in their belts and sacks covering their heads. I stood between them and Berenguer's home—the side street so thin, my body was enough to block the way.

"You don't salute a superior?" I said to Ballester.

"Out of my way."

Well, he did always make a virtue of concision.

"Think about what will happen if you knock down this door and go and kill Berenguer," I said. "Think. He'll be dead, and you'll be hanged. The deputy of the military estate, and one of the city's own heroes, killed by our own side. Just think of what it would do to morale—and how that plays into the enemy's hands. They'll say we're devouring ourselves likes rats in a sack."

Ballester tore his hood off in disgust. "Think I want to kill Berenguer? Do you really think that? No, I didn't want to come back, I'm not one for risking life and limb to squash a cockroach." He jabbed a thumb in the direction of his men behind him. "But they did! I set out with nine men and came back with six. Want them just to forget? Fine, you tell them so!"

Men with blunt characters don't know how to ask for help; pride prevents them. But, weighing Ballester's words, I could see he was asking me to intercede.

I reminded them of all the sleepless nights, the marches and the skirmishes I'd been alongside them on, which was most of them. I made light of the day I enjoined them to leave Barcelona. A lot had happened since.

"Berenguer is a very old man," I said. "He hasn't got long left to live. To make that life slightly shorter, the price is your lives, plus putting the city in danger. Is that really what you want?"

I myself don't know how I managed to get them to accompany me to a tavern. We found one of the few still open in the city. The alcohol cheered them up considerably, as though they'd never really wanted to kill. They laughed, sang songs, and drank until passing out—all except Ballester and me. From far ends of the table, we exchanged glances, sharing something beyond sadness or bitterness.

"You still haven't suffered enough," Don Antonio had said to me. And I swear I had set out on the expedition prepared to face whatever came, in order to strip away my soul's resentment. But what I didn't know was that pain always comes for us when least we expect it. I believed the expedition would be a chance to put my learning into action, and what really happened was that my ideas about the world came tumbling down. The worst thing was, in spite of that, in spite of the downheartedness that came with seeing that the rules governing us are feigning and false, I was no nearer to learning The Word. "You still haven't suffered enough." In that tavern I saw a look different from those on all the other fearful faces I'd seen. For if all the misfortunes, all the terrible sights during the expedition, hadn't changed me sufficiently, what was I going to have to sacrifice in order to see my light?

That night, through jug after jug of wine, conversing silently with Ballester, I didn't yet know the truly terrible, and at the same time unforeseen, thing: that the sky was just about to come crashing down on our heads.

5

Now, all these years later, I look back on Christmas 1713 with more affection than it merits. Being on duty up on the ramparts was freezing work. Below us, the icebound palisade stakes, and beyond them, the enemy cordon. Wind, rain, and, up above, a leaden sky, grayer than a mule's belly. But when we were on guard on the bastions, high on their prowlike edges, there was always one thing we could do to lift our spirits, and that was to look back across the city we were defending.

Throughout the siege, the Red Pelts were consumed with the idea of maintaining calm among the populace. They'd ordered Barcelonans to fill balconies and windows with lamps and candles at nightfall, so the streets wouldn't be as dark. Turning around, you'd be presented with a lit-up Barcelona. During those Christmas nights, there were more lamps than ever, and the shades were made of red, yellow, and green glass, making the city streets wink and glitter like a nocturnal rainbow.

1714 arrived, and everything carried on as it had been. Three, four, five more months passed, and still the same. Spring burst upon us, and everyone, including me, was becoming fed up with the siege. There was nothing to contend with, only the tedium, the occasional skirmish, and the fatigue that affected the free citizens-turned-soldiers. In Bazoches terms, any siege lasting so long would be considered a failure. More than that: an outright aberration, a complete departure from the very definition of a siege. Pópuli would have needed to sweep us aside within a week, yet there we were, and not an Attack Trench in sight.

Anyway, what I mean is that, in the spring of 1714, I'd had nearly all I could take. Everyone had, save one man: Don Antonio de Villarroel. Among my many tasks, one of the most demanding was accompanying him when he was inspecting positions. One bastion, another, the curtain walls covering the stretches between the bastions; Don Antonio was never satisfied. More soldiers were needed here, more cannons there; and over there, that old breach hadn't been closed up entirely. On May 19 that year, I was taking the brunt of one of his tirades when we were interrupted by a heavier than usual artillery bombardment.

Silent explosions could be seen coming from the enemy cannons. Then you'd hear a faint whistling sound, followed, with a sonorous *crrrack*, by the impact of cannonball on ramparts. But it was different on this occasion. They were aiming high, and the cannonballs sailed over the walls and came down inside the city, on the roofs or west faces of civilian buildings.

"Lunatics!" I shouted. "Here, we're here! Are you using your rectal holes to aim with?"

The cannonade continued, more and more off-target shots. I was raging. Don Antonio made me be quiet—he'd understood what was happening long before I had. "They know precisely what they're about," he said.

"But Don Antonio," I protested, "they're missing us by miles."

He turned and went over to the command post. I followed behind. The light finally turned on in my head: They were shelling the city itself!

Years studying in Bazoches to learn how to storm a stronghold with minimal casualties, and here was Pópuli, the butcher, aiming his cannons at civilian houses rather than at the ramparts! It was a feat so unusual, such a departure from the Bazoches precepts, and from the slightest glimmer of human civility, and so flagrant, sordid, and brutal, that I didn't want to believe it was happening. As we ran through the streets, an enormous cannonball landed on a four-story building. The facade crumbled, and as the stones and beams came crashing down, I heard amid the noise the wailing of a child. The sound of a child in pain will always stir up all-consuming hatred. I briefly went back up to the top of the bastion. I remember taking out a telescope and scanning the Bourbon positions. Casting around the *fajina* parapets, among which their cannons were concealed, my lens came to rest on a man standing still between all the smoke and the to-ing and fro-ing of the gunners. He, too, was looking through a telescope. We were looking at each other. He raised an arm in greeting—mockingly, mocking our agony. And then I recognized him: It was Verboom, that utter swine.

The high command, including Costa, were immediately called together in an emergency meeting. Everyone aside from Costa was unsettled; chewing a sprig of parsley and speaking in his usual dispassionate monotone, he seemed almost not to care: "They're using long-range cannons. But even with them, they can't reach all the neighborhoods, only the one nearest the walls, the Ribera barrio. It's only a three-gun battery."

I couldn't help myself from making a selfish comment: "And as luck would have it, Ribera is where my family lives."

Some of the officers called on Don Antonio to send out a couple of battalions against the battery. Others thought the cannonade was an attempt to provoke a large sortie that was doomed to fail. Still others argued for a missive to be sent to Pópuli, threatening the execution of prisoners if the shelling was not called off. Our resident parsley-chewer came up with a simple but brilliant solution: We needed to take our most accurate cannons, the shorter-range ones, closer to the enemy positions, and from there destroy their battery. How? Sallying forth from the city with one whole battery of our own.

"But," I objected, "that will also put the enemy in a position to fire on our cannons."

His answer was very much that of a gunner: "What is infantry for if not to provide cover for artillery?"

You could never tell if Costa was being serious. He fished around in his pouch and looked crestfallen to find himself out of parsley. "Give me and my Mallorcans ten minutes to carry out our own bombardment," he said, looking up. "That's all we'll need."

When it came to it, five minutes was more than enough. Don Antonio sent out two full battalions, and these attacked the cordon in ostentatiously well-ordered ranks, with twenty drummers announcing the onslaught. The Bourbons sent twice their number to tackle them, falling for the trap. Making the most of the diversion, Costa set out with six cannons. Our cannonballs landed right on the heads of that poor Bourbon battery. The Mallorcans hooked the light cannons back onto the carriages and fell back into the city. This was mud in Pópuli's eye—outmaneuvered, and three cannons down.

Infuriated, he brought together all his cannons and pushed the cordon a little closer to the city—close enough to put the whole of Barcelona within range, save the seafront. The attack of May 19 was nothing next to what was about to befall us. The bombardment of the whole urban district commenced. An uninterrupted and systematic barrage, raining down upon us night and day for months.

Such military terror as that has a great fondness for destruction on a grand scale. The tall defiles formed by the city's buildings, along with the narrow streets, were too great a temptation. Missile upon missile they hurled, with all the glee of a child stamping on ant nests. I can still see streets thick with fleeing civilians as the walls around them erupted like pus-filled pimples.

To all Barcelonans, this was the inferno; for Pópuli, a calculated measure. His reasoning being that, in the face of such terror, the people would pressure its government to open the city gates. In a sense, putting all emotion aside, it was the right move from Pópuli. Would it be worth us paying with our homes and our cathedrals, our very lives? The army defending Barcelona was made up of militia fighting to defend their families. Now, with those loved ones coming under fire, if they were going to be killed anyway, where was the sense in continuing the resistance? But Pópuli had acted in anger, and he had miscalculated. The people didn't think along the lines he'd expected. Quite the opposite.

Nor even did Martí Zuviría, an engineer trained in coolheaded decision-making. Precisely because I knew how barbarous the enemy was, and that they would stop at nothing, it was my duty to plead for the white flag to be shown. Why did I not? I don't know. Perhaps we'd gone too far for that. In spite of what I'd learned at Bazoches, beyond its walls, the reality of war was altogether different. The marquis's rationale was not equal to the changes being wrought in the world at that time.

Plus, Pópuli's maneuver merely demonstrated his impotence and frustration. Rather than denting people's faith, the bombardment—by showing that Pópuli didn't believe he could overcome the defenders— was a spur. Further—and something we didn't know yet—Madrid had made it known that, because of his negligence, Pópuli was to be replaced. He'd never have the chance to ride victorious into Barcelona. Pópuli took his frustration out on the Barcelonans. The sustained flurries of missiles came in fifteen-minute intervals, precise and forbidding. So it was for months. Some streets took such a battering, you had to resort to memory to discern where you were.

Old Barcelona, always lighthearted, full of joy and cheer, now coming under aerial torment. Cannonballs that were the enemies of all intelligence, including the printing press: One fell on the offices of the city's most venerable newspaper, the *Diario del Sitio*, killing its entire writing staff as well as the proprietors. Anti-religious cannonballs: One came through the rose window at the Church of Pi during a service, slaughtering the parishioners. Cannonballs, that is to say, that were nocturnal, blind, and deranged, because one also killed three of Philip's agents as they were pinning lampoons to a wall. Poor boys, in quite a state they were. I came across a paintbrush attached to a wall—the point about this brush being that it was also attached to a hand, and that hand to half an arm. Up to the elbow was left. Its owner was putting up lampoons when the cannonball fell on his head. Anyway, the teams of cleaners didn't hurry to take it down, leaving it as an example and a lesson to traitors.

All we could do was evacuate the Barcelonans to the beach or up to the mountain of Montjuic, the only places beyond the cannons' reach. The minority went up to Montjuic—those who had servants they could send back down for provisions. So on the beach, an enormous encampment of exiles was established. First mattresses were laid out, and over those the most sturdy and welcoming tents. The feminine touch was evident in them. They always used their best linens, quilts, and curtains for the awnings—the most visible part of the tent. A kind of unspoken competitiveness broke out, roofs covered with damask silks and colorful cashmere. Around the tents, domestic furniture was placed, some of it baroque in style. It made sense that the owners brought their most precious belongings, so they could keep an eye on them. But what a contrast! Humble cooking fires in the sand, and around them oak tables with spiral legs, fine mirrors, wardrobes taller than a person, upholstered chairs, and even one or two up-to-date lady's dressing tables, *toujours à la mode.*

The massive bombardment had something isocratic about it: In the face of such an onslaught, everyone became equal; where you came from and your social standing ceased to matter. The grouping together on the beaches, the immodesty of contact, provoked the opposite of Pópuli's desire. These people, neighbors but now in a new sense, no longer separated by walls as before, came to form an open-air community. Forced together, they felt more unified than ever. The children ran in the sand, the women cooked together. Elderly men conversed, sitting smoking their pipes; there were not many male adults to be seen besides.

Between the beach and the city ramparts, the city was one of deserted streets and abandoned buildings. And what an unprecedented sight, these streets. The rumbling of the cannonballs opened doors. Many of the buildings' damaged facades had dropped away like masks, exposing three or four storeys with furniture and beds still in place. People couldn't carry everything, and so much unguarded wealth was a considerable temptation. The Red Pelts were nothing if not rigorous, though, and they placed guards on the streets with a license to kill.

One of the first looters to be caught was called Cigalet (a nickname, roughly translatable as "little chicken"). Following a summary trial, he was sentenced to hang—immediately, as an example to others. Cigalet was well known, making it a high-profile case: It so happened that the first person caught with his hand in the silver chest was also the city's main executioner. His assistant, who was betrothed to Cigalet's daughter, had to do the honors. Cigalet was far calmer about it than his future son-in-law. Walking up the scaffold steps, the prisoner joked with the crowd. They said encouraging things, lightly mocking him, halfway between irony and sympathy. "Remember your promotion is down to me," he said as his son-in-law-to-be placed the noose over his head. What a scene! I wonder what the wedding night must have been like.

Poor Cigalet at least got a trial; subsequent looters were never even brought before a tribunal. There were stakes in three different places in the city—the looter would be tied to whichever happened to be nearest to the crime, then shot. No question, any city under siege is subject to extraordinary measures, but it was as though the Red Pelts' regime and the bestiality of the Bourbons had become two wheels on the same axle.

Members of the Civil Guard were recruited from the lowest of the low. There wasn't any choice, given that the honorable citizens were manning the ramparts as part of the Coronela militia. The Red Pelts enlisted the procurers, tricksters, tavern ruffians, masterless goons, back-alley cutthroats, and hallucinating drunkards. And these were the ones charged with upholding the law. The naval blockade had seen food prices soar—most looters were impelled not by greed but by hunger. It meant that, by government edict, criminals were given the right to execute those who were starving.

My dear vile Waltraud bids me not to erupt, but how can I not? Calling together these roving patrols, the Red Pelts appealed to order and public calm: the "Octavian peace," they called it, in their most affected language. I'll tell you now what that Octavian peace consisted of: The sky was tumbling down on our heads—in the most literal sense—and right until the last day, the patrols were standing guard at the homes of wealthy *botifleros* such as the ones who had deserted Mataró. When a skeletal child or an old toothless woman slipped in through a hole in the wall, trying to find food, there those killers were, armed by the government itself, tying the hungry to a post and shooting them dead. Bourbons rained down death from without, and Red Pelts from within. There you have it.

There is no such thing as a fortress fully covered by a roof. And fiery tempests were raining down on us from above. When it was all over, seven in ten of Barcelona's houses were either in ruins or had holes punched through them by cannonballs. In just the first two months of the bombardment, in a city with a population of 50,000, precisely 27,275 cannonballs were said to have fallen. Every Barcelonan, therefore, was treated to half a cannonball each by Philip V.

I wonder to this day who the person might have been to keep such close count. I picture him at the top of a bell tower with tablet and chalk, impassive, bored, noting down the impacts with dashes and scores. Which will be where our proverb comes from: "A man who's out of work counts cannonballs."

Meanwhile, news reached us from the enemy lines. Pópuli was now to be replaced as commander of the besieging army. Strange though it may sound, this was the worst news possible.

To replace the useless Pópuli, Little Philip had asked his grandfather to send French reinforcements, including their best general. Guess who that was. Who else but the faithful, invincible marshal of Almansa, scourge of Louis XIV's enemies: Who else but Jimmy.

According to our spies, he had already crossed the Pyrenees, the cream of the French army in tow. They were advancing slowly because of the poor state of the roads and because—pity for us!—of the heavy artillery they were bringing with them.

It was as though someone had ripped my lungs from my chest when I heard this. Jimmy. His cruel and calculating nature, his inexorable determination. I'd have been far happier taking on Satan. Why? Because Jimmy only ever entered the fray if the odds were in his favor.

Don Antonio gave us the news in a military council with the principal commanders. Our agents must have been professionals when it came to counting things, because he then went on to enumerate, battalion by battalion, the French forces Jimmy was bringing with him. I remember the hush that came down. Any officer with half a brain knew what this meant. Nobody spoke the words, but everyone was thinking: "*Now* what?"

Don Antonio gave me that night off. We'd also moved to the beach, into a basic tent made out of strips of old clothes. To Barcelonans, boredom was like a sickness, and on the beach, they kept it at bay with music. The truth is, dining out in front of the beach, my troop of children, dwarves, and old men around me, I felt a little lighter.

Amelis and I retired soon after. I was too tired for lovemaking. Our bed could not have been more simple: one blanket under us and one on top, the sand itself our mattress. The tent had very few comforts, but Amelis kept her music box beside the pillow. She opened it. There, in that crude beach tent, the melodies it played had an especially consoling air.

I recounted the war council to Amelis. "The good news is that the siege will be over soon," I said.

"We're going to surrender?"

I didn't think she'd understood. "We're already at a disadvantage in every department," I said. "But when these French reinforcements arrive, the mismatch will be too huge. We'll send an emissary to negotiate terms, honorable ones, probably something safeguarding lives and property. Jimmy won't oppose that."

"And that will be that?"

"We've held out admirably," I said with some pride. "Far better than anyone could have asked."

She grimaced but said nothing.

"What?" I protested. "If it comes to an end now, we'll keep the house. Otherwise, sooner or later, this bombardment will knock it down."

She got under the covers, brusquely turning her back. "Some kind of peace," she grouched. "A year up on the ramparts for what? All that, and you're just going to let them in, open the gates to the French rather than the Spanish?"

"Tell it to the Red Pelts!" I spat. "They're the ones stockpiling provisions, selling food to the starving at inflated prices. The poor are already giving in. I was with Castellví yesterday, that Valencian intellectual, and we saw an old woman pass out in the middle of the street. All she knows is that she's hungry."

Amelis rolled over to face me. "And when she came around, you asked her if she wanted to surrender?"

"What she wanted was a bite to eat!"

Amelis blew the candle out.

Good old Zuvi was unusually quiet the next day. Curt orders were the only words I spoke. Ballester noticed. I was standing at the prow of one of the bastions, deep in thought, when he came over to me. With his usual Miquelet soft touch, he said: "What the *cojones* is with you?"

There was no reason to hide the facts from him, and I said what was happening. He answered with typically Miquelet-like bravura: He'd have Berwick for dinner, with a few pears and turnips.

I let out a tired laugh. "You don't know Jimmy—Marshal Berwick," I said, correcting myself.

"And you do?" He snorted.

"A little." I knew him better than I'd wanted to. All that time ago we had been intimate—the memory of the scandal had faded, but his character I never forgot. "Jimmy's an opportunist. He wouldn't have taken on the task if it didn't promise the chance to please his superiors and win further laurels and promotion. He's bringing the elite of the French army—with them as reinforcements, and a capable commander, they'll be unstoppable. It's over."

I didn't expect any answer to that. But Ballester came and stood before me. "Know what?" he said in his usual resentful tone. "I put my trust in you once. I said to myself: 'This one's different. Maybe there are men in Barcelona who aren't like the Red Pelts; maybe the war will be a chance to change things.' That was why we came, so no one could say we weren't here when it counted. I accepted taking orders from you. And now look at you, whimpering like a frightened little bitch. What did you think? This is war! You're going to have good and bad moments, and anyone who gives up at the first sign of trouble, well, that only shows he shouldn't have gotten involved to begin with."

I stood and faced him. "Work it out!" I shouted. "When Berwick comes, it won't be Navarran bumpkins we're up against! He's bringing Louis's finest fighters, along with cannons and tons of ammunition. Dragoons, grenadiers, crack troops from the Rhine. The ramparts are in a state, the city half destroyed. Defended by civilians, not soldiers, and most of them famished and ill. I know precisely how Jimmy will go about things, and trust me, either we send an emissary or he'll crush us."

"I see it now," he scoffed. "It's all still ideas and numbers to you."

That was too much. "Ideas and numbers that take into account how many have died! How many more? You lost three on the expedition—want them all gone?"

Ballester punched the battlement. "I want their deaths not to have been for nothing!"

"The point of defending a city," I cried, even more exasperated, "is to save women and children and the sacred places! If we carry on, they'll all be lost! We fight to safeguard them, not to see them devoured!"

"And the Catalan liberties, the constitutions?" he said. "Who's going to safeguard them?"

"How should I know?" I said, holding my arms out wide. "Ask Casanova, ask the politicians. I'm just an engineer."

He gave me the angriest, most accusing glance. "I don't talk to politicians or engineers," he said. "I only talk to men." Then, lowering his voice, he whispered something deeply philosophical (not that he probably knew). "But such are few and far between in this city."

Before I could manage a response, he turned and walked away.

In the following days, it was tenser than ever between Ballester and me. Rather than trying to do anything about it, I ignored him. When we came into contact, I acted like he wasn't there. I refused an order to lead his men on a job. Which he took as an insult. Which it was. His problem, I thought. But the absence of our usual arguments, of those disputes both surly and lubricating, rather than easing things, increased the tension between us.

In a sense, we were a reflection of the mood of the city. Understandably, the news of Berwick's approach didn't do wonders for morale. And vague promises were all we had from the diplomats outside. Nice little letters from Vienna praising our constancy and fidelity. Doubtless Archduke Charles dictated them while mounting the queen, the two of them doing their utmost to ensure the "so-desired succession."

During that period one day, I went with Don Antonio to a government meeting. He wanted me to help them understand the parlous state of our defenses. His reception was glacial.

It was beyond the Red Pelts' powers of comprehension. They were, as a rule, whiners, consummate defeatists, and I thought my report would be used to win over the reticent few. On the contrary. They didn't want to hear a word of what I had to say. Casanova, in particular, looked straight through me with his dark eyes.

I was very young. The public side of things wasn't my affair; I'd been giving my all to the defense of the city. But that day, I had a chance to consider something that occurs only between political leaders.

Casanova was against the resistance and had always been. If, reader, you've been paying attention, you'll know that he did everything in his power to stop the portcullis from being lowered and the city armed. Why, then, was he now so strongly defending those who wanted to carry on fighting, or why at least did he comply with them?

The answer wasn't above but below. In France, the Beast's subordinates obeyed blindly. But in our old besieged city, with the people in turmoil and a government more akin to Athens's model than Sparta's, it was the other way around: The leaders did what the governed told them to. Casanova knew there was no way he could challenge the popular will, which was in favor of holding out. His innermost thought? Impossible to know. I imagine—and this is mere supposition—that in his opinion, it was better to remain in control, in the hope that some chance to end it all would present itself, thereby avoiding greater ills.

Don Antonio merely backed up what I had already said: Berwick was bringing with him a force that would crush us; the council could draw its own conclusions. Here I ought to point out a minor detail— something, though, that in such a tight situation, had an effect: Don Antonio didn't speak Catalan.

Like all educated Catalans, the Red Pelts spoke perfect Castilian. When addressing Don Antonio, they did so in his language, out of deference. But there is something insuperable in Catalans that prevents them from speaking anything but their own tongue to one another. So fragments of the discussions were lost to Don Antonio. I translated for him, whispering in his ear what they were saying when things became heated, which was often. But you surely know good old Zuvi by now: When whoever was speaking became animated, instead of translating the debate, I'd stick my oar in. The only thing the councilors agreed on was the need for drastic measures. And what they came up with was a plan to attack the enemy positions, to raise morale in the city. What a magnificent idea!

Such an attack would be madness. If it went badly, which it was bound to, morale would plummet still further. But then Don Antonio demonstrated perfectly the position he was in: that of a military commander subordinate to a government. He agreed to follow their orders, for all that he personally disagreed.

As in the human body, the nerves in an army are invisible and run from top to bottom. If the officers were unconvinced about the attack, how could the rank and file possibly feel confident? The whole thing was hastily cobbled together. I was one of those to bear the brunt. Orders were sent out in a hurry and got scrambled along the way. I thought I'd been ordered to take part in the assault, but it turned out Don Antonio wanted me in the rearguard. You know, that abject troupe of priests and surgeons meant for evacuating the wounded, and officers whose job it was to stop any who turned back during the opening exchanges, to send them back into the slaughter.

The troops, a thousand men and more, gathered at three of the city gates. The idea was to charge out, form up, and attack the cordon as one. Overrun it and withdraw. Give them a scare so they knew we weren't intimidated by Berwick. As I say, pure imbecility. Jimmy hadn't arrived yet, and he wouldn't care in the slightest about anything that happened before he got there. The Bourbons knew us by that point, and such a limited attack would achieve nothing, nothing besides a gratuitous bloodbath. Dear God, I couldn't think of anything less lovely than to die on such a beautiful spring day.

There are few feelings to match participating in an attack you feel is bound to fail. The relevant thing was not what the officers said to the men but, rather, what they didn't say: They shouted at the men to line up but had no words to suggest they believed in the endeavor. I accompanied the priests as they went up and down the ranks, sprinkling the men with holy water and spouting phrases in Latin. We came upon Ballester and his men.

"Oh ho! Here's our man," he sneered. "Happy about sending us to certain death?"

"I've never argued for harebrained attacks," I retorted. "That was always you. Or have you forgotten? Attack, attack, attack. Well, here's your attack!"

I shoved him back into line. But Ballester would never tolerate anyone laying a finger on him. He came back at me, lifting his hand to my face and pushing me, and saying a few choice words about my mother. That was the last straw.

I've already mentioned how it had been between Ballester and me before that. Added to that, the night before, Anfán also happened to have put his hand to my face, stroking the same cheek as he sat on my knee and asked me to recount the day's fighting. After all that time of him being pricklier than a hedgehog, he'd heard me come in and had gotten out of bed to show me some affection. "*Jefe, jefe.* How many men did you kill today?" And now, a few hours later, it appeared that my last human contact before I died would be with Ballester's grubby paws.

I hit him with a left. I felt his beard cushion the impact of my knuckles. Ballester, naturally, recovered and came at me. Here was a pretty sight just before an attack: two officers going at it in front of the troops. We fell to the floor and rolled about a bit, kicking and howling. Someone separated us and said: "Shall I arrest him, Colonel?"

"And let him off the hook?" I said, spitting a bolus of blood on the ground. "He's not getting off that easily. He'll join the attack like everyone else!"

And so the attack was launched. Our side, all colors under the rainbow, each battalion with its own distinctive tunics, faced by the dour white wall of the Bourbon troops.

An utter disaster. The drums, instead of seeming encouraging, unsettled me. My heart seemed to be in my mouth every time I heard a drumroll. The cannons on the cordon side began firing at us. In the wake of our advance, men were left screaming where they fell. And the cannonballs whistling by, and you not knowing if yours would be the next head to be pulped by one.

Military discipline and civilian brotherliness will always be very different things. A well-trained soldier will advance, advance no matter what, even in the face of an iron tempest. For the Coronela militia, it was different. Each man would look left and right and see alongside him a parent, a son, or a brother: three generations advancing shoulder to shoulder. When one had his leg blown off, or another fell to the floor with half his head gone, those alongside him would always kneel down and try to help. It was my unhappy task to push them on. "On, on!" I cried. "Don't stop, leave it to the surgeons!"

What they failed to understand was that, by stopping, they were loosening the formation. Distraught, they'd stop and crouch down, and the line behind them would have to break to go around them. It was pointless shouting at them: They couldn't hear. And so the formation began falling apart.

I couldn't have been happier to hear the trumpets sounding the retreat. I had only one thought: We're done, let's get away! Until that moment, I'd kept step with the pace of the advance. But as I turned and tried to hurry home, I realized my left leg wasn't working.

My whole leg was covered in blood. As is so often the case, the heat of battle had meant I hadn't felt the pain. The bullet had gone clean through my thigh. The entry and exit wounds were visible in spite of the blood pumping out. The troops were heading back into the city, and I stayed where I was, flapping like a lame duck, letting out ridiculous sobs and groans. For Ballester, sprinting back to the city, here was his chance to take revenge.

"Now what?" he said. "Think we shouldn't stop for the wounded? Still think we ought to leave them where they lie?"

I ought to have begged for his help but instead opted for a few choice words about the gash he was born out of. A few more cannonballs landed around us, and the rest of our men made themselves scarce. What a calamity, that retreat! Some even tossed their rifles to the ground to help run faster; their only thought was reaching the cover of our cannons, where the enemy cavalry wouldn't dare follow.

By now, Bourbon riders had reached the point where our advance had ceased. There was no chance I was going to make it back to the city gates, not even to the palisades. I dropped into a hollow in the ground, facedown, playing dead. With a little luck, I'd be able to wait for nightfall and then slink back to the city.

Well, fortune wasn't favoring me that day. Out of the corner of my eye, I saw two Bourbon soldiers come up alongside the natural trench I was lying in. They were going around impaling bodies with their bayonets to make sure they were dead, and I was next.

"*Arretez!*" I shouted, rolling over to face them. "I'm a lieutenant colonel in His Majesty Carlos III's army. Take me to your commander, and you'll be rewarded."

I could barely believe it, seeing the barriers to the Bourbon cordon swing shut behind me. I'd breakfasted in my home that morning, and now, just a few hours later, here I was in the enemy camp, a wound in my leg and two enemy soldiers keeping me captive.

There were few prisoners aside from me—which just goes to show that short, frightened legs are better than long, injured ones. The cordon had been refined and reinforced since the beginning of the siege, I noticed.

My captors weren't overly discourteous. Pleased with their find, they were leading me to one of their superiors when we came past a surly-looking French captain. Seeing me, he let loose a few insults against the city and said what he thought should happen to the Barcelona "rebels."

I shrugged. "We'll be dining in Paris before that day comes," I said in French.

I was merely referring to a rumor that had been making the rounds in the city: Catalan diplomats were said to be brokering a truce with the French. This captain, though, took me to mean something else altogether; it seemed he thought good old Zuvi was planning on invading France on his own, or somesuch. He snatched the rifle from one of the soldiers guarding me, and rammed the butt into my kidneys. I fell, letting out a helpless cry. What was he about? I looked him in the eye.

He was resolved to kill me: The look on his face stated this clearly. He might simply have been a madman, or perhaps it was the yearlong siege that had turned him into this bitter brute. I couldn't say. But he began aiming the rifle butt, accurately and extremely painfully, at my ribs. I tried dragging myself out from under this barrage, and I cried out for help, but where to find help in an enemy encampment? It was more a harpooning than a beating. One blow to the base of my spine made my sight swim with yellow dots. He was going to kill me. I tried crawling away and got a kick to the head for my troubles.

I began not to feel the pain. I got to my knees, straightening up my body. Something wooden struck me between my shoulder blades, and I fell to the floor again. Just then, however, I caught a brief glimpse of someone.

On the cordon wall, a man standing on the highest tier, looking out over the city and the now deserted battlefield with a telescope.

I recognized the shape and size of the man. The expression, not so much venial as great: a pose that suggested solemnity in the face of trivialities, a silhouette with an invincible aura. "Martí," I said, "it cannot be. This man is dead." I straightened up again, still on my knees.

Delirious or not, I would lose nothing by calling out to him. I held out my hand and cried: "Monsieur de Vauban!"

Without dropping the telescope, the man slowly turned his head.

"*C'est moi! Votre élève bien aimé de* Bazoches*!*"

He looked down at me, frowning. "*C'est qui?*" he asked.

"*Moi!*" I replied, more a spit than a shout. "Martín Zuviría!"

"Martín? *C'est toi?*"

His penetrating look gave way to astonishment. He descended the tiers and came toward me. A look was enough to send the captain packing. When he knelt down beside me, my vision had begun going blurry, all color gone.

He hesitated. Discreetly, I upturned my wrist and bared my forearm for him to see my Points.

Grabbing hold of his lapel, I said: "*Maréchal, quelle est la Parole? Dites-moi! S'il vous plaît, la Parole.*"

It wasn't the marquis, of course, but, rather, his cousin, Dupuy, whom, if you remember, I met on one of his visits to Bazoches. The one who that day made reference to a "clause" preventing me from ever facing him in battle. Yes, isn't life just like that. And my confusion wasn't at all strange—the family resemblance was strong, even down to the way they carried themselves.

He took me to his tent and gave me some hot wine. He then had his private surgeon come and see to the bullet wound in my leg.

"The wound is clean," said Dupuy. "The bullet has only punctured the thigh flesh. If it had hit the artery, you'd be dead by now."

I rolled up my sleeve. I wanted to tell him about my Points once more, as the first time he'd been able to see only the ones nearest to my wrist.

"Four," I said, preempting him. "The fifth hasn't been validated."

Dupuy was a very eminent man. "Yes, I thought as much," he said. "Don't forget, though: Whether or not it's been validated, the tattoo is still there. And you must show that you deserve it."

I changed the subject. What news?

"Marshal Berwick is yet to arrive," he explained. "I was traveling with him, but what with the artillery train, and Miquelets constantly ambushing us, progress was so slow that he asked me to come ahead. He wants me to weigh up the situation. And from what I can tell, this siege has been managed badly, very badly. All the men are on edge. As your treatment shows very well."

I was about to speak, but he put a finger to his lips. "Listen: I'm not in a position to help you as I'd like, unfortunately. You're outside of what I can control; the siege is still being run by the Spanish. You know how thin-skinned they are. You're a lieutenant colonel, and you're their prisoner; I can't just take you off them."

Again I was going to say something, but Dupuy made me be quiet. "Shut up and listen! This is how it's going to go: They'll interrogate you, but they won't be too rough. Yes, yes, I know we're at war, all courtesy's gone out the window, and torture's become de rigueur. Don't worry, though, I've found someone. He serves King Philip, but he's one of ours. You'll be interrogated, but not roughly. A few days with our man, then you'll be under me."

"Who is this individual?" I asked. "French or Spanish?"

He smiled, pointing at the entrance to the tent. "The first person to come through there and use sign language with you. Whoever that is." Before leaving, he asked me, "Martí, do you mind telling me what you were doing inside a city besieged by the king's forces?"

His look was as withering as that of a Ten Points. Neither did I want to lie, nor could I have lied. I was both honest and concise. "I was working as an engineer," I said.

His reaction was that of someone with more Points than I. "I see," he said simply, and left the tent.

I had reason to fear what was coming to me next. So much had changed in such a short space of time that I couldn't get my thoughts in order. The only people who came into the recently erected tent were Dupuy's legion of servants, bringing in furniture, and one French officer who came hoping to pay his respects to the cousin of the great Vauban. And me in the field bed in one corner, bandaged up and unable to move. I carefully watched everyone who came in, waiting for someone to address me with the sign language of engineers. Nothing.

Midway through the afternoon, four Spanish soldiers came in, sent by a captain. They made me go with them in spite of my protests. Their bearing didn't seem particularly soldierly, which is to say they seemed very slovenly, and everything they did seemed strained, as happens with men unwillingly obeying orders. As they dragged me through camp, they kept glancing from side to side, as though afraid someone else would step in and stop them.

The unfortunate houses on the site of the Bourbon camp had been turned into stores or residences for the high command. They took me into one of the latter. We climbed some steps up to the first floor, and I was locked in a room containing an old table and two shabby-looking chairs. A fine layer of dust covered the floor and furniture. The panes in the single window were smashed. The Bourbon camp was the sack, and this tiny room a sack within the sack. Jonah in the belly of the whale? He had nothing on me then!

"Our man"—in the words of the innocent Dupuy—appeared half an hour later. I saw what had happened. Dupuy, just arrived at the Bourbon encampment, was met by a Points Bearer who showed himself to be compliant and polite. In the belief that the sacred fidelities of Bazoches were still in effect in the world, Dupuy had placed full confidence in the man.

"Our man" came in and immediately reprimanded the soldiers he had with him. Why hadn't his guest, the honorable enemy, been given drink and plenty of food? But with his hands, in our sign language, he said to me: "I've got you, you swine."

"Our man" was none other than Joris Prosperus van Verboom, the Antwerp butcher.

6

When everything was over, after Barcelona had fallen and the war was drawing to its close, Verboom was given some very cushy sinecures indeed by Philip V. He stayed on in Catalonia. Barcelona—defeated, flattened, bloodied—remained a source of unease to the Bourbons. There is a form of submission more absolute than death: endless slavery. Little Philip gave the task to Verboom.

I'm going to include two very rough sketches of the city—if my hairy hippopotamus manages not to lose them, that is. The first one you've already seen; it's of old Barcelona as it was immediately before the siege.

And in this next one, you can see what Verboom did to it.

The star that's been added on, the Citadel, was the work of Verboom. Yes, the Citadel. He leveled a fifth of the city for building materials. A perfect bastioned enclosure, there not for the people's protection but from which to control, subdue, and, if necessary, fire cannons on them. An urban tumor that converted Barcelonans into prisoners in their own city.

But what am I doing talking about what happened after the siege? Held captive behind enemy lines, in the hands of my enemy, I had quite enough on my plate.

My usual quick thinking had deserted me. My only way out was to get in touch with Dupuy. Impossible: Verboom stood in my way; a man capable of plotting my kidnap must have been sufficiently foresighted to hide that fact. Most likely, he was going to kill me there and then. And later, he'd allege that I'd tried to get away, and say to Dupuy that some imbecile soldier had shot me by mistake—anything. Shit.

Verboom had arrived in the night, like a sea mist, or like deathly fevers. I'd managed to make myself a weapon, a knife fashioned out of some wood I'd pulled off the window frame and, for the blade, a shard of glass thrust into it. If worse came to worst, before they tried to kill me, I'd try to take his eye out.

However, I quickly saw that the situation was not as I had imagined. The Antwerp butcher brought one servant soldier with him, and his only weapons were a tray, a bottle, and two glasses. The servant put these down on the table and went out. When Verboom and I were alone, I erupted in indignation. "How dare you lock me up! I defect, I offer my services to King Philip, and this is my reward. You can't imagine what I've been through, coerced by those rebels to take part in their deluded attempts to defend their city!"

Verboom's only response to my theatrics was to take a seat, pour wine into the two glasses, and say: "Drink."

I refused. He could have been planning to poison me, to save himself from having to do something violent and then for Dupuy to find out.

"Come now, don't be ridiculous," he said, grimacing. "Think I'd go so low? This is good port—using it as rat poison would be a waste."

He took my glass and drained it in one go. But it would take more than that to win my trust. The silence was eventually broken by the rumbling of cannons starting up outside. The walls shook, and chalk dust fell across the table. Intuitively, Verboom put a hand over his glass, glancing up, which actually convinced me: No one tries to preserve a drink with poison in it. I poured myself some more port and felt it strip my throat. What was Verboom up to? He wasn't exactly getting to the point.

Jimmy was going to arrive within a matter of days. The person whose Attack Trench design ended up being used to take Barcelona would gain a large share of the praise. When he was released in 1712, Verboom made a plan for a future siege of the city. But Jimmy had sent Dupuy ahead to design another trench. Dupuy was a Seven Points. Jimmy was very likely, in any case, to use the trench of a Vauban family member, which would make all the butcher's efforts for naught. Good-bye, glory, goodbye, rewards!

In a nutshell: Verboom was hoping I'd correct, refine, and improve the trench he'd been planning. I was a Five Points—well, sort of—and had the advantage over Dupuy of having been inside the city and therefore knowing what state the defenses were in.

In spite of my situation, I burst out laughing. Did he really think I was going to help him?

"You're the reason I spent two years locked up," he said. "Two long years."

At this point, his hate for me became more than palpable. Everything about Verboom was large: his body, his head, his teeth, like those of a hippo. I gulped, suddenly very afraid. He paused, letting me savor his intimidating force. I was under lock and key, and I was alone; he could do with me as he pleased. And we are all what we are; Saint Jordi killed the dragon as easily as crushing a cockroach, Roger de Llúria brushed aside a hundred thousand Turks over the course of three breakfasts, and King Jaume took Mallorca and Valencia just because he felt bored with his palaces in Barcelona. But as it turned out, Longlegs Zuvi wasn't Saint Jordi, or Roger de Llúria, or King Jaume. I was simply very, very afraid.

"I did nothing to you. Nothing!" he bellowed. "One day I was at Bazoches castle, courting a lady, and a muddy gardener crossed my path. What have I got against gardeners? Nothing. But that day in

1706, I was slandered—vile slander—and four years later, in 1710, I was captured—again, vilely—and now, another four years on, here's this vile gardener again. Except this time, there's nothing to stop me ridding myself of you. Nothing!" He wagged a finger at me. "And yet there is a small possibility I might let you off. If you do as I tell you, I'll merely exile you to the island of Cabrera or some such godforsaken spot."

He left me alone to think about it. He left the drawings for the trench he'd designed, along with some scraps containing the technical details. I didn't bother looking at them. A prisoner has obligations, and he has rights, which add together to form the only thing he must do: escape.

I looked out of the smashed window. Jumping from the first storey wouldn't kill me. A broken ankle for my freedom seemed like a good exchange. There were two soldiers on guard down there, of course. I didn't need to get back to the city, though—that *would* be impossible—but simply to get hold of Dupuy.

Using that spring sun, the papers on the table, and a bit of the windowpane as a magnifying glass, I could start a fire. Confusion. Guards are always more indulgent if it's a fire an escapee is fleeing. They'd be unsure, even if for a second, whether to help or arrest me. I'd have time to shout at the top of my lungs. Sound carries around a military encampment even more than in echoey mountains, and my strange tidings surely would reach Dupuy. Once Dupuy knew what was happening, Verboom would think twice about killing me. After that, time would tell.

I picked up one of the pieces of paper with Verboom's notes on it, and supported myself against the window frame, waiting for the morning rays to begin pouring in. The black of the ink would go up before the white of the paper. I'd direct the light with a piece of concave glass. Before my eyes, some fragment of Verboom's instructions.

It's strange the things you remember—such as what happened to be on that piece of paper:

. . . on the left side **G**, and if time permits, we construct the return **H** and the redoubt **I**, and build the battery **K** of 10 cannons for the mills **L**, and the bridge at the new port on side **M**, and whatever we can of the defenses of the bastion of Sainte Claire and of the old wall which encloses it. This manoeuvre will require 1,000 armed men and then . . .

I turned my head. The map was there on the table. For a moment, I put off my plan to set the place on fire. Once an engineer, always an engineer. I was magnetized by the map. I began examining it.

It was a representation of Barcelona, with its city center and battered walls. And, on the fields around, the zigzagging trench planned by Verboom. The numbers and initials marked on the map had their key in the notes. I had planned a quick glance but ended up sitting down and studying it closely, cross-checking it with the notes.

I scrutinized Verboom's trench, the instructions for how it should be carried out. I went back to the map. And again.

This wasn't much of a trench. Truly, it wasn't. The sheer weight of Bourbon numbers meant, somehow or other, they were bound to reach the ramparts. With huge losses, yes, but what did that matter? None of this would figure in the end: The point was that Dupuy's design would be better, far better, and Jimmy would opt for that one.

Then something happened. One thought led to another: If that was so obviously the way things were going to turn out, wasn't it my duty to intervene? When the Dutch butcher came back, there was good old Zuvi, sitting and reading over his notes.

"Well?" he said.

"Do you want my opinion or not?" Picking up the sheets of paper, I tore them in half and threw them scornfully on the floor. *"Des ordures."* Before he could become animated, I added: "The problem is not so much the design as the whole basis of your approach."

We argued it over. I, being the superior engineer, prevailed.

Verboom perspired easily. My disquisitions had made him sweatier still. The beads on his upper lip, in particular, made me feel sick. In summary, I said: "Look, I've had a think about what you said, and perhaps you're right: Our issues with each other are based on an old misunderstanding. Let's change the agreement: Don't exile me, promote me, and in exchange, I'll work loyally on your behalf."

"Loyalty?" he said skeptically. "You don't know the meaning of the word."

"You need to design another Attack Trench. And who's going to do a better job than me? We need to start from the beginning."

"Your debt with me," he said, "can't just be wiped clean."

"Even you, who hates me, would find it hard to have me executed when I hand over the plan for this new Attack Trench."

I could see exactly what he was thinking, as though his skull were made of glass: It's so close I can almost touch it! What have I got to lose?

"Ink and paper," I said. "A compass, set squares. That's what I need. And a night to work on it."

It ended up being not one night but two, plus three entire days, shut up in that shabby little room. I didn't even have a chance to shave. The artillery fire made the air in the room constantly thick with floating dust.

I worked harder on that Attack Trench than I ever had on anything, pushing my being to its very limit. Believe me when I say the brain is the most tiring muscle to use. Never, ever, not before then or since, have good old Zuvi's talents been tested so hard. I felt like an architect stubbornly trying to turn a decaying shack into something Rome would bless as a cathedral. My quill attacked the inkwell as I made use of my Bazoches faculties, and every line said to me I'd been born for such a task; all the hours under Vauban's tutelage would be justified in these damned plans. "The optimum defense" had been Vauban's question. And perhaps—time would tell—here was the answer: "The optimum defense consists of an Attack Trench." . . . Because, as you might have guessed, I poured all my effort into jeopardizing, obstructing, and generally making the task of the Bourbon army impossible; to shaft the lot of them, from the wheels of their cannons to the toes of their press-ganged soldiers. My design had to seem brilliant on paper and be a disaster once executed. Verboom was a swine but no fool. He'd pick up on bad faith and obvious defects. So I wrought a very lovely lie, false but seductive, featuring elements that were genuine but, underneath, doomed to fail. It had to be sabotage, while seeming to better whatever Dupuy was going to come up with. To better Dupuy! And with Jimmy's scrutiny to contend with as well! The very thought made my head spin.

Whatever happened, a trench was going to reach Barcelona's ramparts. They had more than enough men, whom their tyrant leader looked upon as nothing but cannon fodder. But a defective trench would delay them, possibly add a week or two to proceedings. And in such a time, this trifling universe of ours could turn fully on its axis. Who was to say? The king of one nation might die, or the queen of another; alliances might change; anything.

Verboom, who went from impatient to extremely impatient, kept coming into the room. "Done yet? Berwick's not far away. Hurry!"

I dragged the table over to the window and the steep, defined shaft of sunlight. Thousands of dust motes floated around, reminding me of jellyfish in crosscurrents. Come the third morning, I felt like my tired, stinging eyes were on the cusp of melting.

Verboom came in, slamming the door behind him and giving me a murderous glance. He'd run out of patience.

"This might settle our account," I said before he could speak.

"Some job you must have done for it to be worth a man's life," he said, flattening out the plan on the table. "Especially yours."

He took a long time looking over the plans, and was expressionless throughout. He read the notes, went back to the map. The eternal inspection. I had no way of knowing what his little grunts and groans meant.

In the end, I couldn't contain myself. "Hopeful about our future trench?"

He didn't answer, as though I weren't there. He peered closely at the map, running a finger over it. Without deigning to look at me, he said: "What do you think?" He finally looked up, facing me. "If I weren't, you'd be dead already."

We spent the whole of the following day together, refining the plans. I was worn out; he oozed energy. He had a rough and limitless sort of strength. And my enemy was no dimwit, I'll give him that. During those twenty-four hours, his attention didn't stray from the table for one moment. My God, I thought, doesn't he need to piss, to sleep, does he never eat? A bit of rusk cake and a bottle of port, and I could imagine him traversing whole deserts.

He harried me with questions. "Too close," he said at one point. "You've got the first parallel starting far too close to the city. The day the work starts, the troops will be at risk of being fired on and destroyed."

"Do you want Berwick to back this? Then give him want he wants. The closer we start, the less time we'll need to reach the walls. Berwick won't be able to resist."

"The three parallels, and the channels between them, they're so wide," he objected. "Why? Digging out that much earth means more effort than is needed, and that way you lose time."

"The width of the trench walls needs to be proportional to that of the defenders' walls," I argued. "For the attack itself, we'll need considerable numbers. Where are you hoping the shock troops will go? And how do you expect soldiers and sappers to circulate in such thin channels? The traffic of men and matériel will all be bumping into each other. In trying to save time, you'll waste it."

"You've also aimed the trench much farther to the left," he said, "closer to the sea."

"The land in that area, if you remember, abounds with dykes and small streams. They'll be dry in the summer. The men digging will be able to use the riverbeds that run parallel to the walls. They'll only have to work the trench a little deeper than the ones naturally there from the watercourses."

I'd done a good job in one sense: An enemy is harder to kill at close quarters. That twenty-four hours sharing such a small space, and the sham solidarity—but solidarity after all—had given me a glimpse of the man. He had a habit of scratching his fleshy cheeks with his ring finger, when it's so much more usual for people to use their forefinger. Verboom ceased to be my mortal enemy and turned into a middle-aged man with a distinguishing characteristic: He scratched his face with his ring finger. Our shared enterprise generated something akin to camaraderie. You don't wish your fellow oarsman dead—at least not until you've reached the shore.

Is it possible to honor one's enemy? I began to question everything. What if, after all, the evil was not in him but in me? There was no way for me to contradict his account of our hostilities. In reality, what ill had Verboom done me? He had been showing off in front of a lady one day when a muddy "gardener" had launched into him. Anyone in his place would have cursed me, as he had. As we went on with our calculations of barrow loads, and as I kept going with my diversions and approximations, drainage depths, cavalry numbers, angles of counter-escarpments, I worked out that my dislike for Verboom was but a manifestation of my love for Jeanne Vauban. Perhaps I hated him only because that was easier than owning up to the truth: I'd lost Jeanne, and I was solely responsible. This new perspective unsettled me.

Understand my situation. Torn from my home, confined but still using my intellect to fight, in secret and against everyone, including my own side, who by now might consider me a deserter. Jimmy about to arrive, a presence to oppose that of Don Antonio. And The Word, drifting around somewhere in that corrupt, dust-filled atmosphere. The disquiet I underwent in those days made my hate for Verboom falter.

No, it isn't that, no. I said I'd be sincere, and I will.

I'll tell you why we hated each other from the moment we set eyes on each other, and why I hated him until I killed him, and why, to this very day, I hate Joris Prosperus van Verboom.

Because! Some things simply are, one doesn't choose them, full stop. And to hell with Verboom!

End of chapter, damn it all.

Or not? Oh, my blond walrus suggests that it might be good to tie it up. Ah, yes, she says I should recount the rest of what happened that evening. Now you see what's going on? You've become this book's engineer, and I've been reduced to a poor sapper.

Once we'd finished the job, we were both utterly mentally exhausted. Verboom sent for drink. Port was his passion, and it was what relieved him. A bottle of that strong wine, he said, cost fortunes. Since the war had begun, Portugal had traded only with England, meaning his reserves had steadily diminished. And in spite of that, he shared it with me. Perhaps, as I say, after our shared endeavor, it was harder for him to show me bad manners that evening than he'd find it to have me killed the next morning.

As with all men when they drink (apart from Jimmy), our talk turned to women. Well, Verboom's talk; I said nothing about how much I missed Amelis. During the time Verboom had been confined in Barcelona, the Red Pelts even let him receive visits from high-class courtesans.

"Well, just the one," he said, as though it were nothing. "A harlot in pay of their magistrates."

"Ha!" I said. "Just one woman to keep you company! Such an eminent hostage, and subjected to the torment of monotony? Doubtless they wanted to make it like being married for you."

We were drunk enough by this point for him not to pick up on my sarcasm.

"Oh, but she knew all the tricks, that one. The first thing I plan to do when we enter the city is to have her found. A dark-haired beauty, a bit too thin. I like them with a bit more flesh on. My, could she wiggle those hips, though, and her tongue was a miracle worker."

"Dark hair?"

"Yes, very dark, her hair, but not her skin," he clarified, rapping the table with his knuckles. "And a body harder than oak. Although, the little slut, she was also stingy as can be." He laughed. "She always came wearing the same dress, a violet one. No jewelry, never any new attire whatsoever. Oh, but do you want to know what the most unusual thing about her was?" As he spoke, he glanced around in the manner of a man reminiscing. The port had gone to his head, and he hadn't noticed me looking at him like an animal. "For a woman, she had quite a brain on her. When I was at my lowest points, it was her, her!, who came up with the way out of my hardships. 'Joris, darling,' she said, 'if you want to get out of here, propose an exchange. Suggest they swap you for another big fish, someone at your level. Like that general, say, Villarroel, the one the Bourbons have captured. The only reason it hasn't happened is because no one's had the idea. Him to Barcelona, you to Madrid. Everyone happy.' " Verboom shook his big head in admiration, like a dog shaking water from its fur. "I just hadn't imagined it would be so easy. I made exactly that suggestion. And here I am."

How can I possibly begin to describe the pain? It was more than I could bear. The way he'd recounted the intimacy of her "Joris, darling . . . " We were drinking from clay cups. I didn't realize I was crushing mine in my hand. Suddenly, it shattered into pieces, making a noise like a cracked nut.

This brought Verboom out of his drunken stupor. Looking at me, he saw it in my face. At which his lit up. "No," he said, "it can't be."

I'm ninety-eight years old. And I could live to a thousand and ninety-eight, and still the way he laughed in that moment would resound in my ears as though it were yesterday.

7

Have any of you ever been dead? I have, several times. And such a benign state it is, such a pleasure to be in, that I can well understand why no one comes back from there. Death only kills desires and obligations. And without desires or obligations, why come back to the trifling circumference of this universe of ours?

To recap: Good old Zuvi behind the Bourbon cordon, locked in a room empty except for the dust, my design for the Attack Trench complete. Cannon fire resounding without, monotone and impersonal, as though it were *le Mystère* itself being racked with laughter. Since I had completed my task, the following dawn was surely to be my last. Verboom consulted me on a last few details, shamelessly scribbling down all my answers. Rubbing his tired eyes, he stowed the notes in a file and then let out a little cry in Dutch.

In came two heavies broader across their backs than I am long of leg. The Antwerp butcher stuffed the sheets of paper into the folder. And as he did so, he coolly leaned his head closer to me.

This small gesture said it all. They were going to kill me there and then. Doubtless they were mercenaries, private thugs hired by Verboom. Four massive hands lifted me up under my arms.

"Wait a moment!" I screeched.

Never has my mind whirred into action so quickly. I elbowed my way out of their grips and forced myself back into my seat. Then, extending a hand across the map, I said in a miserable, pleading tone: *"Monseigneur! Et les moulins?"*

"What mills?"

"We still haven't finished planning the attack on Section L here. The rebels will turn these mills into redoubts."

Verboom blinked. "Ah, yes," he said, "the mills in Section L. We were going to come back to them and forgot. Well, they aren't especially important. The attack won't go very near them."

Though what I heard him saying was: "No, we won't defer your execution." The two mercenaries stood there like hunting dogs straining at their chains. They lifted me out of my seat again. Then I came up with a tall story about the mills: An anonymous genius had come up with a curious system for concealing artillery, I said. The windows in the mills were going to be made into gunwales, and medium-caliber cannons placed inside—inconspicuously, the barrels not sticking out. They weren't windmills, but the idea was to put sails on them like a windmill, and these, turning in the wind in time with the cannon fire, would serve to disperse the gunpowder smoke. The enemy would take a good long while working out where the deadly shots were coming from.

"How original!" exclaimed Verboom, obviously planning to use the idea himself one day. He made a few notes and, thinking out loud, asked: "Do you know the mad genius who had the idea? Perhaps, when we take the city, I'll have him spared and offer him the chance to serve under me." Verboom wasn't the most intelligent of men. But then, swiveling his big head all of a sudden, he looked on me with renewed spite. His own words had led him to the answer. "It was you, of course," he said.

That was the last straw. Well, you can't survive forever, hopping from frying pan to frying pan. Verboom gave the order for me to be taken out, and this time the two giants got a good hold of me.

I had no way of knowing, but my fate had been decided several days earlier. A number of spies who had been caught in Barcelona had been hanged outside the walls as an example. The Bourbons decided to carry out reprisals by hanging prisoners along the cordon. Verboom had my name included in the list. In fact, when I arrived, there was only one noose left, on a fifteen-foot L-shaped stage just behind the edge of the cordon.

There was an uproariousness to this mass execution that didn't seem much suited to the meting out of justice. The sight of the hanged men on the city walls had stirred the troops, and the officers were having trouble containing them. I was jostled and shoved through a sea of arms; if not for my thug escorts, I wouldn't have made it as far as the scaffold. My hands were tied behind my back, the noose was dropped down over my head, and the rope was attached to a wooden contraption designed for hoisting infantry out of the trench.

I could see everything from up there. Everything. A westerly wind was blowing the smoke out to sea. My eyes, free from the dust haze of the previous days, scanned the front.

The cordon, the Bourbon cannons. On that day, their gunners seemed subdued in their work, as though Pópuli's imminent departure had somehow lulled them. Men scurried antlike along the channels that ran from the cordon to the Capuchin convent, arms full of munitions. From the city, Costa's missiles came in a measure rather than a torrential fashion.

The Two Crowns' positions were visible, too, and ours I knew from memory. I was certain that the men of the Coronela were behind every rampart face and manning every bastion. In each of the bell towers nearest to the ramparts, pairs of observers. Repair brigades would be emptying detritus from the moat, shielded by welded-together doors.

The land between the two sides, apparently unpeopled, seethed with secret armies. All the ruined houses, fought over a thousand times, had patrols from both armies hiding inside. I could sense our snipers nestled in rifts and crevices. Thus, at once I saw the hunter and the prey, the reckless foragers and the snipers stalking them. Beyond the palisade, the battered city walls, and beyond them the outline of the city, with dozens of bell towers pointing upward like needles. And beneath it all, our Mediterranean, ever indifferent to the agonies of men. The city put me in mind of a moribund body, which, though going into its death pangs, continually formed new patches of scar tissue.

There is something irremissable about the contact of a noose against one's neck. My final thoughts, little as I like to admit it, were empty, emotionless technicalities. Costa needs to alter his range, I thought. A number of soldiers heaved on the wooden contraption. I felt my feet lift off the platform.

The beauty of this world is hidden from us until the moment we feel disconnected from it. In my final vision of things, all was well, beauteous, in order. There was even orderliness to the destruction of the ramparts, the breaches perfect, like silk cocoons. Infinity resides in every instant, every instant is in itself abundant. How wrong ever to think otherwise! My final thought was: How lovely a siege is. Then, as I was deprived of air, delirium overcame me.

I heard a noise. This: "Wake up. That's an order."

I opened my eyes.

It was Jimmy. He peered at me from very close up. I could even smell the perfume on his wig.

There before me, the Jimmy I knew: he and his conceited self-satisfaction, his little courtier laugh, proud as a peacock. He had a small retinue. Seeing me wake, he turned to them in triumph, twirling his hand affectedly, as if to say: *See? I did it. He's back to life.*

Forgive the digression. I was in a hospital tent for Bourbon officers. Thick bandages swaddled my neck. Most of the beds were empty, but we weren't alone. At the far end, on a rickety field bed, there was a Spanish captain going through death pangs, his wounds too atrocious to be hidden with bandages. He exhaled a musical-sounding death rattle. Jimmy paid him not the slightest attention. He ordered his retinue to leave.

"You're a lucky bird," he said when it was just the two of us and the dying man. "I show up, come to inspect the position, and there I see you, dangling from the scaffold with your cock erect. Another second and even I wouldn't have been able to save you. Can you speak?"

I shook my head.

"Little wonder. Much longer and the noose would have pulled your head clean off your body. Was it Verboom's doing?"

I nodded. Removing his gloves and placing them on the table next to us, Jimmy shook his head in mock astonishment. "Well, well. You two been getting on *that* well?"

I responded with a *bras d'honneur*, though a not very energetic one, given my state. Jimmy's face clouded over in thought. He sat down beside me on the bed. A few breaths. Then he patted the inside of my calf. "I've got a lot of work to do. While you recover, I'll decide whether I ought to enlist you or put you back up on that scaffold. Now sleep."

On my third day of confinement in the field hospital, they came to get me. Jimmy had installed himself in a place called Mas Guinardó, a large country house situated within the Bourbon cordon. Some English mercenaries, doubtless Jimmy's own domestic staff, took me there, and they tossed me into the house like a fish into a barrel.

Jimmy wasn't there; my only company, a couple of servants. A strange, ambiguous state to be in: guest and prisoner. I had no orders, nor could I give any, so I simply roamed the premises. The study was overflowing with a clutter of documents and papers. And, on the table in there, a missive from Little Philip.

Let a cat loose in your house, and it's going to have a sniff around. Jimmy knew that, so I felt sure he'd left the letter knowing I'd read it. It contained the directives for the final attack.

Sure, as I am, of Barcelona's imminent surrender, I have
adjudged it convenient to communicate to you my intentions
with regards the matter. As it stands, there can be no doubt,
the rebels wage war upon us. Any grace afforded them will
be out of the piousness and compassion of my heart, and
thus, should they, repenting of their errors, beg for our mercy
before the trench is embarked upon, you will not cede it them
immediately, but then listen to what they have to say. You
will make them aware of the seriousness of their rebellion and
how undeserving they are of our mercy. You will make them
believe they have hope, by offering to intercede with me on
their behalf, and by saying that you will ask for their lives to
be spared, though that is the only grace you will ask, and only
for the high command. If they fail to understand this and allow
the trench to be begun, in that case you will not listen to any
offer of capitulation except one of outright surrender. If they

continue to resist, and it should come to the final assault, in that case they will no longer be deserving, as I'm sure you see, of the slightest compassion, and must accept the final severities of war. Whichever Spanish officers make it into the city shall then be their masters.

Mother of God. If this was the fate they had planned for the officers, what would they do with the rest of the inhabitants?

Jimmy came in unannounced, so utterly aloof that he didn't even deign to reprimand me for snooping.

"All right," he said, "I'll keep this brief. I'm busy."

Always the same impatient movements, even when he was relaxing. He grabbed an apple from a tray, took a seat in a padded armchair, and began chewing the apple. In private, he had the manners of a child, one leg dangling over the arm of the chair, tipping his head back as he ate.

"You're being paid a pittance by the rebels," he went on. "So you aren't fighting on their side for the money. Nor out of ambition, given how obvious it is that the battle's lost. Tell me: Is there someone inside the city you're being loyal to?"

"Yes," I said. My voice sounded like something being scraped against chalk. But at least it had come back.

"Man or woman?" he asked.

"A child."

He tossed the apple behind him. "Dear God, a child. Every time we meet, you've developed some new perversion."

"And a woman, and an old man, and a dwarf," I said seriously, somewhat ferociously.

"A dwarf—I don't think I can imagine . . ." Then, changing tone, he said: "This is what you get for deserting me. If you'd stayed with me after Almansa, you wouldn't be in this pickle. First I honor you and give you the chance to accompany me, which you reject, and now I save your life. Any chance of a thank-you?"

"No," I said.

"Going to help me crush the rebel scum?"

"No."

He laughed. "I like this, knowing your position. Now I can start my Attack Trench. Let's go back to the beginning. I've done my homework. It seems that in Tortosa, you were the only engineer to act like one. I knew it the moment I laid eyes on you. 'This lad's mind,' I said, 'is worth as much attention as his lovely legs.' I can make double use of you." He laughed at his own joke before adding: "Going to ask to serve under me again?"

I said nothing.

"Good, wonderful, we're making progress," he said. "People who don't know their worth, I tend to get for cheap." He stood and began pacing the room, hands clasped behind his back. He began speaking quickly. "The child, the woman, the old man. I'll promise to get them out of this condemned city alive. Oh, and the dwarf too, let's not forget him. Their kind are wonderfully useful—they don't even have to get on their knees in order to suck you. Plus ten thousand pounds. What am I saying? Five thousand and be grateful. Annually and for life, that is, naturally. And some title or other. And a house, why not? From what I've seen, this country has been so ravaged, there will be empty mansions and seigneuries aplenty." He sat down in another armchair, his chin on his hand. He regarded me as if I were some strange insect. "Although . . . come to think of it, I'm going to increase the offer. This mansion, I'll give it to you, but it won't be your primary abode. You'll install your woman there, the dwarf, the whole coterie. You'll visit from time to time. A bit of rumpy-pumpy with her, everyone's happy, and you can go back to your real home." Then he adopted a vague tone, as though what he was saying now was of no importance. He'd known from the beginning what he was going to say, of course. "I've had word from Bazoches. They say Jeanne Vauban isn't all that happy. You know her, do you not? I think so. Her husband has succumbed to insanity once more." He let out a cruel laugh. "He now thinks the philosopher's stone is hidden up his wife's cunt; tried taking it out with a royal scalpel. You know, that long hooked implement the surgeons use to remove anal tumors? Thank the Lord the servants stopped him in time! He's been locked up. The marriage is on its way to being annulled." He smacked his lips. "So sad! A woman that beautiful, so alone in the world!" Then he turned serious again. "It's my belief that you would be a good candidate for turning the castle at Bazoches into an academy for engineers. I also have a hunch you'd be welcomed as the man to run it."

I looked at him with disgust. "You don't know what you're talking about."

"The one who doesn't know is you, you fool!" he exclaimed, becoming angry. "For instance, did you know that Jeanne is a mother? A boy, six years old. And by my calculations, at the time of the conception, the husband was away in Paris." His tone changed once more. "You know these French aristocrats. Horrid husband off elsewhere, and they get their hands on some stable boy for riding lessons. Oh, yes, they call it love sometimes. Sad thing is, ladies don't marry stable boys. Now, though, a nobleman, even a newly minted one, would be perfectly acceptable. And I am certain you'd be a good father to the boy. What do *you* think?"

Jimmy had the rare talent of making the future seem real. I suppose because of his position. It isn't the same fantasizing and boasting in a tavern as it is in a palace. This was Jimmy, the world at his feet. When people like him promised something, it was because they actually had it, and in abundance. Jeanne. The mere mention of her name seemed to bring her within my reach. For me, unreachable; for him, a mere trifle.

"And all in exchange for what?" he said. "Next to nothing. First: When I say so, you will drop everything, wherever you are, to come and be at my side. Even if we're at the opposite ends of Europe. Two: I'm going to give you an order tomorrow. An order you will carry out diligently and to the best of your abilities."

I hesitated. "What order?"

He took my show of interest to mean I'd given in. "I'll let you know my orders when I choose to, not when you ask me to. Do you submit? Yes or no?"

I hung my head, thinking of Jeanne, thinking of Amelis. Thinking of Anfán, and of a son of my own, a stranger but flesh and blood. This was Jimmy. Mentioning Jeanne had brought her back to life, as he'd done with me. To return to Bazoches. The thought alone unhinged me. No one but Jimmy could think up such a painful, empty-hearted storm. If I swallowed the bait, I'd become the things I hated most in the world: a Bourbon and an aristocrat. If not, my son was set to become one anyway. Only Jimmy had the power to make you feel like an *échauguette* during a bombardment.

"*Merde!*" he said, losing patience. "Answer! I don't have all day."

Jeanne—did I love her? Wrong question: Did I love her *enough* to forget about Amelis, our little home at the top of that building in the Ribera barrio, just behind the Saint Clara bastion? No, that wasn't it, either.

"If you keep your promise," I said, "I'll keep mine."

He gave me an unhurried look. He observed my brow, the tear in my eye. He examined the angle of my lips as though they were those of a bastion to be bombarded. "Good . . . Good . . . "

I could tell he was happy with the way the questioning had gone, because now I saw his body relax.

"And I can see you aren't lying."

Once Pópuli had left, Jimmy inspected the cordon. Good old Zuvi went with him, along with Jimmy's customary English bodyguards, his four black dogs, and a couple of scribblers to note down the great man's words for posterity.

Jimmy stopped at the best-disposed redoubts, observing the defenses with his telescope, finished in a matte black to prevent reflections from the sun, which draw the eye of snipers. He knew what he was doing: Each of his questions was something technical and very much to the point.

"Only interested in the bastions?" I asked.

"What do you mean?" he said, lowering the telescope and looking at me.

"You're an aesthete. Look farther on."

He brought the telescope back up to his eye. "*Mon Dieu, c'est vrai!*" he exclaimed. "*Quelle belle ville!*"

"More so before the bombardment."

He laughed. "None of which makes me any less hungry. Let's have dinner."

As we made our way back to the Guinardó house, Jimmy ruminated aloud to his retinue. "Verily, the king of Spain is the perfect dunderhead. Why destroy a domain this rich? Why do damage to his own interests? Rents, seaports, workshops, and all that commerce paying in to the royal pot. And his warmongering ministers, demanding I raze the entire city and erect a victory statue in the center."

Be in no doubt, Jimmy cared not a jot about the future of the city. He believed what he was saying, so his thinking out loud was merely to exonerate himself should the thing descend into a bloodbath. The Spanish question, in his eyes, was nonsense, a rivalry that would never end and was better not to get involved in. His dogs accompanied him everywhere: four black bitches, large as foals, shorthaired, and with jaws as large as a man's hand. They even followed him to bed, each taking up a position in a corner. I never did feel comfortable around those mongrels—more than merely beastly, they reminded me of black Cerberuses.

Later, Jimmy asked me: "Were you really dead?"

"I think so."

"Death . . ." He sighed. "What's it like?"

"It isn't like anything. Whatever comes next, though, is beyond all comprehension. Time and space fade. A peace beyond words."

"Describe it."

"It can't be described. All I can say is that the most horrific thing isn't to die, it's then coming back."

Jimmy laughed. "You hold it against me that I saved your life?"

Covering my face with a pillow, I answered him: "It's like drinking a million gallons of your own pus."

Jimmy didn't like somber dialogues. And, even less, being on the back foot. "When this is all over, I'll get you some title or other," he said. "Count? Marquis? Baron, let's leave it at baron." He laughed fulsomely. "I *love* being at war. Know why? In peacetime, my family's constantly around me. There's no better excuse for getting away than a good campaign, where I can enjoy time with my dogs *and* my lovers."

Jimmy didn't have any Points on his forearm. He'd had teachers, and he'd been in charge of enough sieges to earn more Points than I had. I asked why.

"It was the first political decision I ever made," he explained. "With time, I'd obviously have become the world's greatest engineer. But a Points Bearer will only ever be a Points Bearer; engineering will absorb him to the exclusion of all else. Kings do not serve engineers but vice versa. And my aim is to be king." He turned to face me. "Why do you ask?"

"If you were an engineer with Points," I said, "I'd have to die for you. Given that you aren't, that means I'm allowed to kill you without the slightest compunction."

This tickled him greatly. "Yes, I had forgotten. Engineers and their hallowed *Mystère*. Do you really think it's those little dots that stop you from stabbing me to pieces? Say if I gave you Verboom, the fact that he has three Points tattooed on his forearm would stop you from ripping his guts out?" He turned serious. "*Le Mystère* is nothing but an old wives' tale, something engineers use to spice up the insipidness of stones and angles. Having your own secret god—or an antigod—makes you feel important, more important than you really are. *Le Mystère*? No such thing." He turned over, resting his head against the pillow and adding: "Snuff out the candles, would you."

8

Jimmy was never one to dawdle. Early the next morning, in his most despotic voice, he said to me: "You said you'd obey my order. The time has come."

I made an exaggerated, courtly bow, and asked: "Your orders?"

He swept the air majestically with one hand and became less tense. "Oh, a trifle," he said. "Have a look at this."

He spread two large maps out on his study table. The first showed the trench designed by Verboom and sabotaged by me, and the second, Dupuy's planned trench. I took my time looking over both. And I can assure you: Sight can be a conduit for great remorse.

I couldn't stop myself from crying. Silent tears that trickled down to my chin and off, pouring onto the maps. Jimmy noticed. "Why do you cry?"

"Such . . . lovely trenches . . ." I said. "What do you know about the feelings of an engineer?"

Whichever Attack Trench Jimmy opted for, our ancient and bat-tered walls would fall. Add any good design to sufficient matériel and the right number of sappers, and there's no way of stopping any Attack Trench; sooner or later, the ramparts will be reached. But if Jimmy went with Dupuy's, which was perfection itself, it would take no time at all: They'd be through in a week. For all that I was a prisoner, I had to do something, anything, to turn Jimmy against Dupuy's. But how was I supposed to do that? How?

Sounding as offhand as I could, I said: "Did Verboom have a chance to look at Dupuy's plan and vice versa?"

Jimmy failed to pick up on the fearfulness underpinning my ques-tion. I'd managed to fool Verboom, a Three Points, with my trench, with some difficulty. But if Dupuy, a Seven Points, looked closely at it, that would be curtains. He'd see the trumpery, all the subversions I'd introduced.

Luckily, though, Jimmy exclaimed: "Please, no! A cockfight is of no interest to me. I want them each to defend his plan, not to knock the other's down. We'll keep it friendly. When you're involved in a siege, the number one thing is to have cohesion in your forces."

If only the Red Pelts had been like Jimmy! Rather than backing Don Antonio, they spent all their time pestering him and having tan-trums. Within the city, a small, divided force; without, Jimmy, an iron fist inside an iron glove.

"I've called them in. To expand on their plans. Of course, I'll have the final say. You know more than I do when it comes to trenches. You can advise me."

"What an honor!" I said. "Little me, judging such esteemed engi-neers. Dupuy is one of your staff officers. You sent him ahead to design an Attack Trench for you. Why wouldn't you just go with his and be done with it?"

"I brought old Dupuy along because he's the greatest living engi-neer. But if there are two offers on the table, why put down money for the horse without hearing about the second?"

He ceased his boyish informalities when the time came to hear the "two peacocks" (as he called them). It was as though he had stepped into a monarch's guise. "We'll hear what they have to say. And remember: You'll be the critic who hides behind the king on the balcony and whispers in his ear. Really, without knowing it, they'll be addressing you. I'll ask your advice when they leave."

He sent me into the room adjacent, the wall so thin that I'd be able to hear, without being seen. There was also a crevice at eye level for me to peep through.

In they came. Jimmy made them sit facing each other and asked them to go through the strong points of their respective plans. Dupuy first, then Verboom. This they did, but inevitably, disagreements arose. The Antwerp butcher was the first to be interrupted.

"Saint Clara?" scoffed Dupuy. "Attack the Saint Clara bastion? A travesty to all ideas of siege warfare!"

"A travesty?" said Verboom. "I've been working on this trench for years. You show up, cobble something together, and dare to say it's better!"

Dupuy turned to Jimmy. "Marshal, please. This city has been besieged on three occasions in recent times. Three! And each time the trenches aimed for the same area—and it was not Saint Clara! Are we to suppose that every one of our illustrious forebears got it so wrong?"

"I may hail from Antwerp," bellowed Verboom, "but I am, have been, and always will be loyal to Philip! God save him! I've suffered captivity for him, and never will I err in my loyalty."

This was an extremely poor line of argument for him to choose. Jimmy could still remember the way Verboom had criticized him before Almansa on the basis of where he came from. Verboom was in for a tongue-lashing now.

"My *dear* Verboom," said Jimmy. "We're not here to discuss our places of birth. Roots, roots, roots . . . Men are not vegetables. Would you suggest I lead an English army against His Majesty Philip V of Spain?"

Verboom imagined plots where there were none. "I see! This meeting is nothing but a formality. I'm an engineer, I was raised by engineers. But evidently, my stock pales in comparison to that of the great Vauban." He got to his feet, fists clenched on the table. "The king of Spain will hear of this! How his true subjects are being overlooked in favor of the French!"

Now Dupuy had taken umbrage; though every inch the gentleman, he also had a volcanic temper. Overly volcanic, really. "Enough, you whore, flaunting your stones and your angles!" he spat, getting up from his seat. "Everyone knows the way you operate, claiming discrimination where there is none, gaining privileges that way. You don't serve any king—you use them one and all."

Jimmy found the slanging match deeply uninteresting and did nothing to hide the fact. I remember the way he gazed at the ceiling, fanning his face with a hand. *Lord, it's warm*, he seemed to be saying, *and how insufferable all this fervor is*. Then a messenger came to the door. The message must have been pressing, to interrupt one of Marshal Berwick's counsels. Jimmy read the letter, utterly uninterested in the cockfight going on in the room.

"Silence, gentlemen!" he said, looking up from the piece of paper. "I have a story for you. The month of July takes its name from Julius Caesar, August from Octavian Augustus. Augustus was succeeded as emperor by a certain Tiberius. The bootlickers in the Roman senate said would he like September to be named after him instead. Tiberius, less of a tyrant than he seemed, derided them: 'What will you do,' he said, 'when you run out of months but still have emperors?'"

Verboom and Dupuy fell quiet, trying to work out the meaning of the Caesarian tale. The room remained silent. Jimmy sent them out with a waft of the hand. Each, a little disoriented, bowed and left the room.

"What did you mean by the parable?" I asked, stepping out from my hiding place.

Jimmy was deep in thought. "Oh, that? No idea. They were about to come to blows, I thought, so why not send them off with something else to think about. Men would rather say nothing and be thought fools than speak and confirm it." He tossed the message to the ground, looking angry. "You won't believe what it says."

It had Philip V's seal on the paper.

"That's right, him, the madman crowned out of sheer luck!" he exclaimed. "He writes to offer me the position of commander in chief of all the armies in Spain. Me, a marshal of Louis XIV of France! What kind of offer is this? For me to abandon Louis? In favor of an unshod army of beggars? Why not name me king of the gypsy armies of Hungary?" He screwed up the paper, enraged. "For the love of God! If a person has Homer, why would he choose Virgil?" He began pacing the room, brooding, with the piece of paper in his hand. He had quite enough problems as it was, and whichever way you looked at it, this put him in a tricky position: Saying no to a king is always dangerous.

"And what have you decided about the trenches?" I asked. "Verboom's or Dupuy's?"

He continued to think and pace, eyes downcast. My heart began to pound. If ever I have prayed—to God or to *le Mystère*—it was then: Please, please, choose my trench, my trench, mine.

Jimmy suddenly halted. Eyes still fixed on the floor, he lifted a forefinger toward the ceiling. "Verboom's. We'll go with Verboom's trench . . . I'll reject Philip's offer, of course," he said, and with truly regal generosity, elucidating, "which will be a snub, and no mistake. If that comes with word that I've also marginalized Verboom, he'll take it even worse. We'll begin work as soon as we have all the matériel. Let's get to it; the sooner we finish with this insane Catalan rabble, the better."

My dear vile Waltraud has told me to stop—she wants to know about Anfán and Amelis. Fatty Waltraud is concerned: Was I really ready to abandon my nearest and dearest? Was I lying to Jimmy? My answer: No, I wasn't lying.

Now for something that, on the face of it, will seem incongruous: The highest love is shown by denying that selfsame love. Jimmy was Jimmy—it would have been impossible to lie to him, he'd have picked up on it in a heartbeat. The only way I could hide my feelings from him was simply not to feel them.

If I truly loved them, I was going to have to postpone that love, supplant my feelings. Fleetingly but believably, to be a different person, transfigured. Overlaying one love with another was the only option. And I assure you, it was as difficult, if not more so, than designing my dissembling Attack Trench. Yes, I'll say it: For a period of forty-eight hours, I surrendered myself. The amount of time needed to dissipate Jimmy's suspicions. Come the third day, he gave me the gift of a French captain's uniform.

Everyone knows the old sailors' saying: A single drop of tar and the whole barrel is corrupt. In the vast Bourbon encampment, I set myself to be that drop. It's amazing the damage that one man, one single man, can do if he sets his mind to it.

I went around proudly in my new French uniform, from one end of the camp to the other. There are captains and then there are captains, and my uniform was white and brand-new: Longlegs Zuvi, looking fine, teaching the rank and file a thing or two about respect. A captain who looked like something straight out of the salons of Versailles, appearing before the grubby troops, knee-deep in mud, brought low by the yearlong siege. I made a nuisance of myself whenever an opportunity presented itself.

I caught sight of a Navarran recruit with a stupid-looking face. I began lecturing him and, when I had cowed him, led him to the artillery depot. Placing a mallet and a scalpel in his hands, I ordered him to get to work on the cannon vents. This would break them, and they could never be used again, but an order's an order. In tyrannical armies, soldiers are meek servants. Unlike men in the Coronela, these never questioned their superiors, let alone talked back. I left him to it. He'd be caught and surely hanged for hammering the cannons like that—but by then at least a few cannons would have been put out of action.

Gunpowder is such a precious resource that, usually, you see a guard posted at the store, and nobody is allowed to move it anywhere unless under express orders. But somewhere in a large siege, you'll always find deposits being moved from one place to another. Should a decent saboteur insert himself in the distribution path, he'll show his worth, ordering the cannon barrels to be taken to the infantry, and the gunpowder for the rifles to the artillery. My dear vile Waltraud doesn't understand. Well, yes, if you spend your days boiling cabbages, what *would* you know about gunpowder? The granulation is different for different weapons—with the wrong powder, the cannonballs shoot all of a foot's distance, and flintlocks explode, blinding the riflemen. Half a grain of gunpowder is enough to scorch a man's eye.

It was when I came across an old acquaintance that I really began to enjoy myself: Captain Antoine Bardonenche. It was inevitable that we'd run into each other sooner or later, somewhere in the camp.

"My fine friend, finally, we meet!" he said. "But you've been demoted. You were lieutenant colonel under King Charles, and they've got you as a captain here."

"*Archduke* Charles," I corrected, fully inhabiting my role as deserter. "Only the rebels call that usurper *King*."

"Ah, yes, well, what does it matter?" said Bardonenche, who couldn't care a pepper about politics. "The point is, we're both captains now. You must come and dine with me."

I managed to make some more mischief before the day was out, and when night fell, I didn't have much choice but to go and join him. It was bittersweet to dine together. The evening concluded over drinks in front of a campfire. The tired blue flames cast a melancholy light on our meeting. The days when we had frolicked around the lakes of Bazoches, alongside Jeanne and her sister, seemed a distant memory.

"Can I admit something to you?" he said, and proceeded with a sentimental nocturnal musing: "I hate this, I hate it all. All these months here, stagnating in this miserable battlefield. Have you ever seen such wretched soldiers? We look like an army of beggars."

"I always thought you felt at home in war, good or bad."

He shook his head. "This isn't war anymore. We're like wolves, circling around some defenseless prey. There's neither honor nor dignity in putting these people to the sword."

Bardonenche had been detailed with protecting the rearguard: whole months escorting supply carts and fighting Miquelets. "Not long ago, near a place called Mataró," he said, "we set fire to an entire forest and drove out a group we'd cornered in there. How those pines blazed! Crackling like grenades, flames as high as the heavens. I called out to them to give themselves up. I gave them my word, four times, that they wouldn't be murdered. It was useless." He paused and then carried on. "When they finally couldn't take it any longer, they came rushing out. And do you know what? Half of them were human torches. Even so, howling, their flesh on fire, they had only one thought: to come and throw themselves at us, to try and take some of us to the inferno with them. I ran one of them through with my saber. Their captain, I think. Look at this." He handed me a small leather pouch. "This is what he was carrying. Strange, don't you think?"

I opened it, finding it full of bullets. A number had flecks of dried blood on them.

"Do you believe in destiny?" he asked me.

"No," I said.

"Nor do I. But it so happens that there are nineteen bullets there, and I in my time have killed nineteen men, in duels or in battle."

"What does that have to do with anything?"

"I ran my saber through his chest, right up to the hilt. The look on his face—it had to be seen to be believed. He tried to say something to me with his last breath. I couldn't make it out."

"Doubtless he was cursing you."

Bardonenche turned to look at the fire again. "Yes, most likely."

"Tiredness" and "Bardonenche" were two words that didn't usually go together. But he seemed exhausted that night, hugging his knees, Busquets's pouch held in one hand. Busquets, the Miquelet captain I met during the expedition, the one who was so intent on liberating Mataró. His superstition was that he wouldn't die until that pouch was full. It seemed Saint Peter had finally opened his gates.

"Why hold on to such a macabre keepsake?" I said, gazing at the pouch as though it were a crystal ball.

"I don't know," he said, groaning. "I feel as though it belongs to me now. I've tried to get rid of it, but I can't."

I smiled incredulously. "Can't? I'll take it from you if you like."

He shook his head once more. "Why could anyone possibly want to carry around a pouch of used bullets?"

"No idea," I said, sighing. "Perhaps the man wanted his killer to have it. Or perhaps it's something more sinister."

"More sinister?"

I tried to put myself in a Miquelet's shoes. "When the Miquelets find a Frenchman or a Spaniard with a rifle whose flint is Catalan, or a sword with a Catalan coat of arms on the cuff, they execute their prisoner using that same stolen weapon. The owner's name is sewn onto the pouch—'Jaume Busquets, *capitá*.' If any friends of the dead man were to capture *you,* they'd make you swallow the contents. That's their way."

The moment I'd spoken, I regretted it. Saying anything cruel to Bardonenche was akin to being nasty to a child, for all that the man was the best swordsman in Europe. Needing to get back to the Guinardó house, I stood up.

"My fine friend," said Bardonenche, bidding me farewell without getting up, "it's wonderful you're serving with us. Do you know what I mean? I've thought on more than one occasion, Dear Lord, if this carries on to the bitter end, there's the chance you're going to have to kill your Bazoches companion."

I wasn't sure what to say. "Antoine," I mused aloud, "it could be that things are a little more complicated than our parents and teachers told us."

The clearsightedness of his answer, when usually, he was so puerile, took me aback. "That would be very sad," he said. "Our love for our betters would mean we've embraced lies. But as good sons and good students, what choice did we have?" In a funereal tone, he added: "I have no desire to kill you."

This sent chills through me; perhaps he wasn't as clueless as he seemed. Our friendship, perhaps, meant he was able to deduce various things. Including the fact that a "rebel" lieutenant colonel, so committed to the defense of his own city, would not so easily switch sides. Perhaps Bardonenche demonstrated the most generous kind of friendship that night: to not betray the traitor.

"Do you believe in premonitions?" he asked me.

"No," I said.

"I do. If Barcelona doesn't surrender, and we embark on the full assault, it will be the death of me. I know it."

Saying this, he turned his gaze back to the fire.

9

The trench was begun on July 11, 1714, in the night.

Jimmy was well stocked on all counts: The first parallel had thirty-five hundred men to dig it, and these received cover from ten infantry battalions and ten companies of grenadiers. Accustomed to war being waged on a shoestring, I couldn't but envy such fabulous resources.

My French captain's uniform made it easy for me to infiltrate myself into the trench. No sooner had the digging begun than I hopped in. And how hard they worked! Thousands of spades, in a line over half a mile long, flinging earth forward, toiling as hard as galley slaves.

The furrow went from knee-deep to chest-deep in a small space of time. Thousands of the *fajina* baskets were being circulated around. These they would line with stones and sand and then place on the front edge of the trench, followed by further reinforcing shovelfuls of earth. I despaired over the Coronela's inaction—What are you waiting for? I thought. Attack, you ought to have attacked already!

You can usually bank on a counter-assault the first day a trench begins. The men working, and the troops providing covering fire, are very exposed. The most common maneuver consists of an artillery bombardment followed by large numbers of men carrying out a lightning sortie. If they plan properly and have fortune on their side, the besieged troops will overrun the men covering the trench; the parallel is not very deep yet and doesn't provide much shelter. The idea of this first sortie is to ruin the works, even fill in what's been dug, then immediately fall back. It doesn't seem like much, but in war, morale is crucial. The city sends the attacking army a message: "What you've done is undone. Come and get us!" The works have to start all over again.

The Bourbons were vulnerable, as is the case on the first day of any siege. But my redesign of Verboom's trench also meant that they'd be beginning particularly close to the ramparts. An unusually short distance, truly. Only two thousand feet, which was one and a half times the distance a rifle could shoot. My secret hope—which, naturally, I didn't communicate to Verboom—was that a general as attentive as Don Antonio would notice the works and attack. Everything would play in our favor. With this first parallel so close to the ramparts, our lads would be able to tackle the trench in an instantaneous charge. If they charged quickly, they'd have no losses until arm-to-arm combat began, and then their zeal would surely be far greater than that of the Beast's French mercenaries or Little Philip's Spanish recruits.

Jimmy gave the order for drums to be played throughout the night, a standard procedure to drown out the sound of the men at work. A waste of time. Even if the works begin in the middle of the night, several thousand men digging are impossible to hide. The next morning is the worst for the sappers: Following a long night's work, they're exhausted, and as the sun comes up, they relax—nothing's happened yet. That's when a lightning attack comes from the besieged army.

But on this occasion, the sun was already up, and there was no sign of any activity on the city walls. Why didn't the Barcelonans attack, why? I broke down inside: Don't you see? I said to myself. Sweet Jesus, attack! And then I experienced the most atrocious feeling, one I'd never wish on another living soul. "My God," I said, "maybe you designed it too well, Martí!"

Of course Don Antonio was planning a lightning attack on the trench the moment it began—which I, not being inside the city, naturally had no way of knowing. So what was going on? The Red Pelts—for a change—had stuck their oars in. Don Antonio spent the night of the twelfth preparing the sortie, and the very first thing on the thirteenth, he sent word to his wife up on Mount Montjuic that he would come to her at nine in the morning and they would later take lunch together. The letter was dictated publicly, so that at eight in the morning the whole city knew that, instead of attacking, General Villarroel was going to spend the entire day dining sumptuously. A truly Homeric snub to the enemy! "They begin their trench? In that case, I shall fill my belly. See how little I care for what they do or do not do!"

Even my dear vile Waltraud can tell that the letter was meant to throw the Bourbon spies off the scent. As we know, there were more spies swarming around the city at that time than flies on a donkey's behind. At nine in the morning, Don Antonio did indeed go up to Montjuic surrounded by a large and visible escort. But his plan was to slip back at eleven, a long while before anyone in the Mediterranean would ever sit down to lunch, and then lead the attack.

Among the ministers, Casanova had been beside himself since the moment he'd received word that the Bourbons had begun their trench. Coming across one of our infantry generals, he lost his temper. "Seeing as you're going to Villarroel's little party in Montjuic," he cried, "you can tell him that the people won't take it all well, not at all well, that the enemy is being allowed to go about its work so freely!"

This general, of course, passed the message on. Appalled at the dressing-down he'd been given, he made out that the *conseller en cap*'s words had been even more injurious. There was nothing Don Antonio could do but defer the attack to go and conciliate the ministers. Not satisfied with having ruined the ploy, Casanova hardly calmed down even when he was made to understand what the plan had been. To top it off, he held forth on what *he* thought the approach should be for the sortie. I still think that no one in besieged Barcelona quite understood to what point a military man like Don Antonio had his patience tested. There were a hundred more darts on the part of Casanova, not one of which is worth recounting.

As Casanova and Don Antonio argued, I was huddled in the first parallel, sheltering as best I could from the cannonade raining down from our parsley-chewing artillery chief, Francesc Costa.

Costa, ever his own man, hadn't waited for any orders to begin firing. Before the sun was up, he'd relocated eight mortars and forty-eight cannons, which then began hurling cannonballs and grapeshot down on the first parallel and my poor head.

If artillery were an art, that dawn bombardment would go down as immortal. The missiles curved perfectly through the air. Smoke trails marked their flight. Some of the shells weighed over a hundred pounds. They flattened everything and raised immense fountains of earth wherever they fell, *fajinas* in pieces, wicker baskets ejected like cutlery.

Costa's Mallorcans alternated stone shells with fused explosive ones—when the latter were two or three meters above the ground, they'd burst open in a flash of white and yellow, spilling red-hot shards onto the heads of everyone in the trench. It was no easy thing to make the fuse exactly the correct length so that it would blow just as it came over the trench, not a moment sooner; too high and the grapeshot wouldn't cause as much damage, too late—once the shell had landed—and the ground would absorb the explosion. If you're facing someone with Costa's skills, the only hope is to dig your trench deep and not too wide, thereby reducing the lethal area. But if you remember, I had convinced Verboom to do the opposite, with very wide and shallow trenches.

As you know, though, I wasn't with our artillery but behind the Bourbon lines. Which twist of fate meant I was on the receiving end of Costa's artistic talents, the cannonballs whooshing and exploding above me. I remember the smell of the warm, wet earth in the trenches, and its still-to-be-braced walls. All around me—crammed beneath and on top of me—dozens of workers were sheltering, as I was, cowering and whimpering in fear of the aerial detonations. The sheer chaos of an Attack Trench means that any survivor has an extreme tale to tell. It is a three-dimensional fight for your life: on the ground, using your hands, in the air, with the bombs; and under the ground, with the mines. Add to that a fourth: You are fighting against time. The advance of a trench is the world's most quantifiable truth. Even so, that's the case only in terms of *le Mystère* or from the perspective of a Ten Points. To the engineer on the side of the besieging army, the advance will always seem to go at a snail's pace; to the one inside the city, faster than a running deer. An Attack Trench is both the most precise human endeavor and that which must take place under the most savage conditions.

Finally, after midday, several thousand men sprang from the city—my neighbors—ready for anything. I peeked over the parapet and saw the bones of the stockade thickening with people on their way to attack the recently begun trench.

Sheer pandemonium. The attack came at all points of the trench, right, left, and center. The cavalry came in support, attacking down the wings. Both armies' artillery fired ceaselessly, and there was so much commotion, smoke, and gunpowder that you didn't know who was killing whom. My initial idea was to hide in some rift in the ground, wait for the wave of attackers to come past my position, identify myself, and go back to the city with them. Good plan, wouldn't you say? Unfortunately, it didn't take into account my proverbial cowardice. Hundreds of men charged in my direction, drunk and screaming like stuck pigs. I thought I recognized them as a unit that had been set up recently, grenadiers under the orders of Captain Castellarnau.

My God, I thought, they seem rather angry. Three Normandy battalions went out to engage them. Castellarnau's men rushed forward like demons, bayoneting the Normans to pieces and moving on. A little closer and I could see their wine-reddened eyes. Terrified, I said to myself: "Martí, they aren't messing around." They advanced, letting out drunken cries, calling Saint Eulalia's name, and bayoneting any fallen men as they came past. The Normans dispatched, there was nothing now between them and the first parallel.

A troop attacking like that will recognize no one. No one! They in a frenzy, me in a white uniform. I then had one of the most bizarre thoughts of my long military life: Mother of God, my allies are nearly upon us. Mercy!

"Run, run!" I bellowed at the workers around me. "Let's go or the rebels will cut us to shreds!"

The men near me were all workers and, seeing me flee, wavered. Castellarnau's drunk grenadiers were nearly upon us, and all the while, the cannonballs continued to fall with devilish precision. If even the officers are fleeing, why would lowly workers, who have no military training, stay?

The entire brigade followed me. (Truly, it was a good thing for them, because as I later found out, the few who did stay were massacred.) Most flung their picks and shovels to the ground, carts and half-full *fajinas*, and sprinted astonishingly quickly—some were so frightened they even overtook me!

The attack fizzled out without any great effect. A spark rather than a full-blown fire, remarkable only for the numbers of dead. And who cares about the dead? The men in the sortie occupied the trench, yes, did as much damage as they could, yes, but the minute they were gone, another four thousand soldiers, workers, and sappers stepped in and renewed the digging effort.

I was handed a report on the day's activity to take to Jimmy. On my way to Mas Guinardó I read it—a punishable offense. Six hundred and forty-eight dead and wounded on a single night and day of trench work. The note came from Verboom himself, and good old Zuvi (what irony!) was the one charged with taking it to Jimmy.

As I entered Mas Guinardó carrying the account, my thoughts were on how many more would have suffered had things gone well. Jimmy was standing in his study, looking out of the window. The carnage that had just taken place was clearly the last thing on his mind. He was lost in thought, gnawing a fist. He turned and looked at me and immediately returned his gaze to the window. His only words were a quiet groaning as he repeated obsessively: "She dies, she dies . . . "

"Who?" I asked.

"The queen, the queen . . . "

I stared in astonishment. "The queen of England! Dying?" I punched the air. "But Jimmy, what marvelous news!"

My God, what a coincidence, and what a disastrous one. Though for diametrically opposed reasons, both Jimmy and I were set to benefit from the news.

The balance of power in England is a very delicate thing, swinging between Tories and Whigs, who alternate in power. With Queen Anne dead, a change of government was inevitable, and with it, a reversal of the policy of conciliating the Beast, of which she had been the principal supporter. And if London turned against Paris, an alliance with Barcelona was also inevitable.

They honor a certain power in England, something unfamiliar in autocracies: that of public opinion. Catcalling critiques of foreign policy are constantly being published in the London gazettes. The "Catalan case" being a glaring example. There were debates about it in their Parliament.

Let's not fool ourselves. Pericles's Greece sent an expedition to Sicily, but not due merely to the goading of the demagogues. England was never altruistic, quite the opposite; public opinion and private interests spurred it on. But if there was a chance that they might come to our aid, what did it matter to us why? England had the strongest navy, and the French blockade would be broken. And as had happened at the first Bourbon siege, in 1706, when the English fleet came into port, they'd inject reinforcements and supplies and do wonders for morale. The besieging of a port that is *not* blockaded is, by nature, unpracticable: *dixit* Vauban.

With Anne's death, it would make sense to defer the sentence. Even two or three days could change everything. And my trench was the deferral.

And Jimmy? That royal death made sense of everything that had happened so far in his life. England in turmoil, the succession to be decided. Jimmy was born to be king, and now that the opportunity had arisen, where was he? Pinned down thousands of miles south by a cause that was anything but close to his heart. Managing a full-blown siege in the south and a dynastic rebellion in the north at the same time—not possible. He would have to choose.

As cosmopolitan as Jimmy seemed, he was also a dyed-in-the-wool Englishman. When his father, the last Catholic king of England, was exiled, Jimmy was raised at the French court. The Beast's ministers were good to him and let his talents develop, in spite of his being a bastard. But as a mercenary in France's pay, he could aspire only to a secondary role, and by 1714 he had all the credentials needed to put himself forward in London. He'd been on the winning side in countless battles, he was a marshal, and he'd seen a few things. He was tolerant of different religious beliefs (he had none), conciliatory to factions (he didn't believe particularly in any one), and would apply himself in the name of any cause that would reflect well on him (he had served, and would be served by, all kinds). Vauban, as politically naive as Cicero, believed in a republic made up of virtuous males. Jimmy didn't believe in any regime that he (along with one or two vicious males) wasn't ruling. His continuing service under the Beast, however, had brought him to Spain. To abandon the siege of Barcelona, just after replacing Pópuli, was unthinkable. Anne's death forced him to decide between obligations he'd accrued in France since childhood, and his destiny.

He had plenty of reason to hate us. The war that had raged across the world for fourteen years was over, to all intents and purposes, but those blind Barcelonans, by refusing to face the truth, were going to hamstring his royal aspirations. Many were the days I spent at his side; I could have tried to understand what made him so fanatical. But I never did. Jimmy began and ended the sieges not bothering to find out who his enemies were or what cause they were fighting for. I believe that he didn't hate us, because he didn't have strong feelings about good and evil. We were an obstacle to him, more than an object of loathing.

And then he fell ill. The doctors failed to see the blindingly obvious: It wasn't so much a bodily sickness as the core of his soul being fractured. He could stay loyal to the Beast and bring the siege to an end. Or he could betray him and go and pursue his destiny in England as a contender for the throne. Finally be a ruler himself, or via one of his mad half brothers. Carry on as a lackey with no future, or try for the ultimate prize.

The tension manifested in a virulent fever, which his military zeal only succeeded in aggravating. He spent his days buzzing around, supervising everything, especially the arrival of the matériel needed for the trench to progress. He'd get back to Mas Guinardó too tired to take off his armor—I had to undo the cinches and straps for him. The sweats had made his chest guard swell and harden, and it was like prising off a tortoise's shell. As I took off his clothes, feeling full of hate for him, he turned and begged me: "You'll never betray me, isn't that right?"

Jimmy's bottomless, insatiable egoism; his despot nature. His whispered fever ravings—*Trench! . . . Go!*—put me on edge.

One morning he couldn't get out of bed. He spent the day there, soaking several changes of sheets. Come nightfall, the officer of the watch arrived to ask for that night's password. He was none other than Bardonenche.

He struck me that day as more committed to service than ever, kindness in his eyes, a total lack of prejudice. When he came in, I was helping the marshal sit up in the bed, my hands bathed in his sweat, our odors intermixed. But not a peep from Bardonenche, no judgment. He took a couple of tentative steps closer, arching his eyebrows, looking at the shivering Jimmy. The only words he had were ones of compassion: "Dear, dear sir," he whispered.

Feeling a sense of urgency, I slapped Jimmy a little. "Jimmy, Jimmy. The army needs the password."

Still writhing, as though possessed, his eyes rolling upward, he half whispered, half gurgled: "Loyalty."

"If he dies," said Bardonenche feelingly, "it will be a disaster. A siege can't withstand three changes at the helm in such a short space of time."

Jimmy's poor state had an outside witness now. After that, it would have been very easy for me to kill him myself; no one would have been able to pin such an inevitable death on me.

But no, I didn't kill him. I couldn't. May my dead forgive me.

His shivers became more and more violent. He spent that final night clinging to me, and he held on so tightly that my ribs hurt for three days after.

"Tell me you'll never leave me, not you," he whispered as the fever took him over. "*Trench . . . Go . . . King . . . Kingdom . . .* "

At around five in the morning, he went slack. I laid a hand against his forehead. The fever had passed. I was thankful and at the same time lamented it. I know that doesn't add up. Put it in, though!

And as he slept, I dressed and left.

There was one thing covering my flight from Mas Guinardó: What castaway abandons ship to go back to the sinking bit of flotsam? No one would suspect a French officer, particularly one as good-looking as me in my new uniform, of wanting to cross the lines to flee to the moribund city.

The first light of dawn had begun to show on the horizon. I walked a long way along the inside edge of the cordon in search of the gate farthest from the trench to my left, which was lit up regularly by the flashes of fire from either side's cannons. Thousands of men were working in the furrows, the bustle of battle concentrated in that one zone. The greater the distance between all that and me, then, the better.

Wandering around inside the Bourbon camp was risky. Finally, I simply had to choose one. There were a number of guards posted there to fend off any sortie from the Barcelonans.

Well, one of the advantages of fleeing from the army headquarters is knowing the password. "Loyalty!" I said.

I didn't break stride, flourishing my hand majestically for them to open the gate. They obeyed. After all, they were there to stop rebels from coming in, not to stop a French captain from leaving to carry out some what secret mission.

Once outside, I could feel the guards' eyes tracking me as I advanced into no-man's-land. (Those white Bourbon uniforms, however shabby and covered in mud they became, always put them at a disadvantage when fighting at night. It made them very fearful of leaving the safety of their little cordon.) I strolled around for a few minutes as if examining the defenses from outside—how deep the ditch around the cordon was, and the piles of firewood piled up at thirty-meter intervals, ready to be set alight to both illuminate and blind any approaching attackers. Once I was a little way away, half enveloped by the predawn darkness, I broke into a run. Use your legs, Zuvi!

No shots rang out. Either they couldn't see me, or they preferred to turn a blind eye. Soldiers, as a rule, know that getting involved with officers only wins you trouble. Which suited me. It would take Jimmy and the others a while longer to find out I'd fled.

Once I was closer to the city, I got down and began crawling; the terrain was a constant up and down, as though you were advancing through a sea swell. I was a way from reaching the city walls when I ran into a soldier dragging himself through no-man's-land, though in the opposite direction. The choppy, broken-up terrain, full of craters from misdirected artillery fire, meant we didn't see each other until the last moment. Down on our bellies like earthworms, we looked at each other, neither of us knowing very well what was supposed to happen next. When work had begun on the trench, the faint hearted and the mercenaries had begun slipping away from the city and making for the cordon. Hardly surprising, given that the city was condemned.

Now, here was a good one for the philosophers of military law: Two deserters meet on a piece of disputed land; is their duty still to kill? We decided not. We pretended not to have seen each other. There were other men, perhaps a dozen, following him, wriggling along like worms. When they came past, they looked at me, not antagonistically, but like I was insane. By this late stage in the siege, almost all the professional soldiers had deserted. The remaining force was an army made up of friends and neighbors.

Our poor bastions and ramparts came into sight, rising up like rotted molar teeth. My senseless return had a lot of Don Antonio about it. Really, the siege of Barcelona was a dispute between two antithetical authorities: Jimmy, subtle, corrupt, a denizen of the higher echelons, the self-interests of Versailles; and Don Antonio, that adorable Castilian maniac, absurdly self-sacrificing, stubborn as a mule, and with the manners of a commoner.

And what of my son, the son I was leaving behind, possibly forever? Returning to the city, I was bidding him, and our chances of ever embracing, farewell. And yet my decision was based on a principle common among the Coronela: Blood ties would always be trumped by the bond between those who spill blood and tears side by side. Am I making myself clear—that conflicts also raged within every combatant? Evil might offer us silks, honors, pleasure, and le Mystère might promise a way out of those bribes in exchange for nothing—or in exchange for a Word. But those internal conflicts were what really urged men on.

They were going to kill me. No, worse. On elbows and knees, I made my way to a darkness more wretched than death. And all for the sake of a crookbacked old man, a deformed dwarf, a savage of a child, and a dark-haired whore. The poets don't dare say it, so I will:

Love's a piece of shit.

10

The moment I arrived back in Barcelona, it was clear how much things had gone downhill during my long absence.

With Jimmy's arrival, the French fleet had been given a boost. Now only the occasional very small ships were managing to make it past the blockade. They had to be small and swift, which meant they could bear only insignificant amounts of cargo. And with the sea supply line definitively strangled, the warehouses in the city were quickly emptied.

Though at exorbitant prices, the Barcelonans had still been able to buy food until that moment. To be clear, a Catalan peso was divided into twenty sueldos, and a typical worker's daily wage was two sueldos. Since January 1714, one liter of wine had cost eight sueldos, and the same amount of liquor, fifteen. A couple of hen eggs (people kept coops on their disintegrating balconies), three sueldos. All meat, from the moment the siege began, had been prohibitively expensive: A couple of hens would set you back two pesos; half a pound of meat, one Catalan peso. A Catalan peso would get you ten pounds of barley or fifteen of corn. To bake a loaf of bread had become a serious challenge.

The first goods to disappear during a siege would be combustibles: firewood and coal. The winter of 1713–1714 had been a cold one, and the reserves had been depleted. People had resorted to burning furniture. As if that weren't enough, rampart defenses also required wood, just as much as they did stone. Things got so dire that we had to dismantle the bridges, or *recs*, that crossed the city canals. Two hundred and five trees once lined the Ramblas, and even they were victim to the voracious efforts of the engineers. The dear Ramblas, that lovely avenue: new trees planted along it after every siege, only to be felled again at the beginning of the next. While I'd been in the Bourbon encampment, the famine had spread. I came back into the city at the beginning of August, when the blockade was at its peak, and at that point even paying astronomical prices wouldn't get you any of the now nonexistent stuffs. What little there was got apportioned to those fighting —so what did the people eat?

In the summer of 1714, the only thing available was a kind of *torta* baked with the husks of beans. The dregs from the storehouse floors, so putrid and foul-smelling that it's hard to believe we managed to swallow that soggy, fetid wheat paste. In Jimmy's company, I'd eaten fillet steaks three times a day. The change of diet was so abrupt that it took me three days to resign myself to it—though, in the end, there being no other option, I did exactly that. The stomach is master to all. Francesc Castellví, our Valencian captain, recounted an experiment he'd carried out using a crust of this husk *torta*: He broke off a little and tried feeding it to one of the few dogs left in the city, only for the dog to run away in disgust.

My thoughts were all of Amelis and Anfán once I entered the city. They'd felt so far away, and it had seemed so unlikely I'd ever see them again, that it had felt like achieving the impossible when I managed to think of anything else. And now, knowing they were close by, I was overcome by the need to take them in my arms. Such are the emotions surrounding a reunion: The closer our loved ones become, the more we fear we're going to lose them.

I found them in the rearguard immediately inside the ramparts, helping with the defense works. Instead of running and embracing them, I watched them from the corner for a few moments. In such abject conditions, you're only too aware of how brief and scarce the good moments are, and it tends to make you content with far less. We were in the midst of the century's most devastating war; we were on the receiving end of it, trapped inside a condemned city. But we were still alive. Our very existence defied the powers that were prevailing, and simply seeing Amelis and Anfán again, I almost broke down and wept.

I was so absorbed in the two of them that it took me a while to comprehend the nature of their task. There were brigades attaching heavy chains to the support beams of buildings, and when the order was given, lines of men and women heaved on these. The houses came crashing down, a great peal of dislodged stone and clouds of masonry. And I saw one of the wrecked houses was ours! I finally went over to them. The recompense was Amelis's face when she saw me—I'd never seen her so happy.

Certain embraces mark out stages in our lives. I'd returned, I was with them again, and as we clasped each other, it was like sealing a bond that even two kings had not been able to break asunder. I could also feel how thin she'd become, her ribs jutting into my fingers.

"For the love of God," I said, "you're pulling out the rubble of our own home."

"Well, there wasn't much left of it anyway," said Peret, who was with them. "We were hit by two cannonballs not long after you were captured."

They were working, as it turned out, on building a "cutting." A draconian measure, I learned, that had been imposed by the government.

When the walls of a sieged city suffer irreparable breaches, there's one emergency course of action: the cutting. Its name comes from what it's intended to do—cut the advance of the besieging army after they've taken control of the ramparts. The idea being to create a zigzag parapet just inside and running parallel with the ramparts. It wants to be as tall as possible, with a ditch dug along it to effectively increase that height. Just as the invaders think they're through, there's one more obstacle for them to get over.

At Bazoches, cuttings were given short shrift. Why? Because they're useless. In all my many days, I've yet to see one fend off any large-scale assault. If Herculean bastions hadn't done the job, why on earth would a puny barricade like that? Before my capture, I'd argued vehemently against the project. And my reasons were many.

First: the adverse effect of a cutting on morale. Knowing there's one more place where they might shelter, the troops manning the rampart have a tendency to submit rather than fight to the death. Second: This second line of defense is less effective, and the invaders, emboldened by having vaulted the first hurdle, will overrun it easily. Third: The way Barcelona was set out meant that our cutting was situated on a plain directly beneath the bastions. The victorious Bourbons would be firing down on us from above, with all the advantages that signifies. Fourth and most important: This terrain also had lots of buildings in it, when what was needed was a clear shot; Barcelona was such a dense urban agglomeration that the buildings virtually hugged the inside of the rampart walls. Whole streets would have to be flattened. And the inhabitants would hardly be thrilled at the government demolishing their homes.

Though as it turned out, at least regarding the last point, I was mistaken. The people living in the houses weren't opposed to the demolitions; they supported them, in the name of saving the city. They were all there, half-starved men and women helping to pull down the roofs beneath which they'd always lived. I couldn't make sense of it. In order to defend their homes, the people of Barcelona were prepared to destroy them.

My Bazoches eyes detected something half buried in the ruins of our building. I went over. It was Amelis's *carillon à musique*. I cradled it like a baby, cleaning off the dirt and muck. It was broken, unsurprisingly—I opened it, but no music came out. I later learned that Peret, who feared thieves more than going hungry, had taken it back to the house when Amelis wasn't looking, thinking that the bolts on our door would be a better protection than the canvas walls at the beach. He seemed to have missed the fact that cannonballs can do slightly more harm than any robber. I took the music box back to Amelis. "It's all right," I said. "We'll find someone to fix it."

I felt somewhat guilty. I'd been taught how to build or repair monumental walls but was helpless in the face of a small box that played music when opened. You could never tell if Amelis was being serious when it came to the box, because what she said was: "No matter."

What is a home, a hearth? Often it's a melody or the memory of a melody. As long as she still had that box, she'd have a home. All that had broken was the outer casing, nothing more.

"No matter," she insisted. "As long as we have the box, the melody will be easier to remember."

I went to see Don Antonio that same afternoon. I had to tell him about Little Philip's letters in support of a wholesale extermination, and about Queen Anne dying. And, of course, the details of the Attack Trench. Thanks to the discipline of the Spherical Room, each and every detail was stored in Zuvi's little head.

Making my way to see him, in that brief journey, I observed the oppressive, filthy atmosphere of the city now. Pyramids of refuse piled up on the beach. The people of Barcelona, always so jovial, all now withdrawn, and the usual merry air replaced by a collective despondency. I saw many more men in the family-run shops than at the start, injured in the fighting, arms and legs missing, convalescing among their loved ones. Women cooking watered-down soups. I saw an argument break out between a couple of them, scratching and pulling each other's hair. As far as I could make out, it was over half a stolen turnip. Entering the streets, I found the very color of the city to have altered, with a gray layer of dust and ash covering everything. And the only battalions not to have deserted, and still in one piece, were those of the Coronela.

Don Antonio was so gaunt, with his clothes hanging off him, that had it not been for his general's uniform, I'd barely have recognized him. He'd hardly slept or eaten since the trench had begun, someone later told me. We sat opposite each other, and he listened at length to what I had to say. A map was spread out, and on it I sketched the features of the trench's progress. The heart can be a stealthy thing sometimes, for the more technical the discussion became, the more I found myself shaken by heinous and disproportionate sentiments.

I'd learned at Bazoches how to focus my mind and put aside my feelings, which cloud clear thinking. But in the Barcelona of 1714, those two opposed poles converged; a deeply rational part of me awoke deep emotions. Who but I, after all, could possibly know the full significance of those ink lines and shapes on the map, apparently so innocuous?

I had set out the line along which the Bourbon trench was advancing, branch by branch. First parallel—there outside the window, growing longer by the hour, while we talked—second parallel, third parallel.

I found myself choking, and as I said the words " . . . and finally, they'll meet the moat, . . . " my voice cracked. I excused myself: "Forgive me, General."

"I want you to go and oversee the cuttings works," he said. "And for the love of God, no blubbing!"

I tried to evince a firmness I utterly did not feel, and before going out, I came up with something in relation to the great question Vauban had one day asked me.

"Who knows," I said, "if we persevere, perhaps we can devise a defense so perfect that the enemy will desist."

But Don Antonio only shook his head. "Son, to come anywhere near perfection, it would be a question of going beyond merely mortal dimensions. And if it's a crime to force professional soldiers into it, what authority could we call on to force an entire city?"

It was a hopeless cause, a fact that no one knew better than Don Antonio. He'd argued a thousand times for the government to negotiate peace. I don't believe any man can ever have suffered a moral quandary such as his then. Persevering with a harebrained defense went against his conscience, when to give up would be an abrogation of his sense of honor. He made several gestures toward throwing in the towel. But he never meant it—he was only using it as a threat in negotiating with the Red Pelts. He was caught in a paradoxical whirlpool: the soldiers blindly obeying him, him obeying the Red Pelts, and the Red Pelts doing as the people wanted. And what was the Coronela, anyway, if not the citizens themselves, armed? Long before the trench had begun, Don Antonio had his eye on a single objective: to avoid a senseless slaughter. A noble ideal, but it was becoming less and less possible with every passing day, particularly as those who sought to save the day were the ones who preferred the idea of self-immolation to surrender.

And me? I'd become an observer of—and at the same time a participator in—that madness of ours. On my first night back, as I lay with Amelis in my arms under the canvas of our tent, we spoke very few words. The broken music box rested on the floor by our bed mat. I preferred not to say too much about what had gone on when I was in the Bourbon encampment. That morning, when the two of us had found each other again, the sight of her hands, bloody from hefting sharp rocks, had made my questions about Verboom feel somewhat less pressing. And now, together, with our naked skin touching, it seemed best just to say nothing.

"A favor" was the one thing I did say. "That Sunday dress of yours, the violet one. Burn it, would you."

She let out a tired laugh. "Martí," she said, "you perfect fool. It's been a long while since I sold that dress, for money to buy food with. "

Jimmy now aimed his artillery—all of it—on the bastions of Portal Nou and Saint Clara and on the stretch of rampart between. Pópuli's murderous but erratic approach was over, replaced with one that was methodical and persistent, as well as adjusted to the way the trench was proceeding. And who had designed it? I found the thought growing and beginning to consume me. The furrow grew closer and closer, day and night, while the cannons sought to create a breach for the final assault.

Naturally, Costa and his Mallorcans did what they could to make life difficult for the enemy gunners. They aimed at the Bourbon cannons and the top of the trench, raining down death on as many sappers and soldiers as possible. The enemy also tried to pick out our cannons, and it was mayhem for all. Cannons from either side seeking each other out, and some of ours belching out grapeshot across their parallels, and some of theirs knocking down our walls and killing our men. Costa was always around, chewing on his parsley sprig, barking orders. Cannons fired, cannons dragged to a new position. And between them, the Coronela rifleman, making sure the soldiers in the trenches kept their heads down.

Those tailors, carpenters, and gardeners knew that until their shift was over, they'd be coming under cannon fire day and night, immured in the pentagonal tomblike bastions. They glanced nervously at the skies, in hope of clouds, as any rain would dampen the gunpowder and thereby slow the Bourbon artillery in their tasks. Alas, this was the peak of summer. The Mediterranean always makes Barcelona's heat humid, and in August, the air turns to a horrible soup. Ah, yes, that blue cloudless sky, no promise of rain, blue, constantly blue: Never has the color blue seemed so uncompromising. And the heat—that of summer, combined with the heat of battle.

The bombardment was so intense that whenever you were up on one of the bastions, you'd constantly be breathing rock dust. Large motes floated on the air: Lifting your hand up was like stirring a dense pollen. A brief stint on Saint Clara or Portal Nou and the gaps between your teeth would fill up with earth; no, something worse, because you knew it was also formed of human remains, ground to stone and dust by the shelling. Some men grew snide, others lost their minds; not a man exists who can resist the effects of an endless bombardment, not a single one. Sometimes they'd crack suddenly, crawl off into a corner, and curl up, not let anyone come near. Their eyes would flutter faster than hummingbird wings, their hands make wringing motions. Madness is always a form of fleeing inside oneself.

The second parallel was reached. This enabled the Bourbons to install artillery that could then attack the ramparts side-on and from far closer. Costa could do little against so many. At this point, they began employing the "Ricochet," a technique invented by none other than Marquis de Vauban himself.

Essentially, the Ricochet meant charging a cannon with only two thirds of the necessary gunpowder. Then the missiles wouldn't punch into or embed in the walls but, rather, skim along like stones over the surface of a stream. It's useful for clearing out cannons installed on ramparts. The missile would run the length of the bastion deck, flattening everything in its path. You'd see the cannonballs, the size of very large watermelons, almost seeming to gambol along and against the stoneworks. Each impact produced a horrifying noise, indifferent to human life. The Ricochet technique converted men into ants and bastions into trodden-on anthills. Hefty stone orbs bouncing, crunching, along the ground.

Left, right, and center they came—and from in front—and at times from all directions at once—and there were constant cries of: "*A terra!*"

If you did get down in time, it was unlikely that the weight of the cannonball would strike you dead—possibly landing on a soft part of your body, break a few ribs, at most. But they were deceptively quick, and their flight was mutilating. If you didn't see one coming, it could tear off a limb and carry on past, impassively bouncing along the cobblestones. The sight of men chopped to pieces is a primordially terrifying one.

The battalions with orders to take their turn up on Portal Nou or Saint Clara would pause before ascending, and kneel down and pray. But they would go up. I'd do anything not to have to order men to occupy the entrances to the bastions. It would have been like supervising an execution of honorable men.

I believed that writing this book would unburden my memory. To let my treachery drain onto the pages, to liberate myself by speaking truth. I thought—oh, vanity—that deploying ink to honor the men and women who fought against all odds, for their liberty, would make me less miserable. But I now see it's an impossible task. Why? Because of our concept of the heroic, which is so elusive, and so degenerate.

Our prototypical hero is proud Achilles. We see him standing victorious over Hector, sword raised. But how can we possibly extol the epic qualities of a filthy group of men when everything they do, their daily functions, is perfectly common? A single act doesn't make a hero; constancy does. It isn't a single bright point but a fine line, indestructibly modest: this ascent up onto inundated ramparts day after day after day. Leaving home and walking into the inferno, then returning home, and in the morning, joining in with death again. And given that so many heroic deeds were constantly being carried out, no one was seen as a hero. But this itself was what made them truly great. Heroes, like traitors, grow old. Those who sacrifice themselves remain; to them goes the glory. It's impossible to live on in glory; only death has the power to confer the stamp of immortality.

Soon the third parallel was under way. I wept to see it, crouching down in a rubble-filled corner of one of the bastions, my hands covering my face, Ballester and his men standing around me. They didn't understand my desolation, and at the same time, they intuited, knew, that my tears pertained to a superior knowledge, something beyond them. The Miquelets hid their feelings, always, and perhaps for that reason admired any open show of emotion.

The third parallel meant the beginning of the end. Goethe once asked me about Vauban's philosophy. I summarized as best I could the basic principle of encircling a place with a trench comprising three large parallels. Goethe thought about it, then said: "It's just as Aristotle said: All dramas consist of three acts." I'd never thought of it like that before.

And on they came. The end of the third parallel would be the end itself. All they had left to do was create the cut that would come through the moat. Then put in place parapets (known as "the gentlemen," in engineering parlance) and, next, to unleash the final assault, using fifty thousand well-drilled assassins.

The Attack Trench was a labyrinth by now, many thousands of feet long, zigzagging, turning corners, contorting in countless directions. Far to our left, we could see Montjuic, shrouded in smoke so that its peak resembled a flying mountain. All my Bazoches faculties were required, just to have a sense of what was going on a few feet in front of my nose. During one of the bombardments, I came to a particularly painful realization.

I was squatting down on the Portal Nou bastion at the time. I felt desperate seeing the breaches widening by the day, as the enemy cannons continued their work, and knowing there was nothing to be done now to plug them. Next to me was a soldier whose name I didn't know. Like me, he was sheltering, just about, from the artillery, one hand gripping his rifle, the other clamping his hat down over his head. He was a nobody. A man dressed in poor, tattered clothes, covered in the dust of the battle. At one point, sneaking a look out through one of the many gaps in the battered wall, he said: "What utter whoreson could have come up with something so twisted?"

Perhaps it was this that dragged me to the edge of true torment: feeling myself to be playing a part in our downfall. Then one day I saw a sign for which I'd been hoping for a long while: buckets being passed over the top of a parapet. They were bailing water from the trench.

I'd designed the trench lines to go near the sea, hoping they'd flood. Jimmy's sappers, trying to dig, suddenly found themselves inundated with salt water. Seeing the buckets, I exploded with glee. I stood up above the rampart and shouted: "Have that! Drown, you rats!"

Ballester yanked me back down. "Lieutenant colonel!" he said, railing at me once I had taken cover again.

I remember that being an extraordinary moment. Why? Because of what I saw in Ballester's eyes: myself.

Until that moment he'd viewed me as someone reliable but lacking in spirit, skittish, and overly cautious. That day saw the culmination of an insane transmutation in each of us. Ballester, a responsible person, in pay of the government, and Lieutenant Colonel Zuviría, a machine, immersed in our murderous task. Yes, the look we shared then lasted a good few moments.

But if the days were hellish, words cannot describe the nights. Once the third parallel had been established, we were sent out on night sorties more often, and they were bloodier than ever. How could I possibly not take part? I knew every nook and cranny of my trench. My presence was crucial in guiding my fellow soldiers. Combat in the pitch black is always a muddled thing, nothing more so, with grenades, knives, and bayonets in a maze of a thousand ditches and branches.

Yes, the night skirmishes were fought with unprecedented ferocity. We'd set out just as it grew dark or, for variation, before dawn. At first I thought Ballester would be in his element in this kind of encounter. Under cover of dark, he could enact the lowest instincts of man, which consists of killing and then running away. The opposite turned out to be true. Those nights ennobled Ballester to the same extent that they made a savage of me.

Swiftness and time efficiency are key in any sortie. The assault squad's only aim was to push as far into the trench as possible, then to dig in and hold off the enemy, while, at their back, a second wave sabotaged other parts. Then they'd both fall back, trying to lose as few men along the way as they could.

A signal would be given (something other than a whistle, which the

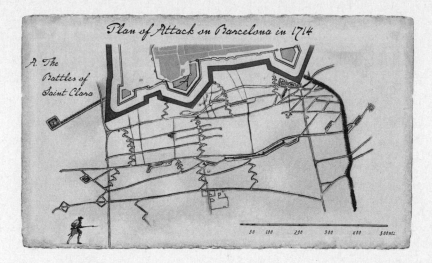

enemy would hear), and we'd run out to the trench, trying to stay low to the ground and silent. Their third parallel was so close by now that it was relatively easy to reach. However watchful the enemy was, we'd be upon them in seconds. Inside the trench, the strangest kind of combat would then commence. First slitting the guard's throat, then, within minutes, securing part of the trench. The darkness of the night, the depths in which we had to maneuver, and the narrowness of the trench, all made it impossible to see anyone, though there were voices aplenty— howls of entreaty and rage. Whistles being blown by Bourbon officers, five or ten different languages being spoken. Our aims on these lightning attacks were to destroy sapping machinery, flood the trench floor and wreck the cannons. And there was good old Zuvi, directing the destruction. Of the cannons, above all.

Our men would climb all over the cannons like monkeys. One would hold a foot-long nail against the fuse entry point, and the other would pound it with a hammer. The cannon would be immobilized; when the enemy retook the terrain, it would be useless. Where possible, we'd steal their tools. The second wave of men was to follow behind, and when they had gathered a good amount of ammunition, including shovels and mattocks, we'd retreat.

We'd occasionally surprise sappers in the trench, and they wouldn't put up any resistance. They'd crowd together, down on their knees, hands raised imploringly to the sky, begging for their lives. The flashes of gunfire, the momentary radiance of grenade explosions here and there, lit up their eyes. The last thing they'd experience would be a typically nightmarish scene: fleeing through the night, boxed in by walls sunk in the earth, reaching a dead end. A pitiless enemy coming after them. The best thing was not to look them in the eye.

"Shoot, Ballester, and be quick about it!" was the order I gave. "Kill them and move forward!"

In August 1714, neither side was taking prisoners. What would be the point? The bitterness we felt overcame us all. Falling back, we wouldn't be able to take our wounded with us. Anyone left behind would be knifed to death by the counterattackers. And in the early hours of the following day, the cadavers would be flung over the front of the trench, and from up on the ramparts, we'd watch them rot in the August sun. A mad time. Everything had grown so dark, we could no longer recognize ourselves.

Anyway, to put aside the darkness for a moment. As an example of le Mystère's constant sense of humor, even when things were at their goriest, here is an anecdote from August 3 of that year.

I'd just gone in to see Don Antonio, my black hair whitened with ash and fragments of rubble. I was interrupted before I began my report, as in came a battalion of Black Pelts—senior priests, that is. They were there to present a Directive for the Assuaging of Divine Wrath.

The Black Pelts have always done a good line in sarcasm, so the only way to take it was as a not very funny joke. Read for yourselves the recipe they'd cooked up to bring about divine mediation and to liberate the city:

> —Permanently put an end to street theater and comedies
> Expel all gypsies from the city
> Gather up the abandoned children which at this time swarm about
> in our streets

Do something about the profane, costly manners of the people of Barcelona
Bring back the veneration and respect of the temples
Hail Marys to be carried out in public places throughout the city

That *Directive for the Assuaging of Divine Wrath* plays in my memory as the perfect conjunction of all that is hypocritical and bizarre. The shelling had long since put an end to street theater, and no one had the energy to go and watch, or take part in, comedies. The poor gypsies, forever scorned, had seen the war as an opportunity to confront the stigma surrounding them: The majority of the drummers in the army had their dark faces. And if children were swarming the devastated streets, like my Anfán, it was because they were looking for food. As for "profane, costly manners," what world were they living in? Our colorful, joyful city had for a long time been deformed and gray. On top of which, what possible link could there be between a siege in progress, divine favor, and silk skirts?

Don Antonio said he was in full agreement with them on every count. The next thing was that he sent them packing, using very florid language. They couldn't have been happier.

Jimmy was a true Coehoornian. I couldn't believe he'd taken so long to begin the assault. The trench wasn't complete, sure enough, but what did that matter to someone who followed Coehoorn's principles? In his hands, the Attack Trench (as my stay in the Mas Guinardó had told me) was nothing but a political instrument. The ramparts had been breached; he had a large, well-disciplined army at his disposal; and he scorned the "rebels," scoundrels, for the larger parts, with very few trained troops among them.

So I failed to understand why the assault was taking so long to begin. My thoughts in designing the trench had been informed in large part by Jimmy's tendencies. A premature attack would put us at an advantage. And there he was, to my dismay, holding his troops back. A strange duel because, even while Jimmy's cannonballs were raining down, even as I was flinging myself to the ground to shelter behind the battlements, I was begging him: "Come on Jimmy, come *on*. Attack at last."

The night of August 11, one of the hottest I can remember, found me behind the walls of Portal Nou. The majority of the militia went bare-chested. I made my way to the most forward position, where the remains of a wall stood like a gigantic corroded tusk, from there looking out at the Bourbons. I had a Coronela man with me, sent by the bastion commander to protect me.

"Quiet!" I said. "Do you not hear that?"

A hammering—thousands of mattocks and hammers. My Bazoches-sharpened hearing meant I could make them out, in spite of them covering the tools with cloth to muffle the sound.

I dashed back to the rearguard, not stopping until I found Don Antonio. I was gasping, having sprinted all the way.

"Carpentry, Don Antonio," I said. "We've heard carpentry from their front line. They're putting in the assault platforms, there's nothing else it can be."

Don Antonio showed no sign of emotion. I remember how he nodded, as though hearing happy news about an old friend. He looked me in the eye, seeking confirmation of the news. Still panting, I said: "They're coming. It's the general assault."

11

To help form an idea of the battle that took place on the twelfth, thirteenth, and fourteenth of August, I here include a group of illustrations.

The below is the Saint Clara bastion and the large breach that had been opened by Jimmy's cannons. The moat, full of rubble dislodged by the shelling, would be easy to traverse. The advance guard was just across from us, positioned on the "gentlemen."

All we could do was create a line of defense inside the bastions themselves. Protecting this exposed line would be suicide, so ten feet or so behind the breaches, we erected barricades. These were of stone and cement, as solid as we were able to make them, and up to chest height.

One of Saint Clara's few advantages was the Saint Joan tower, a tall,

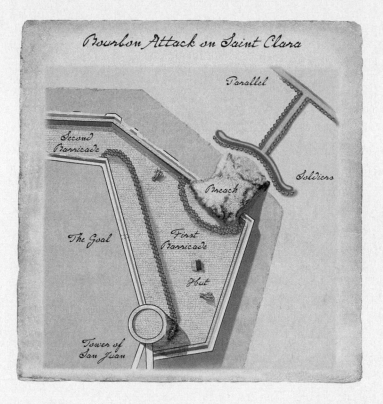

narrow construction behind and to the right of the bastion. Two light cannons had been stationed on it throughout the siege—light but very precise. The height of the tower gave it an excellent shooting angle. Saint Joan harrowed the Bourbons endlessly as they went about their trench works. They developed a loathing for the tower and sent endless cannonballs up at it.

To help people understand the violence of the fighting, I here include three prints of the Saint Joan tower. The first shows what it was like originally, and the second what state it was in on the eve of August 12. (It was so damaged that we'd had to remove the two cannons a few days earlier, as it was on the verge of collapsing.) The last plate is a recreation of what was left of the tower after the siege.

The artist took considerable license. The tower, for example, wasn't square but round, and at this point in the siege, the ramparts were in a far worse state. The prints may not be totally accurate, but they're instructive all the same.

J. Rigaud inv.

The Attack of two Bastio...

The Lodgement being secured on ye Covert way, ye Assailants make a Sap to gain ye Counterscarp
is ye Descent of ye Ditch, we if it be a wet one, they fill it up with Fascines loaded with Stones. As ye the
are several curious ways of covering ye Miner & fixing him to ye wall, while He makes ye Sap. The
they recover out of their confusion, & as they gain upon ym, ye Engineers with all dispatch trace out Lodgeme...
...dants not only counterwork ye Assailants Mine to render it ineffectual, but make Saps of their own to blow up...

4

Parr Sculp.

...eaches being made by the Miner.

...nwards towards y.^e Ditch, & here sometimes they make another Lodgement: their next attempt
...tion is always made upon y.^e ruins of a Breach, this is effected by ye springing of a Mine, & there
...line is ye Signal for ye Assault, ye Troops immediately pass over ye rubbish & push ye besieged before
...to secure themselves behind, taking care to keep a proper communication with their own works. The Defen-
...siegers, when they have penetrated y.^e works, one of wch is represented in y.^e furthermust Bastion in this Print.

J. Rigaud inv.

The Assault on the

The Bastion being taken, the Assailents push Saps forwards to the Wall which shuts i
in the Battlements, & summons the Besieged to deliver the Place, in case of refu
Assault. They spring their Mines, pass over the ruins of the Breaches, & push the
in several parts at once. As the Forces are cut off or advance forwards they are
the Lodgment on the Covert Way: and when the Grand Retrenchment can't be fo

Parr Sculp.

...dy of the Place

...e Bastion, & charge their Mines in readiness: They make breaches with their Cannon
...ot frequent after such Advances are made, the Besiegers prepare for a general
...e Grand Retrenchment, which covers the inside of the place, which they Attack
...r fresh ones, so that there are always Battallions which possess the Breaches, the Ditch,
...e themselves on the Rampart, or at least on the Breach

At dawn on August 12 I was up on Saint Clara. The imminent attack meant I hadn't had a moment's sleep. Those sons of whores, knowing that we knew something was afoot, spent the whole steamy night setting off false alarms. And it was my job to raise the men when the real attack came.

A fine task! Raising the alarm in the city was no easy job. Men were not so much worn out as utterly exhausted. And some officer pissing his pants, rousing the garrison for no good reason, was the last thing they needed. Consider, too, that ours wasn't a professional army but a bunch of civilians with rifles slung over their shoulders. Any alarm would wrench them from their homes, from their beds and their wives' embraces. Jimmy's idea was exactly this: to unnerve the defenders. As I say, the night was one long series of ruses: suddenly, in the pitch dark, trumpet blasts and drumming, and you thought an entire army was pouring down on your head. But nothing happened. Nothing. A few minutes later, there would be a pointless volley of rifle fire. But, counter to expectation, no battalions of grenadiers emerged out of their trenches, no infantry with bayonets mounted, no one. No one. I spent the night gauging the tiniest sounds and thinking of Bazoches: "As long as you are alive, you must pay attention. And as long as you pay attention, you'll stay alive."

At around seven in the morning, a silence came down, a calm so absolute that the absence of noise itself was suspicious. I dashed over and vaulted the first barricade. Then, creeping forward, I dropped down and poked my head over the breach. And what I saw, for all that it was the height of summer, chilled me to the bone.

Hundreds of men were emerging from the "gentlemen." French grenadiers were chosen for their stature, and these were the very tallest of that class of soldier. In place of their usual weapons, unreal sight, they were wearing metal breastplates and brandishing twelve-foot pikes. Just behind this armored urchin came grenadiers, hundreds and hundreds of grenadiers. Ten full companies, at the very least, making their way to the Saint Clara and Portal Nou bastions.

The moat became an ant run of white uniforms, clambering over the rubble in perfect formation. The slope gave way so easily under their feet that it also put you in mind of a herd of elephants parading over gravel.

"This is the end," I said to myself. The cream of the French army was upon us, and all we had to take them on were two Coronela companies, the swordsmiths and the cotton dealers. Fewer than two hundred men, all told.

I ran back the way I'd come, hurdling the barricade. I went and found the commander of the bastion, Lieutenant Colonel Jordi Bastida. "It's the general assault, Bastida!" I cried. "They're lining up!"

Just then we heard an explosion over to our left. The ground trembled. A column of black smoke mushroomed up over the neighboring Portal Nou. The Bourbons had exploded a mine.

"Don Antonio must be informed!" I said, agitated.

Bastida shook me off with disdain. "Well, you'd better go and tell him, then!"

Jordi Bastida was one of our heroes. In 1709 he'd been responsible for repelling the Bourbon assault on Benasque, a small settlement in the Pyrenees. If he'd been in my shoes, have no doubt, he would have interpreted "Well, you'd better go and tell him, then!" to mean, send a messenger; Bastida never would have considered abandoning his post, least of all when a mine had gone off, sending shock waves through the entire city. But I, of course, was not Bastida, and off I ran. And as I ran, I felt sure I'd never see the man alive again.

The Bourbons came at Saint Clara and Portal Nou simultaneously. The latter had just as few men defending it, the tailor and the cup maker companies. But overall, Portal Nou hadn't had it as bad as Saint Clara; it could count on covering fire from either side, and its breaches were not so severe. As for the subterranean mine, it hadn't been well positioned: It took out the forward edge of the pentagon, whereas if the Antwerp butcher had calculated properly and placed it a little farther forward, the entire fortification would have been blown sky-high. Imagine that—could someone possibly have fiddled with the numbers and distances in the plans?

Portal Nou was under Colonel Gregorio de Saavedra y Portugal. (I imagine he was Portuguese, with a surname like that.) For a few long minutes, his tailors and cup makers found themselves blinded by a thick cloud of black smoke. It rained clods of earth and rubble. They must have thought the world had come to an end. But the error in the calculations meant that the vast majority would come away unscathed. And Saavedra, who was a veteran officer, promptly sent his men into the gap.

Which bright Bourbon spark came up with the idea of returning to the time when pikemen were in force, I don't know. (Years later, Jimmy assured me it hadn't been him, but bearing in mind the disaster that took place, and his tendency to never tell the truth, his wanting to deny responsibility would make sense.)

Militiamen from each bastion converged in the breaches and began firing their rifles dementedly. They had covering fire from the ramparts above and were camouflaged by the screen of smoke from the exploded mine below. And the attackers came so thick and fast that they just needed to shoot into the mass of them. The first to fall, logically enough, were the men with the pikes. They were the most strapping men, and their armor was too heavy, and as they went rolling back down the slope they took dozens of others with them.

In the first part of this book, I said a little about the horror of a grenadier attack. I didn't think it necessary to specify at that point that one doesn't need to be a grenadier to use a grenade, and that in Barcelona, we had thousands upon thousands of grenades. A deluge of those black balls now came pouring down on the attackers. That the opposition was so tightly packed together made it many times more effective. At certain points, some of the defenders simply lit a single fuse to one of the grenades in a sack and threw the whole thing. But in spite of the carnage, the Bourbons still made headway.

Meanwhile, good old Zuvi sprinted to find Don Antonio again. I didn't have to go far to find him. He was behind the area under attack, with officers and intermediaries bustling around him. There was nothing I could tell him that he didn't already know, which I found somewhat humiliating.

One of the officers awaiting Don Antonio's orders was Marià Bassons, a law professor who had taken up the position of captain in the Coronela. A small man with a round head and his spectacles firmly in place, even there in the midst of battle, Bassons was one of these men who keep old age at bay by being phlegmatic, making observations on the world as though they themselves are not a part of it.

"Ah, Lieutenant Colonel Zuviría," he said, peering at me through his little glasses. "Tell me, any developments on your legal tribulations? Did you sort it out with those Italians?"

I was out of breath from running, and above our heads, missiles of all calibers were flying to and fro, and Bassons wanted to know about my pending trial. Someone ought to have pointed out to him that most of the courts had been destroyed by the bombardment. I never quite worked out if he was senile or one of these stoic creatures that society props up, as long as there's someone saying it's possible to prop them up.

His company, made up of law students, was nearby, sheltering from stray bullets as they awaited orders. One came over and, both eager and respectful, asked Bassons: "Doctor, are we to attack?"

The law students' company was easily recognizable. Since they were at university, that meant they all came from good families. When enlisting, they each bought themselves not one but two or even three of those uniforms with their long blue jackets. They'd get one dirty during a shift, then have another waiting for them, one of their servants having cleaned it. They struck up an agreement with the tailor company, who would patch their holes for them. I must admit, they never filled me with confidence. The only thing they were any good for was parades, because they scrubbed up so well in their immaculate uniforms with their wide yellow cuffs. The civilians, up on their balconies, found encouragement from seeing them, due to their tendency to confuse a pretty army with a hardened one. My qualms were based on the fact that war and the arts have never been happy bedfellows. "They'll bolt as soon as the first shot is fired" was my view.

Bassons, who always acted like a father with his students, clapped the young soldier on the back. "*Aviat, fill meu, aviat,*" he said. Soon, my boy, very soon. "And remember: *Nihil metuere, nisi turpem famam.*" The only thing to be feared is ill renown.

Old Bassons had enlisted, like many of the people of Barcelona, almost without having to think. For them, war was part of your civic duty, somewhere between paying your taxes and taking part in carnival. Once the *Crida* went out, the students made it clear to the government that their professor was the only man they'd serve under. The Red

Pelts, always very understanding (to the upper classes), made Bassons a captain. (Possibly they worried that if they did otherwise, the students would drag them out and stone them.) In return, Bassons couldn't have felt more proud of the youngsters under his command. *Mon Dieu, quel bon esprit de corps!*

The young soldier went back over to the troop, and Bassons couldn't help but sigh condescendingly. "Youth, always so impatient!" This he said as though my rank somehow meant I wasn't also young.

"Storm," I know, is very overused as a description for battle, but there can be few better ways to describe the situation we were in. Clouds of ash and stone chips came tumbling from the bastions as the cannonballs continued to fall. In our positions just below the ramparts, pulverized fragments rained down on our heads. I didn't want to imagine what it was like inside Saint Clara. With a little luck, I thought, I'll be forgotten about. Ha! I should have been so lucky! One of Villarroel's officers came rushing over: "Zuviría! Is it right you've been up on Saint Clara? You're to show Captain Bassons the way—the students are going as backup for Bastida. Tell them they must hold until further reinforcements arrive!"

I didn't even have time to patch together an excuse.

"Got that?" cried the man. "Hold the position! Hold, or all will be lost!"

I wanted to say no, no, he couldn't send a collection of rosy-cheeked infants to Saint Clara, that the Bourbons would brush them aside in seconds, and it would be of no practical use in the defense of the city. But that would have been to offend Bassons and his hundred or so blue-coats, who were already trotting over. Very enthusiastic about getting themselves killed!

What else could I do but take them to Saint Clara? We crossed the narrows of the gullet, we hurried up the infernal steps. And dear Lord, what a scene we found!

Compared with the deck on Saint Clara at that moment, Golgotha would resemble an English country garden. The surface of that irregular pentagon was entirely carpeted with dead and wounded bodies. A great many of them were close to death, unable to raise an arm to ask for help. All those writhing bodies made me physically sick. Fishermen keep their buckets full of dozens of worms, and you see them squirming around, waiting for the hook to be stuck through them. It was like that.

The Bourbons had taken the first barricade, which we'd erected to encircle the breach, and as a place from which to fire at the invaders when they began slipping through. Take another look at the plate. Now that they were installed there, they were firing on the second barricade, where the small numbers of survivors from Bastida's sword-smiths and cotton dealers were positioned. Twenty or thirty out of the original two hundred remained, and they were firing and reloading ceaselessly, unable to do anything about the fallen men between the two barricades. They'd held off the Bourbon assaults, and had even carried out a number of counterattacks, retaking the first barricade several times. Two hundred versus a thousand, perhaps two thousand!

As the students deployed themselves behind the second barricade, I caught sight of Bastida, who was down. His adjutant, who had propped him up against the battlement wall, was weeping. There was nothing he could do but dab his commander's cheeks with a sponge. Bastida was gazing up at the sky, his eyes half vacant and his mouth open. Kneeling down beside him, I counted six bullet wounds on his body.

I know I can be mean-hearted from time to time, but in that moment, I can assure you, I felt awful at having sidled off. I'd had dealings with Bastida before and found him an honest, decent man. And now here he was lying on the floor with six bits of lead swimming around inside him. Taking his hands in mine, I whispered to him: "Jordi, Jordi, Jordi . . ."

He tried to speak, but I couldn't understand. He gurgled incomprehensibly, the din making everything difficult to hear anyway. It was a miracle he was still breathing.

"Why hasn't he been taken to the hospital?" I yelled at his adjutant.

"He didn't want to be taken, sir!" was the answer. "He gave express orders! There are so few of us that unless we all bear arms, we'll be overrun."

"The student company has come," I said. "Now take him!"

Bastida grabbed my left wrist. His eyes bulged, and the look he gave me—one of stunned lucidity—will stay with me to the day I die. I put my ear to his lips. If he wanted to curse me, I deserved it. His chest contracted, and instead of words, red bubbles cascaded from his mouth. I felt the warmth of his blood spilling over my ear and stood back. He was carried off. He died early the next morning in Saint Creu hospital, after long struggles.

The men on the barricades, separated by that groaning mass of bodies sprawled across the cobbles, continued to exchange fire. More and more of the Bourbon soldiers gathered on the beachhead of the bastion. Once there were enough of them, they would come charging against the baby-faced student company, the bastion would be theirs, and with it, the city.

People unfamiliar with the art of engineering wouldn't have seen that outcome so clearly. The students would load their rifles squatting behind the parapet, turn and aim a single shot over the top, and then kneel back down with a ramrod in one hand and the pouch of gunpowder in the other, again loading their rifles. In their minds, as long as they applied themselves diligently, the result of the battle would not be in doubt. The good Lord would guide their bullets in the same way He did their studies, rewarding constancy, effort, and dedication with a deserving triumph. They failed to understand that behind the small semicircular barricade the enemy was controlling, Jimmy was sending in more and more reinforcements, entire battalions making their way along the trenches from the back. A devastating pool of energy that, at the drop of a hat, would overwhelm anything and everything in its way.

I ought to be clear that, at the time, finding myself at the center of proceedings, I didn't have a clear sense at all of what was going on. Over the following days, I managed to form a general idea.

Jimmy had attacked the bastions of Portal Nou and Saint Clara at the same time. As I've said, he planned to take them, and after that, the city would beg for mercy or else be put to the sword. Siege over. That was if everything went exactly according to plan. When the resistance turned out to be more determined than expected, Jimmy went out onto his balcony at Mas Guinardó and stood by for the messengers to brief him on where things had gotten to.

The first reports perturbed him. The news wasn't bad, it was disastrous: Incredibly, the push for Portal Nou had been repelled.

Jimmy felt annoyed, he felt inconvenienced, but he did not feel dis-
couraged. He had meditated at length on the attack, had an alternative
strategy, and proceeded to put it into effect.

In reality, Jimmy didn't need to take control of two bastions—as
per *les règles*, one was enough. Portal Nou hadn't gone well, so he decided to throw everything he had at Saint Clara. Where good old Zuvi
was, in other words, cowering behind the second barricade.

While Jimmy gave the order for the reserve battalions—all of
them—to make their way to Saint Clara, Dr. Bassons continued going
back and forth along the parapet, exhorting his students. Seemingly
oblivious of the danger, strolling around with his hands clasped behind his back as though it were daisy chains rather than bullets flying
around, and spouting phrases in Latin. Don Antonio had ordered him
to contain the Bourbons, and his lads were making an excellent job of
precisely that. He saw no further; the calculated, catastrophic forces
about to be unleashed were beyond his comprehension. Coming in
my direction and seeing me kneeling close up against the battlement,
keeping my head well down, Bassons stopped and, uncritically, more as
a suggestion than as a recrimination, pointed out: "Lieutenant Colonel,
officers are supposed to set an example."

"Dr. Bassons!" I cried. "Get down!"

According to Bassons's rudimentary military understanding, an officer had to stay on his feet in the face of enemy fire. Truly, he didn't
want for courage, the ignoramus. But we engineers always put staying
alive above honor. Our lot was to build fortresses, the point of which
was to provide protection, not leave people exposed, and unlike in
open battles, in sieges anyone who *doesn't* hide is a fool. Therein one of
the unending sources of mutual disdain between engineers and soldiers.

Zuvi himself had designed and led the construction of the barricades
on the Saint Clara yard. High enough to provide protection from enemy
fire, but at the same time, with gaps to allow rifles to be poked between
the stockades and fired, and low enough that men could get back over in
case of a counterattack. Bassons wasn't a tall man, quite the opposite, but
his head—upon which, absurdly, he still wore a wig—was visible over
the top. That large, round head was a perfect target for any sniper, and
we were in the midst of a firefight as constant as it was chaotic.

"Please, Dr. Bassons!" I again begged him. "Take cover!"

But I was wrong: My warning merely encouraged him to draw his students' attention. Quite a sight: a lieutenant colonel down on his knees, Captain Bassons pontificating on the superiority of intellect and civic pride. He declaimed between bursts of gunfire: "Our grandfathers' grandfathers, and their grandfathers before them, and as far ago as five generations past, lived on the Pyrenean peaks. And they lived like beasts, herding together without order, and without God."

"What are you going on about?" I said, trying to cut him off. "Enough of the sermons!"

He paid me no mind. He was possessed by culture in the same way the preachers are filled by the Holy Spirit. "But then a day came," he said, undaunted by the cascades of bullets flying by, "and they saw a rich country spread out beneath them, a prosperous place for anyone who knew how to work the land, valleys and plains perfect for human civilization. Our ancestors repelled the Moors—that foul-smelling bunch! And it took them generations to do it, establishing their laws, religion, and customs in a new land they named Catalonia."

What nonsense was this? Plus the fact that his rapt students had slowed their firing in order to listen to him. Jumping to my feet, I barked out the order: "Maintain fire! Shoot, load, and shoot!" They didn't listen; my authority was nothing next to that of Marià Bassons, their beloved professor.

Bassons the buffoon carried on with his discoursing: "They created a new order, settling Catalonia and going on to liberate Valencia and Mallorca, populating the lands with our people. And they did not suppress the natives, as is usual in conquered territories, and as is Castile's approach. Rather, they established sibling kingdoms, which, as such, were forever to be our equals and beloved by us. A shared religion, a shared tongue, a shared common law, and each with its own parliament. And what was that law, supreme, absolutely free, and unshakable? Always to serve the king who serves his people." He suddenly became excited, shaking a fist in the air. "And now some French pretender to the Spanish throne wants to trample a thousand years of Catalan liberty because of what some Castilian wrote in his will! Are we going to let them? *Oi que no, nois?*" Not a chance, right, lads?

I remember the way he shouted while shaking his fist, as though rattling a tambourine. I had to bellow to make myself heard over the din: "Dr. Bassons, would you mind getting down?"

I'll never know whether the buffoon heard. He was near enough that I was able to grab him by the tails of his jacket to force him to take cover. But too late. In that instant I saw a white line score the sky, a little comet's tail of smoke behind it. A concave slice of metal, the size of a serving tray, flew toward us and into the side of Bassons's head, embedding in it as though his cranium were soft cheese.

Where had this projectile issued from? No one will ever know. Most likely, it was the remains of a cannonball that had shattered upon impact with the Saint Joan tower behind us to the right. The fragments had flown off in all directions, and the largest nestled in Bassons's head.

He toppled onto me, his head a bloody mess. His body spasmed briefly and then was still. His dead hands were clenched, pawlike. My face was splashed with so much blood, it must have looked like I had measles. I pushed Bassons off me, and before his body hit the ground, almost all of his hundred students, it seemed, had come and crowded around. "Dr. Bassons!"

Panting, I wiped the blood from my face and tried to recover from that sudden death. As I puffed and gasped, they congregated around their professor and me. A collective sobbing started up.

"This is war," I said, trying to console them. "Return to your positions."

The students loved Bassons with that especial, fanatical love that exists between student and teacher. In their shock, they were close to insubordination.

"To your positions," I ordered them, shoving them back, "spread out along the barricade, and fire, damn it, maintain fire! If you let up, they'll gather and charge!"

Now, look, I've never been one to glorify military actions—partly because I've seen so few that have been glorious. Most great military feats are little more than rats being corralled, blind panic. When it comes to battle, men kill to avoid being killed, and that is all. Then a poet shows up, or a historian, or a historian of a poetic bent, and takes that thrusting, thrashing frenzy and puffs it up, imbues it with ideas of valor, calls it glory. And yet, and yet: What happened that day belied my whole logic.

Grief became hate, a repeated cry of "You bastards!" starting up as they fired, loaded, and fired. But to load a rifle, you need a calm head, and their blood was boiling. One among them, the most upset, lost patience; his hands trembled in rage, and the powder poured everywhere apart from down the barrel of his rifle. He let out a strange, female-sounding cry and was suddenly mounting his bayonet and vaulting over the barricade.

I had time only to shout after him: "Eh? Where are you going? Get back here!"

But he wasn't listening. Maddened, he went screaming toward the Bourbon barricade, bayonet at the ready.

"That's it, at them!" some imbecile shouted, encouraged by the mad student's example. "Avenge Don Marià!"

And after him they went! The whole hundred or so of them, following in their comrade's footsteps. Naturally, I tried to hold them back: "Don't, don't! You'll be slaughtered, the lot of you!"

It wasn't just compassion that made me try to stop them. I would have to be the one to tell Don Antonio, our good shepherd of soldiers, that I'd lost the sheep in my care, that they'd gone wandering into a mass suicide. Insults, threats, physically trying to hold them back, all useless. They went over the top, every last one of them. Not me, clearly. I stood with my back against the battlement for a few moments, head in my hands. The only person left was me, me and the body of Bassons the buffoon. *Mon Dieu, quelle catastrophe!*

I turned to watch the massacre through a chink in the barricade. And to this day, I cannot believe the sights I saw.

Spurred on by a very intimate rage, the students covered the distance in the blink of an eye. The Bourbons didn't even have time to unleash an organized volley. There was a scattering of shots, and three or four of the students went down. When they were halfway across, one shouted out the old Barcelonan students' harangue: "Stone them! Stone them!" And that same student stopped in his tracks, striking a flint and putting it to the fuse of a sack full of grenades, before launching it over the top of the enemy barricade. And there we have it: The more loutish a civic tradition, the more use it is to a patriot.

The grenades sent up a cluster of bodies on the other side of the ramparts. The mad youth leading the charge hadn't even stopped to light his grenade but ran on, hoarse from yelling, bayonet out in front. The others followed him, and when they reached the barricade's first wall, they scaled it and began firing and thrusting their rifles into the bodies of the men they found below them.

Beyond, hundreds of Bourbon soldiers were awaiting the order to begin the assault. An attack from the defenders—that was the last thing they were expecting. They were so tightly crammed together that the majority couldn't free their arms to bring out their rifles and fire back. Over the students went, sinking their bayonets into the heads, chests, and backs of their enemies. They were so crazed, and the Bourbons so vulnerable, that the latter panicked and fled. They plunged pell-mell into the moat and back in the direction of the cordon, with the de-mented, braying students hard on their heels.

Once this impossible victory had become reality, I, too, followed after them, crouching low. In the stretch of the bastion between the barricades, my feet crunched over dead and wounded bodies; you couldn't move for them. As I say: To this day, I fail to understand how a handful of scholars could make a thousand or so French grenadiers turn and flee.

I managed, thank heavens, to stop the students from continuing and trying to take on the whole Bourbon encampment. I was helped by the exhaustion that took hold of them, the plumbing of the depths of body and spirit that follows a life-or-death charge. The sound of orders from an officer brought them to their senses again. The first barricade had been taken, and now they needed to man it, reestablishing the situation as it had been before the Bourbon attack. They came meekly back up. Perhaps, as I've suggested elsewhere, because he who returns from a place of madness is more surprised than any by the aberration committed.

I had seen things before then that called into question the teachings at Bazoches. But the students' charge went further: It utterly negated reason. Vauban never would have tolerated such an action, for the inevitable loss of life, and for the fact that it was bound to fail. And yet, and yet, incomprehensible as it was, there was I, standing on a mound of dead French grenadiers and giving orders to the babes who had killed them.

The lad who had initiated the charge had survived. He stood there with a very faraway look in his eyes. The front of his uniform was soaked in blood, top to bottom, and he was gawping at his bayonet, also stained red. He seemed not to understand, as though all the bodies had just appeared and were nothing to do with him. I shook him by the shoulders: "*Noi, noi,* are you all right?"

He didn't recognize me. His mouth opened and shut, and his gaze was otherworldly. "Dr. Bassons," he said. And throughout the rest of the day, he was in another world, and kept on calling me after his departed professor.

12

Jimmy, of course, reduced the human tragedy to numbers. And for a marshal, a number, so long as it is limited to an amount he can justify to his superiors, remains nothing but a number. He could absorb those initial losses, he reasoned, and the next morning, he began the assault again. He threw everything at the battered Saint Clara bastion.

For him, installed on the balcony of his Guinardó country house, watching the battle was no hardship. For the poor beetles of each army fighting over control of Saint Clara, it was like a recurring nightmare: Not twelve hours had passed since the charge of the students, and the situation was exactly as it had been previously, the Bourbons sheltering behind the first barricade, which they had retaken, and our forces behind the second.

Throughout August 13, there was a succession of attacks and counterattacks across the bastion yard. We were one step from the abyss; one step back, just one, and Saint Clara would be in Jimmy's possession. And once he had the bastion, the entire city would inevitably fall. Being the sly fox that he was, Jimmy sent false attacks at other points along the ramparts. They were obviously nothing but feints, but they still meant Don Antonio had to disperse his forces—precisely Jimmy's aim. The key position was protected by no more than a thin screen of men. The city was depending on this handful of combatants, worn out and choking on rifle smoke.

At the very center of the bastion was a small cabin, a munitions store whose construction I myself had overseen. Usually, a good bastion will have gunpowder storerooms underground, but Saint Clara was a woeful bastion, irregular and precarious, and had no basement. In the uproar of battle, prodigious quantities of gunpowder would be spilled. Obviously, the slightest scrap of anything alight would mean catastrophe. Even professional soldiers have trouble reloading a rifle with utter accuracy, and civilian militia more so. To point out the dangers to them, to insist they not rush as they loaded and reloaded, would have been as absurd as asking a child playing with a vase not to break it. This was why I thought it important to build this shelter, to protect the munitions from any stray sparks, and the consequent disaster. If you take a moment to flick back a few pages, you'll see the said cabin on the plate depicting the battle map.

So the day was spent vying for ownership of this insignificant shack halfway between the barricades, an outcrop in the center of the cobbled yard. Now the Coronela would make a push for it, now the Bourbon forces. Unlike Jimmy, Don Antonio was there on the front line, moving between the most perilous positions. The sight of him was a boost to the troops. I can still see him slapping men on the back, chatting with the soldiers, more like a father than a high-up military man.

"My boys," he'd say, "the least of you is worth as much to me as a general. How fortunate I am to have been allowed to lead you."

A moment came when I said to myself: "Enough now." It was well, very well, for him to set an example of fearlessness and self-sacrifice, like generals from antiquity (of course, we saw neither hide nor hair of Casanova), but we hardly wanted our commander in chief to end up like Professor Bassons.

What I couldn't understand was Don Antonio's strategy. Jimmy had a foothold on Saint Clara, meaning the bastion system was no longer to our advantage. Hours passed, and Don Antonio would regularly relieve the half-annihilated forces manning the different outposts, but never initiate any counterattacks. This meant simply accepting the series of bloody clashes in which we'd always be on the losing end. Jimmy was in a position to send wave after wave of men along the trenches to Saint Clara, and to evacuate his wounded; slow and arduous, yes, and the toll considerable, but we were so hugely outnumbered that sooner or later, they would gather together enough men to overrun us.

All the officers, to a man, knew how close we were to the abyss and that time was against us. Lose the second barricade, and it would be good night. The attitude of these officers said everything about the atmosphere in the city: Not a single one was exhorting Don Antonio to try and discuss terms. Far from it! There was a group of captains and colonels constantly asking Don Antonio to sanction a sortie, to let them try and dislodge the Bourbons from the first barricade. From the Catalans, "*si us plau, si us plau*"; from the pro-Charles Castilians who had changed sides, it was "*por favor, por favor*"; and you'd even hear a few Germans with their "*bitte, bitte, herr Ánton!*"

I can still see myself, standing back as officers swarmed around poor Don Antonio, who rejected their ideas one after another. They knew how desperate our situation was. And yet there they were, begging permission to carry out a frontal attack on a position held by several battalions. It was all Don Antonio could do to keep them at bay.

And so it went on until nightfall. The skirmishes continued in the same ferocious vein. Across the city, the bells tolled the warning alarm and didn't abate at sundown. The area where the attack was concentrated stayed brightly lit; we sent up flares so we could see what we were aiming at; the flashes of rifle fire also lit the darkness, like thousands of blinking glowworms. At around four in the morning, I left Saint Clara to go and discuss with Costa which cannons to bring to the bastion, as the embrasures were now in effect. A brief dialogue that saved my life.

I had ordered an old sergeant major, once the general assault was under way, to empty the munitions cabin at the center of the disputed yard. I thought the Bourbons were certain to make gains, and it was imperative that they not seize the contents. What I didn't know was that the old sergeant major had been one of the first to fall. That is, he hadn't lived long enough to gather a group of carriers, go and open the padlocked door with its small firebreak strip of water across the entrance, and empty the store.

I find it amazing when I think how long it took for the catastrophe to come. All day long, each side vied for control of a building they had no idea was brimming with gunpowder, grenades, bullets, and pots and tins containing grapeshot. And nothing had happened. *Le Mystère* must have had a good chortle on our account that day.

One of the survivors later told me the story. Just after I'd left, four in the morning and darkest night, a cry had gone up of: "Forward, for Saint Eulalia, forward!" The Barcelonan troops had held out all that time and resisted their desire to counterattack; in their frustration, a number of them took the prompt of this insane anonymous voice. For the hundredth time, they reached the cabin, repelled the Bourbons who had gathered around it, and then halted before pressing on to the first barricade.

Behind the first assault line, you always had a few men going around with large straw baskets bearing ammunition, particularly grenades, to replenish the troops' supply. At this point, after a day and half a night of constant skirmishing, the bastion yard was almost overflowing with dead bodies and scattered gunpowder. The place reeked of those two things.

Now, I was told, a number of the basket carriers sheltered behind the munitions cabin, and a spark fell from somewhere, setting fire to some gunpowder on the ground. The flame ran along a trail of gunpowder and came to two of the large baskets, which had been put down against the side of the cabin, both containing grenades. You can guess the next part.

I believe this to have been the second largest explosion I've witnessed in all my days. Costa and I were nowhere near Saint Clara and found our discussion interrupted as the shock waves threw us to the ground. Over six hundred feet away, we were. The eruption was red and bloomed upward like a flower. It was followed by an extended rumbling. Up went the flames, and up went the explosions, with half the city bathed in shards and fragments and rubble.

In a daze, I got to my knees. I looked over at Costa; his words came to me as though my head were underwater. I got up and set off for the bastion gullet, stumbling along in zigzags like a drunk.

Le Mystère, I'll give it this much, does at least apportion its humor equally: Both sides suffered roughly the same losses. A little over seventy Coronela men were blown up along with the cabin, and while fewer Bourbons died, the damage was greater to them: Word quickly spread that the explosion had been a rebel mine.

Mines provoke almost uncontrollable terror. An assassin hidden under our feet could at any moment activate many thousands of pounds of explosives, as many as the mind can conceive. Yes, it was a simple accident, the kind that abounds in war, but the Bourbons fell back in droves. How ironic that the two sides, having fought tooth and nail for control of the Saint Clara yard, now abandoned their positions at the same time, as though an agreement had been struck.

The gullet—the entrance to the bastion on the city side—was very narrow precisely to prevent men ever fleeing en masse. There was a captain there, named Jaume Timor, and with his saber drawn, he was stopping anyone who could bear arms. "Quit Saint Clara and the city will be lost!" he roared.

Whole families fought side by side on Saint Clara. As great Herodotus said: "In peace, children bury their parents; war violates the order of nature and causes parents to bury their children." The siege of Barcelona went further, with some burying not only sons but also grandsons. I saw a neighbor of mine named Dídac Pallarès coming along the gullet and Timor standing aside. He had good reason—three good reasons, to be precise: Pallarès was carrying his three sons, all of them injured, in his arms. The skin on their faces was in red and black tatters; I remember one of them in particular, one whom Peret always owed a few sueldos. His were the worst injuries; the flesh on his jaw had come away completely, exposing the bone. It was still raining debris, and Don Antonio was in the vicinity, uttering consoling and encouraging words to the survivors. He and a number of officers tried to reinstate a modicum of order. Well, on this occasion, they didn't manage it.

I was so dazed that I felt like I was seeing with my ears and hearing through my eyes. There were shreds of meat everywhere, remains similar to the formless gobbets you tend to see on the floor of an abattoir. I lifted my gaze. From the top of the bastions, the burning, howling bodies of Coronela men were falling after they leaped off the edge, as if the bastion were a burning ship. I saw all these things and then said to myself: "Ladies and gentlemen, enough. This is more than good old Zuvi can bear. To the hell with the city, the home country, and the constitution." I turned on my heel and ran like a rabbit.

"Fear will rise up into your eyes," I was told in Bazoches, "and do the looking on your behalf. Don't let it." Not bad in the context of a classroom. But when a power comes to bear that can make a bastion lurch and teeter like a paper boat, not even the memory of Bazoches could quash an individual's self-preserving instinct. I wasn't the only one who ran. Dozens of men had been pushed beyond their limits and were fleeing in all directions. I crossed the cutting and entered the city streets before being confronted by a huge crowd.

Women, in droves. They were holding their skirts clear as they ran—but in the opposite direction: toward the walls. Amelis was among them. "What's happening, Martí, what's happening?" she asked, but didn't stop. They'd been drawn by the explosion, and the prevailing chaos had meant there was no one to stop them from reaching the front line. Those of us who had succumbed to panic and fled, now hesitated.

In my view, Barcelona's rescue that night owed more to its women than Timor's saber. We fugitives were deemed cowards, picaroons, eunuchs. Amelis halted and called back at me: "You mean you're going to let the enemy enter?"

Allow me a moment's reflection in place of memories: What ideal was it that motivated the people of Barcelona to keep on going throughout a yearlong siege? Their liberties and constitutions? No, what kept them there was that bond—heavenly or demonic, it matters not—that prevents a man from abandoning the spot he's fighting on. Raw civilians, fourteen-year-old boys, sixty-year-old grandfathers, clung like limpets to the bastions. And why? I'll suggest an answer: because of the overwhelming, unshakable force of the question: "What will people think?" When your whole city's watching, it takes a lot of courage to be a coward.

Thus, even a prissy rat like Longlegs Zuvi went back to his post.

And that whole night we resisted an irresistible force, and through the next morning, and come midday next, good old Zuvi's nerves were utterly shredded, as was the case with the rest of the Coronela.

The center of Saint Clara was now a crater, a solemn gap clung to by what was left of the bastion's five walls. The unutterably mad struggle was for possession of this gap. The hail of rifle volleys was unceasing. And still no offensive from Don Antonio. Throughout this period, Jimmy continued to smugly accumulate men on the first barricade. Time was on his side. He thought (as I did at the time) that Don Antonio had taken leave of his senses—or even his valor—and was relinquishing the defensive positions. Once enough Bourbon battalions had gathered behind the first barricade, there would be no way of stopping an onslaught from them. And there we were, doing nothing but holding the second barricade and firing from Portal Nou and the adjacent sections of the ramparts. A lot of noise but little else came of it: rounds upon rounds of bullets spent while the Bourbons kept their heads down behind the first barricade and in the trench, or came along the cut, digging in deeper and building their parapets higher with every hour that passed.

It had been hell maneuvering the three cannons up to the bastion. And rather than firing those cannons, the Mallorcans wouldn't so much as peek out of the embrasures. As ever, it was as though they were fighting a separate battle from everyone else. They sat around on the bases of the cannons, drinking an abominable liquor from the Balearics—sharing it with none but themselves—and seeming removed from the bedlam surrounding them.

"For the love of God," I said, "fire these cannons, blow up the barricade they're holding! What are you waiting for?"

Their captain shook his head, his only concession being to mutter at me in his islander accent: "*Ses ordres.*" Orders.

There was a considerable stretch of ground between the end of their trench and the bastion because, as per good old Zuvi's modifications to Verboom's plan, the third parallel had been dug as far from the ramparts as possible.

I later learned that it had never been Don Antonio's plan to take back the first barricade. Jimmy was too strong there, it would only have been a bloodbath, so Don Antonio was content to delay them. He waited until the last possible moment before launching his counterattack, anticipating some pause in the assault. Then and only then did he give an order, one that just three officers had been let in on.

Lowering the telescope, he called out in that booming Castilian voice of his: "Do it!"

A flare went up, turning red the thick smoke on and around the bastion and ramparts. The moment he saw this, Costa gave his signal, lowering an arm. I wasn't nearby, but I believe I heard him shout something as well, and within an instant, each and every cannon and mortar began pounding the trenches, creating a barrier of flames.

We saw the explosions hitting the Bourbon lines, and the next two troops charging out from the garrison, one from the left and one from the right. (The arrows on the plate below indicate their trajectories.)

Two hundred previously selected men, under Lieutenant Colonel Tomeu and Colonel Ortiz, attacked each flank. And my God, what a mad dash that was.

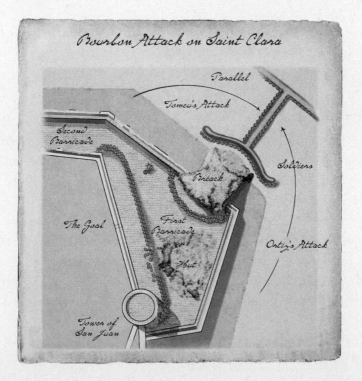

They hurtled out alongside the third parallel, exposing themselves to fire from the trenches. Those four hundred had to be very fast to make the most of Costa's barrage. They converged on the cut, some jumping down inside and others tipping the *fajina* parapets onto the heads of the enemy. Like this:

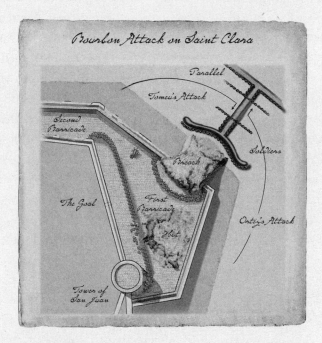

Ortiz was in charge of blocking off the cut on the side of the Bourbon encampment with the *fajinas*, and Tomeu's men did the same on the city side, trapping the enemy in between.

This was one of the swiftest and most exact maneuvers I've ever seen carried out from a besieged position. If Costa hadn't been a superior artilleryman, his cannons and mortars would have been the death of that four hundred. We watched as, having reached the cut, they shot their rifles down into it, annihilating the surprised Bourbons. I still have trouble banishing the memory of that underground wailing.

By the time Jimmy found out, it was too late. With Ortiz blocking the cut, there was no longer any use sending reinforcements.

As for the Bourbons already on Saint Clara, they saw what a sticky position they were in, with Tomeu behind them. And that was when the three cannons manned by the Mallorcans came into play: A large section of the first barricade sank, the brickwork beneath it pummeled so hard that it buckled inward and down.

With cannonballs coming from one side and rifle bullets riddling them from the other, the Bourbons scattered, leaping down into the moat below and sprinting past Tomeu's position, trying to reach the trench. It goes without saying that Ortiz's and Tomeu's men mercilessly gunned them down at close range. The volleys from the rifles up on the Saint Joan tower also intensified, prompted by the sight of the stampede. And then the order came for those of us on the second barricade to charge the first and, finally, unopposed, retake it.

Such is war. In the time it takes to crack your knuckles, the tables turn, and a seemingly hopeless battle that was going nowhere turns into a rout for your enemy. More than four hundred French never made it back to their lines. No prisoners were taken.

I managed to make out a French official through the smoke, standing with his body half out of the third parallel, using his telescope to try to discern what was happening, clearly incredulous at the way the assault had just crumbled. Ballester happened to be next to me, and he was scanning around for a target.

"Give me that!" I said, grabbing his loaded rifle, aiming it at the officer with the telescope, and firing at that reckless figure. The bullet went through his neck, blood gushing out the other side. The man's arms went up, like a pagan hailing an idol, and he fell backward into the trench. I remember the way his telescope, which he'd inadvertently flung upward, twirled around and around in the air. A not insignificant shot: The man I'd taken down was none other than Dupuy.

Still I shudder to think: In all of a yearlong siege, I fired one bullet, just one, and it turned out to be at Dupuy.

Seeing his troops coming pouring back, Jimmy was livid. He lowered his head and contained himself for a moment before exploding. The officers and commanders around him were made aware, in no uncertain terms, of how incompetent they were.

He stormed back into Mas Guinardó with his retinue behind him. He was even angrier than in the critical moments at Almansa.

"The position must be regained!" he howled, shaking his fists. "Even if it means losing the entire army! Or do we want Europe to hear how mighty France has been overturned by a group of rude civilians?"

His generals tried to calm him down, but Jimmy cursed them all. "Silence! I want a report from the horse's mouth. Send me Brigadiers Sauvebouef and Duverger! And Marquis de Polastron!"

Not possible, they said: Sauvebouef and Duverger had both been lost during the assault. Of Polastron there was no word. Well, that was soon to come: Men of the Coronela, still in a frenzy, had decapitated poor Polastron, rammed his head down inside a cannon, and fired him at Mas Guinardó. Hearing that noise, everyone present hung his head. All except Jimmy, who went out on the balcony, there finding Polastron's blackened, smoking head revolving on the balcony floor like a spinning top.

A number of officials appeared whom Jimmy had greater respect for, including Lieutenant Colonel La Motte. Injured, he hobbled in, face soiled and uniform in tatters. "Your Excellence," he argued, "regaining a foothold on Saint Clara would cost us our best troops, a crippling number of casualties and sacrifices. Without reinforcements from France, we'll gain no more than a few feet, and the cost will be terrible . . . The filthy rebel *canaille* are up on the ramparts as we speak, their generals and magistrates are whipping them up, and they mock us with singing and jibes."

All true. The regained positions were teeming with men and women and even some musicians, celebrating the victory. With very little decency, also true. A great display of bare buttocks turned in the direction of the enemy lines.

Even so, it took a report of the losses to change Jimmy's mind. Numbers have the power to cool the most burning passion. In the Saint Clara attack alone, fifteen hundred men had been lost, making a total of five thousand since the beginning of work on the trench: the kind of figures that could no longer be argued away. Most disconcerting of all was the account of officers down. Among them, none other than Dupuy—though, as it turned out, he had survived my bullet through the neck. And there was something further, something Jimmy grasped all too well.

Unlike field battles, in any contest for fortified positions, men have stone and brick to protect them. In Barcelona, thousands upon thousands of bullets were fired, but few ever reached their marks, the bodies of the enemy. The artillery of either side, for their part, were constrained by having to avoid hitting their own men. This meant that bayonet charges were the prime cause of death—which shows, better than any speech ever could, how determined the "rebels" were. There was nothing to suggest that a further assault would be any less bloody or have a different outcome: Breaches stopped, the filthy rebel *canaille* again taking to the rampart tops to sing mock songs.

Jimmy never forgave Don Antonio for humbling him at Saint Clara that day. Having been denied victory, Jimmy now looked to point the finger. Verboom was called in. The Antwerp butcher knew the reason for the summons and began his defense before any attack could come. "I did say that the trench required further tweaking," he said, "and that it meant the assault would be premature."

But Verboom was wrong if he thought Jimmy would be the one to cross-examine him. The next person to speak was Dupuy, who had entered immediately after Verboom: "A bad engineer always blames his trench," he said.

Dupuy was very weak due to the loss of blood, and he had large swathes of bandages around his neck. It was the fifteenth wound he'd suffered in war. Had my bullet entered half an inch to the right, it would have been the last.

With some effort, Dupuy lowered himself into a chair. He opened a rolled-up document he was holding. "Just so you know, I plan to spend my convalescence studying these plans."

For one engineer to appropriate another's plans was beyond bad manners. "Those plans are of *my* trench!" protested Verboom.

"Yours?" said Dupuy. "Are you quite sure? If so, you're going to have to take responsibility for it." In spite of his wound, he spoke with a Bazoches voice, clear and precise. "Water has been found in the trenches; half the days have been spent digging at the earth, half bailing water. Then there is the fact that we have been losing between twenty and thirty dead and wounded a day to artillery fire, an unsustainable figure, and all of them highly trained—that is to say, irreplaceable—sappers. And the reason why? Because, sir, the parallels are excessively wide, and they are insufficiently deep, giving the enemy all the more to aim at. The losses are intolerable."

Verboom's attempts at protest fell on deaf ears.

"I could go on," said Dupuy, "endlessly, in fact, as to the malign subversions contained in these plans. To top it off, the very height of ridiculousness, the cuts between the third parallel and the 'gentlemen' beneath Saint Clara are so long, it's as though they've been designed expressly to invite a sortie against their flanks. You, sir, have created a trench that is akin to the Lord God creating man with the neck of a giraffe, so long and thin that the tiniest nick will mean decapitation." He threw the documents across the floor. "Sir! If you are the author of this trench, it can mean one of only two things: One, you are a negligent hotspur undeserving of the title of engineer, a man who, by some strange twist of fate, is in over his head. Or, even more criminal, if you are the author of this trench, then you are an enemy of the Two Crowns and in service of the archduke. You choose."

Verboom gave Jimmy a pleading look. In such cases, Jimmy's answer was to open his ruthless eyes very wide, not move his body, and let an ominous little smile spread across his lips. A smile, as I can say from experience, that would have made Genghis Khan turn pale. Instead of speaking, he said nothing, giving the floor to his victim to deliver an impossible justification.

"Perhaps . . ." stuttered Verboom, livid, cornered, " . . . perhaps some imposter has meddled with the design!"

"Ho!" said Jimmy, applauding. "Now I've heard it all. The kidnapper was kidnapped!" Jimmy could spit words like icicles when he chose to: "Out of my sight now, dullard."

In private, Jimmy and Dupuy were quite informal with each other. All hierarchy was forgotten.

"He'll be hanged, then?" asked Dupuy.

"No," said Jimmy, casting his gaze out over the embers of the battle. "Philip has already poured twenty million into this siege. Having his chief engineer killed would be too much. But—and you have my word on this—that man will never cross the Pyrenees again. He'll have to make do serving the maniac they've put on the throne in Madrid. Torment enough."

Words that condemned Verboom. Jimmy himself didn't know the extremes of cruelty his sentence would lead to. Thus, the Antwerp butcher, who had always sought to be beloved of his superiors and adored by the soldiery, spent the rest of his days miserably seeking the protection of a mad king against the rank and file, who thought of engineers as bricklayers and meddlers. This was his reward. Well, also, I later went after him and killed him—oh, I've already said?

Dupuy looked over Verboom's (my) plans, smiling and shaking his head.

"What are you smiling at?" said Jimmy scaldingly. "We've had a hiding, and you look as though you couldn't be happier."

Still looking at the paper, Dupuy said: "He was educated by my cousin. What did you expect?"

Jimmy exploded. "I *expected* that you would alter all the stunts hidden in that trench!"

"And I would have," said Dupuy, "if you'd given me time. In that, Verboom was right: A little self-restraint wouldn't have gone amiss in you. But Martí knew that was the one thing you'd lack, that you'd want a swift victory. Again Vauban trumps Coehoorn. And now we have only two options: Either we suspend the trench works, accepting that defeat as well, or we push on and correct the errors that have been made. And you know very well the lives that will cost." Again he tossed down the plans. "This is no trench, it's a labyrinth."

"No," said Jimmy, giving voice to his thoughts. "It's a knot."

13

Jimmy elected to take an ax to it, like the Gordian knot it was. This was Jimmy to a T. He'd been overhasty in unleashing the assault, spurred on both by his Coehoornian spirit and by political expedience.

But he was prepared to rectify the situation. Vauban? Coehoorn? In this instance, he was going to follow neither.

He lined up over a hundred cannons to crush any and every stone that lay in his way. His idea, doing away with any semblance of the art of siege warfare, consisted of flattening what was left of Barcelona's ramparts and bastions, paving the way for the Army of the Two Crowns to march in in battle formation, as in a battle in open country. It would take longer than the initial forecast, but did Jimmy mind that? He had all the time in the world. Saint Clara prompted him to renounce his designs on the throne of England. His place was in London, vying to be king, and yet here he was, his future in ruins because of a city that refused to play along.

There was nothing to be done in the face of such an onslaught; the principles of engineering became meaningless. It was the first time I saw Costa, our stoical parsley-chewing chief of artillery, lose hope. We ran into each other one day, and hunkering down as the walls detonated around us, he grabbed hold of my sleeve, imploring and accusatory, and bellowed in my ear: "I swore I'd hold them off as long as we were three against five. Now they've got nine cannons to every one of ours! For the love of God, what more do you want from us?"

I extricated myself without giving an answer. The Mallorcans carried on working miracles to the end. They'd fire their mortars and, before the enemy had time to pinpoint where the shots were coming from, change position before taking aim once more. They destroyed several Bourbon cannons daily. The shells would go off on the French and Spanish gunners' toes, making a hash of their bodies and lifting the cannons themselves to Babelian heights.

How grand, how majestic a sight: that of heavy artillery tossed in the air! We saw ten-foot iron or bronze barrels twirl through the sky, along with their crews. We saw parabolas of gun carriages lovelier than Jacob's wheel. Up on his balcony, watching with his telescope, being the aesthete he was, Jimmy couldn't have cared less whether they came to land on the broken-down farmhouses of Catalonia, or if they ended up lodged in the sun over France.

And yet, and yet, in the end the skill of the Mallorcans would all be for naught. The Bourbons had inexhaustible resources, of machinery as much as of men. Whereas every one of the Mallorcan gunners we lost was irreplaceable. They were peculiar folk, the Mallorcans, and never said a single word about their dead.

Jimmy resorting to that firestorm took the situation one step closer to the absurd. The siege was no longer a duel between thinking minds but, rather, a steady stream of devastation. I received the order from Don Antonio to withdraw from the front line, and he was quite right: The enemy's new strategy rendered any technical course of action useless. We had gone beyond the civilized and rational. "Perfection can be reached only by going beyond the merely human dimension," Don Antonio had said. Certainly Jimmy's approach, all powerful and at the same time atavistic, destructive, and simply berserk, was dragging the situation beyond all limits. And here is a thing worthy of note: On the first day I was away from the point of attack, I felt a sickness settle on me, as though I were in need of the pain that had been racking me.

So, being of no use to those battered ramparts, I moved back inside the city. We hadn't checked in on the enemy's mining endeavors for a long time. I'd always had a strong dislike for mines. Vauban had no truck with them, and whether we want to or not, we take on the likes and dislikes of our teachers. The marquis saw mines as decoys and therefore ungentlemanly. According to him, the enemy must be beaten head-on; underhand tactics were not acceptable. On top of which, to a mind as supremely rational as his, a *moyen si incertain* was intolerable.

Mines have their fair share of proponents. Should the besieging army succeed in drilling a tunnel underneath the enemy walls and packing it with explosives, the battlements will fall—by surprise, and avoiding all risks. The hardships usually associated with a siege, over in an instant. And in a thundering, apocalyptic manner—not subject to appeal. I've known Maganons who dreamed of packing fifty thousand pounds of explosives into a mine. Proof that even the most exact science can go overboard; were they looking to blow the walls or the entire city, or what?

You can understand the fervor of those who argue for mines. A mine is employed with the certainty of saving time and lives. In practice, and according to what I've seen, this is never the case. Drilling a subterranean tunnel consumes all manner of resources, and without fail, some of those must be taken from the Attack Trench works; in an effort to save time, you only cause delays. Then there is the fact that the besieged will take their own measures. As Vauban put it: on the road to glory, there are no shortcuts.

There was one other reason why Longlegs Zuvi loathed mines. That reason being, of all the ways humans have devised to end one another's lives, there are none more sinister or terrifying than underground combat.

You'd smell miners before you saw them. They spent such long periods underground that their skin gave off a warm stench; you didn't need your senses honed in Bazoches to detect them. They were known as *Los Cucs*—The Worms. What was their brigade leader called? Buggered if I can recall.

Los Cucs hadn't had much success. We knew the enemy was working on a large mine and that it was aiming between Saint Clara and Portal Nou. Knowing Jimmy, if they did reach their destination, the explosion would make that of the night of August 15 seem like a tiny spark off a flint. I asked to be brought up to speed by the captain of *Los Cucs*. What *was* his name? Strange, the things we forget. His men looked haggard and hollow-eyed, and to be presented with reinforcements was a great lift to them.

The objective of countermines is to identify the position of the enemy mine and disable it. Underground labyrinth warfare, this, with far more recourse to fire, smoke, and daggers than rifles and bullets. *Los Cucs* had initiated several tunnels but not yet managed to hit the Bourbon's primary gallery.

"Don't you worry about digging any more galleries," the captain said to me. "Going and sounding out the walls will be more than sufficient. If you find something, you come and let us know. We'll see to the rest."

Men with experience have always commanded my respect—far more than the bookish kind. I nodded and went and spoke with Ballester and his men.

"You come behind me," I said. "Every man is to bring one grenade, a dagger, and two loaded pistols, that's all."

The entrance to our mine was located inside a house that had been blown up, just inside the city walls, the idea being to avoid the prying eyes of any Bourbon spies. The captain of *Los Cucs*—I simply *cannot* recall that man's name—had readied some equipment for us. Very valuable material, and we would need to take care of it. Ignorant Ballester laughed when he saw it. "You're going down there with eight canes and . . . what are those? Plates? Four plates with holes in the middle?"

"These aren't canes and plates," I said, not looking at him. "These are sounding lines, and these are plugs. And extremely valuable they are too."

Down in the narrow confines of the mine, silence was essential. Before descending, I gathered Ballester's men and tried to teach them the rudiments of the sign language of engineers. I could not. I was so afraid that my fingers trembled, and I had to give up on the idea. Very embarrassing. The men, in a circle, regarded me, expecting some kind of instruction that would enable them to face whatever inferno we were about to go down into. I was their most direct line of authority; I was supposed to be showing them the way to return to the world of the living. I looked at that vertical black shaft, and my mind was filled with all the things we might encounter down there: a trench, but maze-like, and beneath the earth, with all kinds of nooks and crannies. And Bourbons who would show no mercy, infinitely more numerous and experienced in underground combat than we were. And even perhaps fifty thousand pounds of gunpowder, ready to go up the very moment we reached the chamber. The thought of it made me shudder violently.

After that time, never have I set foot in a mine or a countermine again. Once, in the Barcelona of 1714, was enough. And that time, in front of those manly Miquelets, I wept like a child. But would you like to guess what happened?

The Miquelets were incredibly good about it. And it wasn't mere tolerance for my bleak view of things—sincerity was far more important to them than any authority. They thought I was afraid because I didn't trust them, and they responded like remorseful children.

"Captain Ballester and I will go first," I said, feigning enthusiasm. "Then the rest of you. Got it?"

Down we went. A ladder, which, to save wood, had been made with fewer rungs than it needed, led us down into the gallery.

All the manuals say that the primary tunnel ought to be wide enough for two miners to move along side by side: one carrying the tools, the other a lamp and a pistol, lighting the way and protecting the other if need be. Manuals! A lot of help they are! The tunnel was so narrow, it pressed against your shoulders. Ballester had to walk behind, with me carrying the tools and the lamp. We shuffled along forty or fifty feet. Feeling stifled, struggling to breathe as if on the gallows once more, I halted.

We were only ten or fifteen feet under the ground, but it was hot as an oven. We could feel the artillery exchanges going on as they reverberated the ground. A fine shower of loose earth was falling from the poorly braced ceiling. I felt sure it was going to cave in.

Zuvi, good old Zuvi, wasn't born to crawl along on his belly. The air became more and more stifling, and I felt invisible pincers gripping my throat. Under the ground, my Bazoches senses were worthless or as good as; the darkness was a leveler, reducing all men to moles. Those guttering lamps in our hands seemed less to light the way than make apparent just how dark it was. And given that my sight could usually take in as much as that of four men at once, to lose it was all the more crippling.

Somehow managing to turn and look behind me, I saw that lunatic Ballester in fits of laughter, though he was keeping his voice down. He pointed around us; it had finally dawned on him why, in the early stages of the siege, I'd insisted on the looting of furniture from houses across the city. The braces for this long, winding tunnel were made from the beams and planks we ourselves had removed. Window frames made the perfect tunnel supports, girding the roof and the sides. Table legs buttressed the walls.

I pushed on, bringing us through into a corridor that seemed to go on forever. Then we came to a fork. I chose the right branch.

I halted somewhere along the way and set one of the plugs against the tunnel wall. Putting my ear against the ceramic part of the large plate and hunching myself over it, I gestured for Ballester to be quiet. His men piled up behind him, their curiosity overcoming any battle seasoning.

It's hard to believe the number of sounds that can travel through earth. They were redoubled by the ceramic, which acted like a micro-scope for acoustics. I introduced the first of the canes through the hole in the center of the plate. The earth was soft, and the cane, or sounding line, passed easily into it, traveling farther and farther into the wall. Once it was all the way in, I screwed the next one onto its bottom and resumed pushing. Then another sounding line, then another. Finally, I could tell, combining my senses of hearing and touch, that the lines in series had come out into a space; the resistance of compacted earth wasn't there anymore. Then I had to feed a thinnish piece of cable down the center of the line, thereby clearing the earth out of it. And when that was done, withdrawing the cable, I could look along the interior of the line, which functioned like a periscope.

The only thing I could tell was that it was an enemy gallery—flickering lights, movements, shadows. I could hear as much as see them. But they were there, all right.

Dark bodies came across my field of vision. I could hear their picks, and the sound of baskets full of earth being dragged along. Their presence became more and more sharply defined, details such as someone clearing his throat.

"What on earth are you doing?" whispered Ballester.

The movements I was making must have struck him as strange. I'd put my eye up to the end of the line for the briefest moment, then pull my head back, and again go to the line—back and forth, like a chicken pecking for seeds. I gestured for him to be quiet.

Too late. Perhaps they heard Ballester, or perhaps they saw my line poking through into their gallery; whatever it was, within moments they had sent a line of their own in our direction, and it emerged into our gallery between Ballester and me. A tubular worm poking through into the space, a metal circle no wider than a thumb and forefinger. And yet what a terrifying thing, for it meant that we'd been discovered.

That little tube of metal—apparently inoffensive—signified death. The men at the far end were killers, and they had sniffed us out. French sappers, veterans of a thousand skirmishes, possibly trained by Vauban himself. And what adeptness they showed: The moment they'd heard or perhaps only sensed us, one sank a sounding line into the wall and located us at the first attempt. I was paralyzed with fear.

Ballester understood what was happening and responded in typical fashion: He inserted his pistol into the opening at the end of the enemy line and pulled the trigger. We heard cries. Ballester's bullet had doubtless hit the enemy sapper in the eye. Perhaps now my chicken-head movements will make sense. Indignation among the dead man's colleagues, shouts, insults. I decided to skip the niceties: "Back, back!" I cried. "Get out, before they smoke us out!"

I by no means ordered the retreat for the sake of it. On top of my habitual cowardice, there was what I'd been taught at Bazoches.

When a brigade of miners locates the opponent's gallery, it will proceed to drill a small *trou*, that is, a hole. Into this hole, a bolus of pine needles will be introduced—the size of a cannonball, smeared with pitch and on fire—and stuffed all the way through. Innocuous it might seem, but far from it. In such narrow spaces, smoke becomes a lethal weapon. In under a minute, all breathable air will have been consumed; the men will pass out and die from suffocation. And if the lack of air doesn't kill them, the enemy will, breaking into the gallery as soon as the smoke has cleared and knifing the fallen bodies.

The French miners had far more expertise than the Miquelets in such matters; they'd be sure to drill a smoke hole far more quickly than we would. And as it says in the manual of good old Zuvi, if you cannot win a race, best to run in the opposite direction. And be quick about it!

We shuffled out of there like centipedes, reaching the ladder just in time. As soon as we were back above earth, the mine shaft began to vomit black smoke, like an underground chimney.

All I said to Ballester was: "How *did* you know it's standard procedure to shoot your pistol along an enemy sounding line like that?"

"I didn't."

Feeling ever bleaker, I went and sat in the corner of the abandoned house, head in hands. The Miquelets, not understanding my despondency, tried to console me. I let out a bitter laugh. "You'll soon get it," I said.

Los Cucs soon showed up, and their captain asked me how it had gone.

"What?" he cried. "You've given away the whereabouts of one of our galleries? And they smoked you out?" He looked despairing. "Do you know what it took for us to make that tunnel? All that work, ruined in half an hour! How am I supposed to lead my men down into a gallery that the enemy has detected? We'll have to block it up and start a whole new one! What kind of imbeciles has the government sent me?"

The final days down in the mine comprised unutterable horrors. Worst of all were the reproachful glances I got from the leader of *Los Cucs* (his name is still a blank!) when we went back down the shaft.

Above, ramparts that might succumb at any moment; below, a hidden deposit of gunpowder, tons of it, that might blow before we found it. One day when we were about to go underground again, I told Ballester's men to wait: There were voices rising up out of the mine, distorted by how far underground they were, but clearly not belonging to *Los Cucs*. The Miquelets pointed their guns down into the shaft.

Everyone was silent. I placed my ear to the entrance of the shaft. Whispers in French and Catalan. The Bourbons had plenty of *botifleros* in their service, so it would make sense to use some of them in the mines.

The Miquelets' fingers were on their triggers, guns encircling the shaft entrance. Then a head appeared, and it had fair and very knotty hair. He looked up at me and said in a happy voice: "Hello, *jefe*! What are you doing here?"

Behind Anfán came Nan, and behind them several *Cucs*. I was speechless. Their leader explained. "The boy and the dwarf save us all kinds of work. They're so small and agile, we can send them into the tiniest shafts and have them listen for enemies. You know them? Why are you looking at me like that?"

This sparked the final fight between Amelis and me. Dashing to the beach with long Zuvi strides, I found her in line at the camp mess.

The only free food provided by the government was a bland fish soup. The line was strictly regimented—the Red Pelts had posted a guard to see that no one got too much—a couple of ladlefuls was the maximum. Amelis ignored me totally. She was so exhausted that her eyes were violet-red, and all her attention was focused on the back of the person in front of her. I grabbed her by the arm and dragged her out of the line. Then she came to life, thrashing around desperately, trying to get clear of me. Her scrawny body felt light as a feather.

Amelis's place in the line was taken immediately by the unscrupulous woman behind her. When Amelis saw she'd lost her place, her legs gave way. She fell to her knees on the sand and wept, her skirts spread out around her like the petals of an open flower.

"Anfán!" I cried. "How could you have let him enlist?"

"*Déu meu, Déu meu,*" she sobbed.

"He's joined up!" I went on. "He'll be killed down in those mines!"

She looked up at me, her face wet with tears. "Want to know how long I've been in line? Since midday yesterday!"

"We took him away from war, from being a trench rat!" I replied. "And all for him to end up dead from an explosion or from a bullet in the head. The French sappers aren't playing games down there!"

She threw her metal bowl in my face. "I was here all yesterday, all last night, and all this morning. And you come and yank me out of the line! What are we supposed to eat? Tell me that!"

It was pointless trying to reason with her—it was the hunger speaking, not Amelis. She barely had the energy to argue. She hung her head like a small dying animal.

Half of the soup rations was apportioned to the wounded and sick in the hospital. It was becoming more watered down daily, and they were using fresh water from the last irrigation canal still coming into the city. The Bourbons had dammed all but one, and that they'd been polluting by placing dead bodies upstream. But the poor gulped it down like nectar—anything to avoid the husk *torta.*

While we'd been arguing, the crowds of people had ebbed away. The woman who had taken Amelis's place in line was the last to be given soup. The people behind her were all protesting. There was uproar, but only in a minor way: The people were so depleted that a couple of blows from the guards dispersed them. Amelis's sobbing gave way to a torrent of tears.

I'd have to take it up with Anfán himself. I ought to point out how much time had passed since I'd encountered him at Tortosa: That was in 1708, and it was now 1714. I roughly estimated that he'd been born at the turn of the century, and that the eight-year-old was now four-teen. He wasn't a child any longer.

When Anfán appeared out of the mineshaft, I begged the leader of the *Cucs* to discharge him. I could hardly blame him for his response, which was one of surprise: "We're so short on troops, why would we turn away anyone of military age?"

Fourteen was the age when a Catalan could legally bear arms. After the years he'd spent under our roof, when we'd taken good care of him and taught him manners, Anfán had turned into quite an impressive young man. I kick myself for not having noticed sooner. If you stare at the grass day after day, you'll miss the fact it's growing. After all, parents always see their children as the babies they once were.

A frontal assault would have been pointless, so I came at him an-other way, with conversation and affection. We had a long discussion about the mining operation. Anfán filled me in at length: *Los Cucs* had been saving time by creating diminutive tunnels on either side of the main mines and sending Nan and Anfán down them. Whenever they found one of the Bourbon galleries, they'd drill through to it, starting overhead and angling the fist-width cavity downward, and then roll two or three grenades in with the fuses lit, before crawling quickly back the way they'd come.

The story made me smile but also shudder. In mine warfare, the combatants, though faceless, soon got to know their opponents by the techniques they used. I felt sure that the Bourbons would have put a price on the heads of these two rats by now.

"So you don't care about Nan, is that right?" I asked, smiling coldly. "At this very moment, there must be dozens of enemy miners thinking of ways to kill the both of you."

Anfán threw his arms wide, ready to take me on. "Dozens? I thought it would be thousands. Casanova's son is fourteen, and he was made drummer of a regiment."

I couldn't contain myself: "And Casanova went and saw him off in person! He pulled some strings so they'd be sent away from the city! They're now garrisoning a place called Cardona!"

And I wasn't lying, either. The Red Pelts loved demonstrating their Homeric virtues: Sending troops out into other parts of Catalonia was like saying to Jimmy that the people of Barcelona had more than enough courage, constancy, and resolve to overcome anything he cared to throw at them. (You can imagine what Don Antonio thought about our own leaders giving men leave.) The fact was, at Cardona, one of the few places the Generalitat still controlled, no fighting was taking place. The Bourbons knew as well as we did that if Barcelona fell, the rest of Catalonia would subside with it, and therefore they dedicated no resources to the outgrowths of "rebellion" elsewhere.

I grabbed Anfán by the arms. "Am I the *jefe*? Say it. Am I or not?"

Truly, he had grown older. He answered me gravely. "Yes, *jefe*, you absolutely are. All right, I won't go back down the mine." He made the sign of the cross. "I swear."

I didn't believe a word of it.

The next day, a small troop of *Cucs,* just four men, finally identified the whereabouts of the primary enemy mine, or Royal Mine, a gallery containing a hundred barrels of gunpowder covered in soaked hide. *Los Cucs* managed to slit the guards' throats and, having set a charge to collapse the ceiling, ghosted the barrels away. Mine found, mine destroyed.

This was the last thing to cheer about. Church bells throughout the city chimed the victory. The *Cucs* heroes' names were Francisco Diago, one of our Aragonese; Josep Mateu, a native of Barcelona; and the man who had led them, the leader of the *Cucs*—what was his name? What a shame not to be able to remember such a sublime warrior! . . . And the fourth of the crew, naturally, was Anfán. Having crawled along one of the small antechambers, he had been the one to hit upon the Royal Mine. How would you have reacted? Would you have told him off or applauded? I chose to do neither.

For the thousandth time, dear vile Waltraud makes me stop. Am I not allowed even a brief moment to enjoy the memory of that rare victory?

What's that you say? How strange that I remember the names of the lower-ranking *Cucs* but not that of the leader? That it's suspicious for a memory as prodigious as mine not to have retained that hero's name, the man who won the city a stay of execution? That maybe I'm pretending and not saying his name because I didn't like the man?

All right, all right!

You are quite right. I set myself to be sincere, fully, and I will be.

The *Cucs* hero was Francesc Molina, and he was the son of a couple who had married in Barcelona but moved back to their native country. They identified so strongly with the city that their son, as did so many other foreigners, had come to fight there, even engaging in mine warfare for the sake of the Catalan capital. He'd fought tooth and nail, day after day, night after night, and finally managed to locate that lethal mound of explosives.

What's that? Where were the Molinas from?

I see, I see, you want me humiliated fully and utterly.

I give in.

The Molinas were from Naples.

14

I, Martí Zuviría, engineer (let's save ourselves the long-winded titles) consent to the following things:

That national extractions are quite random and have no bearing on the character of peoples.

That the vast majority of the Italians I have met are good God-loving creatures, upstanding, trustworthy, decent, and that no one has the right to blame defects or personal slights on whole communities.

And, so that it is set down in writing, I hereby retract any insidious claims there might be in this book with regard to Neapolitans, Italians, and foreigners in general, French, Germans, Castilians, Moors, Jews, Maoris, Oglaga, Dutch, Chinese, Persian.

The other option, correcting the sullied pages, would be a recourse that my parlous finances would not allow.

Happy now? Make you feel good, imposing your will on this shredded bag of bones, as good as on his deathbed? Lo and behold, we end like this: I, the author, begging the forgiveness of the one scribbling down my words.

Yes, all right, you're right: Let's move on. Finish the tale. There's one last tear to cry.

On September 3, 1714, all our seas parted. And the thing that provoked it was neither cannibal hunger, nor an enemy victory, nor an exhausted population giving in. The cause, paradoxically, was a magnanimous gesture by Jimmy.

A messenger came from the enemy encampment that day. Jimmy warned us to surrender or suffer an attack with unimaginable consequences. The text itself was brief and intimidating, with no room for mercy: Give in, or we'd all have our throats cut, right down to the unborn children. But there's one thing I ought to be clear about, to do with the rules that govern a siege.

The ultimate aim of an Attack Trench is to force the besieged city to sue for peace, or, as the French say, *battre la chamade*. In such circumstances, with the trench reaching as far as the city moat, and the ramparts on the verge of collapse, terms are sought to try and safeguard the remaining vestiges. Life, honor, and if possible, a little property. Otherwise the attacking army has every right to enter the city and pillage and rape as much as it pleases. A *chamade* avoids this extreme. War etiquette—which, in my day, was adhered to by all, barring Pópuli, that animal, and his pro-Philip generals—requires that any besieged position that sues for peace will at least keep intact the lives of its remaining population and the honor of its garrison.

It was an unusual thing for Jimmy to do, because it was never the besieging army but the besieged who would carry out a *battre la chamade*. The straits we were in justified Jimmy's decision. But by being the one to send the messenger, and not the other way around, he was opening the door to negotiations. And at that, a negotiation that promised more than the bare minimum. Bravery and constancy always bring some reward: The battle in August had made Jimmy fear that his troops might be massacred. Victory might cost him half the army, and neither Little Philip nor the Beast would be overly pleased at losing their most distinguished officers. Further, if it did come to that, the Bourbon rank and file would be enraged and uncontainable in their desire to take revenge by sacking the city. They would lay waste to Barcelona. And

Jimmy didn't like the idea of the same philosophers he'd been raised among calling him a savage.

The message was written in arrogant and threatening terms, but Don Antonio saw its real meaning. The enemy would discuss terms! Exultant, he called the high command together, looking for them to take a unanimous proposal to the government. As his aide-de-camp, I was also present.

Don Antonio began by pointing out what a unique opportunity it was. It would be beyond insane to let it pass by. We were in a position to save the city, its inhabitants, and even possibly one or two other things besides. Negotiating wasn't a job for the military but for politicians, so our task was to make sure the government understood they couldn't ignore this chance. It would be the last, and it might avert a catastrophe of biblical proportions.

I remember Don Antonio smiling—a rare sight! All our hardships had not been for nothing, all our struggles had borne fruit: The enemy was willing to enter discussions. If our diplomats were worth their salt, the core of the Catalan constitutions and liberties might, might, be upheld.

But the meeting with the high command did not go well. I remember the large rectangular table, packed tightly around with officers. Their uniforms clean but in tatters, and everyone gaunt. Not one of them went along with their commander in chief's suggestion. Not one could look him in the eye. It wasn't that they doubted his authority, he was still revered, but they simply weren't in agreement with the idea of surrendering.

Don Antonio refused to give up yet, and he turned to Casanova to urge a vote in the council. Casanova went along with it, but coolly; he knew better than anyone the leanings of Barcelona's so very isocratic government.

The vote was a landslide—in the wrong direction. Of thirty representatives, only three were in favor of Casanova's motion to negotiate with the Bourbons: It was twenty-six against four. For only three to vote with the head of the government said everything about Casanova's isolated position. In such circumstances, how could policies ever be enforced?

Everything was topsy-turvy now: The only people willing to end the war were the generals.

The news came to us the following day: Don Antonio had stood down. In the face of the inevitable disaster to come, he sent word to the government: Honor prevented him from taking charge of a rout. Therefore, with all military means exhausted, he requested to be put aboard a ship. He'd waive all moneys owed along with all privileges.

I view this as one last attempt to win them over: Either they negotiate or lose him. Unfortunately, the situation had gone beyond all reasonable bounds. The government merely assented: If he wanted to stand down, they would provide him with a couple of swift ships, and he could try and slip through the blockade. Our small, easily maneuverable ships were always used whenever evacuating anyone important, the French ships' hulls being too deep for them to venture into the shallows. The small Catalan vessels would depart under cover of dark, hugging the coast, and sail through the night in the direction of Mallorca.

I was so stunned by the news, I almost thought it was a prank. Don Antonio was leaving us! Dumbfounded, I didn't ask who was replacing him. I could imagine no one capable of taking the role, and indeed, no one was whom they appointed. That is: The Virgin Mary was proclaimed commander in chief.

The Virgin Mary! It had to be a joke. But no, anything but. Martí Zuviría, educated in all the possible nuances of compass and telescope, in precisely displacing exact amounts of earth, would from now on be taking orders from the mother of Jesus.

In the small hours of the next morning, while I was taking an uncomfortable nap against a battlement wall, a liaison officer came and woke me. "Don Antonio is boarding a boat and wishes to see you."

There were chests and trunks piled up in his courtyard, ready to be taken down to the port. Officers hurried in and out of the premises; even at this late stage, Don Antonio was keeping abreast of the situation on the ramparts. I found it strange seeing him dressed in full regalia now that he was no longer general. It is, and always will be, my belief that he clung to the hope that the government would change its mind and reinstate him. To the last instant. Seeing me, he said: "Have you not heard? Then I'll tell you: I'm no longer commanding the forces of Barcelona. Someone else will be giving the orders."

"Who? The Virgin?"

He was moved. Unusually for him, he made the effort to pronounce "son" properly in Catalan. "Be content, *fiyé*. Now that I am a private citizen, you can call me Don Antonio, as you've always wanted."

"Thank you, General," I said, grinding my teeth on the irony in my words. "You can't imagine how happy that makes me."

Unfazed, he adjusted his sword in his belt. "Didn't you hear? I'm not your commander anymore, I'm Don Antonio to you now. All these years I've been slapping your wrist when you have had the impertinence to call me that, and now you can. From now on I am, to you and to anybody else, just another citizen. Don Antonio, if that's what you wish. Understand?"

"Loud and clear, General." And I added: "From today, I'm allowed to address you as a simple fellow citizen, General."

For a brief second, emotion seemed to creep into his mien. The ongoing cannon fire added melancholic urgency to his reflections. For I had spoken on behalf of all who loved him. During the time he had commanded armed civilians, they had considered him one of their own, another Barcelonan. And now that he was leaving, the least obedient of these Barcelonans had shown him his true standing, not so much in a military as a moral sense.

Of course, a man like Don Antonio wouldn't allow himself to be overcome by emotion. He began pacing up and down. As he spoke, he became increasingly incensed. "I've done everything I can, I've argued and begged, I've warned the government of all the ills to come! Defending this city is pure madness now! Staying would mean signing my men's death warrants. Leaving, I abandon them. What have I done to deserve such ignominy?"

I tried to calm him down. It was then that he revealed the real reason he'd sent for me.

"I saved you from bondage once before, at Illueca. I see no reason why I shouldn't do so once more. We'll wake tomorrow in Mallorca, and after that go on to Italy, and from there to court. In Vienna, all your unpaid wages will be seen to: Remember that yours was a royal conscription, not a municipal one. Which means your allegiance is not to Barcelona, and to board a ship would not constitute desertion. And, when I am given a post in the imperial army, I will want an engineer on my staff."

Before I could speak, he went on: "You have a wife and children, as I do. There are a number of spare berths on the ships. Go and gather up your family, and do it now." He bade me hurry with a wave of the hand.

I stayed where I was. Knowing what that meant, he demanded I explain myself. I remember the way my voice didn't seem to belong to me: "General, I cannot," I said.

He looked me up and down, and finally, our eyes met.

"I don't understand. Your temperament is entirely opposed to that of the brave men out there still fighting. The city is being sacrificed, and to what end? Answer me that!"

I did not know what to say.

"So starved you've eaten your own tongue?" he went on, raising his voice. "What makes you want to be a part of the carnage now? You've always been against it. What? You've always been the first to support any retreat! Why stay? Tell me your reasoning!"

In spite of myself, I said nothing. Don Antonio insisted. "Say something, even if just a word. One word, Lord above, at least give me a word!"

One word. Seven years on, and Vauban, in the shape of Don Antonio, was asking me that question again. I blinked, cleared my throat. I racked my brains, but nothing.

I'd unwittingly inflicted more pain on an already suffering soul, an immaculate hero whose very honor was forcing him to depart. Even Martí Zuviría, prince among cowards, had decided to stand and fight. A contrast that undoubtedly would have pained him.

Bewildered, I put my tricorn on my head and, without asking his permission, made to leave. He stopped me: "Wait. You were with me at the Toledo retreat and at Brihuega as well. And you've been with me throughout this siege. It's only right you share in my punishment."

And it was quite some punishment: Before he left, he wanted to bid the troops farewell. Don Antonio de Villarroel, the perfect warrior, had to tell his men that he was abandoning them to the inferno while he sailed away to a palace somewhere. Hard as it would be, nothing in the world would prevent him from bidding that farewell, even if they were going to insult, condemn, and revile him.

We left his residence, and someone brought us horses. We both mounted up, and settling on his saddle, Don Antonio said: "Let's go to it."

Spoken like a martyr. I'm certain that what he wanted was a famous death, the chance to die taking part in some heroic action. Instead, fate had presented him with a pitiful exit through the back door. We rode side by side. As we approached the ramparts, and in breach of all protocol, I grabbed him by the forearm and said: "General, this isn't necessary."

Offended, he threw my hand clear. "Let me go! I have never in all my days fled an enemy. Am I to do so now, from my own men?"

He spurred his horse on, and I followed. I was consumed by worry—not for myself but for Don Antonio. Very few knew the straits he was in, leaving not out of fear but because there was no way for him not to.

We came to the foot of the ramparts. By some miracle, there was a pause in the fighting. Up on Saint Clara, Portal Nou, and the intervening wall, heads turned. At the sight of Don Antonio, they began to gather at the rear of the remaining fortifications. Once they were all there, crammed together and listening, Don Antonio tried to speak, but words failed him. Something in him broke.

His horse began rearing, and Don Antonio barely managed to steady it. Pinching the bridge of his nose as if to stifle the emotions, he again tried to speak. Again the words wouldn't come.

At certain rare moments, time stands still. Up on the bastions and ramparts stood those hundreds of skeletal men, thinner than the rifles they were carrying. Gaunt faces and tricorns tattered and rent by bullets and grapeshot. Uniforms dull with soot and ash, sleeves only barely attached to the rest of their jackets. And the smell. Like long-dead carrion. Right down to the last drummer, they'd heard the news: Their commander was departing. What did he have to say? Hundreds of them, they all kept their eyes fixed on Don Antonio.

And after weeks and weeks in which the sun had beaten down mercilessly and not a cloud had been seen, fat drops of rain began to fall. A great crowd had gathered, and yet you could hear the raindrops land. The stones of the city, warmed by a year of artillery fire, smoldered in the downpour. Nobody blinked.

For the third time, Don Antonio tried to find the words. There was a moment when it seemed like the skin on his face would fall from it. Still mute, he exposed his head, lifting off his tricorn with his right hand, saluting the gathered men. His horse skittered nervously, its rider keeping his hat high in the air as the rain continued to fall. He said nothing; there was nothing more. The only thing left for Don Antonio was to depart. For the men of the Coronela, it was back to manning the walls.

Spurring his horse forward, Don Antonio rode along the interior of the ramparts. His hand still in the air, bearing his tricorn aloft, bidding farewell to the citizen army he'd led for so long. I decided to catch up with him. I rode on his right side, between him and the ramparts. Ridiculous, but I thought by putting my body between him and them, even if there were some soldier in deep despair, it might stop them from shooting the departing general from his saddle. What a difference between this and that long-ago battle of Brihuega in 1710, when Zuvi the rat rode with Don Antonio between *him* and enemy bullets.

I hadn't quite caught him when a roar went up. I lifted my head.

The men of the Coronela, Castilians, Aragonese, Valencians, and Germans, all waving their rifles above their heads. And they weren't cursing Don Antonio but cheering for him. A piecemeal clamor, formless, consisting of just his first name, repeated—*Don Antonio! Don Antonio! Don Antonio!*—that grew louder and louder. The rain intensified, and with it, the commotion. Don Antonio was overcome and spurred his horse on to escape the ovation. Catching up with him, I saw something I thought I'd never see in all my days: The man was crying.

Don Antonio crying! I thought oak trees would dance before it came to that! Noticing that I'd seen his tears, he tried to justify himself: "My one desire is to stay with them, but honor prevents me. I cannot act as commander to a defense that has moved out of the realms of bravery and become sheer recklessness. Nor could I ever forgive myself for putting so many innocent lives at risk."

We left the ramparts behind. The rain continued to fall. Calming his horse with unhappy caresses, Don Antonio whispered to himself, seemingly unaware of me: "I hope those ships never come," he said. "That way I might die shoulder to shoulder with these men, like any other soldier."

Don Antonio bade his men farewell on the eighth, and between then and the eleventh, that dismal September eleventh, the rain fell nonstop, all day and all night.

What a contrast from the inferno that August had been. To begin with, it was a balm, refreshing and relieving us, bringing life where before there had been only the stifling heat. All exposed gunpowder dampened, the Bourbon shelling was briefly suspended. But the downpour also transformed our environment into one of mud and darkness, making the place all the more inhospitable.

The breaches in the walls were a sight to behold. There were five of them, each between a hundred and two hundred feet wide. As many as 687 men would be able to pass through them shoulder to shoulder (don't be surprised at the exactitude of the 687, a Bazoches calculation); that is, roughly two regiments in battle formation.

And there was no way of plugging such gaps. We threw hundreds of spiked wooden bats down into them, spiked with six-inch nails. The workers threw them as far as they could, to try not to expose themselves to enemy fire, even if that meant the placing was not very exact. Thus we made spike-fields of the ground in the gaps.

Dripping wet, beneath dark skies, I continued giving instructions to the living dead manning the defenses. Everyone was worn out, which made it deeply unpleasant having to force them to carry on plugging the gaps. On the city side of each, we dug a ditch and stacked *fajinas* along it, and behind, another ditch, another *fajina* parapet, and another. We made a good number of these, all equally fragile. At certain chosen positions, we placed "organs," which was the name for the invention of a certain local Archimedes.

Essentially, "organs" were wooden platforms with ten or fifteen loaded rifles lined up along them. A thin piece of string ran along all the triggers. A single yank—anyone could do it, even an ancient like

Peret—and a synchronous volley would be fired into the invaded area. It was never likely to be very effective, but at that late stage, we had far more weapons remaining than we did men.

There was one final feat. With Don Antonio gone, I felt free to fight on my own account. I'd learned that, in the desperate defense of a city, everything, rocks, flesh, and even blood are brought to bear. Why not the very elements?

I took aside the workers who were in the best condition. We used the last reserves of wood to create a long canal, paving it with overlapping timbers. The rain meant well water didn't have to be saved, and this aqueduct of ours ran from one of the largest municipal reservoirs out as far as the ramparts. We opened the sluices one night, and a torrent of water inundated the enemy's forward positions. Water gushed over the "gentlemen," and into the cuts, and then the trenches, taking people, *fajina* baskets, and armatures with it. A flood during the night is all the more fearsome. The Bourbons couldn't have known what was going on; besides, what purpose could it possibly serve to shoot at a torrent of water?

The forward part of the trenches became a sewer. At points, the water was chest-deep. A whole day was spent by the enemy bailing out that putrid water. One day, which for us meant one more day in the world of the living. A victory, however brief. Though inside the city, we were so weary, we didn't even have the energy to celebrate it.

While the Bourbons wallowed in the mud, I went and found Costa. I'd never seen him looking so downcast. Francesc Costa, a man who needed nothing but his sprig of parsley to be content.

"Come, Costa," I said, trying to cheer him up. "We've come too far to give up. Prepare guns and munitions."

But he was sitting down, letting the rain fall on his uncovered head, soaked through and hugging himself as though he had a fever. "Munitions. Munitions, you say?" he spat sarcastically. "I haven't even got parsley left to chew. That trench was it for us."

This reference to my handiwork pained me. "The cannons!" I suddenly shouted, and leaving aside all formalities, I went on: "Place them behind the breaches and forget everything else!"

When things become desperate, rumors have the power to displace hope. Dreams. People began saying that an English fleet was on the way and that Charles had sent a German legion. All lies. The anguished multitudes rushed to Plaza del Born, at the center of the city, praying for Barcelona to be saved. Inanities. Deep down, those of us manning the breaches didn't believe in anything, we just fought.

And a good thing that Jimmy's artillery volcano had been extinguished. As I've said, the damp gunpowder prevented them from shelling us for a short time. In place of projectiles, they hurled taunts and threats our way. They were positioned at the crown of the ditch, and their shouts carried across that short distance. They could not have been more than a hundred feet from what remained of the ramparts.

The boldest among them peeked their heads over the tops of the "gentlemen," at the trench's most forward point, and made throat-slitting gestures or waved their fists. And said to us, in grimmest tones: "*Ça va être votre fête!*"

On the night of September 10, I did not sleep. Could not. You didn't need great powers of intuition to guess the final assault would begin at any moment. One of the things we'd done in anticipation was to pull back a number of the most exposed positions. It would be suicide to have groups of men so close to the Bourbon "gentlemen." In the most devastated areas, we chose to create a retreat space for the men who would be receiving the first wave. So that night there was a kind of dead space between our lines and Jimmy's.

I've seen a large number of bombarded landscapes in my time, and the exceptional thing about this one was the outline of the ruins. Even the heaviest artillery usually only pierces rooftops and smashes ramparts, leaving sharp and pointed silhouettes. But when a barrage is so intense and has been carried out over such a long time, the edges take on an undulating bluntness, as though eroded over thousands of years. A very fine drizzle continued to fall over that labyrinth of ruins. The night was black, the moon hidden behind the weeping clouds. My feet slipped among smashed gun carriages, broken rifles, half-buried *fajina* baskets, their wicker mouths gawping ominously from the earth like the faces of drowned people. And thousands of our spiked bats, scattered everywhere. This was a place of such silence, sadness, and ghostliness that even my science was dispelled by its powers.

And then, for no apparent reason, I was overcome by a desire to go back to our tent on the beach.

Amelis was sleeping, unclothed. I awoke her. "Where's Anfán?"

She was subsumed in a drowsiness that was more hunger and exhaustion than sleep. She opened her eyes, those enormous black eyes. I remember being there, in the dark of night, in that meager tent on the beach. Her on the mattress, naked, covered in sweat, while I knelt down and embraced her, less out of love than an urge to protect. She was feverish. I'd woken her from a nightmare. Feeling my hand reaching around her back, she smiled, as though this were some long-awaited reunion. "Martí," she whispered, "you're here."

It was a subdued and queasy feeling of joy.

"For the love of God, Amelis! Where's Anfán?"

If Nan and Anfán were killed, all would have been for absolutely nothing. They'd been part of my household for seven years now, seven. What truly joined us all together were not the transcendent acts but an accumulation of everyday things. There is nothing so significant as a million nothings all joined together.

We were interrupted by an outbreak of shelling, the reverberations of which shook the tent so hard I thought it might take to the air. That could mean only one thing: the general assault being declared. I put my tricorn on my head and made to leave the tent. As I started to duck under the flap, Amelis said something, I don't remember what precisely. Something about Beceite. A very faraway Beceite, that small town in Aragon where we'd met, among rapist Bourbons and murderous Miquelets. Her hunger was making her delirious. Running her finger along her cheek, she begged me in a distant voice: "Martí, it's only mashed raspberry. Don't go, please. It's only raspberry."

She spread her arms wide to me. Duty called, but at the same time here was this woman who had never asked anyone for anything, saying, like a cat mewling the words, *"Si us plau, si us plau."* I went to her.

I embraced her carefully, she was so thin. Otherwise, no exaggeration, I'd have snapped her ribs. Her face was bathed in sweat. The most distressing thing was being able to do nothing to ease her pain. She asked me to get the broken music box. I found it and handed it to her. When she opened it, of course no sound came out. But, smiling, she said: "Do you hear? My father invented this box, he put music in a box. And this was the song he chose. Isn't it lovely?"

I've never liked the idea of lying to the sick. "We'll get it fixed, you'll see."

"Martí!" she cried, her fever going up a notch. "Say you can hear it!"

No, I could not hear it. It was nothing but a broken box, one small scrap among countless objects consigned to oblivion by the enemy bombardment. I said nothing, just sighed. She knew; a high fever can sometimes bring about considerable lucidity. Those vast eyes of hers found mine.

"Shall I tell you something, Martí? The fact that you can't hear the music is what makes you you. This is your great strong point and, at the same time, the thing that limits you. If you *wanted* to hear our music, you'd hear it. But you can't, because you don't believe in it. You don't even try." She added: "You've heard this music a thousand times. Why not now? The box is only a box—one day it was bound to break."

I made her look me in the eye once more. "One thing, Amelis: You're not to leave this beach. Whatever should come to pass, don't go anywhere! If you find yourself walking on anything that isn't sand, you're to turn back."

"*Jefe*, I'll look after her."

Anfán was behind me in the tent, with Nan beside him.

"Where have you been?" I cried. Anfán groaned, impish and reluctant. "For once in your life, pay attention!" I shouted. "Tonight and tomorrow, no one must leave this beach. Not you, not Nan, not Amelis. And it's your job to make sure that's what happens! Understood?" Screaming at Anfán was a waste of time. I changed tack. "Did you know your mother?"

"You know I didn't."

I gestured to Amelis, who was asleep again, or, rather, unconscious, consumed by the fever, delirious. "If you had all the mothers in the world to choose between, is there another you could possibly rather have?"

He looked down at Amelis. The only light was a nearly spent, guttering candle. I'd say, though, that a paltry flame such as that one is capable of feeling emotions.

My Lord, how beautiful a beloved person can seem in her weakness. If it weren't for her, the four of us never would have come together. Our life would have been quite different, and doubtless very much the poorer.

Anfán took a deep breath, and for the first time, I heard the man in him speak: "As you wish, *jefe*. I'll protect her. Whatever should pass, none of us will leave the beach. You have my word."

Chin up, Martí Zuviría, never mind! Never? No, not never.

15

And so, after more than a year under siege, September 11, 1714, finally came around. It began with a forbidding artillery barrage at half past four in the morning, immediately followed by ten thousand men charging at the breaches. Dozens of company banners, officers with their sabers held aloft, the sergeants hefting halberds to show the troops the way. I don't believe there can have been more than five or six hundred haggard militiamen opposing them in the first line.

I find it impossible to recount that September 11 in any kind of coherent order. I myself am unable to comprehend it: Fleeting images are all that remain from that longest of days, not so much a sequence of events as a heap of dismembered images. I left our tent on the beach and made my way back into the city. The church bells were frantically ringing out, all of them. Sheer chaos. What else could it have been, with the Virgin Mary elected commander in chief? Meanwhile, the Bourbons surging up and over ramparts that a child could have kicked aside.

As the sky began growing light, I climbed up onto the terrace of Casa Montserrat, the mansion of a departed *botiflero*, and a vantage point over the area under attack between Saint Clara and Portal Nou. And I saw what, for an engineer, was the most exasperating sight of all: the stretch we'd defended for thirteen long months, overrun by that horde of mindless slaves. A blanket of white uniforms charging in formation across the breaches: *En avant, en avant!* Their numbers were so great that the few being picked off by snipers up on the ramparts didn't make any difference. Was this my fate? Was this what I'd had my senses honed to do? To suffer all the more intensely the fall of Barcelona and the extinction of a people? So that on this, our last day of freedom, I'd hear even more acutely the howls of anguish, cry more tears, and my hands would flail and grasp all the more desperately at the sinking ship?

One of the sights from that day: sections of the ramparts separated from one another by the gigantic breaches, towering up into the sky. Through the telescope, I see a particularly thin stretch of the rampart, either side of which, far below, thousands of enemies are streaming into the city. Just two soldiers are left up there, an old man and a youngster. The old man is loading rifles and handing them to the youngster to fire into the white flood of troops below. The old man isn't quick enough with his reloading. The youngster, impotent and raging, ends up hurling the rifles themselves, the bayonets making primitive spears of them. Another fleeting image, which again comes back to me in the circular telescope sight, is of the second Bourbon wave now having taken this redoubt, and the duo having surrendered, each badly wounded. Up on the battlement, the soldiers force them to their knees before the abyss. Then each of them is kicked over the edge.

A whirl of images. Children pulling the triggers of our "organ" contraptions, point-blank, mowing down whole ranks of grenadiers. Coronela soldiers flinging grenades until the enemy overruns them, and using the last ones to blow themselves up.

A great stack of images, yes, but above and beyond any of them, prevailing in the tragedy, an appearance that enshrined that man in the memory of the righteous: Don Antonio de Villarroel Peláez. Don Antonio! What was he still doing in Barcelona? He was supposed to be miles away, out across the ocean, when he suddenly burst into a meeting between members of the high command. His booming voice.

He was supposed to be in Vienna, safe, covered in praise, and forging a future for himself at Charles's court. But he was here. These are the facts: He had waited until the last possible moment for the government to come to their senses and restore him. But that moment didn't come, and as he walked down to the beach of his salvation, he halted, turned around, and simply returned to the ramparts. He knew very well he was signing his own death warrant. "I wish I could die shoulder to shoulder with these men, like any other soldier," he'd said. Why are there such men as Don Antonio in the world? I don't know the reason why. I only know that, when they appear, it is impossible not to love them.

For a very brief moment, he and I were alone in his study. I didn't know what to say or do. It still pains me that I failed to find the words to tell him what it meant to me that he'd come back. I suppose it doesn't matter. Throughout the rest of the defense, Don Antonio never made a single mention of what he'd given up. Only in that moment, with no one to see or hear, did he let his gaze become abstracted and, smoothing down his uniform, say: "To hell with sailing away."

On that September 11, the head of the government, Rafael Casanova, also played his part, though without attaining the heights of Don Antonio's greatness. Were I an indulgent person, I'd say that Casanova was more of a tragic character than a deplorable one, trapped between his own reasoning, the reasoning of the state, and the people's willingness to go on fighting. But I don't happen to be an indulgent person: If you want to be beloved by your country, you have to be prepared to sacrifice yourself for it. Don Antonio, not even a Catalan, come the final hour, understood this far more clearly than all the Casanovas in the world.

Don Antonio ordered two concentric attacks. He'd lead one and Casanova would lead the other, carrying the Saint Eulalia flag at the head of the troops. Tradition states that that sacred banner should be brought out only if the city is in grave danger. Could there ever be a more grave danger? Don Antonio knew what it would do for the élan of the soldiers to see the Eulalia flying high among them.

The problem was, protocol also demanded that any attack with the sacred ensign had to be led by the city's highest-ranking political representative. The coward Casanova, in other words. I wasn't at the meeting, no, but it most likely took some enraged officer to point a gun at him for Casanova to put on his colonel's uniform. Soldiering and politics don't, or at least shouldn't, mix. But because Casanova was, at least in name, the leader of the Coronela, that meant he really had no choice but to put on that jacket with its golden braids, mount a tired old nag, and head up the attack. His demeanor, it struck me, was like that of an actor being made to play a role he disliked: resigned but at the same time wrapped up in the new part, brandishing his sword above his tricorn, simulating passions he didn't at all feel.

The troop left the Saint Jordi Hall. The roar from the people announced the fact. Desperate, filthy citizens tacked on to the party as it came past. People appeared at balconies and windows, blowing kisses to the violet saint. The same color, as it happened, as the jackets worn by the Sixth Battalion, which was made up of tailors, tavern owners, and tinkers, and which was in the vanguard in front of the banner.

I also remember one of the Red Pelts, still dressed in those claret robes, who rode to one side of the banner. He went along shouting up at the women in the balconies to save their prayers and come and join the sacrifice. I remember the women, who were so weak they could barely stand, propping themselves up on the balcony railings and shouting: *"Doneu-nos pa i hi anirem!"* Give us bread, and we'll come.

It must have been seven in the evening when I saw them pass by on the way to the front, half army, half sword-brandishing mob. The Eulalia banner had returned to the origin of all banners: a nadir that joins men together in a single cause. Once a significant crowd had gathered, a phalanx of bayonets along its front edge, they set out to retake the bastions.

I also say: There are moments when even the stoniest hearts melt. Above the throng, the large rectangular standard rippled in the wind, the Eulalia sewn on it seeming alive. That girl, so young and sad. The banner, drawing nearer to its own demise, fluttered, and it was as though she were looking out at you—and only you.

Fleeting images, yes: I can see Costa, leaning his elbows on the stock of an empty cannon, observing the long column in tears.

"For God's sake!" I cried. "Stop crying and give them some cover."

He shook his head and, turning his palms up, said: "It's over."

So, this jumble of trained soldiers and seething civilians, they attacked. Their objective was to scour the ramparts of enemies, from Portal Nou to Saint Clara. They would have had less of a job tearing the Rock of Gibraltar out of the ocean and bringing it back to exhibit at Saint María del Mar.

Jimmy had already positioned thousands of soldiers and hundreds of sappers on and around the ramparts, in case some lunatic should come and try to retake them. The tragedy was that it wasn't one lunatic but hundreds and hundreds of lunatics. They followed the banner of Saint Eulalia, crushed together like a herd of sheep, more concerned about protecting the standard than killing any enemies. It was a gruesome sight. Rifle fire strafed them from all sides. Dozens fell to the hail of bullets, but still the advance continued.

They came to the ramparts; the walkway around them was perhaps ten feet wide. Like rams, the two vanguards clashed. Another image from that day: the violet uniforms of our Sixth Battalion merging in bayonet combat with the whites of the enemy. Against all expectation, they overran a long stretch of the Bourbon-controlled ramparts. The multitude surrounding the violet girl thinned out as they pushed ahead, shouting battle curses and forcing the enemy back.

I was ordered to make my way to the center point of the Bourbon assault—thankfully, as it meant not having to witness the playing out of that mass suicide. Casanova, who claimed to have been injured in the leg, was evacuated from the fighting a little later. We saw him being carried past on a stretcher. I'm no surgeon, but to me, he seemed only lightly injured. He was more dejected than in physical danger, that much was certain, because when he came past us and people asked what was happening, he raised his head and said: "Go, sirs, and spur on the people, for the dangers are many."

What no one knew at that point was that while a tourniquet was applied to his leg, his doctor was writing a certificate for him so he'd be able to flee the city. Enough about him.

Images, images, a constant stream of them. Barricades at every entrance to every street that fed onto the rampart area, to impede the Bourbon advance into the city center. Against all established siege wisdom, and to Jimmy's surprise, taking the ramparts didn't mean the end of the assault; it was merely the prologue. In any other siege, the defenders would have entered discussions at that point. In Barcelona, people fought on, in street skirmishes and from their windows, converting buildings into ramparts. I became an engineer once more: The streets were so narrow that small barriers could be thrown up in a heartbeat.

While these parapets were being piled up by civilians, soldiers stationed themselves behind and began firing on the approaching Bourbons.

I ran into Ballester behind one of these barricades. He came as backup for the one I was helping erect. Ballester, yes, another image from that September 11, a day that would be his last. He was well aware of the fact, and know what? He seemed almost happy, loading and firing his rifle in unending succession. A kind of festive cheer had come over him, like that of someone who has sworn not to finish the night sober.

Clouds of gunpowder made it impossible to see very far. But just then, Ballester did see something, dropping his ramrod and shoving me. "Your child! And the dwarf! They're between the lines! Look, look!"

Looking up, I could make out the two little monsters scurrying across the open ground between the Bourbon-controlled bastions and the mouth of the street we were on. Thousands of bullets flying, and a voice in my mind screaming: "What are you two doing here?" Only a few hours had passed since Anfán had made a sacred oath to me, and already it was broken. They were running, apparently without a destination, which was unusual; normally, they moved like a pair of hyenas, fixed on their goal as if they had compasses mounted to their noses. Then they went down. Amid flashes of gunfire and gunpowder vapor, I saw them fall. First Nan. Anfán stopped, began to go back for the dwarf, and then was hit himself, letting out a small cry, one more of surprise than of pain. The Bourbon volleys were coming so thick, such a lead hailstorm, that I was able to glance over the barricade for only a moment. Nan and Anfán had disappeared.

I tugged Ballester's sleeve. "Did they get them?" I asked, sobbing. "Did you see it, are you sure?"

Ballester looked me in the eye; his silence said it all. Then a wailing sound reached our ears. Above the sound of the gunfire, the diminishing sound of a death rattle, and the words: *"Father, Father, Father."* With his dying breath, Anfán had become a child once more. He'd fallen down into a rut, out of my field of vision. When Ballester spoke, it only exacerbated the torture; in a small, meek voice, he said: "He's calling for you."

It was all over. The end of the world was no longer only nigh: Your son calling you "Father" for the first time, and it also being the very instant before he passes away. That nameless tension that keeps us all alive then slackened in me. I inhabited an empty body for a time. I don't know how long I was there, down on my knees, feeling that pain. The next thing I remember is Ballester's face in front of mine: "You have to come with me," he said.

All around, the uproar of battle continued, but the bloodbath seemed far away from me, signifying nothing. An obscene, incongruous apathy gripped me. I even burst out laughing. I mocked Ballester as he dragged me away, I mocked everything.

We made for the rearguard. Peret came into view. His very demeanor spoke, and I didn't want to listen. My state was akin to that of a fever dream, when all we see and all we know is turned upside down. I said or perhaps thought: "I told that woman not to leave the beach." Peret spoke, seemingly in unison with a group of people gathered around him like an assembly of ghosts: "We are at the beach, Martí." I looked down at my feet and fell to my knees, which indeed sank into dirty sand. Out of nowhere, a question formed in my mind, one that I should have come up with a long while before: What did Anfán want to say to me? What could have forced him to come in search of me, though it had been emphatically forbidden? Lying in front of me, the body of Amelis.

"A stray bullet," said an old voice, perhaps Peret's.

I didn't try to deny it; we'd seen too many dead bodies. The greenish hue under her fingernails was a clear sign. Even Ballester bit his fist, gasping. We suffered so much that September 11, the pain had to form a line.

I rubbed my cheek against hers, which had begun to turn chill. Yes: Death is a cold nowhere. And no, a cold cadaver does not come back to life. Yet just then she did: She suddenly sat up, like a tail thrashing.

Everyone in the gathering took a step back. I saw Amelis's eyes, which had burst open, and our whole universe, everything, was collected in that look. She grabbed my chest, tried to speak. I knew she was dead, that she had come back to say something to me, only to sink forevermore. And so she did: Though it was only a moment, she came back.

As I remember it, there was a lull in the battle. All the noise was suspended in anticipation of Amelis's words. This, of course, was not what happened. I thought all possible cruelties had occurred. But we still had one coming: the four most terrible words any father could hope to hear.

"Martí," she said imploringly, *"tingues cura d'Anfán."* Take care of Anfán.

And she was gone, a loosening of her soul more than her muscles.

How to face the impossibility of her request, the fact it had come too late? Or that her wish made a connection between me and the world, one of unbearable pain? Amelis couldn't have known that Anfán was dead, that he had died specifically in an attempt to save her, in trying to bring me to help. Even Ballester was moved. His cheeks contracted beneath his beard, and he turned his head away so that I wouldn't see.

Fleeting images: The next finds me at the Fossar de les Moreres, the mass burial ditch. The battle continued to rage, but the only thing concerning me was the bundle I was carrying: Amelis's body covered in a shawl. Ballester was at my side. One of the gravediggers asked me the customary question: "One of ours?" The government had made a decree by which no Bourbon bodies were to be buried. I didn't even bother to answer. Ballester shook his fist at the digger, who fled.

I went down to the ditch. It was a great crater in which bodies were deposited. Wisely, the Red Pelts had ordered it to be built five storeys deep. But at this point in the siege, the pile of bodies was almost up to ground level. I buried Amelis to the sound of cannons thundering. While I knelt down to deposit her body as delicately as I could, Ballester kept an eye out.

A stray bullet. After having made it through a life full of danger, rapes, and destitution, Amelis had been taken by something as ridiculous as a stray bullet. I couldn't prevent the thought: That stray bullet was me.

I fell to my knees and, sobbing uncontrollably, said: "I killed them. Amelis. Anfán. The dwarf. All of them."

Squinting, Ballester asked: "Mind telling me what you're going on about?"

I spoke through gurgles, my face bathed in tears. "I designed the Bourbon trench. While I was over there, on the other side of the cordon. I thought it would be the lesser evil for the city, but I was only fooling myself."

I wished, truly I did, that he would take out a knife and slit my throat, as he should have done in Beceite. The seven intervening years—I saw very clearly now—had all been a dream. But instead of putting an end to me, he reacted with irate skepticism.

"What are you saying?" he shouted. "Who cares about your damned calculations, all those tables and compasses? Get your head out of your books and let's go and fight!"

"I did my best," I said. "And not for the sake of the city, nor for my family, but for engineering. Any Maganon would have dreamed of such a trench. Faced with a recalcitrant city, and provided all the means to create the perfect trench. For all the tricks I included, all I really wanted was to better my teachers, beat Vauban's cousin himself. I let myself be tempted, then hid that fact from myself. There was only one way to erase such a stain, which was coming back to the stronghold I'd condemned, letting the work of my hand lead to my own demise."

Ballester tried to wrestle me to my feet, to urge me back to the front, but I held him off.

"Want to know the worst of it?" I looked for my judgment in Ballester's eyes. Or, rather, that he would execute that judgment. To that end, I concluded: "If I had truly loved my family more than I loved engineering, if I had loved love and not vanity, I'd never have designed any trench. Neither a good one nor a bad one. An honest man serves not the devil—for good or for ill."

"But your work hindered the devil," he said in my defense. "Obstructing the trench, you won us a few more days in this city."

"And for what? Look around you. If I do survive, it will always be hanging over me that I was the architect of its demise." Ballester shook his head, but I refused to listen. "Where is truth, the authentic truth? In our deeds or in the feelings that guide them? I know I didn't design this trench based on love or patriotism but out of vanity. Now the death of my family bears my signature."

I cried so hard, I thought my eyes would drop from my head. Ballester knelt down beside me and, crushing my cheeks in his hands, gave me a hateful look. The world was sinking, and Ballester, I now understand, knew these would be the last words spoken between us.

"Know your problem?" he said. "That you only fight for the living. Between them, the French, the Spanish, and the Red Pelts killed my father, my mother, and my brothers. So many of my people are dead, I've come to terms with the fact that I won't be able to avenge them all. Don't fight for the living, and don't fight for the dead, either. People in the future might speak ill of acts we've committed—because we got things wrong or because we failed. Fine. I'd rather be looked down on for the things I did do than the things I never did."

I was still on my knees, shaken, weeping. He stood up. Ballester standing at his full height made me feel like a child. He added: "Do you truly think the world revolves around your damned trench? Know what I say to that? I hope it was the greatest work of your life. Because if not, what would have been the point in having taken on that bunch of braggarts dressed in white?"

Ballester then did the most loving thing one man can do for another: He lifted me to my feet.

"Let's go, let's go!" he entreated me. And we returned to the fray. I followed him, I think, because at that moment I hadn't the slightest desire to outlive Amelis and Anfán. Or my trench.

A number of units from the Coronela, during their retreat, had taken up positions on the absurd unfinished cutting, the ditch inside the ramparts that had been intended to contain the Bourbon assault. Dozens of the militiamen, covered in mud after all the rain, had taken shelter in it and were leaning out and firing at floor height. The wave of Bourbon soldiers was crashing down on them—they'd end up trapped if they stayed down there. Ballester and I leaped down into the six-foot cutting and began shoving and urging them to get out. "Out of the cutting!" we cried. "Fall back!" Ballester and his men forced them up and out.

I went along shouting, pointing the way to the first line of streets behind us. "To the buildings! Occupy them and shoot from the windows!"

We carried on, forcing them out of the cutting. Before we knew it, the Bourbons were upon us. Dozens, hundreds, of white uniforms jumped down, brandishing their bayonets. They had come from the captured ramparts; it was at least a regiment. Down in the ditch and around it, Barcelonans and Frenchmen gored one another. I now tried to scrabble out myself, but as I was doing so, someone grabbed me by the neck and threw me to the ground. I remember, as I sank into the mud, thinking disparagingly: Why not just knife me in the back? The answer was that the person who had yanked me back down was no other than my good friend Don Antoine Bardonenche.

He'd been tasked with clearing the cutting; the Frenchmen around us wreaking havoc with their bayonets were his escort. It had turned out to be a devastating day even for him. His pristine white uniform was dirty for once, and his face smeared. There were blood spatters all over his chest.

He pointed his sword at my nose and said: "*Mon ami, mon ennemi. Rendez-vous.*"

"*Ah, non!*" I replied in the offended tone of someone asked to pay a debt he does not owe. "*Ça jamais!*"

That's right: Longlegs Zuvi, the rat, refusing the very thing that had been in motion since the siege began. I didn't even have Peret's sword about my person, so, very nobly, I threw a handful of mud in Bardonenche's eyes, turned, and ran. While his and Ballester's men continued laying into one another with bayonets, Bardonenche wiped the mud from his eyes and raced after me. I tripped over a rut, landing face-to-face with a dead soldier. I grabbed the man's rifle and, gasping, turned the bayonet on myself like a spear. Halting, Bardonenche sighed. "Don't," he said.

Pity for Bardonenche—pity for me—pity for all of us. His expression was more than merely downcast: It was commiseration itself. I, of course, felt like a rat cornered by a tiger. Imagine a zero the size of the moon: That was how likely I was to overcome Bardonenche, Europe's finest swordsman.

I still think Martí Zuviría should, by rights, have died that September 11, in that waterlogged cutting. But just then Ballester leaped like a panther from the edge of the ditch, and he and Bardonenche set to tussling in the mud. I wasn't stupid enough to let such a chance go begging, and flexing my long legs, I launched myself out of the cutting.

White uniforms were everywhere; the entire cutting was being overrun by hundreds of Frenchmen. The men accompanying Bardonenche tried to protect their captain, and the Miquelets theirs. Ballester's men fired and thrust their blades in a frenzy, but the cascade of Bourbons intensified. The clamor of the battle was appalling: Across the city, more than forty thousand rifles were exchanging fire, so disorderly and at such a pace that it sounded like a constant drumroll. We had to fall back immediately.

For the second time, I addressed Ballester by his first name. "Esteve!" I howled, on all fours at the edge of the cutting. "Get out, for the love of God, get up here now! You don't know who you're dealing with! *Surti!*"

Ballester had bargained on a French captain being more skilled in martial arts than he was, but by turning it into a brawl in the confines of the cutting, he'd hoped to level the field. Bardonenche's long arms kept hitting up against the walls, preventing him from using his skills. They punched, bit, and scratched each other like wild animals.

Still, not even Ballester could withstand a swordsman like Bardonenche for long. The latter eventually managed to force some space between them and, with a lightning-fast thrust, ran Ballester through at stomach height. The blade entered up to the hilt. Ballester, with half the sword projecting from his lower back, turned his head, looked up, saw me, and said something that I'll take to my grave: "Go! You're more important than we are!"

His last words. Next came a deafening guttural cry that could be heard over and above the din of the battle. His fingers sank into the ground like grappling hooks, and he looked Bardonenche in the eye. Bardonenche threw back his head, but—and this was his error—didn't move away. His most sensible option would have been to let his saber go and kick Ballester's body clear. In Bardonenche's world, I suppose, it was bad form to drop your weapon in such a fashion. Honor was the death of him.

Bardonenche cried out, his chin high, as Ballester, summoning what little strength remained in him, sank his teeth into the Frenchman's neck. They both toppled into the mud. They writhed together, and Ballester's hands came upon something Bardonenche was carrying.

A small leather pouch containing used bullets: the pouch of Busquets, the old Miquelet from Mataró. Ballester took it and forced it into his enemy's mouth, ramming it down his throat with bloodied fingers. Bardonenche, his body in spasms, struggled to get clear.

The rest of the Miquelets had fallen, and several Frenchmen came to their captain's aid, bayoneting Ballester's body. In the melee, and with the two bodies intertwined, they also managed to finish off Bardonenche by stabbing him a few times. By the end, the pair were a single mangled lump enveloped in thick mud. Two men with such different trajectories, so perfectly unalike one from the other, and in their demise, unified by death—as though their destiny had been to end up in each other's arms.

I turned and I ran as never before. *Corre*, Zuvi! Run! Only when there was no breath left in me did I finally come to a halt. Wheezing, with no thought for where I was, I dropped to the ground. I couldn't believe they were all dead. Amelis, Anfán, Nan. Ballester. And still the battle was raging. More images: brave men, the kind I never thought I'd see give in, fleeing home; and cowards, who had never shown their faces anywhere near the ramparts, taking on the enemy armed with hatchets. I'd need a whole page to list the nobles who, back in June 1713, had voted against resisting, and come September 11, 1714, died defending their city.

Questions abound. So many pointless sacrifices—why? Was it worth filling the world with so many tragic, extraordinary tales, all those brilliant, meteoric ends? We know what happened afterward. All officers put in chains, hauled to Castile, and Don Antonio first among them. The Saint Eulalia flag captured and transported to the Atocha shrine in Madrid. The entire country under a military regime for decades. And Barcelona in the hands of that mercenary murderer, the Antwerp butcher, Verboom.

My thoughts turn to another of the Miquelet captains, Josep Moragues. He was tied to the back of a cart and dragged the length and breadth of the city before being decapitated and his arms and legs cut off. They placed his head in a cage and had no qualms about hanging it from one of the city gates. There his bare skull stayed, as mockery of and a warning to the rebels, for twelve long years—twelve, as all the while his widow's protests went unheard.

Could there be any greater ignominy than that of Moragues? Yes, perhaps that of a man named Manuel Desvalls. And not because his body was subjected to torments but because he didn't die from his treatment. Desvalls had commanded troops outside Barcelona. When the victors exiled him, he couldn't have had any idea what the rest of his days would hold. Remarkably, he lived to a hundred. Can you imagine? A larger proportion of his life spent outside his home than in it, his return never allowed. A hundred years—a century. And I'm headed the same way.

Or should I talk about the women, our women, all the women who sustained us and who spat when we said they couldn't fight on the bastions? Or perhaps Castellví, Francesc Castellví, our starry-eyed captain of the Valencian company? When he was exiled, he chose the path of the writer or, more specifically, his own dead end. He stubbornly dedicated his life to chronicling our war, corresponding for decades with participants from either side, men from dozens of countries. He wrote a book five thousand pages long and more, an impartial testimony of all the great deeds. And do you know what happened? No publisher would touch it. He died without a single page making it into the public domain.

But above all, my thoughts turn to Don Antonio, Don Antonio de Villarroel Peláez, renouncing glory and honor, family and even life itself, and all for an allegiance that made no sense—to a group of nameless men. He, a son of Castile, embodying what was good about that harsh land, sacrificing himself for Barcelona, no less. And his reward? Infinite pain, eternal oblivion.

In my delirium, another of my tragedies occurred to me: With Anfán dead, I had a son remaining, one I'd never meet, and who would never learn that his father had fought and died defending the freedoms of a people he'd also never know about. But no, I thought, my pain wasn't unusual: When we lost and all of us perished, all our children would be educated by the victors.

The world: this answerless question. And inhabiting its trifling circumference, the fools who seek the answer. All for nothing.

And yet the doubt remains. The fact is, all those men and women did not have to go up the ramparts. They could have stayed in their houses, let the tyrant in. Resign themselves to it, get down on their knees, beg for their lives. But they didn't. They fought. Knowing full well how slim their chances were, they held out for thirteen months of inexorable terror. Dying for the sake of a word, dying so their children could say for the rest of time, even if only under their breath: "My father defended our bastions." This was the way Ballester—all the Ballesters—thought.

After Ballester's death, I drifted, neither dead nor alive. For how long, and along which streets, I do not know. The gunfire was an innocuous murmur, not worthy of attention. Then someone was beckoning me: "Don Antonio's calling everyone together," the person said. Images, voids, morasses in the memory. But the words "Don Antonio" could bring the dead back to life.

Suddenly, I find myself in Plaza Born, the square at Barcelona's very center. Not heeding the gunfire, Don Antonio is gathering a troop on the cobblestones. And what a troop. The remaining few. Remnants of the Coronela, wounded men dragged from hospital beds, young boys, some women. A couple of priests.

Don Antonio was about to launch the second counterattack, aimed at retaking the ramparts. An absurdity, given that the Bourbons had reached the far side of Plaza Born. There, thousands of white uniforms had gathered, and the first rank was kneeling. For the rest, aside from Don Antonio's steed, I do not believe there were more than a few dozen cavalrymen. The others were lining up like infantry, with one or two officers trying to introduce order to the ranking.

Don Antonio, up on his horse at the front, made a brief speech. But the din was too great for us to hear him. And it made no difference what he had to say. The odd bullet grazed his body, and then one bounced off his saber. Out of the thousands and thousands of shots fired that day, the sound of that one bullet has stayed with me, metal on metal. Don Antonio's response was to raise his saber even higher. I looked at him. And shall I tell you what? He was illuminated.

No, the word "happiness" doesn't fit him. Don Antonio was never happy, just as fish may not see the sun until being torn from the ocean depths. He was about other things. He was going to surpass a threshold that was particular to him, and he had found the opportunity to do so without compromising his honor. That day—finally—it wouldn't be him asking the impossible of his men but the other way around. Joyfully, he led them on their mad sortie.

And The Word? It's ironic, because I began this book prepared to reveal it, and now, after all these pages, this word—this unique word—doesn't matter. Because when it came to that final charge, we were beyond words.

This was The Word. These children, these women, these men from a hundred different places. All united behind Don Antonio's horse. Lining up higgledy-piggledy, about to set out on a cavalry charge without any horses. Fewer than a thousand versus fifty thousand. And yet The Word may be reflected in the dictionaries. A pale reflection, very pale, but a reflection after all.

We attacked, shrieking like the savages who sacked Rome. The Bourbons were in perfect formation on the far side of the square. Their ranks, well stocked with men, reaching a long way back, thousands of rifles pointing straight at us. We were peppered with bullets. Volley after volley, perfectly coordinated. Their officers calling out, *Feu, feu, feu!* My companions falling left and right. The sounds of weeping, wailing, repentance. Don Antonio, like a commander out of antiquity, leading from the front, sheer madness, galloping forward with saber pointed. They shot him down, of course.

His steed was knocked onto its right flank, its huge frame crushing Don Antonio underneath. His knee ended up trapped between the saddle and the Plaza Born cobblestones, his bones snapping like twigs.

The horse thrashed about as though it had been placed over a campfire. It contorted its neck and let out a stream of dung. Goodness knows why, but its whinnying and its shitting remain firmly fixed in my memory. I was the first to go and kneel down next to Don Antonio. I grabbed him under his arms and heaved him out from under the beast. It took me a few moments to notice the look that was in his eye.

It was as though Don Antonio didn't want to be rescued. He just lay there on the ground, half his body trapped beneath the horse. Then I felt one of his large hands grab me by the lapel of my uniform. He gave a violent tug, bringing my face close to his, and then spoke the closest thing to The Word that I would ever hear. And it was spoken not by an emperor in his most august hour but by a general defeated, fallen; I did not hear The Word from the mouth of my own captain but from a man who had crossed over from enemy latitudes, a man who had left everything to join the ranks of the weak and shelterless, the accursed few, and to lay down his life for them.

Don Antonio whispered into my ear: "You must give your whole self."

My head was so empty, my body so detached from my being, that to be quite honest, my memory is a jumble now. I've gone back over this particular moment—everyone galloping forward in the pendulum of death, Don Antonio down on the Plaza Born cobblestones, his steed shitting in death, thousands of bullets zinging past our ears—and perhaps, only perhaps, memory alters what it was that Don Antonio said.

Because sometimes, when I am strolling through autumn fields, I find myself overcome by a burst of memories that are not so bitter. And then I see Don Antonio's large hand on my lapel and hear him speaking incredibly kindly: "Give yourself, *fiyé*." At other times, when I can afford to buy myself a little of that syrupy schnapps, the words I read on Don Antonio's lips are more martial: "Always give yourself, Zuviría, always; that's what matters." At other times, when I am desensitized by foul-smelling liquor, very drunk indeed, the face I see down on the ground of the Plaza Born is not Don Antonio's at all but Vauban's. And it is the marquis who pulls me close, and he says: "Cadet, you have passed."

Yes, I no longer have any sense of who said what or how. All these decades and decades that have gone by, all those many turns around the sun. But what difference does it make, ultimately? Vauban said, "You must know"; Don Antonio said, "Give yourself." And there, in that city square, the detritus of war all around, The Word crumbled under the weight of its own paradox: "You cannot know until you give yourself, and you cannot give yourself until you know."

A number of officers came over to try and help the maimed commander. Don Antonio did finally get up, his splintered leg bone protruding through his breeches, and he started pushing everyone away.

"Don't stop the charge!" he bellowed in his resounding Castilian voice. "Don't stop! No falling back, not as long as I still draw breath. You sons of bitches—no one!"

Dear Don Antonio. How fate scorned him. Even when it came to that September 11, the glorious death he'd hoped for was denied him. Knocked from his horse and severely wounded, he was dragged off to the hospital by his aides. I can still see him struggling to shake off the men who were helping him, as though they were his enemies. Those of us who remained resumed the charge.

During life's worst moments, it is incredible how calm one's thoughts can be. Rightly, perhaps, because once you find yourself on the summit, the mountainsides no longer matter—you'll never be going down them again. As I charged, all I thought was: Very well, at least that Fifth Point is mine now.

Thousands of white beetles raised their rifles in unison, training their sights upon us. We rushed headlong at them. We were no more than fifty in number now, a mix of old men, widows, cavalrymen without horses, horses without riders: my ragged fellow Barcelonans. The Bourbons had brought five cannons and made a battery on a mound of rubble, above and behind the infantry. Grapeshot, was my thought as I continued to hurtle forward, they've loaded them with grapeshot. My other thought being: They'll fire the instant after a volley from these white beetles. I saw one of those round cannon barrels staring me down. I saw a flash of white and yellow.

I was blown backward twenty or thirty feet. All I knew was that something had happened to my face. At first, curiously, it seemed more associated with a feeling of nakedness than death. I was beyond now. And I discovered that Amelis had been right, yes, she had: Anyone who wants to hear a piece of music, hears it. Destroyed, monstrous from that moment forth, I heard that music over the noise of wailing and explosions. "Give yourself, Zuviría, your whole self."

I ought to have understood far sooner—when they put a noose around my neck in the Bourbon camp, or even when I sat beside Vauban on his deathbed. "Summarize the optimum defense." It was this and no more—this was all. We are fallen leaves that linger on. Stars that burst forth in light, fables squandered. Truths whose only reward is lucidity itself. The smell of warm shit running down the legs of ranks of men. Blind telescopes, inane periscopes, lamentations. Funnels imbued with affection, that boy on our prow laughing, like dolphin laughter.

The far side of the river. Admitting that we'll always be looking out at the landscape through the keyhole of the dungeon, knowing that ears of corn fall but do not complain. My shredded spirits, my broken calculations. Give yourself, Zuviría, give.

And discovering—beyond the utmost extreme, beyond the Euphrates and the Rubicon, where there are no longer any tears, oh, the greatness and the consolation of the few and the poor, of the weak and forlorn—that the darker our twilight hours, the more blessed will be the dawn of those who will come after us.

A Historical Note

A few people who read this book in draft form have asked me about the historical basis of the facts that appear in it. I can only answer that I have worked according to the usual conventions of the historical novel, which require that you confine yourself to established pieces of data while at the same time tolerating fiction in the private realm. For all the dates and events relating to historical characters, or to political or military events, I have restricted myself to the facts. Fortunately, the chronicles that cover the Spanish War of Succession and the 1713–1714 Siege of Barcelona are generous enough to make it possible to go into some detail. The parliamentary debates that took place in Barcelona in 1713 have been extracted directly from documents of the period. Even where secondary characters are concerned, I have chosen to follow historical sources: the obsession that seizes Jeanne Vauban's husband over the philosopher's stone, the skirmish in Beceite in which Zuviría meets Ballester, as well as the death of Dr. Bassons and the charge of the law students in the battle of August 1714, or the events relating to the expedition of the military delegate, to cite just a few examples, are all fully evidenced. The words spoken by Berwick, infuriated at the Barcelonans' resistance, with his staff officers, can be pursued in the chronicles and in his own autobiography. A good proportion of the insults aimed by Villarroel at Zuviría are also drawn from a range of documents, though in such cases we know only that they were directed at "a certain officer." As for Zuviría himself, historical chronicles make only a very few elusive references to him, describing him as General Villarroel's aide-de-camp, a translator, a member of a number of different commissions, and even a coordinator of the activities that took place outside the city walls during the course of the siege. In any case, he was one of the few senior officers on the pro-Austrian side who, following his participation in the 1713–1714 siege, managed to get to Vienna and thereby avoid the repression of the Bourbon regime.

The War of the Spanish Succession: A Chronology

SPAIN	EUROPE
1700	
—Charles II of Spain, known as *El Hechizado*, or "The Bewitched," dies.	
1701	
—Philip V is named king.	—The Grand Alliance between Austria, Denmark, England, and Holland is formed.
1702	
	—The Grand Alliance declares war on Spain and France.
1703	
	—Portugal and the House of Savoy join the Grand Alliance.
1704	
—The Austrian pretender to the Spanish throne, Charles III, disembarks in Portugal.	—France loses forty thousand men in the Battle of Blenheim.
—Portuguese Campaign: The Anglo-Portuguese army attacks Spain from Portugal but is repelled by the Franco-Spanish army under the duke of Berwick.	
—Admiral Rooke takes Gibraltar in the name of Charles III of Austria but with the flag of England hoisted.	

SPAIN	EUROPE
1705	
—Treaty of Genoa, by which a group of Catalan leaders make a pact with England to support them in a pro-Charles war effort.	
—Charles III enters Barcelona and establishes it as the provisional capital of his kingdom.	
1706	
—Philip V lays siege to Barcelona, but the arrival of an Anglo-Dutch fleet forces his withdrawal.	—French defeat at the Battle of Ramillies.
—The Allies occupy Madrid, but Charles III's unpopularity leads to the evacuation of the city.	
1707	
—The Army of the Two Crowns defeats the Allies at the Battle of Almansa.	
—The Bourbons occupy Lleida.	
1708	
—The Bourbons besiege and take Tortosa.	
1710	
—Battles of Almenar and Zaragoza.	
—The Allies enter Madrid for the second time, before being forced to evacuate by a Bourbon counteroffensive.	
—Battles of Brihuega and Villaviciosa.	
—Girona taken by the French army.	

SPAIN	EUROPE
1711	
—Emperor Joseph I of Austria dies. Charles, his younger brother, is named as his successor and leaves Barcelona for Vienna.	
1713	
—Signing of the Treaty of Evacuation. The Allied armies commit to withdrawing all troops on the peninsula.	—Treaty of Utrecht: General peace between Europe's powers is sealed. Philip V renounces any claim to the French throne, and Charles III to that of Spain. England reneges on the Treaty of Genoa, by which it had undertaken to uphold the Catalan constitutions in the case of a military defeat.
—June: The Catalan executive declares resistance.	
-—July: Siege of Barcelona begins.	
1714	
—September 11: Final assault on, and fall of, Barcelona. Abolition of the Catalan constitutions and liberties.	
1719	
—War between France and Spain. Marshal Berwick's French army, with five thousand Catalans among its number, takes several strongholds in the Navarran region of Spain.	
—Catalan guerrillas continue to fight the Bourbon forces.	
1725	
	—Treaty is signed between the Spanish and Austrian empires.

The Characters in VICTUS

ALEMANY, FRANCESC: Catalan nobleman who in 1713 argued against defending Barcelona. He did, however, agree to fight, accepting the result of the vote. Died in combat.

AMELIS: Fictional character.

ANFÁN: Fictional character.

BALLESTER, ESTEVE: Miquelet officer. According to the chronicles of the time, he was captured by the Bourbons during a skirmish at Beceite and subsequently rescued by his men in an epic counterattack. Although Ballester is a minor figure in historical terms, in *Victus*, Zuviría dedicates a large number of pages to him, perhaps because he came to consider him a representative of Catalan peasantry taking up arms.

BARDONENCHE, ANTOINE DE: French captain descended from a noble family. Took part in the siege of Barcelona as a member of the French army. According to Castellví's *Crónicas*, he was involved in a rather frivolous and strange episode (which Zuviría does not include): In the early stages of the siege, he entered the city as a "guest," of his own initiative, drawn by the beauties of its architecture. Despite their initial astonishment, the Barcelonans obliged him, and Zuviría was given the task of walking him around the city. He was soon returned, safe and sound, to the Bourbon lines, where the duke of Pópuli reprimanded him for his extravagance, but with no further consequences. Most likely, Waltraud Spöring decided to suppress the pages in question, like so many others, before sending the book to be printed.

BASSONS, MARIÀ: Barcelonan professor of law. He enlisted in the city's militia and took part in its defense as captain to his own students. Died in combat in the battle of Santa Clara (Saint Clara) in August 1714.

BASTIDA, JORDI: Catalan soldier who defended Benasque in 1709. He was in Barcelona during the siege and met a valiant death defending the Santa Clara bastion in August.

BATLLE, BALDIRI: Catalan nobleman. He voted against the decision to defend the city from the Bourbon troops. He accepted the results of the vote, which went against his position. He died defending the city.

BEAST, THE: See Louis XIV.

BERENGUER, ANTONI: Catalan military deputy. Led the disastrous expedition that sought to raise recruits to attack the Bourbon rear immediately afterward. His incompetence led to his arrest upon his return, and to facing justice, albeit with no severe consequences.

BERWICK, JAMES FITZ-JAMES (JIMMY), DUKE OF: French marshal, bastard son of King James of England. Educated in France, where he rose in the social hierarchy thanks to his merits and despite his illegitimacy. The winner of the Battle of Almansa, he stormed Barcelona in 1714, having taken over from the duke of Pópuli. Died in 1734 in mysterious circumstances, during the siege of Philippsburg, in Germany.

BUSQUETS, JAUME: Miquelet leader. His only mention in the histories is by Castellví, according to whom he tried in vain to take the town of Bourbon-controlled Mataró.

CASANOVA, RAFAEL: Catalan lawyer. In 1713 he took over political control of the besieged city of Barcelona. Wounded on September 11, 1714. Survived the period of Bourbon repression and resumed the practice of law.

CASTELLVÍ, FRANCESC DE: Minor Catalan noble who fought in Barcelona at the rank of captain. After 1714 he had to seek exile in Vienna, throwing himself upon the clemency of Emperor Charles. Lived a precarious life, devoting himself to writing the great chronicle of the War of Succession and the siege of Barcelona, his monumental *Narraciones históricas* (Historical narratives). He died without having managed to secure their publication. The original was not recovered until the nineteenth century.

CHARLES III: Austrian pretender to the Spanish throne. From 1705 to 1709, while engaged in his fight for the Spanish crown, he kept his court at Barcelona. In 1711, upon the death of his brother, he left for Vienna to be crowned emperor of the Germanic Holy Roman Empire, abandoning Catalonia to her fate.

CIGALET: Official executioner of the city of Barcelona. During the siege, he was caught looting one of the bombed houses and immediately condemned to death. As it happened, the sentence was carried out by his assistant and future son-in-law, who would take over his position.

COSTA, FRANCESC: Catalan artillery officer whose competence in arms was praised even by his adversaries. Had under his command a large group of Mallorcans, considered the best artillery soldiers of their day. Following the fall of Barcelona, Marshal Berwick offered Costa a position in the French army at a very high salary. Costa fled.

DALMAU, SEBASTIÀ: Member of an affluent Barcelona family who put himself at the service of the Generalitat after the Allies left the peninsula. The Dalmau family depleted their fortune in defense of the city, paying out of their own coffers for the maintenance of an entire regiment. Sebastià took part in the defense, suffered from the repression, and ended his days in Austria, serving Emperor Charles at the rank of lieutenant colonel.

DESVALLS, MANUEL: Governor of Cardona. After September 11, he went into exile in Vienna, like so many other notable pro-Austrians. Desvalls would live to a hundred. The fight in the interior of Catalonia was led by his brother Antoni.

DIAGO, FRANCISCO: Miner of Aragonés origin, a member of the brigade who managed to find the principal Bourbon mine that stretched beneath the walls of Barcelona.

DUCROIX, ARMAND: Fictional character.

DUCROIX, ZENO: Fictional character.

DUPUY: Cousin to Sébastien Vauban, who, like him, devoted himself to military engineering. Dupuy took part in the final stages of the siege of Barcelona and was seriously wounded at the battle of the bastion of Santa Clara. Over the course of his military career, he received as many as sixteen wounds in combat.

DUVERGER: Senior French officer killed in the fighting at the siege of Barcelona.

FERRER, EMMANUEL: Minor Catalan noble who distinguished himself as a councilor in the management of the city of Barcelona. During the 1713 debates, he was the spokesman for those in favor of resisting the Bourbon troops.

FORGOTTEN, MONSIEUR: Although Zuviría refers to Forgotten as "a cousin of the Duc d'Orléans," historians have not been able to agree on which historical figure this might refer to. Some studies of the Zuvirian work have put forward the theory that Forgotten did not really exist but was a synthesis of a number of different characters. Thus Zuviría dramatizes all the contempt he felt for the aristocratic commanders who waged war without any technical knowledge and for their own personal gain.

FIVALLER, CARLES DE: Old Catalan deputy who embodied Catalonia's parliamentary tradition. During the 1713 debates, and contrary to every prediction, he declared himself an ardent supporter of the proposal to attempt a defense of the city, which swayed a large proportion of the votes.

GALWAY, HENRY MASSUE DE RUVIGNY, COUNT OF: English soldier and nobleman of French origin, sent in 1704 to Portugal to command the Allied armies. Defeated by Berwick in 1707 at the decisive Battle of Almansa.

IN-A-TRICE: See Stanhope, James.

JIMMY: See Berwick.

JOSEPH I: Austrian emperor, brother to the pretender, Charles III of Spain. Upon Joseph's death in 1711, Charles left Spain to declare himself the new emperor, which provoked a switch in alliances that led to Catalonia's abandonment by the Allies.

LA MOTTE: French lieutenant colonel injured in the battle for Santa Clara. La Motte was the officer who finally succeeded in persuading Berwick to suspend the attack, even if this was a humiliation for the Army of the Two Crowns.

LITTLE PHILIP: See Philip V.

LOUIS XIV: King of France, nicknamed the Sun King. As the king of France, he launched an imperialist policy that would lead to the Spanish War of Succession. Despite the creation of Versailles and the magnificence of his court, by the end of his kingdom, the country had fallen into ruin. In 1714 the fall of Barcelona was celebrated with a Te Deum in Paris.

MARLBOROUGH: English soldier and aristocrat who, during the War of Succession, managed to defeat the French troops at Blenheim, Schellenberg, and Malplaquet, successively. However, he was accused of embezzling public funds and prolonging the war unnecessarily for his own personal gain, and in 1711 was stripped of his positions. Marlborough was a relative of Berwick, with whom he maintained a private correspondence despite the fact that they were fighting on opposing sides throughout the war.

MASSUE DE RUVIGNY, HENRY: See Galway.

MATEU, JOSEP: Barcelonan miner who was a member of the brigade that managed to find the Bourbon mine stretching beneath the walls of Barcelona just before it was set to explode.

MINAS, MARQUIS DAS: Portuguese general who led his country's troops that took part in the Battle of Almansa. Das Minas was a veteran commander, aged over sixty. Although the role played by the Portuguese battalions at Almansa was subsequently heavily criticized by their English allies, there is no evidence to support their accusations.

MOLINA, FRANCESC: Barcelonan of Italian origin who led Barcelona's mining brigades. During the siege, he led the anti-mine work and found the principal Bourbon mine just as it was about to be blown.

MORAGUES, JOSEP: Catalan leader who fought the Bourbons outside the besieged city of Barcelona. At the end of the war, he was captured and executed. His skull was kept on display for over a decade on one of the gates into the city, as a warning against future rebellions. In the nineteenth century, the character of Moragues was retrieved by the Spanish romantic movement, who converted him into a mythic figure in the story of Catalan liberties.

NAN: Fictional character.

ORLÉANS, DUC D': French aristocrat and soldier who took part in several episodes in the War of Spanish Succession, in Italy as well as in Spain. In 1708 he led the siege of Tortosa, a strategic location in the south of Catalonia. Following the death of Louis XIV, he succeeded him as regent, scandalizing Europe with his private orgies and parties.

ORTIZ: Pro-Austrian colonel who played a significant role in the battle of Santa Clara when his troops contributed toward surrounding the Bourbon vanguard.

PALLARÈS, DÍDAC: Barcelona citizen who was a member of the Coronela, or the city's militia. During the siege, three of his sons, who were also members of that militia, died or were seriously injured.

PERET: Fictional character.

PHILIP V: Duc d'Anjou, grandson of Louis XIV of France, and Bourbon pretender to the Spanish throne following the death of Carlos II. After the retreat of the Allied troops, he considered Catalan resistance a seditious rebellion and decided to deal with the "rebels" with particular viciousness. From a very early age, Philip had shown symptoms of severe mental imbalance. In the final phase of his life, the symptoms of dementia became more acute, to the point where he grew his nails over ten inches long, dressed in rags, and slept in open coffins.

PORKY: Fictional character.

POLASTRON: Senior French officer killed in combat at the siege of Barcelona.

PÓPULI, RESTAINO CANTELMO STUART, DUKE OF: Italian nobleman serving Philip V. Pópuli felt personal ill will toward the Barcelonans because, he claimed, they had mistreated his wife during the disturbances of 1705. In 1713 Philip placed under his command the Franco-Spanish troops who were to begin the occupation of Catalonia. Faced with unexpected resistance from Barcelona, Pópuli laid siege to it. His inability to take the city led to his replacement by Berwick nine months later.

POU, JOSEP: Doctor from Vic who made an offer to the Bourbon troops of the city's surrender, without the Catalan government's knowledge.

ROGER, LLUÍS: Catalan nobleman who voted against Barcelona taking up arms against Philip V. He accepted the result of the final vote, which went in the opposite direction, and took part in the city's defense. Died in combat.

SAAVEDRA Y PORTUGAL, GREGORIO DE: Pro-Austrian who appears at the most critical moments in the story of the siege, such as the battle of Santa Clara. During the final days of the siege, Zuviría was carrying out anti-mine work. This might explain why he does not mention that it was Saavedra tasked with answering the final Bourbon ultimatum to surrender. When the marquis of Tserclaes approached the walls to learn the city's reply, Saavedra said: "The commons have met and have decided as follows: not to listen to any proposals from the enemy. Has Your Excellence anything to say?" "No." "Well then, withdraw, because the fight will go on."

SALA, BENET: Bishop of Barcelona who, in the 1713 debates, intervened behind the scenes for the pro-surrender position but without success. Despite his efforts, at the end of the war, he would face reprisals from the Bourbon regime.

SANT JOAN, NICOLAU DE: Catalan politician who, during the 1713 debates, led the group in favor of surrendering the city.

SANTA CRUZ (FATHER AND SON): Soldiers who held the command of the engineering corps of the besieged city of Barcelona. They deserted and offered their services to the Bourbon leadership, but the offer was not accepted, and father and son were evacuated to Alicante, suggesting that their posts were purely nominal.

SAUVEBOEUF: French soldier killed in combat during the attacks on Barcelona.

SHITSON: Foreign officer, name unknown, who took part with the Catalan troops in the ill-fated expedition by the military deputy. Castellví tells us only that he was an officer repudiated by his former superiors, and that in his flight, the deputy left the troops in his charge.

STANHOPE, JAMES: English aristocrat and soldier who, in 1710, was sent to Spain as commander of the English military force tasked with bringing an end to the war. His performance was heavily criticized, both politically and militarily, and in 1710 he was taken prisoner along with most of his troops. Stanhope would marry the daughter of the governor of Madras and enter a career in politics, and such an unfortunate one that his role as finance minister would coincide with the crisis that came to be known the South Sea Bubble, which ruined the English economy.

STRETCH: Fictional character.

TIMOR, JAUME: Catalan commander who, in 1714, played a significant role in the battle for Santa Clara, managing to prevent the defenders from abandoning the bastion when the situation was at its most desperate.

TOMEU: Colonel who, together with Colonel Ortiz, outflanked the vanguard of the Bourbon trench, a maneuver that completed the Franco-Spanish defeat during the battle of Santa Clara.

VALÈNCIA, ANTONI: Barcelonan nobleman. In 1713 he voted against shutting the city's gates and resisting the Bourbon attack. He died defending the city.

VAN COEHOORN, MENO: Dutch military engineer who developed theories of siege warfare completely opposed to the Vaubanian model. Coehoorn was a contemporary of Vauban's, and they even confronted each other directly in the siege of Namur. Vaubanian, who had been leading the besieging army, received the surrender directly from Coehoorn himself.

VAN VERBOOM, JORIS PROSPERUS: Military engineer of Dutch origin who served the Spanish Bourbons. In 1710 he was wounded in battle and captured by the pro-Austrian troops. He spent two years as a prisoner in Barcelona, where he studied the city's defenses. In 1714 he was indeed the man appointed to design the attack trench that would take the city by storm. Subsequently, he built the Citadel in the interior of the city, as a means to subdue the citizens.

VAUBAN, CHARLOTTE: Elder daughter of Sébastien Vauban.

VAUBAN, JEANNE: Younger daughter of Sébastien Vauban. Married a member of the French nobility who, shortly after the wedding, went mad in his search for the philosopher's stone, although some years later, surprisingly, recovered his wits.

VAUBAN, SÉBASTIEN LE PRESTE: French engineer, marquis, and marshal known for his innovations in the art of fortification and siege warfare including the development of new methods of siege and attack.

VENDÔME: French marshal sent to Spain by Louis XIV to provide military aid to his grandson, Philip. In 1710 he took part in the battles of Brihuega and Villaviciosa, whose results were inconclusive. He died in 1712, in Vinaroz, of indigestion from eating prawns.

VILLARROEL, ANTONIO DE: Spanish soldier who, at the start of the war, served in the Bourbon army. In 1708 he played a notable part in the attack on the strategically important city of Tortosa. In 1710, however, he switched sides and joined the pro-Austrian army at a general's rank. Villarroel's cavalry was decisive in the Battle of Villaviciosa for avoiding defeat. In 1713 he was appointed the commander of Barcelona by the Catalan government. A few days before the attack in 1714, he resigned from his post, believing that resisting to the end would be tantamount to a massacre. Despite this, rather than setting sail, he decided at the last moment to remain in the city. During the fighting of September 11, he was gravely injured, and soon afterward, though this went against terms of the capitulation, he was arrested and imprisoned. He was made to suffer terribly in prison and was not freed until shortly before his death.

VON STARHEMBERG, GUIDO RUDIGER: Austrian soldier sent to Spain by the emperor to help his son Charles, who was pretender to the Spanish throne. Starhemberg was a more than competent soldier, though unable to achieve any genuinely decisive victories for the Austrian forces. In 1713 he was Charles III's viceroy in Catalonia. Following the Treaty of Evacuation, which forced the evacuation of all Allied troops still on Spanish soil, he attempted to bring about the handing over of Barcelona to the Bourbon forces but, faced with strong popular opposition, decided to set sail with his troops and leave the Barcelonans to their fate.

WALTRAUD: Fictional character.

DE ZÚÑIGA, DIEGO: Fictional character.

ZUVIRÍA, MARTÍ: Aide-de-camp to General de Villarroel. In his *Narraciones históricas*, Castellví refers to Zuviría as fulfilling roles as diverse as translator from the French, adjutant to General Villarroel, and taking part in missions outside Barcelona during the siege. It is known that he managed to escape to Vienna, where he shows up on the list of expatriate pro-Austrians.

About the Author

Albert Sánchez Piñol is a best-selling international author. His books have been translated into thirty-seven languages worldwide. An anthropologist by training and a writer by profession, his works are well-researched and historically illuminating. *Victus* is his third novel translated into English.

The Translators

Daniel Hahn is a writer, editor, and translator with some forty books to his name. His translations include fiction from Europe, Africa, and the Americas, and nonfiction by writers ranging from Portuguese Nobel laureate José Saramago to Brazilian footballer Pelé.

Thomas Bunstead was a British Centre for Literary Translation mentee in 2011–12, working with Margaret Jull Costa, and has since translated and co-translated several novels from the Spanish, including work by Eduardo Halfon, Yuri Herrera, and Enrique Vila-Matas. His translation of Aixa de la Cruz's "True Milk" was selected for Dalkey Archive's *Best of European Fiction 2015*.